Wild Western Days

Wild Western Days

The Coming of Cassidy

Bar-20

Hopalong Cassidy

CLARENCE E. MULFORD

A Tom Doherty Associates Book

New York

WILD WESTERN DAYS

The Coming of Cassidy was first published in 1913; *Bar-20* was first published in 1907; *Hopalong Cassidy* was first published in 1910.

A Forge Book
Published by Tom Doherty Associates, LLC
175 Fifth Avenue
New York, NY 10010

www.tor-forge.com

Forge® is a registered trademark of Tom Doherty Associates, LLC.

ISBN 978-0-7653-2307-1

First Edition: April 2010

Printed in the United States of America

0 9 8 7 6 5 4 3 2 1

CONTENTS

The Coming of Cassidy

PREFACE

It was on one of my annual visits to the ranch that Red, whose welcome always seemed a little warmer than that of the others, finally took me back to the beginning. My friendship with the outfit did not begin until some years after the fight at Buckskin, and, while I was familiar with that affair and with the history of the outfit from that time on, I had never seemed to make much headway back of that encounter. And I must confess that if I had depended upon the rest of the outfit for enlightenment I should have learned very little of its earlier exploits. A more secretive and bashful crowd, when it came to their own achievements, would be hard to find. But Red, the big, smiling, under-foreman, at last completely thawed and during the last few weeks of my stay, told me story after story about the earlier days of the ranch and the parts played by each member of the outfit. Names that I had heard mentioned casually now meant something to me; the characters stepped out of the obscurity of the past to act their parts again. To my mind's eye came Jimmy Price, even more mischievous than Johnny Nelson; "Butch" Lynch and Charley James, who erred in judgment; the coming and going of Sammy Porter, and why "You-Bet" Somes never arrived; and others who did their best, or worst, and went their way. The tales will follow, as closely as possible, in chronological order. Between some of them the interval is short; between others, long; the less interesting stories that should fill those gaps may well be omitted.

It was in the '70s, when the buffalo were fast disappearing from the state, and the hunters were beginning to turn to other ways of earning a living, that Buck Peters stopped his wagon on the banks of Snake Creek and built himself a sod dugout in the heart of a country forbidding and full of perils. It was said that he was only the agent for an eastern syndicate that, carried away by the prospects of the cattle industry, bought a "ranch," which later was found to be entirely strange to cattle. As a matter of fact there were no cows within three hundred miles of it, and there never had been. Somehow the syndicate got in touch with Buck and sent him out to look things over and make a report to them. This he did, and in his report he stated that the "ranch" was split in two parts by about forty square miles of public land, which he recommended that he be allowed to buy according to his judgment. When everything was settled the syndicate found that they owned the west, and best, bank of an unfailing river and both banks of an unfailing creek for a distance of about thirty miles. The strip was not very wide then, but it did not need to be, for it cut off the back-lying range from water and rendered it useless to anyone but his employers. Westward there was no water to amount to anything for one hundred miles. When this had been digested thoroughly by the syndicate it caused Buck's next pay check to be twice the size of the first.

He managed to live through the winter, and the following spring a herd of about two thousand or more poor cattle was delivered to him, and he noticed at once that fully half of them were unbranded; but mavericks were cows, and in those days it was not questionable to brand them. Persuading two members of the drive outfit to work for him he settled down to face the work and perils of ranching in a wild country. One of these two men, George Travis, did not work long; the other was the man who told me these tales. Red went back with the drive outfit, but in Buck's wagon, to return in four weeks with it heaped full of necessities, and to find that troubles already had begun. Buck's trust was not misplaced. It was during Red's absence that Bill Cassidy, later to be known by a more descriptive name, appeared upon the scene and played his cards.

C.E.M.

CHAPTER 1

The Coming of Cassidy

The trail boss shook his fist after the departing puncher and swore softly. He hated to lose a man at this time and he had been a little reckless in threatening to "fire" him; but in a gun-fighting outfit there was no room for a hothead. "Cimarron" was boss of the outfit that was driving a large herd of cattle to California, a feat that had been accomplished before, but that no man cared to attempt the second time. Had his soul been enriched by the gift of prophecy he would have turned back. As it was he returned to the work ahead of him. "Aw, let him go," he growled. "He's wuss off'n I am, an' he'll find it out quick. I never did see nobody what got crazy mad so quick as him."

"Bill" Cassidy, not yet of age, but a man in stature and strength, rode north because it promised him civilization quicker than any other way except the back trail, and he was tired of the coast range. He had forgotten the trail boss during the last three days of his solitary journeying and the fact that he was in the center of an uninhabited country nearly as large as a good-sized state gave him no concern; he was equipped for two weeks, and fortified by youth's confidence.

All day long he rode, around mesas and through draws, detouring to avoid canyons and bearing steadily northward with a certainty that was a heritage. Gradually the great bulk of mesas swung off to the west, and to the east the range grew steadily more level as it swept toward the peaceful river lying in the distant valley like a carelessly flung rope of silver. The forest vegetation, so luxuriant along the rivers and draws a day or two before, was now rarely seen, while chaparrals and stunted mesquite became more common.

He was more than twenty-five hundred feet above the ocean, on a great plateau broken by mesas that stretched away for miles in a vast sea of grass. There was just enough tang in the dry April air to make riding a pleasure and

he did not mind the dryness of the season. Twice that day he detoured to ride
around prairie-dog towns and the sight of buffalo skeletons lying in groups was
not rare. Alert and contemptuous gray wolves gave him a passing glance, but
the coyotes, slinking a little farther off, watched him with more interest. Occasionally he had a shot at antelope and once was successful.

Warned by the gathering dusk he was casting about for the most favorable
spot for his blanket and fire when a horseman swung into sight out of a draw
and reined in quickly. Bill's hand fell carelessly to his side while he regarded
the stranger, who spoke first, and with a restrained welcoming gladness in his
voice. "Howd'y, Stranger! You plumb surprised me."

Bill's examination told him that the other was stocky, compactly built, with
a pleasing face and a "good eye." His age was about thirty and the surface indi-
cations were very favorable. "Some surprised myself," he replied. "Ridin' my
way?"

"Far's th' house," smiled the other. "Better join us. Couple of buffalo hunters
dropped in awhile back."

"They'll go a long way before they'll find buffalo," Bill responded, suspiciously. Glancing around he readily picked out the rectangular blot in the valley, though it was no easy feat. "Huntin' or ranchin'?" he inquired in tones
devoid of curiosity.

"Ranchin'," smiled the other. "Hefty proposition, up here, I reckon. Th'
wolves'll walk in under yore nose. But I ain't seen no Injuns."

"You will," was the calm reply. "You'll see a couple, first; an' then th' whole
cussed tribe. *They* ain't got no buffalo no more, neither."

Buck glanced at him sharply and thought of the hunters, but he nodded.
"Yes. But if that couple don't go back?" he asked, referring to the Indians.

"Then you'll save a little time."

"Well, let 'em come. I'm here to stay, one way or th' other. But, anyhow, I ain't
got no border ruffians like they have over in th' Panhandle. They're worse'n Injuns."

"Yes," agreed Bill. "Th' war ain't ended yet for some of them fellers. Ex-
guerrillas, lots of 'em."

When they reached the house the buffalo hunters were arguing about their
next day's ride and the elder, looking up, appealed to Bill. "Howd'y, Stranger.
Ain't come 'cross no buffaler signs, hev ye?"

Bill smiled. "Bones an' old chips. But th' gray wolves was headin' southwest."

"What'd I tell you?" triumphantly exclaimed the younger hunter.

"Well, they ain't much dif'rence, is they?" growled his companion.

Bill missed nothing the hunters said or did and during the silent meal had a good chance to study their faces. When the pipes were going and the supper wreck cleaned away, Buck leaned against the wall and looked across the room at the latest arrival. "Don't want a job, do you?" he asked.

Bill shook his head slowly, wondering why the hunters had frowned at a job being offered on another man's ranch. "I'm headed north. But I'll give you a hand for a week if you need me," he offered.

Buck smiled. "Much obliged, friend; but it'll leave me worse off than before. My other puncher'll be back in a few weeks with th' supplies, but I need four men all year round. I got a thousand head to brand yet."

The elder hunter looked up. "Drive 'em back to cow-country an' sell 'em, or locate there," he suggested.

Buck's glance was as sharp as his reply, for he couldn't believe that the hunter had so soon forgotten what he had been told regarding the ownership of the cattle. "I don't own 'em. This range is bought an' paid for. I won't lay down."

"I done forgot they ain't yourn," hastily replied the hunter, smiling to himself. Stolen cattle cannot go back.

"If they was I'd stay," crisply retorted Buck. "I ain't quittin' nothin' I starts."

"How many'll you have nex' spring?" grinned the younger hunter. He was surprised by the sharpness of the response. "More'n I've got now, in spite of hell!"

Bill nodded approval. He felt a sudden, warm liking for this rugged man who would not quit in the face of such handicaps. He liked game men, better if they were square, and he believed this foreman was as square as he was game. "By th' Lord!" he ejaculated. "For a plugged peso I'd stay with you!"

Buck smiled warmly. "Would *good* money do? But don't you stay if you oughtn't, son."

When the light was out Bill lay awake for a long time, his mind busy with his evening's observations, and they pleased him so little that he did not close his eyes until assured by the breathing of the hunters that they were asleep. His Colt, which should have been hanging in its holster on the wall where he had left it, lay unsheathed close to his thigh and he awakened frequently during the night so keyed was he for the slightest sound. Up first in the morning, he replaced the gun in its scabbard before the others opened their eyes, and it was not until the hunters had ridden out of sight into the southwest that he entirely relaxed his vigilance. Saying good-bye to the two cowmen was not without regrets, but he shook hands heartily with them and swung decisively northward.

He had been riding perhaps two hours, thinking about the little ranch and the hunters, when he stopped suddenly on the very brink of a sheer drop of two hundred feet. In his abstraction he had ridden up the sloping southern face of the mesa without noticing it. "Bet there ain't another like this for a hundred miles," he laughed, and then ceased abruptly and stared with unbelieving eyes at the mouth of a draw not far away. A trotting line of gray wolves was emerging from it and swinging toward the southwest ten abreast. He had never heard of such a thing before and watched them in amazement. "Well, I'm—!" he exclaimed, and his Colt flashed rapidly at the pack. Two or three dropped, but the trotting line only swerved a little without pause or a change of pace and soon was lost in another draw. "Why, they're single hunters," he muttered. "Huh! I won't never tell this. I can't hardly believe it myself. How 'bout you, Ring-Bone?" he asked his horse.

Turning, he rode around a rugged pinnacle of rock and stopped again, gazing steadily along the back trail. Far away in a valley two black dots were crawling over a patch of sand and he knew them to be horsemen. His face slowly reddened with anger at the espionage, for he had not thought the cowmen could doubt his good will and honesty. Then suddenly he swore and spurred forward to cover those miles as speedily as possible. "Come on, ol' Hammer-Head!" he cried. "We're goin' back!"

The hunters had finally decided they would ride into the southwest and had ridden off in that direction. But they had detoured and swung north to see him pass and be sure he was not in their way. Now, satisfied upon that point, they were going back to that herd of cattle, easily turned from skinning buffalo to cattle, and on a large scale. To do this they would have to kill two men and then, waiting for the absent puncher to return with the wagon, kill him and load down the vehicle with skins. "Like hell they will!" he gritted. "Three or none, you piruts. Come on, White-Eye! Don't sleep all th' time; an' don't light often'r once every ten yards, you saddle-galled, barrel-bellied runt!"

Into hollows, out again; shooting down steep-banked draws and avoiding cacti and chaparral with cat-like agility, the much-described little pony butted the wind in front and left a low-lying cloud of dust swirling behind as it whirred at top speed with choppy, tied-in stride in a winding circle for the humble sod hut on Snake Creek. The rider growled at the evident speed of the two men ahead, for he had not gained upon them despite his efforts. "If I'm too late to stop it, I'll clean th' slate, anyhow," he snapped. "Even if I has to ambush! *Will* you run?" he demanded, and the wild-eyed little bundle of whalebone and steel found a little more speed in its flashing legs.

The rider now began to accept what cover he could find and when he neared the hut left the shelter of the last, low hill for that afforded by a draw leading to within a hundred yards of the dugout's rear wall. Dismounting, he ran lightly forward on foot, alert and with every sense strained for a warning.

Reaching the wall he peered around the corner and stifled an exclamation. Buck's puncher, a knife in his back, lay head down the sloping path. Placing his ear to the wall he listened intently for some moments and then suddenly caught sight of a shadow slowly creeping past his toes. Quickly as he sprang aside he barely missed the flashing knife and the bulk of the man behind it, whose hand, outflung to save his balance, accidentally knocked the Colt from Bill's grasp and sent it spinning twenty feet away.

Without a word they leaped together, fighting silently, both trying to gain the gun in the hunter's holster and trying to keep the other from it. Bill, forcing the fighting in hopes that his youth would stand a hot pace better than the other's years, pushed his enemy back against the low roof of the dugout; but as the hunter tripped over it and fell backward, he pulled Bill with him. Fighting desperately they rolled across the roof and dropped to the sloping earth at the doorway, so tightly locked in each other's arms that the jar did not separate them. The hunter, falling underneath, got the worst of the fall but kept on fighting. Crashing into the door head first, they sent it swinging back against the wall and followed it, bumping down the two steps still locked together.

Bill possessed strength remarkable for his years and build and he was hard as iron; but he had met a man who had the sinewy strength of the plainsman, whose greater age was offset by greater weight and the youth was constantly so close to defeat that a single false move would have been fatal. But luck favored him, for as they surged around the room they crashed into the heavy table and fell with it on top of them. The hunter got its full weight and the gash in his forehead filled his eyes with blood. By a desperate effort he pinned Bill's arm under his knee and with his left hand secured a throat grip, but the under man wriggled furiously and bridged so suddenly as to throw the hunter off him and Bill's freed hand, crashing full into the other's stomach, flashed back to release the weakened throat grip and jam the tensed fingers between his teeth, holding them there with all the power of his jaws. The dazed and gasping hunter, bending forward instinctively, felt his own throat seized and was dragged underneath his furious opponent.

In his Berserker rage Bill had forgotten about the gun, his fury sweeping everything from him but the primal desire to kill with his hands, to rend and crush like an animal. He was brought to his senses very sharply by the jarring, crashing roar of the six-shooter, the powder blowing away part of his shirt and burning his side. Twisting sideways he grasped the weapon with one hand, the wrist with the other and bent the gun slowly back, forcing its muzzle farther and farther from him. The hunter, at last managing to free his left hand from the other's teeth, found it useless when he tried to release the younger man's grip of the gun; and the Colt, roaring again, dropped from its owner's hand as he relaxed.

The victor leaned against the wall, his breath coming in great, sobbing gulps, his knees sagging and his head near bursting. He reeled across the wrecked room, gulped down a drink of whisky from the bottle on the shelf and, stumbling, groped his way to the outer air where he flung himself down on the ground, dazed and dizzy. When he opened his eyes the air seemed to be filled with flashes of fire and huge, black fantastic blots that changed form with great swiftness and the hut danced and shifted like a thing of life. Hot bands seemed to encircle his throat and the throbbing in his temples was like blows of a hammer. While he writhed and fought for breath a faint gunshot reached his ears and found him apathetic. But the second, following closely upon the first, seemed clearer and brought him to himself long enough to make him arise and stumble to his horse, and claw his way into the saddle. The animal, maddened by the steady thrust of the spurs, pitched viciously and bolted; but the rider had learned his art in the sternest school in the world, the "busting" corrals of the great Southwest, and he not only stuck to the saddle, but guided the fighting animal through a barranca almost choked with obstructions.

Stretched full length in a crevice near the top of a mesa lay the other hunter, his rifle trained on a smaller boulder several hundred yards down and across the draw. His first shot had been an inexcusable blunder for a marksman like himself and now he had a desperate man and a very capable shot opposing him. If Buck could hold out until nightfall he could slip away in the darkness and do some stalking on his own account.

For half an hour they had lain thus, neither daring to take sight. Buck could not leave the shelter of the boulder because the high ground behind him offered no cover; but the hunter, tiring of the fruitless wait, wriggled back into the crevice, arose and slipped away, intending to crawl to the edge of the mesa further down and get in a shot from a new angle before his enemy learned of the shift; and this shot would not be a blunder. He had just lowered himself down a steep wall when the noise of rolling pebbles caused him to look around, expecting to see his friend. Bill was just turning the corner of the wall and their eyes met at the same instant.

"'Nds up!" snapped the youth, his Colt glinting as it swung up. The hunter, gripping the rifle firmly, looked into the angry eyes of the other, and slowly obeyed. Bill, watching the rifle intently, forthwith learned a lesson he never forgot: never to watch a gun, but the eyes of the man who has it. The left hand of the hunter seemed to melt into smoke, and Bill, firing at the same instant, blundered into a hit when his surprise and carelessness should have cost him dearly. His bullet, missing its intended mark by inches, struck the still moving Colt of the other, knocking it into the air and numbing the hand that held it. A searing pain in his shoulder told him of the closeness of the call and set his lips into a thin, white line. The hunter, needing no words to interpret the look in the youth's eyes, swiftly raised his hands, holding the rifle high above his head, but neglected to take his finger from the trigger.

Bill was not overlooking anything now and he noticed the crooked finger. "Stick th' muzzle *up*, an' pull that trigger," he commanded, sharply. "Now!" he grated. The report came crashing back from half a dozen points as he nodded. "Drop it, an' turn 'round." As the other obeyed he stepped cautiously forward, jammed his Colt into the hunter's back and took possession of a skinning knife. A few moments later the hunter, trussed securely by a forty-foot lariat, lay cursing at the foot of the rock wall.

Bill, collecting the weapons, went off to cache them and then peered over the mesa's edge to look into the draw. A leaden splotch appeared on the rock almost under his nose and launched a crescendo scream into the sky to whine into silence. He ducked and leaped back, grinning foolishly as he realized Buck's error. Turning to approach the edge from another point he felt his sombrero jerk at his head as another bullet, screaming plaintively, followed the first. He dropped like a shot, and commented caustically upon his paucity of brains as he gravely examined the hole in his head gear. "Huh!" he grunted. "I had a fool's luck three times in twenty minutes—damned if I'm goin' to risk th' next turn. *Three* of 'em," he repeated. "I'm a' Injun from now on. An' that foreman shore can shoot!"

He wriggled to the edge and called out, careful not to let any of his anatomy show above the skyline. "Hey, Buck! I ain't no buffalo hunter! This is Cassidy, who you wanted to punch for you. Savvy?" He listened, and grinned at the eloquent silence. "You talk too rapid," he laughed. Repeating his statements he listened again, with the same success. "Now I wonder is he stalkin' *me*? Hey, *Buck*!" he shouted.

"Stick yore hands up an' foller 'em with yore face," said Buck's voice from below. Bill raised his arms and slowly stood up. "Now what'n blazes do *you* want?" demanded the foreman, belligerently.

"Nothin'. Just got them hunters, one of 'em alive. I reckoned mebby you'd sorta like to know it." He paused, cogitating. "Reckon we better turn him loose when we gets back to th' hut," he suggested. "I'll keep his guns," he added, grinning.

The foreman stuck his head out in sight. "Well, I'm damned!" he exclaimed, and sank weakly back against the boulder. "Can you give me a hand?" he muttered.

The words did not carry to the youth on the skyline, but he saw, understood, and, slipping and bumping down the steep wall with more speed than sense, dashed across the draw and up the other side. He nodded sagely as he examined the wound and bound it carefully with the sleeve of his own shirt. " 'T ain't much—loss of blood, mostly. Yo're better off than Travis."

"Travis dead?" whispered Buck. "In th' back! Pore feller, pore feller; didn't have no show. Tell me about it." At the end of the story he nodded. "Yo're all right, Cassidy. He'd 'a' stood a good chance of gettin' me, 'cept for you." A frown clouded his face and he looked weakly about him as if for an answer to the question that bothered him. "Now what am I goin' to do up here with all these cows?" he muttered.

Bill rolled the wounded man a cigarette and lit it for him, after which he fell to tossing pebbles at a rock further down the hill.

"I reckon it *will* be sorta tough," he replied, slowly. "But I sorta reckoned me an' you, an' that other feller, can make a big ranch out of yore little one. Anyhow, I'll bet we can have a mighty big time tryin'. A mighty fine time. What you think?"

Buck smiled weakly and shoved out his hand with a visible effort. "We can! Shake, Bill!" he said, contentedly.

CHAPTER 2

The Weasel

The winter that followed the coming of Bill Cassidy to the Bar-20 ranch was none too mild to suit the little outfit in the cabin on Snake Creek, but it was not severe enough to cause complaint and they weathered it without trouble to speak of. Down on the big ranges lying closer to the Gulf the winter was so mild as to seem but a brief interruption of summer. It was on this warm, southern range that Skinny Thompson, one bright day of early spring, loped along the trail to Scoria, where he hoped to find his friend, Lanky Smith, and where he determined to put an end to certain rumors that had filtered down to him on the range and filled his days with anger.

He was within sight of the little cow-town when he met Frank Lewis, but recently returned from a cattle drive. Exchanging gossip of a harmless nature, Skinny mildly scored his missing friend and complained about his flea-like ability to get scarce. Lewis, laughing, told him that Lanky had left town two days before bound north. Skinny gravely explained that he always had to look after his missing friend, who was childish, irresponsible and helpless when alone. Lewis laughed heartily as he pictured the absent puncher, and he laughed harder as he pictured the two together. Both lean as bean poles, Skinny stood six feet four, while Lanky was fortunate if he topped five feet by many inches. Also they were inseparable, which made Lewis ask a question. "But how does it come you ain't with him?"

"Well, we was punchin' down south an' has a li'l run-in. When I rid in that night I found he had flitted. What I want to know is what business has he got, siftin' out like that an' makin' me chase after him?"

"I dunno," replied Lewis, amused. "You're sort of gardjean to him, hey?"

"Well, he gets sort of homesick if I ain't with him, anyhow," replied Skinny, grinning broadly. "An' who's goin' to look after him when I ain't around?"

"That puts me up a tree," replied Lewis. "I shore can't guess. But you two should ought to 'a' been stuck together, like them other twins was. But if he'd do a thing like that I'd think you wouldn't waste no time on him."

"Well, he *is* too ornery an' downright cussed for any human bein' to worry about very much, or 'sociate with steady an' reg'lar. Why, lookit him gettin' sore on me, an' for nothin'! But I'm so used to bein' abused I get sort of lost when he ain't around."

"Well," smiled Lewis, "he's went up north to punch for Buck Peters on his li'l ranch on Snake Creek. If you want to go after him, this is th' way I told him to go," and he gave instructions hopelessly inadequate to anyone not a plainsman. Skinny nodded, irritated by what he regarded as the other's painful and unnecessary details and wheeled to ride on. He had started for town when Lewis stopped him with a word. "Hey," he called. Skinny drew rein and looked around.

"Better ride in cautious like," Lewis remarked, casually. "Somebody was in town when I left—he shore was thirsty. He ain't drinkin' a drop, which has riled him considerable. So-long."

"Huh!" grunted Skinny. "Much obliged. That's one of th' reasons I'm goin' to town," and he started forward again, tight-lipped and grim.

He rode slowly into Scoria, alert, watching windows, doors and corners, and dismounted before Quigg's saloon, which was the really "high-toned" thirst parlor in the town. He noticed that the proprietor had put black shades to the windows and door and then, glancing quickly around, entered. He made straight for the partition in the rear of the building, but the proprietor's voice checked him. "You needn't bother, Skinny—there ain't nobody in there; an' I locked th' back door an hour ago." He glanced around the room and added, with studied carelessness: "You don't want to get any reckless today." He mopped the bar slowly and coughed apologetically. "Don't get careless."

"I won't—it's me that's doin' th' hunting today," Skinny replied, meaningly. "Him a-hunting for me yesterday, when he shore knowed I wasn't in town, when he knowed he couldn't find me! I was getting good an' tired of him, an' so when Walt rode over to see me last night an' told me what th' coyote was doing yesterday, an' what he was yelling around, I just natchurly had to straddle leather an' come in. I can't let him put that onto me. Nobody can call me a card cheat an' a coward an' a few other choice things like he did without seeing me, an' seeing me quick. An' I shore hope he's sober. Are both of 'em in town, Larry?"

"No; only Dick. But he's making noise enough for two. He shore raised th' devil yesterday."

"Well, I'm goin' North trailin' Lanky, but before I leave I'm shore goin' to sweeten things around here. If I go away without getting him he'll say he scared me out, so I'll have to do it when I come back, anyhow. You see, it might just as well be today. But th' next time I sit in a game with fellers that can't drop fifty dollars without saying they was cheated I'll be a blamed sight bigger fool than I am right now. I shouldn't 'a' taken cards with 'em after what has passed. Why didn't they say they was cheated, then an' there, an' not wait till three days after I left town? All that's bothering me is Sam: if I get his brother when he ain't around, an' then goes North, he'll say I had to jump th' town to get away from him. But I'll stop that by giving him his chance at me when I get back."

"Say, why don't you wait a day an' get 'em both before you go?" asked Quigg hopefully.

"Can't: Lanky's got two days' start on me an' I want to catch him soon as I can."

"I can't get it through my head, nohow," Quigg remarked. "Everybody knows you play square. I reckon they're hard losers."

Skinny laughed shortly: "Why, can't you see it? Last year I beat Dick Bradley out with a woman over in Ballard. Then his fool brother tried to cut in an' beat me out. Cards? Hell!" he snorted, walking toward the door. "You an' everybody else knows—" he stopped suddenly and jerked his gun loose as a shadow fell across the doorsill. Then he laughed and slapped the newcomer on the shoulder: "Hullo, Ace, my boy! You had a narrow squeak then. You want to make more noise when you turn corners, unless somebody's looking for you with a gun. How are you, anyhow? An' how's yore dad? I've been going over to see him regular, right along but I've been so busy I kept putting it off."

"Dad's better, Skinny; an' I'm feeling too good to be true. What'll you have?"

"Reckon it's my treat; you wet last th' other time. Ain't that right, Quigg? Shore, I knowed it was."

"All right, here's luck," Ace smiled. "Quigg, that's better stock; an' would you look at th' style—real curtains?"

Quigg grinned. "Got to have 'em. I'm on th' sunny side of th' street."

"I hear yo're goin' North," Ace remarked.

"Yes, I am; but how'd you know about it?"

"Why, it ain't no secret, is it?" asked Ace in surprise. "If it is, you must 'a' told a woman. I heard of it from th' crowd—everybody seems to know about it. Yo're going up alone, too, ain't you?"

"Well, no, it ain't no secret; an' I am going alone," slowly replied Skinny. "Here, have another."

"All right—this is on me. Here's more luck."

"Where is th' crowd?"

"Keeping under cover for a while to give you plenty of elbow room," Ace replied. "He's sober as a judge, Skinny, an' mad as a rattler. Swears he'll kill you on sight. An' his brother ain't with him; if he does come in too soon I'll see he don't make it two to one. Good luck, an' so-long," he said quickly, shaking hands and walking toward the door. He put one hand out first and waved it, slowly stepping to the street and then walking rapidly out of sight.

Skinny looked after him and smiled. "Larry, there's a blamed fine youngster," he remarked, reflectively. "Well, he ought to be—he had th' best mother God ever put breath into." He thought for a moment and then went slowly towards the door. "I've heard so much about Bradley's gun-play that I'm some curious. Reckon I'll see if it's all true—" and he had leaped through the doorway, gun in hand. There was no shot, no sign of his enemy. A group of men lounged in the door of the "hash house" farther down the street, all friends of his, and he nodded to them. One of them turned quickly and looked down the intersecting street, saying something that made his companions turn and look with him. The man who had been standing quietly by the corner saloon had disappeared. Skinny, smiling knowingly, moved closer to Quigg's shack so as to be better able to see around the indicated corner, and half drew the Colt which he had just replaced in the holster. As he drew even with the corner of the building he heard Quigg's warning shout and dropped instantly, a bullet singing over him and into a window of a near-by store. He rolled around the corner, scrambled to his feet and dashed around the rear of the saloon and the corral behind it, crossed the street in four bounds and began to work up behind the buildings on his enemy's side of the street, cold with anger.

"Pot shooting, hey!" he gritted, savagely.

"Says I'm a-scared to face him, an' then tries *that. There*, damn you!" His Colt exploded and a piece of wood sprang from the corner board of Wright's store. "Missed!" he swore. "Anyhow, I've notified you, you coyote."

He sprang forward, turned the corner of the store and followed it to the street. When he came to the street end of the wall he leaped past it, his Colt preceding him. Finding no one to dispute with him he moved cautiously toward the other corner and stopped. Giving a quick glance around, he smiled suddenly, for the glass in Quigg's half-open door, with the black curtain behind it, made a fair mirror. He could see the reflection of Wright's corral and Ace leaning against it, ready to handle the brother if he should appear as a belligerent; and he could see along the other side of the store, where Dick Bradley, crouched, was half-way to the street and coming nearer at each slow step.

Skinny, remembering the shot which he had so narrowly escaped, resolved that he wouldn't take chances with a man who would pot shoot. He wheeled, slipped back along his side of the building, turned the rear corner and then, spurting, sprang out beyond the other wall, crying: "Here!"

Bradley, startled, fired under his arm as he leaped aside. Turning while in the air, his half-raised Colt described a swift, short arc and roared as he alighted. As the bullet sang past his enemy's ear he staggered and fell—and Skinny's smoking gun chocked into its holster.

"There, you coyote!" muttered the victor. "Yore brother is next if he wants to take it up."

As night fell Skinny rode into a small grove and prepared to camp there. Picketing his horse, he removed the saddle and dropped it where he would sleep, for a saddle makes a fair pillow. He threw his blanket after it and then started a quick, hot fire for his coffee-making. While gathering fuel for it he came across a large log and determined to use it for his night fire, and for that purpose carried it back to camp with him. It was not long before he had reduced the provisions in his saddle-bags and leaned back against a tree to enjoy a smoke. Suddenly he knocked the ashes from his pipe and grew thoughtful, finally slipping it into his pocket and getting up.

"That coyote's brother will know I went North an' all about it," he muttered. "He knows I've got to camp tonight an' he can foller a trail as good as th' next man. An' he knows I shot his brother. I reckon, mebby, he'll be some surprised."

An hour later a blanket-covered figure lay with its carefully covered feet to the fire, and its head, sheltered from the night air by a sombrero, lay on the saddle. A rifle barrel projected above the saddle, the dim flickering light of the greenwood fire and a stray beam or two from the moon glinted from its rustless surface. The fire was badly constructed, giving almost no light, while the leaves overhead shut out most of the moonlight.

Thirty yards away, in another clearing, a horse moved about at the end of a lariat and contentedly cropped the rich grass, enjoying a good night's rest. An hour passed, another, and a third and fourth, and then the horse's ears flicked forward as it turned its head to see what approached.

A crouched figure moved stealthily forward to the edge of the clearing, paused to read the brand on the animal's flank and then moved off toward the fitful light of the smoking fire. Closer and closer it drew until it made out the indistinct blanketed figure on the ground. A glint from the rifle barrel caused it to shrink back deeper into the shadows and raise the weapon it carried. For half a minute it stood thus and then, holding back the trigger of the rifle so there would be no warning clicks, drew the hammer to a full cock and let the trigger fall into place, slowly moving forward all the while. A passing breeze fanned the fire for an instant and threw the grotesque shadow of a stump across the quiet figure in the clearing.

The skulker raised his rifle and waited until he had figured out the exact mark and then a burst of fire and smoke leaped into the brush. He bent low to look under the smoke cloud and saw that the figure had not moved. Another flash split the night and then, assured beyond a doubt, he moved forward quickly.

"First shot!" he exclaimed with satisfaction. "I reckons you won't do no boastin' 'bout killin' Dick, damn you!"

As he was about to drop to his knees to search the body he started and sprang back, glancing fearfully around as he drew his Colt.

"Han's up!" came the command from the edge of the clearing as a man stepped into sight. "I reckon—" Skinny leaped aside as the other's gun roared out and fired from his hip; and Sam Bradley plunged across the blanket-covered log and leaves.

"There," Skinny soliloquized, moving forward. "I knowed they was coyotes, *both* of 'em. Knowed it all th' time."

Two days north of Skinny on the bank of Little Wind River a fire was burning itself out, while four men lay on the sand or squatted on their heels and watched it contentedly. "Yes, I got plumb sick of that country," Lanky Smith was saying, "an' when Buck sent for me to go up an' help him out, I pulls up, an' here I am."

"I never heard of th' Bar-20," replied a little, wizened man, whose eyes were so bright they seemed to be on fire. "Didn't know there was any ranches in that country."

"Buck's got th' only one!" responded Lanky, packing his pipe. "He's located on Snake Creek, an' he's got four thousand head. Reckon there ain't nobody within two hundred mile of him. Lewis said he's got a fine range an' all th' water he can use; but three men can't handle all them cows in *that* country, so I'm goin' up."

The little man's eyes seldom left Lanky's face, and he seemed to be studying the stranger very closely. When Lanky had ridden upon their noon-day camp the little man had not lost a movement that the stranger made and the other two, disappearing quietly, returned a little later and nodded reassuringly to their leader.

The wizened leader glanced at one of his companions, but spoke to Lanky. "George, here, said as how they finally got Butch Lynch. You didn't hear nothin' about it, did you?"

"They was a rumor down on Mesquite range that Butch was got. I heard his gang was wiped out. Well, it had to come sometime—he was carryin' things with a purty high hand for a long time. But I've done heard that before; more'n once, too. I reckon Butch is a li'l too slick to get hisself killed."

"Ever see him?" asked George carelessly.

"Never; an' don't want to. If them fellers can't clean their own range an' perfect their own cows, I ain't got no call to edge in."

"He's only a couple of inches taller'n Jim," observed the third man, glancing at his leader, "an' about th' same build. But he's hell on th' shoot. I saw him twice, but I was mindin' my own business."

Lanky nodded at the leader. "That'd make him about as tall as me. Size don't make no dif'rence no more—King Colt makes 'em look all alike."

Jim tossed away his cigarette and arose, stretching and grunting. "I shore ate too much," he complained. "Well, there's one thing about yore friend's ranch: he ain't got no rustlers to fight, so he ain't as bad off as he might be. I reckon he done named that crick hisself, didn't he? I never heard tell of it."

"Yes; so Lewis says. He says *he'd* called it Split Mesa Crick, 'cause it empties into Mesa River plumb acrost from a big mesa what's split in two as clean as a knife could 'a' done it."

"The Bar-20 expectin' you?" casually asked Jim as he picked up his saddle.

"Shore; they done sent for me. Me an' Buck is old friends. He was up in Montana ranchin' with a pardner, but Slippery Trendley kills his pardner's wife an' drove th' feller loco. Buck an' him hunted Slippery for two years an' finally drifted back south again. I dunno where Frenchy is. If it wasn't for me I reckon Buck'd still be on th' warpath. You bet he's expectin' me!" He turned and threw his saddle on the evil-tempered horse he rode and, cinching deftly, slung himself up by the stirrup. As he struck the saddle there was a sharp report and he pitched off and sprawled grotesquely on the sand. The little man peered through the smoke and slid his gun back into the holster. He turned to his companions, who looked on idly, and with but little interest. "Yo're damned right Butch Lynch is too slick to get killed. I ain't takin' no chances with nobody that rides over my trail these days. An', boys, I got a great scheme! It comes to me like a flash when he's talkin'. Come on, pull out; an' don't open yore traps till I says so. I want to figger this thing out to th' last card. George, shoot his cayuse; an' not another sound."

"But that's a good cayuse; worth easy—"

"Shoot it!" shouted Jim, his eyes snapping. It was unnecessary to add the alternative, for George and his companion had great respect for the lightning-like, deadly-accurate gun hands. He started to draw, but was too late. The crashing report seemed to come from the leader's holster, so quick had been the draw, and the horse sank slowly down, but unobserved. Two pairs of eyes asked a question of the little man and he sneered in reply as he lowered the gun. "It might 'a' been you. Hereafter do what I say. Now, go on ahead, an' keep quiet."

After riding along in silence for a little while the leader looked at his companions and called one of them to him. "George, this job is too big for the three of us; we can handle the ranch end, but not the drive. You know where Longhorn an' his bunch are holdin' out on th' Tortilla? All right; I've got a proposition for 'em, an' you are goin' up with it. It won't take you so long if you wake up an' don't loaf like you have been. Now you listen close, an' don't forget a word": and the little man shared the plan he had worked out, much to his companion's delight. Having made the messenger repeat it, the little man waved him off: "Get a-goin'; you bust some records or I'll bust you, savvy? Charley'll wait for you at that Split Mesa that fool puncher was a-talkin' about. An' don't you ride nowheres near it goin' up—keep to th' east of it. So-long!"

He watched the departing horseman swing in and pass Charley and saw the playful blow and counter. He smiled tolerantly as their words came back to him, George's growing fainter and fainter and Charley's louder and louder until they rang in his ears. The smile changed subtly and cynicism touched his face and lingered for a moment. "Fine, big bodies—nothing else," he muttered. "Big children, with children's heads. A little courage, if steadied; but what a paucity of brains! Good God, what a paucity of brains; what a lack of original thought!"

Of some localities it is said their inhabitants do not die, but dry up and blow away; this, so far as appearances went, seemed true of the horseman who loped along the north bank of Snake Creek, only he had not arrived at the "blow away" period. No one would have guessed his age as forty, for his leathery, wrinkled skin, thin, sun-bleached hair and wizened body justified a guess of sixty. A shrewd observer looking him over would find about the man a subtle air of potential destruction, which might have been caused by the way he wore his guns. A second look and the observer would turn away oppressed by a disquieting feeling that evaded analysis by lurking annoyingly just beyond the horizon of thought. But a man strong in intuition would not have turned away; he would have backed off, alert and tense. Nearing a corral which loomed up ahead, he pulled rein and went on at a walk, his brilliant eyes searching the surroundings with a thoroughness that missed nothing.

Buck Peters was complaining as he loafed for a precious half hour in front of the corral, but Red Connors and Bill Cassidy, his "outfit," discussed the low prices cattle were selling for, the over-stocked southern ranges and the crash that would come to the more heavily mortgaged ranches when the market broke. This was a golden opportunity to stock the little ranch, and Buck was taking advantage of it. But their foreman persisted in telling his troubles and finally, out of politeness, they listened. The burden of the foreman's plaint was the non-appearance of one Lanky Smith, an old friend. When the second herd had been delivered several weeks before, Buck, failing to persuade one of the drive outfit to remain, had asked the trail boss to send up Lanky, and the trail boss had promised.

Red stretched and yawned. "Mebby he's lost th' way."

The foreman snorted. "He can foller a plain trail, can't he? An' if he can ride past Split Mesa, he's a bigger fool than I ever heard of."

"Well, mebby he got drunk an—"

"He don't get that drunk." Astonishment killed whatever else he might have said, for a stranger had ridden around the corral and sat smiling at the surprise depicted on the faces of the three.

Buck and Red, too surprised to speak, smiled foolishly; Bill, also wordless, went upon his toes and tensed himself for that speed which had given to him hands never beaten on the draw. The stranger glanced at him, but saw nothing more than the level gaze that searched his squinting eyes for the soul back of them. The squint increased and he made a mental note concerning Bill Cassidy, which Bill Cassidy already had done regarding him.

"I'm called Tom Jayne," drawled the stranger. "I'm lookin' for Peters."

"Yes?" inquired Buck restlessly. "I'm him."

"Lewis sent me up to punch for you."

"You plumb surprised me," replied Buck. "We don't see nobody up here."

"Reckon not," agreed Jayne smiling. "I ain't been pestered a hull lot by th' inhabitants on my way up. I reckon there's more *buffalo* than men in this country."

Buck nodded. "An' blamed few buffalo, too. But Lewis didn't say nothin' about Lanky Smith, did he?"

"Yes; Smith, he goes up in th' Panhandle for to be a foreman. Lewis missed him. Th' Panhandle must be purty nigh as crowded as this country, I reckon," he smiled.

"Well," replied Buck, "anybody Lewis sends up is good enough for me. I'm payin' forty a month. Some day I'll pay more, if I'm able to an' it's earned."

Jayne nodded. "I'm aimin' to be here when th' pay is raised; an' I'll earn it."

"Then shake han's with Red an' Bill, an' come with me," said Buck. He led the way to the dugout, Bill and Red looking after him and the little newcomer. Red shook his head. "I dunno," he soliloquized, his eyes on the recruit's guns. They were worn low on the thighs, and the lower ends of the holsters were securely tied to the trousers. They were low enough to have the butts even with the swinging hands, so that no time would have to be wasted in reaching for them; and the sheaths were tied down, so they would not cling to the guns and come up with them on the draw. Bill wore his guns the same way for the same reasons. Red glanced at his friend. "He's a queer li'l cuss, Bill," he suggested. Receiving no reply, he grinned and tried again. "I said as how he's a queer li'l cuss." Bill stirred. "Huh?" he muttered. Red snorted. "Why, I says he's a drunk Injun mendin' socks. What in blazes you reckon I'd say!"

"Oh, somethin' like that; but you should 'a' said he's a—a weasel. A cold-blooded, ferocious li'l rat that'd kill for th' joy of it," and Bill moved leisurely to rope his horse.

Red looked after him, cogitating deeply. "Cussed if I hadn't, too! An' so he's a two-gun man, like Bill. Wears 'em plumb low an' tied. Yessir, he's a shore 'nuff weasel, all right." He turned and watched Bill riding away and he grinned as two pictures came to his mind. In the first he saw a youth enveloped in swirling clouds of acrid smoke as two Colts flashed and roared with a speed incredible; in the second there was no smoke, only the flashing of hands and the cold glitter of steel, so quick as to baffle the eye. And even now Bill practiced the draw, which pleased the foreman; cartridges were hard to get and cost money. Red roped his horse and threw on the saddle. As he swung off toward his section of the range he shook his head and scowled.

The Weasel had the eastern section, the wildest part of the ranch. It was cut and seared by arroyos, barrancas and draws; covered with mesquite and chaparral and broken by hills and mesas. The cattle on it were lost in the chaotic roughness and heavy vegetation and only showed themselves when they straggled down to the river or the creek to drink. A thousand head were supposed to be under his charge, but ten times that number would have been but a little more noticeable. He quickly learned ways of riding from one end of the section to the other without showing himself to anyone who might be a hundred yards from any point of the ride; he learned the best grazing portions and the safest trails from them to the ford opposite Split Mesa.

He was very careful not to show any interest in Split Hill Canyon and hardly even looked at it for the first week; then George returned from his journey and reported favorably. He also, with Longhorn's assistance, had picked out and learned a good drive route, and it was decided then and there to start things moving in earnest.

There were two thousand unbranded cattle on the ranch, the entire second drive herd; most of these were on the south section under Bill Cassidy, and the remainder were along the river. The Weasel learned that most of Bill's cows preferred the river to the creek and crossed his section to get there. That few returned was due, perhaps, to their preference for the eastern pasture. In a week the Weasel found the really good grazing portions of his section feeding more cows than they could keep on feeding; but suddenly the numbers fell to the pastures' capacity, without adding a head to Bill's herd.

Then came a day when Red had been riding so near the Weasel's section that he decided to go on down and meet him as he rode in for dinner. When Red finally caught sight of him the Weasel was riding slowly toward the bunkhouse, buried in thought. When his two men had returned from their scouting trip and reported the best way to drive; his and their work had begun in earnest. One small herd had been driven north and turned over to friends not far away, who took charge of the herd for the rest of the drive while the Weasel's companions returned to Split Hill.

Day after day he had noticed the diminishing number of cows on his sections, which was ideally created by nature to hide such a deficit, but from now on it would require all his cleverness and luck to hide the losses and he would be so busy shifting cattle that the rustling would have to ease up. One thing bothered him: Bill Cassidy was getting very suspicious, and he was not altogether satisfied that it was due to rivalry in gun-play. He was so deeply engrossed in this phase of the situation that he did not hear Red approaching over the soft sand and before Red could make his presence known something occurred that made him keep silent.

The Weasel, jarred by his horse, which shied and reared with a vigor and suddenness its rider believed entirely unwarranted under the circumstances, grabbed the reins in his left hand and jerked viciously, while his right, a blur of speed, drew and fired the heavy Colt with such deadly accuracy that the offending rattler's head dropped under its writhing, glistening coils, severed clean.

Red backed swiftly behind a chaparral and cogitated, shaking his head slowly. "Funny how bashful these gun-artists are!" he muttered. "Now has he been layin' for big bets, or was he—?" the words ceased, but the thoughts ran on and brought a scowl to Red's face as he debated the question.

The following day, a little before noon, two men stopped with sighs of relief at the corral and looked around. The little man riding the horse smiled as he glanced at his tall companion. "You won't have to hoof it no more, Skinny," he said gladly. "It's been a' awful experience for both of us, but you had th' worst end."

"Why, you stubborn li'l fool!" retorted Skinny. "I can walk back an' do it all over again!" He helped his companion down, stripped off the saddle and turned the animal loose with a resounding slap. "Huh!" he grunted as it kicked up its heels. "You oughta feel frisky, after loafin' for two weeks an' walkin' for another. Come on, Lanky," he said, turning. "There ain't nobody home, so we'll get a fire goin' an' rustle chuck for all han's.

They entered the dugout and looked around, Lanky sitting down to rest. His companion glanced at the mussed bunks and started a fire to get dinner for six. "Mebby they don't ride in at noon," suggested the convalescent. "Then we'll eat it all," grinned the cook. "It's comin' to us by this time."

The Weasel, riding toward the rear wall of the dugout, increased the pace when he saw the smoke pouring out of the chimney, but as he neared the hut he drew suddenly and listened, his expression of incredulity followed by one of amazement.

A hearty laugh and some shouted words sent him spinning around and back to the chaparral. As soon as he dared he swung north to the creek and risked its quick-sands to ride down its middle. Reaching the river he still kept to the water until he had crossed the ford and scrambled up the further bank to become lost in the windings of the canyon.

Very soon after the Weasel's departure Buck dismounted at the corral and stopped to listen. "Strangers," he muttered. "Glad they got th' fire goin', anyhow." Walking to the hut he entered and a yell met him at the instant recognition.

"Hullo, Buck!"

"Lanky!" he cried, leaping forward.

"Easy!" cautioned the convalescent, evading the hand. "I've been all shot up an' I ain't right yet."

"That so! How'd it happen?"

"Shake han's with Skinny Thompson, my fool nurse," laughed Lanky.

"I'm a fool, all right, helpin' *him*," grinned Skinny, gripping the hand. "But when I picks him up down in th' Li'l Wind River country I was a' angel. Looked after him for two weeks down there, an' put in another gettin' up here. Served him right, too, for runnin' away from me."

"Little Wind River country?" exclaimed Buck. "Why, I thought you was a foreman in th' Panhandle."

"Foreman nothin'," replied Lanky. "I was shot up by a li'l runt of a rustler an' left to die two hundred mile from nowhere. I wasn't expectin' no gun-play."

"He's ridin' up here," explained Skinny. "Meets three fellers an' gets friendly. They learns his business, an' drops him sudden when he's mountin'. Butch Lynch did th' shootin'. Butch got his name butcherin' th' law. He couldn't make a livin' at it. Then he got chased out of New Mexico for bein' mixed up in a free-love sect, an' pulls for Chicago. He reckoned he owned th' West, so he drifts down here again an' turns rustler. I dunno why he plugs Lanky, less'n he thinks Lanky knows him an' might try to hand him over. I'm honin' for to meet Butch."

Buck looked from one to the other in amazement, suspicion raging in his mind. "Why, I heard you went to th' Panhandle!" he ejaculated.

Skinny grinned: "A fine foreman he'd make, less'n for a hawg ranch!"

"Who told you that?" demanded Lanky, with sudden interest.

"Th' feller Lewis sent up in yore place."

"What?" shouted both in one voice, and Lanky gave a terse description of Butch Lynch. "That him?"

"That's him," answered Buck. "But he was alone. He'll be in soon, 'long with Bill an' Red—which way did you come?" he demanded eagerly. "Why, that was through his section—bet he saw you an' pulled out!"

Skinny reached for his rifle: "I'm goin' to see," he remarked.

"I'm with you," replied Buck.

"Me, too," asserted Lanky, but he was pushed back.

"You stay here," ordered Buck. "He might ride in. An' you've got to send Bill an' Red after us."

Lanky growled, but obeyed, and trained his rifle on the door. But the only man he saw was Red, whose exit was prompt when he had learned the facts.

Down on the south section Bill, unaware of the trend of events, looked over the little pasture that nestled between the hills and wondered where the small herd was. Up to within the last few days he always had found it here, loath to leave the heavy grass and the trickling spring, and watched over by "Old Mosshead," a very pugnacious steer. He scowled as he looked east and shook his head. "Bet they're crowdin' on th' Weasel's section, too. Reckon I'll go over and look into it. He'll be passin' remarks about th' way I ride sign." But he reached the river without being rewarded by the sight of many of the missing cows and he became pugnaciously inquisitive. He had searched in vain for awhile when he paused and glanced up the river, catching sight of a horseman who was pushing across at the ford. "Now, what's th' Weasel doin' over there?" he growled. "An' what's his hurry? I never did put no trust in him an' I'm going to see what's up."

Not far behind him a tall, lean man peered over the grass-fringed bank of a draw and watched him cross the river and disappear over the further bank. "Huh!" muttered Skinny, riding forward toward the river. "That *might* be one of Peters' punchers; but I'll trail him to make shore."

Down the river Red watched Bill cross the stream and then saw a stranger follow. "What th' hell!" he growled, pushing on. "That's one of 'em trailin' Bill!" and he, in turn, forded the river, hot on the trail of the stranger.

Bill finally dismounted near the mesa, proceeded on foot to the top of the nearest rise, and looked down into the canyon at a point where it widened into a circular basin half a mile across. Dust was arising in thin clouds as the missing cows, rounded up by three men, constantly increased the rustlers' herd. To the northwest lay the mesa, where the canyon narrowed to wind its tortuous way through; to the southeast lay the narrow gateway, where the towering, perpendicular cliffs began to melt into the sloping sides of hills and changed the canyon into a swiftly widening valley. The sight sent the puncher running toward the pass, for the herd had begun to move toward that outlet, urged by the Weasel and his nervous companions.

Back in the hills Skinny was disgusted and called himself names. To lose a man in less than a minute after trailing him for an hour was more than his sensitive soul could stand without protest. Bill had disappeared as completely as if he had taken wings and flown away. The disgusted trailer, dropping to all-fours because of his great height, went ahead, hoping to blunder upon the man he had lost.

Back of him was Red, whose grin was not so much caused by Skinny's dilemma, which he had sensed instantly, as it was by the inartistic spectacle

Skinny's mode of locomotion presented to the man behind. There was humor a-plenty in Red's make-up and the germ of mischief in his soul was always alert and willing; his finger itched to pull the trigger, and the grin spread as he pondered over the probable antics of the man ahead if he should be suddenly grazed by a bullet from the rear. "Bet he'd go right up on his head an' kick," Red chuckled—and it took all his will power to keep from experimenting. Then, suddenly, Skinny disappeared, and Red's fretful nature clawed at his tropical vocabulary with great success. It was only too true—Skinny had become absolutely lost, and the angry Bar-20 puncher crawled furiously this way and that without success, until Skinny gave him a hot clew that stung his face with grit and pebbles. He backed, sneezing, around a rock and wrestled with his dignity. Skinny, holed up not far from the canyon's rim, was throwing a mental fit and calling himself outrageous names. "An' he's been trailin' *me*! Hell of a fine fool *I* am; I'm awful smart today, *I* am! I done gave up my teethin' ring too soon, *I* did." He paused and scratched his head reflectively. "Huh! *This* is some populous region, an' th' inhabitants have peculiar ways. Now I wonder who's trailin' him? I'm due to get cross-eyed if I try to stalk 'em both."

A bullet, fired from an unexpected direction, removed the skin from the tip of Skinny's nose and sent a shock jarring clean through him. "Is that him, th' other feller, or somebody else?" he fretfully pondered, raising his hand to the crimson spot in the center of his face. He did not rub it—he rubbed the air immediately in front of it, and was careful to make no mistake in distance. The second bullet struck a rock just outside the gully and caromed over his head with a scream of baffled rage. He shrunk, lengthwise and sidewise, wishing he were not so long; but he kept on wriggling, backward. "Not enough English," he muttered. "Thank th' Lord he can't massé!"

The firing put a different aspect on things down in the basin. The Weasel crowded the herd into the gap too suddenly and caused a bad jam, while his companions, slipping away among the boulders and thickets, worked swiftly but cautiously up the cliff by taking advantage of the crevices and seams that scored the wall. Climbing like goats, they slipped over the top and began a game of hide and seek over the boulder-strewn, chaparral-covered plateau to cover the Weasel, who worked, without cover of any kind, in the basin.

Red was deep in some fine calculations of angles when his sombrero slid off his head and displayed a new hole, which edged at him with Cyclopean ferocity. He ducked, and shattered all existing records for the crawl, stopping finally when he had covered twenty yards and collected many thorns and bruises. He had worked close to the edge of the cliff and as he turned to circle back of his enemy he chanced to glance over the rim, swore angrily and fired. The Weasel, saving himself from being pinned under his stricken horse, leaped for the shelter of the cover near the foot of the basin's wall. Red was about to fire again when he swayed and slipped down behind a boulder. The rustler, twenty yards away, began to maneuver for another shot when Skinny's rifle cracked viciously and the cattle thief, staggering to the edge of the cliff, stumbled, fought for his balance, and plunged down into the basin. His companion, crawling swiftly toward Skinny's smoke, showed himself long enough for Red to swing his rifle and shoot offhand. At that moment Skinny caught sight of him and believed he understood the situation. "You Conners or Cassidy?" he demanded over the sights. Red's answer made him leap forward and in a few moments the wounded man, bandaged and supported by his new friend, hobbled to the rim of the basin in time to see the last act of the tragedy.

The gateway, now free of cattle, lay open and the Weasel dashed for it in an attempt to gain the horses picketed on the other side. He had seen George plunge off the cliff and knew that the game was up. As he leaped from his cover Skinny's head showed over the rim of the cliff and his bullet sang shrilly over the rustler's head. The second shot was closer, but before Skinny could try again Red's warning cry made him lower the rifle and stare at the gateway.

The Weasel saw it at the same time, slowed to a rapid walk, but kept on for the pass, his eyes riveted malevolently on the youth who had suddenly arisen from behind a boulder and started to meet him.

"It's easy to get him now," growled Skinny, starting to raise the rifle, a picture of Lanky's narrow escape coming to his mind.

"Bill's right in line," whispered Red, leaning forward tensely and robbing his other senses to strengthen sight. "They're th' best in th' Southwest," he breathed.

Below them Bill and the Weasel calmly advanced, neither hurried nor touching a gun. Sixty yards separated them—fifty—forty—thirty—"God Almighty!" whispered Skinny, his nails cutting into his calloused palms. Red only quivered. Twenty-five—twenty. Then the Weasel slowed down, crouching a little, and his swinging hands kept closer to his thighs. Bill, though moving slowly, stood erect and did not change his pace. Perspiration beaded the faces of the watchers on the cliff and they almost stopped breathing. This was worse than they had expected—forty yards would have been close enough to start shooting. "It's a pure case of speed now," whispered Red, suddenly understanding. The promised lesson was due—the lesson the Weasel had promised to give Bill on the draw. Accuracy deliberately was being eliminated by that cold-blooded advance. Fifteen yards—ten—eight—six—five—and a flurry of smoke. There had been no movement to the eyes of the watchers—just smoke, and the flat reports, that came to them like two beats of a snare drum's roll. Then they saw Bill step back as the Weasel pitched forward. He raised his eyes to meet them and nodded. "Come on, get th' cayuses. We gotta round up th' herd afore it scatters," he shouted.

Red leaned against Skinny and laughed senselessly. "Ain't he a damned fool?"

Skinny stirred and nodded. "He shore is; but come on. I don't want no argument with *him*."

CHAPTER 3

Jimmy Price

On a range far to the north, Jimmy Price, a youth as time measures age, followed the barranca's edge and whistled cheerfully. He had never heard of the Bar-20, and would have showed no interest if he had heard of it, so long as it lay so far away. He was abroad in search of adventure and work, and while his finances were almost at ebb tide he had youth, health, courage and that temperament that laughs at hard luck and believes in miracles. The tide was so low it must turn soon and work would be forthcoming when he needed it. Sitting in the saddle with characteristic erectness he loped down a hill and glanced at the faint trail that led into the hills to the west. Cogitating a moment he followed it and soon saw a cow, and soon after others.

"I'll round up th' ranch house, get a job for awhile an' then drift on south again," he thought, and the whistle rang out with renewed cheerfulness.

He noticed that the trail kept to the low ground, skirting even little hills and showing marked preference for arroyos and draws with but little regard, apparently, for direction or miles. He had just begun to cross a small pasture between two hills when a sharp voice asked a question: "Where you goin'?"

He wheeled and saw a bewhiskered horseman sitting quietly behind a thicket. The stranger held a rifle at the ready and was examining him critically. "Where you goin'?" repeated the stranger, ominously. "An' what's yore business?"

Jimmy bridled at the other's impudent curiosity and the tones in which it was voiced, and as he looked the stranger over a contemptuous smile flickered about his thin lips. "Why, I'm goin' west, an' I'm lookin' for th' sunset," he answered with an exasperating drawl. "Ain't seen it, have you?"

The other's expression remained unchanged, as if he had not heard the flippant and pugnacious answer. "Where you goin' an' what for?" he demanded again.

Jimmy turned further around in the saddle and his eyes narrowed. "I'm goin' to mind my own business, because it's healthy," he retorted. "You th' President, or only a king?" he demanded, sarcastically.

"I'm boss of Tortilla range," came the even reply. "You answer my question."

"Then you can gimme a job an' save me a lot of fool ridin'," smiled Jimmy. "It'll be some experience workin' for a sour dough as ornery as you are. Fifty per', an' all th' rest of it. Where do I eat an' sleep?"

The stranger gazed steadily at the cool, impudent youngster, who returned the look with an ironical smile. "Who sent you out here?" he demanded with blunt directness.

"Nobody," smiled Jimmy. "Nobody sends me nowhere, never, 'less 'n I want to go. Purty near time to eat, ain't it?"

"Come over here," commanded the Boss of Tortilla range.

"It's closer from you to me than from me to you."

"Yo're some sassy, now ain't you? I've got a notion to drop you an' save somebody else th' job."

"He'll be lucky if you do, 'cause when that gent drifts along I'm natchurally goin' to get there first. It's been tried already."

Anger glinted in the Boss's eyes, but slowly faded as a grim smile fought its way into view. "I've a mind to give you a job just for th' great pleasure of bustin' yore spirit."

"If yo're bettin' on that card you wants to have a copper handy," bantered Jimmy. "It's awful fatal when it's played to win."

"What's yore name, you cub?"

"Elijah—ain't I done prophesied? When do I start punchin' yore eight cows, Boss?"

"Right now! I like yore infernal gall; an' there's a pleasant time comin' when I starts again' that spirit."

"Then my name's Jimmy, which is enough for you to know. Which cow do I punch first?" he grinned.

"You ride ahead along th' trail. I'll show you where you eat," smiled the Boss, riding toward him.

Jimmy's face took on an expression of innocence that was ludicrous.

"I allus let age go first," he slowly responded. "I might get lost if I lead. I'm plumb polite, I am."

The Boss looked searchingly at him and the smile faded. "What you mean by that?"

"Just what I said. I'm plumb polite, an' hereby provin' it. I allus insist on bein' polite. Otherwise, gimme my month's pay an' I'll resign. But I'm shore some puncher," he laughed.

"I observed yore politeness. I'm surprised you even know th' term. But are you shore you won't get lost if you foller me?" asked the Boss with great sarcasm.

"Oh, that's a chance I gotta take," Jimmy replied as his new employer drew up alongside. "Anyhow, yo're better lookin' from behind."

"Jimmy, my lad," observed the Boss, sorrowfully shaking his head, "I shore sympathize with th' shortness of yore sweet young life. Somebody's natchurally goin' to spread you all over some dismal landscape one of these days."

"An' he'll be a whole lot lucky if I ain't around when he tries it," grinned Jimmy. "I got a' awful temper when I'm riled, an' I reckons that would rile me up quite a lot."

The Boss laughed softly and pushed on ahead, Jimmy flushing a little from shame of his suspicions. But a hundred yards behind him, riding noiselessly on the sand and grass, was a man who had emerged from another thicket when he saw the Boss go ahead; and he did not for one instant remove his eyes from the new member of the outfit. Jimmy, due to an uncanny instinct, soon realized it, though he did not look around. "Huh! Reckon I'm th' meat in this sandwich. Say, Boss, who's th' Injun ridin' behind me?" he asked.

"That's Longhorn. Look out or he'll gore you," replied the Boss.

"'That'd be a bloody shame,' as th' Englishman said. Are all his habits as pleasant an' sociable?"

"They're mostly worse; he's a two-gun man."

"Now ain't that lovely! Wonder what he'd do if I scratch my laig sudden?"

"Let me know ahead of time, so I can get out of th' way. If you do that it'll save me fifty dollars an' a lot of worry."

"Huh! I won't save it for you. But I wish I could get out my smokin' what's in my hip pocket, without Longhorn gamblin' on th' move."

The next day Jimmy rode the west section harassed by many emotions. He was weaponless, much to his chagrin and rage. He rode a horse that was such a ludicrous excuse that it made escape out of the question, and they even locked it in the corral at night. He was always under the eyes of a man who believed him ignorant of the surveillance. He already knew that three different brands of cattle "belonged" to the "ranch," and his meager experience was sufficient to acquaint him with a blotted brand when the work had been carelessly done. The Boss was the foreman and his outfit, so far as Jimmy knew, consisted of Brazo Charley and Longhorn, both of whom worked nights. The smiling explanation of the Boss, when Jimmy's guns had been locked up, he knew to be only part truth. "Yo're so plumb fighty we dassn't let you have 'em," the Boss had said. "If we got to bust yore high-strung, unlovely spirit without killin' you, you can't have no guns. An' th' corral gate is shore padlocked, so keep th' cayuse I gave you."

Jimmy, enraged, sprang forward to grab at his gun, but Longhorn, dexterously tripping him, leaned against the wall and grinned evilly as the angry youth scrambled to his feet. "Easy, Kid," remarked the gun-man, a Colt swinging carelessly in his hand. "You'll get as you give," he grunted. "Mind yore own affairs an' work, an' we'll treat you right. Otherwise—" the shrugging shoulders made further explanations unnecessary.

Jimmy looked from one to the other and silently wheeled, gained the decrepit horse and rode out to his allotted range, where he saturated the air with impotent profanity. Chancing to look back he saw a steer wheel and face the south; and at other times during the day he saw that repeated by other cattle— nor was this the only sign of trailing. Having nothing to do but ride and observe the cattle, which showed no desire to stray beyond the range allotted to them, he observed very thoroughly; and when he rode back to the bunkhouse that night he had deciphered the original brand on his cows and also the foundation for that worn by Brazo Charley's herd on the section next to him. "I dunno where mine come from, but Charley's uster belong to th' C I, over near Sagebrush basin. That's a good hundred miles from here, too. Just wait till I get a gun! Trip me an' steal my guns, huh? If I had a good cayuse I'd have that C I bunch over here right quick! I reckon they'd like to see this herd."

When he reached the bunkhouse all traces of his anger had disappeared and he ate hungrily during the silent meal.

When Longhorn and Brazo pushed away from the table Jimmy followed suit and talked pleasantly of things common to cowmen, until the two picked up their saddles and rifles and departed in the direction of the corral, the Boss staying with Jimmy and effectually blocking the door. But he could not block Jimmy's hearing so easily and when the faint sound of hoofbeats rolled past the bunkhouse Jimmy knew that there were more than two men doing the riding. He concluded the number to be five, and perhaps six; but his face gave no indication of his mind's occupation.

"Play crib?" abruptly demanded the Boss, taking a well-worn deck of cards from a shelf. Jimmy nodded and the game was soon going on. "Seventeen," grunted the Boss, pegging slowly. "Pair of fools, they are," he growled. "Both plumb stuck on one gal an' they go courtin' together. She reminds *me* of a slab of bacon, she's that homely."

Jimmy laughed at the obvious lie. "Well, a gal's a gal out here," he replied.

"Twenty for a pair," he remarked. He wondered, as he pegged, if it was necessary to take along an escort when one went courting on the Tortilla. The idea of Brazo and Longhorn tolerating any rival or any company when courting struck him as ludicrous. "An' which is goin' to win out, do you reckon?"

"Longhorn—he's bad; an' a better gun-man. Twenty-three for six. Got th' other tray?" anxiously grinned the Boss.

"Nothin' but an eight—that's two for th' go. My crib?"

The Boss nodded. "Ugly as blazes," he mused. "*I* wouldn't court her, not even in th' dark—huh! Fifteen two an' a pair. That's bad goin', very bad goin'," he sighed as he pegged.

"But you can't tell nothin' 'bout wimmen from their looks," remarked Jimmy, with the grave assurance of a man whose experience in that line covered years instead of weeks. "Now I knowed a right purty gal once. She was plumb sweet an' tender an' clingin', she was. An' she had high ideas, she did. She went an' told me she wouldn't have nothin' to do with no man what wasn't honest, an' all that. But when a feller I knowed rid in to her place one night she shore hid him under her bed for three days an' nights. He had got real popular with a certain posse because he was careless with a straight iron. Folks fairly yearned for to get a good look at him. They rid up to her place and she lied so sweet an' perfect they shore apologized for even botherin' her. Who'd 'a' thought to look under *her* bed, anyhow? Some day he'll go back an' natchurally run off with that li'l gal." He scanned his hand and reached for the pegs. "Got eight here," he grunted.

The Boss regarded him closely. "She stood off a posse with her eyes an' mouth, eh?"

"Didn't have to stand 'em off. They was plumb ashamed th' minute they saw her blushes. An' they was plumb sorry for her bein' even a li'l interested in a no-account brand-blotter like—him." He turned the crib over and spread it out with a sort of disgust. "Come purty near bein' somethin' in that crib," he growled.

"An' did you know that feller?" the Boss asked carelessly.

Jimmy started a little. "Why, yes; he was once a pal of mine. But he got so he could blot a brand plumb clever. Us cow-punchers shore like to gamble. We are plumb childish th' way we bust into trouble. I never seen one yet that was worth anythin' that wouldn't take 'most any kind of fool chance just for th' devilment of it."

The Boss ruffled his cards reflectively. "Yes; we are a careless breed. Sort of flighty an' reckless. Do you think that gal's still in love with you? Wimmin' is fickle," he laughed.

"*She* ain't," retorted Jimmy with spirit. "She'll wait all right—for him."

The Boss smiled cynically. "You can't hide it, Jimmy. Yo're th' man what got so popular with th' sheriff. Ain't you?"

Jimmy half arose, but the Boss waved him to be seated again. "Why, you ain't got nothin' to fear out here," he assured him. "We sorta like fellers that'll take a chance. I reckon we all have took th' short end one time or another. An' I got th' idea mebby yo're worth more'n fifty a month. Take any chances for a hundred?"

Jimmy relaxed and grinned cheerfully. "I reckon I'd do a whole lot for a hundred real dollars every month."

"Yo're on, fur's I'm concerned. I'll have to speak to th' boys about it, first. Well, I'm goin' to turn in. You ride Brazo's an' yore own range for th' next couple of days. Good night."

Jimmy arose and sauntered carelessly to the door, watched the Boss enter his own house, and then sat down on the wash bench and gazed contentedly across the moonlit range. "Gosh," he laughed as he went over his story of the beautiful girl with the high ideals. "I'm gettin' to be a sumptuous liar, I am. It comes so easy I gotta look out or I'll get th' habit. I'd do mor'n lie, too, to get my gun back, all right." He stretched ecstatically and then sat up straight. The Boss was coming toward him and something in his hand glittered in the soft moonlight as it swung back and forth. "Forget somethin'?" called Jimmy.

"You better stop watchin' th' moonlight," laughed the Boss as he drew near. "That's a bad sign—'specially while that gal's waitin' for you. Here's yore gun an' belt—I reckoned mebby you might need it."

Jimmy chuckled as he took the weapon. "I ain't so shore 'bout needin' it, but I was plumb lost without it. Kept feelin' for it all th' time an' it was gettin' on my nerves." He weighed it critically and spun the cylinder, carelessly feeling for the lead in the chambers as the cylinder stopped. Every one was loaded and a thrill of fierce joy surged over him. But he was suspicious—the offer was too quick and transparent. Slipping on the belt he let the gun slide into the blackened holster and grinned up at the Boss. "Much obliged. It feels right, now." He drew the Colt again and emptied the cartridges into his hand. "Them's th' only pills as will cure troubles a doctor can't touch," he observed, holding one up close to his face and shaking it at the smiling Boss in the way of emphasis. His quick ear caught the sound he strained to hear, the soft swish inside the shell. "Them's Law in this country," he soliloquized as he slid the tested shell in one particular chamber and filled all the others. "Yessir," he remarked as the cylinder slowly revolved until he had counted the right number of clicks and knew that the tested shell was in the right place. "Yes-sir, them's The Law."

The soft moonlight suddenly kissed the leveled barrel and showed the determination that marked the youthful face behind it. "An' it shore works both ways, Boss," he said harshly. "Put up yore paws!"

As the Boss leaped forward the hammer fell and caused a faint, cap-like report. Then the stars streamed across Jimmy's vision and became blotted out by an inky-black curtain that suddenly enveloped him. The Boss picked up the gun and, tossing it on the bench, waited for the prostrate youth to regain his senses.

Jimmy stirred and looked around, his eyes losing their look of vacancy and slowly filling with murderous hatred as he saw the man above him and remembered what had occurred. "Sand *sounds* like powder, my youthful friend," the Boss was saying, "but it don't *work* like powder. I purty near swallowed yore gal story; but I sorta reckoned mebby I better make shore about you. Yo're clever, Jimmy; so clever that I dassn't take no chances with you. I'll just tie you up till th' boys come back—we both know what they'll say. I'd 'a' done it then only I like you; an' I wish you had been in earnest about joinin' us. Now get up."

Jimmy arose slowly and cautiously and then moved like a flash, only to look down the barrel of a Colt. His clenched hands fell to his side and he bowed his head; but the Boss was too wary to be caught by any pretenses of a broken spirit. "Turn 'round an' hol' up yore han's," he ordered. "I'll blow you apart if you even squirms."

Jimmy obeyed, seething with impotent fury, but the steady pressure of the Colt on his back told him how useless it was to resist. Life was good, even a few hours of it, for in those few hours perhaps a chance would come to him. The rope that had hung on the wall passed over his wrists and in a few moments he was helpless. "Now sit down," came the order and the prisoner obeyed sullenly. The Boss went in the bunkhouse and soon returned, picked up the captive and, carrying him to the bunk prepared for him, dumped him in it, tied a few more knots and, closing the door, securely propped it shut and strode toward his own quarters, swearing savagely under his breath.

An hour later, while a string of horsemen rode along the crooked, low-lying trail across the Tortilla, plain in the moonlight, a figure at the bunkhouse turned the corner, slipped to the door and carefully removed the props.

Waiting a moment it opened the door slowly and slipped into the black interior, and chuckled at the sarcastic challenge from the bunk. "Sneakin' back again, hey?" blazed Jimmy, trying in vain to bridge on his head and heels and turn over to face the intruder. "Turn me loose an' gimme a gun—I oughta have a chance!"

"All right," said a quiet, strange voice. "That's what I'm here for; but don't talk so loud."

"Who're you?"

"My name's Cassidy. I'm from th' Bar-20, what owns them cows you been abusin'. Huh! he shore tied some knots! Wasn't takin' no more chances with you, all right!"

"G'wan! He never did take none."

"So I've observed. Get th' blood circulatin' an' I'll give you some warmedicine for that useless gun of yourn what ain't sand."

"Good for you! I'll sidle up agin' that shack an' fill him so full of lead he won't know what hit him!"

"Well, every man does things in his own way; but I've been thinkin' he oughta have a chance. He shore gave you some, Kid. Longhorn'd 'a' shot you quick tonight."

"Yes; an' I'm goin' to get him, too!"

"Now you ain't got no gratitude," sighed Cassidy. "You want to hog it all. I was figgerin' to clean out this place by myself, but now you cut in an' want to freeze me out. But, Kid, mebby Longhorn won't come back no more. My outfit's a-layin' for his li'l party. I sent 'em down word to expect a call on our north section; an' I reckon they got a purty good idea of th' way up here, in case they don't receive Longhorn an' his friends as per schedule."

"How long you been up here?" asked Jimmy in surprise, pausing in his operation of starting his blood to circulating.

"Long enough to know a lot about this layout. For instance, I know yo're honest. That's why I cut you loose tonight. You see, my friends might drop in here any minute an' if you was in bad company they might make a mistake. They acts some hasty, at times. I'm also offerin' you a good job if you wants it. We need another man."

"I'm yourn, all right. An' I reckon I will give th' Boss a chance. He'll be more surprised, that way."

Cassidy nodded in the dark. "Yes, I reckon so; he'll have time to wonder a li'l. Now you tell me how yo're goin' at this game."

But he didn't get a chance then, for his companion, listening intently, whistled softly and received an answer. In another moment the room was full of figures and the soft buzz of animated conversation held his interest. "All right," said a deep voice. "We'll keep on an' get that herd started back at daylight. If Longhorn shows up you can handle him; if you can't, there's yore friend Jimmy," and the soft laugh warmed Jimmy's heart. "Why, Buck," replied

Jimmy's friend, "he's spoke for that job already." The foreman turned and paused as he stood in the door. "Don't forget; you ain't to wait for us. Take Jimmy, if you wants, an' head for Oleson's. I ain't shore that herd of hissn is good enough for us. We'll handle this li'l drive-herd easy. So-long."

Red Connors stuck his head through a small window: "Hey, if Longhorn shows up, give him my compliments. I shore bungled that shot."

"'Tain't th' first," chuckled Cassidy. But Buck cut short the arguments and led the way to Jimmy's pasture.

At daylight the Boss rolled out of his bunk, started a fire and put on a kettle of water to get hot. Buckling on his gun he opened the door and started toward the bunkhouse, where everything appeared to be as he had left it the night before.

"It's a cussed shame," he growled. "But I can't risk him bringin' a posse out here. *What* th' devil!" he shouted as he ducked. A bullet sang over his head, high above him, and he glanced at the bunkhouse with renewed interest.

Having notified the Boss of his intentions and of the change in the situation, Jimmy walked around the corner of the house and sent one dangerously close to strengthen the idea that sand was no longer sand. But the Boss had surmised this instantly and was greatly shocked by such miraculous happenings on his range. He nodded cheerfully at the nearing youth and as cheerfully raised his gun. "An' he gave me a chance, too! He could 'a' got me easy if he didn't warn me! Well, here goes, Kid," he muttered, firing.

Jimmy promptly replied and scored a hit. It was not much of a hit, but it carried reflection in its sting. The Boss's heart hardened as he flinched instinctively and he sent forth his shots with cool deliberation. Jimmy swayed and stopped, which sent the Boss forward on the jump. But the youth was only further proving his cleverness against a man whom he could not beat at so long a range. As the Boss stopped again to get the work over with, a flash of smoke spurted from Jimmy's hand and the rustler spun half way around, stumbled and fell. Jimmy paused in indecision, a little suspicious of the fall, but a noise behind him made him wheel around to look.

A horseman, having topped the little hill just behind the bunkhouse, was racing down the slope as fast as his worn-out horse could carry him, and in his upraised hand a Colt glittered as it swung down to become lost in a spurt of smoke. Longhorn, returning to warn his chief, felt savage elation at this opportunity to unload quite a cargo of accumulated grouches of various kinds and sizes, which collection he had picked up from the Bar-20 northward in a running fight of twenty miles. Only a lucky cross trail, that had led him off at a tangent and somehow escaped the eyes of his pursuers, had saved him from the fate of his companions.

Jimmy swung his gun on the newcomer, but it only clicked, and the vexed youth darted and dodged and ducked with a speed and agility very creditable as he jammed cartridges into the empty chambers. Jimmy's interest in the new conditions made him forget that he had a gun and he stared in rapt and delighted anticipation at the cloud of dust that swirled suddenly from behind the corral and raced toward the disgruntled Mr. Longhorn, shouting Red's message as it came.

Mr. Cassidy sat jauntily erect and guided his fresh, gingery mount by the pressure of cunning knees. The brim of his big sombrero, pinned back against the crown by the pressure of the wind, revealed the determination and optimism that struggled to show itself around his firmly set lips; his neckerchief flapped and cracked behind his head and the hairs of his snow-white goatskin chaps rippled like a thing of life and caused Jimmy, even in his fascinated interest, to covet them.

But Longhorn's soul held no reverence for goatskin and he cursed harder when Red's compliments struck his ear about the time one of Cassidy's struck his shoulder. He was firing hastily against a man who shot as though the devil had been his teacher. The man from the Bar-20 used two guns and they roared like the roll of a drum and flashed through the heavy, low-lying cloud of swirling smoke like the darting tongue of an angry snake.

Longhorn, enveloped in the acrid smoke of his own gun, which wrapped him like a gaseous shroud, knew that his end had come. He was being shot to pieces by a two-gun man, the like of whose skill he had never before seen or heard of. As the last note of the short, five second, cracking tattoo died away Mr. Cassidy slipped his empty guns in their holsters and turned his pony's head toward the fascinated spectator, whose mouth offered easy entry to smoke and dust. As Cassidy glanced carelessly back at the late rustler Jimmy shut his mouth, gulped, opened it to speak, shut it again and cleared his dry throat. Looking from Cassidy to Longhorn and back again, he opened his mouth once more. "You—you—what'd'ju pay for them chaps?" he blurted, idiotically.

CHAPTER 4

■ ◆◆◆◆◆◆ ■ ◆◆◆◆◆◆◆◆◆◆◆◆◆◆◆◆◆◆◆◆◆◆◆◆◆◆◆◆◆ ■ ◆◆◆◆◆◆ ■

Jimmy Visits Sharpsville

Bill Cassidy rode slowly into Sharpsville and dismounted in front of Carter's Emporium, nodding carelessly to the loungers hugging the shade of the store. "Howd'y," he said. "Seen anything of Jimmy Price—a kid, but about my height, with brown hair and a devilish disposition?"

Carter stretched and yawned, a signal for a salvo of yawns. "Nope, thank God. You needn't describe nothin' about that Price cub to none of us. *We* know him. He spent three days here about a year ago, an' th' town's been sorta restin' up ever since. You don't mean for to tell us he's comin' here again!" he exclaimed, sitting up with a jerk.

Bill laughed at the expression. "As long as you yearn for him so powerful hard, why I gotta tell you he's on his way, anyhow. I had to go east for a day's ride an' he headed this way. He's to meet me here."

Carter turned and looked at the others blankly. Old Dad Johnson nervously stroked his chin. "Well, then he'll git here, all right," he prophesied pessimistically. "He usually gets where he starts for; an' I'm plumb glad I'm goin' on tomorrow."

"Ha, ha!" laughed George Bruce. "So'm I goin' on, by Scott!"

Grunts and envious looks came from the group and Carter squirmed uneasily. "That's just like you fellers, runnin' away an' leavin' me to face it. An' it was you fellers what played most of th' tricks on him last time he was here. Huh! now I gotta pay for 'em," he growled.

Bill glanced over the gloomy circle and laughed heartily. Two faces out of seven were bright, Dad's particularly so. "Well, he seems to be quite a favorite around here," he grinned.

Carter snorted. "Huh! Seems to be nothin'."

"He ain't exactly a favorite," muttered Dawson. "He's a—a—an event; that's what he is!"

Carter nodded. "Yep; that's what he is, 'though you just can't help likin' th' cub, he's that cheerful in his devilment."

Charley Logan stretched and yawned. "Didn't hear nothin' about no Injuns, did you? A feller rid through here yesterday an' said they was out again."

Bill nodded. "Yes; I did. An' there's a lot of rumors goin' around. They've been over in th' Crazy Butte country an' I heard they raided through th' Little Mountain Valley last week. Anyhow, th' Seventh is out after em', in four sections."

"Th' Seventh is *a* regiment," asserted George Bruce. "Leastawise it was when I was in it. It is th' best in th' Service."

Dad snorted. "Listen to him! It was when *he* was in it! Lordy, Lordy, Lordy!" he chuckled.

"There hain't no cavalry slick enough to ketch Apaches," declared Hank, dogmatically. "Troops has too many fixin's an' sech. You gotta travel light an' live without eatin' an' drinkin' to ketch them Injuns; an' then you never hardly sometimes see 'em, at that."

"Lemme tell you, Mosshead, th' Seventh can lick all th' Injuns ever spawned!" asserted Bruce with heat. "It wiped out Black Kettle's camp, in th' dead of winter, too!"

"That was Custer as did that," snorted Carter.

"Well, he was leadin' th' Seventh, same as he is now!"

Charley Logan shook his head. "We are talking about ketchin' 'em, not fightin' 'em. An' no cavalry in th' hull country can ketch 'Paches in *this* country—it's too rough. 'Paches are only scared of punchers."

"Shore," asserted Carter. "Apaches laugh at troops, less'n it's a pitched battle, when they don't. Cavalry chases 'em so fur an' no farther; punchers chase 'em inter hell, out of it an' back again."

"They shore is 'lusive," cogitated Lefty Dawson, carefully deluging a fly ten feet away and shifting his cud for another shot. "An' I, for one, admits I ain't hankerin' for to chase 'em close."

"Wish we could get that cub Jimmy to chase some," exclaimed Carter. "Afore he gits here," he explained, thoughtfully.

"Oh, he's all right, Carter," spoke up Lefty. "We was all of us young and playful onct."

"But we all warn't he-devils workin' day *an'* night tryin' to make our betters miserable!"

"Oh, he's a good kid," remarked Dad. "I sorta hates to miss him. Anyhow, we got th' best of him, last time."

Bill finished rolling a cigarette, lit it and slowly addressed them. "Well, all I got to say is that he suits me right plumb down to th' ground. Now, just lemme tell you somethin' about Jimmy," and he gave them the story of Jimmy's part in the happenings on Tortilla Range, to the great delight of his audience.

"By Scott, it's just like him!" chuckled George Bruce.

"That's shore Jimmy, all right," laughed Lefty.

"What did *I* tell you?" beamed Dad. "He's a heller, he is. He's all right!"

"Then why don't you stay an' see him?" demanded Carter.

"I gotta go on, or I would. Yessir, I would!"

"Reckon them Injuns won't git so fur north as here," suggested Carter hopefully, and harking back to the subject which lay heaviest on his mind. "They've only been here twict in ten years."

"Which was twice too often," asserted Lefty.

"Th' last time they was here," remarked Dad, reminiscently, "they didn't stop long; though where they went to I dunno. We gave 'em more'n they could handle. That was th' time I just bought that new Sharps rifle, an' what I done with that gun was turrible." He paused to gather the facts in the right order before he told the story, and when he looked around again he flushed and swore. The audience had silently faded away to escape the moth-eaten story they knew by heart. The fact that Dad usually improved it and his part in it, each time he told it, did not lure them. "Cussed ingrates!" he swore, turning to Bill. "They're plumb jealous!"

"They act like it, anyhow," agreed Bill soberly. "I'd like to hear it, but I'm too thirsty. Come in an' have one with me?" The story was indefinitely postponed.

An accordion wheezed down the street and a mouth organ tried desperately to join in from the saloon next door, but, owing to a great difference in memory, did not harmonize. A roar of laughter from Dawson's, and the loud clink of glasses told where Dad's would-have-been audience then was. Carter walked around his counter and seated himself in his favorite place against the door jamb. Bill, having eluded Dad, sat on a keg of edibles and smoked in silence and content, occasionally slapping at the flies which buzzed persistently around his head. Knocking the ashes from the cigarette he leaned back lazily and looked at Carter. "Wonder where he is?" he muttered.

"Huh?" grunted the proprietor, glancing around. "Oh, you worryin' about that yearlin'? Well, you needn't! Nothin' never sidetracks Jimmy."

A fusillade of shots made Bill stand up, and Carter leaped to his feet and dashed toward the counter. But he paused and looked around foolishly. "That's his yell," he explained. "Didn't I tell you? He's arrove, same as usual."

The drumming of hoofs came rapidly nearer and heads popped out of windows and doors, each head flanked by a rifle barrel. Above a swirling cloud of dust glinted a spurting Colt and thrust through the smudge was a hand waving a strange collection of articles.

"Hullo, Kid!" shouted Dawson. "What you got? See any Injuns?"

"It's a G-string an' a medicine-bag, by all that's holy!" cried Dad from the harness shop. "Where'd you git 'em, Jimmy?"

Jimmy drew rein and slid to a stand, pricking his nettlesome "Calico" until it pranced to suit him. Waving the Apache breech-cloth, the medicine-bag and a stocking-shaped moccasin in one hand, he proudly held up an old, dirty, battered Winchester repeater in the other and whooped a war-cry.

"Blame my hide!" shouted Dad, running out into the street. "It *is* a G-string! He's gone an' got one of 'em! He's gone an' got a 'Pache! Good boy, Kid! An' how'd you do it?"

Carter plodded through the dust with Bill close behind. "*Where'd* you do it?" demanded the proprietor eagerly. To Carter location meant more than method. He was plainly nervous. When he reached the crowd he, in turn, examined the trophies. They were genuine, and on the G-string was a splotch of crimson, muddy with dust.

"What's in the war-bag, Kid?" demanded Lefty, preparing to see for himself. Jimmy snatched it from his hands. "You never mind what's in it, Freckle-face!" he snapped. "That's my bag, *now*. Want to spoil my luck?"

"How'd you do it?" demanded Dad breathlessly.

"*Where'd* you do it?" snapped Carter. He glanced hurriedly around the horizon and repeated the question with vehemence. "Where'd you get him?"

"In th' groin, first. Then through th'—"

"I don't mean where, I mean *where*—near here?" interrupted Carter.

"Oh, fifteen mile east," answered Jimmy. "He was crawlin' down on a bunch of cattle. He saw me just as I saw him. But he missed an' I didn't," he gloated proudly. "I met a Pawnee scout just afterward an' he near got shot before he signaled. He says hell's a-poppin'. Th' 'Paches are raidin' all over th' country, down—"

"I knowed it!" shouted Carter. "Yessir, I knowed it! I felt it all along! Where you finds one you finds a bunch!"

"We'll give 'em blazes, like th' last time!" cried Dad, hurrying away to the harness shop where he had left his rifle.

"I've been needin' some excitement for a long time," laughed Dawson. "I shore hope they come."

Carter paused long enough to retort over his shoulder: "An' I hopes you drop dead! You never did have no sense! Not nohow!"

Bill smiled at the sudden awakening and watched the scrambling for weapons. "Why, there's enough men here to wipe out a tribe. I reckon we'll stay an' see th' fun. Anyhow, it'll be a whole lot safer here than fightin' by ourselves out in th' open somewhere. What you say?"

"You couldn't drag me away from this town right now with a cayuse," Jimmy replied, gravely hanging the medicine-bag around his neck and then stuffing the gory G-string in the folds of the slicker he carried strapped behind the cantle of the saddle. "We'll see it out right here. But I do wish that 'Pache owned a better gun than this thing. It's most fallin' apart an' ain't worth nothin'."

Bill took it and examined the rifling and the breechblock. He laughed as he handed it back. "You oughta be glad it wasn't a better gun, Kid. I don't reckon he could put two in the same place at two hundred paces with this thing. I ain't even anxious to shoot it off on a bet."

Jimmy gasped suddenly and grinned until the safety of his ears was threatened. "Would you look at Carter?" he chuckled, pointing. Bill turned and saw the proprietor of Carter's Emporium carrying water into his store, and with a speed that would lead one to infer that he was doing it on a wager. Emerging again he saw the punchers looking at him and, dropping the buckets, he wiped his face on his sleeve and shook his head. "I'm fillin' everything," he called. "I reckon we better stand 'em off from my store—th' walls are thicker."

Bill smiled at the excuse and looked down the street at the adobe buildings. "What about th' 'dobes, Carter?" he asked. The walls of some of them were more than two feet thick.

Carter scowled, scratched his head and made a gesture of impatience. "They ain't big enough to hold us all," he replied, with triumph. "This here store is th' best place. An', besides, it's all stocked with water an' grub, an' everything."

Jimmy nodded. "Yo're right, Carter; it's th' best place." To Bill he said in an aside. "He's plumb anxious to protect that shack, now ain't he?"

Lefty Dawson came sauntering up. "Wonder if Carter'll let us hold out in his store?"

"He'll pay you to," laughed Bill.

"It's loop-holed. Been so since th' last raid," explained Lefty. "An' it's chock full of grub," he grinned.

They heard Dad's voice around the corner. "Just like last time," he was say-ing. "We oughta put four men in Dick's 'dobe acrost th' street. Then we'd have a strategy position. You see—oh, hullo," he said as he rounded the corner ahead of George Bruce. "Who's goin' on picket duty?" he demanded.

Under the blazing sun a yellow dog wandered aimlessly down the deserted street, his main interest in life centered on his skin, which he frequently sat down to chew. During the brief respites he lounged in the doors of deserted buildings, frequently exploring the quiet interiors for food. Emerging from the "hotel" he looked across the street at the Emporium and barked tentatively at the man sitting on its flat roof. Wriggling apologetically, he slowly gained the middle of the street and then sat down to investigate a sharp attack. A can sailed out of the open door and a flurry of yellow streaked around the corner of the "hotel" and vanished.

In the Emporium grave men played poker for nails, Bill Cassidy having cor-ralled all the available cash long before this, and conversed in low tones. The walls, reinforced breast high by boxes, barrels and bags, were divided into reg-ular intervals by the open loopholes, each opening further indicated by a lean-ing rifle or two and generous piles of cartridges. Two tubs and half a dozen buckets filled with water stood in the center of the room, carefully covered over with boards and wrapping paper. Clouds of tobacco smoke lay in filmy stratums in the heated air and drifted up the resin-streaked sides of the build-ing. The shimmering, gray sand stretched away in a glare of sunlight and seemed to writhe under the heated air, while droning flies flitted lazily through the windows and held caucuses on the sugar barrel. A slight, grating sound overhead caused several of the more able or energetic men to glance up lazily, grateful they were not in Hank's place. It was hot enough under the roof, and they stretched ecstatically as they thought of Hank. Three days' vigil and anx-iety had become trying even to the most solid.

John Carter fretfully damned solitaire and pushed the cards away to pick up pencil and paper and figure thoughtfully. This seemed to furnish him with even less amusement, for he scowled and turned to watch the poker game. "Huh," he sniffed, "playin' poker for nails! An' you don't even own th' nails," he grinned facetiously, and glanced around to see if his point was taken. He suddenly stiff-ened when he noticed the man who sat on his counter and labored patiently and zealously with a pocket knife. "Hey, you!" he exclaimed excitedly, his wrath quickly aroused. "Ain't you never had no bringin' up? If yo're so plumb sot on whittlin', you tackle that sugar barrel!"

Jimmy looked the barrel over critically and then regarded the peeved proprietor, shaking his head sorrowfully. "This here is a better medjum for the exposition of my art," he replied gravely. "An' as for bringin' up, lemme observe to these gents here assembled that you ain't never had no artistic trainin'. Yore skimpy soul is dwarfed an' narrowed by false weights and dented measures. You can look a sunset in th' face an' not see it for countin' yore profits." Carter glanced instinctively at the figures as Jimmy continued. "An' you can't see no beauty in a daisy's grace—which last is from a book. I'm here carvin' th' very image of my cayuse an' givin' you a work of art, free an' gratis. I'm timid an' sensitive, I am; an' I'll feel hurt if—"

"Stop that noise," snorted a man in the corner, turning over to try again. "Sensitive an' timid? Yes; as a mule! Shut up an' lemme get a little sleep."

"A-men," sighed a poker-player. "An' let him sleep—he's a cussed nuisance when he's awake."

"Two mules," amended the dealer. "Which is worse than one," he added thoughtfully.

"We oughta put four men in that 'dobe—" began Dad persistently.

"An' will you shut up about that 'dobe an' yore four men?" snapped Lefty. "Can't you say nothin' less'n it's about that mud hut?"

Jimmy smiled maddeningly at the irritated crowd. "As I was sayin' before you all interrupted me, I'll feel hurt—"

"You *will*; an' quick!" snapped Carter. "You quit gougin' that counter!"

Bill craned his neck to examine the carving, and forthwith held out a derisively pointing forefinger.

"Cayuse?" he inquired sarcastically. "Looks more like th' map of th' United States, with some almost necessary parts missin'. Your geography musta been different from mine."

The artist smiled brightly. "Here's a man with imagination, th' emancipator of thought. It's crude an' untrained, but it's there. Imagination is a hopeful sign, for it is only given to human bein's. From this we surmise an' must conclude that Bill is human."

"Will somebody be liar enough to say th' same of you?" politely inquired the dealer.

"Will you fools shut up?" demanded the man who would sleep. He had been on guard half the night.

"But you oughta label it, Jimmy," said Bill. "You've got California bulgin' too high up, an' Florida sticks out th' wrong way. Th' Great Lakes is *all* wrong— looks like a kidney slippin' off of Canada. An' where's Texas?"

"Huh! It'd have to be a cow to show Texas," grinned Dad Johnson, who, it appeared, also had an imagination and wanted people to know it.

"You cuttin' in on this teet-a-teet?" demanded Jimmy, dodging the compliments of the sleepy individual.

"As a map it is no good," decided Bill decisively.

"It is no map," retorted Jimmy. "I know where California bulges an' how Florida sticks out. What you call California is th' south end of th' cayuse, above which I'm goin' to put th' tail—"

"Not if I'm man enough, you ain't!" interposed Carter, with no regard for politeness.

"—where I'm goin' to put th' tail," repeated Jimmy. "Florida is one front laig raised off th' ground—"

"Trick cayuse, by Scott!" grunted George Bruce. "No wonder it looks like a map."

"Th' Great Lakes is th' saddle, an' Maine is where th' mane goes—*Ouch!*"

"Mangy pun," grinned Bill.

"Kentucky ought to be under th' saddle," laughed Dad, smacking his lips. "Pass th' bottle, John."

"You take too much an' we'll all be Ill-o'-noise," said Charley Logan alertly.

"Them Injuns can't come too soon to suit *me*," growled Fred Thomas. "Who started this, anyhow?"

The sleepy man arose on one elbow, his eyes glinting. "After th' fight, you ask *me* th' same thing! Th' answer will be ME!" he snapped. "I'm goin' to clean house in about two minutes, an' fire you all out in th' street!"

Jimmy smiled down at him. "Well, you needn't be so sweepin' an' extensive in yore cleanin' operations," he retorted. "All you gotta do is go outside an' roll in th' dust like a chicken."

The crowd roared its appreciation and the sleepy individual turned over again, growling sweeping opinions.

"But if them Injuns are comin' I shore wish they'd hurry up an' do it," asserted Dad. "I ought to 'a' been home three days ago."

"Wish to God you was!" came from the floor.

Bill tossed away his half-smoked cigarette, Carter promptly plunging into the sugar barrel after it. "They ain't comin'," Bill asserted. "Every time some drunk Injun gets in a fight or beats his squaw th' rumor starts. An' by th' time it gets to us it says that all th' Apaches are out follerin' old Geronimo on th' war trail. He can be more places at once than anybody *I* ever heard of. I'm ridin' on tomorrow morning, 'Paches or no 'Paches."

"Good!" exclaimed Jimmy, glancing at Carter. "I'll have this here carving all done by then."

There was a sudden scrambling and thumping overhead and hot exclamations zephyred down to them. Carter dashed to the door, while the others reached for rifles and began to take up positions.

"See 'em, Hank?" cried Carter anxiously.

"See what?" came a growl from above.

"Injuns, of course, you damned fool!"

"Naw," snorted Hank. "There ain't no Injuns out at all, not after Jimmy got that one."

"Then what's th' matter?"

"My dawg's lickin' yore dawg. *Sic* him, Pete! Hi, there! Don't you run!"

"My dawg still gettin' licked?" grinned Carter.

"I'll swap you," offered Hank promptly. "Mine can lick yourn, anyhow."

"In a race, mebby."

"Hell!" growled Hank, cautiously separating himself from a patch of hot resin that had exuded generously from a pine knot. "I'm purty nigh cooked an' I'm comin' down, Injuns or *no* Injuns. If they was comin' this way they'd 'a' been here long afore this."

"But that Pawnee told Price they was out," objected Carter. "Cassidy heard th' same thing, too. An' didn't Jimmy get one!" he finished triumphantly.

"Th' Pawnee was drunk!" retorted Hank, collecting splinters as he slipped a little down the roof. "Great Mavericks! This here is awful!" He grabbed a protruding nail and checked himself. "Price might 'a' shot a 'Pache, or he might not. I don't take him serious no more. An' that feller Cassidy can't help what scared folks tells him. Sufferin' *toads*, what a roof!"

Carter turned and look back in the store. "Jimmy, you shore they are out? An' *will* you quit cuttin' that counter!"

Jimmy slid off the counter and closed the knife. "That's what th' Pawnee said. When I told you fellers about it, you was so plumb anxious to fight, an' eager to interrupt an' ask fool questions that I shore hated to spoil it all. What that scout says was that th' 'Paches was out raidin' down Colby way, an' was headin' south when last re—"

"*Colby!*" yelled Lefty Dawson, as the others stared foolishly. "*Colby!* Why, that's three hundred miles south of here! An' you let us make fools of ourselves for *three* days! I'll bust you open!" and he arose to carry out his threat.

"Where'd you git them trophies?" shouted Dad angrily. "Them was genuine!"

Jimmy slipped through the door as Dawson leaped and he fled at top speed to the corral, mounted in one bound and dashed off a short distance. "Why, I got them trophies in a poker game from that same Pawnee scout, you Mosshead! He couldn't play th' game no better'n you fellers. An' th' blood is snake's blood, fresh put on. You *will* drive me out of town, hey?" he jeered, and, wheeling, forthwith rode for his life. Back in the store Bill knocked aside the rifle barrel that Carter shoved through a loop hole. "A joke's a joke, Carter," he said sternly. "You don't aim to hit him, but you might," and Carter, surprised at the strength of the twist, grinned, muttered something and went to the door without his rifle, which Bill suddenly recognized. It was the weapon that had made up Jimmy's "trophies"!

"Blame his hide!" spluttered Lefty, not knowing whether to shoot or laugh. A queer noise behind him made him turn, a movement imitated by the rest. They saw Bill rolling over and over on the floor in an agony of mirth. One by one the enraged garrison caught the infection and one by one lay down on the floor and wept. Lefty, propping himself against the sugar barrel, swayed to and fro, sense-lessly gasping. "They *allus* are raidin' down Colby way! Blame my hide, *oh*, blame my hide! Ha-ha-ha! Ha-ha-ha! They *allus* are raidin' down *Colby* way!"

"Three days, an' Hank *on* the roof!" gurgled George Bruce. "*Three* days, by Scott!"

"Hank on th' roof," sobbed Carter, "settin' on splinters an hot rosim! Whee-hee-hee! Three-hee-hee days hatchin' pine knots an' rosim!"

"Gimme a drink! Gimme a drink!" whispered Dad, doubled up in a corner. "Gimme a ho-ho-ho!" he roared in a fresh paroxysm of mirth. "Lefty an' George settin' up nights watchin' th' shadders! Ho-ho-ho!"

"An' Carter boardin' us *free*!" yelled Baldy Martin. "Oh, my God! He'll never get over it!"

"Yessir!" squeaked Dad. "*Free*; an' scared we'd let 'em burn his store. 'Bet-ter stand 'em off in my place,' he says. 'It's full of grub,' he says. He-he-he!"

"An' did you see Hank squattin' on th' roof like a horned toad waitin' for his dinner?" shouted Dickinson. "I'm goin' to die! I'm goin' to die!" he sobbed.

"No sich luck!" snorted Hank belligerently. "I'll skin him alive! Yessir; *alive*!"

Carter paused in his calculations of his loss in food and tobacco. "Better let him alone, Hank," he warned earnestly. "Anyhow, we pestered him nigh to death las' time, an' he's shore come back at us. Better let him alone!"

Up the street Jimmy stood beside his horse and thumped and scratched the yellow dog until its rolling eyes bespoke a bliss unutterable and its tail could not wag because of sheer ecstasy.

"Purp," he said gravely, "never play jokes on a pore unfortunate an' git careless.

Don't never forget it. Last time I was here they abused me shameful. Now that th' storm has busted an' this is gettin' calm-like, you an' me'll go back an' get a good look at th' asylum," he suggested, vaulting into the saddle and starting toward the store. No invitation was needed because the dog had adopted him on the spot. And the next morning, when Jimmy and Bill, loaded with poker-gained wealth, rode out of town and headed south, the dog trotted along in the shadow made by Jimmy's horse and glanced up from time to time in hopeful expectancy and great affection.

A distant, flat pistol shot made them turn around in the saddle and look back. A group of the leading citizens of Sharpsville stood in front of the Emporium and waved hats in one last, and glad farewell. Now that Jimmy had left town, they altered their sudden plans and decided to continue to populate the town of Sharpsville.

CHAPTER 5

The Luck of Fools

"Did you ever see a dog like Asylum?" demanded Jimmy, looking fondly at the mongrel as they rode slowly the second day after leaving Sharpsville.

Bill shook his head emphatically. "Never, nowheres."

Jimmy turned reproachfully. "Lookit how he's follered us."

"Follered *you*," hastily corrected Bill. "He ought to. You feed an' scratch him, an' he'll go anywhere for that. But he's big," he conceded.

"Mostly wolf-hound," guessed Jimmy, proudly.

"He looks like a wolf—God help it—at th' end of a hard winter."

"Well, he ain't yourn!"

"An' won't be, not if I can help it."

"He ain't no good, is he?" sneered Jimmy.

"I wouldn't say that, Kid," grunted Bill. "You know there's good *Injuns*; but he looks purty healthy right now. Why didn't you call him Hank? They look— Good God!" he exclaimed as he glanced through an opening in the hills. The ring of ashes that had been a corral still smoldered, and smoke arose fitfully from the caved-in roof of the adobe bunkhouse, whose beams, weakened by fire, had fallen under their heavy load.

"Injuns!" whispered Jimmy. "Not gone long, neither. Mebby they ain't all— ain't all—" he faltered, thinking of what might lie under the roof. Bill, nodding, rode hurriedly to the ruins, wheeled sharply and returned, shaking his head slowly. There was no need to explain Apache methods to his companion, and he spoke of the Indians instead. "They split. About a dozen in th' big party an' about eight in th' other. It looks sorta serious, Kid."

Jimmy nodded. "I reckon so. An' they're usually where nobody wants 'em, anyhow. Wouldn't Sharpsville be disgusted if they went north? But let's get out of here, 'less you got some plan to bag a couple."

"I like you more all th' time," Bill smiled. "But I ain't got no plan, except to move."

"Now, if they ain't funny," muttered Jimmy. "If they only knowed what they was runnin' into!"

Bill turned in surprise. "I reckon I'm easy, but I'll bite: what are they runnin' into?"

"I don't mean th' Injuns; I mean that wagon," replied Jimmy, nodding to a canvas-covered "schooner" on the opposite hill. "Come here, 'Sylum!" he thundered. Bill wheeled, and smothered a curse when he saw the woman. "Fools!" he snarled. "Don't let *her* know," and he was galloping toward the newcomers.

"They shore is innercent," soliloquized Jimmy, following. "Just like a baby chasin' a rattler for to play with it."

Bill drew rein at the wagon and removed his sombrero. "Howd'y," he said. "Where you headin' for?" he asked pleasantly.

Tom French shifted the reins. "Sharpsville. And where in—thunder—is it?"

His brother stuck his head out through the opening in the canvas. "Yes; where?"

"You see, we are lost," explained the woman, glancing from Bill to Jimmy, whose spectacular sliding stop was purely for her benefit, though she knew it not. "We left Logan four days ago and have been wandering about ever since."

"Well, you ain't a-goin' to wander no more, ma'am," smiled Bill. "We're goin' to Logan an' we'll take you as far as th' Logan-Sharpsville trail," he said, wondering where it was. "You must 'a' crossed it without knowin' it."

"Then, thank goodness, everything is all right. We are very fortunate in having met you gentlemen and we will be very grateful to you," she smiled.

"You bet!" exclaimed Tom. "But where *is* Sharpsville?" he persisted.

"Sixty miles north," replied Jimmy, making a great effort to stop with the reins what he was causing with his shielded spur. His horse could cavort beautifully under persuasion. "Logan, ma'am," he said, indifferent to the antics of his horse, "is about thirty miles east. You must 'a' sashayed some to get only this far in four days," he grinned.

"And we would be 'sashaying' yet, if I hadn't found this trail," grunted Tom. There was a sudden disturbance behind his shoulder and the canvas was opened wider. "*You* found it!" snorted George. "You mean, *I* found it. Leave it to Mollie if I didn't! And I told you that you were going wrong. Didn't I?" he demanded.

"Hush, George," chided his sister.

"But *didn't* I? Didn't I say we should have followed that moth-eaten road running—er—north?"

"Did you?" shouted Tom, turning savagely. "You told me so many fool things I couldn't pick out those having a flicker of intelligence hovering around their outer edges. *You* drove two days out of the four, didn't you?"

"Tom!" pleaded Mollie, earnestly.

"Oh, let him rave, Sis," rejoined George, and he turned to the punchers. "Friends, I beg thee to take charge of this itinerant asylum and its charming nurse, for the good of our being and the salvation of our souls. Amen."

Tom found a weak grin. "Yes, so be it. We place ourselves and guide under your orders, though I reserve the right to beat him to a pleasing pulp when he gets sober enough to feel it. At present he reclines ungracefully within."

"You mean you got a drunk guide, in there?" demanded Bill angrily.

"He feels the yearning right away," observed George. "We'll have to take turns thrashing Bacchus, I fear."

"How long's he been that way?" demanded Bill.

"I haven't known him long enough to answer that," responded Tom. "I doubt if he were ever really sober. He is a peripatetic distillery and I believe he lived on blotters even as a child. The first day—"

"—hour," inserted George.

"—he became anxious about the condition of the rear axle and examined it so frequently that by night he had slipped back into the Stone Age—he was ossified and petrified. He could neither see, eat nor talk. Strange creatures peopled his imagination. He shot at one before we could get his gun away from him, and it was our best skillet. How the devil he could hit it is more than I know. At this moment he may be fleeing from green tigers."

"Beg pardon," murmured George. "At this moment I have my foot on his large, unwashed face."

"Why, George! You'll hurt him!" gasped Mollie.

"No such luck. He's beyond feeling."

"But you will! It isn't right to—"

"Don't bother your head about him, Sis," interrupted Tom, savagely.

"Sure," grinned George. "Save your sympathy until he gets sober. He'll need some then."

"Now, George, there is no use of having an argument," she retorted, turning to face him. And as she turned Bill took quick advantage. One finger slipped around his scalp and ended in a jerky, lifting motion that was horribly suggestive. His other hand and arm swept back and around, the gesture taking in the hills; and at the same time he nodded emphatically toward the rear of the wagon, where Jimmy was slowly going. Across the faces of the brothers there flashed in quick succession mystification, apprehensive doubt, fear and again doubt. But a sudden backward jerk of Bill's head made them glance at the ruined 'dobe and the doubt melted into fear, and remained. George was the first to reply and he spoke to his sister. "As long as you fear for his facial beauty, Sis, I'll look for a better place for my foot," and he disappeared behind the drooping canvas. Jimmy's words were powerful, if terse, and George returned to the seat a very thoughtful man. He took instant advantage of his sister's conversation with Bill and whispered hurriedly into his brother's ear. A faint furrow showed momentarily on Tom's forehead, but swiftly disappeared, and he calmly filled his pipe as he replied. "Oh, he'll sober up," he said. "We poured the last of it out. And I have a great deal of confidence in these two gentlemen."

Bill smiled as he answered Mollie's question. "Yes, we did have a bad fire," he said. "It plumb burned us out, ma'am."

"But *how* did it happen?" she insisted.

"Yes, yes; how did it happen—I mean it happened like this, ma'am," he floundered. "You see, I—that is, *we*—*we* had some trouble, ma'am."

"So I surmised," she pleasantly replied. "I presume it was a fire, was it not?"

Bill squirmed at the sarcasm and hesitated, but he was saved by Jimmy, who turned the corner of the wagon and swung into the breach with promptness and assurance. "We fired a Mexican yesterday," he explained. "An' last night th' Mexican slipped back an' fired us. He got away, this time, ma'am; but we're shore comin' back for him, all right."

"But isn't he far away by this time?" she asked in surprise.

"Mexicans, ma'am, are funny people. I could tell you lots of funny things about 'em, if I had time. This particular coyote is nervy an' graspin'. I reckon he was a heap disappointed when he found we got out alive, an' I reckon he's in these hills waitin' for us to go to Logan for supplies. When we do he'll round up th' cows an' run 'em off. Savvy? I means, understand?" he hurriedly explained.

"But why don't you hunt him now?"

Jimmy shook his head hopelessly. "You just don't understand Mexicans, ma'am," he asserted, and looked around. "Does she?" he demanded.

There was a chorus of negatives, and he continued. "You see, he's plannin' to steal our cows."

"That's what he's doin'," cheerfully assented Bill.

"I believe you said that before," smiled Mollie.

"Ha, ha!" laughed Bill. "He shore did!"

"Yes, I did!" snapped Jimmy, glaring at him.

"Then, for goodness' sake, are you going away and let him do it?" demanded Mollie.

Jimmy grinned easily, and drawled effectively. "We're aimin' to stop him, ma'am. You see," he half whispered, whereat Bill leaned forward eagerly to learn the facts. "He won't show hisself an' we can't track him in th' hills without gettin' picked off at long range. It would be us that'd have to do th' movin', an' that ain't healthy in rough country. So we starts to Logan, but circles back an' gets him when he's plumb wrapped up in them cows he's honin' for."

"That's it," asserted Bill, promptly and proudly. Jimmy was the smoothest liar he had ever listened to. "An' th' plan is all Jimmy's, too," he enthused, truthfully.

"Doubtless it is quite brilliant," she responded, "but I certainly wish I were that 'Mexican'!"

"Sis!" exploded George, "I'm surprised!"

"Very well; you may remain so, if you wish. But will someone tell me this: How can these gentlemen take us to Logan if they are going only part way and then returning after that dense, but lucky, 'Mexican'?"

"I should 'a' told you, ma'am," replied Jimmy, "that th' Logan-Sharpsville trail is about half way. We'll put you on it an' turn back."

The strain was telling on Bill and he raised his arm. "Sorry to cut off this interestin' conversation, but I reckon we better move. Jimmy, tie that wolf-hound to th' axle—it won't make *him* drunk—an' then go ahead an' pick a new trail to Logan. Keep north of th' other, an' stay down from sky-lines. I'll foller back a ways. Get a-goin'," and he was obeyed.

Jimmy rode a quarter of a mile in advance, unjustly escaping the remarks that Mollie was directing at him, her brothers, Bill, the dog and the situation in general. A backward glance as he left the wagon apprised him that the dangers of scouting were to be taken thankfully. He rode carelessly up the side of a hill and glanced over the top, ducked quickly and backed down with undignified haste. He fervently endorsed Bill's wisdom in taking a different route to Logan, for the Apaches certainly would strike the other trail and follow hard; and to have run into them would have been disastrous. He approached the wagon leisurely, swept off his sombrero and grinned. "Reckon you could hit any game?" he inquired. The brothers nodded glumly. "Well, get yore guns handy." There was really no need for the order. "There's lots of it, an' fresh meat'll come in good. Don't shoot till I says so," he warned, earnestly.

"O.K., Hawkeye," replied Tom coolly.

"We'll wait for the whites of their eyes, *à la Bunker Hill*," replied George, uneasily, "before we wipe out the game of this large section of God's accusing and forgotten wilderness. Any *big* game loose?"

Jimmy nodded emphatically. "You bet! I just saw a bunch of copperhead snakes that'd give you chills." The tones were very suggestive and George stroked his rifle nervously and felt little drops of cold water trickle from his armpits. Mollie instinctively drew her skirts tighter around her and placed her feet on the edge of the wagon box under the seat. "They can't climb into the wagon, can they?" she asked apprehensively.

"Oh, no, ma'am," reassured Jimmy. "Anyhow, th' dog will keep them away." He turned to the brothers. "I ain't shore about th' way, so I'm goin' to see Bill. Wait till I come back," and he was gone. Tom gripped the reins more firmly and waited. Nothing short of an earthquake would move that wagon until he had been told to drive on. George searched the surrounding country with anxious eyes while his sister gazed fascinatedly at the ground close to the wagon. She suddenly had remembered that the dog was tied.

Bill drummed past, waving his arm, and swept out of sight around a bend, the wagon lurching and rocking after him. Out of the little valley and across a rocky plateau, down into an arroyo and up its steep, further bank went the wagon at an angle that forced a scream from Mollie. The dog, having broken loose, ran with it, eyeing it suspiciously from time to time. Jeff Purdy, the oblivious guide, slid swiftly from the front of the wagon box and stopped suddenly with a thump against the tailboard. George, playing rear guard, managed to hold on and then with a sigh of relief sat upon the guide and jammed his feet against the corners of the box.

"So he—went back for—his friend to—find the way!" gasped Mollie in jerks. "What a pity—he did—it. I could—do better myself. I'm being jolted—into a thousand—pieces!" Her hair, loosening more with each jolt, uncoiled and streamed behind her in a glorious flame of gold. Suddenly the wagon stopped so quickly that she gasped in dismay and almost left the seat. Then she screamed and jumped for the dashboard. But it was only Mr. Purdy sliding back again.

Before them was the perpendicular wall of a mesa and another lay several hundred yards away. Bill, careful of where he walked, led the horses past a boulder until the seat was even with it. "Step on nothing but rock," he quietly ordered, and had lifted Mollie in his arms before she knew it. Despite her protests he swiftly carried her to the wall and then slowly up its scored face to a ledge that lay half way to the top. Back of the ledge was a horizontal fissure that was almost screened from the sight of anyone below. Gaining the cave, he lowered her gently to the floor and stood up. "Do not move," he ordered.

Her face was crimson, streaked with white lanes of anger and her eyes snapped. "What does this mean?" she demanded.

He looked at her a moment, considering. "Ma'am, I wasn't goin' to tell you till I had to. But it don't make no difference now. It's Injuns, close after us. Don't show yoreself."

She regarded him calmly. "I beg your pardon—if I had only known—is there great danger?"

He nodded. "If you show yoreself. There's allus danger with Injuns, ma'am."

She pushed the hair back from her face. "My brothers? Are they coming up?"

Her courage set him afire with rage for the Apaches, but he replied calmly. "Yes. Mebby th' Injuns won't know yo're here, Ma'am. Me an' Jimmy'll try to lead 'em past. Just lay low an' don't make no noise."

Her eyes glowed suddenly as she realized what he would try to do. "But yourself, and Jimmy? Wouldn't it be better to stay up here?"

"Yo're a thoroughbred, ma'am," he replied in a low voice. "Me an' Jimmy has staked our lives more'n onct out of pure devilment, with nothin' to gain. I reckon we got a reason this time, th' best we ever had. I'm most proud, ma'am, to play my cards as I get them." He bent swiftly and touched her head, and was gone.

Meeting the brothers as they toiled up with supplies, he gave them a few terse orders and went on. Taking a handful of sand from behind a boulder and scattering it with judicious care, he climbed to the wagon seat and waited, glancing back at the faint line that marked the arroyo's rim. In a few minutes a figure popped over it and whirled toward him in a high-flung, swirling cloud of dust. Overtaking the lurching wagon, Jimmy shouted a query and kept on, his pony picking its way with the agility and certainty of a mountain cat. The wagon, lurching this way and that, first on the wheels of one side and then on those of the other, bouncing and jumping at such speed that it was a miracle it was not smashed to splinters, careened after the hard-riding horseman. A rifle bounced over the tailboard, followed swiftly by a box of cartridges and an ebony-backed mirror, which settled on its back and glared into the sky like an angry Cyclops.

Mr. Purdy, bruised from head to foot and rapidly getting sober, emitted language in jerks and grabbed at the tailboard as the wagon box dropped two feet, leaving him in the air. But it met him half way and jolted him almost to the canvas top. He slid against the side and then jammed against the tailboard again and reached for it in desperation. Another drop in the trail made him miss it, and as the wagon arose again like a steel spring Mr. Purdy, wondering what caused all the earthquakes, arose on his hands and knees in the dust and spat angrily after the careening vehicle. He scrambled unsteadily to his feet and shook eager fists after the four-wheeled jumping-jack, and gave the Recording Angel great anguish of mind and writer's cramp. Pausing as he caught sight of the objects on the ground, he stared at them thoughtfully. He had seen many things during the past few days and was not to be fooled again. He looked at the sky, and back to the rifle. Then he examined the mesa wall, and quickly looked back at the weapon. It was still there and had not moved. He closed his eyes and opened them suddenly and grunted. "Huh, bet a ten spot it's real." He approached it cautiously, ready to pounce on it if it moved, but it did not and he picked it up. Seeing the cartridges, he secured them and then gasped with fear at the glaring mirror. After a moment's thought he grabbed at it and put it in his pocket just before a sudden, swirling cloud of dust drove him, choking and gasping, to seek the shelter of the boulders close to the wall. When he raised his head again and looked out he caught sight of a sudden movement in the open, and promptly ducked, and swore. Apaches! Twelve of them!

He had seen strange things during the last few days, and just because the rifle and other objects had turned out to be real was no reason that he should absolutely trust his eyes in this particular instance. There was a limit, which in this case was Apaches in full war dress; so he arose swaggeringly and fired at the last, and saw the third from the last slide limply from his horse. As the rest paused and half of them wheeled and started back he rubbed his eyes in amazement, damned himself for a fool and sprinted for the mesa wall, up which he climbed with the frantic speed of fear. He was favored by the proverbial luck of fools and squirmed over a wide ledge without being hit. There was but one way to get him and he knew he could pick them off as fast as they showed above the rim. He rolled over and a look of mystification crept across his face. Digging into his pockets to see what the bumps were, he produced the mirror and a flask. The former he placed carelessly against the wall and the latter he raised hastily to his lips. The mirror glared out over the plain, its rays constantly interrupted by Mr. Purdy's cautious movements as he settled himself more comfortably for defense.

A bullet screamed up the face of the wall and he flattened, intently watching the rim. Chancing to glance over the plain, he noticed that the wagon was still moving, but slowly, while far to the south two horsemen galloped back toward the mesa on a wide circle, six Apaches tearing to intercept them before they could gain cover. "I was shore wise to leave th' schooner," he grinned. "I allus know when to jump," he said, and then swung the rifle toward the rim as a faint sound reached his ears. Its smoke blotted out the piercing black eyes that looked for an instant over the edge and found eternity, and Mr. Purdy grinned when the sound of impact floated up from below. "They won't try that no more," he grunted, and forthwith dozed in a drunken stupor. A sober man might have been tempted to try a shot over the rim, and would have been dead before he could have pulled the trigger. Mr. Purdy was again favored by luck.

Leaving two braves to watch him, the other two searched for a better way up the wall.

The race over the plain was interesting but not deadly or very dangerous for Bill and Jimmy. Armed with Winchesters and wornout Spencer carbines and not able to get close to the two punchers, the Apaches did no harm, and suffered because of Mr. Cassidy's use of a new, long-range Sharps. "You allus want to keep Injuns on long range, Kid," Bill remarked as another fell from its horse. The shot was a lucky one, but just as effective. "They ain't worth a damn figurin' windage an' th' drift of a fast-movin' target, 'specially when it's goin' over ground like this. It's a white man's weapon, Jimmy. Them repeaters ain't no good for over five hundred; they don't use enough powder. An' I reckon them Spencers was wore out long ago. They ain't even shootin' close." He whirled past the projecting spur of the mesa and leaped from his horse, Jimmy following quickly. Three hundred yards down the canyon two Apaches showed themselves for a moment as they squirmed around a projection high up on the wall and not more than ten feet below the ledge. The expressions which they carried into eternity were those of great surprise. The two who kept Mr. Purdy treed on his ledge saw their friends fall, and squirmed swiftly toward their horses. It could only be cowpunchers entering the canyon at the other end and they preferred the company of their friends until they could determine numbers. When half way to the animals they changed their minds and crept toward the scene of action. Mr. Purdy, feeling for his flask, knocked it over the ledge and looked over after it in angry dismay. Then he shouted and pointed down. Bill and Jimmy stared for a moment, nodded emphatically, and separated hastily. Mr. Purdy ducked and hugged the ledge with renewed affection. Glancing around, he was almost blinded by the mirror and threw it angrily into the canyon, and then rubbed his eyes again. Far away on the plain was a moving blot which he believed to be horsemen. He fired his rifle into the air on a chance and turned again to the events taking place close at hand. "Other way, Hombre!" he warned, and Jimmy, obeying, came upon the Apache from the rear, and saved Bill's life. At hide and seek among rocks the Apache has no equal, but here they did not have a chance with Mr. Purdy calling the moves in a language they did not well understand. A bird's-eye view is a distinct asset and Mr. Purdy was playing his novel game with delighted interest and a plainsman's instinct. Consumed with rage, the remaining Indian whirled around and sent the guide reeling against the wall and then down in a limp heap. But Bill paid the debt and continued to worm among the rocks.

There was a sudden report to the westward and Jimmy staggered and dived behind a boulder. The other four, having discovered the trick that had been played upon them on the other side of the mesa, were anxious to pay for it. Bill hurriedly crawled to Jimmy's side as the youth brushed the blood out of his eyes and picked up his rifle. "It's th' others, Kid," said Bill. "An' they're gettin' close. Don't move an inch, for this is their game." A roar above him made him glance upward and swear angrily. "Now they've gone an' done it! After all we've done to hide 'em!" Another shot from the ledge and a hot, answering fire broke out from below. "My God!" said a voice, weakly. Bill shook his head. "That was Tom," he muttered. "Come on, Kid," he growled. "We got to drive 'em out, damn it!" They were too interested in picking their way in the direction of the Apaches to glance at Mr. Purdy's elevated perch or they would have seen him on his knees at the very edge making frantic motions with his one good arm. He was facing the east and the plain. Beaming with joy, he waved his arm toward Bill and Jimmy, shouted instructions in a weak voice, that barely carried to the canyon floor, and collapsed, his duty done.

Bill was surprised fifteen minutes later to hear strange voices calling to him from the rear and he turned like a flash, his Colt swinging first. "Well, I'm damned!" he ejaculated. Four punchers were crawling toward him. "Glad to see you," he said, foolishly.

"I reckon so," came the smiling reply. "That lookin' glass of yourn shore bothered us. We couldn't read it, but we didn't have to. Where are they?"

"Plumb ahead, som'ers. Four of 'em," Bill replied. "There's two tenderfeet up on that ledge, with their sister. We was gettin' plumb worried for 'em."

"Not them as hired Whiskey Jeff for to guide 'em?" asked Dickinson, the leader.

"Th' same. But how'n hell did Logan ever come to let 'em start?" demanded Bill, angrily.

"We didn't pay no attention to th' rumors that has been flyin' around for th' last two months. Nobody had seen no signs of 'em," answered the Logan man. "We didn't reckon there was no danger till last night, when we learned they hadn't showed up in Sharpsville, nor been seen anywheres near th' trail. Then we remembers Jeff's habits, an', while we debates it, we gets word that th' Injuns was seen north of Cook's ranch yesterday. We moves sudden. Here comes th' boys back—I reckon th' job's done. They're a fine crowd, a'right. You should 'a' seen 'em cut loose an' raise th' dust when we saw that lookin' glass a-winkin'. We couldn't read it none, but we didn't have to. We just cut loose."

"Lookin' glass!" exclaimed Bill, staring. "That's twice you've mentioned it. What glass? We didn't have no lookin' glass, nohow."

"Well, Whiskey Jeff had one, a'right. An' he shore keeps her a-talkin', too. Ain't it a cussed funny thing that a feller that's got a hard-boiled face like his'n would go an' tote a lookin' glass around with him? We never done reckoned he was that vain."

Bill shook his head and gave it up. He glanced above him at the ledge and started for it as Jimmy pushed up to him through the little crowd. "Hello, Kid," Bill smiled. "Come on up an' help me get her down," he invited. Jimmy shook his head and refused. "Ah, what's th' use? She'll only gimme hell for handin' her that blamed lie," he snapped. "An' you can do it alone—didn't you tote her up th' cussed wall?" It had been a long-range view, but Jimmy had seen it, just the same, and resented it.

Bill turned and looked at him. "Well, I'm cussed!" he muttered, and forthwith climbed the wall. A few minutes later he stuck his head over the rim of the ledge and looked down upon a good-natured crowd that lounged in the shadow of the wall and told each other all about it. Jimmy was the important center of interest and he was flushed with pride. It would take a great deal to make him cut short his hour of triumph and take him away from the admiring circle that hedged him in and listened intently to his words. "Yessir, by God," he was saying, "just then I looks over th' top of a li'l hill an' what I sees makes me duck a-plenty. There was a dozen of 'em, stringin' south. I knowed they'd shore hit that—"

"Hey, Kid," said a humorous voice from above. Jimmy glanced up, vexed at the interruption. "Well, what?" he growled. Bill grinned down at him in a manner that bid fair to destroy the dignity that Jimmy had striven so hard to build up. "She says all right for you. She's done let you down easy for that whoppin' big lie you went an' spun her. She wants to know ain't you comin' up so she can talk to you? How about it?"

"Go on, Kid," urged a low and friendly voice at his elbow.

"Betcha!" grinned another. "Wish it was me! I done seen her in Logan."

Jimmy loosed a throbbing phrase, but obeyed, whereat Bill withdrew his grinning face from the sight of the grinning faces below. "He's comin' ma'am;

but he's shore plumb bashful." He looked down the canyon and laughed. "There they go to get Purdy off'n his perch. I'm natchurally goin' to lick anybody as tries to thrash that man," he muttered, glancing at George as he passed Jimmy on the ledge. George grinned and shook his head. "I'm going to give him the spree of his sinful, long life," he promised, thoughtfully.

Far to the west, silhouetted for a moment against the crimson sunset, appeared a row of mounted figures. It looked long and searchingly at the mesa and slowly disappeared from view. Bill saw it and pointed it out to Lefty Dickinson. "There's th' other eight," he said, smiling cheerfully. "If it wasn't for Whiskey Jeff's lookin' glass that eight'd mean a whole lot to us. We've had the luck of fools!"

CHAPTER 6

■ ◆◆◆◆◆ ■ ◆◆◆◆◆◆◆◆◆◆◆◆◆◆◆◆◆◆◆◆◆◆◆◆◆◆◆ ■ ◆◆◆◆◆ ■

Hopalong's Hop

Having sent Jimmy to the Bar-20 with a message for Buck Peters and seen the tenderfeet start for Sharpsville on the right trail and under escort, Bill Cassidy set out for the Crazy M ranch, by the way of Clay Gulch. He was to report on the condition of some cattle that Buck had been offered cheap and he was anxious to get back to the ranch. It was in the early evening when he reached Clay Gulch and rode slowly down the dusty, shack-lined street in search of a hotel. The town and the street were hardly different from other towns and streets that he had seen all over the cow-country, but nevertheless he felt uneasy. The air seemed to be charged with danger, and it caused him to sit even more erect in the saddle and assume his habit of indifferent alertness. The first man he saw confirmed the feeling by staring at him insolently and sneering in a veiled way at the low-hung, tied-down holsters that graced Bill's thighs. The guns proclaimed the gunman as surely as it would have been proclaimed by a sign; and it appeared that gun-men were not at that time held in high esteem by the citizens of Clay Gulch. Bill was growing fretful and peevish when the man, with a knowing shake of his head, turned away and entered the harness shop. "Trouble's brewin' some-wheres around," muttered Bill, as he went on. He had singled out the first of two hotels when another citizen, turning the corner, stopped in his tracks and looked Bill over with a deliberate scrutiny that left but little to the imagina-tion. He frowned and started away, but Bill spurred forward, determined to make him speak.

"*Might* I inquire if this is Clay Gulch?" he asked, in tones that made the other wince.

"You might," was the reply. "It is," added the citizen, "an' th' Crazy M lays fif-teen mile west." Having complied with the requirements of common politeness the citizen of Clay Gulch turned and walked into the nearest saloon. Bill squinted after him and shook his head in indecision.

"He wasn't guessin', neither. He shore knowed where I wants to go. I reckon Oleson must 'a' said he was expectin' me." He would have been somewhat surprised had he known that Mr. Oleson, foreman of the Crazy M, had said nothing to anyone about the expected visitor, and that no one, not even on the ranch, knew of it. Mr. Oleson was blessed with taciturnity to a remarkable degree; and he had given up expecting to see anyone from Mr. Peters.

As Bill dismounted in front of the "Victoria" he noticed that two men further down the street had evidently changed their conversation and were examining him with frank interest and discussing him earnestly. As a matter of fact they had not changed the subject of their conversation, but had simply fitted him in the place of a certain unknown. Before he had arrived they discussed in the abstract; now they could talk in the concrete. One of them laughed and called softly over his shoulder, whereupon a third man appeared in the door, wiping his lips with the back of a hairy, grimy hand, and focused evil eyes upon the innocent stranger. He grunted contemptuously and, turning on his heel, went back to his liquid pleasures. Bill covertly felt of his clothes and stole a glance at his horse, but could see nothing wrong. He hesitated: should he saunter over for information or wait until the matter was brought to his attention? A sound inside the hotel made him choose the latter course, for his stomach threatened to become estranged and it simply howled for food. Pushing open the door he dropped his saddle in a corner and leaned against the bar.

"Have one with me to get acquainted?" he invited. "Then I'll eat, for I'm hungry. An' I'll use one of yore beds to-night, too."

The man behind the bar nodded cheerfully and poured out his drink. As he raised the liquor he noticed Bill's guns and carelessly let the glass return to the bar.

"Sorry, sir," he said coldly. "I'm hall out of grub, the fire's hout, *hand* the beds are taken. But mebby 'Awley, down the strite, can tyke care of you."

Bill was looking at him with an expression that said much and he slowly extended his arm and pointed to the untasted liquor.

"Allus finish what you start, English," he said slowly and clearly. "When a man goes to take a drink with me, and suddenly changes his mind, why I gets riled. I don't know what ails this town, an' I don't care; I don't give a cuss about yore grub an' your beds; but if you don't drink that liquor you poured out *to* drink, why I'll natchurally shove it down yore British throat so cussed hard it'll strain yore neck. Get to it!"

The proprietor glanced apprehensively from the glass to Bill, then on to the business-like guns and back to the glass, and the liquor disappeared at a gulp. "W'y," he explained, aggrieved. "There hain't no call for to get riled hup like that, strainger. I bloody well forgot it."

"Then don't you go an' 'bloody well' forget this: Th' next time I drops in here for grub an' a bed, you have 'em both, an' be plumb polite about it. Do you get me?" he demanded icily.

The proprietor stared at the angry puncher as he gathered up his saddle and rifle and started for the door. He turned to put away the bottle and the sound came near being unfortunate for him. Bill leaped sideways, turning while in the air and landed on his feet like a cat, his left hand gripping a heavy Colt that covered the short ribs of the frightened proprietor before that worthy could hardly realize the move.

"Oh, all right," growled Bill, appearing to be disappointed. "I reckoned mebby you was gamblin' on a shore thing. I feels impelled to offer you my sincere apology; you ain't th' kind as would even gamble *on* a shore thing. You'll see me again," he promised. The sound of his steps on the porch ended in a thud as he leaped to the ground and then he passed the window leading his horse and scowling darkly. The proprietor mopped his head and reached twice for the glass before he found it. "Gawd, what a bloody 'eathen," he grunted. "'E won't be as easy as the lawst was, blime 'im."

Mr. Hawley looked up and frowned, but there was something in the suspicious eyes that searched his face that made him cautious. Bill dropped his load on the floor and spoke sharply. "I want supper an' a bed. You ain't full up, an' you ain't out of grub. So I'm goin' to get 'em both right here. Yes?"

"You shore called th' turn, stranger," replied Mr. Hawley in his Sunday voice. "That's what I'm in business for. An' business is shore dull these days."

He wondered at the sudden smile that illuminated Bill's face and half guessed it; but he said nothing and went to work. When Bill pushed back from the table he was more at peace with the world and he treated, closely watching his companion. Mr. Hawley drank with a show of pleasure and forthwith brought out cigars. He seated himself beside his guest and sighed with relief.

"I'm plumb tired out," he offered. "An' I ain't done much. You look tired, too. Come a long way?"

"Logan," replied Bill. "Do *you* know where I'm goin'? An' why?" he asked.

Mr. Hawley looked surprised and almost answered the first part of the question correctly before he thought. "Well," he grinned, "if I could tell where strangers was goin', an' why, I wouldn't never ask 'em where they come from. An' I'd shore hunt up a li'l game of faro, you bet!"

Bill smiled. "Well, that might be a good idea. But, say, what ails this town, anyhow?"

"What ails it? Hum! Why, lack of money for one thing; scenery, for another; wimmin, for another. Oh, hell, I ain't got time to tell you what ails it. Why?"

"Is there anything th' matter with me?"

"I don't know you well enough for to answer that kerrect."

"Well, would you turn around an' stare at me, an' seem pained an' hurt? Do I look funny? Has anybody put a sign on my back?"

"You looks all right to me. What's th' matter?"

"Nothin', yet," reflected Bill slowly. "But there will be, mebby. You was mentionin' faro. Here's a turn you can call: somebody in this wart of a two-by-nothin' town is goin' to run plumb into a big surprise. There'll mebby be a loud noise an' some smoke where it starts from; an' a li'l round hole where it stops. When th' curious delegation now holdin' forth on th' street slips in here after I'm in bed, an' makes inquiries about me, you can tell 'em that. An' if Mr.— Mr. Victoria drops in casual, tell him I'm cleanin' my guns. Now then, show me where I'm goin' to sleep."

Mr. Hawley very carefully led the way into the hall and turned into a room opposite the bar. "Here she is, stranger," he said, stepping back. But Bill was out in the hall listening. He looked into the room and felt oppressed.

"No she ain't," he answered, backing his intuition. "She is upstairs, where there is a li'l breeze. By th' Lord," he muttered under his breath. "This is some puzzle." He mounted the stairs shaking his head thoughtfully. "It shore is, it shore is."

The next morning when Bill whirled up to the Crazy M bunkhouse and dismounted before the door a puncher was emerging. He started to say something, noticed Bill's guns and went on without a word. Bill turned around and looked after him in amazement. "Well, what th' devil!" he growled. Before he could do anything, had he wished to, Mr. Oleson stepped quickly from the house, nodded and hurried toward the ranch house, motioning for Bill to follow. Entering the house, the foreman of the Crazy M waited impatiently for Bill to get inside, and then hurriedly closed the door.

"They've got onto it some way," he said, his taciturnity gone; "but that don't make no difference if you've got th' sand. I'll pay you one hundred an' fifty a month, furnish yore cayuses an' feed you. I'm losin' more 'n two hundred cows every month an' can't get a trace of th' thieves. Harris, Marshal of Clay Gulch, is stumped, too. *He* can't move without proof; *you* can. Th' first man to get is George Thomas, then his brother Art. By that time you'll know how things lay. George Thomas is keepin' out of Harris' way. He killed a man last week over in Tuxedo an' Harris wants to take him over there. He'll not help you, so don't ask him to." Before Bill could reply or recover from his astonishment Oleson continued and described several men. "Look out for ambushes. It'll be th' hardest game you ever went up ag'in, an' if you ain't got th' sand to go through with it, say so."

Bill shook his head. "I got th' sand to go through with anythin' I starts, but I don't start here. I reckon you got th' wrong man. I come up here to look over a herd for Buck Peters; an' here you go shovin' wages like that at me. When I tells Buck what I've been offered he'll fall dead." He laughed. "Now I knows th' answer to a lot of things."

"Here, here!" he exclaimed as Oleson began to rave. "Don't you go an' get all het up like that. I reckon I can keep my face shut. An' lemme observe in yore hat-like ear that if th' rest of this gang is like th' samples I seen in town, a good gun-man would shore be robbin' you to take all that money for th' job. Fifty a month, for two months, would be a-plenty."

Oleson's dismay was fading, and he accepted the situation with a grim smile. "You don't know them fellers," he replied. "They're a bad lot, an' won't stop at nothin'."

"All right. Let's take a look at them cows. I want to get home soon as I can."

Oleson shook his head. "I gave you up, an' when I got a better offer I let 'em go. I'm sorry you had th' ride for nothin', but I couldn't get word to you."

Bill led the way in silence back to the bunkhouse and mounted his horse. "All right," he nodded. "I shore was late. Well, I'll be goin'."

"That gun-man is late, too," said Oleson. "Mebby he ain't comin'. You wan th' job at *my* figgers?"

"Nope. I got a better job, though it don't pay so much money. It's steady, an' a hull lot cleaner. So-long," and Bill loped away, closely watched by Shorty Allen from the corral. And after an interval, Shorty mounted and swung out of the other gate of the corral and rode along the bottom of an arroyo until he felt it was safe to follow Bill's trail. When Shorty turned back he was almost to town, and he would not have been pleased had he known that Bill knew of the trailing for the last ten miles. Bill had doubled back and was within a hundred yards of Shorty when that person turned ranchward.

"Huh! I must be popular," grunted Bill. "I reckon I will stay in Clay Gulch til t'morrow mornin'; an' at the Victoria," he grinned. Then he laughed heartily. "Victoria! I got a better name for it than that, all right."

When he pulled up before the Victoria and looked in the proprietor scowled at him, which made Bill frown as he went on to Hawley's. Putting his horse in the corral he carried his saddle and rifle into the barroom and looked around. There was no one in sight, and he smiled. Putting the saddle and rifle back in one corner under the bar and covering them with gunny sacks he strolled to the Victoria and entered through the rear door. The proprietor reached for his gun but reconsidered in time and picked up a glass, which he polished with exaggerated care. There was something about the stranger that obtruded upon his peace of mind and confidence. He would let someone else try the stranger out.

Bill walked slowly forward, by force of will ironing out the humor in his face and assuming his sternest expression. "I want supper an' a bed, an' don't forget to be plumb polite," he rumbled, sitting down by the side of a small table in such a manner that it did not in the least interfere with the movement of his right hand. The observing proprietor observed and gave strict attention to the preparation of the meal. The gun-man, glancing around, slowly arose and walked carelessly to a chair that had blank wall behind it, and from where he could watch windows and doors.

When the meal was placed before him he glanced up. "Go over there an' sit down," he ordered, motioning to a chair that stood close to the rifle that leaned against the wall. "Loaded?" he demanded. The proprietor could only nod. "Then sling it acrost yore knees an' keep still. Well, start movin'."

The proprietor walked as though he were in a trance but when he seated himself and reached for the weapon a sudden flash of understanding illu-mined him and caused cold sweat to bead upon his wrinkled brow. He put the weapon down again, but the noise made Bill look up.

"Acrost yore knees," growled the puncher, and the proprietor hastily obeyed, but when it touched his legs he let loose of it as though it were hot. He felt a great awe steal through his fear, for here was a gun-man such as he had read about. This man gave him all the best of it just to tempt him to make a break. The rifle had been in his hands, and while it was there the gun-man was calmly eating with both hands on the table and had not even looked up until the noise of the gun made him!

"My Gawd, 'e must be a wizard with 'em. I 'opes I don't forget!" With the thought came a great itching of his kneecap; then his foot itched so as to make him squirm and wear horrible expressions. Bill, chancing to glance up carelessly, caught sight of the expressions and growled, whereupon they became angelic. Fearing that he could no longer hold in the laughter that tortured him, Bill arose.

"Shoulder, *arms!*" he ordered, crisply. The gun went up with trained precision. "Been a sojer," thought Bill. "Carry, *arms!* About, *face!* To a bedroom, *march!*" He followed, holding his sides, and stopped before the room. "This th' best?" he demanded. "Well, it ain't good enough for *me.* About, *face!* Forward, *march!* Column, *left!* Ground, *arms!* Fall out." Tossing a coin on the floor as payment for the supper Bill turned sharply and went out without even a backward glance.

The proprietor wiped the perspiration from his face and walked unsteadily to the bar, where he poured out a generous drink and gulped it down. Peering out of the door to see if the coast was clear, he scurried across the street and told his troubles to the harness-maker.

Bill leaned weakly against Hawley's and laughed until the tears rolled down his cheeks. Pushing weakly from the building he returned to the Victoria to play another joke on its proprietor. Finding it vacant he slipped upstairs and hunted for a room to suit him. The bed was the softest he had seen for a long time and it lured him into removing his boots and chaps and guns, after he had propped a chair against the door as a warning signal, and stretching out flat on his back, he prepared to enjoy solid comfort. It was not yet dark, and as he was not sleepy he lay there thinking over the events of the past twenty-four hours, often laughing so hard as to shake the bed. What a reputation he would have in the morning! The softness of the bed got in its work and he fell asleep, for how long he did not know; but when he awakened it was dark and he heard voices coming up from below. They came from the room he had refused to take. One expression banished all thoughts of sleep from his mind and he listened intently. "'Red-headed Irish gun-man.' Why, they means me! 'Make him hop into hell.' I don't reckon I'd do that for anybody, even my friends."

"I tried to give 'im this room, but 'e wouldn't tyke *it,*" protested the proprietor, hurriedly. "'E says the bloody room wasn't good enough for 'im, and 'e marches me out and makes off. Likely 'e's in 'Awley's."

"No, he ain't," growled a strange voice. "You've gone an' bungled th' whole thing."

"But I s'y I didn't, you know. I tries to give 'im this werry room, George, but 'e wouldn't 'ave it. D'y think I wants 'im running haround this blooming town? 'E's worse nor the other, *hand* Gawd knows 'e was bad enough. 'E's a cold-*blooded* beggar, 'e *is!*"

"You missed yore chance," grunted the other. "Wish *I* had that gun you had."

"I was wishing to Gawd you *did*," retorted the proprietor. "It never looked so bloody big before, damn 'is 'ide!'"

"Well, his cayuse is in Hawley's corral," said the first speaker. "If I ever finds Hawley kept him under cover I'll blow his head off. Come on; we'll get Harris first. He ought to be gettin' close to town if he got th' word I sent over to Tuxedo. He won't let us call him. He's a man of his word."

"He'll be here, all right. Fred an' Tom is watchin' his shack, an' we better take th' other end of town—there's no tellin' how he'll come in now," suggested Art Thomas. "But I wish I knowed where that cussed gun-man is."

As they went out Bill, his chaps on and his boots in his hand, crept down the stairs, and stopped as he neared the hall door. The proprietor was coming back. The others were outside, going to their stations and did not hear the choking gasp that the proprietor made as a pair of strong hands reached out and throttled him. When he came to he was lying face down on a bed, gagged and bound by a rope that cut into his flesh with every movement. Bill, waiting a moment, slipped into the darkness and was swallowed up. He was looking for Mr. Harris, and looking eagerly.

The moon arose and bathed the dusty street and its crude shacks in silver, cunningly and charitably hiding its ugliness; and passed on as the skirmishing rays of the sun burst into the sky in close and eternal pursuit. As the dawn spread swiftly and long, thin shadows sprang across the sandy street, there arose from the dissipated darkness close to the wall of a building an armed man, weary and slow from a tiresome vigil. Another emerged from behind a pile of boards that faced the marshal's abode, while down the street another crept over the edge of a dried-out water course and swore softly as he stood up slowly to flex away the stiffness of cramped limbs. Of vain speculation he was empty; he had exhausted all the whys and hows long before and now only muttered discontentedly as he reviewed the hours of fruitless waiting. And he was uneasy; it was not like Harris to take a dare and swallow his own threats without a struggle. He looked around apprehensively, shrugged his shoulders and stalked behind the shacks across from the two hotels.

Another figure crept from the protection of Hawley's corral like a slinking coyote, gun in hand and nervously alert. He was just in time to escape the challenge that would have been hurled at him by Hawley, himself, had that gentleman seen the skulker as he grouchily opened one shutter and scowled sleepily at the kindling eastern sky. Mr. Hawley was one of those who go to bed with regret and get up with remorse, and his temper was always easily disturbed before breakfast. The skulker, safe from the remorseful gentleman's eyes, and gun, kept close to the building as he walked and was again fortunate, for he had passed when Mr. Hawley strode heavily into his kitchen to curse the cold, rusty stove, a rite he faithfully performed each morning. Across the street George and Art Thomas walked to meet each other behind the row of shacks and stopped near the harness shop to hold a consultation. The subject was so interesting that for a few moments they were oblivious to all else.

A man softly stepped to the door of the Victoria and watched the two across the street with an expression on his face that showed his smiling contempt for them and their kind. He was a small man, so far as physical measurements go, but he was lithe, sinewy and compact. On his opened vest, hanging slovenly and blinking in the growing light as if to prepare itself for the blinding glare of midday, glinted a five-pointed star of nickel, a lowly badge that every rural community knows and holds in an awe far above the metal or design. Swinging low on his hip gleamed the ivory butt of a silver-plated Colt, the one weakness that his vanity seized upon. But under the silver and its engraving, above and before the cracked and stained ivory handles, lay the power of a great force; and under the casing of the marshal's small body lay a virile manhood, strong in courage and determination. Toby Harris watched, smilingly; he loved the dramatic and found keen enjoyment in the situation. Out of the corner of his eye he saw a carelessly dressed cowpuncher slouching indolently along close to the buildings on the other side of the street with the misleading sluggishness of a panther. The red hair, kissed by the slanting rays of the sun where it showed beneath the soiled sombrero, seemed to be a flaming warning; the half-closed eyes, squinting under the brim of the big hat, missed nothing as they darted from point to point.

The marshal stepped silently to the porch and then on to the ground, his back to the rear of the hotel, waiting to be discovered. He had been in sight perhaps a minute. The cow-puncher made a sudden, eye-baffling movement and smoke whirled about his hips. Fred, turning the corner behind the marshal, dropped his gun with a scream of rage and pain and crashed against the window in sudden sickness, his gunhand hanging by a tendon from his wrist. The marshal stepped quickly forward at the shot and for an instant gazed deeply into the eyes of the startled rustlers. Then his Colt leaped out and crashed a fraction of a second before the brothers fired. George Thomas reeled, caught sight of the puncher and fired by instinct. Bill, leaving Harris to watch the other side of the street, was watching the rear corner of the Victoria and was unprepared for the shot. He crumpled and dropped and then the marshal, enraged, ended the rustler's earthly career in a stream of flame and smoke. Tom, turning into the street further down, wheeled and dashed for his horse, and Art, having leaped behind the harness shop, turned and fled for his life. He had nearly reached his horse and was going at top speed with great leaps when the prostrate man in the street, raising on his elbow, emptied his gun after him, the five shots sounding almost as one. Art Thomas arose convulsively, steadied himself and managed to gain the saddle. Harris looked hastily down the street and saw a cloud of dust racing northward, and grunted. "Let them go—*they* won't never come back no more." Running to the cowpuncher he raised him after a hurried examination of the wounded thigh. "Hop along, Cassidy," he smiled in encouragement. "You'll be a better man with one good laig than th' whole gang was all put together."

The puncher smiled faintly as Hawley, running to them, helped him toward his hotel. "Th' bone is plumb smashed. I reckon I'll hop along through life. It'll be hop along, for me, all right. That's *my* name, all right. Huh! Hopalong Cassidy! But I didn't hop into hell, did I, Harris?" he grinned bravely.

And thus was born a nickname that found honor and fame in the cowcountry—a name that stood for loyalty, courage and most amazing gun-play. I have Red's word for this, and the endorsement of those who knew him at the time. And from this on, up to the time he died, and after, we will forsake "Bill" and speak of him as Hopalong Cassidy, a cowpuncher who lived and worked in the days when the West was wild and rough and lawless; and who, like others, through the medium of the only court at hand, Judge Colt, enforced justice as he believed it should be enforced.

CHAPTER 7

"Dealing the Odd"

Faro-bank is an expensive game when luck turns a cold shoulder on any player, and "going broke" is as easy as ruffling a deck. When a man finds he has two dollars left out of more than two months' pay and that it has taken him less than thirty minutes to get down to that mark, he cannot be censored much if he rails at that Will-o'-the-wisp, the Goddess of Luck. Put him a good ten days' ride from home, acquaintances and money and perhaps he will be justified in adding heat in plenty to his denunciation. He had played to win when he should have coppered, coppered when he should have played to win, he had backed both ends against the middle and played the high card as well—but only when his bets were small did the turn show him what he wanted to see. Perhaps the case-keeper had hoodooed him, for he never did have any luck at cards when a tow-headed man had a finger in the game.

Fuming impotently at his helplessness, a man limped across the main street in Colby, constrained and a little awkward in his new store clothes and new, squeaking boots that were clumsy with stiffness. The only things on him that he could regard as old and tried friends were the battered sombrero and the heavy, walnut-handled Colt's .45 which rubbed comfortably with each movement of his thigh. The weapon, to be sure, had a ready cash value—but he could not afford to part with it. The horse belonged to his ranch, and the saddle must not be sold; to part with it would be to lose his mark of caste and become a walking man, which all good punchers despised.

"Ten days from home, knowin' nobody, two measly dollars in my pocket, an' luck dead agin me," he growled with pugnacious pessimism. "Oh, I'm a wise old bird, I am! A hell of a wise bird. Real smart an' cute an' shiny, a cache of wisdom, a real, bonyfied Smart Aleck with a head full of spavined brains. I copper th' deuce an' th' deuce wins; I play th' King to win for ten dollars when I ought to copper it. I lay two-bits and it comes right—ten dollars an' I see my guess go *loco*. Reckon I better slip these here twin bucks down in my kill-me-soon boots afore some blind papoose takes 'em away from me. Wiser'n Solomon, I am; I've got old Caesar climbin' a cactus for pleasure an' joy. S-u-c-k-e-r is my middle name—an' I'm busted."

He almost stumbled over a little tray of a three-legged table on the corner of the street and his face went hard as he saw the layout. Three halves of English walnut shells lay on the faded and soiled green cloth and a blackened, shriveled pea was still rolling from the shaking he had given the table. He stopped and regarded it gravely, jingling his two dollars disconsolately. "Don't this town do nothin' else besides gamble?" he muttered, looking around.

"Howd'y, stranger!" cheerfully cried a man who hastened up. "Want to see me fool you?"

The puncher's anger was aroused to a thin, licking flame; but it passed swiftly and a cold, calculating look came into his eyes. He glanced around swiftly, trying to locate the cappers, but they were not to be seen, which worried him a little. He always liked to have possible danger where he could keep an eye on it. Perhaps they were eating or drinking—the thought stirred him again to anger: two dollars would not feed him very long, nor quench his thirst.

"Pick it out, stranger," invited the proprietor, idly shifting the shells. "It's easy if yo're right smart—but lots of folks just can't do it; they can't seem to get th' hang of it, somehow. That's why it's a bettin' proposition. Here it is, right before yore eyes! One little pea, three little shells, right here plumb in front of yore eyes! Th' little pea hides under one of th' little shells, right in plain sight: But can you tell which one? That's th' whole game, right there. See how it's done?" and the three little shells moved swiftly but clumsily and the little pea disappeared. "Now, then; where would *you* say it was?" demanded the hopeful operator, genially.

The puncher gripped his two dollars firmly, shifted his weight as much as possible on his sound leg, and scowled: he knew where it was. "Do I look like a kid? Do you reckon you have to coax like a fool to get me all primed up to show how re-markably smart an' quick I am? You don't; I know how smart I am. Say, you ain't, not by any kinda miracle, a blind papoose, are you?" he demanded.

"What you mean?" asked the other, smiling as he waited for the joke. It did not come, so he continued. "Don't take no harm in my fool wind-jammin', stranger. It's in th' game. It's a habit; I've said it so much I just can't help it no more—I up an' says it at a funeral once; that is, part of it—th' first part. That's dead right! But I reckon I'm wastin' my time—unless you happen to feel coltish an' hain't got nothin' to do for an age. I've been playin' in hard luck th' last week or so—you see, I ain't as good as I uster be. I ain't quite so quick, an' a little bit off my quickness is a whole lot off my chances. But th' game's square—an' that's a good deal more'n you can say about most of 'em."

The puncher hesitated, a grin flickering about his thin lips and a calm joy warming him comfortably. He knew the operator. He knew that face, the peculiar, crescent-shaped scar over one brow, and the big, blue eyes that years of life had not entirely robbed of their baby-like innocence. The past, sorted thoroughly and quickly by his memory, shoved out that face before a crowd of others. Five years is not a long time to remember something unpleasant; he had reasons to remember that countenance. Knowing the face he also knew that the man had been, at one time, far from "square." The associations and means of livelihood during the past five years, judging from the man's present occupation, had not been the kind to correct any evil tendency. He laid a forefinger on the edge of the tray. "Start th' machinery—I'll risk a couple of dollars, anyhow. That ain't much to lose. I bet two dollars I can call it right," he said, watching closely.

He won, as he knew he would; and the result told him that the gambler had not reformed. The dexterous fingers shifting the shells were slower than others he had seen operate and when he had won again he stopped, as if to leave. "When I hit town a short time ago I didn't know I'd be so lucky. I went an' drawed two months' pay when I left th' ranch; I shore don't need it. Shuffle 'em again—it's yore money, anyhow," he laughed. "You should 'a' quit th' game before you got so slow."

"Goin' back to work purty soon?" queried the shell-man, wondering how much this "sucker" had left unspent.

"Not me! I've only just had a couple of drinks since I hit town—an' *I'm* due to celebrate."

The other's face gave no hint of his thoughts, which were that the fool before him had about a hundred dollars on his person. "Well, luck's with you today—you've called it right twice. I'll bet you a cool hundred that you can't call it th' third time. It's th' quickness of my hands agin yore eyes—an' you can't beat me three straight. Make it a hundred? I hate to play all day."

"I'll lay you my winnin's an' have some more of yore money," replied the puncher, feverishly. "Ain't scared, are you?"

"Don't know what it means to be scared," laughed the other. "But I ain't got no small change, nothin' but tens. Play a hundred an' let's have some real excitement."

"Nope; eight or nothin'.'"

He won again. "Now, sixteen even. Come on; I've got you beat."

"But what's th' use of stringin' 'long like that?" demanded the shell-man.

"Gimme a chance to get my hand in, won't you?" retorted the puncher.

"Well, all right," replied the gambler, and he lost the sixteen.

"Now thirty," suggested the puncher. "Next time all I've got, every red cent. Once more to practice—then every red," he repeated, shifting his feet nervously. "I'll clean you out an' have a real, genuine blow-out on yore money. Come on, I'm in a hurry."

"I'll fool you *this* time, by th' Lord!" swore the gambler, angrily. "You've got more luck than sense. An' I'll fool you next time, too. Yo're quicker'n most men I've run up agin, but I can beat you, shore as shootin'. Th' game's square, th' play fair—my hand agin yore eye. Ready? Then watch me!"

He swore luridly and shoved the money across the board to the winner, bewailing his slowness and getting angrier every moment. "Yo're th' cussedest man I ever bet agin! But I'll get you *this* time. You can't guess right all th' time, an' I know it."

"There she is; sixty-two bucks, three score an' two dollars; all I've got, every cent. Let's see you take it away from me!"

The gambler frowned and choked back a curse. He had risked sixty dollars to win two, and the fact that he had to let this fool play again with the fire hurt his pride. He had no fear for his money—he knew he could win at every throw—but to play that long for two dollars! And suppose the sucker had quit with the sixty!

"Do you get a dollar a month?" he demanded, sarcastically. "Well, I reckon you earn it, at that. Thought you had money, thought you drew down two months' pay an' hain't had nothin' more'n two drinks? Did you go an' lose it on th' way?"

"Oh, I drew it a month ago," replied the sucker, surprised. "I've only had two drinks in this town, which I hit 'bout an hour ago. But I shore lost a wad playin' faro-bank agin a towhead. Come on—lemme take sixty more of yore money, anyhow."

"Sixty-*two!*" snapped the proprietor, determined to have those two miserable dollars and break the sucker for revenge. "Every cent, you remember."

"*All* right; I don't care! I ain't no tin-horn," grumbled the other. "Think I care 'bout two dollars?" But he appeared to be very nervous, nevertheless.

"Well, put it on th' table."

"After you put yourn down."

"There it is. Now watch me close!" A gleam of joy flashed up in the angry man's eyes as he played with the shells. "Watch me close! Mebby it is, an' mebby it ain't—th' game's square, th' play's fair. It's my hand agin yore eye. Watch me close!"

"Oh, go ahead! I'm watchin', all right. Think I'd go to sleep now!"

The shifting hands stopped, the shells lay quiet, and the gambler gazed blankly down the unsympathetic barrel of a Colt.

"Now, Thomas, old thimble-rigger," crisply remarked the supposed sucker as he cautiously slid the money off the table, to be picked up later when conditions would be more favorable. "Th' little pea ain't under *no* shell. *Stop!* Step back one pace an' elevate them paws. Don't make no more funny motions with that hand, savvy? But you can drop th' pea if it hurts them two fingers. Now we'll see if I win; I allus like to be shore," and he cautiously turned over the shells, revealing nothing but the dirty green cloth. "I win; it ain't there—just like I thought."

"Who are you, an' how'd you know my name?" demanded the gambler, mentally cursing his two missing cappers. They were drinking once too often and things were going to happen in their vicinity, and very soon.

"Why, you took twenty-five dollars from me up in Alameda onct, when I couldn't afford to lose it," grinned the puncher. "I was something of a kid then. I remember you, all right. My foreman told me about yore bang-up fight agin th' Johnson brothers, who gave you that scar. I thought then that you were a great man—now I know you ain't. I wouldn't 'a' played at all if I hadn't knowed how crooked you was. Take yore layout an' yore crookedness, find th' pea an' yore cappers, an' clear out. An' if anybody asks you if you've seen Hopalong Cassidy you tell 'em I'm up here in Colby makin' some easy money beatin' crooked games. So-long, an' *don't* look back!"

Hopalong watched him go and then went to the nearest place where he could get something to eat. In due time, having disposed of a square meal, Hopalong called for a drink and a cigar, and sat quietly smoking for nearly half an hour, so lost in thought that his cigar went out repeatedly. As he reviewed his disastrous play at faro many small details came to him and now he found them interesting. The dealer was not a master at his trade and Hopalong had seen many better; in fact the man was not even second class, and this fact hurt his pride. He had played a careful game, and the great majority of his small bets had won—it was only when he risked twenty or thirty dollars that he lost. The only big bet that he had been at all lucky on was one where doubles showed on the turn and he had been split, losing half of his stake. But when he had played his last fifty dollars on the Jack, open, the final blow fell and he had left the table in disgust.

Why weren't there cue-cards, so the players could keep their own tally of the cards instead of having to depend on the cue-box kept by the case-keeper? This made him suspicious; a crooked dealer and case-keeper can trim a big bet at will, unless the players keep their own cases or are exceptionally wise; and even then a really good dealer will get away with his play nine times out of ten. While he seldom played a system, he had backed one that morning; but he was cured of that weakness now. If the game were square he figured he could get at least an even break; if crooked, nothing but a gun could beat it, and he had a very good gun. When he thought of the gun, he reviewed the arrangement of the room and estimated the weight of the rough, deal table on which rested the faro layout. He smiled and turned to the bartender. "Hey, barkeeper! Got any paper an' a pencil?"

After some rummaging the taciturn dispenser of liquid forget-it produced the articles in question and Hopalong, drawing some hurried lines, paid his bill, treated, kept the pencil and headed for the faro game across the street.

When he entered the room the table was deserted and he nodded to the dealer as he seated himself at the right of the case-keeper, who now took his place, and opposite the dealer and the lookout. He was not surprised to find no other players in the room, for the hour was wrong; later in the afternoon there would be many and at night the place would be crowded. This suited him perfectly and he settled himself to begin playing.

When the deck was shuffled and placed in the deal box Hopalong put his ruled paper in front of him on the table, tallied once against the King for the soda card and started to play quarters and half dollars. He caught the fugitive look that passed between the men as they saw his cue-card but he gave no sign of having observed it. After that he never looked up from the cards while his bets were small. Two deals did not alter his money much and he knew that so far the game was straight. If it were not to remain straight the crookedness would not come more than once in a deal if the frame-up was "single-odd" and then not until the bet was large enough to practically break him. His high-card play ran in his favor and kept him gradually drawing ahead. He lost twice in calling the last turn and guessed it right once, at four to one, which made him win in that department of the game.

When the fifth deal began he was quite a little ahead and his play became bolder, some of the bets going as high as ten dollars. He broke even and then played heavier on the following deal. His first high bet, twenty dollars, was on the eight, open, only one eight having shown. Double eights showed on the next turn and he was split, losing half the stake.

It was about this time that the lookout discovered that Mr. Cassidy was getting a little excited and several times had nearly forgotten to keep his cases. This information was cautiously passed to the dealer and case-keeper and from then on they evinced a little more interest in the game. Finally the player, after studying his cue-card, placed fifty dollars on the Queen, open, and coppered the deuce, a case-card, and then put ten more on the high card. This came in the middle of the game and he was prepared for trouble as the turn was made, but fortune was kind to him and he raked in sixty dollars. He was mildly surprised that he had won, but explained it to himself by thinking that the stakes were not yet high enough. From then on he was keenly alert, for the crookedness would come soon if it ever did, but he strung small sums on the next dozen turns and waited for a new deal before plunging.

As the dealer shuffled the cards the door opened and closed noisily and a surprised and doubting voice exclaimed: "Ain't you Hopalong Cassidy? Cassidy, of th' Bar-20?"

Hopalong glanced up swiftly and back to the cards again: "Yes; what of it?"

"Oh, nothin'. I saw you onct an' I wondered if I was right."

"Ain't got time now; see you later, mebby. You might stick around outside so I can borrow some money if I go broke." The man who knew Mr. Cassidy silently faded, but did not stick around, thereby proving that the player knew human nature and also how to get rid of a pest.

When the dealer heard the name he glanced keenly at the owner of it, exchanged significant looks with the case-keeper and faltered for an instant as he shoved the cards together. He was not sure that he had shuffled them right, and an anxious look came into his eyes as he realized that the deal must go on. It was far from reassuring to set out to cheat a man so well known for expert short-gun work as the Bar-20 puncher and he wished he could be relieved. There was no other dealer around at that time of the day and he had to go through with it. He did not dare to shuffle again and chance losing the card beyond hope, and for the reason that the player was watching him like a hawk.

A ten lay face up on the deck and Hopalong, tallying against it on his sheet, began to play small sums. Luck was variable and remained so until the first twenty dollar bet, when he reached out excitedly and raked in his winnings, his coat sleeve at the same time brushing the cue-card off the table. But he had forgotten all about the tally sheet in his eagerness to win and played several more cards before he noticed it was missing and sought for it. Smothering a curse he glanced at the case-keeper's tally and went on with the play. He did not see the look of relief that showed momentarily on the faces of the dealer and his associates, but he guessed it.

He had no use for cue-cards when he felt like doing without them; he liked to see them in use by the players because it showed the game to be more or less straight, and it also saved him from over-heating his memory. When he had brushed his tally sheet off the table he knew what he was doing, and he knew every card that had been drawn out of the box. So far he had seen no signs of cheating and he wished to give the dealer a chance. There should now remain in the deal box three cards, a deuce, five and a four, with a Queen in sight as the last winner. He knew this to be true because he had given all his attention to memorizing the cards as they showed in the deal box, and had made his bets small so he would not have to bother about them. As he had lost three times on a four he now believed it was due to win.

Taking all his money he placed it on the four: "Two hundred and seventy on th' four to win," he remarked, crisply.

The dealer sniffed almost inaudibly and the case-keeper prepared to cover him on the cue-rack under cover of the excitement of the turn. If the four lay under the Queen, Cassidy lost; if not he either won or was in hock. The dealer was unusually grave as he grasped the deal box to make the turn and as the Queen slid off a five-spot showed.

The dealer's hand trembled as he slid the five off, showing a four, and a winner for Hopalong. He went white—he had bungled the shuffle in his indecision and now he didn't know what might develop. And in his agitation he exposed the hock card before he realized what he was doing, and showed another five. He had made the mistake of showing the "odd."

Hopalong, ready for trouble, was more prepared than the others and he was well under way before they started. His left hand swung hard against the case-keeper's jaw, his Colt roared at the drawing bartender, crumpling the trouble-hunter into a heap on the floor dazed from shock of a ball that "creased" his head. He had done this as he sprang to his feet and his left hand, dropping swiftly to the heavy table, threw it over onto the lookout and the dealer at the instant their hands found their guns. Caught off their balance they went down under it and before they could move sufficiently to do any damage, Hopalong vaulted the table and kicked their guns out of their hands. When they realized just what had happened a still-smoking Colt covered them. Many of Hopalong's most successful and spectacular plays had been less carefully thought out beforehand than this one and he laughed sneeringly as he looked at the men who had been so greedy as to try to clean him out the second time.

"Get up!" he snarled.

They crawled out of their trap and sullenly obeyed his hand, backing against the wall. The case-keeper was still unconscious and Hopalong, disarming him, dragged him to the wall with the others.

"I wondered where that deuce had crawled to," Mr. Cassidy remarked, grimly, "an' I was goin' to see, only it's plain now. I knowed you was clumsy, but my God! Any man as can't deal 'single-odd' ought to quit th' business, or play straight. So you had five fives agin me, eh? Instead of keepin' th' five under th' Queen, you bungled th' deuce in its place. When you went to pull off th' Queen an' five like they was one card, you had th' deuce under her. You see, I keep cases in my old red head an' I didn't have to believe what th' cue-rack was all fixed to show me. An' I was waitin', all ready for th' play that'd make me lose.

"As long as this deal was framed up, we'll say it was this mornin'. You cough up th' hundred an' ten I lost then, an' another hundred an' ten that I'd won if it wasn't crooked. An' don't forget that two-seventy I just pulled down, neither. Make it in double eagles an' don't be slow 'bout it. Money or lead—with *you* callin' th' turn." It was not a very large amount and it took only a moment to count it out. The eleven double eagles representing the morning's play seemed to slide from the dealer's hand with reluctance—but a man lives only once, and they slid without stopping.

The winner, taking the money, picked up the last money he had bet and, distributing it over his person to equalize the weight, gathered up the guns from the floor. Backing toward the door he noticed that the bartender moved and a keen glance at that unfortunate assured him that he would live.

When he reached the door he stopped a moment to ask a question, the tenseness of his expression relaxing into a broad, apologetic grin. "Would you mind tellin' me where I can find some more frame-ups? I shore can use th' money."

The mumbled replies mentioned a locality not to be found on any map of the surface of the globe, and grinning still more broadly, Mr. Cassidy sidestepped and disappeared to find his horse and go on his way rejoicing.

CHAPTER 8

The Norther

Johnny knew I had a notebook crammed with the stories his friends had told me; but Johnny, being a wise youth, also knew that there was always room for one more. Perhaps that explains his sarcasm, for, as he calmly turned his back on his fuming friend, he winked at me and sauntered off, whistling cheerfully.

Red spread his feet apart, jammed his fists against his thighs and stared after the youngster. His expression was a study and his open mouth struggled for a retort, but in vain. After a moment he shook his head and slowly turned to me. "Hear th' fool? He's from *Idyho*, he is. It never gets cold nowhere else on earth. Ain't it terrible to be so ignorant?" He glanced at the bunkhouse, into which Johnny had gone for dry clothing. "So I ain't never seen no cold weather?" he mused thoughtfully. Snapping his fingers irritably, he wheeled toward the corral. "I'm goin' down to look at th' dam—there's been lots of water leanin' ag'in it th' last week. Throw th' leather on Saint, if you wants, an' come along. I'll tell you about some cold weather that had th' *Idyho* brand faded. *Cold weather!* Huh!"

As he swung past the bunkhouse we saw Johnny and Billy Jordan leaning in the doorway ragging each other, as cubs will. Johnny grinned at Red and executed a one-hand phrase of the sign language that is universally known, which Red returned with a chuckle. "Wish he'd been here th' time God took a hand in a big game on this ranch," he said. "I'm minus two toes on each foot in consequence thereof. They can't scare me none by preachin' a red-hot hell. No, sir; not any."

He was silent a moment. "Mebby it ain't so bad when a feller is used to it; but we ain't. An' it frequent hits us goin' over th' fence, with both feet off th' ground. Anyhow, that Norther wasn't no storm—it was th' attendant agitation caused by th' North Pole visitin' th' Gulf.

"Cowan had just put Buckskin on th' map by buildin' th' first shack. John Bartlett an' Shorty Jones, damn him, was startin' th' Double Arrow with two hundred head. When th' aforementioned agitation was over they had less'n one hundred. We lost a lot of cows, too; but our range is sheltered good, an' that rock wall down past Meeker's bunkhouse stopped our drifts, though lots of th' cows died there.

"We'd had a mild winter for two weeks, an' a lot of rain. We was chirpin' like li'l fool birds about winter bein' over. Ever notice how many times winter is over before it is? But Buck didn't think so; an' he shore can smell weather. We was also discussin' a certain campin' party Jimmy had discovered across th' river. Jimmy was at th' bunkhouse that shift an' he was a great hand for snoopin' around kickin' up trouble. He reports there's twelve in th' party an' they're camped back of Split Hill. Now, Split Hill is no place for a camp, even in th' summer; an' what got us was th' idea of campin' at all in th' winter. It riled Buck till he forgot to cross off three days on th' calendar, which we later discovered by help of th' almanac an' th' moon. Buck sends Hoppy over to scout around Split Hill. You know Hoppy. He scouted for two days without bein' seen, an' without discoverin' any lawful an' sane reason why twelve hard-lookin' fellers should be campin' back of Split Hill in th' winter time. He also found they had come from th' south, an' he swore there wasn't no cow tracks leadin' toward them from our range. But there was lots of hoss tracks back and forth. An' when he reports that th' campers had left an' gone on north we all feel better. Then he adds they turned east below th' Double Arrow an' went back south again. That's different. It's plain to some of us they was lookin' us over for future use; learnin' our ways an' th' lay of th' land. There was seven of us at th' time, but we could 'a' licked 'em in a fair fight.

"In them days we only had two line houses. Number One was near Big Coulee, with Cowan's at th' far end of its fifteen miles of north line; th' west line was a twenty-five mile ride south to Lookout Peak. Number Two was where th' Jumpin' Bear empties into th' river, now part of Meeker's range. From it th' riders went west twenty-five miles to th' Peak an' north from it twenty-five miles along th' east line. There was a hundred thousan' acres in Conroy Valley an' thirty thousan' in th' Meeker triangle, which made up Section Two. At that time mebby ten thousan' cows was on this section—two-thirds of all of 'em. When we built Number Three on th' Peak this section was cut down to a reasonable size. Th' third headquarters then was th' bunkhouse, with only th' east line to ride. One part, th' shortest, ran north to Cowan's; th' other run about seventeen miles south to Li'l Timber, where th' line went on as part of Number Two's. We paired off an' had two weeks in each of 'em in them days.

"When we shifted at th' end of that week Jimmy Price an' Ace Fisher got Number One; Skinny an' Lanky was in Number Two; an' me an' Buck an' Hoppy took life easy in th' bunkhouse, with th' cook to feed us. Buck, he scouted all over th' ranch between th' lines an' worked harder than any of us, spendin' his nights in th' nearest house.

"One mornin', about a week after th' campers left, Buck looked out of th' bunkhouse door an' cautions me an' Hoppy to ride prepared for cold weather. I can see he's worried, an' to please him we straps a blanket an' a buffalo robe behind our saddles, cussin' th' size of 'em under our breath. I've got th' short ride that day, an' Buck says he'll wait for me to come back, after which we'll scout around Medicine Bend. He's still worried about them campers. In th' Valley th' cows are thicker'n th' other parts of th' range, an' it wouldn't take no time to get a big herd together. He's got a few things to mend, so he says he'll do th' work before I get back.

"Down on Section Two things is happenin' fast, like they mostly do out here. Twelve rustlers can do a lot if they have things planned, an' 'most any fair plan will work once. They only wanted one day—after that it would be a runnin' fight, with eight or nine of 'em layin' back to hold us off while th' others drove th' cows hard. Why, Slippery Trendley an' Tamale Jose was th' only ones that ever slid across our lines with that many men.

"Three rustlers slipped up to Number Two at night an' waited. When Skinny opened th' door in th' mornin' he was drove back with a hole in his shoulder. Then there was hell a-poppin' in that li'l mud shack. But it didn't do no good, for neither of 'em could get out alive until after dark. They learned that with sorrow, an' pain. An' they shore was het up about it. Ace Fisher, ridin' along th' west line from Number One, was dropped from ambush. Two more rustlers lay back of Medicine Bend lookin' for any of us that might ride down from the bunkhouse. An' they sent two more over to Li'l Timber to lay under that ledge of rock that sticks out of th' south side of th' bluff like a porch roof. Either me or Hoppy would be ridin' that way. They stacked th' deck clever; but Providence cut it square.

"Th' first miss-cue comes when a pert gray wolf lopes past ahead of Hoppy when he's quite some distance above Li'l Timber. This gray wolf was a whopper, an' Hoppy was all set to get him. He wanted that sassy devil more'n he wanted money just then, so he starts after it. Mr. Gray Wolf leads him a long chase over th' middle of th' range an' then suddenly disappears. Hoppy hunts around quite a spell, an' then heads back for th' line. While he's huntin' for th' wolf it gets cold, an' it keeps on gettin' colder fast.

"Me, I leaves later'n usual that mornin'. An' I don't get to Cowan's until late. I'm there when I notices how cussed cold it's got all of a sudden. Cowan looks at his thermometer, which Jimmy later busts, an' says she has gone down thirty degrees since daylight. He gives me a bottle of liquor Buck wanted, an' I ride west along th' north line, hopin' to meet Jimmy or Ace for a short talk.

"All at once I notice somebody's pullin' a slate-covered blanket over th' north sky, an' I drag *my* blanket out an' wrap it around me. I'm gettin' blamed cold, an' also a li'l worried. Shall I go back to Cowan's or head straight for th' bunkhouse? Cowan's the nearest by three miles, but what's three miles out here? It's got a lot colder than it was when I was at Cowan's, an' while I'm debatin' about it th' wind dies out. I look up an' see that th' slate-covered blanket has traveled fast. It's 'most over my head, an' th' light is gettin' poor. When I look down again I notice my cayuses's ears movin' back an' forth, an' he starts pawin' an' actin' restless. That settles it. I'm backin' instinct just then, an' I head for home. I ain't cussin' that blanket none now, an' I'm glad I got th' robe handy; an' that quart of liquor ain't bulky no more.

"All at once th' bottom falls out of that lead sky, an' flakes as big as quarters sift down so fast they hurts my eyes, an' so thick I can't see twenty feet. In ten minutes everythin' is white, an' in ten more I'm in a strange country. My hands an' feet ache with cold, an' I'm drawin' th' blanket closer, when there's a puff of wind so cold it cuts into my back like a knife. It passes quick, but it don't fool me. I know what's behind it. I reach for th' robe an' has it 'most unfastened when there's a roar an' I'm 'most unseated by th' wind before I can get set. I didn't know then that it's goin' to blow that hard for three days, an' it's just as well. It's full of ice—li'l slivers that are sharp as needles an' cut an' sting till they make th' skin raw. I let loose of th' robe an' tie my bandanna around my face, so my nose an' mouth is covered. My throat burns already almost to my lungs. Good Lord, but it *is* cold! My hands are stiff when I go back for th' robe, an' it's all I can do to keep it from blowin' away from me. It takes me a long time to get it over th' blanket, an' my hands are 'most froze when it's fastened. That was a good robe, but it didn't make much difference that day. Th' cold cuts through it an' into my back as if it wasn't there. My feet are gettin' worse all th' time, an' it ain't long before I ain't got none, for th' achin' stops at th' ankles. Purty soon only my knees ache, an' I know it won't be long till they won't ache no more.

"I'm squirmin' in my clothes tryin' to rub myself warm when I remember that flask of liquor. Th' cork was out far enough for my teeth to get at it, an' I drink a quarter of it quick. It's an awful load—any other time it would 'a' knocked me cold, for Cowan sold a lot worse stuff then than he does now. But it don't phase me, except for takin' most of th' linin' out of my mouth an' throat. It warms me a li'l, an' it makes my knees ache a li'l harder. But it don't last long—th' cold eats through me just as hard as ever a li'l later, an' then I begin to see things an' get sleepy. Cows an' cayuses float around in th' air, an' I'm countin' money, piles of it. I get warm an' drowsy an' find myself noddin'. That scares me a li'l, an' I fight hard ag'in it. If I go to sleep it's all over. It keeps gettin' worse, an' I finds my eyes shuttin' more an' more frequent, an' more an' more frequent thinkin' I don't care, anyhow. An' so I drifts along pullin' at th' bottle till it's empty. That should 'a' killed me, then an' there—but it don't even make me real drunk. Mebby I spilled some of it, my hands bein' nothin' but sticks. I can't see more'n five feet now, an' my eyes water, which freezes on 'em. I've given up all hope of hearin' any shootin'. So I close th' peekhole in th' blanket an' robe, drawin' 'em tight to keep out some of th' cold. I am sittin' up stiff in th' saddle, like a soldier, just from force of habit, and after a li'l while I don't know nothin' more. Pete says I was a corpse, froze stiff as a ramrod, an' he calls me ghost for a long time in fun. But Pete wasn't none too clear in his head about that time.

"Down at Li'l Timber, Hoppy managed to get under th' shelter of that projectin' ledge of rock on th' south side of th' bluff. Th' snow an' ice is whirlin' under it because of a sort of back draft, but th' wind don't hit so hard. He's fightin' that cayuse every foot, tryin' to get to th' cave at th' west end, an' disputin' th' right of way with th' cows that are packed under it. There's firewood under that ledge an' there's food on th' hoof, an' snow water for drink; so if he can make th' cave he's safe. He's more worried about his supply of smokin' tobacco than anythin' else, so far as he's concerned.

"All at once he runs onto four men huddled half-froze in a bunch right ahead of him. He knows in a flash who they are, an' he draws fumblingly, an' holds th' gun in his two hands, they are so cold. One clean hit an' five clean misses in twenty feet! They're gropin' for their guns when a sudden gust of wind whirls down from th' top of th' hill, pilin' snow an' ice on 'em till they can't see nor breathe. An' a couple of old trees come down to make things nicer. Hoppy is blinded, an' when he gets so he can see again there's one rustler's arm stickin' up out of th' snow, but no signs of th' other three. They blundered out into th' open tryin' to get away from th' stuff comin' down on 'em, an' that means they won't be back no more.

"Hoppy manages to get to th' cave, tie his cayuse to a fallen tree, an' gather enough firewood for a good blaze, which he puts in front of th' cave. It takes him a long time to use up his matches one by one, an' then he pulls th' lead out of a cartridge with his teeth, shakes th' powder loose in it an' along th' barrel. Usin' his cigarette papers for tinder he gets th' fire started an' goin' good an' is feelin' some cheerful when he remembers th' three rustlers driftin' south. They was bound to hit a big arroyo that would lead 'em almost ag'in' Number Two's door. With th' wind drivin' 'em straight for it, Hoppy thinks it might mean trouble for Lanky or Skinny. He didn't think about 'em only havin' wool-lined slickers on, or he'd 'a' knowed they couldn't live till they got halfway. They left their blankets in camp so they could work fast.

"People have called us clannish, an' said we was a 'lovin' bunch' because we stick together so tight. We've faced so much together that us of th' old bunch has got th' same blood in our veins. We ain't eight men—we're one man in eight different kinds of bodies. God help anybody that tries to make us less! It's one thing to stand up an' swap shots with a gunman; but it's another to turn yore back on a cave an' a fire like that an' go out into what is purty nigh shore death on a long chance of helpin' a couple of friends that was able to take care of themselves. That's one of th' things that explains why we made Shorty Jones an' his eleven men pay with their lives for takin' Jimmy's life. Twelve for one! That fight at Buckskin ain't generally understood, even by our friends. An' Hoppy crowns his courage twice in that one storm. Ain't he an old son-of-a-gun?

"He leaves that fire an' forces his cayuse to take him out in th' storm again, finds that th' arroyo is level full of snow, but has both banks swept bare. He passes them three rustlers in th' next ten minutes—they won't do no more cow-liftin'. Then he tries to turn back, but that's foolish. So he drifts on, gettin' a li'l loco by now. He's purty near asleep when he thinks he hears a shot. He fights his cayuse again, but can't stop it, so he falls off an' lets it drift, an' crawls an' fights his way back to where that shot was fired from. God only knows how he does it, but he falls over a cow an' sees Lanky huggin' its belly for th' li'l warmth in th' carcass. An' he ought to 'a' found him, after leavin' his cayuse an' turnin' back on foot in that hell storm! Th' drifts was beginnin' to make then—when th' storm was over I saw drifts thirty feet high in th' open; an' in th' valley there was some that run 'most to th' top of th' bluffs, an' they're near sixty feet high.

"Well, Lanky is as crazy as him, an' won't let go of that cow, an' they have a fight, which is good for both of 'em. Finally Lanky gets some sense in his head an' realizes what Hoppy is tryin' to do for him, an' they go staggerin' down wind, first one fallin' an' then th' other. But they keep fightin' like th' game boys they are, neither givin' a cuss for himself, but shore obstinate that he's goin' to get th' other out of it. That's *our* spirit; an' we're proud of it, by God! Hoppy wraps th' robe around Lanky, an' so they stagger on, neither one knowin' very much by that time. Th' Lord must 'a' pitied that pair, an' admired th' stuff He'd put in 'em, for they bump into th' line house kerslam, an' drop, all done an' exhausted.

"Meanwhile Skinny's hoppin' around inside, prayin' an' cussin' by streaks, every five minutes openin' th' door an' firin' off his Colt. He has tied th' two ropes together, an' frequent he ties one end to th' door, th' other to hisself, an' goes out pokin' around in th' snow, hopin' to stumble over his pardner. He's plumb forgot his bad shoulder long ago. Purty soon he opens th' door again to shoot off th' gun, an' in streaks somethin' between his laigs. He slams th' door as he jumps aside, an' then looks scared at Lanky's sombrero! Mebby he's slow hoppin' outside an' diggin' them out of th' drift that's near covered 'em! Now, don't think bad of Skinny. He dassn't leave th' house to search any distance, even if he could 'a' seen anythin'. His best play is to stick there an' shoot off his gun—Lanky might drift past if he was not there to signal. Skinny thought more of Lanky any time than he did of hisself, th' emaciated match!

"It don't take long to kick in a lot of snow with that wind blowin' an' he rubs them two till he's got tears in his eyes. Then he fills 'em with hot stew an' whisky, rolls 'em up together an' leaves 'em in th' same bunk. It ain't warm enough in that house, even with th' fire goin', to make 'em lose no arms or laigs.

"It seems that Lanky, watchin' his chance as soon as th' snow fell heavy enough to cover his movements, slipped out of th' house an' started to circle out around them festive rustlers that held him an' his friend prisoners. He made Skinny stay behind to hold th' house an' keep a gun poppin'. Lanky has worked up behind where th' rustlers was layin' when th' Norther strikes full force. It near blows him over, an', not havin' on nothin' but an old army overcoat that was wore out, th' cold gets him quick. He can't see, an' he can't hear Skinny's shots no more! He does th' best he can an' tries to fight back along his trail, but in no time there ain't no tracks to follow. Then he loses his head an' starts wanderin' until a cow blunders down on him. He shoots th' cow an' hugs its belly to keep warm an' then he don't really remember nothin' 'till he wakes up in th' bunk alongside of Hoppy, both gettin' over an awful drunk. Skinny kept feedin' liquor to 'em till it was gone, an' he had a plenty when he began.

"Jimmy Price was at Number One when th' blow started, an' Buck was in th' bunkhouse, an' it was three weeks before they could get out an' around, on account of th' snow fallin' so steady an' hard they couldn't see nothin'.

"Well, getting back to me explains how Pete Wilson came to th' Bar-20. He is migratin' south, just havin' had th' pleasure of learnin' that his wife sloped with a better-lookin' man. He was scared she might get tired of th' other feller an' sift back, so he sells out his li'l store, loads a waggin with blankets, grub, an' firewood, an' starts south, winter or no winter. He moves fast for a new range, where he can make a new beginnin' an' start life fresh, with five years of burnin' matrimonial experience as his valuablest asset. Pete says he reckoned mebby he wouldn't have so many harness sores if he run single th' rest of his life; heretofore he'd been so busy applyin' salve that he didn't have time to find out just what was th' trouble with th' double harness. Lots of men feel that way, but they ain't got Pete's unlovely outspoken habit of thought. We used to reckon mebby he wasn't as smart as th' rest of us, him bein' slow an' blunderin' in his retorts. We've played that with coppers lots of times since, though. While he ain't what you'd call quick at retortin', his retorts usually is heard by th' whole county. It ain't every collar-galled husband that's got th' gumption or smartness to jump th' minute th' hat is lifted. Pete had.

"He's drivin' across our range, an' when th' wind dies out sudden an' th' snow sifts down, he's just smart enough to get out his beddin' an' wrap it around him till he looks like a bale of cotton. An' even at that he's near froze an' lookin' for a place to make a stand when he feels a bump. It's me, fallin' off my cayuse, against his front wheel. He emerges from his beddin', lifts me into th' waggin, puts most of his blankets around me, an' stops. Knowin' he can't save th' cayuses, he shoots 'em. That means grub for us, anyhow, if we run short of th' good stuff. Nobody but Pete could 'a' got th' canvas off that waggin in such a gale, but he did it. He busts th' arches an' slats off th' top of th' waggin an' uses 'em for firewood. Th' canvas he drapes over th' box, lettin' it hang down on both sides to th' ground. An' in about five minutes th' whole thing was covered over with snow. Pete's the strongest man we ever saw, an' we've seen some good ones. Wrastlin' that canvas with stiff hands was a whole lot more than what he done to Big Sandy up there on Thunder Mesa.

"Pete says I was dead when he grabbed me, an' smellin' disgraceful of liquor. But th' first thing I know is lookin' up in th' gloom at a ceilin' that's right close to my head, an' at a sorta rafter. That rafter gives me a shock. It don't even touch th' ceilin', but runs along 'most a foot below it. I close my eyes an' do a lot of thinkin'. I remember freezin' to death, but that's all. An' just then I hears a faint voice say: 'He shore was dead.' I don't know Pete then, or that he talked to his-self sometimes. An' I reckon I was a li'l off in my head, at that. I begin to won-der if he means me, an' purty soon I'm shore of it. An' don't I sympathize with myself? I'm dead an' gone somewhere; but no preacher I ever heard ever de-scribed no place like this. Then I smell smoke an' burnin' meat—which gives me a clew to th' range I'm on. Mebby I'm shelved in th' ice box, waitin' my turn, or somethin'. I knew I'd led a sinful life. But there wasn't no use of rubbin' it in—it's awful to be dead an' know it.

"Th' next time I opens my eyes I can't see nothin'; but I can feel somethin' layin' alongside of me. It's breathin' slow an' regular, an it bothers me till I get th' idea all of a sudden. It's another dead one, cut out of th' herd an' shoved in my corral to wait for subsequent events. I felt sorry for him, an' lay there tryin' to figger it out, an' I'm still figgerin' when it starts to get light. Th' other feller grunts an' sits up, bumpin' his head solid against that fool rafter. No dead man that was shoved in a herd consigned to heaven ever used such language, which makes me all the shorer of where I am. But if hell's hot we've still got a long way to go.

"He sits there rubbin' his head an' cussin' steadily, an' I'm so moved by it that I compliments him. He jumps an' bumps his head again, an' looks at me close. 'Damned if you ain't a husky corpse,' he says. That settles it. I ain't crazy, like I was hopin', but I'm dead. 'You an' me is on th' ragged edge of hell,' he adds.

"'But who tipped *you* off?' I asks. 'They just shoved me in here an' didn't tell me nothin' at all.'

"'Crazy as th' devil,' he grunts, lookin' at me harder.

"'Yo're a liar,' I replies. 'I may be dead, but damned if I'm crazy!'

"'An' I don't blame you, either,' he mused, sorrowful. 'Now you keep quiet till I gets somethin' to eat,' an' he crawls into a li'l round hole at th' other end of th' room.

"Purty soon I smell smoke again, an' after a long time he comes back with some hot coffee an' burned meat. I grab for th' grub, an' while I'm eatin' I de-mands to know where I am.

"He laughs, real cheerful, an' tells me. I'm under his waggin, surrounded by canvas an' any God's quantity of snow. Th' drift over us is fifteen foot high, th' wind had died down, an' it's still snowin' so hard he can't see twenty feet. It is also away down below freezin'.

"We stayed under that drift 'most three weeks, livin' on raw meat after our firewood gave out. We didn't suffer none from th' cold, though, under all that snow an' with all th' blankets we had. When it stopped snowin' we discovered a drift shamefully high about a mile northeast of us, an' from th' smoke comin' out of it I knew it was th' bunkhouse.

"Well, to cut it short, it was. An' mebby Buck wasn't glad to see me! He was worried 'most sick an' as soon as we could, we got cayuses and started out to look for th' others, scared stiff at what we expected to find."

He paused and was silent a moment. "But only Ace was missin'," he added. "We found him an' th' rustlers later, when th' snow went off."

He paused again and shook his head. "It shore was a miracle that we didn't go with 'em, all of us, except Buck. Pete was so plumb disgusted with travelin' in th' winter, an' had lost his cayuses, that when Buck offers him Ace's bunk he stays. An' he ain't never left us since. Huh! Cold? That cub don't know nothin'— mebby he will when he grows up, but I dunno, at that. *Idyho!*"

CHAPTER 9

The Drive

The Norther was a thing of the past, but it left its mark on Buck Peters, whose grimness of face told what the winter had been to him. His daily rides over the range, the reports of his men since that deadly storm had done a great deal to lift the sagging weight that rested on his shoulders; but he would not be sure until the round-up supplied facts and figures.

That the losses had not been greater he gave full credit to the valley with its arroyos, rock walls, draws, heavily grassed range and groves of timber; for the valley, checking the great southward drift by its steep ridges of rock, sheltered the herds in timber and arroyos and fed them on the rich profusion of its grasses, which, by some trick of the rushing winds, had been whirled clean of snow.

But over the cow-country, north, east, south and west, where vast ranges were unprotected against the whistling blasts from the north, the losses had been stupendous, appalling, stunning. Outfits had been driven on and on before the furious winds, sleepy and apathetic, drifting steadily southward in the white, stinging shroud to a drowsy death. Whole herds, blindly moving before the wind, left their weaker units in constantly growing numbers to mark the trail, and at last lay down to a sleep eternal. And astonishing and incredible were the distances traveled by some of those herds.

Following the Norther came another menace and one which easily might surpass the worst efforts of the blizzard. Warm winds blew steadily, a hot sun glared down on the snow-covered plain and then came torrents of rain which continued for days, turning the range into a huge expanse of water and mud and swelling the watercourses with turgid floods that swirled and roared above their banks. Should this be quickly followed by cold, even the splendid valley would avail nothing. Ice, forming over the grasses, would prove as deadly as a pestilence; the cattle, already weakened by the hardships of the Norther, and not having the instinct to break through the glassy sheet and feed on the grass underneath, would search in vain for food, and starve to death. The week that followed the cessation of the rains started gray hairs on the foreman's head; but a warm, constant sun and warm winds dried off the water before the return of freezing weather. The herds were saved.

Relieved, Buck reviewed the situation. The previous summer had seen such great northern drives to the railroad shipping points in Kansas that prices fell until the cattlemen refused to sell. Rather than drive home again, the great herds were wintered on the Kansas ranges, ready to be hurled on the market when Spring came with better prices. Many ranches, mortgaged heavily to buy cattle, had been on the verge of bankruptcy, hoping feverishly for better prices the following year. Buck had taken advantage of the situation to stock his ranch at a cost far less than he had dared to dream. Then came the Norther and in the three weeks of devastating cold and high winds the Kansas ranges were swept clean of cattle, and even the ranges in the South were badly crippled. Knowing this, Buck also knew that the following Spring would show record high prices. If he had the cattle he could clean up a fortune for his ranch; and if his herd was the first big one to reach the railroad at Sandy Creek it would practically mean a bonus on every cow.

Under the long siege of uncertainty his impatience smashed through and possessed him as a fever and he ordered the calf round-up three weeks earlier than it ever had been held on the ranch. There was no need of urging his men to the task—they, like himself, sprang to the call like springs freed from a restraining weight, and the work went on in a fever of haste. And he took his place on the firing line and worked even harder than his outfit of fanatics.

One day shortly after the work began a stranger rode up to him and nodded cheerfully. "Li'l early, ain't you?" Buck grunted in reply and sent Skinny off at top speed to close a threatened gap in the lengthy driving line. "Goin' to git 'em on th' trail early this year?" persisted the stranger. Buck, swayed by some swift intuition, changed his reply. "Oh, I dunno; I'm mainly anxious to see just what that storm did. An' I hate th' calf burnin' so much I allus like to get it over quick." He shouted angrily at the cook and waved his arms frantically to banish the chuck wagon. "He can make more trouble with that waggin than anybody I ever saw," he snorted. "Get out of there, you fool!" he yelled, dashing off to see his words obeyed. The cook, grinning cheerfully at his foreman's language and heat, forthwith chose a spot that was not destined to be the center of the cut-out herd. And when Buck again thought of the stranger he saw a black dot moving toward the eastern skyline.

The crowded days rolled on, measured full from dawn to dark, each one of them a panting, straining, trying ordeal. Worn out, the horses were turned back into the temporary corral or to graze under the eyes of the horse wranglers, and fresh ones took up their work; and woe unto the wranglers if the supply fell below the demand. For the tired men there was no relief, only a shifting in the kind of work they did, and they drove themselves with grave determination, their iron wills overruling their aching bodies. First came the big herds in the valley; then, sweeping north, they combed the range to the northern line in one grand, mad fury of effort that lasted day after day until the tally man joyously threw away his chewed pencil and gladly surrendered the last sheet to the foreman. The first half of the game was over. Gone as if it were a nightmare was the confusion of noise and dust and cows that hid a remarkable certainty of method. But as if to prove it not a dream, four thousand cows were held in three herds on the great range, in charge of the extra men.

Buck, leading the regular outfit from the north line and toward the bunkhouse, added the figures of the last tally sheet to the totals he had in a little book, and smiled with content. Behind him, cheerful as fools, their bodies racking with weariness, their faces drawn and gaunt, knowing that their labors were not half over, rode the outfit, exchanging chaff and banter in an effort to fool themselves into the delusion that they were fresh and "chipper." Nearing the bunkhouse they cheered lustily as they caught sight of the hectic cook laboring profanely with two balking pintos that had backed his wagon half over the edge of a barranca and then refused to pull it back again. Cookie's reply, though not a cheer, was loud and pregnant with feeling. To think that he had driven those two animals for the last two weeks from one end of the ranch to the other without a mishap, and then have them balance him and his wagon on the crumbling edge of a twenty-foot drop when not a half mile from the bunkhouse, thus threatening the loss of the wagon and all it contained and the mangling of his sacred person! And to make it worse, here came a crowd of whooping idiots to feast upon his discomfiture.

The outfit, slowing so as not to frighten the devilish pintos and start them backing again, drew near; and suddenly the air became filled with darting ropes, one of which settled affectionately around Cookie's apoplectic neck. In no time the strangling, furious dough-king was beyond the menace of the crumbling bank, flat on his back in the wagon, where he had managed to throw himself to escape the whistling hoofs that quickly turned the dashboard into matchwood. When he managed to get the rope from his neck he arose, unsteady with rage, and choked as he tried to speak before the grinning and advising outfit. Before he could get command over his tongue the happy bunch wheeled and sped on its way, shrieking with mirth unholy. They had saved him from probable death, for Cookie was too obstinate to have jumped from the wagon; but they not only forfeited all right to thanks and gratitude, but deserved horrible deaths for the conversation they had so audibly carried on while they worked out the cook's problem. And their departing words and gestures made homicide justifiable and a duty. It was in this frame of mind that Cookie watched them go.

Buck, emerging from the bunkhouse in time to see the rescue, leaned against the door and laughed as he had not laughed for one heartbreaking winter. Drying his eyes on the back of his hand, he looked at the bouncing, happy crowd tearing southward with an energy of arms and legs and lungs that seemed a miracle after the strain of the round-up. Just then a strange voice made him wheel like a flash, and he saw Billy Williams sitting solemnly on his horse near the corner of the house.

"Hullo, Williams," Buck grunted, with no welcoming warmth in his voice. "What th' devil brings *you* up here?"

"I want a job," replied Billy. The two, while never enemies nor interested in any mutual disagreements, had never been friends. They never denied a nodding acquaintance, nor boasted of it. "That Norther shore raised hell. There's ten men for every job, where I came from."

The foreman, with that quick decision that was his in his earlier days, replied crisply. "It's your'n. Fifty a month, to start."

"Keno. Lemme chuck my war-bag through that door an' I'm ready," smiled Billy. He believed he would like this man when he knew him better. "I thought th' Diamond Bar, over east a hundred mile, had weathered th' storm lucky. You got 'em beat. They're movin' heaven an' earth to get a herd on the trail, but they didn't have no job for *me*," he laughed, flushing slightly. "Sam Crawford owns it," he explained naïvely.

Buck laughed outright. "I reckon you didn't have much show with Sam, after that li'l trick you worked on him in Fenton. So Sam is in this country? How are they fixed?"

"They aims to shove three thousan' east right soon. It's fancy prices for th' first herd that gets to Sandy Creek," he offered. "I heard they're havin' lots of wet weather along th' Comanchee; mebby Sam'll have trouble a-plenty gettin' his herd acrost. Cows is plumb aggervatin' when it comes to crossin' rivers," he grinned.

Buck nodded. "See that V openin' on th' skyline?" he asked, pointing westward. "Ride for it till you see th' herd. Help 'em with it. We'll pick it up t'morrow."

He turned on his heel and entered the house, grave with a new worry. He had not known that there was a ranch where Billy had said the Diamond Bar was located; and a hundred miles handicap meant much in a race to Sandy Creek. Crawford was sure to drive as fast as he dared. He was glad that Billy had mentioned it, and the wet weather along the Comanchee—Billy already had earned his first month's pay.

All that day and the next the consolidation of the three herds and the preparation for the drive went on. Sweeping up from the valley the two thousand three- and four-year-olds met and joined the thousand that waited between Little Timber and Three Rocks; and by nightfall the three herds were one by the addition of the thousand head from the Big Coulee. Four thousand head of the best cattle on the ranch spent the night within gunshot of the bunkhouse and corrals on Snake Creek.

Buck, returning from the big herd, smiled as he passed the chuck-wagon and heard Cookie's snores, and went on, growing serious all too quickly. At the bunkhouse he held a short consultation with his regular outfit and then returned to the herd again while his drive crew turned eagerly to their bunks. Breakfast was eaten by candle light and when the eastern sky faded into a silver gray Skinny Thompson vaulted into the saddle and loped eastward without a backward glance. The sounds of his going scarcely had died out before Hopalong, relieved of the responsibilities of trail boss, shouldered others as weighty and rode into the northeast with Lanky at his side. Behind him, under charge of Red, the herd started on its long and weary journey to Sandy Creek, every man of the outfit so imbued with the spirit of the race that even with its hundred miles' advantage the Diamond Bar could not afford to waste an hour if it hoped to win.

Out of the side of a verdant hill, whispering and purling, flowed a small stream and shyly sought the crystal depths of a rock-bound pool before gaining courage enough to flow gently over the smooth granite lip and scurry down the gentle slope of the arroyo. To one side of it towered a splinter of rock, slender and gray, washed clean by the recent rains. To the south of it lay a baffling streak a little lighter than the surrounding grass lands. It was, perhaps, a quarter of a mile wide and ended only at the horizon. This faint band was the Dunton trail, not used enough to show the strong characteristics of the depressed bands found in other parts of the cow-country. If followed it would lead one to Dunton's Ford on the Comanchee, forty miles above West Bend, where the Diamond Bar aimed to cross the river.

The shadow of the pinnacle drew closer to its base and had crossed the pool when Skinny Thompson rode slowly up the near bank of the ravine, his eyes fixed smilingly on the splinter of rock. He let his mount nuzzle and play with the pool for a moment before stripping off the saddle and turning the animal loose to graze. Taking his rifle in the hope of seeing game, he went up to the top of the hill, glanced westward and then turned and gazed steadily into the northeast, sweeping slowly over an arc of thirty degrees. He stood so for several minutes and then grunted with satisfaction and returned to the pool. He had caught sight of a black dot far away on the edge of the skyline that split into two parts and showed a sidewise drift. Evidently his friends would be on time. Of the herd he had seen no sign, which was what he had expected.

When at last he heard hoofbeats he arose lazily and stretched, chiding himself for falling asleep, and met his friends as they turned into sight around the bend of the hill. "Reckoned you might 'a' got lost," he grinned sleepily.

"G'wan!" snorted Lanky.

"What'd you find?" eagerly demanded Hopalong.

"Three thousan' head on th' West Bend trail five days ahead of us," replied Skinny. "Ol' Sam is drivin' hard." He paused a moment. "Acts like he knows we're after him. Anyhow, I saw that feller that visited us on th' third day of th' round-up. So I reckon Sam knows."

Lanky grinned. "He won't drive so hard later. I'd like to see him when *he* sees th' Comanchee! Bet it's a lake south of Dunton's 'cordin' to what he found. But it ain't goin' to bother us a whole lot."

Hopalong nodded, dismounted and drew a crude map in the sand of the trail. Skinny watched it, grave and thoughtful until, all at once, he understood. His sudden burst of laughter startled his companions and they exchanged foolish grins. It appeared that from Dunton's Ford north, in a distance of forty miles, the Comanchee was practically born. So many feeders, none of them formidable, poured into it that in that distance it attained the dignity of a river. Hopalong's plan was to drive off at a tangent running a little north from the regular trail and thus cross numerous small streams in preference to going on straight and facing the swollen Comanchee at Dunton's Ford. As the regular trail turned northward when not far from Sandy Creek they were not losing time. Laughing gaily they mounted and started west for the herd which toiled toward them many miles away. Thanks to the forethought that had prompted their scouting expedition the new trail was picked out in advance and there would be no indecision on the drive.

Eighty miles to the south lay the fresh trail of the Diamond Bar herd, and five days' drive eastward on it, facing the water-covered lowlands at West Bend, Sam Crawford held his herd, certain that the river would fall rapidly in the next two days. It was the regular ford, and the best on the river. The water did fall, just enough to lure him to stay; but, having given orders at dark on the second night for an attempt at crossing at daylight the next morning, he was amazed when dawn showed him the river was back to its first level.

Sam was American born, but affected things English and delighted in spelling "labor" and like words with a "u." He hated hair chaps and maintained that the gun-play of the West was mythical and existed only in the minds of effete Easterners. Knowing that, it was startling to hear him tell of Plummer, Hickock, Roberts, Thompson and a host of other gunmen who had splotched the West with blood. Not only did every man of that section pack a gun, but Crawford, himself, packed one, thus proving himself either a malicious liar or an imbecile. He acted as though the West belonged to him and that he was the arbiter of its destiny and its chosen historian—which made him troublesome on the great, free ranges. Only that his pretensions and his crabbed, irascible, childish temper made him ludicrous he might have been taken seriously, to his sorrow. Failing miserably at law, he fled from such a precarious livelihood, beset with a haunting fear that he had lost his grip, to an inherited ranch. This fear that pursued him turned him into a carping critic of those who excelled him in most things, except in fits of lying about the West as it existed at that time.

When he found that the river was over the lowlands again he became furious and, carried away by rage, shouted down the wiser counsel of his clear-headed night boss and ordered the herd into the water. Here and there desperate, wide-eyed steers wheeled and dashed back through the cordon of riders, their numbers constantly growing as the panic spread. The cattle in the front ranks, forced into the swirling stream by the pressure from the rear, swam with the current and clambered out below, adding to the confusion. Steers fought throughout the press and suddenly, out of the right wing of the herd, a dozen crazed animals dashed out in a bunch for the safety of the higher ground; and after them came the herd, an irresistible avalanche of maddened beef. It was not before dark that they were rounded up into a nervous, panicky herd once more. The next morning they were started north along the river, to try again at Dunton's Ford, which they reached in three days, and where another attempt at crossing the river proved in vain.

Meanwhile the Bar-20 herd pushed on steadily with no confusion. It crossed the West Run one noon and the upper waters of the Little Comanchee just before dark on the same day. Next came East Run, Pawnee Creek and Ten Mile

Creek, none of them larger than the stream the cattle were accustomed to back on the ranch. Another day's drive brought them to the west branch of the Comanchee itself, the largest of all the rivers they would meet. Here they were handled cautiously and "nudged" across with such care that a day was spent in the work. The following afternoon the east branch held them up until the next day and then, with a clear trail, they were sent along on the last part of the long journey.

When Sam Crawford, forced to keep on driving north along the Little Comanchee, saw that wide, fresh trail, he barely escaped apoplexy and added the finishing touches to the sullenness of his outfit. Seeing the herd across, he gave orders for top speed and drove as he never had driven before; and when the last river had been left behind he put the night boss in charge of the cattle and rode on ahead to locate his rivals of the drive. Three days later, when he returned to his herd, he was in a towering fury and talked constantly of his rights and an appeal to law, and so nagged his men that mutiny stalked in his shadow.

When the Bar-20 herd was passing to the south of the little village of Depau, Hopalong turned back along the trail to find the Diamond Bar herd. So hard had Sam pushed on that he was only two days' drive behind Red and his outfit when Hopalong rode smilingly into the Diamond Bar camp. He was talking pleasantly of shop to some of the Diamond Bar punchers when Sam dashed up and began upbraiding him and threatening dire punishment. Hopalong, maintaining a grave countenance, took the lacing meekly and humbly as he winked at the grinning punchers. Finally, after exasperating Sam to a point but one degree removed from explosion, he bowed cynically, said "so-long" to the friendly outfit and loped away toward his friends. Sam, choking with rage, berated his punchers for not having thrown out the insulting visitor and commanded more speed, which was impossible. Reporting to Red the proximity of their rivals, Hopalong fell in line and helped drive the herd a little faster. The cattle were in such condition from the easy traveling of the last week that they could easily stand the pace if Crawford's herd could. So the race went on, Red keeping the same distance ahead day after day.

Then came the night when Sandy Creek lay but two days' drive away. A storm had threatened since morning and the first lightning of the drive was seen. The cattle were mildly restless when Hopalong rode in at midnight and he was cheerfully optimistic. He was also very much awake, and after trying in vain to get to sleep he finally arose and rode back along the trail toward the stragglers, which Jimmy and Lanky were holding a mile away. Red had pushed on to the last minute of daylight and Lanky had decided to hold the stragglers instead of driving them up to the main herd so they would start even with it the following morning. It was made up of the cattle that had found the drive too much for them and was smaller than the outfit had dared to hope for.

Hopalong had just begun to look around for the herd when it passed him with sudden uproar. Shouting to a horseman who rode furiously past, he swung around and raced after him, desperately anxious to get in front of the stampede to try to check it before it struck the main herd and made the disaster complete. For the next hour he was in a riot of maddened cattle and shaved death many times by the breadth of a hand. He could hear Jimmy and Lanky shouting in the black void, now close and now far away. Then the turmoil gradually ceased and the remnant of the herd paused, undecided whether to stop or go on. He flung himself at it and by driving cleverly managed to start a number of cows to milling, which soon had the rest following suit. The stampede was over. A cursing blot emerged from the darkness and hailed. It was Lanky, coldly ferocious. He had not heard Jimmy for a long time and feared that the boy might be lying out on the black plain, trampled into a shapeless mass of flesh. One stumble in front of the charging herd would have been sufficient.

Daylight disclosed the missing Jimmy hobbling toward the breakfast fire at the cook wagon. He was bruised and bleeding and covered with dirt, his clothes ripped and covered with mud; and every bone and muscle in his body was alive with pain.

The Diamond Bar's second squad had ridden in to breakfast when a horseman was seen approaching at a leisurely lope. Sam, cursing hotly, instinctively fumbled at the gun he wore at his thigh in defiance to his belief concerning the wearing of guns. He blinked anxiously as the puncher stopped at the wagon and smiled a heavy-eyed salutation. The night boss emerged from the shelter of the wagon and grinned a sheepish welcome. "Well, Cassidy, you fellers got th' trail somehow. We was some surprised when we hit yore trail. How you makin' it?"

"All right, up to last night," replied Hopalong, shaking hands with the night boss. "Got a match, Barnes?" he asked, holding up an unlighted cigarette. They talked of things connected with the drive and Hopalong cautiously swung the conversation around to mishaps, mentioning several catastrophes of past years. After telling of a certain stampede he had once seen, he turned to Barnes and asked a blunt question. "What would you do to anybody as stampeded yore stragglers within a mile of th' main herd on a stormy night?" The answer was throaty and rumbling. "Why, shoot him, I reckon." The others intruded their ideas and Crawford squirmed, his hand seeking his gun under the pretense of tightening his belt.

Hopalong arose and went to his horse, where a large bundle of canvas was strapped behind the saddle. He loosened it and unrolled it on the ground. "Ever see this afore, boys?" he asked, stepping back. Barnes leaped to his feet with an ejaculation of surprise and stared at the canvas. "Where'd you git it?" he demanded. "That's our old wagon cover!"

Hopalong, ignoring Crawford, looked around the little group and smiled grimly. "Well, last night our stragglers was stampeded. Lanky told me he saw somethin' gray blow past him in th' darkness, an' then th' herd started. We managed to turn it from th' trail an' so it din't set off our main herd. Jimmy was near killed—well, you know what it is to ride afore stampeded cows. I found this cover blowed agin' a li'l clump of trees, an' when I sees yore mark, I reckoned I ought to bring it back." He dug into his pocket and brought out a heavy clasp knife. "I just happened to see this not far from where th' herd started from, so I reckoned I'd return it, too." He held it out to Barnes, who took it with an oath and wheeled like a flash to face his employer.

Crawford was backing toward the wagon, his hand resting on the butt of his gun, and a whiteness of face told of the fear that gripped him. "I'll take my time, right now," growled Barnes. "Damned if I works another day for a low-lived coyote that'd do a thing like that!" The punchers behind him joined in and demanded their wages. Hopalong, still smiling, waved his hand and spoke. "Don't leave him with all these cows on his hands, out here on th' range. If you quits him, wait till you get to Sandy Creek. He ain't no man, he ain't; he's a nasty li'l brat of a kid that couldn't never grow up into a man. So, that bein' true, he ain't goin' to get handled like a man. I'm goin' to lick him, 'stead of shootin' him like he was a man. You know," he smiled, glancing around the little circle, "us cowpunchers don't never carry guns. We don't swear, nor wear chaps, even if all of us has got 'em on right now. We say 'please' an' 'thank you' an' never get mad. Not never wearin' a gun I can't shoot him; but, by God, I can lick him th' worst he's ever been licked, an' I'm goin' to do it right now." He wheeled to start after the still-backing cowman, and leaped sideways as a cloud of smoke swirled around his hips. Crawford screamed with fear and pain as his Colt tore loose from his fingers and dropped near the wheel of the wagon. Terror gripped him and made him incapable of flight. Who was this man, *what* was he, when he could draw and fire with such speed and remarkable accuracy? Crawford's gun had been half raised before the other had seen it. And before his legs could perform one of their most cherished functions the limping cowpuncher was on him, doing his best to make good his promise. The other half of the Diamond Bar drive crew, attracted by the commotion at the chuck wagon, rode in with ready guns, saw their friends making no attempt at interference, asked a few terse questions and, putting up their guns, forthwith joined the circle of interested and pleased spectators to root for the limping red-head.

Red, back at the Bar-20 wagon, inquired of Cookie the whereabouts of Hopalong. Cookie, still smarting under Jimmy's galling fire of language, grunted ignorance and a wish. Red looked at him, scowling. "You can talk to th' Kid like that, mebby; but you get a civil tongue in yore head when any of us grown-ups ask questions." He turned on his heel, looked searchingly around the plain and mounting, returned to the herd, perplexed and vexed. As he left the camp, Jimmy hobbled around the wagon and stared after him. "Kid!" he snorted. "Grown-ups!" he sneered. "Huh!" He turned and regarded Cookie evilly. "Yo're gonna get a good lickin' when I get so I can move better," he promised. Cookie lifted the red flannel dish-rag out of the pan and regarded it thoughtfully. "You better wait," he agreed pleasantly. "You can't run now. I'm honin' for to drape this mop all over yore wall-eyed face; but I can wait." He sighed and went back to work. "Wish Red would shove you in with th' rest of th' cripples back yonder, an' get you off'n my frazzled nerves."

Jimmy shook his head sorrowfully and limped around the wagon again, where he resumed his sun bath. He dozed off and was surprised to be called for dinner. As he arose, grunting and growling, he chanced to look westward, and his shout apprised his friends of the return of the missing red-head.

Hopalong dismounted at the wagon and grinned cheerfully, despite the suspicious marks on his face. Giving an account of events as they occurred at the Diamond Bar chuck wagon, he wound up with: "Needn't push on so hard, Red. Crawford's herd is due to stay right where it is an' graze peaceful for a week. I heard Barnes give th' order before I left. How's things been out here while I was away?"

Red glared at him, ready to tell his opinion of reckless fools that went up against a gun-packing crowd alone when his friends had never been known to refuse to back up one of their outfit. The words hung on his lips as he waited for a chance to launch them. But when that chance came he had been disarmed by the cheerfulness of his happy friend. "Hoppy," he said, trying to be severe, "yo're nothing' but a crazy, damned fool. But what did they say when you started for huffy Sam like that?"

CHAPTER 10

The Hold-up

The herd delivered at Sandy Creek had traveled only half way, for the remaining part of the journey would be on the railroad. The work of loading the cars was fast, furious fun to anyone who could find humor enough in his make-up to regard it so. Then came a long, wearying ride for the five men picked from the drive outfit to attend to the cattle on the way to the cattle pens of the city. Their work at last done, they "saw the sights" and were now returning to Sandy Creek.

The baggage smoking-car reeked with strong tobacco, the clouds of smoke shifting with the air currents, and dimly through the haze could be seen several men. Three of these were playing cards near the baggage-room door, while two more lounged in a seat half way down the aisle and on the other side of the car. Across from the card-players, reading a magazine, was a fat man, and near the water cooler was a dyspeptic-looking individual who was grumbling about the country through which he was passing.

The first five, as their wearing apparel proclaimed, were not of the kind usually found on trains, not the drummer, the tourist, or the farmer. Their heads were covered with heavy sombreros, their coats were of thick, black woolens, and their shirts were also of wool. Around the throat of each was a large handkerchief, knotted at the back; their trousers were protected by "chaps," of which three were of goatskin. The boots were tight-fitting, narrow, and with high heels, and to them were strapped heavy spurs. Around the waist, hanging loosely from one hip, each wore a wide belt containing fifty cartridges in the loops, and supporting a huge Colt's revolver, which rested against the thigh.

They were happy and were trying to sing but, owing to different tastes, there was noticeable a lack of harmony. "Oh Susanna" never did go well with

"Annie Laurie," and as for "Dixie," it was hopelessly at odds with the other two. But they were happy, exuberantly so, for they had enjoyed their relaxation in the city and now were returning to the station where their horses were waiting to carry them over the two hundred miles which lay between their ranch and the nearest railroad-station.

For a change the city had been pleasant, but after they had spent several days there it lost its charm and would not have been acceptable to them even as a place in which to die. They had spent their money, smoked "top-notcher" cigars, seen the "shows" and feasted each as his fancy dictated, and as behooved cowpunchers with money in their pockets. Now they were glad that every hour reduced the time of their stay in the smoky, jolting, rocking train, for they did not like trains, and this train was particularly bad. So they passed the hours as best they might and waited impatiently for the stop at Sandy Creek, where they had left their horses. Their trip to the "fence country" was now a memory, and they chafed to be again in the saddle on the open, wind-swept range, where miles were insignificant and the silence soothing.

The fat man, despairing of reading, watched the card-players and smiled in good humor as he listened to their conversation, while the dyspeptic, nervously twisting his newspaper, wished that he were at his destination. The baggage-room door opened and the conductor looked down on the card-players and grinned. Skinny moved over in the seat to make room for the genial conductor.

"Sit down, Simms, an' take a hand," he invited. Laughter arose continually and the fat man joined in it, leaning forward more closely to watch the play.

Lanky tossed his cards face down on the board and grinned at the onlooker.

"Billy shore bluffs more on a varigated flush than any man I ever saw."

"Call him once in a while and he'll get cured of it," laughed the fat man, bracing himself as the train swung around a sharp turn.

"He's too smart," growled Billy Williams. "He tried that an' found I didn't have no varigated flushes. Come on, Lanky, if yo're playing cards, put up."

Farther down the car, their feet resting easily on the seat in front of them, Hopalong and Red puffed slowly at their large, black cigars and spoke infrequently, both idly watching the plain flit by in wearying sameness, and both tired and lazy from doing nothing but ride.

"Blast th' cars, anyhow," grunted Hopalong, but he received no reply, for his companion was too disgusted to say anything.

A startling, sudden increase in the roar of the train and a gust of hot, sulphurous smoke caused Hopalong to look up at the brakeman, who came down the swaying aisle as the door slammed shut.

"Phew!" he exclaimed genially. "Why in thunder don't you fellows smoke up?"

Hopalong blew a heavy ring, stretched energetically and grinned: "Much farther to Sandy Creek?"

"Oh, you don't get off for three hours yet," laughed the brakeman.

"That's shore a long time to ride this bronc train," moodily complained Red as the singing began again. "She shore pitches a-plenty," he added.

The train-hand smiled and seated himself on the arm of the front seat: "Oh, it might be worse."

"Not this side of hades," replied Red with decision, watching his friend, who was slapping the cushions to see the dust fly out: "Hey, let up on that, will you! There's dust a-plenty without no help from you!"

The brakeman glanced at the card-players and then at Hopalong.

"Do your friends always sing like that?" he inquired.

"Mostly, but sometimes it's worse."

"On the level?"

"Shore enough; they're singing 'Dixie,' now. It's their best song."

"That ain't 'Dixie!'"

"Yes it is: that is, most of it."

"Well, then, what's the rest of it?"

"Oh, them's variations of their own," remarked Red, yawning and stretching. "Just wait till they start something sentimental; you'll shore weep."

"I hope they stick to the variations. Say, you must be a pretty nifty gang on the shoot, ain't you?"

"Oh, some," answered Hopalong.

"I wish you fellers had been aboard with us one day about a month ago. We was the wrong end of a hold-up, and we got cleaned out proper, too."

"An' how many of 'em did you get?" asked Hopalong quickly, sitting bolt upright.

The fat man suddenly lost his interest in the card-game and turned an eager ear to the brakeman, while the dyspeptic stopped punching holes in his time-card and listened. The card-players glanced up and then returned to their game, but they, too, were listening.

The brakeman was surprised: "How many did we get! Gosh! we didn't get none! They was six to our five."

"How many cards did you draw, you Piute?" asked Lanky.

"None of yore business; I ain't dealing, an' I wouldn't tell you if I was," retorted Billy.

"Well, I can ask, can't I?"

"Yes—you can, an' did."

"You didn't get none?" cried Hopalong, doubting his ears.

"I should say not!"

"An' they owned th' whole train?"

"They did."

Red laughed. "Th' cleaning-up must have been sumptuous an' elevating."

"Every time I holds threes he allus has better," growled Lanky to Simms.

"On th' level, we couldn't do a thing," the brakeman ran on. "There's a water tank a little farther on, and they must 'a' climbed aboard there when we stopped to connect. When we got into the gulch the train slowed down and stopped and I started to get up to go out and see what was the matter; but I saw *that* when I looked down a gun-barrel. The man at the throttle end of it told me to put up my hands, but they were up as high then as I could get 'em without climbin' on the top of the seat."

"Can't you listen and play at th' same time?" Lanky asked Billy.

"I wasn't countin' on takin' the gun away from him," the brakeman continued, "for I was too busy watchin' for the slug to come out of the hole. Pretty soon somebody on the outside whistled and then another feller come in the car; he was the one that did the cleanin' up. All this time there had been a lot of shootin' outside, but now it got worse. Then I heard another whistle and the engine puffed up the track, and about five minutes later there was a big explosion, and then our two robbers backed out of the car among the rocks shootin' back regardless. They busted a lot of windows."

"An' you didn't git none," grumbled Hopalong, regretfully.

"When we got to the express-car, what had been pulled around the turn," continued the brakeman, not heeding the interruption, "we found a wreck. And we found the engineer and fireman standin' over the express-messenger, too scared to know he wouldn't come back no more. The car had been blowed up with dynamite, and his fighting soul went with it. He never knowed he was licked."

"An' nobody tried to help him!" Hopalong exclaimed, wrathfully now.

"Nobody wanted to die with him," replied the brakeman.

"Well," cried the fat man, suddenly reaching for his valise, "I'd like to see anybody try to hold me up!" Saying which he brought forth a small revolver.

"You'd be praying out of your bald spot about that time," muttered the brakeman.

Hopalong and Red turned, perceived the weapon, and then exchanged winks.

"That's a fine shootin'-iron, stranger," gravely remarked Hopalong.

"You bet it is!" purred the owner, proudly. "I paid six dollars for that gun."

Lanky smothered a laugh and his friend grinned broadly: "I reckon that'd kill a man—if you stuck it in his ear."

"Pshaw!" snorted the dyspeptic, scornfully. "You wouldn't have time to get it out of that grip. Think a train-robber is going to let you unpack? Why don't you carry it in your hip-pocket, where you can get at it quickly?"

There were smiles at the stranger's belief in the hip-pocket fallacy but no one commented upon it.

"Wasn't there no passengers aboard when you was stuck up?" Lanky asked the conductor.

"Yes, but you can't count passengers in on a deal like that."

Hopalong looked around aggressively: "We're passengers, ain't we?"

"You certainly are."

"Well, if any misguided maverick gets it into his fool head to stick *us* up, you see what happens. Don't you know th' fellers outside have all th' worst o' th' deal?"

"They have not!" cried the brakeman.

"They've got all the best of it," asserted the conductor emphatically. "I've been inside, and I know."

"Best nothing!" cried Hopalong. "They are on th' ground, watching a danger-line over a hundred yards long, full of windows and doors. Then they brace th' door of a car full of people. While they climb up the steps they can't see inside, an' then they go an' stick their heads in plain sight. It's an even break who sees th' other first, with th' men inside training their guns on th' glass in th' door!"

"Darned if you ain't right!" enthusiastically cried the fat man.

Hopalong laughed: "It all depends on th' men inside. If they ain't used to handling guns, 'course they won't try to fight. We've been in so many gun-festivals that we wouldn't stop to think. If any coin-collector went an' stuck his ugly face against th' glass in that door he'd turn a back-flip off'n th' platform before he knowed he was hit. Is there any chance for a stick-up to-day, d'y think?"

"Can't tell," replied the brakeman. "But this is about the time we have the section-camps' pay on board," he said, going into the baggage end of the car.

Simms leaned over close to Skinny. "It's on this train now, and I'm worried to death about it. I wish we were at Sandy Creek."

"Don't you go worryin' none, then," the puncher replied. "It'll get to Sandy Creek all right."

Hopalong looked out of the window again and saw that there was a gradual change in the nature of the scenery, for the plain was becoming more broken each succeeding mile. Small woods occasionally hurtled past and banks of cuts flashed by like mottled yellow curtains, shutting off the view. Scrub timber stretched away on both sides, a billow sea of green, and miniature valleys lay under the increasing number of trestles twisting and winding toward a high horizon.

Hopalong yawned again: "Well, it's none o' our funeral. If they let us alone I don't reckon we'll take a hand, not even to bust up this monotony."

Red laughed derisively: "Oh, no! Why, you couldn't sit still nohow with a fight going on, an' you know it. An' if it's a stick-up! Wow!"

"Who gave you any say in this?" demanded his friend. "Anyhow, you ain't no angel o' peace, not nohow!"

"Mebby they'll plug yore new sombrero," laughed Red.

Hopalong felt of the article in question: "If any two-laigged wolf plugs my war-bonnet he'll be some sorry, an' so'll his folks," he asserted, rising and going down the aisle for a drink.

Red turned to the brakeman, who had just returned: "Say," he whispered, "get off at th' next stop, shoot off a gun, an' yell, just for fun. Go ahead, it'll be better'n a circus."

"Nix on the circus, says I," hastily replied the other. "I ain't looking for no excitement, an' I ain't paid to amuse th' passengers. I hope we don't even run over a track-torpedo this side of Sandy Creek."

Hopalong returned, and as he came even with them the train slowed.

"What are we stopping for?" he asked, his hand going to his holster.

"To take on water; the tank's right ahead."

"What have you got?" asked Billy, ruffling his cards.

"None of yore business," replied Lanky. "You call when you gets curious."

"Oh, th' devil!" yawned Hopalong, leaning back lazily. "I shore wish I was on my cayuse pounding leather on th' home trail."

"Me, too," grumbled Red, staring out of the window. "Well, we're moving again. It won't be long now before we gets out of this."

The card-game continued, the low-spoken terms being interspersed with casual comment; Hopalong exchanged infrequent remarks with Red, while the brakeman and conductor stared out of the same window. There was noticeable an air of anxiety, and the fat man tried to read his magazine with his thoughts far from the printed page. He read and re-read a single paragraph several times without gaining the slightest knowledge of what it meant, while the dyspeptic passenger fidgeted more and more in his seat, like one sitting on hot coals, anxious and alert.

"We're there now," suddenly remarked the conductor, as the bank of a cut blanked out the view. "It was right here where it happened; the turn's farther on."

"How many cards did you draw, Skinny?" asked Lanky.

"Three; drawin' to a straight flush," laughed the dealer.

"Here's the turn! We're through all right," exclaimed the brakeman.

Suddenly there was a rumbling bump, a screeching of air-brakes and the grinding and rattle of couplings and pins as the train slowed down and stopped with a suddenness that snapped the passengers forward and back. The conductor and brakeman leaped to their feet, where the latter stood quietly during a moment of indecision.

A shot was heard and the conductor's hand, raised quickly to the whistle-rope sent blast after blast shrieking over the land. A babel of shouting burst from the other coaches and, as the whistle shrieked without pause, a shot was heard close at hand and the conductor reeled suddenly and sank into a seat, limp and silent.

At the first jerk of the train the card-players threw the board from across their knees, scattering the cards over the floor, and crouching, gained the center of the aisle, intently peering through the windows, their Colts ready for instant use. Hopalong and Red were also in the aisle, and when the conductor had reeled Hopalong's Colt exploded and the man outside threw up his arms and pitched forward.

"Good boy, Hopalong!" cried Skinny, who was fighting mad.

Hopalong wheeled and crouched, watching the door, and it was not long before a masked face appeared on the farther side of the glass. Hopalong fired and a splotch of red stained the white mask as the robber fell against the door and slid to the platform.

"Hear that shooting?" cried the brakeman. "They're at the messenger. They'll blow him up!"

"Come on, fellers!" cried Hopalong, leaping toward the door, closely followed by his friends.

They stepped over the obstruction on the platform and jumped to the ground on the side of the car farthest from the robbers.

"Shoot under the cars for legs," whispered Skinny. "That'll bring 'em down where we can get 'em."

"Which is a good idea," replied Red, dropping quickly and looking under the car.

"Somebody's going to be surprised, all right," exulted Hopalong.

The firing on the other side of the train was heavy, being for the purpose of terrifying the passengers and to forestall concerted resistance. The robbers could not distinguish between the many reports and did not know they were being opposed, or that two of their number were dead.

A whinny reached Hopalong's ears and he located it in a small grove ahead of him: "Well, we know where th' cayuses are in case they make a break."

A white and scared face peered out of the cab-window and Hopalong stopped his finger just in time, for the inquisitive man wore the cap of fireman.

"You idiot!" muttered the gunman, angrily. "Get back!" he ordered.

A pair of legs ran swiftly along the other side of the car and Red and Skinny fired instantly. The legs bent, their owner falling forward behind the rear truck, where he was screened from sight.

"They had it their own way before!" gritted Skinny. "Now we'll see if they can stand th' iron!"

By this time Hopalong and Red were crawling under the express-car and were so preoccupied that they did not notice the faint blue streak of smoke immediately over their heads. Then Red glanced up to see what it was that sizzled, saw the glowing end of a three-inch fuse, and blanched. It was death not to dare and his hand shot up and back, and the dynamite cartridge sailed far behind him to the edge of the embankment, where it hung on a bush.

"Good!" panted Hopalong. "We'll pay 'em for that!"

"They're worse'n rustlers!"

They could hear the messenger running about over their heads, dragging and up-ending heavy objects against the doors of the car, and Hopalong laughed grimly: "Luck's with this messenger, all right."

"It ought to be—he's a fighter."

"Where are they? Have they tumbled to our game?"

"They're waiting for the explosion, you chump."

"Stay where you are then. Wait till they come out to see what's th' matter with it."

Red snorted: "Wait nothing!"

"All right, then; I'm with you. Get out of my way."

"I've been in situations some peculiar, but this beats 'em all," Red chuckled, crawling forward.

The robber by the car truck revived enough to realize that something was radically wrong, and shouted a warning as he raised himself on his elbow to fire at Skinny but the alert puncher shot first.

As Hopalong and Red emerged from beneath the car and rose to their feet there was a terrific explosion and they were knocked to the ground, while a sudden, heavy shower of stones and earth rained down over everything. The two punchers were not hurt and they arose to their feet in time to see the engineer and fireman roll out of the cab and crawl along the track on their hands and knees, dazed and weakened by the concussion.

Suddenly, from one of the day-coaches, a masked man looked out, saw the two punchers, and cried: "It's all up! Save yourselves!"

As Hopalong and Red looked around, still dazed, he fired at them, the bullet singing past Hopalong's ear. Red smothered a curse and reeled as his friend grasped him. A wound over his right eye was bleeding profusely and Hopalong's face cleared of its look of anxiety when he realized that it was not serious.

"They creased you! Blamed near got you for keeps!" he cried, wiping away the blood with his sleeve.

Red, slightly stunned, opened his eyes and looked about confusedly. "Who done that! Where is he?"

"Don't know, but I'll shore find out," Hopalong replied. "Can you stand alone?"

Red pushed himself free and leaned against the car for support: "Course I can! Git that cuss!"

When Skinny heard the robber shout the warning he wheeled and ran back, intently watching the windows and doors of the car for trouble.

"We'll finish yore tally right here!" he muttered.

When he reached the smoker he turned and went toward the rear, where he found Lanky and Billy lying under the platform. Billy was looking back and guarding their rear, while his companion watched the clump of trees where the second herd of horses was known to be. Just as they were joined by their foreman, they saw two men run across the track, fifty yards distant, and into the grove, both going so rapidly as to give no chance for a shot at them.

"There they are!" shouted Skinny, opening fire on the grove.

At that instant Hopalong turned the rear platform and saw the brakeman leap out of the door with a Winchester in his hands. The puncher sprang up the steps, wrenched the rifle from its owner, and, tossing it to Skinny, cried: "Here, this is better!"

"Too late," grunted the puncher, looking up, but Hopalong had become lost to sight among the rocks along the right of way. "If I only had this a minute ago!" he grumbled.

The men in the grove, now in the saddle, turned and opened fire on the group by the train, driving them back to shelter. Skinny, taking advantage of the cover afforded, ran toward the grove, ordering his friends to spread out and surround it; but it was too late, for at that minute galloping was heard and it grew rapidly fainter.

Red appeared at the end of the train: "Where's th' rest of the coyotes?"

"Two of 'em got away," Lanky replied.

"Ya-ho!" shouted Hopalong from the grove. "Don't none of you fools shoot! I'm coming out. They plumb got away!"

"They near got *you*, Red," Skinny cried.

"Nears don't count," Red laughed.

· "Did you ever notice Hopalong when he's fighting mad?" asked Lanky, grinning at the man who was leaving the woods. "He allus wears his sombrero hanging on one ear. Look at it now!"

"Who touched off that cannon some time back?" asked Billy.

"I did. It was an anti-gravity cartridge what I found sizzling on a rod under th' floor of th' express car," replied Red.

"Why didn't you pinch out th' fuse 'stead of blowing everything up?" Lanky asked.

"I reckon I was some hasty," grinned Red.

"It blowed me under th' car an' my lid through a windy," cried Billy. "An' Skinny, he went up in th' air like a shore-'nough grasshopper."

Hopalong joined them, grinning broadly: "Hey, reckon ridin' in th' cars ain't so bad after all, is it?"

"Holy smoke!" cried Skinny. "What's that a-popping?"

Hopalong, Colt in hand, leaped to the side of the train and looked along it, the others close behind him, and saw the fat man with his head and arm out of the window, blazing away into the air, which increased the panic in the coaches. Hopalong grinned and fired into the ground, and the fat man nearly dislocated parts of his anatomy by his hasty disappearance.

"Reckon he plumb forgot all about his fine, six-dollar gun till just now," Skinny laughed.

"Oh, he's making good," Red replied. "He said he'd take a hand if anything busted loose. It's a good thing he didn't come to life while me an' Hoppy was under his windy looking for laigs."

"Reckon some of us better go in th' cars an' quiet th' stampede," Skinny remarked, mounting the steps, followed by Hopalong. "They're shore *loco*."

The uproar in the coach ceased abruptly when the two punchers stepped through the door, the inmates shrinking into their seats, frightened into silence. Skinny and his companion did not make a reassuring sight, for they were grimy with burned powder and dust, and Hopalong's sleeve was stained with Red's blood.

"Oh, my jewels, my pretty jewels," sobbed a woman, staring at Skinny and wringing her hands.

"Ma'am, we shore don't want yore jewelry," replied Skinny, earnestly. "Ca'm yoreself; we don't want nothin'."

"*I* don't want that!" growled Hopalong, pushing a wallet from him. "How many times do you want us to tell you we don't want nothin'? We ain't robbers; we licked th' robbers."

Suddenly he stooped and, grasping a pair of legs which protruded into the aisle obstructing the passage, straightened up and backed toward Red, who had just entered the car, dragging into sight a portly gentleman, who kicked and struggled and squealed, as he grabbed at the stanchions of seats to stay his progress. Red stepped aside between two seats and let his friend pass, and then leaned over and grasped the portly gentleman's coat-collar. He tugged energetically and lifted the frightened man clear of the aisle and deposited him across the back of a seat, face down, where he hung balanced, yelling and kicking.

"Shut yore face, you cave-hunter!" cried Red in disgust. "Stop that infernal noise! You fat fellers make all yore noise after th' fighting is all over!"

The man on the seat, suddenly realizing what a sight he made, rolled off his perch and sat up, now more angry than frightened. He glared at Red's grinning face and sputtered: "It's an outrage! It's an outrage! I'll have you hung for this day's work, young man!"

"That's right," grinned Hopalong. "He shore deserves it. I told him more'n once that he'd get strung up some day."

"Yes, and you, too!"

"Please don't," begged Hopalong. "I don't want t' die!"

Tense as the past quarter of an hour had been a titter ran along the car and, fuming impotently, the portly gentleman fled into the smoker.

"I'll bet he had a six-dollar gun, too," laughed Red.

"I'll bet he's calling hisself names right about now," Hopalong replied. Then he turned to reply to a woman: "Yes, ma'am, we did. But they wasn't real badmen."

At this a young woman, who was about as pretty as any young woman could be, arose and ran to Hopalong and, impulsively throwing her arms around his neck, cried: "You brave man! You hero! You dear!"

"Skinny! Red! Help!" cried the frightened and embarrassed puncher, struggling to get free.

She kissed him on the cheek, which flamed even more red as he made frantic efforts to keep his head back.

"Ma'am!" he cried, desperately. "Leggo, ma'am! Leggo!"

"Oh! Ho! Ho!" roared Red, weak from his mirth and, not looking to see what he was doing, he dropped into a seat beside another woman. He was on his feet instantly; fearing that he would have to go through the ordeal his friend was going through, he fled down the aisle, closely followed by Hopalong, who by this time had managed to break away. Skinny backed off suspiciously and kept close watch on Hopalong's admirer.

Just then the brakeman entered the car, grinning, and Skinny asked about the condition of the conductor.

"Oh, he's all right now," the brakeman replied. "They shot him through the arm, but he's repaired and out bossin' the job of clearin' the rocks off the track. He's a little shaky yet, but he'll come around all right."

"That's good. I'm shore glad to hear it."

"Won't you wear this pin as a small token of my gratitude?" asked a voice at Skinny's shoulder.

He wheeled and raised his sombrero, a flush stealing over his face: "Thank you, ma'am, but I don't want no pay. We was plumb glad to do it."

"But this is not pay! It's just a trifling token of my appreciation of your courage, just something to remind you of it. I shall feel hurt if you refuse."

Her quick fingers had pinned it to his shirt while she spoke and he thanked her as well as his embarrassment would permit. Then there was a rush toward him and, having visions of a shirt looking like a jeweler's window, he turned and fled from the car, crying: "Pin 'em on th' brakeman!"

He found the outfit working at a pile of rocks on the track, under the supervision of the conductor, and Hopalong looked up apprehensively at Skinny's approach.

"Lord!" he ejaculated, grinning sheepishly, "I was some scairt you was a woman."

Red dropped the rock he was carrying and laughed derisively.

"Oh, yo're a brave man, you are! Scared to death by a purty female girl! If I'd 'a' been you I wouldn't 'a' run, not a step!"

Hopalong looked at him witheringly: "Oh, no! You wouldn't 'a' run! You'd dropped dead in your tracks, you would!"

"You was both of you a whole lot scared," Skinny laughed. Then, turning to the conductor: "How do you feel, Simms?"

"Oh, I'm all right: but it took the starch out of me for awhile."

"Well, I don't wonder, not a bit."

"You fellows certainly don't waste any time getting busy," Simms laughed.

"That's the secret of gun-fightin'," replied Skinny.

"Well, you're a fine crowd all right. Any time you want to go any place when you're broke, climb aboard my train and I'll see't you get there."

"Much obliged."

Simms turned to the express-car: "Hey, Jackson! You can open up now if you want to."

But the express-messenger was suspicious, fearing that the conductor was talking with a gun at his head: "You go to hell!" he called back.

"Honest!" laughed Simms. "Some cowboy friends o' mine licked the gang. Didn't you hear that dynamite go off? If they hadn't fished it out from under your feet you'd be communing with the angels 'bout now."

For a moment there was no response, and then Jackson could be heard dragging things away from the door. When he was told of the cartridge and Red had been pointed out to him as the man who had saved his life, he leaped to the ground and ran to where that puncher was engaged in carrying the ever-silenced robbers to the baggage-car. He shook hands with Red, who laughed deprecatingly, and then turned and assisted him.

Hopalong came up and grinned: "Say, there's some cayuses in that grove up th' track; shall I go up an' get 'em?"

"Shore! I'll go an' get 'em with you," replied Skinny.

In the grove they found seven horses picketed, two of them being pack-animals, and they led them forth and reached the train as the others came up.

"Well, here's five saddled cayuses, an' two others," Skinny grinned.

"Then we can ride th' rest of th' way in th' saddle instead of in that blamed train," Red eagerly suggested.

"That's just what we can do," replied Skinny. "Leather beats car-seats any time. How far are we from Sandy Creek, Simms?"

"About twenty miles."

"An' we can ride along th' track, too," suggested Hopalong.

"We shore can," laughed Skinny, shaking hands with the train-crew: "We're some glad we rode with you this trip: we've had a fine time."

"And we're glad you did," Simms replied, "for that ain't no joke, either."

Hopalong and the others had mounted and were busy waving their sombreros and bowing to the heads and handkerchiefs which were decorating the car-windows.

"All aboard!" shouted the conductor, and cheers and good wishes rang out and were replied to by bows and waving of sombreros. Then Hopalong jerked his gun loose and emptied it into the air, his companions doing likewise. Suddenly five reports rang out from the smoker and they cheered the fat man as he waved at them. They sat quietly and watched the train until the last handkerchief became lost to sight around a curve, but the screeching whistle could be heard for a long time.

"Gee!" laughed Hopalong as they rode on after the train, "won't th' fellers home on th' ranch be a whole lot sore when they hears about the good time what they missed!"

CHAPTER 11

Sammy Finds a Friend

The long train ride and the excitement were over and the outfit, home-ward bound, loped along the trail, noisily discussing their exciting and humorous experiences and laughingly commented upon Hopalong's decision to follow them later. They could not understand why he should be interested in a town like Sandy Creek after a week spent in the city.

Back in the little cow-town their friend was standing in the office of the ho-tel, gazing abstractedly out of the window. His eyes caught and focused on a woman who was walking slowly along the other side of the square and finally paused before McCall's "Palace," a combination saloon, dance and gambling hall. He smiled cynically as his memory ran back over those other women he had seen in cow-towns and wondered how it was that the men of the ranges could rise to a chivalry that was famed. At that distance she was strikingly pretty. Her complexion was an alluring blend of color that the gold of her hair crowned like a burst of sunshine. He noticed that her eyebrows were too prominent, too black and heavy to be Nature's contribution. And there was about her a certain forwardness, a dash that bespoke no bashful Miss; and her clothes, though well-fitting, somehow did not please his untrained eye. A sudden impulse seized him and he strode to the door and crossed the dusty square, avoiding the piles of rusted cans, broken bottles and other rubbish that littered it.

She had become interested in a dingy window but turned to greet him with a resplendent smile as he stepped to the wooden walk. He noted with displea-sure that the white teeth displayed two shining panels of gold that drew his eyes irresistibly; and then and there he hated gold teeth.

"Hello," she laughed. "I'm glad to see somebody that's alive in this town. Ain't it awful?"

He instinctively removed his sombrero and was conscious that his habitual bashfulness in the presence of members of her sex was somehow lacking. "Why, I don't see nothin' extra dead about it," he replied. "Most of these towns are this way in daylight. Th' moths ain't out yet. You should 'a' been here last night!"

"Yes? But you're out; an' you look like you might be able to fly," she replied.

"Yes; I suppose so," he laughed.

"I see you wear *two* of 'em," she said, glancing at his guns. "Ain't one of them things enough?"

"One usually is, mostly," he assented. "But I'm pigheaded, so I wears two."

"Ain't it awful hard to use two of 'em at once?" she asked, her tone flattering. "Then you're one of them two-gun men I've heard about, ain't you?"

"An' seen?" he smiled.

"Yes, I've seen a couple. Where you goin' so early?"

"Just lookin' th' town over," he answered, glancing over her shoulder at a cub of a cow-puncher who had opened the door of the "Retreat," but stopped in his tracks when he saw the couple in front of McCall's. There was a look of surprised interest on the cub's face, and it swiftly changed to one of envious interest. Hopalong's glance did not linger, but swept carelessly along the row of shacks and back to his companion's face without betraying his discovery.

"Well; you can look it over in about ten seconds, from th' outside," she rejoined. "An' it's so dusty out here. My throat is awful dry already."

He hadn't noticed any dust in the air, but he nodded. "Yes; thirsty?"

"Well, it ain't polite or ladylike to say yes," she demurred, "but I really am."

He held open the door of the "Palace" and preceded her to the dance hall, where she rippled the keys of the old piano as she swept past it. The order given and served, he sipped at his glass and carried on his share of a light conversation until, suddenly, he arose and made his apologies. "I got to attend to somethin'," he regretted as he picked up his sombrero and turned. "See you later."

"Why!" she exclaimed. "I was just beginnin' to get acquainted!"

"A moth without money ain't no good," he smiled. "I'm goin' out to find th' money. When I'm in good company I like to spend. See you later?" He bowed as she nodded, and departed.

Emerging from McCall's he glanced at the "Retreat" and sauntered toward it. When he entered he found the cub resting his elbows on the pine bar, arguing with the bartender about the cigars sold in the establishment. The cub glanced up and appealed to the newcomer. "Ain't they?" he demanded.

Hopalong nodded. "I reckon so. But what is it about?"

"These cigars," explained the cub, ruefully. "I was just sayin' there ain't a good one in town."

"You lose," replied Hopalong. "Are you shore you knows a good cigar when you smokes it?"

"I know it so well that I ain't found one since I left Kansas City. You said I lose. Do *you* know one well enough to be a judge?"

Hopalong reached to his vest pocket, extracted a cigar and handed it to the cub, who took it hesitatingly. "Why, I'm much obliged. I—I didn't mean that—you know."

Hopalong nodded and rearranged the cigar's twin-brothers in his pocket. He would be relieved when they were smoked, for they made him nervous with their frailty. The cub lighted the cigar and an unaffected grin of delight wreathed his features as the smoke issued from his nostrils. "Who sells 'em?" he demanded, excitedly.

"Corson an' Lukins, up th' hill from th' depot," answered Hopalong. "Like it?"

"Like it! Why, stranger, I used to spend most of my week's pocket money for these." He paused and stared at the smiling puncher. "Did you say Corson an' Lukins?" he demanded incredulously. "Well, I'll be hanged! When was you there?"

"Last week. Here, bartender; liquor for all hands."

The cub touched the glass to his lips and waved his hand at a table. Seated across from the stranger with the heaven-sent cigars he ordered the second round, and when he went to pay for it he drew out a big roll of bills and peeled off the one on the outside.

Hopalong frowned. "Sonny," he said in a low voice, "it ain't none of my affair, but you oughta put that wad away an' forget you have it when out in public. You shouldn't tempt yore feller men like that."

The cub laughed: "Oh, I had my eye teeth cut long ago. Play a little game?"

Hopalong was amused. "Didn't I just tell you not to tempt yore feller men?"

The cub grinned. "I reckon it'll fade quick, anyhow; but it took me six months' hard work to get it together. It'll last about six days, I suppose."

"Six hours, if you plays every man that comes along," corrected Hopalong.

"Well, mebby," admitted the cub. "Say: that was one fine girl you was talkin' to, all right," he grinned.

Hopalong studied him a moment. "Not meanin' no offense, what's yore name?"

"Sammy Porter; why?"

"Well, Sammy," remarked Hopalong as he arose. "I reckon we'll meet again before I leave. You was remarkin' she was a fine girl. I admit it; she was. So-long," and he started for the door.

Sammy flushed. "Why, I—I didn't mean nothin'!" he exclaimed. "I just happened to think about her—that's all! You know, I saw you talkin' to her. Of course, you saw her first," he explained.

Hopalong turned and smiled kindly. "You didn't say nothin' to offend me. I was just startin' when you spoke. But as long as you mentioned it I'll say that my interest in th' lady was only brief. Her interest in me was th' same. Beyond lettin' you know that I'll add that I don't generally discuss wimmin. I'll see you later," and, nodding cheerily, he went out and closed the door behind him.

Hopalong leaned lazily against the hotel, out of reach of the spring wind, which was still sharp, and basked in the warmth of the timid sun. He regarded the little cow-town cynically but smilingly and found no particular fault with it. Existing because the railroad construction work of the season before had chanced to stop on the eastern bank of the deceptive creek, and because of the nearness of three drive trails, one of them important, the town had sprung up, mushroom-like, almost in a night. Facing on the square were two general stores, the railroad station and buildings, two restaurants, a dozen saloons where gambling either was the main attraction or an ambitious side-line, McCall's place and a barber shop with a dingy, bullet-peppered red-and-white pole set close to the door. Between the barber shop and McCall's was a narrow space, and the windows of the two buildings, while not opposite, opened on the little strip of ground separating them.

Rubbing a hand across his chin he regarded the barber shop thoughtfully and finally pushed away from the sun-warmed wall of the hotel and started lazily toward the red-and-white pole. As he did so the tin-panny notes of a piano redoubled and a woman's voice shrilly arose to a high note, flatted, broke and swiftly dropped an octave. He squirmed and looked speculatively along the westward trail, wondering how far away his outfit was and why he had not gone with them. Another soaring note that did not flat and a crashing chord from the piano were followed by a burst of uproarious, reckless laughter. Hopalong frowned, snapped his fingers in sudden decision and stepped briskly toward the barber shop as the piano began anew.

Entering quietly and closing the door softly, he glanced appraisingly through the windows and made known his wants in a low voice. "I want a shave, haircut, shampoo, an' anythin' else you can think of. I'm tired an' don't want to talk. Take yore own time an' do a good job; an' if I'm asleep when yo're through, don't wake me till somebody else wants th' chair. Savvy? All right— start in."

In McCall's a stolid bartender listened to the snatches of conversation that filtered under the door to the dance hall alongside and on his face there at times flickered the suggestion of a cynical smile. A heavy, dark complexioned man entered from the street and glanced at the closed door of the dance hall. The bartender nodded and held up a staying hand, after which he shoved a drink across the bar. The heavy-set man carefully wiped a few drops of spilled liquor from his white, tapering hands and seated himself with a sigh of relief, and became busy with his thoughts until the time should come when he would be needed.

On the other side of that door a little comedy was being enacted. The musician, a woman, toyed with the keys of the warped and scratched piano, the dim light from the shaded windows mercifully hiding the paint and the hardness of her face and helping the jewelry, with which her hands were covered, keep its tawdry secret.

"I don't see what makes you so touchy," grumbled Sammy in a pout. "I ain't goin' to hurt you if I touch yore arm." He was flushed and there was a suspicious unsteadiness in his voice.

She laughed. "Why, I thought you wanted to talk?"

"I did," he admitted, sullenly; "but there's a limit to most wants. Oh, well: go ahead an' play. That last piece was all right; but give us a gallop or a mazurka—anything lively. Better yet, a caprice: it's in keepin' with yore temperament. If you was to try to interpert mine you'd have to dig it out of Verdi an' toll a funeral bell."

"Say; who told you so much about music?" she demanded.

"Th' man that makes harmonicas," he grinned. He arose and took a step toward her, but she retreated swiftly, smiling. "Now behave yourself, for a little while, at least. What's th' matter with you, anyhow? What makes you so silly?"

"You, of course. I don't see no purty wimmin out on th' range, an' you went to my head th' minute I laid eyes on you. *I* ain't in no hurry to leave this town, now nohow."

"I'm afraid you're going to be awful when you grow up. But you're a nice boy to say such pretty things. Here," she said, filling his glass and handing it to him, "let's drink another toast—you know such nice ones."

"Yes; an' if I don't run out of 'em purty soon I'll have to hunt a solid, immovable corner somewheres; an' there ain't nothin' solid or immovable about *this* room at present," he growled. "What you allus drinkin' to somethin' for? Well, here's a toast—I don't know any more fancy ones. Here's to—*you!*"

"That's nicer than—oh, pshaw!" she exclaimed, pouting. "An' you wouldn't drink a full glass to *that* one. You must think I'm nice, when you renig like that! Don't tell me any more pretty things—an' stop right where you are! Think you can hang onto me after that? Well, that's better; why didn't you do it th' first time? You can be a nice boy when you want to."

He flushed angrily. "Will you stop callin' me a boy?" he demanded unsteadily. "I ain't no kid! I do a man's work, earn a man's pay, an' I spend it like a man."

"An' drink a boy's drink," she teased. "You'll grow up some day." She reached forward and filled his glass again, for an instant letting her cheek touch his. Swiftly evading him she laughed and patted him on the head. "Here, *man*," she taunted, "drink this if you dare!"

He frowned at her but gulped down the liquor. "There, like a fool!" he grumbled, bitterly. "You tryin' to get me drunk?" he demanded suddenly in a heavy voice.

She threw back her head and regarded him coldly. "It will do me no good. Why should I? I merely wanted to see if you would take a dare, if you were a man. You are either not sober now, or you are insultingly impolite. I don't care to waste any more words or time with you," and she turned haughtily toward the door.

He had leaned against the piano, but now he lurched forward and cried out. "I'm sorry if I hurt yore feelin's that way—I shore didn't mean to. Ain't we goin' to make up?" he asked, anxiously.

"Do you mean that?" she demanded, pausing and looking around.

"You know I do, Annie. Le's make up—come on; le's make up."

"Well; I'll try you, an' see."

"Play some more. You play beautiful," he assured her with heavy gravity.

"I'm tired of—but, say: Can you play poker?" she asked, eagerly.

"Why, shore; who can't?"

"Well, I can't, for one. I want to learn, so I can win my money back from Jim. He taught me, but all I had time to learn was how to lose."

Sammy regarded her in puzzled surprise and gradually the idea became plain. "Did he teach you, an' win money from you? Did he *keep* it?" he finally blurted, his face flushed a deeper red from anger.

She nodded. "Why, yes; why?"

He looked around for his sombrero, muttering savagely.

"Where you goin'?" she asked in surprise.

"To get it back. He ain't goin' to keep it, th' coyote!"

"Why, he won't give it back to you if he wouldn't to me. Anyhow, he won it."

"*Won* it!" he snapped. "He stole it, that's how much he won it. He'll give it back or get shot."

"Now look here," she said, quickly. "You ain't goin' gunnin' for no friend of mine. If you want to get that money for me, an' I certainly can use it about now, you got to try some other way. Say! Why don't you win it from him?" she exulted. "That's th' way—get it back th' way it went."

He weighed her words and a grin slowly crept across his face. "Why, I reckon you called it, that time, Annie. That's th' way I'll try first, anyhow, Li'l Girl. Where is this good friend of yourn that steals yore money? Where is this feller?"

As if in answer to his inquiry the heavy-set man strolled in, humming cheerily. And as he did so the sleepy occupant of the barber's chair slowly awoke, rubbed his eyes, stretched luxuriously and, paying his bill, loafed out and lazily sauntered down the street, swearing softly.

"Why, here he is now," laughed the woman. "You must 'a' heard us talkin' about you, Jim. I'm goin' to get my money back—this is Mr. Porter, Jim, who's goin' to do it."

The gambler smiled and held out his hand. "Howd'y, Mr. Porter," he said.

Sammy glared at him: "Put yore paw down," he said, thickly. "I ain't shakin' han's with no dogs or tin-horns."

The gambler recoiled and flushed, fighting hard to repress his anger. "What you mean?" he growled, furiously.

"What I said. If you want revenge sit down there an' play, if you've got th' nerve to play with a man. I never let no coyote steal a woman's money, an' I'm goin' to get Annie her twenty. Savvy?"

The gambler's reply was a snarl. "Play!" he sneered. "I'll play, all right. It'll take more'n a sassy kid to get that money back, too. I'm goin' to take yore last red cent. You can't talk to me like that an' get it over. An' don't let me hear you call her 'Annie' no more, neither. Yo're too cussed familiar!"

Her hand on Sammy's arm stopped the draw and he let the gun drop back into the holster. "*No!*" she whispered. "Make a fool of him, Sammy! Beat him at his own game."

Sammy nodded and scowled blackly. "I call th' names as suits me," he retorted. "When I see you on th' street I'm goin' to call you some that I'm savin' up now because a lady's present. They're hefty, too."

At first he won, but always small amounts. Becoming reckless, he plunged heavily on a fair hand and lost. He plunged again on a better hand and lost. Then he steadied as much as his befuddled brain would permit and played a careful game, winning a small pot. Another small winning destroyed his caution and he plunged again, losing heavily. Steadying himself once more he began a new deal with excess caution and was bluffed out of the pot, the gambler sneeringly showing his cards as he threw them down. Sammy glanced around to say something to the woman, but found she had gone. "Aw, never mind her!" growled his opponent. "She'll be back—she can't stay away from a kid like you."

The woman was passing through the barroom and, winking at the bartender, opened the door and stepped to the street. She smiled as she caught sight of the limping stranger coming toward her. He might have found money, but she was certain he had found something else and in generous quantities. He removed his sombrero with an exaggerated sweep of his hand and hastened to meet her, walking with the conscious erectness of a man whose feet are the last part of him to succumb. "Hullo, Sugar," he grinned. "I found some, a'right. Now we'll have some music. Come 'long."

"There ain't no hurry," she answered. "We'll take a little walk first."

"No, we won't. We'll have some music an' somethin' to drink. If you won't make th' music, I will; or shoot up th' machine. Come 'long, Sugar," he leered, pushing open the door with a resounding slam. He nodded to the bartender and apologized. "No harm meant, Friend. It sorta slipped; jus' slipped, tha's all. Th' young lady an' me is goin' to have some music. What? All right for you, Sugar! Then I'll make it myself," and he paraded stiffly toward the inner door.

The bartender leaned suddenly forward. "Keep out of there! You'll bust that pianner!"

The puncher stopped with a jerk, swung ponderously on his heel and leveled a forefinger at the dispenser of drinks. "I won't," he said. "An' if I do, I'll pay for it. Come on, Sugar—le's play th' old thing, jus' for spite." Grasping her arm he gently but firmly escorted her into the dance hall and seated her at the piano. As he straightened up he noticed the card players and, bowing low to her, turned and addressed them.

"Gents," he announced, bowing again, "we are goin' to have a li'l music an' we hopes you won't objec'. Not that we gives a damn, but we jus' hopes you won't." He laughed loudly at his joke and leaned against the piano. "Let 'er go," he cried, beating time. "Allaman lef' an' ladies change! Swing yore partner's gal—I mean, swing some other gal: but what's th' diff'rence? All join han's an' hop to th' middle—nope! It's all han's roun' an' swing 'em again. But it don't make no diff'rence, does it, Lulu?" He whooped loudly and marched across the room, executed a few fancy steps and marched back again. As he passed the card table Sammy threw down his hand and arose with a curse. The marcher stopped, fiddled a bit with his feet until obtaining his balance, and then regarded the youth quizzically. "S'matter, Sonny?" he inquired.

Sammy scowled, slowly recognized the owner of the imported cigars and shook his head. "Big han's, but not big enough; an' I lost my pile." Staggering to the piano he plumped down on a chair near it and watched the rippling fingers of the player in drunken interest.

The hilarious cowpuncher, leaning backward perilously, recovered his poise for a moment and then lurched forward into the chair the youth had just left. "Come on, pardner," he grinned across at the gambler. "Le's gamble. I been honin' for a game, an' here she is." He picked up the cards, shuffled them clumsily and pushed them out for the cut. The gambler hesitated, considered and then turned over a jack. He lost the deal and shoved out a quarter without interest.

The puncher leaned over, looked at it closely and grinned. "Two bits? That ain't poker; that's—that's dominoes!" he blurted, angrily, with the quick change of mood of a man in his cups.

"I ain't anxious to play," replied the gambler. "I'll kill a li'l time at a two-bit game, though. Otherwise I'll quit."

"A'right," replied the dealer. "I didn't expec' nothin' else from a tin-horn, no how. I want two cards after you get yourn." The gambler called on the second raise and smiled to himself when he saw that his opponent had drawn to a pair and an ace. He won on his own deal and on the one following.

The puncher increased the ante on the fourth deal and looked up inquiringly, a grin on his face. "Le's move out th' infant class," he suggested.

The gambler regarded him sharply. "Well, th' other *was* sorta tender," he admitted, nodding.

The puncher pulled out a handful of gold coins and clumsily tried to stack them, which he succeeded in doing after three attempts. He was so busy that he did not notice the look in the other's eyes. Picking up his hand he winked at it and discarded one. "Goin' to raise th' ante a few," he chuckled. "I got a feelin' I'm goin' t' be lucky." When the card was dealt to him he let it lay and bet heavily. The gambler saw it and raised in turn, and the puncher, frowning in indecision, nodded his head wisely and met it, calling as he did so. His four fives were just two spots shy to win and he grumbled loudly at his luck. "Huh," he finished, "she's a jack pot, eh?" He slid a double eagle out to the center of the table and laughed recklessly. The deals went around rapidly, each one calling for a ten-dollar sweetener and when the seventh hand was dealt the puncher picked his cards and laughed. "She's open," he cried, "for fifty," and shoved out the money with one hand while he dug up a reserve pile from his pocket with the other.

The gambler saw the opener and raised it fifty, smiling at his opponent's expression. The puncher grunted his surprise, studied his hand, glanced at the pot and shrugging his shoulders, saw the raise. He drew two cards and chuckled as he slid them into his hand; but before the dealer could make his own draw the puncher's chuckle died out and he stared over the gambler's shoulder. With an oath he jerked out his gun and fired. The gambler leaped to his feet and whirled around to look behind. Then he angrily faced the frowning puncher. "What you think yo're doin'?" he demanded, his hand resting inside his coat, the thumb hooked over the edge of the vest.

The puncher waved his hand apologetically. "I never have no luck when I sees a cat," he explained. "A black cat is worse; but a yaller one's bad enough. I'll bet that yaller devil won't come back in a hurry—judgin' by th' way it started. I won't miss him, if he does."

The gambler, still frowning, glanced at the deck suspiciously and saw that it lay as he had dropped it. The bartender, grinning at them from the door, cracked a joke and went back to the bar. Sammy, after a wild look around, settled back in his chair and soothed the pianist a little before going back to sleep.

Drawing two cards the gambler shoved them in his hand without a change in his expression—but he was greatly puzzled. It was seldom that he bungled and he was not certain that he had. The discard contained the right number of cards and his opponent's face gave no hint to the thoughts behind it. He hesitated before he saw the bet—ten dollars was not much, for the size of the pot justified more. He slowly saw it, willing to lose the ten in order to see his opponent's cards. There was something he wished to know, and he wanted to know it as soon as he could. "I call that," he said. The puncher's expression of tenseness relaxed into one of great relief and he hurriedly dropped his cards. Three kings, an eight, and a deuce was his offering. The gambler laid down a pair of queens, a ten, an eight and a four, waved his hand and smiled. "It's just as well I didn't draw another queen," he observed, calmly. "I might 'a' raised once for luck."

The puncher raked in the pot and turned around in his chair. "I cleaned up that time," he exulted to the woman. She had stopped playing and was stroking Sammy's forehead. Smiling at the exuberant winner she nodded. "You should have let the cat stay—I think it really brought you luck." He shook his head emphatically. "*No*, ma'am! It was chasin' it away as did that. That's what did it, a'right."

The gambler glanced quickly at the two top cards on the deck and was picking up those scattered on the table when his opponent turned around again. How that queen and ten had got two cards too deep puzzled him greatly—he was willing to wager even money that he would not look away again until the game was finished, not if all the cats in the world were being slaughtered. One hundred and ninety dollars was too much money to pay for being caught off his guard, as he was tempted to believe he had been. He did not know how much liquor the other had consumed, but he seemed to be sobering rapidly.

The next few deals did not amount to much. Then a jackpot came around and was pushed hard. The puncher was dealing and as he picked up the deck after the cut he grinned and winked. "Th' skirmishin' now bein' over, th' battle begins. If that cat stays away long enough mebby I'll make a killin'.'"

"All right; but don't make no more gun-plays," warned the gambler, coldly. "I allus get excited when I smells gun powder an' I do reckless things sometimes," he added, significantly.

"Then I shore hopes you keep ca'm," laughed the puncher, loud enough to be heard over the noise of the piano, which was now going again.

The pot was sweetened three times and then the gambler dealt his opponent openers. The puncher looked anxiously through the door, grinning coltishly. He slowly pushed out twenty dollars. "There's th' key," he grunted. "A'right; see that an' raise you back. Good for you! I'm stayin' an' boostin' same as ever. Fine! See it again, an' add this. I'm playin' with yore money, so I c'n afford to be reckless. All right; I'm satisfied, too. Gimme one li'l card. I shore am glad I don't need th' king of hearts—that was shore on th' bottom when th' deal *begun*."

The gambler, having drawn, cursed and reached swiftly toward his vest pocket; but he stopped suddenly and contemplated the Colt that peeked over the edge of the table. It looked squarely at his short ribs and was backed by a sober, angry man who gazed steadily into his eyes. "Drop that hand," said the puncher in a whisper just loud enough to be heard by the other over the noise of the piano. "I never did like them shoulder holsters—I carry my irons where everybody can see 'em." Leaning forward swiftly he reached out his left hand and cautiously turned over the other's cards. The fourth one was the king of hearts. "Don't move," he whispered, not wishing to have the bartender take a hand from behind. "An' don't talk," he warned as he leaned farther forward and shoved his Colt against the other's vest and with his left hand extracted a short-barreled gun from the sheath under the gambler's armpit. Sinking back in his chair he listened a moment and, raking in the pot, stowed it away with the other winnings in his pockets.

The gambler stirred, but stopped as the Colt leaped like a flash of light to the edge of the table. "Tin-horn," said the puncher, softly, "you ain't slick enough. I didn't stop you when you wanted that queen an' ten because I wanted you to go on with th' crookedness. Yaller cats is more unlucky to you than they are to me. But when I saw that last play I lost my temper; an' I stopped you. Now if you'll cheat with me, you'll cheat with a drunk boy. So, havin' cheated him, you really stole his money away from him. That bein' so, you will dig up six months' wages at about fifty per month. I'd shoot you just as quick as I'd shoot a snake; so don't get no fool notions in yore head. Dig it right up."

The gambler studied the man across from him, but after a moment he silently placed some money on the table. "It was only two forty," he observed, holding to three double eagles. The puncher nodded: "I'll take yore word for that. Now, in th' beginnin' I only wanted to get th' boy his money; but when you started cheatin' against me I changed my mind. I played fair. Now here's your short-five," he said as he slid the gun across the table. "Mebby you might want to use it sometime," he smiled. "Now you vamoose; an' if I see you in town after th' next train leaves, I'll *make* you use that shoulder holster. An' tell yore friends that Hopalong Cassidy says, that for a country where men can tote their hardware in plain sight, a shoulder lay-out ain't no good: you gotta reach too high. Adios."

He watched the silent, philosophical man-of-cards walk slowly toward the door, upright, dignified and calm. Then he turned and approached the piano. "Sister," he said, politely, "yore gamblin' friend is leavin' town on th' next train. He has pressin' business back east a couple of stations an' wonders if you'll join him at th' depot in time for th' next train."

She had stopped playing and was staring at him in amazement. "Why didn't he come an' tell me himself, 'stead of sneakin' away an' sendin' you over?" she at last demanded, angrily.

"Well, he wanted to, but he saw a man an' slipped out with his gun in his hand. Mebby there'll be trouble; but I dunno. I'm just tellin' you. Gee," he laughed, looking at the snoring youth in the chair, "he got *that* quick. Why, I saw him less'n two hours ago an' he was sober as a judge. Reckon I'll take him over to th' hotel an' put him to bed." He went over to the helpless Sammy, shook him and made him get on his feet. "Come along, Kid," he said, slipping his arm under the sagging shoulder. "We'll get along. Good-by, Sugar," and, supporting the feebly protesting cub, he slowly made his way to the rear door and was gone, a grin wreathing his face as he heard the chink of gold coins in his several pockets.

CHAPTER 12

Sammy Knows the Game

A clean-cut, good-looking young cow-puncher limped slightly as he passed the post office and found a seat on a box in front of the store next door. He sighed with relief and gazed cheerfully at the littered square as though it was something worth looking at. The night had not been a pleasant one because Sammy Porter had insisted upon either singing or snoring; and when breakfast was announced the youth almost had recovered his senses and was full of remorse and a raging thirst. Being flatly denied the hair of the dog that bit him he grew eloquently profane and very abusive. Hence Mr. Cassidy's fondness for the box.

Sounds obtruded. They were husky and had dimensions and they came from the hotel bar. After increasing in volume and carrying power they were followed to the street by a disheveled youth who kicked open the door and blinked in the sunlight. Espying the contented individual on the box he shook an earnest fist at that person and tried next door. In a moment he followed a new burst of noise to the street and shook the other fist. Trying the saloon on the other side of the hotel without success he shook both fists and once again tried the hotel bar, where he proceeded along lines tactful, flattering and diplomatic. Only yesterday he had owned a gun, horse and other personal belongings; he had possessed plenty of money, a clear head and his sins sat lightly on his youthful soul. He still had the sins, but they had grown in weight. Tact availed him nothing, flattery was futile and diplomacy was in vain. To all his arguments the bartender sadly shook his head, not because Sammy had no money, which was the reason he gave, but because of vivid remembrance of the grimness with which a certain red-haired, straight-lipped, two-gun cowpuncher had made known his request. "Let him suffer," had said the gunman. "It'll be a good lesson for him. Understand; not a drop!" And the bartender had understood. To the drink-dispenser's refusal

Sammy replied with a masterpiece of eloquence and during its delivery the bartender stood with his hand on a mallet, but too spellbound to throw it. Wheeling at the close of a vivid, soaring climax, Sammy yanked open the door again and stood transfixed with amazement and hostile envy. His new and officious friend surely knew the right system with women. To the burning indignities of the morning this added the last straw and Sammy bitterly resolved not to forget his wrongs.

Had Mr. Cassidy been a kitten he would have purred with delight as he watched his youthful friend's vain search for the hair of the dog, and his grin was threatening to engulf his ears when the Cub slammed into the hotel. Hearing the beating of hoofs he glanced around and saw a trim, pretty young lady astride a trim, high-spirited pony; and both were thoroughbreds if he was any judge. They bore down upon him at a smart lope and stopped at the edge of the walk. The rider leaped from the saddle and ran toward him with her hand outstretched and her face aglow with a delighted surprise. Her eyes fairly danced with welcome and relief and her cheeks, reddened by the thrust of the wind for more than twenty miles, flamed a deeper red, through which streaks of creamy white played fascinatingly. "Dick Ellsworth!" she cried. "When did you get here?"

Mr. Cassidy stumbled to his feet, one hand instinctively going out to the one held out to him, the other fiercely gripping his sombrero. His face flamed under its tan and he mumbled an incoherent reply.

"Don't you remember *me*?" she chided, a roguish, half-serious expression flashing over her countenance. "Not little Annie, whom you taught to ride? I used to think I needed you then, Dick; but oh, how I need you now. It's Providence, nothing else, that sent you. Father's gone steadily worse and now all he cares for is a bottle. Joe, the new foreman, has full charge of everything and he's not only robbing us right and left, but he's—he's bothering *me*! When I complain to father of his attentions all I get is a foolish grin. If you only knew how I have prayed for you to come back, Dick! Two bitter years of it. But now everything is all right. Tell me about yourself while I get the mail and then we'll ride home together. I suppose Joe will be waiting for me somewhere on the trail; he usually does. Did you ever hate anyone so much you wanted to kill him?" she demanded fiercely, beside herself for the moment.

Hopalong nodded. "Well, yes; I have," he answered. "But you mustn't. What's his name? We'll have to look into this."

"Joe Worth; but let's forget him for awhile," she smiled. "I'll get the mail while you go after your horse."

He nodded and watched her enter the post office and then turned and walked thoughtfully away. She was mounted when he returned and they swung out of the town at a lope.

"Where have you been, and what have you been doing?" she asked as they pushed along the firm, hard trail.

"Punchin' for th' Bar-20, southwest of here. I wouldn't 'a' been here today only I let th' outfit ride on without me. We just got back from Kansas City a couple of days back. But let's get at this here Joe Worth prop'sition. I'm plumb curious. How long's he been pesterin' you?"

"Nearly two years—I can't stand it much longer."

"An' th' outfit don't cut in?"

"They're his friends, and they understand that father wants it so. You'll not know father, Dick: I never thought a man could change so. Mother's death broke him as though he were a reed."

"Hum!" he grunted. "You ain't carin' how this coyote is stopped, just so he is?"

"No!" she flashed.

"An' he'll be waitin' for you?"

"He usually is."

He grinned. "Le's hope he is this time." He was silent a moment and looked at her curiously. "I don't know how you'll take it, but I got a surprise for you—a big one. I'm shore sorry to admit it, but I ain't th' man you think. I ain't Dick What's-his-name, though it shore ain't *my* fault. I reckon I must look a heap like him; an' I hope I can *act* like him in this here matter. I want to see it through like *he* would. I can do as good a job, too. But it ain't nowise fair nor right to pretend I'm him. I ain't."

She was staring at him in a way he did not like. "Not Dick Ellsworth!" she gasped. "You are *not* Dick?"

"I'm shore sorry—but I'd like to play his cards. I'm honin' for to see this here Joe Worth," he nodded, cheerfully.

"And you let me believe you were?" she demanded coldly. "You deliberately led me to talk as I did?"

"Well, now; I didn't just know what to do. You shore was in trouble, which was bad. I reckoned mebby I could get you out of it an' then go along 'bout my business. You ain't goin' to stop me a-doin' it, are you?" he asked anxiously.

Her reply was a slow, contemptuous look that missed nothing and that left nothing to be said. Her horse did not like to stand, anyway, and sprang eagerly forward in answer to the sudden pressure of her knees. She rode the high-strung bay with superb art, angry, defiant, and erect as a statue. Hopalong, shaking his head slowly, gazed after her and when she had become a speck on the plain he growled a question to his horse and turned sullenly toward the town. Riding straight to the hotel he held a short, low-voiced conversation with the clerk and then sought his friend, the Cub. This youthful grouch was glaring across the bar at the red-faced, angry man behind it, and the atmosphere was not one of peace. The Cub turned to see who the newcomer was and thereupon transferred his glare to the smiling puncher.

"Hullo, Kid," breezed Hopalong.

"You go to hell!" growled Sammy, remembering to speak respectfully to his elders. He backed off cautiously until he could keep both of his enemies under his eyes.

Hopalong's grin broadened. He dug into his pockets and produced a large sum of money. "Here, Kid," said he, stepping forward and thrusting it into Sammy's paralyzed hands. "Take it an' buy all th' liquor you wants. You can get yore gun off'n th' clerk, an' he'll tell you where to find yore cayuse an' other belongings. I gotta leave town."

Sammy stared at the money in his hand. "What's this?" he demanded, his face flushing angrily.

"Money," replied Hopalong. "It's that shiny stuff you buys things with. Spondulix, cash, mazuma. You spend it, you know."

Sammy sputtered. He might have frothed had his mouth not been so dry. "Is it?" he demanded with great sarcasm. "I thought mebby it was cows, or buttons. What you handin' it to me for? I ain't no damned beggar!"

Hopalong chuckled. "That money's yourn. I pried it loose from th' tin-horn that stole it from you. I also, besides, pried off a few chunks more; but them's mine. I allus pays myself good wages; an' th' aforesaid chunks is plenty an' generous. Amen."

Sammy regarded his smiling friend with a frank suspicion that was brutal. The pleasing bulge of the pockets reassured him and he slowly pocketed his rescued wealth. He growled something doubtless meant for thanks and turned to the bar. "A large chunk of th' Mojave Desert slid down my throat las' night an' I'm so dry I rustles in th' breeze. Let's wet down a li'l." Having extracted some of the rustle he eyed his companion suspiciously. "Thought you was a stranger hereabouts?"

"You've called it."

"Huh! Then I'm goin' to stick close to you an get acquainted with th' female population of th' towns we hit. An' I had allus reckoned lightnin' was quick!" he soliloquized, regretfully. "How'd you do it?" he demanded.

Hopalong was gazing over his friend's head at a lurid chromo portraying the Battle of Bull Run and he pursed his lips thoughtfully. "That shore was some slaughter," he commented. "Well, Kid," he said, holding out his hand, "I'm leavin'. If you ever gets down my way an' wants a good job, drop in an' see us. Th' clerk'll tell you how to get there. An' th' next time you gambles, stay sober."

"Hey! Wait a minute!" exclaimed Sammy. "Goin' home now?"

"Can't say as I am, direct."

"Comin' back here before you do?"

"Can't say that, neither. Life is plumb on-certain an' gunplay's even worse. Mebby I will if I'm alive."

"Who you gunnin' for? Can't I take a hand?"

"Reckon not, Sammy. Why, I'm cuttin' in where I ain't wanted, even if I am needed. But it's my duty. It's a hell of a community as waits for a total stranger to do its work for it. If yo're around an' I come back, why I'll see you again. Meanwhile, look out for tin-horns."

Sammy followed him outside and grasped his arm. "I can hold up my end in an argument," he asserted fiercely. "You went an' did me a good turn— lemme do *you* one. If it's anythin' to do with that li'l girl you met to-day I won't cut in—only on th' trouble end. I'm particular strong on th' trouble part. Look here: Ain't a friend got no rights?"

Hopalong warmed to the eager youngster—he was so much like Jimmy; and Jimmy, be it known, could bedevil Hopalong as much as any man alive and not even get an unkind word for it. "I'm scared to let you come, Kid; she'd fumigate th' ranch when you left. Th' last twenty-four hours has outlawed you, all right. You keep to th' brush trails in th' draws—don't cavort none on sky-lines till you lose that biled owl look." He laughed at the other's expression and placed his hands on the youth's shoulders. "That ain't it, Kid; I never apologizes, serious, for th' looks of my friends. They're my friends, drunk or sober, in hell or out of it. I just can't see how you can cut in proper. Better wait for me here—I'll turn up, all right. Meanwhile, as I says before, look out for tin-horns."

Sammy watched him ride away, and then slammed his sombrero on the ground and jumped on it, after which he felt relieved. Procuring his gun from the clerk he paused to cross-examine, but after a fruitless half hour he sauntered out, hiding his vexation, to wrestle with the problem in the open. Passing the window of a general store he idly glanced at the meager display behind the dusty glass and a sudden grin transfigured his countenance. He would find out about the girl first and that would help him solve the puzzle. Thinking thus he wandered in carelessly and he wandered out again gravely clutching a small package. Slipping behind the next building he tore off the paper and carefully crumpled and soiled with dust the purchase. Then he went down to the depot and followed the railroad tracks toward the other side of the square. Reaching the place where the south trail crossed the tracks he left them and walked slowly toward a small depression that was surrounded by hoofprints. He stooped quickly and straightened up with a woman's handkerchief dangling from his fingers. He grinned foolishly, examined it, sniffed at it and scratched his head while he cogitated. A decisive wave of his hand apprised the two spectators that he had arrived at a conclusion, which he bore out by heading straight for the post office, which was a part of the grocery store. The postmaster and grocer, in person one, watched his approach with frank curiosity.

Sammy nodded and went in the store, followed by the proprietor. "Howd'y," he remarked, producing the handkerchief. "Just picked this up over on th' trail. Know who dropped it?"

"Annie Allison, I reckon," replied the other. "She came in that way from th' Bar-U. Want to leave it?"

Sammy considered. "Why, I might as well take it to her—I'm going down there purty soon. Don't know any other ranch that might use a broncho-buster, do you?"

The proprietor shook his head. "No; most folks 'round here bust their own. Perfessional?"

Sammy nodded. "Yes. Here, gimme two-bits' worth of them pep'mint lozengers. Yes, it shore is fine; but it'll rain before long. Well, by-by."

The bartender of the "Retreat" sniffed suspiciously and eyed the open door thoughtfully, holding aloft the barmop while he considered. Then he put the mop on the bar and went to the door, where he peered out. "Huh!" he grunted. "Hogin' that?" he sarcastically inquired. Sammy held out the bag and led the way to the bar. "Where's th' Bar-U? Yes? Do their own broncho-bustin'? Who, me? Ain't nothin' on laigs can throw me, includin' humans an' bartenders. What? Well, what you want to get all skinned up for, for nothin'? Five dollars? If you must lose it I might as well have it. One fall? All right; come out here an' get it."

The bartender chuckled and vaulted the counter as advance notice of his agility and physical condition, and immediately there ensued a soft shuffling.

Suddenly the building shook and dusted itself and Sammy arose and stepped back, smiling at his victim. "Thanks," he remarked. "Good money was spent on part of my education—boxin' bein' th' other half. Now, for five more, where can't I hit you?"

"Behind th' bar," grinned the other; "I got deadly weapons there. Look here!" he exclaimed hurriedly as a great idea struck him. "Everybody 'round here will back their wrastlin' reckless; le's team up an' make some easy money. I'll make th' bets an' you win 'em. Split even. What say?"

"Later on, mebby. What'd you say that Bar-U foreman's name was?"

The bartender's reply was supplemented by a pious suggestion. "An' if you wrastles *him*, bust his cussed neck!"

"Why this friendship?" queried Sammy, laughing.

"Oh, just for general principles."

Sammy bought cigars, left some lozenges and went out to search for his horse, which he duly found. Inwardly he was elated and he flexed his muscles and made curious motions with his arms, which caused the pie-bald to show the whites of its eyes wickedly and flatten its ragged ears. Its actions were justified, for a left hand darted out and slapped the wrinkling muzzle, deftly escaping the clicking teeth. Then the warlike piebald reflected judiciously as it chewed the lozenge. The eyes showed less white and the ears, moving forward and back, compromised by one staying forward. The candy was old and stale and the sting of the mint was negligible, but the sugar was much in evidence. When the hand darted out again the answering nip was playful and the ears were set rigidly forward. Sammy laughed, slipped several more lozenges into the ready mouth, vaulted lightly to the saddle and rode slowly toward the square. The piebald kicked mildly and reached around to nip at the stirrup, and then went on about its business as any well-broken cow pony should.

Reaching the square Sammy drew rein suddenly and watched a horseman who was riding away from the "Retreat." Waiting a few minutes Sammy spurred forward to the saloon and called the bartender out to him. "Who was that feller that just left?" he asked, curiously.

"Joe Worth, th' man yo're goin' to strike for that job. Why don't you catch him now an' mebby save yoreself a day's ride?"

"Good idea," endorsed Sammy. "See you later," and the youth wheeled and loped toward the trail, but drew rein when hidden from the "Retreat" by some buildings. He watched the distant horseman until he became a mere dot and then Sammy pushed on after him. There was a satisfied look on his face and he chuckled as he cogitated. "I shore got th' drift of this; I know th' game!

Wonder how Cassidy got onto it?" He laughed contentedly. "Well, five hundred ain't too little to split two ways; an' mebby it *is* a two-man job. Mr. Joe Worth, who was once Mr. George Atkins, I wouldn't give a peso for yore chances after I get th' lay of th' ground an' find out yore habits. Yo're goin' back to Willow Springs as shore as 'dogies' hang 'round water holes. An' you'll shore dance their tune when you gets there."

Mr. Cassidy, arriving at the Bar-U, asked for the foreman and was told that the boss was in town, but would be back sometime in the afternoon. The newcomer replied that he would return later and, carefully keeping out of sight of the ranch house as well as he could, he wheeled and rode back the way he had come, being very desirous to have a good look at the foreman before they met. Arriving at an arroyo several miles north of the ranch he turned into it, and, leaving his horse picketed on good grass along the bottom, he climbed to a position where he could see the trail without being seen. Having settled himself comfortably he improved the wait by trying to think out the best way to accomplish the work he had set himself to do. Shooting was too common and hardly justifiable unless Mr. Worth forced the issue with weapons of war.

The time passed slowly and he was relieved when a horseman appeared far to the north and jogged toward him, riding with the careless grace of one at home in the saddle. Being thoroughly familiar with the trail and the surrounding country the rider looked straight ahead as if attention to the distance yet untraveled might make it less. He passed within twenty feet of the watcher and went on his way undisturbed. Hopalong waited until he was out of sight around a hill and then, vaulting into the saddle, rode after him, still puzzled as to how he would proceed about the business in hand. He dismounted at the bunkhouse and nodded to those who lingered near the wash bench awaiting their turn.

"Just in time to feed," remarked one of the punchers. "Watch yore turn at th' basins—every man for hisself's th' rule."

"All right," Hopalong laughed. "But is there any chance to get a job here?" he asked, anxiously.

"You'll have to quiz th' Ol' Man—here he comes now," and the puncher waved at the approaching foreman. "Hey, Joe! Got a job for this *hombre*?" he called.

The foreman keenly scrutinized the newcomer, as he always examined strangers. The two guns swinging low on the hips caught his eyes instantly but he showed no particular interest in them, notwithstanding the fact that they proclaimed a gunman. "Why I reckon I got a job for you," he said. "I been waitin' to keep somebody over on Cherokee Range. But it's time to eat: we'll talk later."

After the meal the outfit passed the time in various ways until bed-time, the foreman talking to the new member of his family. During the night the foreman awakened several times and looked toward the newcomer's bunk but found nothing suspicious. After breakfast he called Hopalong and one of the others to him. "Ned," he said, "take Cassidy over to his range and come right back. Hey, Charley! You an' Jim take them poles down to th' ford an' fence in that quicksand just south of it. Ben says he's been doin' nothin' but pullin' cows outen it. All right, Tim; comin' right away."

Ned and the new puncher lost no time but headed east at once with a pack-horse carrying a week's provisions for one man. The country grew rougher rapidly and when they finally reached the divide a beautiful sight lay below them, stretching as far as eye could see to the east. In the middle distance gleamed the Cherokee, flowing toward the south through its valley of rocks, canyons, cliffs, draws and timber.

"There's th' hut," said Ned, pointing to a small gray blot against the dead black of a towering cliff. "Th' spring's just south of it. Bucket Hill, up north there, is th' north boundary; Twin Spires, south yonder is th' other end; an' th' Cherokee will stop you on th' east side. You ride in every Sat'day if you wants. Don't get lonesome," he grinned and, wheeling abruptly, went back the way they had come.

Hopalong shook his head in disgust. To be sidetracked like this was maddening. It had taken three hours of hard traveling over rough country to get where he was and it would take as long to return; and all for nothing! He regarded the pack animal with a grin, shrugged his shoulders and led the way toward the hut, the pack horse following obediently. It was another hour before he finally reached the little cabin, for the way was strange and rough. During this time he had talked aloud, for he had the tricks of his kind and when alone he talked to himself. When he reached the hut he relieved the pack horse of its load, carrying the stuff inside. Closing the door and blocking it with a rock he found the spring, drank his fill and then let the horses do likewise. Then he mounted and started back over the rough trail, thinking out loud and confiding to his horse and he entered a narrow defile close to the top of the divide, promising dire things to the foreman. Suddenly a rope settled over him, pinned his arms to his sides and yanked him from the saddle before he had time to think. He landed on his head and was dazed as he sat up and looked around. The foreman's rifle confronted him, and behind the foreman's feet were his two Colts.

"You talks too much," sneered the man with the drop. "I suspicioned you th' minute I laid eyes on you. It'll take a better man than you to get that five hundred reward. I reckon th' Sheriff was too scared to come hisself."

Hopalong shook his head as if to clear it. What was the man talking about? Who was the sheriff? He gave it up, but would not betray his ignorance. Yes: he had talked too much. He felt of his head and was mildly surprised to see his hand covered with blood when he glanced at it. "Five hundred's a lot of money," he muttered.

"Blood money!" snapped the foreman. "You had a gall tryin' to get me. Why, I been lookin' for somebody to try it for two years. An' I was ready every minute of all that time."

Slowly it came to Hopalong and with it the realization of how foolish it would be to deny the part ascribed to himself. The rope was loose and his arms were practically free; the foreman had dropped the lariat and was depending upon his gun. The captive felt of his head again and, putting his hands behind him for assistance in getting up, arose slowly to his feet. In one of the hands was a small rock that it had rested upon during the effort of rising. At the movement the foreman watched him closely and ordered him not to take a step if he wanted to live a little longer.

"I reckon I'll have to shoot you," he announced. "I dassn't let you loose to foller me all over th' country. Anyhow, I'd have to do it sooner or later. I wish you was Phelps, damn him; but he's a wise sheriff. Better stand up agin' that wall. I gotta do it; an' you deserve it, you Judas!"

"Meanin' yo're Christ?" sneered Hopalong. "Did you kill th' other feller like that? If I'd 'a' knowed that I'd 'a' slapped yo're dawg's face at th' bunkhouse an' made you take an even break. Shore you got nerve enough to shoot straight if I looks at you while yo're aimin'?" He laughed cynically. "I don't want to close my eyes."

The foreman's face went white and he half lowered the rifle as he took a step forward. Hopalong leaped sideways and his arm straightened out, the other staggering under the blow of the missile. Leaping forward Hopalong ran into a cloud of smoke and staggered as he jumped to close quarters. His hand smashed full in the foreman's face and his knee sank in the foreman's groin. They went down, the foreman weak from the kick and Hopalong sick and weak from the bullet that had grazed the bone of his bad thigh. And lying on the ground they fought in a daze, each incapable of inflicting serious injury for awhile. But the foreman grew stronger as his enemy grew weaker from loss of blood and, wriggling from under his furious antagonist, he reached for his Colt. Hopalong threw himself forward and gripped the gun wrist between his teeth and closed his jaws until they ached. But the foreman, pounding cease-lessly on the other's face with his free hand, made the jaws relax and drew the weapon. Then he saw all the stars in the heavens as Hopalong's head crashed full against his jaw and before he could recover the gun was pinned under his enemy's knee. Hopalong's head crashed again against the foreman's jaw and his right hand gripped the corded throat while the left, its thumb inside the foreman's cheek and its fingers behind an ear, tugged and strained at the dis-torted face. Growling like wild beasts they strained and panted, and then, sud-denly, Hopalong's grip relaxed and he made one last, desperate effort to bring his strength back into one furious attack; but in vain. The battered foreman, quick to sense the situation, wrestled his adversary to one side long enough to grab the Colt from under the shifting knee. As he clutched it a shot rang out and the weapon dropped from his nerveless hand before he could pull the trig-ger. An exulting, savage yell roared in his ears and in the next instant he seemed to leave the ground and soar through space. He dropped ten feet away and lay dazed and helpless as a knee crashed against his chest. Sammy Porter, his face working curiously with relief and rage, rolled him against the wall of the defile and struck him over the head with a rifle, first disarming him.

Hopalong opened his eyes and looked around, dazed and sick. The fore-man, bound hand and foot by a forty-five-foot lariat, lay close to the base of the wall and stared sullenly at the sky. Sammy was coming up the trail with a drip-ping sombrero held carefully in his hands and was growling and talking it all over. Hopalong looked down at his thigh and saw a heavy, blood-splotched bandage fastened clumsily in place. Glancing at Sammy again he idly noted that part of the youth's blue-flannel shirt was missing. Curiously, it matched the bandage. He closed his eyes and tried to think what it was all about.

Sammy ambled up to him, threw some water in the bruised face and then grinned cheerfully at the language he evoked. Producing a flask and holding it up to the light, Sammy slid his thumb to a certain level and then shoved the bottle against his friend's teeth. "Huh!" he chuckled, yanking the bottle away. "You'll be all right in a couple of days. But you shore are one hell of a sight— it's a toss-up between you an' Atkins."

It was night. Hopalong stirred and arose on one elbow and noticed that he was lying on a blanket that covered a generous depth of leaves and pine boughs. The sap-filled firewood crackled and popped and hissed and whistled under the licking attack of the greedy flames, which flared up and died down in endless alternation, and which grotesquely revealed to Hopalong's throbbing eyes a bound figure lying on another blanket. That, he decided, was the foreman. Letting his gaze wander around the lighted circle he made out a figure squatting on the other side of the fire, and concluded it was Sammy Porter. "What you doin', Kid?" he asked.

Sammy arose and walked over to him. "Oh, just watchin' a fool puncher an' five hundred dollars," he grinned. "How you feelin' now, you ol' sage hen?"

"Good," replied the invalid, and, comparatively, it was the truth. "Fine an' strong," he added, which was not the truth.

"That's the way to talk," cheered the Cub. "You shore had one fine séance. You earned that five hundred, all right."

Hopalong reflected and then looked across at the prisoner. "He can fight like the devil," he muttered. "Why, I kicked him hard enough to kill anybody else." He turned again and looked Sammy in the eyes, smiling as best he could. "There ain't no five hundred for me, Kid. I didn't come for that, didn't know nothin' about it. An' it's blood money, besides. We'll turn him loose if he'll get out of the country, hey? We'll give him a chance; either that or you take th' reward."

Sammy stared, grunted and stared again. "What you ravin' about?" he demanded. "An' you didn't come after him for that money?" he asked, sarcastically.

Hopalong nodded and smiled again. "That's right, Kid," he answered, thoughtfully. "I come down to make him get out of th' country. You let him go after we get out of this. I reckon I got yore share of the reward right here in my pocket; purty near that much, anyhow. You take it an' let him vamoose. What you say?"

Sammy rose, angry and disgusted. His anger spoke first. "You go to hell with yore money! I don't want it!" Then, slowly and wonderingly spoke his disgust. "He's yourn; do what you want. But I here remarks, frank an' candid, open an' so all may hear, that yo're a large, puzzlin' damned fool. Now lay back on that blanket an' go to sleep afore I changes my mind!"

Sammy drifted past the prisoner and looked down at him. "Hear that?" he demanded. There was no answer and he grunted. "Huh! You heard it, all right; an' it plumb stunned you." Passing on he grabbed the last blanket in sight, it was on the foreman's horse, and rolled up in it, feet to the fire. His gun he placed under the saddle he had leaned against, which now made his pillow. As he squirmed into the most comfortable position he could find under the circumstances he raised his head and glanced across at his friend. "Huh!" he growled softly. "That's th' worst of them sentimental fellers. That gal shore wrapped him 'round her li'l finger all right. Oh, well," he sighed. "Tain't none of my doin's, thank the Lord; I got sense!" And with the satisfaction of this thought still warm upon him he closed his eyes and went to sleep, confident that the slightest sound would awaken him; and fully justified in his confidence.

CHAPTER 13

His Code

Mr. "Youbet" Somes, erstwhile foreman of the Two-X-Two ranch, in Arizona, and now out of a job, rode gloomily toward Kit, a town between him and his destination.

Needless to say, he was a cowman through and through. More than that, he was so saturated with cowmen's traditions as to resent pugnaciously anything which flouted them.

He was of the old school, and would not submit quietly to two things, among others, which an old-school cowman hated—wire fences and sheep. To this he owed his present ride, for he hated wire fences cordially. They meant the passing of the free, open range, of straight trails across country; they meant a great change, an intolerable condition.

"Yessir, bronch! Things are gettin' damnabler every year, with th' railroads, tourists, nesters, barb' wire, an' sheep. Last year, it was a windmill, that screeched till our hair riz up. It wouldn't work when we wanted it to, an' we couldn't stop it when it once got started.

"It gave us no sleep, no peace; an' it killed Bob Cousins—swung round with th' wind an' knocked him off'n th' platform, sixty feet, to th' ground. Bob allus did like to monkey with th' buzz saw. I shore told him not to go up there, because th' cussed thing was loaded; but, bein' mule-headed, he knowed more'n me.

"But this year! Lord—but that was an awful pile of wire, bronch! Three strands high, an' over a hundred an' fifty miles round that pasture. That was a' insult, bronch; an' I never swaller 'em. That's what put me an' you out here, in th' middle of nowhere, tryin' to find a way out. G'wan, now! You ain't goin' to rest till I gets off you. G'wan, I told you!"

Mr. Somes was riding east, bound for the Bar-20, where he had friends. For a year or two, he had heard persistent rumors to the effect that Buck Peters had more cows than he knew what to do with; and he argued rightly that the Bar-20 foreman could find a place for an old friend, whose ability was unquestioned. Of one thing he was certain—there were no wire fences, down there.

It was dusk when he dismounted in front of Logan's, in Kit, and went inside. The bartender glanced up, reaching for a bottle on the shelf beside him.

Youbet nodded. "You got it first pop. Have one with me. I'm countin' on staying over in town tonight. Got a place for me?"

"Shore have—upstairs in th' attic. Want grub, too?"

"Well, I sorter hope to have somethin' to eat afore I pull out. Here's how!" And when Mr. Somes placed his empty glass on the bar, he smiled good-naturedly. "That's good stuff. Much goin' on in town?"

"Reckon you can get a game most anywhere."

"Where do I get that grub? Here?"

"No—down th' street. Ridin' far?"

"Yes—a little. Goin' down to th' Bar-20 for a job punchin'. I hear Peters has got more cows than he can handle. Know anybody down there you wants to send any word to?"

"I'll be hanged if I know," laughed the bartender. "I know a lot of fellers, but they shift so I can't keep track of 'em, nohow."

A man in a far corner pushed back his chair, and approached the bar, scowling as he glanced at Youbet. "Gimme another," he ordered.

"Why, hullo, stranger!" exclaimed Youbet. "I didn't see you before. Have one with me."

The other looked him squarely in the eyes. "Ex-cuse me, stranger—I'm a sheepman, an' I don't drink with cowmen."

"Well, ex-cuse *me*!" retorted Youbet, like a flash. "If I'd 'a' knowed you was a sheepman, I wouldn't 'a' asked you!"

The sheepman drank his liquor and, returning to his corner, placed his elbows on the table, and his chin in his hands, apparently paying no further attention to the others.

"If I can't get a job with Peters, I can try th' C-80 or Double Arrow," continued Youbet, as he toyed with his glass. "If I can't get on with one of them, I reckons Waffles, of th' O-Bar-O, will find a place for me, though I don't like that country a whole lot."

The bartender hesitated for a moment. "Do you know Waffles?" he asked.

"Shore—know 'em all. Why? Do you know him, too?"

"No; but I've heard of him."

"That so? He's a good feller, he is. I've punched with both him an' Peters."

"I heard he wasn't," replied the bartender, slowly but carelessly.

"Then you heard wrong, all right," rejoined Youbet. "He's one of us old fellers—hates sheep, barb' wire, an' nesters as bad as I do; an' sonny," he continued, warming as he went on. "Th' cow country ain't what it used to be—not no way. I can remember when there warn't no wires, no nesters, an' no sheep. An', between you and me, I don't know which is th' worst. Every time I runs up agin' one of 'em, I says it's th' worst; but I guess it's just about a even break."

"I heard about yore friend Waffles through sheep," replied the bartender. "He chased a sheep outfit out of a hill range near his ranch, an' killed a couple of 'em, a-doin' it."

"Served 'em right—served 'em right," responded Youbet, turning and walking toward the door. "They ain't got no business on a cattle range—not nohow."

The man in the corner started to follow, half raising his hand, as though to emphasize something he was about to say; but changed his mind, and sullenly resumed his brooding attitude.

"Reckon I'll put my cayuse in yore corral, an' look th' town over," Youbet remarked, over his shoulder. "Remember, yo're savin' a bed for me."

As he stepped to the street, the man in the corner lazily arose and looked out of the window, swearing softly while he watched the man who hated sheep.

"Well, there's another friend of yore business," laughed the bartender, leaning back to enjoy the other's discomfiture. "*He* don't like 'em, neither."

"He's a fool of a mossback, so far behind th' times he don't know who's President," retorted the other, still staring down the street.

"Well, he don't know that this has got to be a purty fair sheep town—that's shore."

"He'll find out, if he makes many more talks like that—an' that ain't no dream, neither!" snapped the sheepman. He wheeled, and frowned at the man behind the bar. "You see what he gets, if he opens his cow mouth in here tonight. Th' boys hate this kind real fervent; an' when they finds out that he's a side pardner of that coyote Waffles, they won't need much excuse. You wait— that's all!"

"Oh, what's th' use of gettin' all riled up about it?" demanded the bartender easily. "He didn't know *you* was a sheepman, when he made his first break. An' lemme tell you somethin' you want to remember—them old-time cowmen can use a short gun somethin' slick. They've got 'em trained. Bet *he* can work th' double roll without shootin' hisself full of lead." The speaker grinned exasperatingly.

"Yes!" exploded the sheepman, who had tried to roll two guns at once, and had spent ten days in bed as a result of it.

The bartender laughed softly as he recalled the incident. "Have you tried it since?" he inquired.

"Go to th' devil!" grinned the other, heading for the door. "But he'll get in trouble, if he spouts about hatin' sheep, when th' boys come in. You better get him drunk an' lock him in th' attic, before then."

"G'wan! I ain't playin' guardian to nobody," rejoined the bartender. "But remember what I said—them old fellers can use 'em slick an' rapid."

The sheepman went out as Youbet returned; and the latter seated himself, crossing his legs and drawing out his pipe.

The bartender perfunctorily drew a cloth across the bar, and smiled. "So you don't like wire, sheep, or nesters," he remarked.

Mr. Somes looked up, in surprise, forgetting that he held a lighted match between thumb and finger. "Like 'em! Huh, I reckon not. I'm lookin' for a job because of wire. Hell!" he exclaimed, dropping the match, and rubbing his finger. "That's twice I did that fool thing in a week," he remarked, in apology and self-condemnation, and struck another match.

"I was foreman of my ranch for nigh onto ten years. It was a good ranch, an' I was satisfied till last year, when they made me put up a a windmill that didn't mill, but screeched awful. I stood for that because I could get away from it in th' daytime.

"But this year! One day, not very long ago, I got a letter from th' owners, an' it says for me to build a wire fence around our range. It went on to say that there was two carloads of barb' wire at Mesquite. We was to tote that wire home, an' start in. If two carloads wasn't enough, they'd send us more. We had one busted-down grub waggin, an' Mesquite shore was fifty miles away— which meant a whoppin' long job totin'.

"When I saw th' boys, that night, I told 'em that I'd got orders to raise their pay five dollars a month—which made 'em cheer. Then I told 'em that was so providin' they helped me build a barb' wire fence around th' range—which didn't make 'em cheer.

"Th' boundary lines of th' range we was usin' was close onto a hundred an' fifty miles long, an' three strands of wire along a trail like that is some job. We was to put th' posts twelve feet apart, an' they was to be five feet outen th' ground an' four feet in it—which makes 'em nine feet over all.

"There wasn't no posts at Mesquite. Them posts was supposed to be growin' freelike on th' range, just waitin' for us to cut 'em, skin 'em, tote an' drop 'em every twelve feet along a line a hundred an' fifty miles long. An' then there was to be a hole dug for every post, an' tampin', staplin', an' stringin' that hell-wire. An' don't forget that lone, busted-down grub waggin that was to do that totin'!

"There was some excitement on th' Two-X-Two that night, an' a lot of fig- gerin'; us bein' some curious about how many posts was needed, an' how many holes we was to dig to fit th' aforesaid posts. We made it sixty-six thousand. Think of it! An' only eight of us to tackle a job like that, an' ride range at th' same time!"

"Oh, ho!" roared the bartender, hugging himself, and trying to carry a drink to the narrator at the same time. "Go on! That's good!"

"Is, is it?" snorted Youbet. "Huh! You wouldn't 'a' thought so, if you was one of us eight. Well, I set right down an' writ a long letter—took six cents' worth of stamps—an' gave our views regardin' wire fences in general an' this one of ourn in particular. I hated fences, an' do yet; an' so'd my boys hate 'em, an' they do yet.

"In due time, I got a answer, which come for two cents. It says: 'Build that fence.'

"I sent Charley over to Mesquite to look over them cars of wire. He saw 'em, both of 'em. An' th' agent saw him.

"Th' agent was a' important man, an' he grabs Charley quick. 'Hey, you Two-X-Two puncher—you get that wire home quick. It went past here three times before they switched it, an' I've been gettin' blazes from th' company ever since. We needs th' cars.'

"'Don't belong to me,' says Charley. 'I shore don't want it. I'm eatin' beans an' bacon instead.'

"'You send for that wire!' yells th' agent, wild-like.

"Charley winks. 'Can't you keep it passin' this station till it snows hard? Have a drink.'

"Well, th' agent wouldn't drink, an' he wouldn't send that pore wire out into a cold world no more; an' so Charley comes home an' reports, him lookin' wan- like. When he told us, he looked sort of funny, an' blurts out that his mother went an' died in Laramie, an' he must shore 'nuff rustle up there an' bury her. He went.

"Then Fred Ball begun to have pains in his stomach, an' said it was appen- dix somethin', what he had been readin' about in th' papers. He had to go to Denver, an' get a good doctor, or he'd shore die. He went.

"Carson had to go to Santa Fé to keep some of his numerous city lots from bein' sold off by th' sheriff. He went.

"Th' rest, bein' handicapped by th' good start th' others had made in cor-rallin' all th' excuses, said they'd go for th' wire. They went.

"I waited four days, an' then I went after 'em. When I got to th' station, I sees th' agent out sizin' up our wire; an' when I hails, he jumps my way quick, an' grabs my laig tight.

"'You take that wire home!' he yells.

"'Shore,' says I soothingly. 'You looks mad,' I adds.

"'Mad! Mad!' he shouts, hoppin' round, but hangin' onto my laig like grim death. 'Mad! I'm goin' *loco*—crazy! I can't sleep! There's twenty letters an' messages on my table, tellin' me to get that wire off'n th' cars an' send th' emp-ties back on th' next freight! You've got to take it—*got to!*'"

The bartender shocked his nervous system by drinking plain water by mis-take, but he listened eagerly. "Yes? What then?"

"Well, then I asks him where I can find my men, an' team, an' waggin'. He tells me. Th' team an' waggin is in a corral down th' street, but he don't know where th' men are. They held a gun to his head, an' said they'd kill him if he didn't flag th' next train for 'em. Th' next train was a through express, carryin' mail. He wasn't dead.

"He showed me ten more letters an' messages, regardin' th' flaggin' of a contract-mail train for four fares; an' some of them letters must 'a' been writ-ten by a old-time cowman, they was that eloquent an' God-fearin'. Then I went.

"Why, Charley was twenty years old; an' we figgered that, when th' last staple was drove in th' last post, he'd 'a' been dead ten years! Where did I come in, the—?"

"Oh, Lord!" sighed the bartender, holding his sides, and trying to straighten his face so that he could talk out of the middle of it. "That's th' best ever! Have another drink!"

"I ain't tellin' my troubles for liquor," snorted Youbet. "You have one with me. Here comes some customers down th' street, I reckon."

"Say!" exclaimed the bartender hurriedly. "You keep mum about sheep. This is a red-hot sheep town, an' it hates Waffles an' all his friends. Hullo, boys!" he called to four men, who filed into the room. "Where's th' rest of you?"

"Comin' in later. Same thing, Jimmy," replied Clayton, chief herder. "An' give us th' cards."

"Have you seen Price?" asked Towne.

"Yes; he was in here a few minutes ago. What'd you say, Schultz?" the bar-tender asked, turning to the man who pulled at his sleeve.

"I said dot you vas nod right aboud vat you said de odder day. Chust now I ask Glayton, und he said you vas nod."

"All right, Dutchy—all right!" laughed the bartender. "Then it's on me this time, ain't it?"

Youbet walked to the bar. "Say, where do I get that grub? It's about time for me to mosey off an' feed."

"Next building—and you'll take mutton if yo're wise," replied the bartender, in a low voice. "Th' hash is awful, an' the beef is tough," he added, a little louder.

"Mutton be damned!" snorted Youbet, stamping out. "I eat what I punch!" And his growls became lost in the street.

Schultz glanced up. "Yah! Und he shoot vat *I* eat, tam him, ven he gan!"

"Oh, put yore ante in, an' don't talk so much!" rejoined Towne. "He ain't going to shoot *you*."

"It'll cost you two bits to come in," remarked Clayton.

"An' two more," added Towne, raising the ante.

"Goot! I blay mit you. But binochle iss der game!"

"I'll tell you a good story about a barb' wire fence tomorrow, fellers," promised the bartender, grinning.

The poker game had been going for some time before further remarks were made about the cowman who had left, and then it was Clayton who spoke.

"Say, Jimmy!" he remarked, as Schultz dealt. "Who is yore leather-pants friend who don't like mutton?"

The bartender lifted a bottle, and replaced it with great care. "Oh, just a ranch foreman, out of a job. He's a funny old feller."

"So? An' what's so funny about him? Get in there, Towne, if you wants to do any playin' with us."

"Why, he was ordered to build a hundred an' fifty miles of wire fence around his range, an' he jumped ruther than do it."

"Yas—an' most of it government land, I reckon," interposed Towne.

"Pshaw! It's an old game with them," laughed Clayton. "Th' law don't get to them; an' if they've got a good outfit, nobody has got any chance agin 'em."

"Py Gott, dot's right!" grunted Schultz.

"Shore, it is," responded Towne, forgetting the game. "Take that Apache Hills run-in. Waffles didn't have no more right to that range than anybody else, but that didn't make no difference. He threw a couple of outfits in there, penned us in th' cabin, killed MacKay, an' shot th' rest of us up plenty. Then he threatened to slaughter our herd if we didn't pull out. By God, I'd like to get a cowman like him up here, where th' tables are turned around on th' friends proposition."

"Hullo, boys!" remarked the bartender to the pair who came in.

"Just in time. Get chairs, an' take hands," invited Clayton, moving over.

"Who's th' cowman yo're talkin' about?" asked Baxter, as he leaned lazily against the bar.

"Oh, all of 'em," rejoined Towne surlily. "There's one in town, now, who don't like sheep."

"That so?" queried Baxter slowly. "I reckon he better keep his mouth shut, then."

"Oh, he's all right! He's a jolly old geezer," assured the bartender. "He just talks to hear hisself—one of them old-timers what can't get right to th' way things has changed on th' range. It was them boys that did great work when th' range was wild."

"Yes, an' it's them bull-headed old fools what are raisin' all th' hell with th' sheep," retorted Towne, frowning darkly as he remembered some of the indignities he had borne at the hands of cowmen.

"I wish his name was Waffles." Clayton smiled significantly.

"Rainin' again," remarked a man in the doorway, stamping in. "Reckon it ain't never goin' to stop."

"Where you been so long, Price?" asked Clayton, as a salutation.

"Oh, just shiftin' about. That cow wrastler raised th' devil in th' hotel," Price replied. "Old fool! They brought him mutton, an' he wanted to clean out th' place. Said he'd as soon eat barb' wire. They're feedin' him hash an' canned stuff, now."

"He'll get hurt, if he don't look out," remarked Clayton. "Who is he, anyhow, Price?"

"Don't know his name; but he's from Arizona, on his way to th' Pecos country. Says he's a friend of Buck Peters an' Waffles. To use one of his own expressions, he's a old mosshead."

"Friend of Waffles, hey?" exclaimed Towne.

"Yumpin' Yimminy!" cried Oleson, in the same breath.

"Well, if he knows when he's well off, he'll stay away from here, an' keep his mouth closed," said Clayton.

"Aw, let him alone! He's one agin' th' whole town—an' a good old feller, at that," hastily assured the bartender. "It ain't his fault that Waffles buffaloed you fellers out of th' Hills, is it? He's goin' on early tomorrow; so let him be."

"You'll get yoreself in trouble, Jimmy, m' boy, if you inserts yoreself in this," warned Towne. "It was us agin' a whole section, an' we got ours. Let him take his, if he talks too much."

"Shore," replied Price. "I heard him shoot off his mouth, an hour ago, an' he's got altogether too much to say. You mind th' bar an' yore own business, Jimmy. We ain't kids."

"Go you two bits better," said Clayton, shoving out a coin. "Gimme some cards, Towne. It'll cost you a dollar to see our raises."

Baxter walked over to watch the play. "I'm comin' in next game. Who's winnin', now?"

"Reckon I am; but we ain't much more'n got started," Clayton replied. "Did you call, Towne? Why, I've got three little tens. You got anythin' better?"

"Never saw such luck!" exclaimed Towne disgustedly. "Dutchy, yo're a Jonah."

"Damn th' mutton, says I. It was even in that hash!" growled a voice, just outside the door.

A moment later, Youbet Somes entered, swinging his sombrero energetically to shake off the water.

"Damn th' rain, too, an' this wart of a town. A man can't get nothin' fit to eat for love or money, on a sheep range. Gimme a drink, sonny! Mebby it'll cut th' taste of that rank tallow out'n my mouth. Th' reason there is sheep on this earth of our'n is that th' devil chased 'em out 'n his place—an' no blame to him."

He drank half his liquor, and, placing the glass on the bar beside him, turned to watch the game. "Ah, strangers—that's th' only game, after all. I've dabbled in 'em all from faro to roulette, but that's th' boss of 'em all."

"See you an' call," remarked Clayton, ignoring the newcomer. "What you got, you Dutch pagan?"

"*Zwei Kaisers* und a bair of chackasses, mit a deuce."

"Kings up!" exclaimed Clayton. "Why, say—you bet th' worst of anybody I ever knew! You'll balk on bettin' two bits on threes, and plunge on a bluff. I reckoned you didn't have nothin'. Why ain't you more consistent?" he asked, winking at Towne.

"Gonsisdency iss no chewel in dis game—it means go broke," placidly grunted Schultz, raking in his winnings.

His friend Schneider smiled.

Coyotes are gettin' too numerous, this year," Baxter remarked, shuffling.

Youbet pushed his sombrero back on his head. "They don't get numerous on a cow range," he said significantly.

"Huh!" snorted Baxter. "They've got too much respect to stay on one longer than they've got to."

"They'd rather be with their woolly-coated cousins," rejoined the cowman quietly. It was beneath his dignity as a cowman to pay much attention to what sheepmen said, yet he could not remain silent under such a remark.

He regarded sheep herders, those human beings who walked at their work, as men who had reached the lowest rung in the ladder of human endeavors. His belief was not original with him, but was that of many of his school. He was a horseman, a mounted man, and one of the aristocracy of the range; they were, to him, the rabble, and almost beneath his contempt.

Besides, it was commonly believed by cowmen that sheep destroyed the grass as far as cattle grazing was concerned—and this was the chief reason for the animosity against sheep and their herders, which burned so strongly in the hearts of cattle owners and their outfits.

Youbet drained his glass, and continued: "The coyote leaves th' cattle range for th' same good reason yore sheep leave it—because they are chased out, or killed. Naturally, blood kin will hang together in banishment."

"You know a whole lot, don't you?" snorted Clayton, with sarcasm. "Yo're shore wise, you are!"

"He is so vise as a—a gow," remarked Schultz, grinning.

"You'll know more, when you get as old as me," replied the ex-foreman, carefully placing the empty glass on the bar.

"I don't want to get as old as you, if I have to lose all my common sense," retorted Clayton angrily.

"An' be a damned nuisance generally," observed Towne.

"I've seen a lot of things in my life," Youbet began, trying to ignore the tones of the others. They were young men, and he knew that youth grew unduly heated in argument. "I saw th' comin' of th' Texas drive herds, till th' range was crowded where th' year before there was nothin'. I saw th' comin' of th' sheep— an' barb' wire, I'm sorry to say. Th' sheep came like locusts, leavin' a dyin' range behind 'em. Thin, half-starved cattle showed which way they went. You can't tell me nothin' I don't know about sheep."

"An' I've seen sheep dyin' in piles on th' open range," cried Clayton, his own wrongs lashing him into a rage. "I've seen 'em dynamited, an' drowned and driven hell-to-split over canyons! I've had my men taunted, an' chased, an' killed— *killed*, by God!—just because they tried to make a' honest livin'! Who did it all? Who killed my men an' my sheep? *Who did it?*" he shouted, taking a short step forward, while an endorsing growl ran along the line of sheepmen at his side.

"Cowpunchers—they did it! They killed 'em—an' why? Because we tried to use th' grass that we had as much right to as they had—*that's* why!"

"Th' cows was here first," replied Youbet, keenly alert, but not one whit abashed by the odds, long as they were. "It was theirs because they was there first."

"It was not theirs, no more'n th' sun was!" cried Towne, unable to allow his chief to do all the talking.

"You said you knowed Waffles," continued Clayton loudly. "Well, he's another of you old-time cowmen! He killed MacKay—murdered him—because we was usin' a hill range a day's ride from his own grass! He had twenty men like hisself to back him up. If we'd been as many as them, they wouldn't 'a' tried it—an' you know it!"

"I don't know anything of th' kind, but I do know—" began Youbet; but Schultz interrupted him with a remark intended to contain humor.

"Ven you say you doand know anyt'ing, you know somedings; ven you know dot you doand know noddings, den you know somedings. Und das iss so—yah."

"Who th' devil told you to stick yore Dutch mouth—" retorted Youbet; but Clayton cut him short.

"So *yo're* a old-timer, hey?" cried the sheepman. "Well, by God, yore old-time friend Waffles is a coward, a murderer, an'—"

"Yo're a liar!" rang out the vibrant voice of the cowman, his gun out and leveled in a flash. The seven had moved forward as one man, actuated by the same impulse; and their hands were moving toward their guns when the crashes of Youbet's weapon reverberated in the small room, the acrid smoke swirling around him as though to shield him from the result of his folly—a result which he had weighed and then ignored.

Clayton dropped, with his mouth still open. Towne's gun chocked back in the scabbard as its owner stumbled blindly over a chair and went down, never to rise. Schultz fired once, and fell back across the table.

The three shots had followed one another with incredible quickness; and the seven, not believing that one man would dare attack so many, had not expected his play. Before the stunned sheepmen could begin firing, three were dead.

Price, badly wounded, fired as he plunged to the wall for support; and the other three were now wrapped in their own smoke.

Wounded in several places, with his gun empty, Youbet hurled the weapon at Price, and missed by so narrow a margin that the sheepman's aim was spoiled. Youbet now sprang to the bar, and tried to vault over it, to get to the gun which he knew always lay on the shelf behind it. As his feet touched the upper edge of the counter, he grunted and, collapsing like a jackknife, loosed his hold, and fell to the floor.

"Mein Gott!" groaned Schneider, as he tried to raise himself. He looked around in a dazed manner, hardly understanding just what had happened. "He vas mat; crazy mat!"

Oleson arose unsteadily to his feet, and groped his way along the wall to where Price lay.

The fallen man looked up, in response to the touch on his shoulder; and he swore feebly: "Damn that fool—that idiot!"

"Shut up, an' git out!" shouted the bartender, standing rigidly upright, with a heavy Colt in his upraised hand. There were tears in his eyes, and his voice broke from excitement. "He wouldn't swaller yore insults! He knowed he was a better man! Get out of here, every damned one of you, or I'll begin where he stopped. G 'wan—*get out!*"

The four looked at him, befuddled and sorely hurt; but they understood the attitude, if they did not quite grasp the words—and they knew that he meant what he looked. Staggering and hobbling, they finally found the door, and plunged out to the street, to meet the crowd of men who were running toward the building.

Jimmy, choking with anger and with respect for the man who had preferred death to insults, slammed shut the door and, dropping the bar into place, turned and gazed at the quiet figure huddled at the base of the counter.

"Old man," he muttered, "now I understands why th' sheep don't stay long on a cattle range."

CHAPTER 14

Sammy Hunts a Job

Sammy Porter, detailed by Hopalong, the trail-boss, rode into Truxton three days before the herd was due, to notify the agent that cars were wanted. Three thousand three-year-olds were on their way to the packing houses and must be sent through speedily. Sammy saw the agent and, leaving him much less sweeter in temper than when he had found him, rode down the dismal street kicking up a prodigious amount of dust. One other duty demanded attention and its fulfillment was promised by the sign over the faded pine front of the first building.

"Restaurant," he read aloud. "That's mine. Beans, bacon an' biscuits for 'most a month! But now I'm goin' to forget that Blinky Thompkins ever bossed a trail wagon an' tried to cook."

Dismounting, he glanced in the window and pulled at the downy fuzz trying to make a showing on his upper lip. "Purty, all-right. Brown hair an' I reckon brown eyes. Nice li'l girl. Well, they don't make no dents on *me* no more," he congratulated himself, and entered. His twenty years fairly sagged with animosity toward the fair sex, the intermittent smoke from the ruins of his last love affair still painfully in evidence at times. But careless as he tried to be he could not banish the swaggering mannerisms of Youth in the presence of Maid, or change his habit of speech under such conditions.

"Well, well," he smiled. "Here I 'are' again. Li'l Sammy in search of his grub. An' if it's as nice as you he'll shore have to flag his outfit an' keep this town all to hisself. Got any chicken?"

The maid's nose went up and Sammy noticed that it tilted a trifle, and he cocked his head on one side to see it better. And the eyes were brown, very big and very deep—they possessed a melting quality he had never observed before.

The maid shrugged her shoulders and swung around, the tip-tilt nose going a bit higher.

Sammy leaned back against the door and nodded approval of the slender figure in spic-and-span white. "Li'l Sammy is a fer-o-cious cow-punch from a chickenless land," he observed, sorrowfully. "There ain't *no* kinds of chickens. Nothin' but men an' cattle an' misguided cooks; an' beans, bacon an' biscuits. Li'l Miss, have you a chicken for me?"

"No!" The head went around again, Sammy bending to one side to see it as long as he could. The pink, shell-like ear that flirted with him through the loosely-gathered, rebellious hair caught his attention and he leveled an accusing finger at it. "Naughty li'l ear, peekin' at Sammy that-a-way! Oh, you stingy girl!" he chided as the back of her head confronted him. "Well, Sammy don't like girls, no matter how pink their ears are, or turned up their noses, or wonderful their eyes. He just wants chicken, an' all th' fixin's. He'll be very humble an' grateful to Li'l Miss if she'll tell him what he can have. An' he'll behave just like a Sunday-school boy.

"Aw, you don't want to get mad at only me," he continued after she refused to answer. "Got any chicken? Got any—eggs? Lucky Sammy! An' some nice ham? Two lucky Sammies. An' some mashed potatoes? Fried? Good. An' will Li'l Miss please make a brand new cup of strong coffee? Then he'll go over an' sit in that nice chair an' watch an' listen. But you oughtn't get mad at him. Are you really-an'-truly mad?"

She swept down the room, into the kitchen partitioned off at the farther end and slammed the door. Sammy grinned, tugged at his upper lip and fancy-stepped to the table. He smoothed his tumbled hair, retied his neck-kerchief and dusted himself off with his red bandanna handkerchief. "Nice li'l town," he soliloquized. "*Fine* li'l town. Dunno as I ought to go back to th' herd—Hoppy didn't tell me to. Reckon I'll stick in town an' argue with th' agent. If I argue with th' agent I'll be busy; an' I can't leave while I'm busy." He leaned back and chuckled. "Lucky me! If Hoppy had gone an' picked Johnny to argue with th' agent for three whole days where would *I* be? But I gotta keep Johnny outa here, th' son-of-a-gun. He ain't like me—he *likes* girls; an' he ain't bashful."

He picked up a paper lying on a chair near him and looked it over until the kitchen door squeaked. She carried a tray covered with a snow-white napkin which looked like a topographical map with its mountains and valleys and plains. His chuckle was infectious to the extent of a smile and her eyes danced as she placed his dinner before him.

"Betcha it's fine," he grinned, shoveling sugar into the inky coffee. "Blinky oughta have a good look at *this* layout."

"Don't be too sure," she retorted. "Mrs. Olmstead is sick and I'm taking charge of things for her. I'm not a good cook."

"Nothin's th' matter with this," he assured her between bites. "Lots better'n most purty girls can do. If Hopalong goes up against this he'll offer you a hundred a month an' throw Blinky in to wash th' dishes. But he'd have to 'point me guard, or you wouldn't have no time to do no cookin'."

"You'd make a fine guard," she retorted.

"Don't believe it, huh? Jus' wait till you know me better."

"How do you know I'm going to?"

"I'm a good guesser. Jus' put a li'l pepper right there on that yalla spot. Say, any chance to get a job in this town?"

"Why, I don't know."

"Goin' to stay long?"

"I can't stay. I won't go till Mrs. Olmstead is well."

"Not meanin' no harm to Mrs. Olmstead, of course—but you don't *have* to go, do you?"

"I do as I please."

"So I was thinkin'. Now, 'bout that job: any chance? Any ranches near here?"

"Several. But they want *men*. Are you a real cowboy?"

Sammy folded his hands and shook his head sorrowfully. "Huh! Want *men*! Now if I only had whiskers like Blinky. Why, 'course I'm a cowboy. Regular one—but I can outgrow it easy. I'm a sorta maverick an' I'm willin' to wear a nice brand. My name's Sammy Porter," he suggested.

"That's nice. Mine isn't nice."

"Easy to change it. Really like mine?"

"Coffee strong enough?"

"Sumptious. How long's Mrs. Olmstead going to be sick?"

Her face clouded. "I don't know. I hope it will not be for long. She's had *so* much trouble the past year. Oh, wait! I forgot the toast!" and she sped lightly away to rescue the burning bread.

The front door opened and slammed shut, the newcomer dropping into the nearest chair. He pounded on the table. "Hello, there! I want somethin' to eat, quick!"

Sammy turned and saw a portly, flashily dressed drummer whose importance was written large all over him. "Hey!" barked the drummer, "gimme something to eat. I can't wait all day!"

A vicious clang in the kitchen told that his presence was known and resented.

As Sammy turned from the stranger he caught sight of a pretty flushed face disappearing behind the door jamb, the brown eyes snapping and the red lips straight and compressed. His glance, again traveling to the drummer, began with the dusty patent leathers and went slowly upward, resting boldly on the heavy face. Sammy's expression told nothing and the newcomer, glaring at him for an instant, looked over the menu card and then stared at the partition, fidgeting in his chair, thumping meanwhile on the table with his fingers.

At a sound from the kitchen Sammy turned back to his table and smiled reassuringly as the toast was placed before him. "I burned it and had to make new," she said, the pink spots in her cheeks a little deeper in color.

"Why, th' other was good enough for me," he replied. "Know Mrs. Olmstead a long time?" he asked.

"Ever since I was a little girl. She lived near us in Clev—"

"Cleveland," he finished. "State of Ohio," he added, laughingly. "I'll get it all before I go."

"Indeed you won't!"

"Miss," interrupted the drummer, "if you ain't *too* busy, would you mind gettin' me a steak an' some coffee?" The tones were weighted with sarcasm and Sammy writhed in his chair. The girl flushed, turned abruptly and went slowly into the kitchen, from where considerable noise now emanated. In a short time she emerged with the drummer's order, placed it in front of him and started back again. But he stopped her. "I said I wanted it rare an' it's well done. An' also that I wanted fried potatoes. Take it back."

The girl's eyes blazed: "You gave no instructions," she retorted.

"Don't tell me that! I know what I said!" snapped the drummer. "I won't eat it an' I won't pay for it. If you wasn't so *busy* you'd heard what I said."

Sammy was arising before he saw the tears of vexation in her eyes, but they settled it for him. He placed his hand lightly on her shoulder. "You get me some pie an' take a li'l walk. Me an' this here gent is goin' to hold a palaver. Ain't we, stranger?"

The drummer glared at him. "We ain't!" he retorted.

Sammy grinned ingratiatingly. "Oh, my; but we are." He slung a leg over a chair back and leaned forward, resting his elbow on his knee. "Yes, indeed we are—least-a-wise, *I* am." His tones became very soft and confiding. "An' I'm shore goin' to watch you eat that steak."

"What's that you're going to do?" the drummer demanded, half rising.

"Sit down," begged Sammy, his gun swinging at his knee. He picked up a toothpick with his left hand and chewed it reflectively. "These here Colts make a' awful muss, sometimes," he remarked. "'Specially at close range. Why," he confided, "I once knowed a man what was shot 'most in two. He was a mosshead an' wouldn't do what he was told. Better sorta lead off at that steak, *hombre*," he suggested, chewing evenly on the toothpick. Noticing that the girl still lingered, hypnotized by fear and curiosity, he spoke to her over his shoulder. "Won't you please get me that pie, or somethin'? Run out an' borrow a pan, or somethin'," he pleaded. "I don't like to be handicapped when I'm feedin' cattle."

The drummer's red face paled a little and one hand stole cautiously under his coat—and froze there. Sammy hardly had moved, but the Colt was now horizontal and glowered at the gaudy waistcoat. He was between it and the girl and she did not see the movement. His smile was placid and fixed and he spoke so that she should get no inkling of what was going on. "Never drink on an empty stomach," he advised. "After you eat that meal, then you can fuss with yore flask all you wants." He glanced out of the corner of his eye at the girl and nodded. "Still there! Oh, I most forgot, stranger. You take off yore hat an' 'pologize, so she can go. Jus' say yo're a dawg an never did have no manners. *Say* it!" he ordered, softly. The drummer gulped and muttered something, but the Colt, still hidden from the girl by its owner's body, moved forward a little and Sammy's throaty growl put an end to the muttering. "Say it plain," he ordered, the color fading from his face and leaving pink spots against the white. "That's better—now, Li'l Miss, you get me that pie—please!" he begged.

When they were alone Sammy let the gun swing at his knee again. "I don't know how they treats wimmin where you came from, stranger; but out here we're plumb polite. 'Course you didn't know that, an' that's why you didn't get all mussed up. Yo're jus' plain ignorant an' can't help yore bringin' up. Now, you eat that steak, *pronto!*"

"It's too cold, now," grumbled the drummer, fidgeting in the chair.

The puncher's left hand moved to the table again and when it returned to his side there was a generous layer of red pepper on the meat. "Easy to fix things when you know how," he grinned. "If it gets any colder I'll fix it some more." His tones became sharper and the words lost their drawled softness. "You goin' to start ag'in that by yoreself, or am I goin' to help you?" he demanded, lifting his leg off the chair and standing erect. All the humor had left his face and there was a grimness about the tight lips and a menace in the squinting eyes that sent a chill rippling down the drummer's spine. He tasted a forkful of the meat and gulped hastily, tears welling into his eyes. The puncher moved a little nearer and watched the frantic gulps with critical attention. "'Course, you can eat any way you wants—yo're payin' for it; but boltin' like a coyote ain't good for th' stummick. Howsomever, it's yore grub," he admitted.

A cup of cold coffee and a pitcher of water followed the meat in the same gulping haste. Tears streamed down the drummer's red face as he arose and turned toward the door. "Hol' on, stranger!" snapped Sammy. "That costs six bits," he prompted. The coins rang out on the nearest table, the door slammed and the agonized stranger ran madly down the street, cursing at every jump. Sammy sauntered to the door and craned his neck. "Somebody's jus' naturally goin' to bust him wide open one of these days. He ain't got no sense," he muttered, turning back to get his pipe.

A cloud of dust rolled up from the south, causing Briggs a little uneasiness, and he scowled through the door at the long empty siding and the pens sprawled along it.

Steps clacked across the platform and a grinning cowpuncher stopped at the open window. "They're here," he announced. "How 'bout th' cars?"

Briggs looked around wearily. For three days his life had been made miserable by this pest, who carried a laugh in his eyes, a sting on his tongue and a chip on his shoulder. "They'll be here soon," he replied, with little interest. "But there's th' pens."

"Yes, there's th' pens," smiled Sammy. "They'll hold 'bout one-tenth of that herd. Ain't I been pesterin' you to get them cars?"

The agent sighed expressively and listened to the instrument on his table. When it ceased he grabbed the key and asked a question. Then he smiled for the first time that day. "They're passing Franklin. Be here in two hours. Now get out of here or I'll lick you."

"There's a nice place in one of them pens," smiled Sammy.

"I see you're eating at Olmstead's," parried the agent.

"Yea."

"Nice girl. Come up last summer when Mrs. Olmstead petered out. I ate there last winter."

Sammy grinned at him. "Why'd you stop?"

Briggs grew red and glanced at the nearing cloud of dust. "Better help your outfit, hadn't you?"

Sammy was thoughtful. "Say, that's a plumb favorite eatin' place, ain't it?"

Briggs laughed. "Wait till Saturday when th' boys come in. There's a dozen shinin' up to that girl. Tom Clarke is real persistent."

Sammy forsook the building as a prop. "Who's he? Puncher?"

"Yes; an' bad," replied the agent. "But I reckon she don't know it."

Sammy looked at the dust cloud and turned to ask one more question. "What does this persistent gent look like, an' where's he hang out?" He nodded at the verbose reply and strode to his horse to ride toward the approaching herd. He espied Red first, and hailed. "Cars here in two hours. Where's Hoppy?"

"Back in th' dust. But what happened to *you*?" demanded Red, with virile interest. Sammy ignored the challenge and loped along the edge of the cloud until he found the trail boss. "Them cars'll be here in two hours," he reported.

"Take you three days to find it out?" snapped Hopalong.

"Took me three days to get 'em. I just about unraveled that agent. He swears every time he hears a noise, thinkin' it's me."

"Broke?" demanded Hopalong.

Sammy flushed. "I ain't gambled a cent since I hit town. An' say, them pens won't hold a tenth of 'em," he replied, looking over the dark blur that heaved under the dust cloud like a fog-covered, choppy sea.

"I'm goin' to hold 'em on grass," replied the trail boss. "They ain't got enough cars on this toy road to move all them cows in less'n a week. I ain't goin' to let 'em lose no weight in pens. Wait a minute! You're on night herd for stayin' away."

When Sammy rode into camp the following morning he scorned Blinky's food, much to the open-mouthed amazement of that worthy and Johnny Nelson. Blinky thought of doctors and death; but Johnny, noticing his bunkmate's restlessness and careful grooming of his person, had grave suspicions. "Good grub in this town?" he asked, saddling to go on his shift.

Sammy wiped a fleck of dust off his boot and looked up casually. "Shore. Best is at the Dutchman's at th' far end of th' street."

Johnny mounted, nodded and departed for the herd, where Red was pleasantly cursing his tardiness. Red would eat Blinky's grub and gladly. Johnny was cogitating. "There's a girl in this town, an' he's got three days' head start. No wonder them cars just got here!" Red's sarcastic voice intruded. "Think I eat grass, or my stummick's made of rubber?" he snapped. "Think I feed onct a month like a snake?"

"No, Reddie," smiled Johnny, watching the eyebrows lift at the name. "More like a hawg."

Friday morning, a day ahead of the agent's promise, the cars backed onto the siding and by noon the last cow of the herd was taking its first—and last—ride. Sammy slipped away from the outfit at the pens and approached the restaurant from the rear. He would sit behind the partition this time and escape his friends.

The soft sand deadened his steps and when he looked in at the door, a cheery greeting on the tip of his tongue, he stopped and stared unnoticed by the sobbing girl bent over the table. One hand, outflung in dejected abandon, hung over the side and Sammy's eyes, glancing at it, narrowed as he looked. His involuntary, throaty exclamation sent the bowed head up with a jerk, but the look of hate and fear quickly died out of her eyes as she recognized him.

"An' all th' world tumbled down in a heap," he smiled. "But it'll be all right again, same as it allus was," he assured her. "Will Li'l Miss tell Sammy all about it so he can put it together again?"

She looked at him through tear-dimmed eyes, the sobs slowly drying to a spasmodic catching in the rounded throat. She shook her head and the tears welled up again in answer to his sympathy. He walked softly to the table and placed a hand on her bowed head. "Li'l Miss will tell Sammy all about it when she dries her eyes an' gets comfy. Sammy will make things all right again an' laugh with her. Don't you mind him a mite—jus' cry hard, an' when all th' tears are used up, then you tell Sammy what it's all about." She shook her head and would not look up. He bent down carefully and examined the bruised wrist—and his eyes glinted with rage; but he did not speak. The minutes passed in silence, the girl ashamed to show her reddened and tear-stained face; the boy stubbornly determined to stay and learn the facts. He heard his friends tramp past, wondering where he was, but he did not move.

Finally she brushed back her hair and looked up at him and the misery in her eyes made him catch his breath. "Won't you go?" she pleaded.

He shook his head.

"Please!"

"Not till I find out whose fingers made them marks," he replied. The look of fear flashed up again, but he checked it with a smile he far from felt. "Nobody's goin' to make you cry, an' get away with it," he told her. "Who was it?"

"I won't tell you. I can't tell you! I don't know!"

"Li'l Miss, look me in th' eyes an' say it again. I thought so. You mustn't say things that ain't true. Who did that?"

"What do you want to know for?"

"Oh, jus' because."

"What will you do?"

"Oh, I'll sorta talk to him. All I want to know is his name."

"I won't tell you; you'll fight with him."

He turned his sombrero over and looked gravely into its crown. "Well," he admitted, "he *might* not like me talkin' 'bout it. Of course, you can't never tell."

"But he didn't mean to hurt me. He's only rough and boisterous; and he wasn't himself," she pleaded, looking down.

"Uh-huh," grunted Sammy, cogitating. "So'm I. *I'm* awful rough an' boisterous, *I* am; only I don't hurt wimmin. What's his name?"

"I'll not tell you!"

"Well, all right; but if he ever comes in here again an' gets rough an' boisterous he'll lose a hull lot of future. I'll naturally blow most of his head off, which is frequent fatal. What's that? Oh, he's a bad man, is he? Uh-huh; so'm I. Well, I'm goin' to run along now an' see th' boss. If you won't tell, you won't. I'll be back soon," and he sauntered to the street and headed for Pete's saloon, where the agent had said Mr. Clarke was wont to pass his fretful hours.

As he turned the corner he bumped into Hopalong and Johnny, who grabbed at him, and missed. He backed off and rested on his toes, gingery and alert. "Keep yore dusty han's off'n me," he said, quietly. "I'm goin' down to palaver with a gent what I don't like."

Hopalong's shrewd glance looked him over. "What did this gent do?" he asked, and he would not be evaded.

"Oh, he insulted a nice li'l girl, an' I'm in a hurry."

"G'way!" exclaimed Johnny. "That straight?"

"Too damn straight," snapped Sammy. "He went an' bruised her wrists an' made her cry."

"Lead th' way, Kid," rejoined Johnny, readjusting his belt. "Mebby he's got some friends," he suggested, hopefully.

"Yes," smiled Hopalong, "mebby he has. An' anyhow, Sammy; you *know* yo're plumb careless with that gun. You might miss him. Lead th' way."

As they started toward Pete's Johnny nudged his bunkmate in the ribs: "Say; she ain't got no sisters, has she?" he whispered.

. . .

One hour later Sammy, his face slightly scratched, lounged into the kitchen and tossed his sombrero on a chair, grinning cheerfully at the flushed, saucy face that looked out from under a mass of rebellious, brown hair. "Well, I saw th' boss, an' I come back to make everythin' well again," he asserted, laughing softly. "That rough an' boisterous Mr. Clarke has sloped. He won't come back no more."

"Why, *Sammy!*" she cried, aghast. "What *have* you done?"

"Well, for one thing, I've got you callin' me Sammy," he chuckled, trying to sneak a hand over hers. "I told th' boss I'm goin' to get a job up here, so I'll know Mr. Clarke won't come back. But you know, he only thought he was bad. I shore had to take his ol' gun away from him so he wouldn't go an' shoot hisself, an' when las' seen he was feelin' for his cayuse, intendin' to leave these parts. That's what I *done*," he nodded, brightly. "Now comes what I'm goin' to do. Oh, Li'l Miss," he whispered, eagerly. "I'm jus' all mixed up an' millin'. My own feet plumb get in my way. So I jus' gotta stick aroun' an' change yore name, what you don't like. Uh-huh; that's jus' what I gotta do," he smiled.

She tossed her head and the tip-tilt nose went up indignantly. "Indeed you'll do nothing of the kind, Sammy Porter!" she retorted. "I'll choose my own name when the time comes, and it will not be Porter!"

He arose slowly and looked around. Picking up the pencil that lay on the shelf he lounged over to the partition and printed his name three times in large letters. "All right, Li'l Miss," he agreed. "I'll jus' leave a list where you can see it while you're selectin'. I'm now goin' out to get that job we spoke about. You have th' name all picked out when I get back," he suggested, waving his hand at the wall. "An' did anybody ever tell you it was plumb risky to stick yore li'l nose up thataway?"

"Sammy Porter!" she stormed, stamping in vexation near the crying point. "You get right out of here! I'll *never* speak to you again!"

"You won't get a chance to talk much if you don't sorta bring that snubby nose down a li'l lower. I'm plumb weak at times." He laughed joyously and edged to the door. "Don't forget that list. I'm goin' after that job. So-long, Li'l Miss."

"Sammy!"

"Oh, all right; I'll go after it later on," he laughed, returning.

CHAPTER 15

When Johnny Sloped

Johnny Nelson hastened to the corner of the bunkhouse and then changed his pace until he seemed to ooze from there to the cook shack door, where he lazily leaned against the door jamb and ostentatiously picked his teeth with the negative end of a match. The cook looked up calmly, and calmly went on with his work; but if there was anything rasping enough to cause his calloused soul to quiver it was the aforesaid calisthenics executed by Johnny and the match; for Cookie's blunt nature hated hints. If Johnny had demanded, even profanely and with large personal animus, why meals were not ahead of time, it would be a simple matter to heave something and enlarge upon his short cut speech. But the subtleties left the cook floundering in a mire of rage—which he was very careful to conceal from Johnny. The youthful nuisance had been evincing undue interest in early suppers for nearly a month; and judging from the lightness of his repasts he was entirely unjustified in showing any interest at all in the evening meal. So Cookie strangled the biscuit in his hand, but smiled blandly at his tormentor.

"Well, all through?" he pleasantly inquired, glancing carelessly at Johnny's clothes.

"I'm hopin' to begin," retorted Johnny, and the toothpick moved rapidly up and down.

Cookie condensed another biscuit and gulped. "That's shore some stone," he said, enviously, eying the two-caret diamond in Johnny's new, blue tie. Johnny never had worn a tie before he became owner of the diamond, but with the stone came the keen realization of how lost it was in a neck-kerchief, how often covered by the windblown folds; so he had hastened to Buckskin and spent a dollar that belonged to Red for the tie, thus exhausting both the supply of ties and Red's dollars. The honor of wearing the only tie and diamond in that section of the cow-country brought responsibilities, for he had spoken hastily to several humorous friends and stood a good chance of being soundly thrashed therefor.

He threw away the match and scratched his back ecstatically on the door jamb while he strained his eyes trying to look under his chin. Fixed chins and short ties are trials one must learn to accept philosophically—and Johnny might have been spared the effort were it not for the fact that the tie had been made for a boy, and was awesomely shortened by encircling a sixteen-inch neck. Evidently it had been made for a boy violently inclined toward a seafaring life, as suggested by the anchors embroidered in white down its middle.

"Lemme see it," urged Cookie, sighing because its owner had resolutely refused to play poker when he had no cash. This had become a blighting sorrow in the life of a naturally exuberant and very fair cook.

"An' for how long?" demanded Johnny, a cold and calculating light glinting in his eyes.

"Oh, till supper's ready," replied Cookie with great carelessness.

"Nix; but you can wear it twenty minutes if you'll get my grub quick," he replied. "Got to meet Lucas at half-past five." He cautiously dropped the match he had thoughtlessly produced.

The cook tried to look his belief and accepted the offer. Johnny's remarkably clean face, plastered hair and general gala attire suggested that Lucas was a woman—which Lucas profanely would have denied. Also, Johnny had been seen washing Ginger, and when a puncher washes a cayuse it's a sign of insanity. Besides, Ginger belonged to Red, who also had owned that lone dollar. Red's clothes did not fit Johnny.

"Goin' to surprise Lucas?" inquired the cook.

"What you mean?"

Cookie glanced meaningly at the attire: "Er—you ain't in th' habit of puttin' on war paint for to see Lucas, are you?"

Johnny's mental faculties produced: "Oh, we're goin' to a dance."

"Where 'bouts?" exploded the cook.

"*Way* up north!" One's mind needs to be active as a flea to lie properly to a man like the cook. He had made a ghastly mistake.

"By golly! I'll give th' boys cold grub an' go with you," and the cook began to save time.

Johnny gulped and shook his head: "Got a invite?"

Cookie caught the pan on his foot before it struck the floor and gasped: "Invite? Ain't it free-fer-all?"

"No; this is a high-toned thing-a-bob. Costs a dollar a head, too."

"High-toned?" snorted the cook, derisively. "Don't they know you? An' I thought Red was broke. Show me that permit!"

"Lucas's got it—that's why I've got to catch him."

"Oh! An' is *he* goin' all feathered up, too?"

"Shore, he's got to."

"Huh! He wouldn't dress like that to see a *fight*. Has she got any sisters?" Cookie finished, hopefully.

"Now what you talkin' about?"

"Why, Lucas," answered the cook, placidly. "Lemme tell you something. When you want to lose me have a invite to a water-drinkin' contest. An' before you go, be shore to rub Hoppy's boots some more; that's such a pasty shine it'll look like sand-paper before you get to th'—dance. You want to make it hard an' slippery. An' I've read som'ers that only wimmin ought to smell like a drugstore. You better let her do th' fumigatin'."

Johnny surrendered and dolefully whiffed the crushed violets he had paid two bits a pint for at El Paso—it was not necessary to whiff them, but he did so.

"You ought to hone yore razor, too," continued the cook, critically.

"I told Buck it was dull, I ain't goin' to sharpen it for him. But, say, are you shore about th' perfumery?"

"Why, of course."

"But how'll I git it off?"

"Bury th' clothes," suggested Cookie, grinning.

"I like your gall! Which clothes are best, Pete's or Billy's?"

"Pete's would fit you like th' wide, wide world. You don't want blankets on when you go courtin'. Try Billy's. An' I got a pair of socks, though one's green— but th' boots'll hide it."

"I didn't put none on my socks, you chump!"

"How'd *I* know? But, say! Has she got any sisters?"

"No!" yelled Johnny, halfway through the gallery in search of Billy's clothes. When he emerged Cookie looked him over. "Ain't it funny, Kid, how a pipe'll stink up clothes?" he smiled. Johnny's retort was made over several yards of ground and when he had mounted Cookie yelled and waved him to return. When Johnny had obeyed and impatiently demanded the reason, Cookie pleasantly remarked: "Now, be shore an' give her my love, Kid."

Johnny's reply covered half a mile of trail.

.   .   .

Johnny rode alertly through Perry's Bend, for Sheriff Nolan was no friend of his; and Nolan was not only a discarded suitor of Miss Joyce, but a warm personal friend of George Greener, the one rival Johnny feared. Greener was a widower as wealthy as he was unscrupulous, and a power on that range: when he said "jump," Nolan soared.

The sheriff was standing before the Palace saloon when Johnny rode past, and he could not keep quiet. His comment was so judiciously chosen as to bring white spots on Johnny's flushed cheeks. The Bar-20 puncher was not famed for his self-control, and, wheeling in the saddle, he pointed a quivering forefinger at Mr. Nolan's badge of office, so conspicuously displayed: "Better men than you have hid behind a badge and banked on a man's regard for th' law savin' 'em from their just deserts. Politics is a hell of a thing when it opens th' door to anything that might roll in on th' wind. You come down across th' line tomorrow an' see me, without th' nickel-plated ornament you disgraces," he invited. "Any dog can tell a lie in his kennel, but it takes guts to bark outside th' yard."

Mr. Nolan flushed, went white, hesitated, and walked away. To fight in defense of the law was his duty; but no sane man warred on the Bar-20 unless he must. Mr. Nolan was a man whose ideas of necessity followed strange curves, and not to his credit. One might censure Mr. Cassidy or Mr. Connors, or pick a fight with some of the others of that outfit and not get killed; but he must not harm their protégé. Mr. Nolan not only walked away but he sought the darkest shadows and held conversation with himself. If it were only possible to get the pugnacious and very much spoiled Mr. Nelson to fracture, smash, pulverize some law! This, indeed, would be sweet.

Meanwhile Johnny, having watched the sheriff slip away, loosed a few more words into the air and went on his way, whistling cheerfully. Reaching the Joyce cottage he was admitted by Miss Joyce herself and at sight of her blushing face his exuberant confidence melted and left him timid. This he was wont to rout by big words and a dashing air he did not feel.

"Oh! Come right in," she invited. "But you are late," she laughed, chidingly.

He critically regarded the dimples, while he replied that he had drawn rein to slay the sheriff but, knowing that it would cost him more valuable time, he had consented with himself to postpone the event.

"But you must not do that!" she cried. "Why, that's terrible! You shouldn't even think of such things."

"Well, of course—if yo're agin' it I won't."

"But what did he do?"

"Oh, I don't reckon I can tell that. But do you really want him to live?"

"Why, certainly! What a foolish question."

"But why do you? Do you—*like* him?"

"I like everybody."

"Yes; an' everybody likes you, too," he growled, the smile fading. "That's th' trouble. Do you like him very much?"

"I wish you wouldn't ask such foolish questions."

"Yes; I know. But do you?"

"I prefer not to answer."

"Huh! That's an answer in itself. You do."

"I don't think you're very nice tonight," she retorted, a little pout spoiling the bow in her lips. "You're awfully jealous, and I don't like it."

"Gee! Don't like it! I should think you'd want me to be jealous. I only wish you was jealous of *me*. Norah, I've just got to say it now, an' find out—"

"Yes; tell me," she interrupted eagerly. "What *did* he do?"

"Who?"

"Mr. Nolan, of course."

"Nolan?" he demanded in surprise.

"Yes, yes; tell me."

"I ain't talking about *him*. I was goin' to tell you something that I've—"

"That you've done and now regret? Have you ever—ever killed a man?" she breathed. "Have you?"

"No; *yes*! Lots of 'em," he confessed, remembering that once she had expressed admiration for brave and daring men. "Most half as many as Hopalong; an' I ain't near as old as him, neither."

"You mean Mr. Cassidy? Why don't you bring him with you some evening? I'd like to meet him."

"Not *me*. I went an' brought a friend along once, an' had to lick him th' next day to keep him away from here. He'd 'a' camped right out there in front if I hadn't. No, ma'am; not any."

"Why, the idea! But Mr. Greener's very much like your friend, Mr. Cassidy. He's very brave, and a wonderful shot. He told me so himself."

"What! He told you so hisself! Well, well. Beggin' yore pardon, he ain't nowise like Hoppy, not even in th' topics of his conversation. Why, he's a child; an' blinks when he shoots off a gun. Here—can he show a gun like mine?" and forthwith he held out his Colt, butt foremost, and indicated the notches he had cut that afternoon. A fleeting doubt went through his mind at what his outfit would say when it saw those notches. The Bar-20 cut no notches. It wanted to forget.

She looked at them curiously and suddenly drew back. "Oh! Are they—*are* they?" she whispered.

He nodded: "They are. There is plenty of room for Nolan's, an' mebby his owner, too," he suggested. "Can't you see, Norah?" he asked in a swift change of tone. "Can't you see? Don't you know how much I—"

"Yes. It must be terrible to have such remorse," she quickly interposed. "And I sympathize with you deeply, too."

"Remorse nothin'! Them fellers was lookin' for it, an' they got just what they deserved. If I hadn't 'a' done it somebody else would."

"And *you* a murderer! I never thought that of *you*. I can hardly believe it of you. And you calmly confess it to me as though it were nothing!"

"Why, I—I—"

"Don't talk to me! To think you have human blood on your hands. To think—"

"Norah! Norah, listen; won't you?"

"—that you are that sort of a man! How dare you call here as you have? How dare you?"

"But I tell you they were tryin' to get *me*! I just *had* to. Why, I didn't do it for nothin'. I've got a right to defend myself, ain't I?"

"You *had* to? Is that true?" she demanded.

"Why, shore! Think I go 'round killin' men, like Greener does, just for th' fun of it?"

"He doesn't do anything of the kind," she retorted. "You know he doesn't! Didn't you just say he blinks when he shoots off a gun?"

"Yes; I did. But I didn't want you to think he was a murderer like Nolan," he explained. Even Cookie, he thought, would find it hard to get around that neat little effort.

"I'm so relieved," she laughed, delighted at her success in twisting him. "I am so glad he doesn't blink when he shoots. I'd hate a man who was afraid to shoot."

Johnny's chest arose a little. "Well, how 'bout me?"

"But you've killed men; you've shot down your fellow men; have ghastly marks on your revolver to brag about."

"Well—say—but how can I shoot without shootin' or kill without killin'?" he demanded. "An' I don't brag about 'em, neither; it makes me feel too sad to do any braggin'. An' Greener's killed 'em, too; an' he brags about it."

"Yes; but he doesn't blink!" she exclaimed triumphantly.

"Neither do *I*."

"Yes; but you shoot to kill."

"Lord pity us—don't *he*?"

"Y-e-s, but that's different," she replied, smiling brightly.

Johnny looked around the room, his eyes finally resting on his hat.

"Yes, I see it's different. Greener can kill, an' blink! I can't. If he kills a man he's a hero; I'm a murderer. I kinda reckon he's got th' trail. But I love you, an' you've got to pick my trail—does it lead up or down?"

"Johnny Nelson! What are you saying?" she demanded, arising.

"Something turrible, mebby. I don't know; an' I don't care. It's true—so there you are. Norah, can't you see I do?" he pleaded, holding out his hands. "Won't you marry me?"

She looked down, her cheeks the color of fire, and Johnny continued hurriedly: "I've loved you a whole month! When I'm ridin' around I sorta' see you, an' hear you. Why, I talk to you lots when I'm alone. I've saved up some money, an' I had to work hard to save it, too. I've got some cows runnin' with our'n—in a little while I'll have a ranch of my own. Buck'll let me use th' east part of th' ranch, an' there's a hill over there that'd look fine with a house on it. I can't wait no longer, Norah, I've got to know. Will you let me put this on yore finger?" He swiftly bent the pin into a ring and held it out eagerly: "Can I?"

She pushed him away and yielded to a sudden pricking of her conscience, speaking swiftly, as if forcing herself to do a disagreeable duty, and hating herself at the moment. "Johnny, I've been a—a flirt! When I saw you were beginning to care too much for me I should have stopped it; but I didn't. I amused myself—but I want you to believe one thing; I never thought what it might mean to you. It was carelessness with me. But I was flirting, just the same— and it hurts to admit it. I'm not good enough for you, Johnny Nelson; it's hard to say, but it's true. Can you, *will* you forgive me?"

He choked and stepped forward holding out his hands imploringly, but she eluded him. When he saw the shame in her face, the tears in her eyes, he stopped and laughed gently: "But we can begin right, now, can't we? I don't care, not if you'll let me see you same as ever. You might get to care for me. And, anyhow, it ain't yore fault. I reckon it's me that's to blame."

At that moment he was nearer to victory than he had ever been; but he did not realize it and opportunity died when he failed to press his advantage.

"I *am* to blame," she said, so low he could hardly catch the words. When she continued it was with a rush: "I am not free—I haven't been for a week. I'm not free any more—and I've been leading you on!"

His face hardened, for now the meaning of Greener's sneering laugh came to him, and a seething rage swept over him against the man who had won. He knew Greener, knew him well—the meanness of the man's nature, his cold cruelty; the many things to the man's discredit loomed up large against the frailty of the woman before him.

Norah stepped forward and laid a pleading hand on his arm, for she knew the mettle of the men who worked under Buck Peters: "What are you thinking? Tell me!"

"Why, I'm thinking what Nolan said. An', Norah, listen. You say you want me to forgive you? Well, I do, if there's anything to forgive. But I want you to primise me that if Greener don't treat you right you'll tell me."

"What do you mean?"

"Only what I said. Do you promise?"

"Perhaps you would better speak to him about it!" she retorted.

"I will—an' plain. But don't worry 'bout me. It was my fault for bein' a tenderfoot. I never played this game before, an' don't know th' cards. Good-by."

He rode away slowly, and made the rounds, and by the time he reached Lacey's he was so unsteady that he was refused a drink and told to go home. But he headed for the Palace instead, and when he stepped high over the doorsill Nolan was seated in a chair tipped back against one of the side walls, and behind the bar on the other side of the room Jed Terry drummed on the counter and expressed his views on local matters. The sheriff was listening in a bored way until he saw Johnny enter and head his way, feet high and chest out; and at that moment Nolan's interest in local affairs flashed up brightly.

Johnny lost no time: "Nolan," he said, rocking on his heels, "tell Greener I'll kill him if he marries that girl. He killed his first wife by abuse an' he don't kill no more. Savvy?"

The sheriff warily arose, for here was the opportunity he had sought. The threat to kill had a witness.

"An' if you opens your toad's mouth about her like you did tonight, I'll kill you, too." The tones were dispassionate, the words deliberate.

"Hear that, Jed?" cried the sheriff, excitedly. "Nelson, yo're under ar—"

"Shut up!" snapped Johnny loudly, this time with feeling. "When yo're betters are talkin' you keep your face closed. Now, it ain't hardly healthy to slander wimmin in this country, 'specially *good* wimmin. You lied like a dog to me tonight, an' I let you off; don't try it again."

"I told th' truth!" snapped Nolan, heatedly. "I said she was a flirt an' by th' great horned spoon she is a flirt, an' you—"

The sheriff prided himself upon his quickness, but the leaping gun was kicked out of his hand before he knew what was coming; a chair glanced off Jed's face and wrapped the front window about itself in its passing, leaving the bartender in the throbbing darkness of interplanetary space; and as the sheriff opened his eyes and recovered from the hard swings his face had stopped, a galloping horse drummed southward toward the Bar-20; and the silence of the night was shattered by lusty war-whoops and a spurting .45.

When the sheriff and his posse called at the Bar-20 before breakfast the following morning they found a grouchy outfit and learned some facts.

"Where's Johnny?" repeated Hopalong, with a rising inflection. "Only wish I knowed!"

A murmur of wistful desire arose and Lanky Smith restlessly explained it: "He rampages in 'bout midnight an' wakes us up with his racket. When we asks what he's doin' with *our* possessions he suggests we go to hell. He takes *his* rifle, Pete's rifle, Buck's brand new canteen, 'bout eighty pounds of catridges an' other useful duffle, *all* th' tobacco, an' blows away quick."

"On my cayuse," murmured Red.

"Wearin' my *good* clothes," added Billy, sorrowfully.

"An' *my* boots," sighed Hopalong.

"I ain't got no field glasses no more," grumbled Lanky.

"But he only got one laig of my new pants," chuckled Skinny. "I was too strong for him."

"He yanked my blanket off'n me, which makes me steal Red's," grinned Pete.

"Which you didn't keep very long!" retorted Red, with derision.

"Which makes us all peevish," plaintively muttered Buck.

"Now ain't it a hell of a note?" laughed Cookie, loudly, forthwith getting scarce. He had nothing good enough to be taken.

"An' whichever was it run ag'in' yore face, Sheriff?" sympathetically inquired Hopalong. "Mighty good thing it stopped," he added thoughtfully.

"Never mind my face!" snorted the peace officer hotly as his deputies smoothed out their grins. "I want to know where Nelson is, an' damned quick! We'll search the house first."

"Hold on," responded Buck. "North of Salt Spring Creek yo're a sheriff; down here yo're nothin'. Don't search no house. He ain't here."

"How do I know he ain't?" snapped Nolan.

"My word's good; or there'll be another election stolen up in yore county," rejoined Buck ominously. "An' I wouldn't hunt him too hard, neither. We'll punish him."

Nolan wheeled and rode toward the hills without another word, his posse pressing close behind. When they entered Apache Pass one of them accidentally exploded his rifle, calling forth an angry tirade from the sheriff. Johnny heard it, and cared little for the warning from his friend Lucas; he waited and then rode down the rocky slope of the pass on the trail of the posse, squinting wickedly at the distant group as he caught glimpses of them now and again, and with no anxiety regarding backward glances. "Lot's wife'll have nothing on them if they look back," he muttered, fingering his rifle lovingly. At nightfall he watched them depart and grinned at the chase he would lead them when they returned.

But he did not see them again, although his friends reported that they were turning the range upside down to find him. One of his outfit rode out to him with supplies and information every few days and it was Pete who told him that six posses were in the hills. "An' you can't leave, 'cause one of th' cordon would get you shore. I had a hell of a time getting in today." Red reported that the sheriff had sworn to take him dead or alive. Then came the blow. The sheriff was at the point of death from lockjaw caused by complete paralysis of the curea-frend nerve just above the phlagmatic diaphragm, which Johnny had fractured. It was Hopalong who imparted this sad news, and withered Johnny's hope of returning to a comfortable bunkhouse and square meals. So the fugitive clung to the hills, shunned sky-lines and wondered if the sheriff would recover before snow flew. He was hungry most of the time now because the outfit was getting stingy with the food supplies—and he dared not shoot any game.

Four weeks passed, weeks of hunger and nervous strain, and he was getting desperate. He had learned that Greener and his fiancée were going down to Linnville soon, since Perry's Bend had no parson; and his cup of bitterness, overflowing, drove him to risk an attempt to leave that part of the country. He had seen none of Pete's "cordon" although he had looked for them, and he believed he could get away. So he rode cautiously down Apache Pass one noon, thoughtfully planning his flight. The sand, washed down the rock walls by the last rain, deadened all sounds of his progress, and as he turned a sharp bend in the cut he almost bumped into Greener and Norah Joyce. They were laughing at how they had eluded the crowd of friends who were eager to accompany them—but the laughter froze when Johnny's gun swung up.

"'Nds up, Greener!" he snapped, viciously, remembering his promise to Sheriff Nolan. "Miss Joyce, if you make any trouble it'll cost him his life."

"Turned highwayman, eh?" sneered Greener, keenly alert for the necessary fraction of a second's carelessness on the part of the other. He was gunman enough to need no more.

"Miss Joyce, will you please ride along? I want to talk to him alone," said Johnny, his eyes fastened intently on those of his enemy.

"Yes, Norah; that's best. I'll join you in a few minutes," urged Greener, smiling at her.

Johnny had a sudden thought and his warning was grave and cold. "Don't get very far away an' don't make no sounds, or signals; if you do it'll be th' quickest way to *need* 'em. He'll pay for any mistakes like that."

"You coward!" she cried, angrily, and then delivered an impromptu lecture that sent the blood surging into the fugitive's wan cheeks. But she obeyed, slowly, at Greener's signal, and when she was out of sight Johnny spoke.

"Greener, yo're not going to marry her. You know what you are, you know how yore first wife died—an' I don't intend that Norah shall be abused as the other was. I'm a fugitive, hard pressed; I'm weak from want of food, and from hardships; all I have left is a slim chance of gettin' away. I've reached the point where I can't harm myself by shooting you an' I'm goin' to do it rather than let any trouble come to her. But you'll get an even break, because I ain't never going to shoot a man when he's helpless. Got anything to say?"

"Yes; yo're th' biggest fool I ever saw," replied Greener. "Yo're locoed through an' through; an' I'm goin' to take great pleasure in putting you away. But I want to thank you for one thing you did. You were drunk at the time an' may not remember it. When you hit Nolan for talking like he did I liked you for it, an' I'm goin' to tell you so. Now we'll get at th' matter before us so I can move along."

Neither had paid any attention to Norah in the earnestness and keen-eyed scrutiny of each other and the first sign they had of her actions was when she threw her arms around Greener's neck and shielded him. He was too much of a man to fire from cover and Johnny realized it while the other tried to get her to leave the scene.

"I won't leave you to be murdered—I *know* what it means, I *know* it," she cried. "My place is here, and you can't deny your wife's first request! What will I do without you! Oh, dear, let me stay! I *will* stay! What woman ever had such a wedding day before! Dear, dear, what can I do? Tell me what to do!"

Johnny sniffled and wished the posse had taken him. This was a side he had never thought of. His wife! Greener's wife! Then he was too late, and to go on would be a greater evil than the one he wished to eliminate. When she turned on him like a tigress and tore him to pieces word by word, tears rolling down her pallid cheeks and untold misery in her eyes, he shook his head and held up his hand.

"Greener, you win; I can't stop what's happened," he said slowly. "But I'll tell you this, an' I mean every word: If you don't treat her like she deserves, I'll come back some of these days and kill you *shore*. Nolan got his because he talked ill of her; an' you'll get yours if I die the next minute, if you ain't square with her."

"I don't need no instructions on how to treat my wife," retorted the other. "An' I'm beginnin' to see th' cause of yore insanity, and it pardons you as nothing else will. Put up yore gun an' get back to th' ranch, where you belong—an' *keep away from me*. Savvy?"

"Not much danger of me gettin' in yore way," growled Johnny, "when I'm hunted like a dog for doing what any man would 'a' done. When th' sheriff gets well, if he ever does, mebby I'll come back an' take my medicine. How was he, anyhow, when you left?"

"Dead tired, an' some under th' influence of liquor," replied Greener, a smile breaking over his frown. He knew the whole story well, as did the whole range, and he had laughed over it with the Bar-20 outfit.

"What's that? Ain't he near dead?" cried Johnny, amazed.

"Well, purty nigh dead of fatigue dancin' at our weddin' last night; but I reckon he'll be driftin' home purty soon, an' all recovered." Greener suddenly gave way and roared with laughter. There was a large amount of humor in his make-up and it took possession of him, shaking him from head to foot. He had always liked Johnny, not because he ever wanted to but because no one could know the Bar-20 protégé and keep from it. This climax was too much for him, and his wife, gradually recovering herself, caught the infection and joined in.

Johnny's eyes were staring and his mouth wide open, but Greener's next words closed the eyes to a squint and snapped shut the open mouth.

"That there paralysis of th' cure-a-friend nerve didn't last; an' when I heard why you licked him I said a few words that made him a wiser man. He didn't hunt you after th' first day. Now you go up an' shake han's with him. He knows he got what was coming to him and so does everybody else know it. Go home an' quit playin' th' fool for th' whole blamed range to laugh at."

Johnny stirred and came back to the scene before him. His face was livid with rage and he could not speak at first. Finally, however, he mastered himself and looked up: "I'm cured, all right, but *they* ain't! Wait till my turn comes!

What a fool I was to believe 'em; but they usually tell th' truth. 'Cure-a-friend nerve'! They'll pay me dollar for cent before I'm finished!" He caught the sparkle of his diamond pin, the pin he had won, when drunk, at El Paso, and a sickly grin flickered over the black frown. "I'm a little late, I reckon; but I'd like to give th' bride a present to show there ain't no hard feelin's on my part, an' to bring her luck. This here pin ain't no fit ornament for a fool like me, so if it's all right, I'll be plumb tickled to see her have it. How 'bout it, Greener?"

The happy pair exchanged glances and Mrs. Greener, hesitating and blushing, accepted the gift: "You can bend it into a ring easy," Johnny hastily remarked, to cut off her thanks.

Greener extended his hand: "I reckon we can be friends, at that, Nelson. You squared up with me when you licked Nolan. Come up an' see us when you can."

Johnny thanked him and shook hands and then watched them ride slowly down the canyon, hand in hand, happy as little children. He sat silently, lost in thought, his anger rising by leaps and bounds against the men who had kept him on the anxious seat for a month. Straightening up suddenly, he tore off the navy blue necktie and, hurling it from him, fell into another reverie, staring at the canyon wall, but seeing in his mind's eye the outfit planning his punishment; and his eyes grew redder and redder with fury. But it was a long way home and his temper cooled as he rode; that is why no one knew of his return until they saw him asleep in his bunk when they awakened at daylight the following morning. And no one ever asked about the diamond, or made any explanations—for some things are better unmentioned. But they paid for it all before Johnny considered the matter closed.

Bar-20

CHAPTER 1

Buckskin

The town lay sprawled over half a square mile of alkali plain, its main street depressing in its width, for those who were responsible for its inception had worked with a generosity born of the knowledge that they had at their immediate and unchallenged disposal the broad lands of Texas and New Mexico on which to assemble a grand total of twenty buildings, four of which were of wood. As this material was scarce, and had to be brought from where the waters of the Gulf lapped against the flat coast, the last-mentioned buildings were a matter of local pride, as indicating the progressiveness of their owners. These creations of hammer and saw were of one story, crude and unpainted; their cheap weather sheathing warped and shrunken by the pitiless sun, curled back on itself and allowed unrestricted entrance to alkali dust and air. The other shacks were of adobe and owned by Indians and Mexicans.

It was an incident of the Cattle Trail, that most unique and stupendous of all modern migrations, and its founders must have been inspired with a malicious desire to perpetrate a crime against geography, or else they reveled in a perverse cussedness, for within a mile on every side lay broad prairies, and two miles to the east flowed the indolent waters of the Rio Pecos itself. The distance separating the town from the river was excusable, for at certain seasons of the year the placid stream swelled mightily and swept down in a broad expanse of turbulent, yellow flood.

Buckskin was a town of one hundred inhabitants, located in the valley of the Rio Pecos fifty miles south of the Texas–New Mexico line. The census claimed two hundred, but it was a well-known fact that it was exaggerated. One instance of this is shown at the name of Tom Flynn. Those who once knew Tom Flynn, alias Johnny Redmond, alias Bill Sweeney, alias Chuck Mullen, by all four names, could find them in the census list. Furthermore, he had been shot and killed in the March of the year preceding the census, and now occupied a grave in the young but flourishing cemetery. Perry's Bend, twenty miles up the river, was cognizant of this and other facts, and, laughing in open derision at the padded list, claimed to be the better town in all ways, including marksmanship.

One year before this tale opens, Buck Peters, an example for the more recent Billy the Kid, had paid Perry's Bend a short but busy visit. He had ridden in at the north end of Main Street and out at the south. As he came in he was fired at by a group of ugly cowboys from a ranch known as the C-80. He was hit twice, but he unlimbered his artillery, and before his horse had carried him, half dead, out on the prairie, he had killed one of the group. Several citizens had joined the cowboys and added their bullets against Buck. The deceased had been the best bartender in the country, and the rage of the suffering citizens can well be imagined. They swore vengeance on Buck, his ranch, and his stamping ground.

The difference between Buck and Billy the Kid is that the former never shot a man who was not trying to shoot him, or who had not been warned by some action against Buck that would call for it. He minded his own business, never picked a quarrel, and was quiet and pacific up to a certain point. After that had been passed he became like a raging cyclone in a tenement house, and storm cellars were much in demand.

"Fanning" is the name of a certain style of gun-play and was universal among the bad men of the West. While Buck was not a bad man, he had to rub elbows with them frequently, and he believed that the sauce for the goose was the sauce for the gander. So he had removed the trigger of his revolver and worked the hammer with the thumb of the "gun hand" or the thumb of the unencumbered hand. The speed thus acquired was greater than that of the more modern double-action weapon. Six shots in three seconds was his average speed when that number was required, and when it is thoroughly understood that at least five of them found their intended billets it is not difficult to realize that fanning was an operation of danger when Buck was doing it.

He was a good rider, as all cowboys are, and was not afraid of anything that lived. At one time he and his chums, Red Connors and Hopalong Cassidy, had successfully routed a band of fifteen Apaches who wanted their scalps. Of these, twelve never hunted scalps again, nor anything else on this earth, and the other three returned to their tribe with the report that three evil spirits had chased them with "wheel guns" (cannons).

So now, since his visit to Perry's Bend, the rivalry of the two towns had turned to hatred and an alert and eager readiness to increase the inhabitants of each other's graveyard. A state of war existed, which for a time resulted in nothing worse than acrimonious suggestions. But the time came when the score was settled to the satisfaction of one side, at least.

Four ranches were also concerned in the trouble. Buckskin was surrounded by two, the Bar-20 and the Three Triangle. Perry's Bend was the common point for the C-80 and the Double Arrow. Each of the two ranch contingents accepted the feud as a matter of course, and as a matter of course took sides with their respective towns. As no better class of fighters ever lived, the trouble assumed Homeric proportions and insured a danger zone well worth watching.

Bar-20's northern line was C-80's southern one, and Skinny Thompson took his turn at outriding one morning after the season's roundup. He was to follow the boundary and turn back stray cattle. When he had covered the greater part of his journey he saw Shorty Jones riding toward him on a course parallel to his own and about long revolver range away. Shorty and he had "crossed trails" the year before and the best of feelings did not exist between them.

Shorty stopped and stared at Skinny, who did likewise at Shorty. Shorty turned his mount around and applied the spurs, thereby causing his indignant horse to raise both heels at Skinny. The latter took it all in gravely and, as Shorty faced him again, placed his left thumb to his nose, wiggling his fingers suggestively. Shorty took no apparent notice of this but began to shout:

"Yu wants to keep yore busted-down cows on yore own side. They was all over us day afore yesterday. I'm goin' to salt any more what comes over, and don't yu fergit it, neither."

Thompson wigwagged with his fingers again and shouted in reply: "Yu c'n salt all yu wants to, but if I ketch yu adoin' it yu won't have to work no more. An' I kin say right here thet they's more C-80 cows over here than they's Bar-20's over there."

Shorty reached for his revolver and yelled, "Yore a liar!"

Among the cowboys in particular and the Westerners in general at that time, the three suicidal terms, unless one was an expert in drawing quick and shooting straight with one movement, were the words "liar," "coward," and "thief." Any man who was called one of these in earnest, and he was the judge, was expected to shoot if he could and save his life, for the words were seldom used without a gun coming with them. The movement of Shorty's hand toward his belt before the appellation reached him was enough for Skinny, who let go at long range—and missed.

The two reports were as one. Both urged their horses nearer and fired again. This time Skinny's sombrero gave a sharp jerk and a hole appeared in the crown. The third shot of Skinny's sent the horse of the other to its knees and then over on its side. Shorty very promptly crawled behind it and, as he did so, Skinny began a wide circle, firing at intervals as Shorty's smoke cleared away.

Shorty had the best position for defense, as he was in a shallow coulée, but he knew that he could not leave it until his opponent had either grown tired of the affair or had used up his ammunition. Skinny knew it, too. Skinny also knew that he could get back to the ranch house and lay in a supply of food and ammunition and return before Shorty could cover the twelve miles he had to go on foot.

Finally Thompson began to head for home. He had carried the matter as far as he could without it being murder. Too much time had elapsed now, and, besides, it was before breakfast and he was hungry. He would go away and settle the score at some time when they would be on equal terms.

He rode along the line for a mile and chanced to look back. Two C-80 punchers were riding after him, and as they saw him turn and discover them they fired at him and yelled. He rode on for some distance and cautiously drew his rifle out of its long holster at his right leg. Suddenly he turned around in the saddle and fired twice. One of his pursuers fell forward on the neck of his horse, and his comrade turned to help him. Thompson wigwagged again and rode on, reaching the ranch as the others were finishing their breakfast.

At the table Red Connors remarked that the tardy one had a hole in his sombrero, and asked its owner how and where he had received it.

"Had a argument with C-80 out'n th' line."

"Go 'way! Ventilate enny?"

"One."

"Good boy, sonny! Hey, Hopalong, Skinny perforated C-80 this mawnin'!"

Hopalong Cassidy was struggling with a mouthful of beef. He turned his eyes toward Red without ceasing, and grinning as well as he could under the circumstances managed to grunt out "Gu—," which was as near to "Good" as the beef would allow.

Lanky Smith now chimed in as he repeatedly stuck his knife into a reluctant boiled potato, "How'd yu do it, Skinny?"

"Bet he sneaked up on him," joshed Buck Peters; "did yu ask his pardin, Skinny?"

"Ask nothin'," remarked Red, "he jest nachurly walks up to C-80 an' sez, 'Kin I have the pleasure of ventilatin' yu?' an' C-80 he sez, 'If yu do it easy like,' sez he. Didn't he, Thompson?"

"They'll be some ventilatin' under th' table if yu fellows don't lemme alone; I'm hungry," complained Skinny.

"Say, Hopalong, I bets yu I kin clean up C-80 all by my lonesome," announced Buck, winking at Red.

"Yah! Yu onct tried to clean up the Bend, Buckie, an' if Pete an' Billy hadn't afound yu when they come by Eagle Pass that night yu wouldn't be here eatin' beef by th' pound," glancing at the hard-working Hopalong. "It was plum' lucky fer yu that they was acourtin' that time, wasn't it, Hopalong?" suddenly asked Red. Hopalong nearly strangled in his efforts to speak. He gave it up and nodded his head.

"Why can't yu git it straight, Connors? I wasn't doin' no courtin', it was Pete. I runned into him on th' other side o' th' pass. I'd look fine acourtin', wouldn't I?" asked the downtrodden Williams.

Pete Wilson skillfully flipped a potato into that worthy's coffee, spilling the beverage of the questionable name over a large expanse of blue flannel shirt. "Yu's all right, yu are. Why, when I meets yu, yu was lost in th' arms of yore lady-love. All I could see was yore feet. Go an' git tangled up with a two hundred and forty pound half-breed squaw an' then try to lay it onter me! When I proposed drownin' yore troubles over at Cowan's, yu went an' got mad over what yu called th' insinooation. An' yu shore didn't look any too blamed fine, neither."

"All th' same," volunteered Thompson, who had taken the edge from his appetite, "we better go over an' pay C-80 a call. I don't like what Shorty said about saltin' our cattle. He'll shore do it, unless I camps on th' line, which same I hain't hankerin' after."

"Oh, he wouldn't stop th' cows that way, Skinny; he was only afoolin'," exclaimed Connors meekly.

"Foolin' yore gran'mother! That there bunch'll do anything if we wasn't lookin'," hotly replied Skinny.

"That's shore nuff gospel, Thomp. They's sore fer mor'n one thing. They got aplenty when Buck went on th' warpath, an' they's hankerin' to git square," remarked Johnny Nelson, stealing the pie, a rare treat, of his neighbor when that unfortunate individual was not looking. He had it halfway to his mouth when its former owner, Jimmy Price, a boy of eighteen, turned his head and saw it going.

"Hi-yi! Yu clay-bank coyote, drap thet pie! Did yu ever see such a son-of-a-gun fer pie?" he plaintively asked Red Connors, as he grabbed a mighty handful of apples and crust. "Pie'll kill yu some day, yu bobtailed jack! I had an uncle that died onct. He et too much pie an' he went an' turned green, an' so'll yu if yu don't let it alone."

"Yu ought'r seed th' pie Johnny had down in Eagle Flat," murmured Lanky Smith reminiscently. "She had feet that'd stop a stam*pede*. Johnny was shore loco about her. Swore she was the finest blossom that ever growed." Here he choked and tears of laughter coursed down his weather-beaten face as he pictured her. "She was about fifteen han's high an' about sixteen han's around. Johnny used to chalk off when he hugged her, usen't yu, Johnny? One night when he had got purty well around on th' second lap he run inter a man jest startin' out on his fust. They hain't caught that Mexican yet."

Nelson was pelted with everything in sight. He slowly wiped off the pie crust and bread and potatoes. "Anybody'd think I was a busted grub wagon," he grumbled. When he had fished the last piece of beef out of his ear he went out and offered to stand treat. As the roundup was over, they slid into their saddles and raced for Cowan's saloon at Buckskin.

CHAPTER 2

The Rashness of Shorty

Buckskin was very hot; in fact it was never anything else. Few people were on the streets and the town was quiet. Over in the Houston hotel a crowd of cowboys was lounging in the barroom. They were very quiet—a condition as rare as it was ominous. Their mounts, twelve in all, were switching flies from their quivering skins in the corral at the rear. Eight of these had a large C-80 branded on their flanks; the other four, a Double Arrow.

In the barroom a slim, wiry man was looking out of the dirty window up the street at Cowan's saloon. Shorty was complaining, "They shore oughter be here now. They rounded up last week." The man nearest assured him that they would come. The man at the window turned and said, "They's yer now."

In front of Cowan's a crowd of nine happy-go-lucky, daredevil riders were sliding from their saddles. They threw the reins over the heads of their mounts and filed in to the bar. Laughter issued from the open door and the clink of glasses could be heard. They stood in picturesque groups, strong, self-reliant, humorous, virile. Their expensive sombreros were pushed far back on their heads and their hairy chaps were covered with the alkali dust from their ride.

Cowan, bottle in hand, pushed out several more glasses. He kicked a dog from under his feet and looked at Buck. "Rounded up yet?" he inquired.

"Shore, day afore yisterday," came the reply. The rest were busy removing the dust from their throats, and gradually drifted into groups of two or three. One of these groups strolled over to the solitary card table, and found Jimmy Price resting in a cheap chair, his legs on the table.

"I wisht yu'd extricate yore delicate feet from off'n this hyar table, James," humbly requested Lanky Smith, morally backed up by those with him.

"Ya-as, they shore is delicate, Mr. Smith," responded Jimmy, without moving.

"We wants to play draw, Jimmy," explained Pete.

"Yore shore welcome to play if yu wants to. Didn't I tell yu when yu growed that mustache that yu didn't have to ask me anymore?" queried the placid James, paternally.

"Call 'em off, sonny. Pete sez he kin clean me out. Anyhow, yu kin have the fust deal," compromised Lanky.

"I'm shore sorry fer Pete if he cayn't. Yu don't reckon I has to have fust deal to beat yu fellers, do yu? Go way an' lemme alone; I never seed such a bunch fer buttin' in as yu fellers."

Billy Williams returned to the bar. Then he walked along it until he was behind the recalcitrant possessor of the table. While his aggrieved friends shuffled their feet uneasily to cover his approach, he tiptoed up behind Jimmy and, with a nod, grasped that indignant individual firmly by the neck while the others grabbed his feet. They carried him, twisting and bucking, to the middle of the street and deposited him in the dust, returning to the now-vacant table.

Jimmy rested quietly for a few seconds and then slowly arose, dusting the alkali from him. "Th' wall-eyed piruts," he muttered, and then scratched his head for a way to "play hunk." As he gazed sorrowfully at the saloon he heard a snicker from behind him. He, thinking it was one of his late tormentors, paid no attention to it. Then a cynical, biting laugh stung him. He wheeled, to see Shorty leaning against a tree, a sneering leer on his flushed face. Shorty's right hand was suspended above his holster, hooked to his belt by the thumb—a favorite position of his when expecting trouble.

"One of yore reg'lar habits?" he drawled.

Jimmy began to dust himself in silence, but his lips were compressed to a thin white line.

"Does they hurt yu?" pursued the onlooker.

Jimmy looked up. "I heard tell that they make glue outen cayuses, sometimes," he remarked.

Shorty's eyes flashed. The loss of the horse had been rankling in his heart all day.

"Does they git yu frequent?" he asked. His voice sounded hard.

"Oh, 'bout as frequent as yu lose a cayuse, I reckon," replied Jimmy hotly.

Shorty's hand streaked to his holster and Jimmy followed his lead. Jimmy's Colt was caught. He had bucked too much. As he fell Shorty ran for the Houston House.

Pistol shots were common, for they were the universal method of expressing emotions. The poker players grinned, thinking their victim was letting off his indignation. Lanky sized up his hand and remarked half audibly, "He's a shore good kid."

The bartender, fearing for his new beveled, gilt-framed mirror, gave a hasty glance out the window. He turned around, made change and remarked to Buck, "Yore kid, Jimmy, is plugged." Several of the more credulous craned their necks to see, Buck being the first. "Hell!" he shouted, and ran out to where Jimmy lay coughing, his toes twitching. The saloon was deserted and a crowd of angry cowboys surrounded their chum—a boy. Buck had seen Shorty enter the door of the Houston House and he swore. "Chase them damn cayuses behind th' saloon, Pete, an' git under cover."

Jimmy was choking and he coughed up blood. "He's shore—got me. My—gun stuck," he added apologetically. He tried to sit up, but was not able and he looked surprised. "It's purty—damn hot—out here," he suggested. Johnny and Billy carried him in the saloon and placed him by the table, in the chair he had previously vacated. As they stood up he fell across the table and died.

Billy placed the dead boy's sombrero on his head and laid the refractory revolver on the table. "I wonder who th' shooter was." He looked at the slim figure and started to go out, followed by Johnny. As he reached the threshold a bullet zipped past him and thudded into the frame of the door. He backed away and looked surprised. "That's Shorty's shootin'—he allus misses 'bout that much." He looked out and saw Buck standing behind the live oak that Shorty had leaned against, firing at the hotel. Turning around he made for the rear, remarking to Johnny that "they's in th' Houston." Johnny looked at the quiet figure in the chair and swore softly. He followed Billy. Cowan, closing the door and taking a .60-caliber buffalo gun from under the bar, went out also and slammed the rear door forcibly.

CHAPTER 3

The Argument

Up the street two hundred yards from the Houston House Skinny and Pete lay hidden behind a boulder. Three hundred yards on the other side of the hotel Johnny and Billy were stretched out in an arroyo. Buck was lying down now, and Hopalong, from his position in the barn belonging to the hotel, was methodically dropping the horses of the besieged, a job he hated as much as he hated poison. The corral was their death trap. Red and Lanky were emitting clouds of smoke from behind the store, immediately across the street from the barroom. A .60-caliber buffalo gun roared down by the plaza and several Sharps cracked a protest from different points. The town had awakened and the shots were dropping steadily.

Strange noises filled the air. They grew in tone and volume and then dwindled away to nothing. The hum of the buffalo gun and the sobbing *pi-in-in-ing* of the Winchesters were liberally mixed with the sharp whines of the revolvers.

There were no windows in the hotel now. Raw furrows in the bleached wood showed yellow, and splinters mysteriously sprang from the casings. The panels of the door were producing cracks and the cheap door handle flew many ways at once. An empty whisky keg on the stoop boomed out mournfully at intervals and finally rolled down the steps with a rumbling protest. Wisps of smoke slowly climbed up the walls and seemed to be waving defiance to the curling wisps in the open.

Pete raised his shoulder to refill the magazine of his smoking rifle and dropped the cartridges all over his lap. He looked sheepishly at Skinny and began to load with his other hand.

"Yore plum' loco, yu are. Don't yu reckon they kin hit a blue shirt at two hundred?" Skinny cynically inquired. "Got one that time," he announced a second later.

"I wonder who's got th' buffalo," grunted Pete. "Mus' be Cowan," he replied to his own question and settled himself to use his left hand.

"Don't yu git Shorty; he's my meat," suggested Skinny.

"Yu better tell Buck—he ain't got no love fer Shorty," replied Pete, aiming carefully.

The panic in the corral ceased and Hopalong was now sending his regrets against the panels of the rear door. He had cut his last initial in the near panel and was starting a wobbly "H" in its neighbor. He was in a good position. There were no windows in the rear wall, and as the door was a very dangerous place he was not fired at.

He began to get tired of this one-sided business and crawled up on the window ledge, dangling his feet on the outside. He occasionally sent a bullet at a different part of the door, but amused himself by annoying Buck.

"Plenty hot down there?" he pleasantly inquired, and as he received no answer he tried again. "Better save some of them cartridges fer some other time, Buck."

Buck was sending .45 Winchesters into the shattered window with a precision that presaged evil to any of the defenders who were rash enough to try to gain the other end of the room.

Hopalong bit off a chew of tobacco and drowned a green fly that was crawling up the side of the barn. The yellow liquid streaked downward a short distance and was eagerly sucked up by the warped boards.

A spurt of smoke leaped from the battered door and the bored Hopalong promptly tumbled back inside. He felt of his arm, and then, delighted at the notice taken of his artistic efforts, shot several times from a crack on his right. "This yer's shore gittin' like home," he gravely remarked to the splinter that whizzed past his head. He shot again at the door and it sagged outward, accompanied by the thud of a falling body. "Pies like mother used to make," he announced to the empty loft as he slipped the magazine full of .45's. "An' pills like popper used to take," he continued when he had lowered the level of the liquor in his flask.

He rolled a cigarette and tossed the match into the air, extinguishing it by a shot from his Colt.

"Got any cigarettes, Hoppy?" said a voice from below.

"Shore," replied the joyous puncher, recognizing Pete; "how'd yu git here?"

"Like a cow. Busy?"

"None whatever. Comin' up?"

"Nope. Skinny wants a smoke too."

Hopalong handed tobacco and papers down the hole. "So long."

"So long," replied the daring Pete, who risked death twice for a smoke.

The hot afternoon dragged along and about three o'clock Buck held up an empty cartridge belt to the gaze of the curious Hopalong. That observant worthy nodded and threw a double handful of cartridges, one by one, to the patient and unrelenting Buck, who filled his gun and piled the few remaining ones up at his side. "Th' lives of mice and men gang aft all wrong," he remarked at random.

"Th' son-of-a-gun's talkin' Shakespeare," marveled Hopalong.

"Satiate any, Buck?" he asked as that worthy settled down to await his chance.

"Two," he replied, "Shorty an' another. Plenty damn hot down here," he complained. A spurt of alkali dust stung his face but the hand that made it never made another. "Three," he called. "How many, Hoppy?"

"One. That's four. Wonder if th' others got any?"

"Pete said Skinny got one," replied the intent Buck.

"Th' son-of-a-gun, he never said nothin' about it, an' me a fillin' his ornery paws with smokin'." Hopalong was indignant.

"Bet yu ten we don't git 'em afore dark," he announced.

"Got yu. Go yu ten more I gits another," promptly responded Buck.

"That's a shore cinch. Make her twenty."

"She is."

"Yu'll have to square it with Skinny, he shore wanted Shorty plum' bad," Hopalong informed the unerring marksman.

"Why didn't he say suthin' about it? Anyhow, Jimmy was my bunkie."

Hopalong's cigarette disintegrated and the board at his left received a hole. He promptly disappeared and Buck laughed. He sat up in the loft and angrily spat the soaked paper out from between his lips.

"All that trouble fer nothin', th' white-eyed coyote," he muttered. Then he crawled around to one side and fired at the center of his "C." Another shot hurtled at him and his left arm fell to his side. "That's funny—wonder where th' damn pirut is?" He looked out cautiously and saw a cloud of smoke over a knothole which was situated close up under the eaves of the barroom; and it was being agitated. Someone was blowing at it to make it disappear. He aimed very carefully at the knot and fired. He heard a sound between a curse and a squawk and was not molested any further from that point.

"I knowed he'd git hurt," he explained to the bandage, torn from the edge of his kerchief, which he carefully bound around his last wound.

Down in the arroyo Johnny was complaining.

"This yer's a no-good bunk," he plaintively remarked.

"It shore ain't—but it's th' best we kin find," apologized Billy.

"That's th' sixth that feller sent up there. He's a damn poor shot," observed Johnny; "must be Shorty."

"Shorty kin shoot plum' good—tain't him," contradicted Billy.

"Yas—with a six-shooter. He's off'n his feed with a rifle," explained Johnny.

"Yu wants to stay down from up there, yu ijit," warned Billy as the disgusted Johnny crawled up the bank. He slid down again with a welt on his neck.

"That's somebody else now. He oughter a done better'n that," he said.

Billy had fired as Johnny started to slide and he smoothed his aggrieved chum. "He could onct, yu means."

"Did yu git him?" asked the anxious Johnny, rubbing his welt.

"Plum' center," responded the businesslike Billy. "Go up agin, mebby I kin git another," he suggested tentatively.

"Mebby you kin go to hell. I ain't no gallery," grinned the now-exuberant owner of the welt.

"Who's got th' buffalo?" he inquired as the .60 caliber roared.

"Mus' be Cowan. He's shore all right. Sounds like a bloomin' cannon," replied Billy. "Lemme alone with yore fool questions, I'm busy," he complained as his talkative partner started to ask another. "Go an' git me some water—I'm alkalied. An' git some .45's, mine's purty near gone."

Johnny crawled down the arroyo and reappeared at Hopalong's barn.

As he entered the door a handful of empty shells fell on his hat and dropped to the floor. He shook his head and remarked, "That mus' be that fool Hopalong."

"Yore shore right. How's business?" inquired the festive Cassidy.

"Purty fair. Billy's got one. How many's gone?"

"Buck's got three, I got two and Skinny's got one. That's six, an' Billy's is seven. They's five more," he replied.

"How'd yu know?" queried Johnny as he filled his flask at the horse trough.

"Because they's twelve cayuses behind th' hotel. That's why."

"They might git away on 'em," suggested the practical Johnny.

"Can't. They's all cashed in."

"Yu said that they's five left," ejaculated the puzzled water-carrier.

"Yah; yore a smart cuss, ain't yu?"

Johnny grinned and then said, "Got any smokin'?"

Hopalong looked grieved. "I ain't no store. Why don't yu git generous and buy some?"

He partially filled Johnny's hand, and as he put the sadly depleted bag away he inquired, "Got any papers?"

"Nope."

"Got any matches?" he asked cynically.

"Nope."

"Kin yu smoke 'em?" he yelled, indignantly.

"Sure nuff," placidly replied the unruffled Johnny. "Billy wants some .45's."

Hopalong gasped. "Don't he want my gun, too?"

"Nope. Got a better one. Hurry up, he'll git mad."

Hopalong was a very methodical person. He was the only one of his crowd to carry a second cartridge strap. It hung over his right shoulder and rested on his left hip, holding one hundred cartridges and his second Colt. His waist belt held fifty cartridges and all would fit both the rifle and revolvers. He extracted twenty from that part of the shoulder strap hardest to get at, the back, by simply pulling it over his shoulder and plucking out the bullets as they came into reach.

"That's all yu kin have. I'm *Buck's* ammernition jackass," he explained. "Bet yu ten we gits 'em afore dark"—he was hedging.

"Any fool knows that. I'll take yu if yu bets th' other way," responded Johnny, grinning. He knew Hopalong's weak spot.

"Yore on," promptly responded Hopalong, who would bet on anything.

"Well, so long," said Johnny as he crawled away.

"Hey, yu, Johnny!" called out Hopalong, "don't yu go an' tell anybody I got any pills left. I ain't no ars'nal."

Johnny replied by elevating one foot and waving it. Then he disappeared.

Behind the store, the most precarious position among the besiegers, Red Connors and Lanky Smith were ensconced and commanded a view of the entire length of the barroom. They could see the dark mass they knew to be the rear door and derived a great amount of amusement from the spots of light which were appearing in it.

They watched the "C" (reversed to them) appear and be completed. When the wobbly "H" grew to completion they laughed heartily. Then the hardwood bar had been dragged across their field of vision and up to the front windows, and they could only see the indiscriminate holes which appeared in the upper panels at frequent intervals.

Every time they fired they had to expose a part of themselves to a return shot, with the result that Lanky's forearm was seared its entire length. Red had been more fortunate and only had a bruised ear.

They laboriously rolled several large rocks out in the open, pushing them beyond the shelter of the store with their rifles. When they had crawled behind them they each had another wound. From their new position they could see Hopalong sitting in his window. He promptly waved his sombrero and grinned.

They were the most experienced fighters of all except Buck, and were saving their shots. When they did shoot they always had some portion of a man's body to aim at, and the damage they inflicted was considerable. They said nothing, being older than the rest and more taciturn, and they were not reckless. Although Hopalong's antics made them laugh, they grumbled at his recklessness and were not tempted to emulate him. It was noticeable, too, that they shoved their rifles out simultaneously and, although both were aiming, only one fired. Lanky's gun cracked so close to the enemy's that the whirr of the bullet over Red's head was merged in the crack of his partner's reply.

When Hopalong saw the rocks roll out from behind the store he grew very curious. Then he saw a flash, followed instantly by another from the second rifle. He saw several of these follow shots and could sit in silence no longer. He waved his hat to attract attention and then shouted, "How many?" A shot was sent straight up in the air and he notified Buck that there were only four left.

The fire of these four grew less rapid—they were saving their ammunition. A potshot at Hopalong sent that gentleman's rifle hurtling to the ground. Another tore through his hat, removing a neat amount of skin and hair and giving him a lifelong part. He fell back inside and proceeded to shoot fast and straight with his revolvers, his head burning as though on fire. When he had vented the dangerous pressure of his anger he went below and tried to fish the rifle in with a long stick. It was obdurate, so he sent three more shots into the door, and, receiving no reply, ran out around the corner of his shelter and grasped the weapon. When halfway back he sank to the ground. Before another shot could be fired at him with any judgment a ripping, spitting rifle was being frantically worked from the barn. The bullets tore the door into seams and gaps; the lowest panel, the one having the "H" in it, fell inward in chunks. Johnny had returned for another smoke.

Hopalong, still grasping the rifle, rolled rapidly around the corner of the barn. He endeavored to stand, but could not. Johnny, hearing rapid and fluent swearing, came out.

"Where'd they git yu?" he asked.

"In th' off leg. Hurts like hell. Did yu git him?"

"Nope. I jest come fer another cig; got any left?"

"Up above. Yore gall is shore appallin'. Help me in, yu two-laigged jackass."

"Shore. We'll shore pay our 'tentions to that door. She'll go purty soon—she's as full of holes as th' Bad Lan's," replied Johnny. "Git aholt an' hop along, Hopalong."

He helped the swearing Hopalong inside, and then the lead they pumped into the wrecked door was scandalous. Another panel fell in and Hopalong's "C" was destroyed. A wide crack appeared in the one above it and grew rapidly. Its mate began to gape and finally both were driven in. The increase in the light caused by these openings allowed Red and Lanky to secure better aim and soon the fire of the defenders died out.

Johnny dropped his rifle and, drawing his six-shooter, ran out and dashed for the dilapidated door, while Hopalong covered that opening with a fusillade.

As Johnny's shoulder sent the framework flying inward he narrowly missed sudden death. As it was he staggered to the side, out of range, and dropped full-length to the ground, flat on his face. Hopalong's rifle cracked incessantly, but to no avail. The man who had fired the shot was dead. Buck got him immediately after he had shot Johnny.

Calling to Skinny and Red to cover him, Buck sprinted to where Johnny lay gasping. The bullet had entered his breast, just missed his lungs and had passed out his back. Buck, Colt in hand, leaped through the door, but met with no resistance. He signaled to Hopalong, who yelled, "They's none left."

The trees and rocks and gullies and buildings yielded men who soon crowded around the hotel. A young doctor, lately graduated, appeared. It was his first case, but he eased Johnny and saved his life. Then he went over to Hopalong, who was now raving, and attended to him. The others were patched up as well as possible and the struggling young physician had his pockets crammed full of gold and silver coins.

The scene of the wrecked barroom was indescribable. Holes, furrows, shattered glass and bottles, the liquor oozing down the walls of the shelves and running over the floor; the ruined furniture, a wrecked bar, seared and shattered and covered with blood; bodies as they had been piled in the corners; ropes, shells, hats; and liquor everywhere, over everything, met the gaze of those who had caused the chaos.

Perry's Bend had failed to wipe out the score.

CHAPTER 4

The Vagrant Sioux

Buckskin gradually readjusted itself to the conditions which had existed before its sudden leap into the limelight as a town which did things. The soirée at the Houston House had drifted into the past, and was now substantially established as an epoch in the history of the town. Exuberant joy gave way to dignity and deprecation, and to solid satisfaction; and the conversations across the bar brought forth parallels of the affair to be judged impartially—and the impartial judgment was, unanimously, that while there had undoubtedly been good fights before Perry's Bend had disturbed the local quiet, they were not quite up to the new standard of strenuous hospitality. Finally the heat blistered everything back into the old state, and the shadows continued to be in demand.

One afternoon, a month after the reception of the honorable delegation from Perry's Bend, the town of Buckskin seemed desolated, and the earth and the buildings thereon were as huge furnaces radiating a visible heat, but when the blazing sun had begun to settle in the west it awoke with a clamor which might have been laid to the efforts of a zealous Satan. At this time it became the Mecca of two score or more joyous cowboys from the neighboring ranches, who livened things as those knights of the saddle could.

In the scant but heavy shadow of Cowan's saloon sat a picturesque figure from whom came guttural, resonant rumblings which mingled in a spirit of loneliness with the fretful sighs of a flea-tormented dog. Both dog and master were vagrants, and they were tolerated because it was a matter of supreme indifference as to who came or how long they stayed as long as the ethics and the unwritten law of the cow country were inviolate. And the breaking of these caused no unnecessary anxiety, for justice was both speedy and sure.

When the outcast Sioux and his yellow dog had drifted into town some few months before they had caused neither expostulation nor inquiry, as the cardinal virtue of that whole broad land was to ask a man no questions which might prove embarrassing to all concerned; judgment was of observation, not of history, and a man's past would reveal itself through actions. It mattered little whether he was an embezzler or the wild chip from some prosperous eastern block, as men came to the range to forget and to lose touch with the pampered East; and the range absorbed them as its own. A man was only a man when he had the qualities necessary; and the illiterate who could ride and shoot and live to himself was far more esteemed than the educated who could not do those things. The more a man depends upon himself and the closer is his contact to a quick judgment the more laconic and even-poised he becomes. And the knowledge that he is himself a judge tends to create caution and judgment. He has no court to uphold his honor and to offer him protection, so he must be quick to protect himself and to maintain his own standing. His nature saved him, or it executed; and the range absolved him of all unpaid penalties of a careless past. He became a man born again and he took up his burden, the exactions of a new environment, and he lived as long as those exactions gave him the right to live. He must tolerate no restrictions of his natural rights, and he must not restrict; for the one would proclaim him a coward, the other a bully; and both received short shrifts in that land of the self-protected. The basic law of nature is the survival of the fittest.

So, when the wanderers found their level in Buckskin they were not even asked by what name men knew them. Not caring to hear a name which might not harmonize with their idea of the fitness of things, the cowboys of the Bar-20 had, with a freedom born of excellent livers and fearless temperaments, bestowed names befitting their sense of humor and adaptability. The official title of the Sioux was By-and-by; the dog was known as Fleas. Never had names more clearly described the objects to be represented, for they were excellent examples of cowboy discernment and aptitude.

In their eyes By-and-by was a man. He could feel and he could resent insults. With them he had a right to enjoy his life as he saw fit so long as he did not trespass on or restrict the rights of others. They were not analytic in temperament, neither were they moralists. He was not a menace to society, because society had superb defenses. So they vaguely recognized his many poor qualities and clearly saw his few good ones. He could shoot, when permitted, with the best; no horse, however refractory, had ever been known to throw him; he was an adept at following the trails left by rustlers, and that was an asset; he became of value to the community; he was an economic factor. His ability to consume liquor with indifferent effects raised him another notch in their estimation. He was not always talking when someone else wished to—another count. There remained about him that stoical indifference to the petty; that observant nonchalance; and a dignity common to chieftains. He was a log of grave deference which tossed on their sea of mischievous hilarity.

He wore a pair of corduroy trousers, known to the carefree as "pants," which were held together by numerous patches of what had once been brilliantly colored calico. A pair of suspenders, torn into two separate straps, made a belt for himself and a collar for his dog. The trousers had probably been secured during a fit of absentmindedness on his part when their former owner had not been looking. Tucked at intervals in the top of the corduroys (the exceptions making convenient shelves for alkali dust) was what at one time had been a stiff-bosomed shirt. This was open down the front and back, the weight of the trousers on the belt holding it firmly on the square shoulders of the wearer, thus precluding the necessity of collar buttons. A pair of moccasins, beautifully worked with wampum, protected his feet from the onslaughts of cacti and the inquisitive and pugnacious sand flies; and lying across his lap was a repeating Winchester rifle.

The two were contented and happy. They had no cares nor duties, and their pleasures were simple and easily secured, as they consisted of sleep and a proneness to avoid moving. Like the untrammeled coyote, their bed was where sleep overtook them; their food, what the night wrapped in a sense of security, or the generosity of the cowboys of the Bar-20. No cowboy ever knew so little of responsibility or as much unadulterated content. There is a penalty even to civilization and ambition.

When the sun had cast its shadows beyond By-and-by's feet the air became charged with noise; shouts, shots and the rolling thunder of madly pounding hoofs echoed flatly throughout the town. By-and-by yawned, stretched and leaned back, reveling in the semiconscious ecstasy of the knowledge that he did not have to immediately get up. Fleas opened one eye and cocked an ear in inquiry, and then rolled over on his back, squirmed and sighed contentedly and long. The outfit of the Bar-20 had come to town.

The noise came rapidly nearer and increased in volume as the riders turned the corner and drew rein suddenly, causing their mounts to slide on their haunches in ankle-deep dust.

"Hullo, old Buck-with-th'-pants, how's yore liver?"

"Come up an' irrigate, old tank!"

"Chase th' flea ranch an' trail along!"

These were a few of the salutations discernible among the medley of playful yells, the safety valves of supercharged good-nature.

"Skr-e-e!" yelled Hopalong Cassidy, letting off a fusillade of shots in the vicinity of Fleas, who rapidly retreated around the corner, where he wagged his tail in eager expectation. He was not disappointed, for a cow pony tore around in pursuit and Hopalong leaned over and scratched the yellow back, thumping it heartily, and, tossing a chunk of beef into the open jaws of the delighted dog, departed as he had come. The advent of the outfit meant a square meal, and the dog knew it.

In Cowan's, lined up against the bar, the others were earnestly and assiduously endeavoring, with a promise of success, to get By-and-by drunk, which endeavors coincided perfectly with By-and-by's idea of the fitness of things. The fellowship and the liquor combined to thaw out his reserve and to loosen his tongue. After gazing with an air of injured surprise at the genial loosening of his knees he gravely handed his rifle with an exaggerated sweep of his arm, to the cowboy nearest him, and wrapped his arms around the recipient to insure his balance. The rifle was passed from hand to hand until it came to Buck Peters, who gravely presented it to its owner as a new gun.

By-and-by threw out his stomach in an endeavor to keep his head in line with his heels, and grasping the weapon with both hands turned to Cowan, to whom he gave it.

"Yu hab this un. Me got two. Me keep new un, mebbyso." Then he loosened his belt and drank long and deep.

A shadow darkened the doorway and Hopalong limped in. Spying By-and-by pushing the bottle into his mouth, while Red Connors propped him, he grinned and took out five silver dollars, which he jingled under By-and-by's eyes, causing that worthy to lay aside the liquor and erratically grab for the tantalizing fortune.

"Not yet," said Hopalong, changing the position of the money. "If yu wants to corral this here herd of simoleons yu has to ride a cayuse what Red bet me yu can't ride. Yu has got to grow on that there saddle and stayed growed for five whole minutes by Buck's ticker. I ain't a-goin' to tell yu he's any sawhorse, and yu'd know better, as yu reckons Red wouldn't bet on no losin' proposition if he knowed better, which same he don't. Yu straddles that four-laigged cloudburst an' yu gets these. I ain't seen th' cayuse yet that yu couldn't freeze to, an' I'm backin' my opinions with my moral support an' one month's pay."

By-and-by's eyes began to glitter as the meaning of the words sifted through his befuddled mind. Ride a horse—five dollars—then he straightened up and began to speak in an incoherent jumble of Sioux and bad English. He, the mighty rider of the Sioux; he, the bravest warrior and the greatest hunter; could he ride a horse for five dollars? Well, he rather thought he could. Grasping Red by the shoulder, he tacked for the door and narrowly missed hitting the bottom step first, landing, as it happened, in the soft dust. Somewhat sobered by the jar, he stood up and apologized to the crowd.

The outfit of the Bar-20 was, perhaps, the most famous of all from Canada to the Rio Grande. The foreman, Buck Peters, controlled a crowd of men (who had all the instincts of boys) that had shown no quarter to many rustlers, and who, while always carefree and easygoing (even fighting with great good humor and carelessness), had established the reputation of being the most reckless gang of daredevil gunfighters that ever pounded leather. Crooked gaming houses, from El Paso to Cheyenne and from Phoenix to Leavenworth, unanimously and enthusiastically damned them from their boots to their sombreros, and the sheriffs and marshals of many localities had received from their hands most timely assistance—and some trouble. Wiry, indomitable, boyish and generous, they were splendid examples of virile manhood; and, surrounded as they were with great dangers and a unique civilization, they should not, in justice, be judged by opinions born of the commonplace.

They were real cowboys, which means, public opinion to the contrary notwithstanding, that they were not lawless, nor drunken, shooting bullies who held life cheaply, as their kin has been unjustly pictured; but while these men were naturally peaceable they had to continually rub elbows with men who were not. Gamblers, criminals, bullies and the riffraff that fled from the protected East had drifted among them in great numbers, and it was this class that caused the trouble. The hardworking "cowpunchers" lived according to the law of the land, and they obeyed that greatest of all laws, that of self-preservation. Their fun was boisterous, but they paid for all the damage they inflicted; their work was one continual hardship, and the reaction of one extreme swings far toward the limit of its antithesis. Go back to the Apple if you would trace the beginning of self-preservation and the need.

Buck Peters was a man of mild appearance, somewhat slow of speech and correspondingly quick of action, who never became flurried. His was the master hand that controlled, and his Colts enjoyed the reputation of never missing when a hit could have been expected with reason. Many floods, stampedes and blizzards had assailed his nerves, but he yet could pour a glass of liquor, held at arm's length, through a knothole in the floor without wetting the wood.

Next in age came Lanky Smith, a small, undersized man of retiring disposition. Then came Skinny Thompson, six feet four on his bared soles, and true to his name; Hopalong described him as "th' shadow of a chalk mark." Pete Wilson, the slow-witted and very taciturn, and Billy Williams, the wavering pessimist, were of ordinary height and appearance. Red Connors, with hair that shamed the name, was the possessor of a temper which was as dry as tinder; his greatness weakness was his regard for the rifle as a means of preserving peace. Johnny Nelson was the protégé, and he could do no wrong. The last, Hopalong Cassidy, was a combination of irresponsibility, humor, good nature, love of fighting, and nonchalance when face-to-face with danger. His most prominent attribute was that of always getting into trouble without any intention of so doing; in fact, he was much aggrieved and surprised when it came. It seemed as though when any "bad man" desired to add to his reputation he invariably selected Hopalong as the means (a fact due, perhaps, to the perversity of things in general). Bad men became scarce soon after Hopalong became a fixture in any locality. He had been crippled some years before in a successful attempt to prevent the assassination of a friend, Sheriff Harris, of Albuquerque, and he still possessed a limp.

When Red had relieved his feelings and had dug the alkali out of his ears and eyes, he led the Sioux to the rear of the saloon, where a "pinto" was busily engaged in endeavoring to pitch a saddle from his back, employing the intervals in trying to see how much of the picket rope he could wrap around his legs.

When By-and-bye saw what he was expected to ride he felt somewhat relieved, for the pony did not appear to have more than the ordinary amount of cussedness. He waved his hand, and Johnny and Red bandaged the animal's eyes, which quieted him at once, and then they untangled the rope from around his legs and saw that the cinches were secure. Motioning to By-and-by that all was ready, they jerked the bandage off as the Indian settled himself in the saddle.

Had By-and-by been really sober he would have taken the conceit out of that pony in chunks, and as it was he experienced no great difficulty in holding his seat; but in his addled state of mind he grasped the end of the cinch strap in such a way that when the pony jumped forward in its last desperate effort the buckle slipped and the cinch became unfastened; and By-and-by, still seated in the saddle, flew headforemost into the horse trough, where he spilled much water.

As this happened Cowan turned the corner, and when he saw the wasted water (which he had to carry, bucketful at a time, from the wells a good quarter of a mile away) his anger blazed forth, and yelling, he ran for the drenched Sioux, who was just crawling out of his bath. When the unfortunate saw the irate man bearing down on him he sputtered in rage and fear, and, turning, he ran down the street, with Cowan thundering flat-footedly behind on a fat man's gallop, to the hysterical cheers of the delighted outfit, who saw in it nothing but a good joke.

When Cowan returned from his hopeless task, blowing and wheezing, he heard sundry remarks, which were not calculated to increase his opinion of his physical condition.

"Seems to me," remarked the irrepressible Hopalong, "that one of those cayuses has got th' heaves."

"It shore sounds like it," acquiesced Johnny, red in the face from holding in his laughter, "an' say, somebody interferes."

"All knock-kneed animals do, yu heathen," supplied Red.

"Hey, yu, let up on that an' have a drink on th' house," invited Cowan. "If I gits that damn Sioux I'll make yu think there's been a cyclone. I'll see how long that bum hangs around this here place, I will."

Red's eyes narrowed and his temper got the upper hand. "He ain't no bum when yu gives him rotgut at a quarter of a dollar a glass, is he? Anytime that 'bum' gits razzled out for nothin' more'n this, why, I goes too; an' I ain't sayin' nothin' about goin' peaceable-like, neither."

"I knowed somethin' like this 'ud happen," dolefully sang out Billy Williams, strong on the side of his pessimism.

"For th' Lord's sake, have yu broke out?" asked Red, disgustedly. "I'm goin' to hit the trail—but just keep this afore yore mind: if By-and-by gits in any accidents or ain't in sight when I comes to town again, this here climate'll be a damn sight hotter'n it is now. No hard feelings? It's just a casual bit of advice. Come on, fellows, let's amble—I'm hungry."

As they raced across the plain toward the ranch a pair of beady eyes, snapping with a drunken rage, watched them from an arroyo; and when Cowan entered the saloon the next morning he could not find By-and-by's rifle, which he had placed behind the bar. He also missed a handful of cartridges from the box near the cash drawer; and had he looked closely at his bottled whiskey he would have noticed a loss there. A horse was missing from a Mexican's corral and there were rumors that several Indians had been seen far out on the plain.

CHAPTER 5

The Law of the Range

Phew! I'm shore hungry," said Hopalong, as he and Red dismounted at the ranch the next morning for breakfast. "Wonder what's good for it?"

"They's three things that's good for famine," said Red, leading the way to the bunkhouse. "Yu can pull in yore belt, yu can drink, an' yu can eat. Yore getting as bad as Johnny—but he's young yet."

The others met their entrance with a volley of good-humored banter, some of which was so personal and evoked such responses that it sounded like the preliminary skirmish to a fight. But under all was that soft accent, that drawl of humorous appreciation and eyes twinkling in suppressed merriment. Here they were thoroughly at home and the spirit of comradeship manifested itself in many subtle ways; the wit became more daring and sharp. Billy lost some of his pessimism, and the alertness disappeared from their manner.

Skinny left off romping with Red and yawned. "I wish that cook'ud wake up an' git breakfast. He's the cussedest thing I ever saw—he kin go to sleep standin' up an' not know it. *Johnny's* th' boy that worries him—th' kid comes in an' whoops things up till he's gorged himself."

"Johnny's got th' most appallin' feel for grub of anybody I knows," added Red. "I wonder what's keepin' him—he's usually bangin' around here bawlin' for his grub like a spoiled calf, long afore Cookie's got th' fire goin'."

"Mebby he rustled some grub out with him—I saw him tiptoein' out of th' gallery this mornin' when I come back for my cigs," remarked Hopalong, glancing at Billy.

Billy groaned and made for the gallery. Emerging half a minute later he blurted out his tale of woe: "Every time I blows myself an' don't drink it all in town some slab-sided maverick freezes to it. It's gone," he added, dismally.

"Too bad, Billy—but what is it?" asked Skinny.

"What is it? Wha'd yu think it was, yu emaciated match? *Jewelry? Cayuses?* It's whisky—two dollars' worth. Somethin's allus wrong. This here whole yearth's wrong."

"Will yu let up?" yelled Red, throwing a sombrero at the grumbling unfortunate. "Yu ask Buck where yore tanglefoot is."

"I'd shore look nice askin' th' *boss* if he'd rustled my whisky, *wouldn't I?* An' would yu mind throwin' somebody else's hat? I paid twenty wheels for that eight years ago, and I don't want it mussed none."

"Gee, yore easy! Why, Ah Sing, over at Albuquerque, gives them away every time yu gits yore shirt washed," gravely interposed Hopalong as he went out to cuss the cook.

"Well, what'd yu think of that?" exclaimed Billy in an injured tone.

"Oh, yu needn't be hikin' for Albuquerque—Washee-Washee'ud charge yu double for washin' yore shirt. Yu ought to fall in th' river someday—then he might talk business," called Hopalong over his shoulder as he heaved an old boot into the gallery. "Hey, yu hibernatin' son of morphine, if yu don't git them flapjacks in here pretty sudden-like I'll scatter yu all over th' landscape. Yu just wait till Johnny comes!"

"Wonder where th' kid is?" asked Lanky, rolling a cigarette.

"Off somewhere lookin' at th' sun through th' bottom of my bottle," grumbled Billy.

Hopalong started to go out, but halted on the sill and looked steadily off toward the northwest. "That's funny. Hey, fellows, here comes Buck an' Johnny ridin' double—on a walk, too!" he exclaimed. "Wonder what th'—thunder! Red, Buck's carryin' him! Somethin's busted!" he yelled, as he dashed for his pony and made for the newcomers.

"I told yu he was hittin' my bottle," pertly remarked Billy, as he followed the rest outside.

"Did yu ever see Johnny drunk? Did yu ever see him drink more'n two glasses? Shut yore wailin' face—they's somethin' worse'n that in this here," said Red, his temper rising. "Hopalong an' me took yore cheap liquor—it's under Pete's bunk," he added.

The trio approached on a walk and Johnny, delirious and covered with blood, was carried into the bunkhouse. Buck waited until all had assembled again and then, his face dark with anger, spoke sharply and without the usual drawl: "Skragged from behind, damn them! Get some grub an' water an' be quick. We'll see who the gent with th' grudge is."

At this point the expostulations of the indignant cook, who, not under-standing the cause, regarded the invasion of china-shop bulls as sacrilegious, came to his ears. Striding quickly to the door, he grabbed the pan the Mexican was about to throw and, turning the now frightened man around, thundered, "Keep quiet an' get 'em some grub."

When rifles and ammunition had been secured they mounted and followed him at a hard gallop along the back trail. No words were spoken, for none were necessary. All knew that they would not return until they had found the man for whom they were looking, even if the chase led to Canada. They did not ask Buck for any of the particulars, for the foreman was not in the humor to talk, and all, save Hopalong, whose curiosity was always on edge, recognized only two facts and cared for nothing else: Johnny had been ambushed and they were going to get the one who was responsible. They did not even conjecture as to who it might be, because the trail would lead them to the man himself, and it mattered nothing who or what he was—there was only one course to take with an assassin. So they said nothing, but rode on with squared jaws and set lips, the seven ponies breast to breast in a close arc.

Soon they came to an arroyo which they took at a leap. As they approached it they saw signs in the dust which told them that a body had lain there huddled up; and there were brown spots on the baked alkali. The trail they followed was now single, Buck having ridden along the bank of the arroyo when hunting for Johnny, for whom he had orders. This trail was very irregular, as if the horse had wan-dered at will. Suddenly they came upon five tracks, all pointing one way, and four of these turned abruptly and disappeared in the northwest. Half a mile beyond the point of separation was a chaparral, which was an important factor to them.

Each man knew just what had taken place as if he had been an eyewitness, for the trail was plain. The assassins had waited in the chaparral for Johnny to pass, probably having seen him riding that way. When he had passed and his back had been turned to them they had fired and wounded him severely at the first volley, for Johnny was of the stuff that fights back and his revolvers had showed full chambers and clean barrels when Red had examined them in the bunkhouse. Then they had given chase for a short distance and, from some in-explicable motive, probably fear, they had turned and ridden off without know-ing how bad he was hit. It was this trail that led to the northwest, and it was this trail that they followed without pausing.

When they had covered fifty miles they sighted the Cross Bar O ranch, where they hoped to secure fresh mounts. As they rode up to the ranch house the owner, Bud Wallace, came around the corner and saw them.

"Hullo, boys! What deviltry are yu up to now?" he asked.

Buck leaped from his mount, followed by the others, and shoved his sombrero back on his head as he started to remove the saddle.

"We're trailin' a bunch of murderers. They ambushed Johnny an' damn near killed him. I stopped here to get fresh cayuses."

"Yu did right!" replied Wallace heartily. Then raising his voice he shouted to some of his men who were near the corral to bring up the seven best horses they could rope. Then he told the cook to bring out plenty of food and drink.

"I got four punchers what ain't doin' nothin' but eat," he suggested.

"Much obliged, Wallace, but there's only four of 'em, an' we'd rather get 'em ourselves—Johnny'ud feel better," replied Buck, throwing his saddle on the horse that was led up to him.

"How's yore cartridges—got plenty?" persisted Wallace.

"Two hundred apiece," responded Buck, springing into his saddle and riding off. "So long," he called.

"So long, an' plug hell out of them," shouted Wallace as the dust swept over him.

At five in the afternoon they forded the Black River at a point where it crossed the state line from New Mexico, and at dusk camped at the base of the Guadalupe Mountains. At daybreak they took up the chase, grim and merciless, and shortly afterward they passed the smoldering remains of a campfire, showing that the pursued had been in a great hurry, for it should have been put out and masked. At noon they left the mountains to the rear and sighted the Barred Horseshoe, which they approached.

The owner of the ranch saw them coming, and from their appearance surmised that something was wrong.

"What is it?" he shouted. "Rustlers?"

"Nope. Murderers. I wants to swap cayuses quick," answered Buck.

"There they are. Th' boys just brought 'em in. Anything else I can let yu have?"

"Nope," shouted Buck as they galloped off.

"Somebody's goin' to get plugged full of holes," murmured the ranch owner as he watched them kicking up the dust in huge clouds.

After they had forded a tributary of the Rio Penasco near the Sacramento Mountains and had surmounted the opposite bank, Hopalong spurred his horse to the top of a hummock and swept the plain with Pete's field glasses, which he had borrowed for the occasion, and returned to the rest, who had kept on without slacking the pace. As he took up his former position he grunted, "Indians" and unslung his rifle, an example followed by the others. The ponies were now running at top speed, and as they shot over a rise their riders saw their quarry a mile and a half in advance. One of the Indians looked back and discharged his rifle in defiance, and it now became a race worthy of the name—Death fled from Death. The fresher mounts of the cowboys steadily cut down the distance and, as the rifles of the pursuers began to speak, the hard-pressed Indians made for the smaller of two knolls, the plain leading to the larger one being too heavily strewn with boulders to permit speed.

As the fugitives settled down behind the rocks which fringed the edge of their elevation a shot from one of them disabled Billy's arm, but had no other effect than to increase the score to be settled. The pursuers rode behind a rise and dismounted, from where, leaving their mounts protected, they scattered out to surround the knoll.

Hopalong, true to his curiosity, finally turned up on the highest point of the other knoll, a spur of the range in the west, for he always wanted to see all he could. Skinny, due to his fighting instinct, settled one hundred yards to the north and on the same spur. Buck lay hidden behind an enormous boulder eight hundred yards to the northeast of Skinny, and the same distance southeast of Buck was Red Connors, who was crawling up the bed of an arroyo. Billy, nursing his arm, lay in front of the horses, and Pete, from his position between Billy and Hopalong, was crawling from rock to rock in an endeavor to get near enough to use his Colts, his favorite and most effective weapons. Intermittent puffs of smoke arising from a point between Skinny and Buck showed where Lanky Smith was improving each shining hour.

There had been no directions given, each man choosing his own position, yet each was of strategic worth. Billy protected the horses, Hopalong and Skinny swept the knoll with a plunging fire, and Lanky and Buck lay in the course the besieged would most likely take if they tried a dash. Off to the east Red barred them from creeping down the arroyo, and from where Pete was he could creep up to within sixty yards if he chose the right rocks. The ranges varied from four hundred yards for Buck to sixty for Pete, and the others averaged close to three hundred, which allowed very good shooting on both sides.

Hopalong and Skinny gradually moved nearer to each other for companionship, and as the former raised his head to see what the others were doing he received a graze on the ear.

"Wow!" he yelled, rubbing the tingling member.

Two puffs of smoke floated up from the knoll, and Skinny swore.

"Where'd he get yu, Fat?" asked Hopalong.

"G'wan, don't get funny, son," replied Skinny.

Jets of smoke arose from the north and east, where Buck and Red were stationed, and Pete was halfway to the knoll. So far he hadn't been hit as he dodged in and out, and, emboldened by his luck, he made a run of five yards and his sombrero was shot from his head. Another dash and his empty holster was ripped from its support. As he crouched behind a rock he heard a yell from Hopalong, and saw that interested individual waving his sombrero to cheer him on. An angry *pang!* from the knoll caused that enthusiastic rooter to drop for safety.

"Locoed son-of-a-gun," complained Pete. "He'll shore git potted." Then he glanced at Billy, who was the center of several successive spurts of dust.

"How's business, Billy?" he called pleasantly.

"Oh, they'll git me yet," responded the pessimist. "Yu needn't git anxious. If that off buck wasn't so green he'd 'a' had me long ago."

"Ya-*hoo!* Pete! Oh, Pete!" called Hopalong, sticking his head out at one side and grinning as the wondering object of his hail craned his neck to see what the matter was.

"Huh?" grunted Pete, and then remembering the distance he shouted, "What's th' matter?"

"Got any cigarettes?" asked Hopalong.

"Yu damn sheep!" said Pete, and turning back to work he drove a .44 into a yellow moccasin.

Hopalong began to itch and he saw that he was near an ant hill. Then the cactus at his right boomed out mournfully and a hole appeared in it. He fired at the smoke and a yell informed him that he had made a hit. "Go 'way!" he complained as a green fly buzzed past his nose. Then he scratched each leg with the foot of the other and squirmed incessantly, kicking out with both feet at once. A warning metallic *whir-r-r!* on his left caused him to yank them in again, and turning his head quickly he had the pleasure of lopping off the head of a rattlesnake with his Colt's.

"Glad yu wasn't a copperhead," he exclaimed. "Somebody had ought 'a' shot that fool Noah. Damn the ants!" He drowned with a jet of tobacco juice a Gila monster that was staring at him and took a savage delight in its frantic efforts to bury itself.

Soon he heard Skinny swear and he sung out: "What's the matter, Skinny? Git plugged again?"

"Naw, bugs—ain't they hell?" plaintively asked his friend.

"They ain't none over here. What kind of bugs?"

"Sufferin' Moses, I ain't no bugologist! All kinds!"

But Hopalong got it at last. He had found tobacco and rolled a cigarette, and in reaching for a match exposed his shoulder to a shot that broke his collarbone. Skinny's rifle cracked in reply and the offending brave rolled out from behind a rock. From the fuss emanating from Hopalong's direction Skinny knew that his neighbor had been hit.

"Don't yu care, Hoppy. I got th' cuss," he said consolingly. "Where'd he git yu?" he asked.

"In th' heart, yu pie-faced nuisance. Come over here an' corral this cussed bandage an' gimme some water," snapped the injured man.

Skinny wormed his way through the thorny chaparral and bound up the shoulder. "Anything else?" he asked.

"Yes. Shoot that bunch of warts an' blow that tobacco-eyed Gila to Cheyenne. This here's worse than the time we cleaned out th' C-80 outfit!" Then he kicked the dead toad and swore at the sun.

"Close yore yap; yore worse than a kid! Anybody'd think yu never got plugged afore," said Skinny indignantly.

"I can cuss all I wants," replied Hopalong, proving his assertion as he grabbed his gun and fired at the dead Indian. A bullet whined above his head and Skinny fired at the smoke. He peeped out and saw that his friends were getting nearer to the knoll.

"They's closin' in now. We'll soon be gittin' home," he reported.

Hopalong looked out in time to see Buck make a dash for a boulder that lay ten yards in front of him, which he reached in safety. Lanky also ran in and Pete added five more yards to his advance. Buck made another dash but leaped into the air, and, coming down as if from an intentional high jump, staggered and stumbled for a few paces and then fell flat, rolling over and over toward the shelter of a split rock, where he lay quiet. A leering red face peered over the rocks on the knoll, but the whoop of exultation was cut short, for Red's rifle cracked and the warrior rolled down the steep bank, where another shot from the same gun settled him beyond question.

Hopalong choked and, turning his face away, angrily dashed his knuckles into his eyes. "Damn 'em! Damn 'em! They've got Buck! They've got Buck, damn 'em! They've got Buck, Skinny! Good old Buck! They've got him! Jimmy's gone, Johnny's plugged, and now Buck's gone! Come on!" he sobbed in a frenzy of vengeance. "Come on, Skinny! We'll tear their cussed hides into a deeper red than they are now! Oh, damn it, I can't see—where's my gun?" He groped for the rifle and fought Skinny when the latter, red-eyed but cool, endeavored to restrain him. "Lemme go, curse yu! Don't yu know they got Buck? Lemme go!"

"Down! Red's got th' skunk. Yu can't do nothin'—they'd drop yu afore yu took five steps. *Red's* got him, I tell yu! We'll pay 'em with th' coals of hell if yu'll keep yore head!" exclaimed Skinny, throwing the crazed man heavily.

Musical tones, rising and falling in weird octaves, whining pityingly, diabolically, sobbing in a fascinating monotone and slobbering in ragged chords, calling as they swept over the plain, always calling and exhorting, they mingled in barbaric discord with the defiant barks of the six-shooters and the inquiring cracks of the Winchesters. High up in the air several specks sailed and drifted, more coming up rapidly from all directions. Buzzards know well where food can be found.

As Hopalong leaned back against a rock he was hit in the thigh by a ricochet that tore its way out, whirling like a circular saw, a span above where it entered. The wound was very nasty, being ripped twice the size made by an ordinary shot, and it bled profusely. Skinny crawled over and attended to it, making a tourniquet of his neckerchief and clumsily bandaging it with a strip torn from his shirt.

"Yore shore lucky, yu are," he grumbled as he made his way back to his post, where he vented his rancor by emptying the semi-depleted magazine of his Winchester at the knoll.

Hopalong began to sing and shout and he talked of Jimmy and his childhood, interspersing the broken narrative with choice selections as sung in the music halls of Leavenworth and Abilene. He wound up by yelling and struggling, and Skinny had his hands full in holding him.

"Hopalong! Cassidy! Come out of that! Keep quiet—yu'll shore git plugged if yu don't stop that plungin'. For God's sake, did yu hear that?" A bullet viciously hissed between them and flattened out on a nearby rock; others cut their way through the chaparral to the sound of falling twigs, and Skinny threw himself on the struggling man and strapped Hopalong with his belt to the base of a honey mesquite that grew at his side.

"Hold still, now, and let that bandage alone. Yu allus goes off th' range when yu gets plugged," he complained. He cut down a cactus and poured the sap over the wounded man's face, causing him to gurgle and look around. His eyes had a sane look now and Skinny slid off his chest.

"Git that—belt loose; I ain't—no cow," brokenly blazed out the picketed Hopalong. Skinny did so, handed the irate man his Colts and returned to his own post, from where he fired twice, reporting the shots.

"I'm tryin' to get him on th' glance—th' first one went high an' th' other fell flat," he explained.

Hopalong listened eagerly, for this was shooting that he could appreciate.

"Lemme see," he commanded. Skinny dragged him over to a crack and settled down for another try.

"Where is he, Skinny?" asked Hopalong.

"Behind that second big one. No, over on this here side. See that smooth granite? If I can get her there on th' right spot he'll shore know it." He aimed carefully and fired.

Through Pete's glasses Hopalong saw a leaden splotch appear on the rock and he notified the marksman that he was shooting high. "Put her on that bump closer down," he suggested. Skinny did so and another yell reached their ears.

"That's a dandy. Yore shore all right, yu old cuss," complimented Hopalong, elated at the success of the experiment.

Skinny fired again and a brown arm flopped out into sight. Another shot struck it and it jerked as though it were lifeless.

"He's cashed. See how she jumped? Like a rope," remarked Skinny with a grin. The arm lay quiet.

Pete had gained his last cover and was all eyes and Colts. Lanky was also very close in and was intently watching one particular rock. Several shots echoed from the far side of the knoll and they knew that Red was all right. Billy was covering a cluster of rocks that protruded above the others and, as they looked, his rifle rang out and the last defender leaped down and disappeared in the chaparral. He wore yellow trousers and an old boiled shirt.

"By-an'-by, by all that's bad!" yelled Hopalong. "Th' measly coyote! An' me a-fillin' his ornery hide with liquor. Well, they'll have to find him all over again now," he complained, astounded by the revelation. He fired into the chaparral to express his pugnacious disgust and scared out a huge tarantula, which alighted on Skinny's chaps, crawling rapidly toward the unconscious man's neck. Hopalong's face hardened and he slowly covered the insect and fired, driving it into the sand, torn and lifeless. The bullet touched the leathern garment and Skinny remonstrated, knowing that Hopalong was in no condition for fancy shooting.

"Huh!" exclaimed Hopalong. "That was a tarantula what I plugged. He was headin' for yore neck," he explained, watching the chaparral with apprehension.

"Go 'way, was it? Bully for yu!" exclaimed Skinny, tarantulas being placed at par with rattlesnakes, and he considered that he had been saved from a horrible death. "Thought yu said they wasn't no bugs over here," he added in an aggrieved tone.

"They wasn't none. Yu brought 'em. I only had th' main show—Gilas, rattlers an' toads," he replied, and then added, "Ain't it cussed hot up here?"

"She is. Yu won't have no cinch ridin' home with that leg. Yu better take my cayuse—he's busted more'n yourn," responded Skinny.

"Yore cayuse is at th' Cross Bar O, yu wall-eyed pirute."

"Shore 'nuff. Funny how a feller forgets sometimes. Lemme alone now, they's goin' to git By-an'-by. Pete an' Lanky has just went in after him."

That was what had occurred. The two impatient punchers had grown tired of waiting, and risked what might easily have been death in order to hasten matters. The others kept up a rapid fire, directed at the far end of the chaparral on the knoll, in order to mask the movements of their venturesome friends, intending also to drive By-and-by toward them so that he would be the one to get picked off as he advanced.

Several shots rang out in quick succession on the knoll and the chaparral became agitated. Several more shots sounded from the depth of the thicket and a mounted Indian dashed out of the northern edge and headed in Buck's direction. His course would take him close to Buck, whom he had seen fall, and would let him escape at a point midway between Red and Skinny, as Lanky was on the knoll and the range was very far to allow effective shooting by these two.

Red saw him leave the chaparral and in his haste to reload jammed the cartridge, and By-and-by swept on toward temporary safety, with Red dancing in a paroxysm of rage, swelling his vocabulary with words he had forgotten existed.

By-and-by, rising to his full height in the saddle, turned and wiggled his fingers at the frenzied Red and made several other signs that the cowboy was in the humor to appreciate to the fullest extent. Then he turned and shook his rifle at the marksmen on the larger knoll, whose best shots kicked up the dust fully fifty yards too short. The pony was sweeping toward the reservation and friends only fifteen miles away, and By-and-by knew that once among the mountains he would be on equal footing at least with his enemies. As he passed the rock behind which Buck lay sprawled on his face he uttered a piercing whoop of triumph and leaned forward on his pony's neck. Twenty leaps farther and the spiteful crack of an unerring rifle echoed from where the foreman was painfully supporting himself on his elbows. The pony swept on in a spurt of nerve-racking speed, but alone. By-and-by shrieked again and crashed heavily to the ground, where he rolled inertly and then lay still. Men like Buck are dangerous until their hearts have ceased to beat.

CHAPTER 6

Trials of the Convalescent

The days at the ranch passed in irritating idleness for those who had obstructed the flight of hostile lead, and worse than any of the patients was Hopalong, who fretted and fumed at his helplessness, which retarded his recovery. But at last the day came when he was fit for the saddle again, and he gave notice of his joy in whoops and forthwith announced that he was entitled to a holiday; and Buck had not the heart to refuse him. So he started forth in his quest of peace and pleasure, but instead had found only trouble and had been forced to leave his card at almost every place he had visited.

There was that affair in Red Hot Gulch, Colorado, where, under pressure, he had invested sundry pieces of lead in the persons of several obstreperous citizens and then had paced the zealous and excitable sheriff to the state line.

He next was noticed in Cheyenne, where his deformity was vividly dwelt upon, to the extent of six words, by one Tarantula Charley, the aforesaid Charley not being able to proceed to greater length on account of heart failure. As Charley had been a ubiquitous nuisance, those present availed themselves of the opportunity offered by Hopalong to indulge in a free drink.

Laramie was his next stopping place, and shortly after his arrival he was requested to sing and dance by a local terror, who informed all present that he was the only seventeen-buttoned rattlesnake in the cow country. Hopalong, hurt and indignant at being treated like a common tenderfoot, promptly knocked the terror down. After he had irrigated several square feet of parched throats belonging to the audience he again took up his journey and spent a day at Denver, where he managed to avoid any further trouble.

Santa Fé loomed up before him several days later and he entered it shortly before noon. At this time the old Spanish city was a bundle of high-strung nerves, and certain parts of it were calculated to furnish any and all kinds of excitement except revival meetings and church fairs. Hopalong straddled a lively nerve before he had been in the city an hour. Two local bad men, Slim Travennes and Tex Ewalt, desiring to establish the fact that they were roaring prairie fires, attempted to consume the placid and innocent stranger as he limped across the plaza in search of a game of draw poker at the Black Hills Emporium, with the result that they needed repairs, to the chagrin and disgust of their immediate acquaintances, who endeavored to drown their mortification and sorrow in rapid but somewhat wild gunplay, and soon remembered that they had pressing engagements elsewhere.

Hopalong reloaded his guns and proceeded to the Emporium, where he found a game all prepared for him in every sense of the word. On the third deal he objected to the way in which the dealer manipulated the cards, and when the smoke cleared away he was the only occupant of the room, except a dog belonging to the bartender that had intercepted a stray bullet.

Hunting up the owner of the hound, he apologized for being the indirect cause of the animal's death, deposited a sum of Mexican dollars in that gentleman's palm and went on his way to Alameda, which he entered shortly after dark, and where an insult, simmering in its uncalled-for venom, met him as he limped across the floor of the local dispensary on his way to the bar. There was no time for verbal argument and precedent had established the manner of his reply, and his repartee was as quick as light and most effective. Having resented the epithets he gave his attention to the occupants of the room.

Smoke drifted over the table in an agitated cloud and dribbled lazily upward from the muzzle of his six-shooter, while he looked searchingly at those around him. Strained and eager faces peered at his opponent, who was sliding slowly forward in his chair, and for the length of a minute no sound but the guarded breathing of the onlookers could be heard. This was broken by a nervous cough from the rear of the room, and the faces assumed their ordinary nonchalant expressions, their rugged lines heavily shadowed in the light of the flickering oil lamps, while the shuffling of cards and the clink of silver became audible. Hopalong Cassidy had objected to insulting remarks about his affliction.

Hopalong was very sensitive about his crippled leg and was always prompt to resent any scorn or curiosity directed at it, especially when emanating from strangers. A young man of twenty-three years, when surrounded by nearly perfect specimens of physical manhood, is apt to be painfully self-conscious of any such defect, and it reacted on his nature at times, even though he was well known for his happy-go-lucky disposition and playfulness. He consoled himself with the knowledge that what he lost in symmetry was more than balanced by the celerity and certainty of his gun hand, which was right or left, or both, as the occasion demanded.

Several hours later, as his luck was vacillating, he felt a heavy hand on his shoulder, and was overjoyed at seeing Buck and Red, the latter grinning as only Red could grin, and he withdrew from the game to enjoy his good fortune.

While Hopalong had been wandering over the country the two friends had been hunting for him and had traced him successfully, that being due to the trail he had blazed with his six-shooters. This they had accomplished without harm to themselves, as those of whom they inquired thought that they must want Hopalong "bad," and cheerfully gave the information required.

They had started out more for the purpose of accompanying him for pleasure, but that had changed to an urgent necessity in the following manner:

While on the way from Denver to Santa Fé they had met Pete Willis of the Three Triangle, a ranch that adjoined their own, and they paused to pass the compliments of the season.

"Purty far from th' grub wagon, Pie," remarked Buck.

"Oh, I'm only goin' to Denver," responded Pie.

"Purty hot," suggested Red.

"She shore is. Seen anybody yu knows?" Pie asked.

"One or two—Billy of th' Star Crescent an' Panhandle Lukins," answered Buck.

"That so? Panhandle's goin' to punch for us next year. I'll hunt him up. I heard down south of Albuquerque that Thirsty Jones an' his brothers are lookin' for trouble," offered Pie.

"Yah! They ain't lookin' for no trouble—they just goes around blowin' off. Trouble? Why, they don't know what she is," remarked Red contemptuously.

"Well, they's been dodgin' th' sheriff purty lively lately, an' if that ain't trouble I don't know what is," said Pie.

"It shore is, an' hard to dodge," acquiesced Buck.

"Well, I has to amble. Is Panhandle in Denver? Yes? I calculates as how me an' him'll buck th' tiger for a whirl—he's shore lucky. Well, so long," said Pie as he moved on.

"So long," responded the two.

"Hey, wait a minute," yelled Pie after he had ridden a hundred yards. "If yu sees Hopalong yu might tell him that th' Joneses are goin' to hunt him up when they gits to Albuquerque. They's shore sore on him. 'Tain't none of my funeral, only they ain't always a-carin' how they goes after a feller. So long," and soon he was a cloud of dust on the horizon.

"Trouble!" snorted Red; "well, between dodgin' Harris an' huntin' Hopalong I reckons they'll shore find her." Then to himself he murmured, "Funny how everthin' comes his way."

"That's gospel shore enough, but, as Pie said, they ain't a whole lot particular as how they deal th' cards. We better get a move on an' find that ornery little cuss," replied Buck.

"O.K., only I ain't losin' no sleep about Hoppy. His gun's too lively for me to do any worryin'," asserted Red.

"They'll get lynched sometime, shore," declared Buck.

"Not if they find Hoppy," grimly replied Red.

They tore through Santa Fé, only stopping long enough to wet their throats, and after several hours of hard riding entered Alameda, where they found Hopalong in the manner narrated.

After some time the three left the room and headed for Albuquerque, twelve miles to the south. At ten o'clock they dismounted before the Nugget and Rope, an unpainted wooden building supposed to be a clever combination of barroom, dance and gambling hall and hotel. The cleverness lay in the man who could find the hotel part.

■ ◆ ◆ ◆ ◆ ◆ ■ ◆ ■ ◆ ◆ ◆ ◆ ◆ ■

CHAPTER 7

The Open Door

The proprietor of the Nugget and Rope, a German named Baum, not being troubled with police rules, kept the door wide open for the purpose of inviting trade, a proceeding not to the liking of his patrons for obvious reasons. Probably not one man in ten was fortunate enough to have no one "looking for him," and the lighted interior assured good hunting to anyone in the dark street. He was continually opening the door, which every newcomer promptly and forcibly slammed shut. When he saw men walk across the room for the express purpose of slamming it he began to cherish the idea that there was a conspiracy on foot to anger him and thus force him to bring about his own death. After the door had been slammed three times in one evening by one man, the last slam being so forcible as to shake two bottles from the shelf and to crack the door itself, he became positive that his suspicions were correct, and so was very careful to smile and take it as a joke. Finally, wearied by his vain efforts to keep it open and fearing for the door, he hit upon a scheme, the brilliancy of which inflated his chest and gave him the appearance of a prize-winning bantam. When his patrons strolled in that night there was no door to slam, as it lay behind the bar.

When Buck and Red entered, closely followed by Hopalong, they elbowed their way to the rear of the room, where they could see before being seen. As yet they had said nothing to Hopalong about Pie's warning and were debating in their minds whether they should do so or not, when Hopalong interrupted their thoughts by laughing. They looked up and he nodded toward the front, where they saw that anxious eyes from all parts of the room were focused on the open door. Then they noticed that it had been removed. The air of semi-hostile, semianxious inquiry of the patrons and the smile of satisfaction covering the face of Baum appealed to them as the most ludicrous sight their eyes had seen for months, and they leaned back and roared with laughter, thus calling forth sundry looks of disapproval from the innocent causers of their merriment. But they were too well known in Albuquerque to allow the disapproval to approach a serious end, and finally, as the humorous side of the situation dawned on the crowd, they joined in the laugh and all went merrily.

At the psychologic moment someone shouted for a dance and the suggestion met with uproarious approval. At that moment Harris, the sheriff, came in and volunteered to supply the necessary music if the crowd would pay the fine against a straying fiddler he had corralled the day before. A hat was quickly passed and a sum was realized which would pay several fines to come and Harris departed for the music.

A chair was placed on the bar for the musician and, to the tune of "Old Dan Tucker" and an assortment of similar airs, the board floor shook and trembled. It was a comical sight and Hopalong, the only wallflower besides Baum and the sheriff, laughed until he became weak. Cowpunchers play as they work, hard and earnestly, and there was plenty of action. Sombreros flapped like huge wings and the baggy chaps looked like small, distorted balloons.

The Virginia reel was a marvel of supple, exaggerated grace and the quadrille looked like a free-for-all for unbroken colts. The honor of prompter was conferred upon the sheriff, and he gravely called the changes as they were usually called in that section of the country:

"Oh, th' ladies trail in
    An' th' gents trail out,
An' all stampede down th' middle.
    If yu ain't got th' tin
        Yu can dance an' shout,
But yu must keep up with th' fiddle."

As the dance waxed faster and the dancers grew hotter Hopalong, feeling lonesome because he wouldn't face ridicule, even if it was not expressed, went over and stood by the sheriff. He and Harris were good friends, for he had received the wound that crippled him in saving the sheriff from assassination. Harris killed the man who had fired that shot, and from this episode on the burning desert grew a friendship that was as strong as their own natures.

Harris was very well liked by the majority and feared by the rest, for he was a "square" man and the best sheriff the county had ever known. Quiet and unassuming, small of stature and with a kind word for everyone, he was a universal favorite among the better class of citizens. Quick as a flash and unerring in his shooting, he was a nightmare to the "bad men." No profane word had ever been known to leave his lips, and he was the possessor of a widespread reputation for generosity. His face was naturally frank and open; but when his eyes narrowed with determination it became blank and cold. When he saw his young friend sidle over to him he smiled and nodded a hearty welcome.

"They's shore cuttin' her loose," remarked Hopalong.

"First two pairs forward an' back!—they shore is," responded the prompter.

"Who's th' gent playin' lady to Buck?" queried Hopalong.

"Forward again an' ladies change!—Billy Jordan."

Hopalong watched the couple until they swung around and then he laughed silently. "Buck's got too many feet," he seriously remarked to his friend.

"Swing th' girl yu loves th' best!—he ain't lonesome, look at that—"

Two shots rang out in quick succession and Harris stumbled, wheeled and pitched forward on his face as Hopalong's sombrero spun across his body. For a second there was an intense silence, heavy, strained and sickening. Then a roar broke forth and the crowd of frenzied merrymakers, headed by Hopalong, poured out into the street and spread out to search the town. As daylight dawned the searchers began to straggle back with the same report of failure. Buck and Red met on the street near the door and each looked questioningly at the other. Each shook his head and looked around, their fingers toying absentmindedly at their belts. Finally Buck cleared his throat and remarked casually, "Mebby he's following 'em."

Red nodded and they went over toward their horses. As they were hesitating which route to take, Billy Jordan came up.

"Mebby yu'd like to see yore pardner—he's out by Buzzard's Spring. We'll take care of *him*," jerking his thumb over his shoulder toward the saloon where Harris's body lay. "And we'll *all* git th' *others* later. They can't git away for long."

Buck and Red nodded and headed for Buzzard's Spring. As they neared the water hole they saw Hopalong sitting on a rock, his head resting in one hand while the other hung loosely from his knee. He did not notice them when they arrived, and with a ready tact they sat quietly on their horses and looked in every direction except toward him. The sun became a ball of molten fire and the sand flies annoyed them incessantly, but still they sat and waited, silent and apologetic.

Hopalong finally arose, reached for his sombrero, and, finding it gone, swore long and earnestly at the scene its loss brought before him. He walked over to his horse and, leaping into the saddle, turned and faced his friends. "Yu old sons-of-guns," he said. They looked sheepish and nodded negatively in answer to the look of inquiry in his eyes. "They ain't got 'em yet," remarked Red slowly. Hopalong straightened up, his eyes narrowed and his face became hard and resolute as he led the way back toward the town.

Buck rode up beside him and, wiping his face with his shirtsleeve, began to speak to Red. "We *might* look up th' Joneses, Red. They had been dodgin' th' sheriff purty lively lately, an' they was huntin' Hopalong. Ever since we had to kill their brother in Buckskin they has been yappin' as how they was goin' to wipe us out. Hopalong an' Harris was standin' clost together an' they tried for both. They shot twice, one for Harris an' one for Hopalong, an' what more do yu want?"

"It shore looks thataway, Buck," replied Red, biting into a huge plug of tobacco which he produced from his chaps. "Anyhow, they wouldn't be no loss if they didn't. 'Member what Pie said?"

Hopalong looked straight ahead, and when he spoke the words sounded as though he had bitten them off: "Yore right, Buck, but I gits first try at Thirsty. He's my meat an' I'll plug th' fellow what says he ain't. Damn him!"

The others replied by applying their spurs, and in a short time they dismounted before the Nugget and Rope. Thirsty wouldn't have a chance to not care how he dealt the cards.

Buck and Red moved quickly through the crowd, speaking fast and earnestly. When they returned to where they had left their friend they saw him half a block away and they followed slowly, one on either side of the street. There would be no bullets in his back if they knew what they were about, and they usually did.

As Hopalong neared the corner, Thirsty and his two brothers turned it and saw him. Thirsty said something in a low voice, and the other two walked across the street and disappeared behind the store. When assured that they were secure, Thirsty walked up to a huge boulder on the side of the street farthest from the store and turned and faced his enemy, who approached rapidly until about five paces away, when he slowed up and finally stopped.

For a number of seconds they sized each other up, Hopalong quiet and deliberate with a deadly hatred; Thirsty pale and furtive with a sensation hitherto unknown to him. It was Right meeting Wrong, and Wrong lost confidence. Often had Thirsty Jones looked death in the face and laughed, but there was something in Hopalong's eyes that made his flesh creep.

He glanced quickly past his foe and took in the scene with one flash of his eyes. There was the crowd, eager, expectant, scowling. There were Buck and Red, each lounging against a boulder, Buck on his right, Red on his left. Before him stood the only man he had ever feared. Hopalong shifted his feet and Thirsty, coming to himself with a start, smiled. His nerve had been shaken, but he was master of himself once more.

"Well!" he snarled, scowling.

Hopalong made no response, but stared him in the eyes.

Thirsty expected action, and the deadly quiet of his enemy oppressed him. He stared in turn, but the insistent searching of his opponent's eyes scorched him and he shifted his gaze to Hopalong's neck.

"Well!" he repeated uneasily.

"Did yu have a nice time at th' dance last night?" asked Hopalong, still searching the face before him.

"Was there a dance? I was over in Alameda," replied Thirsty shortly.

"Ya-as, there was a dance, an' yu can shoot purty damn far if yu was in Alameda," responded Hopalong, his voice low and monotonous.

Thirsty shifted his feet and glanced around. Buck and Red were still lounging against their boulders and apparently were not paying any attention to the proceedings. His fickle nerve came back again, for he knew he would receive fair play. So he faced Hopalong once more and regarded him with a cynical smile.

"Yu seems to worry a whole lot about me. Is it because yu has a tender feelin', or because it's none of yore damn business?" he asked aggressively.

Hopalong paled with sudden anger, but controlled himself.

"It's because yu murdered Harris," he replied.

"An how does yu figger it out?" asked Thirsty, jauntily.

"He was huntin' yu hard an' yu thought yu'd stop it, so yu came in to lay for him. When you saw me an' him together yu saw th' chance to wipe out another score. That's how I figger it out," replied Hopalong quietly.

"Yore a reg'lar 'tective, ain't yu?" Thirsty asked ironically.

"I've got common sense," responded Hopalong.

"Yu has? Yu better tell th' rest that, too," replied Thirsty.

"I know yu shot Harris, an' yu can't get out of it by makin' funny remarks. Anyhow, yu won't be much loss, an' th' stage company'll feel better, too."

"An' suppose I did shoot him, I done a good job, didn't I?"

"Yu did the worst job you could do, yu highway robber," softly said Hopalong, at the same time moving nearer. "Harris knew yu stopped th' stage last month, an' that's why yu've been dodgin' him."

"Yore a liar!" shouted Thirsty, reaching for his gun.

The movement was fatal, for before he could draw, the Colt in Hopalong's holster leaped out and flashed from its owner's hip and Thirsty fell sideways, facedown in the dust of the street.

Hopalong started toward the fallen man, but as he did so a shot rang out from behind the store and he pitched forward, stumbled and rolled behind the boulder. As he stumbled his left hand streaked to his hip, and when he fell he had a gun in each hand.

As he disappeared from sight Goodeye and Bill Jones stepped from behind the store and started to run away. Not able to resist the temptation to look again, they stopped and turned and Bill laughed.

"Easy as hell," he said.

"Run, yu fool—Red an' Buck'll be here. Want to git plugged?" shouted Goodeye angrily.

They turned and started for a group of ponies twenty yards away, and as they leaped into the saddles two shots were fired from the street. As the reports died away Buck and Red turned the corner of the store, Colts in hand, and, checking their rush as they saw the saddles emptied, they turned toward the street and saw Hopalong, with blood oozing from an abrasion on his cheek, sitting up cross-legged, with each hand holding a gun, from which came thin wisps of smoke.

"Th' son-of-a-gun!" cried Buck, proud and delighted.

"Th' son-of-a-gun!" echoed Red, grinning.

CHAPTER 8

Hopalong Keeps His Word

The waters of the Rio Grande slid placidly toward the Gulf, the hot sun branding the sleepy waters with streaks of molten fire. To the north arose from the gray sandy plain the Quitman Mountains, and beyond them lay Bass Cañon. From the latter emerged a solitary figure astride a broncho, and as he ascended the topmost rise he glanced below him at the placid stream and beyond it into Mexico. As he sat quietly in his saddle he smiled and laughed gently to himself. The trail he had just followed had been replete with trouble which had suited the state of his mind and he now felt humorous, having cleaned up a pressing debt with his six-shooter. Surely there ought to be a mild sort of excitement in the land he faced, something picturesque and out of the ordinary. This was to be the finishing touch to his trip, and he had left his two companions at Albuquerque in order that he might have to himself all that he could find.

Not many miles to the south of him lay the town which had been the rendezvous of Tamale José, whose weakness had been a liking for other people's cattle. Well he remembered his first manhunt: the discovery of the theft, the trail and pursuit and—the ending. He was scarcely eighteen years of age when that event took place, and the wisdom he had absorbed then had stood him in good stead many times since. He had even now a touch of pride at the recollection how, when his older companions had failed to get Tamale José, he with his undeveloped strategy had gained that end. The fight would never be forgotten, as it was his first, and no sight of wounds would ever affect him as did those of Red Connors as he lay huddled up in the dark corner of that old adobe hut.

He came to himself and laughed again as he thought of Carmencita, the first girl he had ever known—and the last. With a boy's impetuosity he had wooed her in a manner far different from that of the peons who sang beneath her window and talked to her mother. He had boldly scaled the wall and did his courting in her house, trusting to luck and to his own ability to avoid being seen. No hidden meaning lay in his words; he spoke from his heart and with no concealment. And he remembered the treachery that had forced him, fighting, to the camp of his outfit; and when he had returned with his friends she had disappeared. To this day he hated that mud-walled convent and those sisters who so easily forgot how to talk. The fragrances of the old days wrapped themselves around him, and although he had ceased to pine for his black-eyed Carmencita—well, it would be nice if he chanced to see her again. Spurring his mount into an easy canter he swept down to and across the river, fording it where he had crossed it when pursuing Tamale José.

The town lay indolent under the Mexican night, and the strumming of guitars and the tinkle of spurs and tiny bells softly echoed from several houses. The convent of St. Maria lay indistinct in its heavy shadows and the little church farther up the dusty street showed dim lights in its stained windows. Off to the north became audible the rhythmic beat of a horse and soon a cowboy swept past the convent with a mocking bow. He clattered across the stone-paved plaza and threw his mount back on its haunches as he stopped before a house. Glancing around and determining to find out a few facts as soon as possible, he rode up to the low door and pounded upon it with the butt of his Colt. After waiting for possibly half a minute and receiving no response he hammered a tune upon it with two Colts and had the satisfaction of seeing half a score of heads protrude from the windows in the nearby houses.

"If I could scare up another gun I might get th' whole blamed town up," he grumbled whimsically, and fell on the door with another tune.

"Who is it?" came from within. The voice was distinctly feminine and Hopalong winked to himself in congratulation.

"Me," he replied, twirling his fingers from his nose at the curious, forgetting that the darkness hid his actions from sight.

"Yes, I know; but who is 'me'?" came from the house.

"Ain't I a fool!" he complained to himself, and raising his voice he replied coaxingly, "Open th' door a bit an' see. Are yu Carmencita?"

"O-o-o! But you must tell me who it is first."

"Mr. Cassidy," he replied, flushing at the 'mister,' "an' I wants to see Carmencita."

"Carmencita who?" teasingly came from behind the door.

Hopalong scratched his head. "Gee, yu've roped me—I suppose she has got another handle. Oh, yu know—she used to live here about seven years back. She had great big black eyes, pretty cheeks an' a mouth that 'ud stampede anybody. Don't yu know now? She was about so high," holding out his hands in the darkness.

The door opened a trifle on a chain and Hopalong peered eagerly forward.

"Ah, it is you, the brave Americano! You must go away quick or you will meet with harm. Manuel is awfully jealous and he will kill you! Go at once, please!"

Hopalong pulled at the half-hearted down upon his lip and laughed softly. Then he slid the guns back in their holsters and felt of his sombrero.

"Manuel wants to see me first, Star Eyes."

"No! no!" she replied, stamping upon the floor vehemently. "You must go now—at once!"

"I'd shore look nice hittin' th' trail because Manuel Somebody wants to get hurt, wouldn't I? Don't yu remember how I used to shinny up this here wall an' skin th' cat gettin' through that hole up there what yu said was a window? Ah, come on an' open th' door—I'd shore like to see yu again!" pleaded the irrepressible.

"No! no! Go away. Oh, won't you please go away!"

Hopalong sighed audibly and turned his horse. As he did so he heard the door open and a sigh reached his ears. He wheeled like a flash and found the door closed again on its chain. A laugh of delight came from behind it.

"Come out, please!—just for a minute," he begged, wishing that he was brave enough to smash the door to splinters and grab her.

"If I do, will you go away?" asked the girl. "Oh, what will Manuel say if he comes? And all those people, they'll tell him!"

"Hey, yu!" shouted Hopalong, brandishing his Colts at the protruding heads. "Git scarce! I'll shore plug th' last one in!" Then he laughed at the sudden vanishing.

The door slowly opened and Carmencita, fat and drowsy, wobbled out to him. Hopalong's feelings were interfering with his breathing as he surveyed her. "Oh, yu shore are mistaken, Mrs. Carmencita. I wants to see yore *daughter!*"

"Ah, you have forgotten the little Carmencita who used to look for you. Like all the men, you have forgotten," she cooed reproachfully. Then her fear predominated again and she cried, "Oh, if my husband should see me now!"

Hopalong mastered his astonishment and bowed. He had a desire to ride madly into the Rio Grande and collect his senses.

"Yu are right—this *is* too dangerous—I'll amble on some," he replied hastily.

Under his breath he prayed that the outfit would never learn of this. He turned his horse and rode slowly up the street as the door closed.

Rounding the corner he heard a soft footfall, and swerving in his saddle he turned and struck with all his might in the face of a man who leaped at him, at the same time grasping the uplifted wrist with his other hand. A curse and the tinkle of thin steel on the pavement accompanied the fall of his opponent. Bending down from his saddle he picked up the weapon and the next minute the enraged assassin was staring into the unwavering and, to him, growing muzzle of a Colt's .45.

"Yu shore had a bum teacher. Don't you know better'n to *push* it in? An' me a cowpuncher, too! I'm most grieved at yore conduct—it shows you don't appreciate cow-wrastlers. This is safer," he remarked, throwing the stilleto through the air and into a door, where it rang out angrily and quivered. "I don't know as I wants to ventilate yu; we mostly poisons coyotes up my way," he added. Then a thought struck him. "Yu must be that dear Manuel I've been hearin' so much about?"

A snarl was the only reply and Hopalong grinned.

"Yu shore ain't got no call to go loco that way, none whatever. I don't want yore Carmencita. I only called to say hulloo," responded Hopalong, his sympathies being aroused for the wounded man before him from his vivid recollection of the woman who had opened the door.

"Yah!" snarled Manuel. "You wants to poison my little bird. You with your fair hair and your cursed swagger!"

The six-shooter tentatively expanded and then stopped six inches from the Mexican's nose. "Yu wants to ride easy, hombre. I ain't no angel, but I don't poison no woman; an' don't yu amble off with th' idea in yore head that she wants to be poisoned. Why, she near stuck a knife in me!" he lied.

The Mexican's face brightened somewhat, but it would take more than that to wipe out the insult of the blow. The horse became restless, and when Hopalong had effectively quieted it he spoke again.

"Did yu ever hear of Tamale José?"

"Yes."

"Well, I'm th' fellow that stopped him in th' 'dobe hut by th' arroyo. I'm tellin' yu this so yu won't do nothin' rash an' leave Carmencita a widow."

The hate on the Mexican's face redoubled and he took a short step forward, but stopped when the muzzle of the Colt kissed his nose. He was the brother of Tamale José. As he backed away from the cool touch of the weapon he thought out swiftly his revenge. Some of his brother's old companions were at that moment drinking mescal in a saloon down the street, and they would be glad to see this Americano die. He glanced past his house at the saloon and Hopalong misconstrued his thoughts.

"Shore, go home. I'll just circulate around some for exercise. No hard feelings, only yu better throw it next time," he said as he backed away and rode off. Manuel went down the street and then ran into the saloon, where he caused an uproar.

Hopalong rode to the end of the plaza and tried to sing, but it was a dismal failure. Then he felt thirsty and wondered why he hadn't thought of it before. Turning his horse and seeing the saloon he rode up to it and in, lying flat on the animal's neck to avoid being swept off by the door frame. His entrance scared white some half a dozen loungers, who immediately sprang up in a decidedly hostile manner. Hopalong's Colts peeped over the ears of his horse and he backed into a corner near the bar.

"One, two, three—now, altogether, *breathe*! Yu acts like yu never saw a real puncher afore. All th' same," he remarked, nodding at several of the crowd, "I've seen yu afore. Yu are th' gents with th' hotfoot getaway that vamoosed when we got Tamale."

Curses were flung at him and only the humorous mood he was in saved trouble. One, bolder than the rest, spoke up: "The señor will not see any 'hotfoot getaway,' as he calls it, now! The señor was not wise to go so far away from his friends!"

Hopalong looked at the speaker and a quizzical grin slowly spread over his face. "They'll shore feel glad when I tells them yu was askin' for 'em. But didn't yu see too much of 'em once, or was yu poundin' leather in the other direction? Yu don't want to worry none about me—*an' if yu don't get yore hands closter to yore neck they'll be hell to pay!* There, that's more like home," he remarked, nodding assurance.

Reaching over he grasped a bottle and poured out a drink, his Colt slipping from his hand and dangling from his wrist by a thong. As the weapon started to fall several of the audience involuntarily moved as if to pick it up. Hopalong noticed this and paused with the glass halfway to his lips. "Don't bother yoreselves none; I can git it again," he said, tossing off the liquor.

"Wow! Holy smoke!" he yelled. "This ain't drink! Sufferin' coyotes, nobody can accuse yu of sellin' liquor! Did yu make this all by yoreself?" he asked incredulously of the proprietor, who didn't know whether to run or to pray. Then he noticed that the crowd was spreading out and his Colts again became the center of interest.

"Yu with th' lovely face, *sit down!*" he ordered as the person addressed was gliding toward the door. "I ain't a-goin' to let you pot me from th' street. Th' first man who tries to get scarce will stop somethin' hot. An' yu *all* better sit down," he suggested, sweeping them with his guns. One man, more obdurate than the rest, was slow in complying and Hopalong sent a bullet through the top of his high sombrero, which had a most gratifying effect.

"You'll regret this!" hissed a man in the rear, and a murmur of assent arose. Someone stirred slightly in searching for a weapon and immediately a blazing Colt froze him into a statue.

"Yu shore looks funny; eeny, meeny, miny, mo," counted off the daring horseman; "move a bit an' off yu go," he finished. Then his face broke out in another grin as he thought of more enjoyment.

"That there gent on th' left," he said, pointing out with a gun the man he meant. "Yu sing us a song. Sing a nice little song."

As the object of his remarks remained mute he let his thumb ostentatiously slide back with the hammer of the gun under it. "Sing! Quick!" The man sang.

As Hopalong leaned forward to say something a stiletto flashed past his neck and crashed into the bottle beside him. The echo of the crash was merged into a report as Hopalong fired from his waist. Then he backed out into the street and, wheeling, galloped across the plaza and again faced the saloon. A flash split the darkness and a bullet hummed over his head and thudded into an adobe wall at his back. Another shot and he replied, aiming at the flash. From down the street came the sound of a window opening and he promptly caused it to close again. Several more windows opened and hastily closed, and he rode slowly toward the far end of the plaza. As he faced the saloon once more he heard a command to throw up his hands and saw the glint of a gun, held by a man who wore the insignia of sheriff. Hopalong complied, but as his hands went up two spurts of fire shot forth and the sheriff dropped his weapon, reeled and sat down. Hopalong rode over to him and, swinging down, picked up the gun and looked the officer over.

"Shoo, yu'll be all right soon—yore only plugged in th' arms," he remarked as he glanced up the street. Shadowy forms were gliding from cover to cover and he immediately caused consternation among them by his accuracy.

"Ain't it hell?" he complained to the wounded man. "I never starts out but what somebody makes me shoot 'em. Came down here to see a girl an' find she's married. Then when I moves on peaceable-like her husband makes me hit him. Then I wants a drink an' he goes an' fans a knife at me, an' me just teachin' him how! Then yu has to come along an' make more trouble. Now look at them fools over there," he said, pointing at a dark shadow some fifty paces off. "They're pattin' their backs because I don't see 'em, an' if I hurts them they'll git mad. Guess I'll make 'em dust along," he added, shooting into the spot. A howl went up and two men ran away at top speed.

The sheriff nodded his sympathy and spoke. "I reckons you had better give up. You can't get away. Every house, every corner and shadow holds a man. You are a brave man—but, as you say, unfortunate. Better help me up and come with me—they'll tear you to pieces."

"Shore I'll help yu up—I ain't got no grudge against nobody. But my friends know where I am an' they'll come down here an' raise a ruction if I don't show up. So, if it's all th' same to you, I'll be ambling right along," he said as he helped the sheriff to his feet.

"Have you any objections to telling me your name?" asked the sheriff as he looked himself over.

"None whatever," answered Hopalong heartily. "I'm Hopalong Cassidy of th' Bar-20, Texas."

"You don't surprise me—I've heard of you," replied the sheriff wearily. "You are the man who killed Tamale José, whom I hunted for unceasingly. I found him when you had left and I got the reward. Come again sometime and I'll divide with you; two hundred and fifty dollars," he added craftily.

"I shore will, but I don't want no money," replied Hopalong as he turned away. "Adios, señor," he called back.

"Adios," replied the sheriff as he kicked a nearby door for assistance.

The cow pony tied itself up in knots as it pounded down the street toward the trail, and although he was fired on he swung into the dusty trail with a song on his lips. Several hours later he stood dripping wet on the American side of the Rio Grande and shouted advice to a score of Mexican cavalrymen on the opposite bank. Then he slowly picked his way toward El Paso for a game at Faro Dan's.

The sheriff sat in his easy chair one night some three weeks later, gravely engaged in rolling a cigarette. His arms were practically well, the wounds being in the fleshy parts. He was a philosopher and was disposed to take things easy, which accounted for his being in his official position for fifteen years. A gentleman at the core, he was well educated and had visited a goodly portion of the world. A book of Horace lay open on his knees and on the table at his side lay a shining new revolver, Hopalong having carried off his former weapon. He read aloud several lines and in reaching for a light for his cigarette noticed the new six-shooter. His mind leaped from Horace to Hopalong, and he smiled grimly at the latter's promise to call.

Glancing up, his eyes fell on a poster which conveyed the information in Spanish and in English that there was offered and which gave a good description of that gentleman.

> **FIVE HUNDRED DOLLARS ($500)**
> **REWARD**
> **For Hopalong Cassidy, of the Ranch**
> **Known as the Bar-20, Texas, U.S.A.**

Sighing for the five hundred, he again took up his book and was lost in its pages when he heard a knock, rather low and timid. Wearily laying aside his reading, he strode to the door, expecting to hear a lengthy complaint from one of his townsmen. As he threw the door wide open the light streamed out and lighted up a revolver and behind it the beaming face of a cowboy, who grinned.

"Well, I'll be damned!" ejaculated the sheriff, starting back in amazement.

"Don't say that, sheriff; you've got lots of time to reform," replied a humorous voice. "How's th' wings?"

"Almost well: you were considerate," responded the sheriff.

"Let's go in—somebody might see me out here an' get into trouble," suggested the visitor, placing his foot on the sill.

"Certainly—pardon my discourtesy," said the sheriff. "You see, I wasn't expecting you tonight," he explained, thinking of the elaborate preparations that he would have gone to if he had thought the irrepressible would call.

"Well, I was down this way, an' seeing as how I had promised to drop in I just natchurally dropped," replied Hopalong as he took the chair proferred by his host.

After talking awhile on everything and nothing the sheriff coughed and looked uneasily at his guest.

"Mr. Cassidy, I am sorry you called, for I like men of your energy and courage and I very much dislike to arrest you," remarked the sheriff. "Of course you understand that you are under arrest," he added with anxiety.

"Who, me?" asked Hopalong with a rising inflection.

"Most assuredly," breathed the sheriff.

"Why, this is the first time I ever heard anything about it," replied the astonished cowpuncher. "I'm an American—don't that make any difference?"

"Not in this case, I'm afraid. You see, it's for manslaughter."

"Well, don't that beat th' devil, now?" said Hopalong. He felt sorry that a citizen of the glorious United States should be prey for troublesome sheriffs, but he was sure that his duty to Texas called upon him never to submit to arrest at the hands of a Mexican. Remembering the Alamo, and still behind his Colt, he reached over and took up the shining weapon from the table and snapped it open on his knee. After placing the cartridges in his pocket he tossed the gun over on the bed and, reaching inside his shirt, drew out another and threw it after the first.

"That's yore gun; I forgot to leave it," he said, apologetically. "Anyhow yu needs two," he added.

Then he glanced around the room, noticed the poster and walked over and read it. A full swift sweep of his gloved hand tore it from its fastenings and crammed it under his belt. The glimmer of anger in his eyes gave way as he realized that his head was worth a definite price, and he smiled at what the boys would say when he showed it to them. Planting his feet far apart and placing his arms akimbo he faced his host in grim defiance.

"Got any more of these?" he inquired, placing his hand on the poster under his belt.

"Several," replied the sheriff.

"Trot 'em out," ordered Hopalong shortly.

The sheriff sighed, stretched and went over to a shelf, from which he took a bundle of the articles in question. Turning slowly he looked at the puncher and handed them to him.

"I reckons they's all over this here town," remarked Hopalong.

"They are, and you may never see Texas again."

"So? Well, yu tell yore most particular friends that the job is worth five thousand, and that it will take so many to do it that when th' money is divided up it won't buy a meal. There's only one man in this country tonight that can earn that money, an' that's me," said the puncher. "An' I don't need it," he added, smiling.

"But you are my prisoner—you are under arrest," enlightened the sheriff, rolling another cigarette. The sheriff spoke as if asking a question. Never before had five hundred dollars been so close at hand and yet so unobtainable. It was like having a checkbook but no bank account.

"I'm shore sorry to treat yu mean," remarked Hopalong, "but I was paid a month in advance an' I'll have to go back an' earn it."

"You can—if you say that you will return," replied the sheriff tentatively. The sheriff meant what he said and for the moment had forgotten that he was powerless and was not the one to make terms.

Hopalong was amazed and then he smiled sympathetically.

"Never like to promise nothin'," he replied. "I might get plugged, or something might happen that wouldn't let me." Then his face lighted up as a thought came to him. "Say, I'll cut th' cards with yu to see if I comes back or not."

The sheriff leaned back and gazed at the cool youngster before him. A smile of satisfaction, partly at the self-reliance of his guest and partly at the novelty of his situation, spread over his face. He reached for a pack of Mexican cards and laughed. "God! You're a cool one—I'll do it. What do you call?"

"Red," answered Hopalong.

The sheriff slowly raised his hand and revealed the ace of hearts.

Hopalong leaned back and laughed, at the same time taking from his pocket the six extracted cartridges. Arising and going over to the bed he slipped them in the chambers of the new gun and then placed the loaded weapon at the sheriff's elbow.

"Well, I reckon I'll amble, sheriff," he said as he opened the door. "If yu ever sifts up my way drop in an' see me—th' boys'll give yu a good time."

"Thanks; I will be glad to," replied the sheriff. "You'll take your pitcher to the well once too often someday, my friend. This courtesy," glancing at the restored revolver, "might have cost you dearly."

"Shoo! I did that once an' th' feller tried to use it," replied the cowboy as he backed through the door. "Some people are awfully careless," he added. "So long—"

"So long," replied the sheriff, wondering what sort of a man he had been entertaining.

The door closed softly and soon after a joyous whoop floated in from the street. The sheriff toyed with the new gun and listened to the low caress of a distant guitar.

"Well, don't that beat hell?" he ejaculated.

CHAPTER 9

The Advent of McAllister

The blazing sun shone pitilessly on an arid plain which was spotted with dust-gray clumps of mesquite and thorny chaparral. Basking in the burning sand and alkali lay several Gila monsters, which raised their heads and hissed with wide-open jaws as several faint, whip-like reports echoed flatly over the desolate plain, showing that even they had learned that danger was associated with such sounds.

Off to the north there became visible a cloud of dust and at intervals something swayed in it, something that rose and fell and then became hidden again. Out of that cloud came sharp, splitting sounds, which were faintly responded to by another and larger cloud in its rear. As it came nearer and finally swept past, the Gilas, to their terror, saw a madly pounding horse, and it carried a man. The latter turned in his saddle and raised a gun to his shoulder and the thunder that issued from it caused the creeping audience to throw up their tails in sudden panic and bury themselves out of sight in the sand.

The horse was only a broncho, its sides covered with hideous yellow spots, and on its near flank was a peculiar scar, the brand. Foam flecked from its crimsoned jaws and found a resting place on its sides and on the hairy chaps of its rider. Sweat rolled and streamed from its heaving flanks and was greedily sucked up by the drought-cursed alkali. Close to the rider's knee a bloody furrow ran forward and one of the broncho's ears was torn and limp. The broncho was doing its best—it could run at that pace until it dropped dead. Every ounce of strength it possessed was put forth to bring those hind hoofs well in front of the forward ones and to send them pushing the sand behind in streaming clouds. The horse had done this same thing many times—when would its master learn sense?

The man was typical in appearance with many of that broad land. Lithe, sinewy and bronzed by hard riding and hot suns, he sat in his Cheyenne saddle like a centaur, all his weight on the heavy, leather-guarded stirrups, his body rising in one magnificent straight line. A bleached mustache hid the thin lips, and a gray sombrero threw a heavy shadow across his eyes. Around his neck and over his open, blue flannel shirt lay loosely a knotted silk kerchief, and on his thighs a pair of open-flapped holsters swung uneasily with their ivory-handled burdens. He turned abruptly, raised his gun to his shoulder and fired, then he laughed recklessly and patted his mount, which responded to the confident caress by lying flatter to the earth in a spurt of heartbreaking speed.

"I'll show 'em who they're trailin'. This is th' second time I've started for Muddy Wells, an' I'm goin' to git there, too, for all th' Apaches out of Hades!"

To the south another cloud of dust rapidly approached and the rider scanned it closely, for it was directly in his path. As he watched it he saw something wave and it was a sombrero! Shortly afterward a real cowboy yell reached his ears. He grinned and slid another cartridge in the greasy, smoking barrel of the Sharp's and fired again at the cloud in his rear. Some few minutes later a whooping, bunched crowd of madly riding cowboys thundered past him and he was recognized.

"Hullo, Frenchy!" yelled the nearest one. "Comin' back?"

"Come on, McAllister!" shouted another; "we'll give 'em blazes!" In response the straining broncho suddenly stiffened, bunched and slid on its haunches, wheeled and retraced its course. The rear cloud suddenly scattered into many smaller ones and all swept off to the east. The rescuing band overtook them and, several hours later, when seated around a table in Tom Lee's saloon, Muddy Wells, a count was taken of them, which was pleasing in its facts.

"We was huntin' coyotes when we saw yu," said a smiling puncher who was known as Salvation Carroll chiefly because he wasn't.

"Yep! They've been stalkin' Tom's chickens," supplied Waffles, the champion poker player of the outfit. Tom Lee's chickens could whip anything of their kind for miles around and were reverenced accordingly.

"Sho! Is that so?" asked Frenchy with mild incredulity, such a state of affairs being deplorable.

"She shore is!" answered Tex Le Blanc, and then, as an afterthought, he added, "Where'd yu hit th' Indians?"

"'Bout four hours back. This here's th' second time I've headed for this place—last time they chased me to Las Cruces."

"That so?" asked Bigfoot Baker, a giant. "Ain't they *allus* interferin', now? Anyhow, they're better 'n coyotes."

"They was purty well heeled," suggested Tex, glancing at a bunch of repeating Winchesters of late model which lay stacked in a corner. "Charley here said he thought they was from th' way yore cayuse looked, didn't yu, Charley?" Charley nodded and filled his pipe.

"'Pears like a feller can't amble around much nowadays without havin' to fight," grumbled Lefty Allen, who usually went out of his way hunting up trouble.

"We're goin' to th' Hills as soon as our cookie turns up," volunteered Tenspot Davis, looking inquiringly at Frenchy. "Heard any more news?"

"Nope. Same old story—lots of gold. Shucks, I've bit on so many of them rumors that they don't feaze me no more. One man who don't know nothin' about prospectin' goes an' stumbles over a fortune an' those who know it from A to Izzard goes 'round pullin' in their belts."

"*We* don't pull in no belts—*we* knows just where to look, *don't* we, Tenspot?" remarked Tex, looking very wise.

"Ya-as we do," answered Tenspot, "if yu hasn't dreamed about it, we do."

"Yu wait; I wasn't dreamin', none whatever," assured Tex. "I *saw* it!"

"Ya-as, I saw it too onct," replied Frenchy with sarcasm. "Went and lugged fifty pound of it all th' way to th' assay office—took me two days; an' that there four-eyed cuss looks at it and snickers. Then he takes me by th' arm an' leads me to th' window. 'See that pile, my friend? That's all like yourn,' sez he. 'It's worth about one dollar a ton at th' coast. They use it for ballast.'"

"Aw! But this what *I* saw was *gold!*" exploded Tex.

"So was mine, for a while!" laughed Frenchy, nodding to the bartender for another round.

"Well, we're tired of punchin' cows! Ride sixteen hours a day, year in an' year out, an' what do we get? Fifty a month an' no chance to spend it, an' grub that 'd make a coyote sniffle! I'm for a vacation, an' if I goes broke, why, I'll punch again!" asserted Waffles, the foreman, thus revealing the real purpose of the trip.

"What'd yore boss say?" asked Frenchy.

"Whoop! What didn't he say! Honest, I never thought he had it in him. It was fine. He cussed an hour frontways an' then trailed back on a dead gallop, with us a-laughin' fit to bust. *Then* he rustles for his gun an' we rustles for town," answered Waffles, laughing at his remembrance of it.

As Frenchy was about to reply his sombrero was snatched from his head and disappeared. If he "got mad" he was to be regarded as not sufficiently well acquainted for banter and he was at once in hot water; if he took it good-naturedly he was one of the crowd in spirit; but in either case he didn't get his hat without begging or fighting for it. This was a recognized custom among the O-Bar-O outfit and was not intended as an insult.

Frenchy grabbed at the empty air and arose. Punching Lefty playfully in the ribs he passed his hands behind that person's back. Not finding the lost headgear he laughed and, tripping Lefty up, fell with him and, reaching up on the table for his glass, poured the contents down Lefty's back and arose.

"Yu son-of-a-gun!" indignantly wailed that unfortunate. "Gee, it feels funny," he added, grinning as he pulled the wet shirt away from his spine.

"Well, I've got to be amblin'," said Frenchy, totally ignoring the loss of his hat. "Goin' down to Buckskin," he offered, and then asked, "When's yore cook comin'?"

"Day after tomorrow, if he don't get loaded," replied Tex.

"Who is he?"

"A one-eyed Mexican—Antonio."

"*I* used to know him. He's a hell of a cook. Dished up th' grub one season when I was punchin' for th' Tin-Cup up in Montana," replied Frenchy.

"Oh, he kin cook *now*, all right," replied Waffles.

"That's about all he can cook. Useter wash his knives in th' coffeepot an' blow on th' tins. I chased him a mile one night for leavin' sand in th' skillet. Yu can have him—I don't envy yu none whatever."

"He don't sand no skillet when little Tenspot's around," assured that person, slapping his holster. "Does he, Lefty?"

"If he does, yu oughter be lynched," consoled Lefty.

"Well, so long," remarked Frenchy, riding off to a small store, where he bought a cheap sombrero.

Frenchy was a jack-of-all-trades, having been cowpuncher, prospector, proprietor of a "hotel" in Albuquerque, foreman of a ranch, sheriff, and at one time had played angel to a venturesome but poor show troupe. Besides his versatility he was well known as the man who took the stage through the Sioux country when no one else volunteered. He could shoot with the best, but his one pride was the brand of poker he handed out. Furthermore, he had never been known to take an unjust advantage over any man and, on the contrary, had frequently voluntarily handicapped himself to make the event more interesting. But he must not be classed as being hampered with self-restraint.

His reasons for making this trip were twofold: he wished to see Buck Peters, the foreman of the Bar-20 outfit, as he and Buck had punched cows together twenty years before and were firm friends; the other was that he wished to get square with Hopalong Cassidy, who had decisively cleaned him out the year before at poker. Hopalong played either in great good luck or the contrary, while Frenchy played an even, consistent game and usually left off richer than when he began, and this decisive defeat bothered him more than he would admit, even to himself.

The roundup season was at hand and the Bar-20 was short of ropers, the rumors of fresh gold discoveries in the Black Hills having drawn all the more restless men north. The outfit also had a slight touch of the gold fever, and only their peculiar loyalty to the ranch and the assurance of the foreman that when the work was over he would accompany them, kept them from joining the rush of those who desired sudden and much wealth as the necessary preliminary of painting some cow town in all the "bang-up" style such an event would call for. Therefore they had been given orders to secure the required assistance, and they intended to do so, and were prepared to kidnap, if necessary, for the glamour of wealth and the hilarity of the vacation made the hours falter in their speed.

As Frenchy leaned back in his chair in Cowan's saloon, Buckskin, early the next morning, planning to get revenge on Hopalong and then to recover his sombrero, he heard a medley of yells and whoops and soon the door flew open before the strenuous and concentrated entry of a mass of twisting and kicking arms and legs, which magically found their respective owners and reverted to the established order of things. When the alkali dust had thinned he saw seven cowpunchers sitting on the prostrate form of another, who was earnestly engaged in trying to push Johnny Nelson's head out in the street with one foot as he voiced his lucid opinion of things in general and the seven in particular. After Red Connors had been stabbed in the back several times by the victim's energetic elbow he ran out of the room and presently returned with a pleased expression and a sombrero full of water, his finger plugging an old bullet hole in the crown.

"Is he any better, Buck?" anxiously inquired the man with the reservoir.

"About a dollar's worth," replied the foreman. "Jest put a little right here," he drawled as he pulled back the collar of the unfortunate's shirt.

"Ow! wow! WOW!" wailed the recipient, heaving and straining. The unengaged leg was suddenly wrested loose, and as it shot up and out Billy Williams, with his pessimism aroused to a blue-ribbon pitch, sat down forcibly in an adjacent part of the room, from where he lectured between gasps on the follies of mankind and the attributes of army mules.

Red tiptoed around the squirming bunch, looking for an opening, his pleased expression now having added a grin.

"Seems to be gittin' violent-like," he soliloquized, as he aimed a stream at Hopalong's ear, which showed for a second as Pete Wilson strove for a half-nelson, and he managed to include Johnny and Pete in his effort.

Several minutes later, when the storm had subsided, the woeful crowd enthusiastically urged Hopalong to the bar, where he "bought."

"Of all th' ornery outfits I ever saw—" began the man at the table, grinning from ear to ear at the spectacle he had just witnessed.

"Why, hullo, Frenchy! Glad to see yu, yu old son-of-a-gun! What's th' news from th' Hills?" shouted Hopalong.

"Rather locoed, an' there's a locoed gang that's headin' that way. Goin' up?" he asked.

"Shore, after roundup. Seen any punchers trailin' around loose?"

"Ya-as," drawled Frenchy, delving into the possibilities suddenly opened to him and determining to utilize to the fullest extent the opportunity that had come to him unsought. "There's nine over to Muddy Wells that yu might git if yu wants them bad enough. They've got a sombrero of mine," he added deprecatingly.

"Nine! Twisted Jerusalem, Buck! Nine whole cowpunchers a-pinin' for work," he shouted, but then added thoughtfully, "Mebby they's engaged," it being one of the courtesies of the land not to take another man's help.

"Nope. They've stampeded for th' Hills an' left their boss *all* alone," replied Frenchy, well knowing that such desertion would not, in the minds of the Bar-20 men, add any merits to the case of the distant outfit.

"Th' sons-of-guns," said Hopalong, "let's go an' get 'em," he suggested, turning to Buck, who nodded a smiling assent.

"Oh, what's the hurry?" asked Frenchy, seeing his projected game slipping away into the uncertain future and happy in the thought that he would be avenged on the O-Bar-O outfit. "They'll be there till tomorrow noon—they's waitin' for their cookie, who's goin' with them."

"A cook! A cook! Oh, joy, a cook!" exulted Johnny, not for one instant doubting Buck's ability to capture the whole outfit and seeing a whirl of excitement in the effort.

"Anybody we knows?" inquired Skinny Thompson.

"Shore. Tenspot Davis, Waffles, Salvation Carroll, Bigfoot Baker, Charley Lane, Lefty Allen, Kid Morris, Curley Tate an' Tex Le Blanc," responded Frenchy.

"Umm-m. Might as well rope a blizzard," grumbled Billy. "Might as well try to git th' Seventh Cavalry. We'll have a pious time corralling that bunch.

Them's th' fellows that hit that bunch of inquirin' Crow braves that time up in th' Bad Lands an' then said by-bye to th' Ninth."

"Aw, shut up! They's only two that's very much, an' Buck an' Hopalong can sing 'em to sleep," interposed Johnny, afraid that the expedition would fall through.

"How about Curley and Tex?" pugnaciously asked Billy.

"Huh, jest because they buffaloed yu over to Las Vegas yu needn't think they's dangerous. Salvation an' Tenspot are th' only ones who can shoot," stoutly maintained Johnny.

"Here yu, get mum," ordered Buck to the pair. "When this outfit goes after anything it generally gets it. All in favor of kidnappin' that outfit signify th' same by kickin Billy," whereupon Bill swore.

"Do yu want yore hat?" asked Buck, turning to Frenchy.

"I shore do," answered that individual.

"If yu helps us at th' roundup we'll get it for yu. Fifty a month an' grub," offered the foreman.

"O.K.," replied Frenchy, anxious to even matters.

Buck looked at his watch. "Seven o'clock—we ought to get there by five if we relays at th' Barred-Horseshoe. Come on."

"How are we goin' to git them?" asked Billy.

"Yu leave that to me, son. Hopalong an' Frenchy 'll tend to that part of it," replied Buck, making for his horse and swinging into the saddle, an example which was followed by the others, including Frenchy.

As they swung off Buck noticed the condition of Frenchy's mount and halted. "Yu take that cayuse back an' get Cowan's," he ordered.

"That cayuse is good for Cheyenne—she eats work, an' besides I wants my own," laughed Frenchy.

"Yu must had a reg'lar picnic from th' looks of that crease," volunteered Hopalong, whose curiosity was mastering him.

"Shoo! I had a little argument with some feather dusters—th' O-Bar-O crowd cleaned them up."

"That so?" asked Buck.

"Yep! They sorter got into th' habit of chasin' me to Las Cruces an' forgot to stop."

"How many 'd yu get?" asked Lanky Smith.

"Twelve. Two got away. I got two before th' crowd showed up—that makes fo'teen."

"Now th' cavalry 'll be huntin' yu," croaked Billy.

"Hunt nothin'! They was in war paint—think I was a target?—think I was goin' to call off their shots for 'em?"

They relayed at the Barred-Horseshoe and went on their way at the same pace. Shortly after leaving the last-named ranch Buck turned to Frenchy and asked, "Any of that outfit think they can play poker?"

"Shore. Waffles."

"Does th' reverend Mr. Waffles think so very hard?"

"He shore does."

"Do th' rest of them mavericks think so too?"

"They'd bet their shirts on him."

At this juncture all were startled by a sudden eruption from Billy. "Haw! Haw! Haw!" he roared as the drift of Buck's intentions struck him. "Haw! Haw! Haw!"

"Here, yu long-winded coyote," yelled Red, banging him over the head with his quirt, "If yu don't 'Haw! Haw!' away from my ear I'll make it a Wow! Wow! What d'yu mean? Think I am a echo cliff? Yu slab-sided doodlebug, yu!"

"G'way, yu crimson topknot, think my head's a hunk of quartz? Fer a plugged peso I'd strew yu all over th' scenery!" shouted Billy, feigning anger and rubbing his head.

"There ain't no scenery around here," interposed Lanky. "This here beutiful prospect is a sublime conception of th' devil."

"Easy, boy! Them highfalutin' words 'll give yu a cramp someday. Yu talk like a newly made sergeant," remarked Skinny.

"He learned them words from that sky pilot over at El Paso," volunteered Hopalong, winking at Red. "He used to amble down th' aisle afore the lights was lit so's he could get a front seat. That was all hunky for a while, but every time he'd go out to irrigate, that female organ-wrastler would seem to call th' music off for his special benefit. So in a month he'd sneak in an' freeze to a chair by th' door, an' after a while he'd shy like blazes every time he got within eye range of th' church."

"Shore. But do yu know what made him get religion all of a sudden? He used to hang around on th' outside after th' joint let out an' trail along behind th' music-slinger, lookin' like he didn't know what to do with his hands. Then when he got woozy one time she up an' told him that she had got a nice long letter from her hubby. Then Mr. Lanky hit th' trail for Santa Fé so hard that there wasn't hardly none of it left. I didn't see him for a whole month," supplied Red innocently.

"Yore shore funny, ain't yu?" sarcastically grunted Lanky. "Why, I can tell things on yu that'd make yu stand treat for a year."

"I wouldn't sneak off to Santa Fé an' cheat yu out of them. Yu ought to be ashamed of yoreself."

"Yah!" snorted the aggrieved little man. "I had business over to Santa Fé!"

"Shore," endorsed Hopalong. "We've all had business over to Santa Fé. Why, about eight years ago I had business—"

"Choke up," interposed Red. "About eight years ago yu was washin' pans for Cookie an' askin' me for cartridges. Buck used to larrup yu about four times a day eight years ago."

To their roars of laughter Hopalong dropped to the rear, where, red-faced and quiet, he bent his thoughts on how to get square.

"We'll have a *pleasant* time corralling that gang," began Billy for the third time.

"For heaven's sake get off that trail!" replied Lanky. "We ain't goin' to hold 'em up. De-plomacy's th' game."

Billy looked dubious and said nothing. If he hadn't proven that he was as nervy as any man in the outfit they might have taken more stock in his grumbling.

"What's the latest from Abilene way?" asked Buck of Frenchy.

"Nothin' much 'cept th' barb-wire ruction," replied the recruit.

"What's that?" asked Red, glancing apprehensively back at Hopalong.

"Why, th' settlers put up barb-wire fence so's th' cattle wouldn't get on their farms. That would a been all right, for there wasn't much of it. But some Britishers who own a couple of big ranches out there got smart all of a sudden an' strung wire all along their lines. Punchers crossin' th' country would run plumb into a fence an' would have to ride a day an' a half, mebby, afore they found th' corner. Well, naturally, when a man has been used to ridin' where he blame pleases an' as straight as he pleases he ain't goin' to chase along a five-foot fence to 'Frisco when he wants to get to Waco. So th' punchers got to totin' wire-snips, an' when they runs up agin a fence they cuts down half a mile or so. Sometimes they'd tie their ropes to a strand an' pull off a couple of miles an' then go back after th' rest. Th' ranch bosses sent out men to watch th' fences an' told 'em to shoot any festive puncher that monkeyed with th' hardware. Well, yu know what happens when a puncher gets shot at."

"When fences grow in Texas there'll be th' devil to pay," said Buck. He hated to think that someday the freedom of the range would be annulled, for he knew that it would be the first blow against the cowboys' occupation. When a man's cattle couldn't spread out all over the land he wouldn't have to keep so many men. Farms would spring up and the sun of the free-and-easy cowboy would slowly set.

"I reckons th' cutters are classed th' same as rustlers," remarked Red with a gleam of temper.

"By th' owners, but not by th' punchers; an' it's th' punchers that count," replied Frenchy.

"Well, we'll give them a fight," interposed Hopalong, riding up. "When it gets so I can't go where I please I'll start on th' warpath. I won't buck the cavalry, but I'll keep it busy huntin' for me an' I'll have time to 'tend to th' wire-fence men, too. Why, we'll be told we can't tote our guns!"

"They're sayin' that now," replied Frenchy. "Up in Topeka, Smith, who's now marshal, makes yu leave 'em with th' bartenders."

"I'd like to see any two-laigged cuss get my guns if I didn't want him to!" began Hopalong, indignant at the idea.

"Easy, son," cautioned Buck. "Yu would do what th' rest did because yu are a square man. I'm about as hardheaded a puncher as ever straddled leather an' I've had to use my guns purty considerable, but I reckons if any decent marshal asked me to cache them in a decent way, why, I'd do it. An' let me brand somethin' on yore mind—I've heard of Smith of Topeka, an' he's mighty nifty with his hands. He don't stand off an' tell yu to unload yore lead-ranch, but he ambles up close an' taps yu on yore shirt; if yu makes a gunplay he naturally knocks yu clean across th' room an' unloads yu afore yu gets yore senses back. He weighs about a hundred an' eighty an' he's shore got sand to burn."

"Yah! When I makes a gunplay she plays! I'd look nice in Abilene or Paso or Albuquerque without my guns, wouldn't I? Just because I totes them in plain sight I've got to hand 'em over to some liquor-wrastler? I reckons not! Some hip-pocket skunk would plug me afore I could wink. I'd shore look nice loping around a keno layout without my guns, in th' same town with some cuss huntin' me, wouldn't I? A whole lot of good a marshal would a done Jimmy, an' didn't Harris get his from a cur in th' dark?" shouted Hopalong, angered by the prospect.

"We're talkin' about Topeka, where everybody has to hang up their guns," replied Buck. "An' there's th' law—"

"To blazes with th' law!" whooped Hopalong in Red's ear as he unfastened the cinch of Red's saddle and at the same time stabbing that unfortunate's mount with his spurs, thereby causing a hasty separation of the two. When Red had picked himself up and things had quieted down again the subject was changed, and several hours later they rode into Muddy Wells, a town with a little more excuse for its existence than Buckskin. The wells were in an arid valley west of Guadaloupe Pass, and were not only muddy but more or less alkaline.

CHAPTER 10

Peace Hath Its Victories

As they neared the central group of buildings they heard a hilarious and assertive song which sprang from the door and windows of the main saloon. It was in jig time, rollicking and boisterous, but the words had evidently been improvised for the occasion, as they clashed immediately with those which sprang to the minds of the outfit, although they could not be clearly distinguished. As they approached nearer and finally dismounted, however, the words became recognizable and the visitors were at once placed in harmony with the air of jovial recklessness by the roaring of the verses and the stamping of the time.

> *Oh we're red-hot cowpunchers playin' on our luck,*
> *An' there ain't a proposition that we won't buck;*
> *From sunrise to sunset we've ridden on the range,*
> *But now we're off for a howlin' change.*

> Chorus.
> *Laugh a little, sing a little, all th' day;*
> *Play a little, drink a little—we can pay;*
> *Ride a little, dig a little an' rich we'll grow.*
> *Oh, we're that bunch from th' O-Bar-O!*

> *Oh, there was a little tenderfoot an' he had a little gun,*
> *An' th' gun an' him went a-trailin' up some fun.*
> *They ambles up to Santa Fé to find a quiet game,*
> *An' now they're planted with some more of th' same!*

As Hopalong, followed by the others, pushed open the door and entered he took up the chorus with all the power of Texan lungs and even Billy joined in. The sight that met their eyes was typical of the men and the mood and the place. Leaning along the walls, lounging on the table and straddling chairs with their forearms crossed on the backs were nine cowboys, ranging from old twenty to young fifty in years, and all were shouting the song and keeping time with their hands and feet. In the center of the room was a large man dancing a fair buck-and-wing to the time so uproariously set by his companions. Hatless, neckerchief loose, holsters flapping, chaps rippling out and close, spurs clinking and perspiration streaming from his tanned face, danced Bigfoot Baker as though his life depended on speed and noise. Bottles shook and the air was fogged with smoke and dust. Suddenly, his belt slipping and letting his chaps fall around his ankles, he tripped and sat down heavily. Gasping for breath, he held out his hand and received a huge plug of tobacco, for Bigfoot had won a contest.

Shouts of greeting were hurled at the newcomers and many questions were fired at them regarding "th' latest from th' Hills." Waffles made a rush for Hopalong, but fell over Bigfoot's feet and all three were piled up in a heap. All were beaming with good nature, for they were as so many schoolboys playing truant. Prosaic cowpunching was relegated to the rear and they looked eagerly forward to their several missions. Frenchy told of the barb-wire fence war and of the new regulations of "Smith of Topeka" regarding cowpunchers' guns, and from the caustic remarks explosively given it was plain to be seen what a wire fence could expect, should one be met with, and there were many imaginary Smiths put *hors de combat.*

Kid Morris, after vainly trying to slip a bluebottle fly inside of Hopalong's shirt, gave it up and slammed his hand on Hopalong's back instead, crying: "Well, I'll be doggoned if here ain't Hopalong! How's th' missus an' th' deacon an' all th' folks to hum? I hears yu an' Frenchy's reg'lar poker fiends!"

"Oh, we plays onct in a while, but we don't want none of yore dust. Yu'll shore need it all afore th' Hills get through with yu," laughingly replied Hopalong.

"Oh, yore shore kind! But I was a sort of reckonin' that we needs some more. Perfesser P. D. Q. Waffles is our poker man an' he shore can clean out anything I ever saw. Mebby yu fellers feel reckless-like an' would like to make a pool," he cried, addressing the outfit of the Bar-20, "an' back yore boss of th' full house agin ourn?"

Red turned slowly around and took a full minute in which to size the Kid up. Then he snorted and turned his back again.

The Kid stared at him in outraged dignity. "Well, what t'ell!" he softly murmured. Then he leaped forward and walloped Red on the back. "Hey, yore royal highness!" he shouted. "Yu-yu-yu—oh, hang it—*yu*! Yu slab-sided, ringboned, saddle-galled shade of a coyote, do yu think I'm only meanderin' in th' misty vales of—of—"

Suggestions intruded from various sources. "Hades?" offered Hopalong. "Cheyenne?" murmured Johnny. "Misty mistiness of misty?" tentatively supplied Waffles.

Red turned around again. "Better come up an' have somethin'," he sympathetically invited, wiping away an imaginary tear.

"An' he's so young!" sobbed Frenchy.

"An' so fair!" wailed Tex.

"An' so ornery!" howled Lefty, throwing his arms around the discomfited youngster. Other arms went around him, and out of the sobbing mob could be heard earnest and heartfelt cussing, interspersed with imperative commands, which were gradually obeyed.

The Kid straightened up his wearing apparel. "Come on, yu locoed—"

"Angels?" queried Charley Lane, interrupting him. "Sweet things?" breathed Hopalong in hopeful expectancy.

"Oh, damn it!" yelled the Kid as he ran out into the street to escape the persecution.

"Good Kid, all right," remarked Waffles. "He'll go around an' lick someone an' come back sweet as honey."

"Did somebody say poker?" asked Bigfoot, digressing from the Kid.

"Oh, yu fellows don't want no poker. Of course yu don't. Poker's mighty uncertain," replied Red.

"Yah!" exclaimed Tex Le Blanc, pushing forward. "I'll just bet you to a standstill that Waffles an' Salvation 'll round up all th' festive dollars yu can get together! An' I'll throw in Frenchy's hat as an inducement."

"Well, if yore shore set on it make her a pool," replied Red, "an' th' winners divide with their outfit. Here's a starter," he added, tossing a buckskin bag on the table. "Come on, pile 'em up."

The crowd divided as the players seated themselves at the table, the O-Bar-O crowd grouping themselves behind their representatives; the Bar-20 behind theirs. A deck of cards was brought and the game was on.

Red, true to his nature, leaned back in a corner, where, hands on hips, he awaited any hostile demonstration on the part of the O-Bar-O; then, suddenly remembering, he looked half ashamed of his warlike position and became a peaceful citizen again. Buck leaned with his broad back against the bar, talking over his shoulder to the bartender, but watching Tenspot Davis, who was assiduously engaged in juggling a handful of Mexican dollars. Up by the door Bigfoot Baker, elated at winning the buck-and-wing contest, was endeavoring to learn a new step, while his late rival was drowning his defeat at Buck's elbow. Lefty Allen was softly singing a Mexican love song, humming when the words would not come. At the table could be heard low-spoken card terms and good-natured banter, interspersed with the clink of gold and silver and the soft pat-pat of the onlookers' feet unconsciously keeping time to Lefty's song. Notwithstanding the grim assertiveness of belts full of .45's and the peeping handles of long-barreled Colts, set off with picturesque chaps, sombreros and tinkling spurs, the scene was one of peaceful content and good-fellowship.

"Ugh!" grunted Johnny, walking over to Red and informing that person that he, Red, was a worm-eaten prune and that for half a wink he, Johnny, would prove it. Red grabbed him by the seat of his corduroys and the collar of his shirt and helped him outside, where they strolled about, taking potshots at whatever their fancy suggested.

Down the street in a cloud of dust rumbled the Las Cruces–El Paso stage and the two punchers went up to meet it. Raw furrows showed in the woodwork, one mule was missing and the driver and guard wore fresh bandages. A tired tenderfoot leaped out with a sigh of relief and hunted for his baggage, which he found to be generously perforated. Swearing at the godforsaken land where a man had to fight highwaymen and Indians inside of half a day he grumblingly lugged his valise toward a forbidding-looking shack which was called a hotel.

The driver released his teams and then turned to Red. "Hullo, old hoss, how's th' gang?" he asked genially. "We've had a hell of a time this yere trip," he went on without waiting for Red to reply. "Five miles out of Las Cruces we stood off a son-of-a-gun that wanted th' dude's wealth. Then just this side of the San Andre foothills we runs into a bunch of young bucks who turned us off this yere way an' gave us a runnin' fight purty near all th' way. I'm a whole lot farther from Paso now than I was when I started, an' seein' as I lost a jack I'll be some time gittin' there. Yu don't happen to know of a jack I can borrow, do yu?"

"I don't know about no jack, but I'll rope yu a bronch," offered Red, winking at Johnny.

"I'll pull her myself before I'll put dynamite in th' traces," replied the driver.

"Yu fellers might amble back a ways with me—them buddin' warriors 'll be layin' for me."

"We shore will," responded Johnny eagerly. "There's nine of us now an' there'll be nine more an' a cook tomorrow, mebby."

"Gosh, yu grows some," replied the guard. "Eighteen'll be a plenty for them glory hunters."

"We won't be able to," contradicted Red, "for things are peculiar."

At this moment the conversation was interrupted by the tenderfoot, who sported a new cheap sombrero and also a belt and holster complete.

"Will you gentlemen join me?" he asked, turning to Red and nodding at the saloon. "I am very dry and much averse to drinking alone."

"Why, shore," responded Red heartily, wishing to put the stranger at ease.

The game was running about even as they entered and Lefty Allen was singing "The Insult," the rich tenor softening the harshness of the surroundings.

THE INSULT

I've swum th' Colorado where she runs down clost to hell,
   I've braced th' faro layouts in Cheyenne;
I've fought for muddy water with a howlin' bunch of Sioux,
   An' swallowed hot tamales, an' cayenne.

I've rid a pitchin' broncho 'till th' sky was underneath,
   I've tackled every desert in th' land;
I've sampled XXXX whiskey 'till I couldn't hardly see,
   An' dallied with th' quicksands of the Grande.

I've argued with th' marshals of a half-a-dozen burgs,
   I've been dragged free an' fancy by a cow;
I've had three years' campaignin' with th' fightin', bitin' Ninth,
   An' never lost my temper 'till right now.

I've had the yaller fever an' I've been shot full of holes,
   I've grabbed an army mule plumb by its tail;
I've never been so snortin', really highfalutin' mad
   As when y'u up an' hands me ginger ale!

Hopalong laughed joyously at a remark made by Waffles and the stranger glanced quickly at him. His merry, boyish face, underlined by a jaw showing great firmness and set off with an expression of aggressive self-reliance, impressed the stranger and he remarked to Red, who lounged lazily near him, that he was surprised to see such a face on so young a man and he asked who the player was.

"Oh, his name's Hopalong Cassidy," answered Red. "He's th' cuss that raised that ruction down in Mexico last spring. Rode his cayuse in a saloon and played with the loungers and had to shoot one before he got out. When he did get out he had to fight a whole bunch of Mexicans an' even potted their marshal, who had th' drop on him. Then he returned and visited the marshal about a month later, took his gun away from him an' then cut th' cards to see if he was a prisoner or not. He's a shore funny cuss."

The tenderfoot gasped his amazement. "Are you not fooling with me?" he asked.

"Tell him yu came after that five hundred dollars reward and see," answered Red good-naturedly.

"Holy smoke!" shouted Waffles as Hopalong won his sixth consecutive pot. "Did yu ever see such luck?" Frenchy grinned and some time later raked in his third. Salvation then staked his last cent against Hopalong's flush and dropped out.

Tenspot flipped to Waffles the money he had been juggling and Lefty searched his clothes for wealth. Buck, still leaning against the bar, grinned and winked at Johnny, who was pouring hair-raising tales into the receptive ears of the stranger. Thereupon Johnny confided to his newly found acquaintance the facts about the game, nearly causing that person to explode with delight.

Waffles pushed back his chair, stood up and stretched. At the finish of a yawn, he grinned at his late adversary. "I'm all in, yu old son-of-a-gun. Yu shore can play draw. I'm goin' to try yu again sometime. I was beat fair an' square an' I ain't got no kick comin', none whatever," he remarked, as he shook hands with Hopalong.

"'Oh, we're that gang from th' O-Bar-O,'" hummed the Kid as he sauntered in. One cheek was slightly swollen and his clothes shed dust at every step. "Who wins?" he inquired, not having heard Waffles.

"They did, damn it!" exploded Bigfoot.

One of the Kid's peculiarities was revealed in the unreasoning and hasty conclusions he arrived at. From no desire to imply unfairness, but rather because of his bitterness against failure of any kind and his loyalty to Waffles, came his next words: "Mebby they skinned yu."

Like a flash Waffles sprang before him, his hand held up, palm out. "He don't mean nothin'—he's only a damn-fool kid!" he cried.

Buck smiled and wrested the Colt from Johnny's ever-ready hand. "Here's another," he said. Red laughed softly and rolled Johnny on the floor. "Yu jackass," he whispered, "don't yu know better'n to make a gunplay when we needs them all?"

"What are we goin' to do?" asked Tex, glancing at the bulging pockets of Hopalong's chaps.

"We're goin' to punch cows again, that's what we're goin' to do," answered Bigfoot dismally.

"An' whose are we goin' to punch? We can't go back to the old man," grumbled Tex.

Salvation looked askance at Buck and then at the others. "Mebby," he began, "mebby we kin git a job on th' Bar-20." Then turning to Buck again he bluntly asked, "Are yu short of punchers?"

"Well, I might use some," answered the foreman, hesitating. "But I ain't got only one cook, an'—"

"We'll git yu th' cook all O.K.," interrupted Charley Lane vehemently. "Hi, yu cook!" he shouted, "amble in here an' git a rustle on!"

There was no reply, and after waiting for a minute he and Waffles went into the rear room, from which there immediately issued great chunks of profanity and noise. They returned looking pugnacious and disgusted, with a wildly fighting man who was more full of liquor than was the bottle which he belligerently waved.

"This here animated distillery what yu sees is our cook," said Waffles. "*We eats his grub, nobody else. If he gits drunk that's *our* funeral; *but he won't get drunk*! If yu wants us to punch for yu say so an' we does; if yu don't, we don't."

"Well," replied Buck thoughtfully, "mebby I *can* use yu." Then with a burst of recklessness he added, "Yes, if I lose my job! But yu might sober that cook up if yu let him fall in th' horse trough."

As the procession wended its way on its mission of wet charity, carrying the cook in any manner at all, Frenchy waved his long-lost sombrero at Buck, who stood in the door, and shouted, "Yu old son-of-a-gun, I'm proud to know yu!"

Buck smiled and snapped his watch shut. "Time to amble," he said.

CHAPTER 11

Holding the Claim

O h, we're that gang from th' O-Bar-O," hummed Waffles, sinking the branding iron in the flank of a calf. The scene was one of great activity and hilarity. Several fires were burning near the huge corral and in them half a dozen irons were getting hot. Three calves were being held down for the brand of the "Bar-20" and two more were being dragged up on their sides by the ropes of the cowboys, the proud cow ponies showing off their accomplishments at the expense of the calves' feelings. In the corral the dust arose in steady clouds as calf after calf was "cut out" by the ropers and dragged out to get "tagged." Angry cows fought valiantly for their terrorized offspring, but always to no avail, for the hated rope of some perspiring and dust-grimed rider sent them crashing to earth. Over the plain were herds of cattle and groups of madly riding cowboys, and two cook wagons were stalled a short distance from the corral. The roundup of the Bar-20 was taking place, and each of the two outfits tried to outdo the other and each individual strove for a prize. The man who cut out and dragged to the fire the most calves in three days could leave for the Black Hills at the expiration of that time, the rest to follow as soon as they could.

In this contest Hopalong Cassidy led his nearest rival, Red Connors, both of whom were Bar-20 men, by twenty cut-outs, and there remained but half an hour more in which to compete. As Red disappeared into the sea of tossing horns Hopalong dashed out with a whoop, dragging a calf at the end of his rope.

"Hi, yu trellis-built rack of bones, come along there! Whoop!" he yelled, turning the prisoner over to the squad by the fire. "Chalk up this here insignificant wart of cross-eyed perversity: an' how many?" he called as he galloped back to the corral.

"One ninety-eight," announced Buck, blowing the sand from the tally sheet. "That's shore goin' some," he remarked to himself.

When the calf sprang up it was filled with terror, rage and pain, and charged at Billy from the rear as that pessimistic soul was leaning over and poking his finger at a somber horned toad. "Wow!" he yelled as his feet took huge steps up in the air, each one strictly on its own course. "Woof!" he grunted in the hot sand as he arose on his hands and knees and spat alkali.

"What's s'matter?" he asked dazedly of Johnny Nelson. "*Ain't* it funny!" he yelled sarcastically as he beheld Johnny holding his sides with laughter. "*Ain't* it funny!" he repeated belligerently. "Of course that four-laigged, knock-kneed, wobblin' son-of-a-Piute had to cut *me* out. They wasn't *nobody* in sight but Billy! Why didn't yu *say* he was comin'? Think I can see four ways to once? Why *didn't*—" At this point Red cantered up with a calf, and by a quick maneuver, drew the taut rope against the rear of Billy's knees, causing that unfortunate to sit down heavily. As he arose choking with broken-winded profanity Red dragged the animal to the fire, and Billy forgot his grievances in the press of labor.

"How many, Buck?" asked Red.

"One-eighty."

"How does she stand?"

"Yore eighteen to th' bad," replied the foreman.

"Th' son-of-a-gun!" marveled Red, riding off.

Another whoop interrupted them, and Billy quit watching out of the corner eye for pugnacious calves as he prepared for Hopalong.

"Hey, Buck, this here cuss was with a Barred-Horseshoe cow," he announced as he turned it over to the branding man. Buck made a tally in a separate column and released the animal. "Hullo, Red! Workin'?" asked Hopalong of his rival.

"Some, yu little cuss," answered Red with all the good nature in the world. Hopalong was his particular "side partner," and he could lose to him with the best of feelings.

"Yu looks so nice an' cool, an' clean, I didn't know," responded Hopalong, eyeing a streak of sweat and dust which ran from Red's eyes to his chin and then on down his neck.

"What yu been doin'? Plowin' with yore nose?" returned Red, smiling blandly at his friend's appearance.

"Yah!" snorted Hopalong, wheeling toward the corral. "Come on, yu pie-eatin' doodlebug; I'll beat yu to th' gate!"

The two ponies sent showers of sand all over Billy, who eyed them in pugnacious disgust. "Of all th' locoed imps that ever made life miserable fer a man, them's th' worst! Is there any piece of fool nonsense they hain't harnessed me with?" he beseeched of Buck. "Is there anything they hain't done to me? They hides my liquor; they stuffs th' sweatband of my hat with rope; they ties up my pants; they puts *water* in my *boots* an' *toads* in my *bunk*—ain't they *never* goin' to get sane?"

"Oh, they're only kids—they can't help it," offered Buck. "Didn't they hobble my cayuse when I was on him an' near bust my neck?"

Hopalong interrupted the conversation by bringing up another calf, and Buck, glancing at his watch, declared the contest at an end.

"Yu wins," he remarked to the newcomer. "An' now yu get scarce or Billy will shore straddle yore nerves. He said as how he was goin' to get square on yu tonight."

"I didn't, neither, Hoppy!" earnestly contradicted Billy, who had visions of a night spent in torment as a reprisal for such a threat. "Honest I didn't, did I, Johnny?" he asked appealingly.

"Yu shore did," lied Johnny, winking at Red, who had just ridden up.

"I don't know what yore talkin' about, but yu shore did," replied Red.

"If yu did," grinned Hopalong, "I'll shore make yu hard to find. Come on, fellows," he said; "grub's ready. Where's Frenchy?"

"Over chewin' th' rag with Waffles about his hat—he's lost it again," answered Red.

"He needs a guardian fer that bonnet. Th' Kid an' Salvation has jammed it in th' corral fence an' Waffles has to stand fer it."

"Let's put it in th' grub wagon an' see him cuss Cookie," suggested Hopalong.

"Shore," endorsed Johnny; "Cookie'll feed him bum grub for a week to get square."

Hopalong and Johnny ambled over to the corral and after some trouble located the missing sombrero, which they carried to the grub wagon and hid in the flour barrel. Then they went over by the excited owner and dropped a few remarks about how strange the cook was acting and how he was watching Frenchy.

Frenchy jumped at the bait and tore over to the wagon, where he and the cook spent some time in mutual recrimination. Hopalong nosed around and finally dug up the hat, white as new-fallen snow.

"Here's a hat—found it in th' dough barrel," he announced, handing it over to Frenchy, who received it in open-mouthed stupefaction.

"Yu pie-makin' pirate! *Yu* didn't know where my lid was, *did* yu! Yu cross-eyed lump of hypocrisy!" yelled Frenchy, dusting off the flour with one full-armed swing on the cook's face, driving it into that unfortunate's nose and eyes and mouth. "Yu whitewashed pirate, yu—rub yore face with water an' yu've got pancakes."

"Hey! What you doin'!" yelled the cook, kicking the spot where he had last seen Frenchy. "Don't yu know better'n that!"

"Yu live close to yoreself or I'll throw yu so high th' sun'll duck," replied Frenchy, a smile illuminating his face.

"Hey, Cookie," remarked Hopalong confidentially, "I know who put up this joke on yu. Yu ask Billy who hid th' hat," suggested the tease. "Here he comes now—see how queer he looks."

"Th' mournful Piute," ejaculated the cook. "I'll shore make him wish he'd kept on his own trail. I'll flavor his slush (coffee) with year-old dishrags!"

At this juncture Billy ambled up, keeping his weather eye peeled for trouble. "Who's a dishrag?" he queried. The cook mumbled something about crazy hens not knowing when to quit cackling and climbed up in his wagon. And that night Billy swore off drinking coffee.

When the dawn of the next day broke, Hopalong was riding toward the Black Hills, leaving Billy to untie himself as best he might.

The trip was uneventful and several days later he entered Red Dog, a rambling shantytown, one of those western mushrooms that sprang up in a night. He took up his stand at the Miner's Rest, and finally secured six claims at the cost of nine hundred hard-earned dollars, a fund subscribed by the outfits, as it was to be a partnership affair.

He rode out to a staked-off piece of hillside and surveyed his purchase, which consisted of a patch of ground, six holes, six piles of dirt and a log hut. The holes showed that the claims had been tried and found wanting.

He dumped his pack of tools and provisions, which he had bought on the way up, and lugged them into the cabin. After satisfying his curiosity he went outside and sat down for a smoke, figuring up in his mind how much gold he could carry on a horse. Then, as he realized that he could get a pack mule to carry the surplus, he became aware of a strange presence near at hand and looked up into the muzzle of a Sharp's rifle. He grasped the situation in a flash and calmly blew several heavy smoke rings around the frowning barrel.

"Well?" he asked slowly.

"Nice day, stranger," replied the man with the rifle, "but don't yu reckon yu've made a mistake?"

Hopalong glanced at the number burned on a nearby stake and carelessly blew another smoke ring. He was waiting for the gun to waver.

"No, I reckons not," he answered. "Why?"

"Well, I'll jest tell yu since yu asks. This yere claim's mine an' I'm a reg'lar terror, I am. That's why; an' seein' as it is, yu better amble some."

Hopalong glanced down the street and saw an interested group watching him, which only added to his rage for being in such a position. Then he started to say something, faltered and stared with horror at a point several feet behind his opponent. The "terror" sprang to one side in response to Hopalong's expression, as if fearing that a snake or some such danger threatened him. As he alighted in his new position he fell forward and Hopalong slid a smoking Colt in its holster.

Several men left the distant group and ran toward the claim. Hopalong reached his arm inside the door and brought forth his Sharp's rifle, with which he covered their advance.

"Anything yu want?" he shouted savagely.

The men stopped and two of them started to sidle in front of two others, but Hopalong was not there for the purpose of permitting a move that would screen any gunplay and he stopped the game with a warning shout. Then the two held up their hands and advanced.

"We wants to git Dan," called out one of them, nodding at the prostrate figure.

"Come ahead," replied Hopalong, substituting a Colt for the rifle.

They carried their badly wounded and insensible burden back to those whom they had left, and several curses were hurled at the cowboy, who only smiled grimly and entered the hut to place things ready for a siege, should one come. He had one hundred rounds of ammunition and provisions enough for two weeks, with the assurance of reinforcements long before that time would expire. He cut several rough loopholes and laid out his weapons for quick handling. He knew that he could stop any advance during the day and planned only for night attacks. How long he could go without sleep did not bother him, because he gave it no thought, as he was accustomed to short naps and could awaken at will or at the slightest sound.

As dusk merged into dark he crept forth and collected several handfuls of dry twigs, which he scattered around the hut, as the cracking of these would warn him of an approach. Then he went in and went to sleep.

He awoke at daylight after a good night's rest, and feasted on canned beans and peaches. Then he tossed the cans out of the door and shoved his hat out. Receiving no response he walked out and surveyed the town at his feet. A sheepish grin spread over his face as he realized that there was no danger.

Several red-shirted men passed by him on their way to town, and one, a grizzled veteran of many gold camps, stopped and sauntered up to him.

"Mornin'," said Hopalong.

"Mornin'," replied the stranger. "I thought I'd drop in an' say that I saw that gunplay of yourn yesterday. Yu ain't got no reason to look for a rush. This camp is half decent men an' half bullies, an' th' decent men won't stand fer no play like that. Them fellers that jest passed are neighbors of yourn, an' they won't lay abed if yu needs them. But yu wants to look out fer th' joints in th' town. Guess this business is out of yore line," he finished as he sized Hopalong up.

"She shore is, but I'm here to stay. Got tired of punchin' an' reckoned I'd git rich." Here he smiled and glanced at the hole. "How're yu makin' out?" he asked.

"'Bout five dollars a day apiece, but that ain't nothin' when grub's so high. Got reckless th' other day an' had a egg at fifty cents."

Hopalong whistled and glanced at the empty cans at his feet. "Any marshal in this burg?"

"Yep. But he's one of th' gang. No good, an' drunk half th' time an' half drunk th' rest. Better come down an' have something," invited the miner.

"I'd shore like to, but I can't let no gang get in that door," replied the puncher.

"Oh, that's all right; I'll call my pardner down to keep house till yu gits back. He can hold her all right. Hey, Jake!" he called to a man who was some hundred paces distant; "come down here an' keep house till we gits back, will yu?"

The man lumbered down to them and took possession as Hopalong and his newly found friend started for the town.

They entered the "Miner's Rest" and Hopalong fixed the room is his mind with one swift glance. Three men—and they looked like the crowd he had stopped before—were playing poker at a table near the window. Hopalong leaned with his back to the bar and talked, with the players always in sight.

Soon the door opened and a bewhiskered, heavyset man tramped in, and walking up to Hopalong, looked him over.

"Huh," he sneered, "yu are th' gent with th' festive guns that plugged Dan, ain't yu?"

Hopalong looked at him in the eyes and quietly replied: "An' who th' hell are yu?"

The stranger's eyes blazed and his face wrinkled with rage as he aggressively shoved his jaw close to Hopalong's face.

"Yu runt, I'm a better man than yu even if yu do wear hair pants," referring to Hopalong's chaps. "Yu cow-wrastlers make me tired, an' I'm goin' to show yu that this town is too good for you. Yu can say it right now that yu are a ornery, game-leg—"

Hopalong, blind with rage, smashed his insulter squarely between the eyes with all the power of his sinewy body behind the blow, knocking him in a heap under the table. Then he quickly glanced at the cardplayers and saw a hostile movement. His gun was out in a flash and he covered the trio as he walked up to them. Never in all his life had he felt such a desire to kill. His eyes were diamond points of accumulated fury, and those whom he faced quailed before him.

"Yu scum of th' earth! Draw, please draw! Pull yore guns an' gimme my chance! Three to one, an' I'll lay my guns here," he said, placing them on the bar and removing his hands. "'Nearer My God to Thee' is purty appropriate fer yu just now! Yu seem to be a-scared of yore own guns. Git down on yore dirty knees an' say good an' loud that yu eats dirt! Shout out that yu are too currish to live with decent men," he said, even-toned and distinct, his voice vibrant with passion as he took up his Colts. "Get down!" he repeated, shoving the weapons forward and pulling back the hammers.

The trio glanced at each other, and all three dropped to their knees and repeated in venomous hatred the words Hopalong said for them.

"Now git! An' if I sees yu when I leaves I'll send yu after yore friend. I'll shoot on sight now. Git!" He escorted them to the door and kicked the last one out.

His miner friend still leaned against the bar and looked his approval.

"Well done, youngster! But yu wants to look out—that man," pointing to the now-groping victim of Hopalong's blow, "is th' marshal of this town. He or his pals will get yu if yu don't watch th' corners."

Hopalong walked over to the marshal, jerked him to his feet and slammed him against the bar. Then he tore the cheap badge from its place and threw it on the floor. Reaching down, he drew the marshal's revolver from its holster and shoved it in its owner's hand.

"Yore th' marshal of this place an' it's too good for me, but yore goin' to pick up that tin lie," pointed at the badge, "an' yore goin' to do it right now. Then yore goin' to get kicked out of that door, an' if yu stops runnin' while I can see yu I'll fill yu so full of holes yu'll catch cold. Yore a sumptious marshal, yu are! Yore th' snortingest ki-yi that ever stuck its tail atween its laigs, yu are. Yu wants to keep to yoreself or some papoose or I'll slide yu over th' Divide so fast yu won't have time to grease yore pants. Pick up that license-tag an' let me see you perculate so lively that yore back 'll look like a ten-cent piece in five seconds. Flit!"

The marshal, dazed and bewildered, stooped and fumbled for the badge. Then he stood up and glanced at the gun in his hand and at the eager man before him. He slid the weapon in his belt and drew his hand across his fast-closing eyes. Cursing streaks of profanity, he staggered to the door and landed in a heap in the street from the force of Hopalong's kick. Struggling to his feet, he ran unsteadily down the block and disappeared around a corner.

The bartender, cool and unperturbed, pushed out three glasses on his treat: "I've seen yu afore, up in Cheyenne—'member? How's yore friend Red?" he asked as he filled the glasses with the best the house afforded.

"Well, shore 'nuff! Glad to see yu, Jimmy! What yu doin' away off here?" asked Hopalong, beginning to feel at home.

"Oh, jest filterin' round like. I'm awful glad to see yu—this yere wart of a town needs siftin' out. It was only last week I was wishin' one of yore bunch 'ud show up—that ornament yu jest buffaloed shore raised th' devil in here, an' I wished I had somebody to prospect his anatomy for a lead mine. But he's got a tough gang circulating with him. Ever hear of Dutch Shannon or Blinky Neary? They's with him."

"Dutch Shannon? Nope," he replied.

"Bad eggs, an' not a-carin' how they gits square. Th' feller yu' salted yesterday was a bosom friend of th' marshal's, an' he passed in his chips last night."

"So?"

"Yep. Bought a bottle of ready-made nerve an' went to his own funeral. Aristotle Smith was lookin' fer him up in Cheyenne last year. Aristotle said he'd give a century fer five minutes' palaver with him, but he shied th' town an' didn't come back. Yu know Aristotle, don't yu? He's th' geezer that made fame up to Poison Knob three years ago. He used to go to town ridin' astride a log on th' lumber flume. Made four miles in six minutes with th' promise of a ruction when he stopped. Once when he was loaded he tried to ride back th' same way he came, an' th' first thing he knowed he was three miles farther from his supper an' a-slippin' down that valley like he wanted to go somewhere. He swum out at Potter's Dam an' it took him a day to walk back. But he didn't make that play again, because he was frequently sober, an' when he wasn't he'd only stand off an' swear at th' slide."

"That's Aristotle, all hunk. He's th' chap that used to play checkers with Deacon Rawlins. They used empty an' loaded shells for men, an' when they got a king they'd lay one on its side. Sometimes they'd jar th' board an' they'd all be kings an' then they'd have a cussin' match," replied Hopalong, once more restored to good humor.

"Why," responded Jimmy, "he counted his wealth over twice by mistake an' shore raised a howl when he went to blow it—thought he'd been robbed, an' laid behind th' houses fer a week lookin' fer th' feller that done it."

"I've heard of that cuss—he shore was th' limit. What become of him?" asked the miner.

"He ambled up to Laramie an' stuck his head in th' window of that joint by th' plaza an' hollered 'Fire,' an' they did. He was shore a good feller, all th' same," answered the bartender.

Hopalong laughed and started for the door. Turning around he looked at his miner friend and asked: "Comin' along? I'm goin' back now."

"Nope. Reckon I'll hit th' tiger a whirl. I'll stop in when I passes."

"All right. So long," replied Hopalong, slipping out of the door and watching for trouble. There was no opposition shown him, and he arrived at his claim to find Jake in a heated argument with another of the gang.

"Here he comes now," he said as Hopalong walked up. "Tell him what yu said to me."

"I said yu made a mistake," said the other, turning to the cowboy in a half apologetic manner.

"An' what else?" insisted Jake.

"Why, ain't that all?" asked the claim-jumper's friend in feigned surprise, wishing that he had kept quiet.

"Well I reckons it is if yu can't back up yore words," responded Jake in open contempt.

Hopalong grabbed the intruder by the collar of his shirt and hauled him off the claim. "Yu keep off this, understand? I just kicked yore marshal out in th' street, an' I'll pay yu th' next call. If yu rambles in range of my guns yu'll shore get in th' way of a slug. Yu an' yore gang wants to browse on th' far side of th' range or yu'll miss a sunrise some mornin'. Scoot!"

Hopalong turned to his companion and smiled. "What 'd he say?" he asked genially.

"Oh, he jest shot off his mouth a little. They's all no good. I've collided with lots of them all over this country. They can't face a good man an' keep their nerve. What'd yu say to th' marshal?"

"I told him what he was an' threw him outen th' street," replied Hopalong. "In about two weeks we'll have a new marshal an' he'll shore be a dandy."

"Yes? Why don't yu take th' job yoreself? We're with yu."

"Better man comin'. Ever hear of Buck Peters or Red Connors of th' Bar-20, Texas?"

"Buck Peters? Seems to me I have. Did he punch fer th' Tin-Cup up in Montana, 'bout twenty years back?"

"Shore! Him and Frenchy McAllister punched all over that country an' they used to paint Cheyenne, too," replied Hopalong, eagerly.

"I knows him, then. I used to know Frenchy, too. Are they comin' up here?"

"Yes," responded Hopalong, struggling with another can while waiting for the fire to catch up. "Better have some grub with me—don't like to eat alone," invited the cowboy, the reaction of his late rage swinging him to the other extreme.

When their tobacco had got well started at the close of the meal and content had taken possession of them Hopalong laughed quietly and finally spoke: "Did yu ever know Aristotle Smith when yu was up in Montana?"

"Did I! Well, me an' Aristotle prospected all through that country till he got so locoed I had to watch him fer fear he'd blow us both up. He greased th' fryin' pan with dynamite one night, an' we shore had to eat jerked meat an' canned stuff all th' rest of that trip. What made yu ask? Is he comin' up too?"

"No, I reckons not. Jimmy, th' bartender, said that he cashed in up at Laramie. Wasn't he th' cuss that built that boat out there on th' Arizona desert because he was scared that a flood might come? Th' sun shore warped that punt till it wasn't even good for a hencoop."

"Nope. That was Sister-Annie Tompkins. He was purty near as bad as Aristotle, though. He roped a puma up on th' Sacramentos, an' didn't punch no more fer three weeks. Well, here comes my pardner an' I reckons I'll amble right along. If yu needs any referee or a side pardner in any ruction yu has only got to warble up my way. So long."

The next ten days passed quietly and on the afternoon of the eleventh Hopalong's miner friend paid him a visit.

"Jake recommends yore peaches," he laughed as he shook Hopalong's hand. "He says yu boosted another of that crowd. That bein' so I thought I would drop in an' say that they're comin' after yu tonight, shore. Just heard of it from yore friend Jimmy. Yu can count on us when th' rush comes. But why didn't yu say yu was a pard of Buck Peters'? Me an' him used to shoot up Laramie together. From what yore friend James says, yu can handle this gang by yore lonesome, but if yu needs any encouragement yu make some sign an' we'll help th' event along some. They's eight of us that'll be waitin' up to get th' returns an' we're shore goin' to be in range."

"Gee, it's nice to run across a friend of Buck's! Ain't he a son-of-a-gun?"

asked Hopalong, delighted at the news. Then, without waiting for a reply, he went on: "Yore shore square, all right, an' I hates to refuse yore offer, but I got eighteen friends comin' up an' they ought to get here by tomorrow. Yu tell Jimmy to head them this way when they shows up an' I'll have th' claim for them. There ain't no use of yu fellers gettin' mixed up in this. Th' bunch that's comin' can clean out any gang this side of sunup, an' I expects they'll shore be anxious to begin when they finds me eatin' peaches an' wastin' my time shootin' bums. Yu pass th' word along to yore friends, an' tell them to lay low an' see th' Arory Boerallis hit this town with its tail up. Tell Jimmy to do it up good when he speaks about me holdin' th' claim—I likes to see Buck an' Red fight when they're good an' mad."

The miner laughed and slapped Hopalong on the shoulder. "Yore all right, youngster! Yore just like Buck was at yore age. Say now, I reckons he wasn't a reg'lar terror on wheels! Why, I've seen him do more foolish things than any man I knows of, an' I calculate that if Buck pals with yu there ain't no water in yore sand. My name's Tom Halloway," he suggested.

"An' mine's Hopalong Cassidy," was the reply. "I've heard Buck speak of yu."

"Has yu? Well, don't it beat all how little this world is? Somebody allus turnin' up that knows somebody yu knows. I'll just amble along, Mr. Cassidy, an' don't yu be none bashful about callin' if yu needs me. Any pal of Buck's is my friend. Well, so long," said the visitor as he strode off. Then he stopped and turned around. "Hey, mister!" he called. "They are goin' to roll a fire barrel down agin yu from behind," indicating by an outstretched arm the point from where it would start. "If it burns yu out I'm goin' to take a hand from up there," pointing to a cluster of rocks well to the rear of where the crowd would work from, "an' I don't care whether yu likes it or not," he added to himself.

Hopalong scratched his head and then laughed. Taking up a pick and shovel, he went out behind the cabin and dug a trench parallel with and about twenty paces away from the rear wall. Heaping the excavated dirt up on the near side of the cut, he stepped back and surveyed his labor with open satisfaction. "Roll yore fire barrel an' be damn," he muttered. "Mebby she won't make a bully light for potshots, though," he added, grinning at the execution he would do.

Taking up his tools, he went up to the place from where the gang would roll the barrel, and made half a dozen mounds of twigs, being careful to make them very flimsy. Then he covered them with earth and packed them gently. The mounds looked very tempting from the viewpoint of a marksman in search of cover, and appeared capable of stopping any rifle ball that could be fired against them. Hopalong looked them over critically and stepped back.

"I'd like to see th' look on th' face of th' son-of-a-gun that uses them for cover—won't he be surprised?" and he grinned gleefully as he pictured his shots boring through them. Then he placed in the center of each a chip or a pebble or something that he thought would show up well in the firelight.

Returning to the cabin, he banked it up well with dirt and gravel, and tossed a few shovelfuls up on the roof as a safety valve to his exuberance. When he entered the door he had another idea, and fell to work scooping out a shallow cellar, deep enough to shelter him when lying at full length. Then he stuck his head out of the window and grinned at the false covers with their prominent bull's-eyes.

"When that prize-winnin' gang of ossified idiots runs up agin' these fortifications they shore will be disgusted. I'll bet four dollars an' seven cents they'll think their medicine man's no good. I hopes that puff-eyed marshal will pick out that hump with th' chip on it," and he hugged himself in anticipation.

He then cut down a sapling and fastened it to the roof and on it he tied his neckerchief, which fluttered valiantly and with defiance in the light breeze. "I shore hopes they appreciates that," he remarked whimsically, as he went inside the hut and closed the door.

The early part of the evening passed in peace, and Hopalong, tired of watching in vain, wished for action. Midnight came, and it was not until half an hour before dawn that he was attacked. Then a noise sent him to a loophole, where he fired two shots at skulking figures some distance off. A fusillade of bullets replied; one of them ripped through the door at a weak spot and drilled a hole in a can of the everlasting peaches. Hopalong set the can in the frying pan and then flitted from loophole to loophole, shooting quick and straight. Several curses told him that he had not missed, and he scooped up a finger of peach juice. Shots thudded into the walls of his fort in an unceasing stream, and, as it grew lighter, several whizzed through the loopholes. He kept close to the earth and waited for the rush, and when it came sent it back, minus two of its members.

As he reloaded his Colts a bullet passed through his shirtsleeve and he promptly nailed the marksman. He looked out of a crack in the rear wall and saw the top of an adjoining hill crowned with spectators, all of whom were armed. Some time later he repulsed another attack and heard a faint cheer from his friends on the hill. Then he saw a barrel, blazing from end to end, roll out from the place he had so carefully covered with mounds. It gathered speed and bounded over the rough ground, flashed between two rocks and leaped into the trench, where it crackled and roared in vain.

"Now," said Hopalong, blazing at the mounds as fast as he could load and fire his Sharp's, "we'll just see what yu thinks of yore nice little covers."

Yells of consternation and pain rang out in a swelling chorus, and legs and arms jerked and flopped, one man, in his astonishment at the shot that tore open his cheek, sitting up in plain sight of the marksman. Roars of rage floated up from the main body of the besiegers, and the discomfited remnant of barrel-rollers broke for real cover.

Then he stopped another rush from the front, made upon the supposition that he was thinking only of the second detachment. A hearty cheer arose from Tom Halloway and his friends, ensconced in their rocky position, and it was taken up by those on the hill, who danced and yelled their delight at the battle, to them more humorous than otherwise.

This recognition of his prowess from men of the caliber of his audience made him feel good, and he grinned: "Gee, I'll bet Halloway an' his friends is shore itchin' to get in this," he murmured, firing at a head that was shown for an instant. "Wonder what Red 'll say when Jimmy tells him—bet he'll plow dust like a cyclone," and Hopalong laughed, picturing to himself the satiation of Red's anger. "Old redheaded son-of-a-gun," murmured the cowboy affectionately, "he shore can fight."

As he squinted over the sights of his rifle his eye caught sight of a moving body of men as they cantered over the flats about two miles away. In his eagerness he forgot to shoot and carefully counted them. "Nine," he grumbled. "Wonder what's th' matter?"—fearing that they were not his friends. Then a second body numbering eight cantered into sight and followed the first.

"Whoop! There's th' Redhead!" he shouted, dancing in his joy. "Now," he shouted at the peach can joyously, "yu wait about thirty minutes an' yu'll shore reckon Hades has busted loose!"

He grabbed up his Colts, which he kept loaded for repelling rushes, and recklessly emptied them into the bushes and between the rocks and trees, searching every likely place for a human target. Then he slipped his rifle in a loophole and waited for good shots, having worked off the dangerous pressure of his exuberance.

Soon he heard a yell from the direction of the "Miner's Rest," and fell to jamming cartridges into his revolvers so that he could sally out and join in the fray by the side of Red.

The thunder of madly pounding hoofs rolled up the trail, and soon a horse and rider shot around the corner and headed for the copse. Three more raced close behind and then a bunch of six, followed by the rest, spread out and searched for trouble.

Red, a Colt in each hand and hatless, stood up in his stirrups and sent shot after shot into the fleeing mob, which he could not follow on account of the nature of the ground. Buck wheeled and dashed down the trail again with Red a close second, the others packed in a solid mass and after them. At the first level stretch the newcomers swept down and hit their enemies, going through them like a knife through cheese. Hopalong danced up and down with rage when he could not find his horse, and had to stand and yell, a spectator.

The fight drifted in among the buildings, where it became a series of isolated duels, and soon Hopalong saw panic-stricken horses carrying their riders out of the other side of the town. Then he went gunning for the man who had rustled his horse. He was unsuccessful and returned to his peaches.

Soon the riders came up, and when they saw Hopalong shove a peach into his powder-grimed mouth they yelled their delight.

"Yu old maverick! Eatin' peaches like yu was afraid we'd git some!" shouted Red indignantly, leaping down and running up to his pal as though to thrash him.

Hopalong grinned pleasantly and fired a peach against Red's eye. "I was savin' that one for yu, Reddie," he remarked, as he avoided Buck's playful kick. "Yu fellers git to work an' dig up some wealth—I'm hungry." Then he turned to Buck: "Yore th' marshal of this town, an' any son-of-a-gun what don't like it had better write. Oh, yes, here comes Tom Halloway—'member him?"

Buck turned and faced the miner and his hand went out with a jerk.

"Well, I'll be locoed if I didn't punch with yu on th' Tin-Cup!" he said.

"Yu shore did an' yu was purty devilish, but that there Cassidy of yourn beats anything I ever seen."

"He's a good kid," replied Buck, glancing to where Red and Hopalong were quarreling as to who had eaten the most pie in a contest held some years before.

Johnny, nosing around, came upon the perforated and partially scattered piles of earth and twigs, and vented his disgust of them by kicking them to pieces. "Hey! Hoppy! Oh, Hoppy!" he called, "what are these things?"

Hopalong jammed Red's hat over that person's eyes and replied: "Oh, them's some loaded dice I fixed for them."

"Yu son-of-a-gun!" sputtered Red, as he wrestled with his friend in the exuberance of his pride. "Yu son-of-a-gun! Yu shore ought to be ashamed to treat 'em that way!"

"Shore," replied Hopalong. "But I ain't!"

CHAPTER 12

The Hospitality of Travennes

Mr. Buck Peters rode into Alkaline one bright September morning and sought refreshment at the Emporium. Mr. Peters had just finished some business for his employer and felt the satisfaction that comes with the knowledge of work well done. He expected to remain in Alkaline for several days, where he was to be joined by two of his friends and punchers, Mr. Hopalong Cassidy and Mr. Red Connors, both of whom were at Cactus Springs, seventy miles to the east. Mr. Cassidy and his friends had just finished a nocturnal tour of Santa Fé and felt somewhat peevish and dull in consequence, not to mention the sadness occasioned by the expenditure of the greater part of their combined capital on such foolishness as faro, roulette and wet-goods.

Mr. Peters and his friends had sought wealth in the Black Hills, where they had enthusiastically disfigured the earth in the fond expectation of uncovering vast stores of virgin gold. Their hopes were of an optimistic brand and had existed until the last canister of cornmeal flour had been emptied by Mr. Cassidy's burro, which waited not upon its master's pleasure nor upon the ethics of the case. When Mr. Cassidy had returned from exercising the animal and himself over two miles of rocky hillside in the vain endeavor to give it his opinion of burros and sundry chastisements, he was requested, as owner of the beast, to give his counsel as to the best way of securing eighteen breakfasts. Remembering that the animal was headed north when he last saw it and that it was too old to eat, anyway, he suggested a plan which had worked successfully at other times for other ends, namely, poker. Mr. McAllister, an expert at the great American game, volunteered his service in accordance with the spirit of the occasion and, half an hour later, he and Mr. Cassidy drifted into Pell's poker parlors, which were located in the rear of a Chinese laundry, where they gathered unto themselves the wherewithal for the required breakfasts. An hour spent in the card room of the "Hurrah" convinced its proprietor that they had wasted their talents for the past six weeks in digging for gold. The proof of this permitted the departure of the outfits with their customary éclat.

At Santa Fé the various individuals had gone their respective ways, to re-assemble at the ranch in the near future, and for several days they had been drifting south in groups of twos and threes and, like chaff upon a stream, had eddied into Alkaline, where Mr. Peters had found them arduously engaged in postponing the final journey. After he had gladdened their hearts and soothed their throats by making several pithy remarks to the bartender, with whom he established their credit, he cautioned them against letting anyone harm them and, smiling at the humor of his warning, left abruptly.

Cactus Springs was burdened with a zealous and initiative organization known as vigilantes, whose duty it was to extend the courtesies of the land to cattle thieves and the like. This organization boasted of the name of Travennes' Terrors and of a muster roll of twenty. There was also a boast that no one had ever escaped them which, if true, was in many cases unfortunate. Mr. Slim Travennes, with whom Mr. Cassidy had participated in an extemporaneous ex-change of Colt's courtesies in Santa Fé the year before, was the head of the or-ganization and was also chairman of the committee on arrivals, and the two gentlemen of the Bar-20 had not been in town an hour before he knew of it. Being anxious to show the strangers every attention and having a keen recol-lection of the brand of gunplay commanded by Mr. Cassidy, he planned a smoother method of procedure and one calculated to permit him to enjoy the pleasures of a good old age. Mr. Travennes knew that horse thieves were re-garded as social enemies, that the necessary proof of their guilt was the finding of stolen animals in their possession, that death was the penalty and that every man, whether directly concerned or not, regarded himself as judge, jury and ex-ecutioner. He had several acquaintances who were bound to him by his knowl-edge of crimes they had committed and who could not refuse his slightest wish. Even if they had been free agents they were not above causing the death of an innocent man. Mr. Travennes, feeling very self-satisfied at his cleverness, arranged to have the proof placed where it would do the most harm and in-tended to take care of the rest by himself.

Mr. Connors, feeling much refreshed and very hungry, arose at daylight the next morning, and dressing quickly, started off to feed and water the horses. After having several tilts with the landlord about the bucket he took his depar-ture toward the corral at the rear. Peering through the gate, he could hardly believe his eyes. He climbed over it and inspected the animals at close range, and found that those which he and his friend had ridden for the last two months were not to be seen, but in their places were two better animals, which concerned him greatly. Being fair and square himself, he could not understand the change and sought enlightenment of his more imaginative and suspicious friend.

"Hey, Hopalong!" he called, "come out here an' see what th' devil has happened!"

Mr. Cassidy stuck his auburn head out of the wounded shutter and complacently surveyed his companion. Then he saw the horses and looked hard.

"Quit yore foolin', yu old cuss," he remarked pleasantly, as he groped around behind him with his feet, searching for his boots. "Anybody would think yu was a little boy with yore fool jokes. Ain't yu ever goin' to grow up?"

"They've got our bronchs," replied Mr. Connors in an injured tone. "Honest, I ain't kiddin' yu," he added for the sake of peace.

"Who has?" came from the window, followed immediately by, "Yu've got my boots!"

"I ain't—they're under th' bunk," contradicted and explained Mr. Connors. Then, turning to the matter in his mind he replied, "I don't know who's got them. If I did do yu think I'd be holdin' hands with myself?"

"Nobody'd accuse yu of anything like that," came from the window, accompanied by an overdone snicker.

Mr. Connors flushed under his accumulated tan as he remembered the varied pleasures of Santa Fé, and he regarded the bronchos in anything but a pleasant state of mind.

Mr. Cassidy slid through the window and approached his friend, looking as serious as he could.

"Any tracks?" he inquired, as he glanced quickly over the ground to see for himself.

"Not after that wind we had last night. They might have growed there for all I can see," growled Mr. Connors.

"I reckon we better hold a powwow with th' foreman of this shack an' find out what he knows," suggested Mr. Cassidy. "This looks too good to be a swap."

Mr. Connors looked his disgust at the idea and then a light broke in upon him. "Mebby they was hard pushed an' wanted fresh cayuses," he said. "A whole lot of people get hard pushed in this country. Anyhow, we'll prospect th' boss."

They found the proprietor in his stocking feet, getting the breakfast, and

Mr. Cassidy regarded the preparations with open approval. He counted the tin plates and found only three, and, thinking that there would be more plates if there were others to feed, glanced into the landlord's room. Not finding signs of other guests, on whom to lay the blame for the loss of his horse, he began to ask questions.

"Much trade?" he inquired solicitously.

"Yep," replied the landlord.

Mr. Cassidy looked at the three tins and wondered if there had ever been any more with which to supply his trade. "Been out this morning?" he pursued.

"Nope."

"Talks purty nigh as much as Buck," thought Mr. Cassidy, and then said aloud, "Anybody else here?"

"Nope."

Mr. Cassidy lapsed into a painful and disgusted silence and his friend tried his hand.

"Who owns a mosaic bronch, Chinee flag on th' near side, Skillet brand?" asked Mr. Connors.

"Quien sabe?"

"Gosh, he can nearly keep still in two lingoes," thought Mr. Cassidy.

"Who owns a bobtailed pinto, saddle-galled, cast in th' near eye, Star Diamond brand, white stockin' on th' off front prop, with a habit of scratchin' itself every other minute?" went on Mr. Connors.

"Slim Travennes," replied the proprietor, flopping a flapjack.

Mr. Cassidy reflectively scratched the back of his hand and looked innocent, but his mind was working overtime.

"Who's Slim Travennes?" asked Mr. Connors, never having heard of that person, owing to the reticence of his friend.

"Captain of th' vigilantes."

"What does he look like on th' general run?" blandly inquired Mr. Cassidy, wishing to verify his suspicions. He thought of the trouble he had with Mr. Travennes up in Santa Fé and of the reputation that gentleman possessed. Then the fact that Mr. Travennes was the leader of the local vigilantes came to his assistance and he was sure that the captain had a hand in the change. All these points existed in misty groups in his mind, but the next remark of the landlord caused them to rush together and reveal the plot.

"Good," said the landlord, flopping another flapjack, "and a warnin' to hoss thieves."

"Ahem," coughed Mr. Cassidy and then continued, "is he a tall, lanky, yaller-headed son-of-a-gun, with a big nose an' lots of ears?"

"Mebby so," answered the host.

"Um, slopping over into bad Sioux," thought Mr. Cassidy, and then said aloud, "How long has he hung around this here layout?" at the same time passing a warning glance at his companion.

The landlord straightened up. "Look here, stranger, if yu hankers after his pedigree so all-fired hard yu had best pump him."

"I told yu this here feller wasn't a man what would give away all he knowed," lied Mr. Connors, turning to his friend and indicating the host. "He ain't got time for that. Anybody can see that he is a powerful busy man. An' then he ain't no child."

Mr. Cassidy thought that the landlord could tell all he knew in about five minutes and then not break any speed records for conversation, but he looked properly awed and impressed. "Well, yu needn't go an' get mad about it! I didn't know, did I?"

"Who's gettin' mad?" pugnaciously asked Mr. Connors. After his injured feelings had been soothed by Mr. Cassidy's sullen silence he again turned to the landlord.

"What did this Travennes look like when yu saw him last?" coaxed Mr. Connors.

"Th' same as he does now, as yu can see by lookin' out of th' window. That's him down th' street," enlightened the host, thawing to the pleasant Mr. Connors.

Mr. Cassidy adopted the suggestion and frowned. Mr. Travennes and two companions were walking toward the corral and Mr. Cassidy once again slid out of the window, his friend going by the door.

CHAPTER 13

■❖❖❖❖❖■ ❖❖❖❖❖❖❖❖❖❖❖❖❖❖❖❖❖❖❖❖❖❖❖ ❖❖❖❖❖■

Travennes' Discomfiture

When Mr. Travennes looked over the corral fence he was much chagrined to see a man and a Colt's .45, both paying strict attention to his nose.

"Mornin', Duke," said the man with the gun. "Lose anything?"

Mr. Travennes looked back at his friends and saw Mr. Connors sitting on a rock holding two guns. Mr. Travennes' right and left wings were the targets and they pitted their frowns against Mr. Connors' smile.

"Not that I knows of," replied Mr. Travennes, shifting his feet uneasily.

"Find anything?" came from Mr. Cassidy as he sidled out of the gate.

"Nope," replied the captain of the Terrors, eyeing the Colt.

"Are yu in th' habit of payin' early mornin' calls to this here corral?" persisted Mr. Cassidy, playing with the gun.

"Ya-as. That's my business—I'm th' captain of th' vigilantes."

"That's too bad," sympathized Mr. Cassidy, moving forward a step.

Mr. Travennes looked put out and backed off. "What yu mean, stickin' me up thisaway?" he asked indignantly.

"Yu needn't go an' get mad," responded Mr. Cassidy. "Just business. Yore cayuse an' another shore climbed this corral fence last night an' ate up our bronchs, an' I just nachurlly want to know about it."

Mr. Travennes looked his surprise and incredulity and craned his neck to see for himself. When he saw his horse peacefully scratching itself he swore and looked angrily up the street. Mr. Connors, behind the shack, was hidden to the view of those on the street, and when two men ran up at a signal from Mr. Travennes, intending to insert themselves in the misunderstanding, they were promptly lined up with the first two by the man on the rock.

"Sit down," invited Mr. Connors, pushing a chunk of air out of the way with his guns. The last two felt a desire to talk and to argue the case on its merits, but refrained as the black holes in Mr. Connors' guns hinted at eruption. "Every time yu opens yore mouths yu get closer to th' Great Divide," enlightened that person, and they were childlike in their belief.

Mr. Travennes acted as though he would like to scratch his thigh where his Colt's chafed him, but postponed the event and listened to Mr. Cassidy, who was asking questions.

"Where's our cayuses, General?"

Mr. Travennes replied that he didn't know. He was worried, for he feared that his captor didn't have a secure hold on the hammer of the ubiquitous Colt's.

"Where's *my* cayuse?" persisted Mr. Cassidy.

"I don't know, but I wants to ask yu how yu got mine," replied Mr. Travennes.

"Yu tell me how mine got out an' I'll tell yu how yourn got in," countered Mr. Cassidy.

Mr. Connors added another to his collection before the captain replied.

"Out in this country people get in trouble when they're found with other folks' cayuses," Mr. Travennes suggested.

Mr. Cassidy looked interested and replied: "Yu shore ought to borrow some experience, an' there's lots floating around. More than one man has smoked in a powder mill, an' th' number of them planted who looked in th' muzzle of a empty gun is scandalous. If my remarks don't perculate right smart I'll explain."

Mr. Travennes looked down the street again, saw number five added to the lineup, and coughed up chunks of broken profanity, grieving his host by his lack of courtesy.

"Time," announced Mr. Cassidy, interrupting the round. "I wants them cayuses an' I wants 'em right now. Yu an' me will amble off an' get 'em. I won't bore yu with tellin' yu what'll happen if yu gets skittish. Slope along an' don't be scared; I'm with yu," assured Mr. Cassidy as he looked over at Mr. Connors, whose ascetic soul pined for the flapjacks of which his olfactories caught intermittent whiffs.

"Well, Red, I reckons yu has got plenty of room out here for all yu may corral; anyhow there ain't a whole lot more. My friend Slim an' I are shore going to have a devil of a time if we can't find them cussed bronchs. Whew, them flapjacks smell like a plain trail to payday. Just think of th' nice maple juice we used to get up to Cheyenne on them frosty mornings."

"Get out of here an' lemme alone! What do yu allus want to go an' make a feller unhappy for? Can't yu keep still about grub when yu knows I ain't had my morning's feed yet?" asked Mr. Connors, much aggrieved.

"Well, I'll be back directly an' I'll have them cayuses. Yu tend to business an' watch th' herd. That shorthorn yearling at th' end of th' line"—pointing to a young man who looked capable of taking risks—"he looks like he might take a chance an' gamble with yu," remarked Mr. Cassidy, placing Mr. Travennes in front of him and pushing back his own sombrero. "Don't put too much maple juice on them flapjacks, Red," he warned as he poked his captive in the back of the neck as a hint to get along. Fortunately Mr. Connors' closing remarks are lost to history.

Observing that Mr. Travennes headed south on the quest, Mr. Cassidy reasoned that the missing bronchos ought to be somewhere in the north, and he postponed the southern trip until such time when they would have more leisure at their disposal. Mr. Travennes showed a strong inclination to shy at this arrangement, but quieted down under persuasion, and they started off toward where Mr. Cassidy firmly believed the North Pole and the cayuses to be.

"Yu has got quite a metropolis here," pleasantly remarked Mr. Cassidy as under his direction they made for a distant corral. "I can see four different types of architecture, two of 'em on one residence," he continued as they passed a wood and adobe hut. "No doubt the railroad will put a branch down here someday an' then yu can hire their old cars for yore public buildings. Then when yu gets a post office yu will shore make Chicago hustle some to keep her end up. Let's assay that hollow for horsehide; it looks promisin'.'"

The hollow was investigated but showed nothing other than cactus and baked alkali. The corral came next, and there too was emptiness. For an hour the search was unavailing, but at the end of that time Mr. Cassidy began to notice signs of nervousness on the part of his guest, which grew less as they proceeded. Then Mr. Cassidy retraced their steps to the place where the nervousness first developed and tried another way and once more returned to the starting point.

"Yu seems to hanker for this fool exercise," quoth Mr. Travennes with much sarcasm. "If yu reckons I'm fond of this locoed ramblin' yu shore needs enlightenment."

"Sometimes I do get these fits," confessed Mr. Cassidy, "an' when I do I'm dead sore on objections. Let's peek in that there hut," he suggested.

"Huh; yore ideas of cayuses are mighty peculiar. Why don't you look for 'em up on those cactuses or behind that mesquite? *I* wouldn't be a heap surprised if they was roostin' on th' roof. They are mighty knowing animals, cayuses. I once saw one that could figger like a schoolmarm," remarked Mr. Travennes, beginning sarcastically and toning it down as he proceeded, out of respect for his companion's gun.

"Well, they might be in th' shack," replied Mr. Cassidy. "Cayuses know so much that it takes a month to unlearn them. I wouldn't like to bet they ain't in that hut, though."

Mr. Travennes snickered in a manner decidedly uncomplimentary and began to whistle, softly at first. The gentleman from the Bar-20 noticed that his companion was a musician; that when he came to a strong part he increased the tones until they bid to be heard at several hundred yards. When Mr. Travennes had reached a most passionate part in "Juanita" and was expanding his lungs to do it justice he was rudely stopped by the insistent pressure of his guard's Colt's on the most ticklish part of his ear.

"I shore wish yu wouldn't strain yoreself thataway," said Mr. Cassidy, thinking that Mr. Travennes might be endeavoring to call assistance. "I went an' promised my mother on her deathbed that I wouldn't let nobody whistle out loud like that, an' th' opery is hereby stopped. Besides, somebody might hear them mournful tones an' think that something is th' matter, which it ain't."

Mr. Travennes substituted heartfelt cursing, all of which was heavily accented.

As they approached the hut Mr. Cassidy again tickled his prisoner and insisted that he be very quiet, as his cayuse was very sensitive to noise and it might be there. Mr. Cassidy still thought Mr. Travennes might have friends in the hut and wouldn't for the world disturb them, as he would present a splendid target as he approached the building.

CHAPTER 14

The Tale of a Cigarette

The open door revealed three men asleep on the earthen floor, two of whom were Mexicans. Mr. Cassidy then for the first time felt called upon to relieve his companion of the Colt's which so sorely itched that gentleman's thigh and then disarmed the sleeping guards.

In the far corner of the room were two bronchos, one of which tried in vain to kick Mr. Cassidy, not realizing that he was ten feet away. The noise awakened the sleepers, who sat up and then sprang to their feet, their hands instinctively streaking to their thighs for the weapons which peeked contentedly from the bosom of Mr. Cassidy's open shirt. One of the Mexicans made a lightning-like grab for the back of his neck for the knife which lay along his spine and was shot in the front of his neck for his trouble. The shot spoiled his aim, as the knife flashed past Mr. Cassidy's arm, wide by two feet, and thudded into the door frame, where it hummed angrily.

"Th' only man who could do that right was th' man who invented it, Mr. Bowie, of Texas," explained Mr. Cassidy to the other Mexican. Then he glanced at the broncho, that was squealing in rage and fear at the shot, which sounded like a cannon in the small room, and laughed.

"That's my cayuse all right, an' he wasn't up no cactus nor roostin' on th' roof, neither. He's th' most affectionate beast I ever saw. It took me nigh onto six months afore I could ride him without fighting him to a standstill," said Mr. Cassidy to his guest. Then he turned to the horse and looked it over. "Come here! What d'yu mean, acting thataway? Yu ragged end of nothin' wobbling in space! Yu wall-eyed, ornery, locoed guide to Hades! Yu won't be so frisky when yu've made them seventy hot miles between here an' Alkaline in five hours," he promised, as he made his way toward the animal.

Mr. Travennes walked over to the opposite wall and took down a pouch of

tobacco which hung from a peg. He did this in a manner suggesting ownership, and after he had deftly rolled a cigarette with one hand he put the pouch
in his pocket and, lighting up, inhaled deeply and with much satisfaction. Mr.
Cassidy turned around and glanced the group over, wondering if the tobacco
had been left in the hut on a former call.

"Did yu find yore makings?" he asked, with a note of congratulation in his
voice.

"Yep. Want one?" asked Mr. Travennes.

Mr. Cassidy ignored the offer and turned to the guard whom he had found
asleep.

"Is that his tobacco?" he asked, and the guard, anxious to make everything
run smoothly, told the truth and answered: "Shore. He left it here last night,"
whereupon Mr. Travennes swore and Mr. Cassidy smiled grimly.

"Then yu knows how yore cayuse got in an' how mine got out," said the latter. "I wish yu would explain," he added, fondling his Colt's.

Mr. Travennes frowned and remained silent.

"I can tell yu, anyhow," continued Mr. Cassidy, still smiling, but his eyes
and jaw belied the smile. "Yu took them cayuses out because yu wanted yourn
to be found in their places. Yu remembered Santa Fé an' it rankled in yu. Not
being man enough to notify me that yu'd shoot on sight an' being afraid my
friends would get yu if yu plugged me on th' sly, yu tried to make out that me
an' Red rustled yore cayuses. That meant a lynching with me an' Red in th'
places of honor. Yu never saw Red afore, but yu didn't care if he went with me.
Yu don't deserve fair play, but I'm going to give it to yu because I don't want
anybody to say that any of th' Bar-20 ever murdered a man, not even a skunk
like yu. My friends have treated me too square for that. Yu can take this gun
an' yu can do one of three things with it, which are: walk out in th' open a hundred paces an' then turn an' walk toward me—after you face me yu can set it
a-going whenever yu want to; th' second is, put it under yore hat an' I'll put
mine an' th' others back by th' cayuses. Then we'll toss up an' th' lucky man
gets it to use as he wants. Th' third is, shoot yourself."

Mr. Cassidy punctuated the close of his ultimatum by handing over the
weapon, muzzle first, and, because the other might be an adept at "twirling,"
he kept its recipient covered during the operation. Then, placing his second
Colt's with the captured weapons, he threw them through the door, being very
careful not to lose the drop on his now-armed prisoner.

Mr. Travennes looked around and wiped the sweat from his forehead, and
being an observant gentleman, took the proffered weapon and walked to the

east, directly toward the sun, which at this time was halfway to the meridian. The glare of its straight rays and those reflected from the shining sand would, in a measure, bother Mr. Cassidy and interfere with the accuracy of his aim, and he was always thankful for small favors.

Mr. Travennes was the possessor of accurate knowledge regarding the lay of the land, and the thought came to him that there was a small but deep hole out toward the east and that it was about the required distance away. This had been dug by a man who had labored all day in the burning sun to make an oven so that he could cook mesquite root in the manner he had seen the Apaches cook it. Mr. Travennes blessed hobbies, specific and general, stumbled thoughtlessly and disappeared from sight as the surprised Mr. Cassidy started forward to offer his assistance. Upon emphatic notification from the man in the hole that his help was not needed, Mr. Cassidy wheeled around and in great haste covered the distance separating him from the hut, whereupon Mr. Travennes swore in self-congratulation and regret. Mr. Cassidy's shots barked a cactus which leaned near Mr. Travennes' head and flecked several clouds of alkali near that person's nose, causing him to sneeze, duck, and grin.

"It's his own gun," grumbled Mr. Cassidy as a bullet passed through his sombrero, having in mind the fact that his opponent had a whole belt full of .41's. If it had been Mr. Cassidy's gun that had been handed over he would have enjoyed the joke on Mr. Travennes, who would have had five cartridges between himself and the promised eternity, as he would have been unable to use the .41's in Mr. Cassidy's .45, while the latter would have gladly consented to the change, having as he did an extra .45. Never before had Mr. Cassidy looked with reproach upon his .45-caliber Colt's, and he sighed as he used it to notify Mr. Travennes that arbitration was not to be considered, which that person endorsed, said endorsement passing so close to Mr. Cassidy's ear that he felt the breeze made by it.

"He's been practicin' since I plugged him up in Santa Fé," thought Mr. Cassidy, as he retired around the hut to formulate a plan of campaign.

Mr. Travennes sang "Hi-le, hi-lo," and other selections, principally others, and wondered how Mr. Cassidy could hoist him out. The slack of his belt informed him that he was in the middle of a fast, and suggested starvation as the derrick that his honorable and disgusted adversary might employ.

Mr. Cassidy, while figuring out his method of procedure, absentmindedly jabbed a finger in his eye, and the ensuing tears floated an idea to him. He had always had great respect for ricochet shots since his friend Skinny Thompson had proved their worth on the hides of Sioux. If he could disturb the sand and convey several grains of it to Mr. Travennes' eyes the game would be much simplified. While planning for the proposed excavation, *à la* Colt's, he noticed several stones lying near at hand, and a new and better scheme presented itself for his consideration. If Mr. Travennes could be persuaded to get out of—well, it was worth trying.

Mr. Cassidy lined up his gloomy collection and tersely ordered them to turn their backs to him and to stay in that position, the suggestion being that if they looked around they wouldn't be able to dodge quickly enough. He then slipped bits of his lariat over their wrists and ankles, tying wrists to ankles and each man to his neighbor. That finished to his satisfaction, he dragged them in the hut to save them from the burning rays of the sun. Having performed this act of kindness, he crept along the hot sand, taking advantage of every bit of cover afforded, and at last he reached a point within a hundred feet of the besieged. During the trip Mr. Travennes sang to his heart's content, some of the words being improvised for the occasion and were not calculated to increase Mr. Cassidy's respect for his own wisdom if he should hear them. Mr. Cassidy heard, however, and several fragments so forcibly intruded on his peace of mind that he determined to put on the last verse himself and to suit himself.

Suddenly Mr. Travennes poked his head up and glanced at the hut. He was down again so quickly that there was no chance for a shot at him and he believed that his enemy was still sojourning in the rear of the building, which caused him to fear that he was expected to live on nothing as long as he could and then give himself up. Just to show his defiance he stretched himself out on his back and sang with all his might, his sombrero over his face to keep the glare of the sun out of his eyes. He was interrupted, however, forgot to finish a verse as he had intended, and jumped to one side as a stone bounced off his leg. Looking up, he saw another missile curve into his patch of sky and swiftly bear down on him. He avoided it by a hair's breadth and wondered what had happened. Then what Mr. Travennes thought was a balloon, being unsophisticated in matters pertaining to aerial navigation, swooped down upon him and smote him on the shoulder and also bounced off. Mr. Travennes hastily laid music aside and took up elocution as he dodged another stone and wished that the mesquite-loving crank had put on a roof. In evading the projectile he let his sombrero appear on a level with the desert, and the hum of a bullet as it passed through his headgear and into the opposite wall made him wish that there had been constructed a cellar, also.

"Hi-le, hi-lo" intruded upon his ear, as Mr. Cassidy got rid of the surplus of his heart's joy. Another stone the size of a man's foot shaved Mr. Travennes' ear and he hugged the side of the hole nearest his enemy.

"Hibernate, blank yu!" derisively shouted the human catapult as he released a chunk of sandstone the size of a quail. "Draw in yore laigs an' buck," was his God-speed to the missile.

"Hey, yu!" indignantly yowled Mr. Travennes from his defective storm cellar. "Don't yu know any better'n to heave things thataway?"

"Hi-le, hi-lo," sang Mr. Cassidy, as another stone soared aloft in the direction of the complainant. Then he stood erect and awaited results with a Colt's in his hand leveled at the rim of the hole. A hat waved and an excited voice bit off chunks of expostulation and asked for an armistice. Then two hands shot up and Mr. Travennes, sore and disgusted and desperate, popped his head up and blinked at Mr. Cassidy's gun.

"Yu was fillin' th' hole up," remarked Mr. Travennes in an accusing tone, hiding the real reason for his evacuation. "In a little while I'd a been th' top of a pile instead of th' bottom of a hole," he announced, crawling out and rubbing his head.

Mr. Cassidy grinned and ordered his prisoner to one side while he secured the weapon which lay in the hole. Having obtained it as quickly as possible he slid it in his open shirt and clambered out again.

"Yu remind me of a feller I used to know," remarked Mr. Travennes, as he led the way to the hut, trying not to limp. "Only he throwed dynamite. That was th' way he cleared off chaparral—blowed it off. He got so used to heaving away everything he lit that he spoiled three pipes in two days."

Mr. Cassidy laughed at the fiction and then became grave as he pictured Mr. Connors sitting on the rock and facing down a line of men, any one of whom was capable of his destruction if given the interval of a second.

When they arrived at the hut Mr. Cassidy observed that the prisoners had moved considerably. There was a cleanly swept trail four yards long where they had dragged themselves, and they sat in the end nearer the guns. Mr. Cassidy smiled and fired close to the Mexican's ear, who lost in one frightened jump a little of what he had so laboriously gained.

"Yu'll wear out yore pants," said Mr. Cassidy, and then added grimly, "an' my patience."

Mr. Travennes smiled and thought of the man who had so ably seconded Mr. Cassidy's efforts and who was probably shot by this time. The outfit of the Bar-20 was so well known throughout the land that he was aware the name of the other was Red Connors. An unreasoning streak of sarcasm swept over him and he could not resist the opportunity to get in a stab at his captor.

"Mebby yore pard has wore out somebody's patience, too," said Mr. Travennes, suggestively and with venom.

His captor wheeled toward him, his face white with passion, and Mr. Travennes shrank back and regretted the words.

"I ain't shootin' dogs this here trip," said Mr. Cassidy, trembling with scorn and anger, "so yu can pull yourself together. I'll give yu another chance, but yu wants to hope almighty hard that Red is O.K. If he ain't, I'll blow yu so many ways at once that if yu sprouts yu'll make a good acre of weeds. If he *is* all right yu'd better vamoose this range, for there won't be no hole for yu to crawl into next time. What friends yu have left will have to tote yu off an' plant yu," he finished with emphasis. He drove the horses outside, and, after severing the bonds on his prisoners, lined them up.

"Yu," he began, indicating all but Mr. Travennes, "yu amble right smart toward Canada," pointing to the north. "Keep a-going till yu gets far enough away so a Colt's won't find yu." Here he grinned with delight as he saw his Sharp's rifle in its sheath on his saddle and, drawing it forth, he put away his Colt's and glanced at the trio, who were already industriously plodding northward. "Hey!" he shouted, and when they sullenly turned to see what new idea he had found he gleefully waved his rifle at them and warned them farther: "This is a Sharp's an' it's good for half a mile, so don't stop none too soon."

Having sent them directly away from their friends so they could not have him "potted" on the way back, he mounted his broncho and indicated to Mr. Travennes that he, too, was to ride, watching that that person did not make use of the Winchester which Mr. Connors was foolish enough to carry around on his saddle. Winchesters were Mr. Cassidy's pet aversion and Mr. Connors' most prized possession, this difference of opinion having upon many occasions caused hasty words between them. Mr. Connors, being better with his Winchester than Mr. Cassidy was with his Sharp's, had frequently proved that his choice was the wiser, but Mr. Cassidy was loyal to the Sharp's and refused to be convinced. Now, however, the Winchester became pregnant with possibilities and, therefore, Mr. Travennes rode a few yards to the left and in advance, where the rifle was in plain sight, hanging as it did on the right of Mr. Connors' saddle, which Mr. Travennes graced so well.

The journey back to town was made in good time and when they came to the buildings Mr. Cassidy dismounted and bade his companion do likewise, there being too many corners that a fleeing rider could take advantage of. Mr. Travennes felt of his bumps and did so, wishing hard things about Mr. Cassidy.

CHAPTER 15

The Penalty

While Mr. Travennes had been entertained in the manner narrated, Mr. Connors had passed the time by relating stale jokes
to the uproarious laughter of his extremely bored audience, who had heard the
aged efforts many times since they had first seen the light of day, and most of
whom earnestly longed for a drink. The landlord, hearing the hilarity, had
taken advantage of the opportunity offered to see a free show. Not being able
to see what the occasion was for the mirth, he had pulled on his boots and
made his way to the show with a flapjack in the skillet, which, in his haste, he
had forgotten to put down. He felt sure that he would be entertained, and he
was not disappointed. He rounded the corner and was enthusiastically welcomed by the hungry Mr. Connors, whose ubiquitous guns coaxed from the
skillet its dyspeptic wad.

"Th' saints be praised!" ejaculated Mr. Connors as a matter of form, not
having a very clear idea of just what saints were, but he knew what flapjacks
were and greedily overcame the heroic resistance of the one provided by
chance and his own guns. As he rolled his eyes in ecstatic content the very
man Mr. Cassidy had warned him against suddenly arose and in great haste
disappeared around the corner of the corral, from which point of vantage he
vented his displeasure at the treatment he had received by wasting six shots at
the mortified Mr. Connors.

"Steady!" sang out that gentleman as the lineup wavered. "He's a precedent
to hell for yu fellers! Don't yu get ambitious, none whatever." Then he wondered how long it would take the fugitive to secure a rifle and return to release
the others by drilling him at long range.

His thoughts were interrupted by the vision of a red head that climbed into
view over a rise a short distance off and he grinned his delight as Mr. Cassidy

loomed up, jaunty and triumphant. Mr. Cassidy was executing calisthenics with a Colt's in the rear of Mr. Travennes' neck and was leading the horses.

Mr. Connors waved the skillet and his friend grinned his congratulation at what the token signified.

"I see yu got some more," said Mr. Cassidy, as he went down the lineup from the rear and collected nineteen revolvers of various makes and conditions, this number being explained by the fact that all but one of the prisoners wore two. Then he added the five that had kicked against his ribs ever since he had left the hut, and carefully threaded the end of his lariat through the trigger guards.

"Looks like we stuck up a government supply mule, Red," he remarked, as he fastened the whole collection to his saddle. "Fourteen Colt's, six Steven's, three Remington's an' one puzzle," he added, examining the "puzzle." "'Made in Germany,' it says, an' it shore looks like it. It's got little pins stickin' out of th' cylinder, like yu had to swat it with a hammer or a rock, or something. It's real dangerous—warranted to go off, but mostly by itself, I reckon. It looks more like a cactus than a six-shooter—gosh, it's an eight-shooter! I allus said them Dutchmen were bloody-minded cusses—think of being able to shoot yoreself eight times before th' blamed thing stops!" Then, looking at the lineup for the owner of the weapon, he laughed at the woeful countenances displayed. "Did they sidle in by companies or squads?" he asked.

"By twos, mostly. Then they parade-rested an' got discharged from duty. I had eleven, but one got homesick, or disgusted, or something, an' deserted. It was that cussed flapjack," confessed and explained Mr. Connors.

"What!" said Mr. Cassidy in a loud voice. "Got away! Well, we'll have to make our getaway plumb sudden or we'll never go."

At this instant the escaped man again began his bombardment from the corner of the corral and Mr. Cassidy paused, indignant at the fusillade which tore up the dust at his feet. He looked reproachfully at Mr. Connors and then circled out on the plain until he caught a glimpse of a fleeing cowpuncher, whose back rapidly grew smaller in the fast-increasing distance.

"That's yore friend, Red," said Mr. Cassidy as he returned from his reconnaissance. "He's that shorthorn yearling. Mebby he'll come back again," he added hopefully. "Anyhow, we've got to move. He'll collect reinforcements an' mebby they all won't shoot like him. Get up on yore Clarinda an' hold th' fort for me," he ordered, pushing the farther horse over to his friend. Mr. Connors proved that an agile man can mount a restless horse and not lose the drop, and backed off three hundred yards, deftly substituting his Winchester for the

Colt's. Then Mr. Cassidy likewise mounted with his attention riveted else-where and backed off to the side of his companion.

The bombardment commenced again from the corral, but this time Mr. Connors' rifle slid around in his lap and exploded twice. The bellicose gentle-man of the corral yelled in pain and surprise and vanished.

"Purty good for a Winchester," said Mr. Cassidy in doubtful congratulation.

"That why I got him," snapped Mr. Connors in brief reply, and then he laughed. "Is them th' vigilantes what never let a man get away?" he scornfully asked, backing down the street and patting his Winchester.

"Well, Red, they wasn't all there. They was only twelve all told," excused Mr. Cassidy. "An' then we was two," he explained, as he wished the collection of six-shooters was on Mr. Connors' horse so they wouldn't bark his shin.

"An' we still are," corrected Mr. Connors, as they wheeled and galloped for Alkaline.

As the sun sank low on the horizon Mr. Peters finished ordering provisions at the general store, the only one Alkaline boasted, and sauntered to the saloon where he had left his men. He found them a few dollars richer, as they had borrowed ten dollars from the bartender on their reputations as poker players and had used the money to stake Mr. McAllister in a game against the local poker champion.

"Has Hopalong an' Red showed up yet?" asked Mr. Peters, frowning at the delay already caused.

"Nope," replied Johnny Nelson, as he paused from tormenting Billy Williams.

At that minute the doorway was darkened and Mr. Cassidy and Mr. Con-nors entered and called for refreshments. Mr. Cassidy dropped a huge bundle of six-shooters on the floor, making caustic remarks regarding their utility.

"What's th' matter?" inquired Mr. Peters of Mr. Cassidy. "Yu looks mad an' anxious. An *where in hell did yu corral them guns?*"

Mr. Cassidy drank deep and then reported with much heat what had oc-curred at Cactus Springs and added that he wanted to go back and wipe out the town, said desire being luridly endorsed by Mr. Connors.

"Why, shore," said Mr. Peters, "we'll *all* go. Such doings must be stopped instanter." Then he turned to the assembled outfits and asked for a vote, which was unanimous for war.

Shortly afterward eighteen angry cowpunchers rode to the east, two red-haired gentlemen well in front and urging speed. It was 8 P.M. when they left Al-kaline, and the cool of the night was so delightful that the feeling of ease which came upon them made them lax and they lost three hours in straying from the dim trail. At eight o'clock the next morning they came in sight of their destination and separated into two squads, Mr. Cassidy leading the northern division and Mr. Connors the one which circled to the south. The intention was to attack from two directions, thus taking the town from front and rear.

Cactus Springs lay gasping in the excessive heat and the vigilantes who had toed Mr. Connors' line the day before were lounging in the shade of the "Palace" saloon, telling what they would do if they ever faced the same man again. Half a dozen sympathizers offered gratuitous condolence and advice and all were positive that they knew where Mr. Cassidy and Mr. Connors would go when they died.

The rolling thunder of madly pounding hoofs disturbed their postmortem and they arose in a body to flee from half their number, who, guns in hands, charged down upon them through clouds of sickly white smoke. Travennes' Terrors were minus many weapons and they could not be expected to give a glorious account of themselves. Windows rattled and fell in and doors and walls gave off peculiar sounds as they grew full of holes. Above the riot rattled the incessant crack of Colt's and Winchester, emphasized at close intervals by the assertive roar of .60-caliber buffalo guns. Off to the south came another rumble of hoofs and Mr. Connors, leading the second squad, arrived to participate in the payment of the debt.

Smoke spurted from windows and other points of vantage and hung wavering in the heated air. The shattering of woodwork told of .60 calibers finding their rest, and the whines that grew and diminished in the air sang the course of .45's.

While the fight raged hottest Mr. Nelson sprang from his horse and ran to the "Palace," where he collected and piled a heap of tinderlike wood, and soon the building burst out in flames, which, spreading, swept the town from end to end.

Mr. Cassidy fired slowly and seemed to be waiting for something. Mr. Connors laid aside his hot Winchester and devoted his attention to his Colt's. A spurt of flame and smoke leaped from the window of a 'dobe hut and Mr. Connors sat down, firing as he went. A howl from the window informed him that he had made a hit, and Mr. Cassidy ran out and dragged him to the shelter of a nearby boulder and asked how much he was hurt.

"Not much—in th' calf," grunted Mr. Connors. "He was a bad shot—must have been the cuss that got away yesterday," speculated the injured man as he

slowly arose to his feet. Mr. Cassidy dissented from force of habit and returned to his station.

Mr. Travennes, who was sleeping late that morning, coughed and fought
for air in his sleep, awakened in smoke, rubbed his eyes to make sure and,
scorning trousers and shirt, ran clad in his red woolen undergarments to the
corral, where he mounted his scared horse and rode for the desert and safety.

Mr. Cassidy, swearing at the marksmanship of a man who fired at his head
and perforated his sombrero, saw a crimson rider sweep down upon him, said
rider being heralded by a blazing .41.

"Gosh!" ejaculated Mr. Cassidy, scarcely believing his eyes. "Oh, it's my
friend Slim going to hell," he remarked to himself in audible and relieved explanation. Mr. Cassidy's Colt's cracked a protest and then he joined Mr. Peters
and the others and with them fought his way out of the flame-swept town of
Cactus Springs.

An hour later Mr. Connors glanced behind him at the smoke silhouetted
on the horizon and pushed his way to where Mr. Cassidy rode in silence. Mr.
Connors grinned at his friend of the red hair, who responded in the same
manner.

"Did yu see Slim?" casually inquired Mr. Connors, looking off to the south.

Mr. Cassidy sat upright in his saddle and felt of his Colt's. "Yes," he replied,
"I saw him."

Mr. Connors thereupon galloped on in silence.

CHAPTER 16

Rustlers on the Range

The affair at Cactus Springs had more effect on the life at the Bar-20 than was realized by the foreman. News travels rapidly, and certain men, whose attributes were not of the sweetest, heard of it and swore vengeance, for Slim Travennes had many friends, and the result of his passing began to show itself. Outlaws have as their strongest defense the fear which they inspire, and little time was lost in making reprisals, and these caused Buck Peters to ride into Buckskin one bright October morning and then out the other side of the town. Coming to himself with a start he looked around shamefacedly and retraced his course. He was very much troubled, for, as foreman of the Bar-20, he had many responsibilities, and when things ceased to go aright he was expected not only to find the cause of the evil, but also the remedy. That was what he was paid seventy dollars a month for and that was what he had been endeavoring to do. As yet, however, he had only accomplished what the meanest cook's assistant had done. He knew the cause of his present woes to be rustlers (cattle thieves), and that was all.

Riding down the wide, quiet street, he stopped and dismounted before the ever-open door of a ramshackle one-story frame building. Tossing the reins over the flattened ears of his vicious pinto he strode into the building and leaned easily against the bar, where he drummed with his fingers and sank into a reverie.

A shining bald pate, bowed over an open box, turned around and revealed a florid face, set with two small, twinkling blue eyes, as the proprietor, wiping his hands on his trousers, made his way to Buck's end of the bar.

"Mornin', Buck. How's things?"

The foreman, lost in his reverie, continued to stare out the door.

"Mornin'," repeated the man behind the bar. "How's things?"

"Oh!" ejaculated the foreman, smiling, "purty cussed."

"Anything new?"

"Th' C-80 lost another herd last night."

His companion swore and placed a bottle at the foreman's elbow, but the latter shook his head. "Not this mornin'—I'll try one of them vile cigars, however."

"Them cigars are th' very best that—" began the proprietor, executing the order.

"Oh, hell!" exclaimed Buck with weary disgust. "Yu don't have to palaver none: I shore knows all that by heart."

"Them cigars—" repeated the proprietor.

"Yas, yas; them cigars—I know all about them cigars. Yu gets them for twenty dollars a thousand an' hypnotizes us into payin' yu a hundred," replied the foreman, biting off the end of his weed. Then he stared moodily and frowned. "I wonder why it is?" he asked. "We punchers like good stuff an' we pays good prices with good money. What do we get? Why, cabbage leaves an' leather for our smokin' an' alcohol an' extract for our drink. Now, up in Kansas City we goes to a sumptious layout, pays less an' gets bang-up stuff. If yu smelled one of them K. C. cigars yu'd shore have to ask what it was, an' as for th' liquor, why, yu'd think St. Peter asked yu to have one with him. It's shore wrong somewhere."

"They have more trade in K. C.," suggested the proprietor.

"An' help, an' taxes, an' a license, an' rent, an' brass, cut glass, mahogany an' French mirrors," countered the foreman.

"They have more trade," reiterated the man with the cigars.

"Forty men spend thirty dollars apiece with yu every month."

The proprietor busied himself under the bar. "Yu'll feel better tomorrow. Anyway, what do yu care, yu won't lose yore job," he said, emerging.

Buck looked at him and frowned, holding back the words which formed in anger. What was the use, he thought, when every man judged the world in his own way.

"Have yu seen any of th' boys?" he asked, smiling again.

"Nary a boy. Who do yu reckon's doin' all this rustlin'?"

"I'm reckonin', not shoutin'," responded the foreman.

The proprietor looked out the window and grinned: "Here comes one of yourn now."

The newcomer stopped his horse in a cloud of dust, playfully kicked the animal in the ribs and entered, dusting the alkali from him with a huge sombrero. Then he straightened up and sniffed: "What's burnin'?" he asked, simulating alarm. Then he noticed the cigar between the teeth of his foreman and grinned: "Gee, but yore a brave man, Buck."

"Hullo, Hopalong," said the foreman. "Want a smoke?" waving his hand toward the box on the bar.

Mr. Hopalong Cassidy side-stepped and began to roll a cigarette: "Shore, but I'll burn my own—I know what it is."

"What was yu doin' to my cayuse afore yu come in?" asked Buck.

"Nothin'," replied the newcomer. "That was mine what I kicked in th' corrugations."

"How is it yore ridin' th' calico?" asked the foreman. "I thought yu was dead stuck on that piebald."

"That piebald's a goat; he's been livin' off my pants lately," responded Hopalong. "Every time I looks th' other way he ambles over and takes a bite at me. Yu just wait 'til this rustler business is roped, an' branded, an' yu'll see me eddicate that blessed scrapheap into eatin' grass again. He swiped Billy's shirt th' other day—took it right off th' corral wall, where Billy'd left it to dry." Then, seeing Buck raise his eyebrows, he explained: "Shore, he washed it again. That makes three times since last fall."

The proprietor laughed and pushed out the ever-ready bottle, but Hopalong shoved it aside and told the reason: "Ever since I was up to K. C. I've been spoiled. I'm drinkin' water an' slush."

"For Gawd's sake, has any more of yu fellers been up to K. C.?" queried the proprietor in alarm.

"Shore; Red an' Billy was up there, too," responded Hopalong. "Red's got a few remarks to shout to yu about yore painkiller. Yu better send for some decent stuff afore he comes to town," he warned.

Buck swung away from the bar and looked at his dead cigar. Then he turned to Hopalong. "What did you find?" he asked.

"Same old story: nice wide trail up to th' Staked Plain—then nothin'."

"It shore beats me," soliloquized the foreman. "It shore beats me."

"Think it was Tamale José's old gang?" asked Hopalong.

"If it was they took th' wrong trail home—that ain't th' way to Mexico."

Hopalong tossed aside his half-smoked cigarette. "Well, come on home; what's th' use stewin' over it? It'll come out all O.K. in th' wash." Then he laughed: "There won't be no piebald waitin' for it."

Evading Buck's playful blow he led the way to the door, and soon they were a cloud of dust on the plain. The proprietor, despairing of customers under the circumstances, absentmindedly wiped off the bar, and sought his chair for a nap, grumbling about the way his trade had fallen off, for there were few customers, and those who did call were heavy with loss of sleep, and with anxiety, and only paused long enough to toss off their drink. On the ranges there were occurrences which tried men's souls.

For several weeks cattle had been disappearing from the ranges and the losses had long since passed the magnitude of those suffered when Tamale José and his men had crossed the Rio Grande and repeatedly levied heavy toll on the sleek herds of the Pecos Valley. Tamale José had raided once too often, and prosperity and plenty had followed on the ranches and the losses had been forgotten until the fall roundups clearly showed that rustlers were again at work.

Despite the ingenuity of the ranch owners and the unceasing vigilance and night rides of the cowpunchers, the losses steadily increased until there was promised a shortage which would permit no drive to the western terminals of the railroad that year. For two weeks the banks of the Rio Grande had been patrolled and sharp-eyed men searched daily for trails leading southward, for it was not strange to think that the old raiders were again at work, notwithstanding the fact that they had paid dearly for their former depredations. The patrols failed to discover anything out of the ordinary and the searchers found no trails. Then it was that the owners and foremen of the four central ranches met in Cowan's saloon and sat closeted together for all of one hot afternoon.

The conference resulted in riders being dispatched from all the ranches represented, and one of the couriers, Mr. Red Connors, rode north, his destination being faraway Montana. All the ranches within a radius of a hundred miles received letters and blanks and one week later the Pecos Valley Cattle-Thief Elimination Association was organized and working, with Buck as Chief Ranger.

One of the outcomes of Buck's appointment was a sudden and marked immigration into the affected territory. Mr. Connors returned from Montana with Mr. Frenchy McAllister, the foreman of the Tin-Cup, who was accompanied by six of his best and most trusted men. Mr. McAllister and party were followed by Mr. You-bet Somes, foreman of the Two-X-Two of Arizona, and five of his punchers, and later on the same day Mr. Pie Willis, accompanied by Mr. Billy Jordan and his two brothers, arrived from the Panhandle. The O-Bar-O, situated close to the town of Muddy Wells, increased its payroll by the addition of nine men, each of whom bore the written recommendation of the foreman of the Bar-20. The C-80, Double Arrow and the Three Triangle also received heavy reinforcements, and even Carter, owner of the Barred Horse-shoe, far removed from the zone of the depredations, increased his outfits by half their regular strength. Buck believed that if a thing was worth doing at all that it was worth doing very well, and his acquaintances were numerous and loyal. The collection of individuals that responded to the call were noteworthy examples of "gunplay" and their aggregate value was at par with twice their numbers in cavalry.

Each ranch had one large ranch house and numerous line-houses scattered along the boundaries. These latter, while intended as camps for the outriders, had been erected in the days, none too remote, when Apaches, Arrapahoes, Sioux and even Cheyennes raided southward, and they had been constructed with the idea of defense paramount. Upon more than one occasion a solitary line-rider had retreated within their adobe walls and had successfully resisted all the cunning and ferocity of a score of paint-bedaubed warriors and, when his outfit had rescued him, emerged none the worse for his ordeal.

On the Bar-20, Buck placed these houses in condition to withstand seige. Twin barrels of water stood in opposite corners, provisions were stored on the hanging shelves and the bunks once again reveled in untidiness. Spare rifles, in pattern ranging from long-range Sharp's and buffalo guns to repeating carbines, leaned against the walls, and unbroken boxes of cartridges were piled above the bunks. Instead of the lonesome outrider, he placed four men to each house, two of whom were to remain at home and hold the house while their companions rode side by side on their multi-mile beat. There were six of these houses and, instead of returning each night to the same line-house, the outriders kept on and made the circuit, thus keeping everyone well informed and breaking the monotony. These measures were expected to cause the rustling operations to cease at once, but the effect was to shift the losses to the Double Arrow, the line-houses of which boasted only one puncher each. Unreasonable economy usually defeats its object.

The Double Arrow was restricted on the north by the Staked Plain, which in itself was considered a superb defense. The White Sand Hills formed its eastern boundary and were thought to be second only to the northern protection. The only reason that could be given for the hitherto comparative immunity from the attacks of the rustlers was that its cattle clung to the southern confines where there were numerous springs, thus making imperative the crossing of its territory to gain the herds.

It was in line-house No. 3, most remote of all, that Johnny Redmond fought his last fight and was found facedown in the half-ruined house with a hole in the back of his head, which proved that one man was incapable of watching all the loopholes in four walls at once. There must have been some casualities on the other side, for Johnny was reputed to be very painstaking in his "gunplay," and the empty shells which lay scattered on the floor did not stand for as many ciphers, of that his foreman was positive. He was buried the day he was found, and the news of his death ran quickly from ranch to ranch and made more than one careless puncher arise and pace the floor in anger. More men came to the Double Arrow and its sentries were doubled. The depredations continued, however, and one night a week later Frank Swift reeled into the ranch house and fell exhausted across the supper table. Rolling hoof-beats echoed flatly and died away on the plain, but the men who pursued them returned empty-handed. The wounds of the unfortunate were roughly dressed and in his delirium he recounted the fight. His companion was found literally shot to pieces twenty paces from the door. One wall was found blown in, and this episode, when coupled with the use of dynamite, was more than could be tolerated.

When Buck had been informed of this he called to him Hopalong Cassidy, Red Connors and Frenchy McAllister, and the next day the three men rode north and the contingents of the ranches represented in the Association were divided into two squads, one of which was to remain at home and guard the ranches; the other, to sleep fully dressed and armed and never to stray far from their ranch houses and horses. These latter would be called upon to ride swiftly and far when the word came.

CHAPTER 17

Mr. Trendley Assumes Added Importance

That the rustlers were working under a well-organized system was evident. That they were directed by a master of the game was ceaselessly beaten into the consciousness of the Association by the diversity, dash and success of their raids. No one, save the three men whom they had destroyed, had ever seen them. But, like Tamale José, they had raided once too often.

Mr. Trendley, more familiarly known to men as "Slippery," was the possessor of a biased conscience, if any at all. Tall, gaunt and weather-beaten and with coal-black eyes set deep beneath hairless eyebrows, he was sinister and forbidding. Into his forty-five years of existence he had crowded a century of experience, and unsavory rumors about him existed in all parts of the great West. From Canada to Mexico and from Sacramento to Westport his name stood for brigandage. His operations had been conducted with such consummate cleverness that in all the accusations there was lacking proof. Only once had he erred, and then in the spirit of pure deviltry and in the days of youthful folly, and his mistake was a written note. He was even thought by some to have been concerned in the Mountain Meadow Massacre; others thought him to have been the leader of the band of outlaws that had plundered along the Santa Fé Trail in the late '60's. In Montana and Wyoming he was held responsible for the outrages of the band that had descended from the Holes-in-the-Wall territory and for over a hundred miles carried murder and theft that shamed as being weak the most assiduous efforts of zealous Cheyennes. It was in this last raid that he had made the mistake and it was in this raid that Frenchy McAllister had lost his wife.

When Frenchy had first been approached by Buck as to his going in search of the rustlers he had asked to go alone. This had been denied by the foreman of the Bar-20 because the men whom he had selected to accompany the scout were of such caliber that their presence could not possibly form a hindrance. Besides being his most trusted friends they were regarded by him as being the two best exponents of "gunplay" that the West afforded. Each was a specialist: Hopalong, expert beyond belief with his Colt's six-shooters, was only approached by Red, whose Winchester was renowned for its accuracy. The three made a perfect combination, as the rashness of the two younger men would be under the controlling influence of a man who could retain his coolness of mind under all circumstances.

When Buck and Frenchy looked into each other's eyes there sprang into the mind of each the same name—Slippery Trendley. Both had spent the greater part of a year in fruitless search for that person, the foreman of the Tin-Cup in vengeance for the murder of his wife, the blasting of his prospects and the loss of his herds; Buck, out of sympathy for his friend and also because they had been partners in the Double Y. Now that the years had passed and the long-sought-for opportunity was believed to be at hand, there was promised either a cessation of the outrages or that Buck would never again see his friends.

When the three mounted and came to him for final instructions Buck forced himself to be almost repellent in order to be capable of coherent speech. Hopalong glanced sharply at him and then understood, Red was all attention and eagerness and remarked nothing but the words.

"Have yu ever heard of Slippery Trendley?" harshly inquired the foreman.

They nodded, and on the faces of the younger men a glint of hatred showed itself, but Frenchy wore his poker countenance.

Buck continued: "Th' reason I asked yu was because I don't want yu to think yore goin' on no picnic. I ain't shore it's him, but I've had some hopeful information. Besides, he is th' only man I knows of who's capable of th' plays that have been made. It's hardly necessary for me to tell yu to sleep with one eye open and never to get away from yore guns. Now I'm goin' to tell yu th' hardest part: yu are goin' to search th' Staked Plain from one end to th' other, an' that's what no white man's ever done to my knowledge.

"Now, listen to this an' don't forget it: Twenty miles north from Last Stand Rock is a spring; ten miles south of that bend in Hell Arroyo is another. If yu gets lost within two days from th' time yu enters th' Plain, put yore left hand on a cactus sometime between sunup an' noon, move around until yu are over its shadow an' then ride straight ahead—that's south. If you goes loco beyond Last Stand Rock, follow th' shadows made before noon—that's th' quickest way to th' Pecos. Yu all knows what to do in a sandstorm, so I won't bore yu with that. Repeat all I've told yu," he ordered and they complied.

"I'm tellin' yu this," continued the foreman, indicating the two auxiliaries, "because yu might get separated from Frenchy. Now I suggests that yu look around near th' Devil's Rocks: I've heard that there are several water holes among them, an' besides, they might be turned into fair corrals. Mind yu, I know what I've said sounds damned idiotic for anybody that has had as much experience with th' Staked Plain as I have, but I've had every other place searched for miles around. Th' men of all th' ranches have been scoutin' an' th' Plain is th' only place left. Them rustlers has got to be found if we have to dig to hell for them. They've taken th' pot so many times that they reckons they owns it, an' we've got to at least make a bluff at drawin' cards. Mebby they're at th' bottom of th' Pecos," here he smiled faintly, "but wherever they are, we've *got* to find them. I want to holler 'Keno.'

"If yu finds where they hangs out come away instanter," here his face hardened and his eyes narrowed, "for it'll take more than yu three to deal with them th' way I'm a-hankerin' for. Come right back to th' Double Arrow, send me word by one of their punchers an' get all the rest yu can afore I gets there. It'll take me a day to get th' men together an' to reach yu. I'm goin' to use smoke signals to call th' other ranches, so there won't be no time lost. Carry all th' water yu can pack when yu leaves th' Double Arrow an' don't depend none on cactus juice. Yu better take a packhorse to carry it, an' yore grub—yu can shoot it if yu have to hit th' trail real hard."

The three riders felt of their accouterments, said "So long," and cantered off for the packhorse and extra ammunition. Then they rode toward the Double Arrow, stopping at Cowan's long enough to spend some money, and reached the Double Arrow at nightfall. Early the next morning they passed the last linehouse and, with the profane well-wishes of its occupants ringing in their ears, passed onto one of Nature's worst blunders—the Staked Plain.

CHAPTER 18

❖❖❖❖❖ ❖❖❖❖❖❖❖❖❖❖❖❖❖❖❖❖❖❖❖❖❖❖ ❖❖❖❖❖

The Search Begins

As the sun arose it revealed three punchers riding away from civilization. On all sides, stretching to the evil-appearing horizon, lay vast blotches of dirty-white and faded yellow alkali and sand. Occasionally a dwarfed mesquite raised its prickly leaves and rustled mournfully. With the exception of the riders and an occasional Gila monster, no life was discernible. Cacti of all shapes and sizes reared aloft their forbidding spines or spread out along the sand. All was dead, ghastly; all was oppressive, startlingly repellent in its sinister promise; all was the vastness of desolation.

Hopalong knew this portion of the desert for ten miles inward—he had rescued straying cattle along its southern rim—but once beyond that limit they would have to trust to chance and their own abilities. There were water holes on this skillet, but nine out of ten were death traps, reeking with mineral poisons, colored and alkaline. The two mentioned by Buck could not be depended on, for they came and went, and more than one luckless wanderer had depended on them to allay his thirst, and had died for his trust. So the scouts rode on in silence, noting the half-buried skeletons of cattle which were strewn plentifully on all sides. Nearly three percent of the cattle belonging to the Double Arrow yearly found death on this tableland, and the herds of that ranch numbered many thousand heads. It was this which made the Double Arrow the poorest of the ranches, and it was this which allowed insufficient sentries in its line-houses. The skeletons were not all of cattle, for at rare intervals lay the sand-worn frames of men.

On the morning of the second day the oppression increased with the wind and Red heaved a sigh of restlessness. The sand began to skip across the plain in grains at first and hardly noticeable. Hopalong turned in his saddle and regarded the desert with apprehension. As he looked he saw that where grains had shifted handfuls were now moving. His mount evinced signs of uneasiness and was hard to control. A gust of wind, stronger than the others, pricked his face and grains of sand rolled down his neck. The leather of his saddle emitted strange noises as if a fairy tattoo was being beaten upon it and he raised his hand and pointed off toward the east. The others looked and saw what appeared to be a fog rise out of the desert and intervene between them and the sun. As far as eye could reach small whirlwinds formed and broke and one swept down and covered them with stinging sand. The day became darkened and their horses whinnied in terror and the clumps of mesquite twisted and turned to the gusts.

Each man knew what was to come upon them and they dismounted, hobbled their horses and threw them bodily to the earth, wrapping a blanket around the head of each. A rustling as of paper rubbing together became noticeable and they threw themselves flat upon the earth, their heads wrapped in their coats and buried in the necks of their mounts. For an hour they endured the tortures of hell and then, when the storm had passed, raised their heads and cursed Creation. Their bodies burned as though they had been shot with fine needles and their clothes were meshes where once was tough cloth. Even their shoes were perforated and the throat of each ached with thirst.

Hopalong fumbled at the canteen resting on his hip and gargled his mouth and throat, washing down the sand which wouldn't come up. His friends did likewise and then looked around. After some time had elapsed the loss of their packhorse was noticed and they swore again. Hopalong took the lead in getting his horse ready for service and then rode around in a circle half a mile in diameter, but returned empty-handed. The horse was gone and with it went their main supply of food and drink.

Frenchy scowled at the shadow of a cactus and slowly rode toward the northeast, followed closely by his friends. His hand reached for his depleted canteen, but refrained—water was to be saved until the last minute.

"I'm goin' to build a shack out here an' live in it, *I* am!" exploded Hopalong in withering irony as he dug the sand out of his ears and also from his six-shooter. "I just nachurally dotes on this, *I* do!"

The others were too miserable to even grunt and he neatly severed the head of a Gila monster from its scaly body as it opened its venomous jaws in rage at this invasion of its territory. "Lovely place!" he sneered.

"Yu better save them cartridges, Hoppy," interposed Red as his companion fired again, feeling that he must say something.

"An' what for?" blazed his friend. "To plug sandstorms? Anybody what we

find on this godforsaken layout won't have to be shot—they will commit sui-
cide an' think it's fun! Tell yu what, if them rustlers hangs out on this sand
range they're better men than I reckons they are. Anybody what hides up here
shore earns all he steals." Hopalong grumbled from force of habit and because
no one else would. His companions understood this and paid no attention to
him, which increased his disgust.

"What are we up here for?" he asked, belligerently. "Why, because them
Double Arrow idiots can't even watch a desert! We have to do their work for
them an' they hangs around home an' gets slaughtered! Yes, sir!" he shouted,
"they can't even take care of themselves when they're in line-houses what are
forts. Why, that time we cleaned out them an' th' C-80 over at Buckskin they
couldn't help runnin' into singin' lead!"

"Yas," drawled Red, whose recollection of that fight was vivid. "Yas, an'
why?" he asked, and then replied to his own question. "Because yu sat up in a
barn behind them, Buck played his gun on th' side window, Pete an' Skinny lay
behind a rock to one side of Buck, me an' Lanky was across th' street in front
of them, an' Billy an' Johnny was in th' arroyo on th' other side. Cowan laid on
his stummick on th' roof of his place with a .60-caliber buffalo gun, an' th'
whole blamed town was agin them. There wasn't five seconds passed that lead
wasn't rippin' through th' walls of their shack. Th' Houston House wasn't
made for no fort, an' besides, they wasn't like th' gang that's punchin' now.
That's why."

Hopalong became cheerful again, for here was a chance to differ from his
friend. The two loved each other the better the more they squabbled.

"Yas!" responded Hopalong with sarcasm. "Yas!" he reiterated, drawling it
out. "Yu was in front of them, an' with what? Why, an' old, white-haired, interfering Winchester, that's what! Me an' my Sharp's—"

"Yu and yore Sharp's!" exploded Red, whose dislike for that rifle was very
pronounced. "Yu and yore Sharp's—"

"Me an' my Sharp's, as I was palaverin' before bein' interrupted," continued
Hopalong, "did more damage in five min—"

"Played hell!" snapped Red with heat. "All yu an yore Sharp's could do was
to cut yore initials in th' back door of their shack an'—"

"Did more damage in five minutes," continued Hopalong, "than all th'
blasted Winchesters in th' whole damned town. Why—"

"An' then they was cut blamed poor. Every time that cannon of yourn exploded I shore thought th'—"

"Why, Cowan an' his buffalo did more damage (Cowan was reputed to be a very poor shot) than yu an'—"

"I thought th' artillery was comin' into th' disturbance. I could see yore red head—"

"MY red head!" exclaimed Hopalong, sizing up the crimson warlock of his companion. "MY red head!" he repeated, and then turned to Frenchy: "Hey, Frenchy, whose got th' reddest hair, me or Red?"

Frenchy slowly turned in his saddle and gravely scrutinized them. Being strictly impartial and truthful, he gave up the effort of differentiating and smiled. "Why, if th' tops of yore heads were poked through two holes in a board an' I didn't know which was which, I'd shore make a mistake if I tried to name 'em."

Thereupon the discussion was directed at the judge, and the forenoon passed very pleasantly, Frenchy even smiling in his misery.

CHAPTER 19

Hopalong's Decision

Shortly after noon, Hopalong, who had ridden with his head bowed low in meditation, looked up and slapped his thigh. Then he looked at Red and grinned.

"Look ahere, Red," he began, "there ain't no rustlers with their headquarters on this godforsaken sand heap, an' there never was. They have to have water an' lots of it, too, an' th' nearest of any account is th' Pecos, or some of them streams over in th' Panhandle. Th' Panhandle is th' best place. There are lots of streams an' lakes over there an' they're right in a good grass country. Why, an army could hide over there an' never be found unless it was hunted for blamed good. Then, again, it's close to th' railroad. Up north aways is th' south branch of th' Santa Fé Trail an' it's far enough away not to bother anybody in th' middle Panhandle. Then there's Fort Worth purty near, an' other trails. Didn't Buck say he had all th' rest of th' country searched? He meant th' Pecos Valley an' th' David Mountains country. All th' rustlers would have to do if they were in th' Panhandle would be to cross th' Canadian an' th' Cimarron an' hit th' trail for th' railroad. Good fords, good grass an' water all th' way, cattle fat when they are delivered an' plenty of room. Th' more I thinks about it th' more I cottons to the Panhandle."

"Well, it shore does sound good," replied Red, reflectively. "Do yu mean th' Cunningham Lake region or farther north?"

"Just th' other side of this blasted desert: anywhere where there's water," responded Hopalong, enthusiastically. "I've been doin' some hot reckonin' for th' last two hours an' this is th' way it looks to me: they drives th' cows up on this skillet for a ways, then turns east an' hits th' trail for home an' water. They can get around th' cañon near Thatcher's Lake by a swing of th' north. I tell yu that's th' only way out'n this. Who could tell where they turned with th' wind raisin' th' devil with th' trail? Didn't we follow a trail for a ways, an' then what? Why, there wasn't none to follow. We can ride north 'till we walk behind ourselves an' never get a peek at them. I am in favor of headin' for th' Sulphur Spring Creek district. We can spend a couple of weeks, if we has to, an' prospect that whole region without havin' to cut our water down to a smell an' a taste an' live on jerked beef. If we investigates that country we'll find something else than sandstorms, poisoned water holes an' blisters."

"Ain't th' Panhandle full of nesters (farmers)?" inquired Red, doubtfully.

"Along th' Canadian an' th' edges, yas; in th' middle, no," explained Hopalong. "They hang close together on account of th' Indians, an' they like th' trails purty well because of there allus bein' somebody passin'."

"Buck ought to send some of th' Panhandle boys up there," suggested Red. "There's Pie Willis an' th' Jordans—they knows th' Panhandle like yu knows poker."

Frenchy had paid no apparent attention to the conversation up to this point, but now he declared himself. "Yu heard what Buck said, didn't yu?" he asked. "We were told to search th' Staked Plains from one end to th' other an' I'm goin' to do it if I can hold out long enough. I ain't goin' to palaver with yu because what yu say can't be denied as far as wisdom is concerned. Yu may have hit it plumb center, but I knows what I was ordered to do, an' yu can't get me to go over there if you shouts all night. When Buck says anything, she goes. He wants to know where th' cards are stacked an' why he can't holler 'Keno,' an' I'm goin' to find out if I can. Yu can go to Patagonia if yu wants to, but yu go alone as far as I am concerned."

"Well, it's better if yu don't go with us," replied Hopalong, taking it for granted that Red would accompany him. "Yu can prospect this end of th' game an' we'll be takin' care of th' other. It's two chances now where we only had one afore."

"Yu go east an' I'll hunt around as ordered," responded Frenchy.

"East nothin'," replied Hopalong. "Yu don't get me to wallow in hot alkali an' lose time ridin' in ankle-deep sand when I can hit th' south trail, skirt th' White Sand Hills an' be in God's country again. I ain't goin' to wrastle with no cañon this here trip, none whatever. I'm goin' to travel in style, get to Big Spring by ridin' two miles to where I could only make one on this stove. Then I'll head north along Sulphur Spring Creek an' have water an' grass all th' way, barrin' a few stretches. While you are bein' fricassed I'll be streakin' through cottonwood groves an' ridin' in th' creek."

"Yu'll have to go alone, then," said Red, resolutely. "Frenchy ain't a-goin' to die of lonesomeness on this desert if I knows what I'm about, an' I reckon I do, some. Me an' him'll follow out what Buck said, hunt around for a while an' then Frenchy can go back to th' ranch to tell Buck what's up an' I'll take th' trail yu are a-scared of an' meet yu at th' east end of Cunningham Lake three days from now."

"Yu better come with me," coaxed Hopalong, not liking what his friend had said about being afraid of the trail past the cañon and wishing to have someone with whom to talk on his trip. "I'm goin' to have a nice long swim tomorrow night," he added, trying bribery.

"An' I'm goin' to try to keep from hittin' my blisters," responded Red. "I don't want to go swimmin' in no creek full of moccasins—I'd rather sleep with rattlers or copperheads. Every time I sees a cottonmouth I feels like I had just sit down on one."

"I'll flip a coin to see whether yu comes or not," proposed Hopalong.

"If yu wants to gamble so bad I'll flip yu to see who draws our pay next month, but not for what yu said," responded Red, choking down the desire to try his luck.

Hopalong grinned and turned toward the south. "If I sees Buck afore yu do, I'll tell him yu an' Frenchy are growin' watermelons up near Last Stand Rock an' are waitin' for rain. Well, so long," he said.

"Yu tell Buck we're obeyin' orders!" shouted Red, sorry that he was not going with his bunkie.

Frenchy and Red rode on in silence, the latter feeling strangely lonesome, for he and the departed man had seldom been separated when journeys like this were to be taken. And when in search of pleasure they were nearly always together. Frenchy, while being very friendly with Hopalong, a friendship that would have placed them side by side against any odds, was not accustomed to his company and did not notice his absence.

Red looked off toward the south for the tenth time and for the tenth time thought that his friend might return. "He's a son-of-a-gun," he soliloquized.

His companion looked up: "He shore is, an' he's right about this rustler business, too. But we'll look around for a day or so an' then yu raise dust for th' lake. I'll go back to th' ranch an' get things primed, so there'll be no time lost when we get th' word."

"I'm sorry I went an' said what I did about me takin' th' trail he was a-scared of," confessed Red, after a pause. "Why, he ain't a-scared of nothin'."

"He got back at yu about them watermelons, so what's th' difference?" asked Frenchy. "He don't owe yu nothin'."

An hour later they searched the Devil's Rocks, but found no rustlers. Filling their canteens at a tiny spring and allowing their mounts to drink the remainder of the water, they turned toward Hell Arroyo, which they reached at nightfall. Here, also, their search availed them nothing and they paused in indecision. Then Frenchy turned toward his companion and advised him to ride toward the lake in the night when it was comparatively cool.

Red considered and then decided that the advice was good. He rolled a cigarette, wheeled and faced the east and spurred forward: "So long," he called.

"So long," replied Frenchy, who turned toward the south and departed for the ranch.

The foreman of the Bar-20 was cleaning his rifle when he heard the hoofbeats of a galloping horse and he ran around the corner of the house to meet the newcomer, whom he thought to be a courier from the Double Arrow. Frenchy dismounted and explained why he returned alone.

Buck listened to the report and then, noting the fire which gleamed in his friend's eyes, nodded his approval to the course. "I reckon it's Trendley, Frenchy—I've heard a few things since yu left. An' yu can bet that if Hopalong an' Red have gone for him he'll be found. I expect action any time now, so we'll light th' signal fire." Then he hesitated; "Yu light it—yu've been waiting a long time for this."

The balls of smoke which rolled upward were replied to by other balls at different points on the plain, and the Bar-20 prepared to feed the numbers of hungry punchers who would arrive within the next twenty-four hours.

Two hours had not passed when eleven men rode up from the Three Triangle, followed eight hours later by ten from the O-Bar-O. The outfits of the Star Circle and the Barred Horseshoe, eighteen in all, came next and had scarcely dismounted when those of the C-80 and the Double Arrow, fretting at the delay, rode up. With the sixteen from the Bar-20 the force numbered seventy-five resolute and pugnacious cowpunchers, all aching to wipe out the indignities suffered.

CHAPTER 20

■◆◆◆◆◆■ ◆◆◆◆◆◆◆◆◆◆◆◆◆◆◆◆◆◆◆◆◆◆◆■ ◆◆◆◆◆◆■

A Problem Solved

Hopalong worried his way out of the desert on a straight line, thus cutting in half the distance he had traveled when going into it. He camped that night on the sand and early the next morning took up his journey. It was noon when he began to notice familiar sights, and an hour later he passed within a mile of line-house No. 3, Double Arrow. Half an hour later he espied a cowpuncher riding like mad. Thinking that an investigation would not be out of place, he rode after the rider and overtook him, when that person paused and retraced his course.

"Hullo, Hopalong!" shouted the puncher, and he came near enough to recognize his pursuer. "Thought yu was farmin' up on th' Staked Plain?"

"Hullo, Pie," replied Hopalong, recognizing Pie Willis. "What was yu chasin' so hard?"

"Coyote—damn 'em, but can't they go some? They're gettin' so thick we'll shore have to try strichnine an' thin 'em out."

"I thought anybody that had been raised in th' Panhandle would know better'n to chase greased lightnin'," rebuked Hopalong. "Yu has got about as much show catchin' one of them as a tenderfoot has of bustin' an outlawed cayuse."

"Shore; I know it," responded Pie, grinning. "But it's fun seein' them hunt th' horizon. What are yu doin' down here an' where are yore pardners?"

Thereupon Hopalong enlightened his inquisitive companion as to what had occurred and as to his reasons for riding south. Pie immediately became enthusiastic and announced his intention of accompanying Hopalong on his quest, which intention struck that gentleman as highly proper and wise. Then Pie hastily turned and played at chasing coyotes in the direction of the line-house, where he announced that his absence would be accounted for by the fact that he and Hopalong were going on a journey of investigation into the

Panhandle. Billy Jordan, who shared with Pie the accommodations of the house, objected and showed, very clearly, why he was eminently better qualified to take up the proposed labors than his companion. The suggestions were fast getting tangled up with the remarks, when Pie, grabbing a chunk of jerked beef, leaped into his saddle and absolutely refused to heed the calls of his former companion and return. He rode to where Hopalong was awaiting him as if he were afraid he wasn't going to live long enough to get there. Confiding to his companion that Billy was a "locoed sage hen," he led the way along the base of the White Sand Hills and asked many questions. Then they turned toward the east and galloped hard.

It had been Hopalong's intention to carry out what he had told Red and to go to Big Spring first and thence north along Sulphur Spring Creek, but to this his guide strongly dissented. There was a shortcut, or several of them for that matter, was Pie's contention, and any one of them would save a day's hard riding. Hopalong made no objection to allowing his companion to lead the way over any trail he saw fit, for he knew that Pie had been born and brought up in the Panhandle, the Cunningham Lake district having been his backyard, as it were. So they followed the shortcut having the most water and grass, and pounded out a lively tattoo as they raced over the stretches of sand which seemed to slide beneath them.

"What do yu know about this here business?" inquired Pie, as they raced past a chaparral and onto the edge of a grassy plain.

"Nothin' more'n yu do, only Buck said he thought Slippery Trendley is at th' bottom of it."

"What!" ejaculated Pie in surprise. "Him!"

"Yore on. An' between yu an' me an' th' Devil, I wouldn't be a heap surprised if Deacon Rankin is with him, neither."

Pie whistled: "Are him an' th' Deacon pals?"

"Shore," replied Hopalong, buttoning up his vest and rolling a cigarette. "Didn't they allus hang out together! One watched that th' other didn't get plugged from behind. It was a sort of yu-scratch-my-back-an'-I'll-scratch-yourn arrangement."

"Well, if they still hangs out together, I know where to hunt for our cows," responded Pie. "Th' Deacon used to range along th' headwaters of th' Colorado—it ain't far from Cunningham Lake. Thunderation!" he shouted, "I knows th' very ground they're on—I can take yu to th' very shack!" Then to himself he muttered: "An' that doodlebug Billy Jordan thinkin' he knowed more about th' Panhandle than me!"

Hopalong showed his elation in an appropriate manner and his companion drank deeply from the proffered flask. Thereupon they treated their mounts to liberal doses of strap-oil and covered the ground with great speed.

They camped early, for Hopalong was almost worn out from the exertions of the past few days and the loss of sleep he had sustained. Pie, too excited to sleep and having had unbroken rest for a long period, volunteered to keep guard, and his companion eagerly consented.

Early the next morning they broke camp and the evening of the same day found them fording Sulphur Spring Creek, and their quarry lay only an hour beyond, according to Pie. Then they forded one of the streams which form the headwaters of the Colorado, and two hours later they dismounted in a cotton-wood grove. Picketing their horses they carefully made their way through the timber, which was heavily grown with brush, and, after half an hour's maneu-vering, came within sight of the further edge. Dropping down on all fours, they crawled to the last line of brush and looked out over an extensive bottoms. At their feet lay a small river, and in a clearing on the farther side was a rough camp, consisting of about a dozen lean-to shacks and log cabins in the main collection, and a few scattered cabins along the edge. A huge fire was blazing before the main collection of huts, and to the rear of these was an indistinct black mass, which they knew to be the corral.

At a rude table before the fire more than a score of men were eating supper and others could be heard moving about and talking at different points in the background. While the two scouts were learning the lay of the land, they saw Mr. Trendley and Deacon Rankin walk out of the cabin most distant from the fire, and the latter limped. Then they saw two men lying on rude cots, and they wore bandages. Evidently Johnny Redmond had scored in his fight.

The odor of burning cowhide came from the corral, accompanied by the squeals of cattle, and informed them that brands were being blotted out. Hopalong longed to charge down and do some blotting out of another kind, but a heavy hand was placed on his shoulder and he silently wormed his way after Pie as that person led the way back to the horses. Mounting, they picked their way out of the grove and rode over the plain at a walk. When far enough away to insure that the noise made by their horses would not reach the ears of those in the camp they cantered toward the ford they had taken on the way up.

After emerging from the waters of the last forded stream, Pie raised his hand and pointed off toward the northwest, telling his companion to take that course to reach Cunningham Lake. He himself would ride south, taking, for the saving of time, a yet shorter trail to the Double Arrow, from where he would ride to Buck. He and the others would meet Hopalong and Red at the split rock they had noticed on their way up.

Hopalong shook hands with his guide and watched him disappear into the night. He imagined he could still catch whiffs of burning cowhide and again the picture of the camp came to his mind. Glancing again at the point where Pie had disappeared, he stuffed his sombrero under a strap on his saddle and slowly rode toward the lake. A coyote slunk past him on a time-destroying lope and an owl hooted at the foolishness of men. He camped at the base of a cottonwood and at daylight took up his journey after a scanty breakfast from his saddlebags.

Shortly before noon he came in sight of the lake and looked for his friend. He had just ridden around a clump of cottonwoods when he was hit on the back with something large and soft. Turning in his saddle, with his Colt's ready, he saw Red sitting on a stump, a huge grin extending over his features. He replaced the weapon, said something about fools and dismounted, kicking aside the bundle of grass his friend had thrown.

"Yore shore easy," remarked Red, tossing aside his cold cigarette. "Suppose I was Trendley, where would yu be now?"

"Diggin' a hole to put yu in," pleasantly replied Hopalong. "If I didn't know he wasn't around this part of the country I wouldn't a rode as I did."

The man on the stump laughed and rolled a fresh cigarette. Lighting it, he inquired where Mr. Trendley was, intimating by his words that the rustler had not been found.

"About thirty miles to th' southeast," responded the other. "He's figurin' up how much dust he'll have when he gets our cows on th' market. Deacon Rankin is with him, too."

"Th' devil!" exclaimed Red, in profound astonishment.

"Yore right," replied his companion. Then he explained all the arrangements and told of the camp.

Red was for riding to the rendezvous at once, but his friend thought otherwise and proposed a swim, which met with approval. After enjoying themselves in the lake they dressed and rode along the trail Hopalong had made in coming for his companion, it being the intention of the former to learn more thoroughly the lay of the land immediately surrounding the camp. Red was pleased with this, and while they rode he narrated all that had taken place since the separation on the Plain, adding that he had found the trail left by the rustlers after they had quitted the desert and that he had followed it for the last two hours of his journey. It was well beaten and an eighth of a mile wide.

At dark they came within sight of the grove and picketed their horses at the place used by Pie and Hopalong. Then they moved forward and the same sight greeted their eyes that had been seen the night before. Keeping well within the edge of the grove and looking carefully for sentries, they went entirely around the camp and picked out several places which would be of strategic value later on. They noticed that the cabin used by Slippery Trendley was a hundred paces from the main collection of huts and that the woods came to within a tenth part of that distance of its door. It was heavily built, had no windows and faced the wrong direction.

Moving on, they discovered the storehouse of the enemy, another tempting place. It was just possible, if a siege became necessary, for several of the attacking force to slip up to it and either destroy it by fire or take it and hold it against all comers. This suggested a look at the enemy's water supply, which was the river. A hundred paces separated it from the nearest cabin and any rustler who could cross that zone under the fire of the besiegers would be welcome to his drink.

It was very evident that the rustlers had no thought of defense, thinking, perhaps, that they were immune from attack with such a well-covered trail between them and their foes. Hopalong mentally accused them of harboring suicidal inclinations and returned with his companion to the horses. They mounted and sat quietly for a while, and then rode slowly away and at dawn reached the split rock, where they awaited the arrival of their friends, one sleeping while the other kept guard. Then they drew a rough map of the camp, using the sand for paper, and laid out the plan of attack.

As the evening of the next day came on they saw Pie, followed by many punchers, ride over a rise a mile to the south and they rode out to meet him.

When the force arrived at the camp of the two scouts they were shown the plan prepared for them. Buck made a few changes in the disposition of the men and then each member was shown where he was to go and was told why. Weapons were put in a high state of efficiency, canteens were refilled and haversacks were somewhat depleted. Then the newcomers turned in and slept while Hopalong and Red kept guard.

CHAPTER 21

The Call

At three o'clock the next morning a long line of men slowly filed into the cottonwood grove, being silently swallowed up by the dark. Dismounting, they left their horses in the care of three of their number and disappeared into the brush. Ten minutes later forty of the force were distributed along the edge of the grove fringing on the bank of the river and twenty more minutes gave ample time for a detachment of twenty to cross the stream and find concealment in the edge of the woods which ran from the river to where the corral made an effective barrier on the south. Eight crept down on the western side of the camp and worked their way close to Mr. Trendley's cabin door, and the seven who followed this detachment continued and took up their positions at the rear of the corral, where, it was hoped, some of the rustlers would endeavor to escape into the woods by working their way through the cattle in the corral and then scaling the stockade wall. These seven were from the Three Triangle and the Double Arrow, and they were positive that any such attempt would not be a success from the viewpoint of the rustlers.

Two of those who awaited the pleasure of Mr. Trendley crept forward, and a rope swished through the air and settled over the stump which lay most convenient on the other side of the cabin door. Then the slack moved toward the woods, raised from the ground as it grew taut and, with the stump for its axis, swung toward the door, where it rubbed gently against the rough logs. It was made of braided horsehair, was half an inch in diameter and was stretched eight inches above the ground.

As it touched the door, Lanky Smith, Hopalong and Red stepped out of the shelter of the woods and took up their positions behind the cabin, Lanky behind the northeast corner where he would be permitted to swing his right arm. In his gloved right hand he held the carefully arranged coils of a fifty-foot lariat, and should the chief of the rustlers escape tripping he would have to avoid the cast of the best roper in the southwest. The two others took the northwest corner and one of them leaned slightly forward and gently twitched the tripping-rope. The man at the other end felt the signal and whispered to a companion, who quietly disappeared in the direction of the river and shortly afterward the mournful cry of a whippoorwill dirged out on the early morning air. It had hardly died away when the quiet was broken by one terrific crash of rifles, and the two camp guards asleep at the fire awoke in another world.

Mr. Trendley, sleeping unusually well for the unjust, leaped from his bed to the middle of the floor and alighted on his feet and wide-awake. Fearing that a plot was being consummated to deprive him of his leadership, he grasped the Winchester which leaned at the head of his bed and, tearing open the door, crashed headlong to the earth. As he touched the ground, two shadows sped out from the shelter of the cabin wall and pounced upon him. Men who can rope, throw and tie a wild steer in thirty seconds flat do not waste time in trussing operations, and before a minute had elapsed he was being carried into the woods, bound and helpless. Lanky sighed, threw the rope over one shoulder and departed after his friends.

When Mr. Trendley came to his senses he found himself bound to a tree in the grove near the horses. A man sat on a stump not far from him, three others were seated around a small fire some distance to the north, and four others, one of whom carried a rope, made their way into the brush. He strained at his bonds, decided that the effort was useless and watched the man on the stump, who struck a match and lit a pipe. The prisoner watched the light flicker up and go out and there was left in his mind a picture that he could never forget. The face which had been so cruelly, so grotesquely revealed was that of Frenchy McAllister, and across his knees lay a heavy caliber Winchester. A curse escaped from the lips of the outlaw; the man on the stump spat at a firefly and smiled.

From the south came the crack of rifles, incessant and sharp. The reports rolled from one end of the clearing to the other and seemed to sweep in waves from the center of the line to the ends. Faintly in the infrequent lulls in the firing came an occasional report from the rear of the corral, where some desperate rustler paid for his venture.

Buck went along the line and spoke to the riflemen, and after some time had passed and the light had become stronger, he collected the men into groups of five and six. Taking one group and watching it closely, it could be seen that there was a world of meaning in this maneuver. One man started firing at a particular window in an opposite hut and then laid aside his empty gun and waited. When the muzzle of his enemy's gun came into sight and lowered until it had nearly gained its sight level, the rifles of the remainder of the group crashed out in a volley and usually one of the bullets, at least, found its intended billet. This volley firing became universal among the besiegers and the effect was marked.

Two men sprinted from the edge of the woods near Mr. Trendley's cabin and gained the shelter of the storehouse, which soon broke out in flames. The burning brands fell over the main collection of huts, where there was much confusion and swearing. The early hour at which the attack had been delivered at first led the besieged to believe that it was an Indian affair, but this impression was soon corrected by the volley firing, which turned hope into despair. It was no great matter to fight Indians, that they had done many times and found more or less enjoyment in it; but there was a vast difference between brave and puncher, and the chances of their salvation became very small. They surmised that it was the work of the cow-men on whom they had preyed and that vengeful punchers lay hidden behind that death-fringe of green willow and hazel.

Red, assisted by his inseparable companion, Hopalong, laboriously climbed up among the branches of a black walnut and hooked one leg over a convenient limb. Then he lowered his rope and drew up the Winchester which his accommodating friend fastened to it. Settling himself in a comfortable position and sheltering his body somewhat by the tree, he shaded his eyes by a hand and peered into the windows of the distant cabins.

"How is she, Red?" anxiously inquired the man on the ground.

"Bully: want to come up?"

"Nope. I'm goin' to catch yu when yu lets go," replied Hopalong with a grin.

"Which same I ain't goin' to," responded the man in the tree.

He swung his rifle out over a forked limb and let it settle in the crotch. Then he slewed his head around until he gained the bead he wished. Five minutes passed before he caught sight of his man and then he fired. Jerking out the empty shell he smiled and called out to his friend: "One."

Hopalong grinned and went off to tell Buck to put all the men in trees.

Night came on and still the firing continued. Then an explosion shook the woods. The storehouse had blown up and a sky full of burning timber fell on the cabins and soon three were half consumed, their occupants dropping as they gained the open air. One hundred paces makes fine potshooting, as Deacon Rankin discovered when evacuation was the choice necessary to avoid cremation. He never moved after he touched the ground and Red called out: "Two," not knowing that his companion had departed.

The morning of the next day found a wearied and hopeless garrison, and shortly before noon a soiled white shirt was flung from a window in the nearest cabin. Buck ran along the line and ordered the firing to cease and caused to be raised an answering flag of truce. A full minute passed and then the door slowly opened and a leg protruded, more slowly followed by the rest of the man, and Cheyenne Charley strode out to the bank of the river and sat down. His example was followed by several others and then an unexpected event occurred. Those in the cabins who preferred to die fighting, angered at this desertion, opened fire on their former comrades, who barely escaped by rolling down the slightly inclined bank into the river. Red fired again and laughed to himself. Then the fugitives swam down the river and landed under the guns of the last squad. They were taken to the rear and, after being bound, were placed under a guard. There were seven in the party and they looked worn out.

When the huts were burning the fiercest the uproar in the corral arose to such a pitch as to drown all other sounds. There were left within its walls a few hundred cattle whose brands had not yet been blotted out, and these, maddened to frenzy by the shooting and the flames, tore from one end of the enclosure to the other, crashing against the alternate walls with a noise which could be heard far out on the plain. Scores were trampled to death on each charge and finally the uproar subsided in sheer want of cattle left with energy enough to continue. When the corral was investigated the next day there were found the bodies of four rustlers, but recognition was impossible.

Several of the defenders were housed in cabins having windows in the rear walls, which the occupants considered fortunate. This opinion was revised, however, after several had endeavored to escape by these openings. The first thing that occurred when a man put his head out was the hum of a bullet, and in two cases the experimenters lost all need of escape.

The volley firing had the desired effect, and at dusk there remained only one cabin from which came opposition. Such a fire was concentrated on it that before an hour had passed the door fell in and the firing ceased. There was a rush from the side, and the Barred Horseshoe men who swarmed through the cabins emerged without firing a shot. The organization that had stirred up the Pecos Valley ranches had ceased to exist.

CHAPTER 22

The Showdown

A fire burned briskly in front of Mr. Trendley's cabin that night and several punchers sat around it occupied in various ways. Two men leaned against the wall and sang softly of the joys of the trail and the range. One of them, Lefty Allen, of the O-Bar-O, sang in his sweet tenor, and other men gradually strolled up and seated themselves on the ground, where the fitful gleam of responsive pipes and cigarettes showed like fireflies. The songs followed one after another, first a lover's plea in soft Spanish and then a rollicking tale of the cowtowns and men. Supper had long since been enjoyed and all felt that life was, indeed, well worth living.

A shadow loomed against the cabin wall and a procession slowly made its way toward the open door. The leader, Hopalong, disappeared within and was followed by Mr. Trendley, bound and hobbled and tied to Red, the rear being brought up by Frenchy, whose rifle lolled easily in the crotch of his elbow. The singing went on uninterrupted and the hum of voices between the selections remained unchanged. Buck left the crowd around the fire and went into the cabin, where his voice was heard assenting to something. Hopalong emerged and took a seat at the fire, sending two punchers to take his place. He was joined by Frenchy and Red, the former very quiet.

In the center of a distant group were seven men who were not armed. Their belts, half full of cartridges, supported empty holsters. They sat and talked to the men around them, swapping notes and experiences, and in several instances found former friends and acquaintances. These men were not bound and were apparently members of Buck's force. Then one of them broke down, but quickly regained his nerve and proposed a game of cards. A fire was started and several games were immediately in progress. These seven men were to die at daybreak.

As the night grew older man after man rolled himself in his blanket and lay down where he sat, sinking off to sleep with a swiftness that bespoke tired muscles and weariness. All through the night, however, there were twelve men on guard, of whom three were in the cabin.

At daybreak a shot from one of the guards awakened every man within hearing, and soon they romped and scampered down to the river's edge to indulge in the luxury of a morning plunge. After an hour's horseplay they trooped back to the cabin and soon had breakfast out of the way.

Waffles, foreman of the O-Bar-O, and Youbet Somes strolled over to the seven unfortunates who had just completed a choking breakfast and nodded a hearty "Good morning." Then others came up and finally all moved off toward the river. Crossing it, they disappeared into the grove and all sounds of their advance grew into silence.

Mr. Trendley, escorted outside for the air, saw the procession as it became lost to sight in the brush. He sneered and asked for a smoke, which was granted. Then his guards were changed and the men began to straggle back from the grove.

Mr. Trendley, with his back to the cabin, scowled defiantly at the crowd that hemmed him in. The coolest, most damnable murderer in the West was not now going to beg for mercy. When he had taken up crime as a means of livelihood he had decided that if the price to be paid for his course was death, he would pay like a man. He glanced at the cottonwood grove, wherein were many ghastly secrets, and smiled. His hairless eyebrows looked like livid scars and his lips quivered in scorn and anger.

As he sneered at Buck there was a movement in the crowd before him and a pathway opened for Frenchy, who stepped forward slowly and deliberately, as if on his way to some bar for a drink. There was something different about the man who had searched the Staked Plain with Hopalong and Red: he was not the same puncher who had arrived from Montana three weeks before. There was lacking a certain air of carelessness and he chilled his friends, who looked upon him as if they had never really known him. He walked up to Mr. Trendley and gazed deeply into the evil eyes.

Twenty years before, Frenchy McAllister had changed his identity from a happy-go-lucky, devil-may-care cowpuncher and became a machine. The grief that had torn his soul was not of the kind which seeks its outlet in tears and wailing: it had turned and struck inward, and now his deliberate ferocity was icy and devilish. Only a glint in his eyes told of exultation, and his words were sharp and incisive; one could well imagine one heard the click of his teeth as they bit off the consonants: every letter was clear-cut, every syllable startling in its clearness.

"Twenty years and two months ago today," he began, "you arrived at the ranch house of the Double Y, up near the Montana–Wyoming line. Everything was quiet, except, perhaps, a woman's voice, singing. You entered, and before you left you pinned a note to that woman's dress. I found it, and it is due."

The air of carelessness disappeared from the members of the crowd and the silence became oppressive. Most of those present knew parts of Frenchy's story, and all were in hearty accord with anything he might do. He reached within his vest and brought forth a deerskin bag. Opening it, he drew out a package of oiled silk and from that he took a paper. Carefully replacing the silk and the bag, he slowly unfolded the sheet in his hand and handed it to Buck, whose face hardened. Two decades had passed since the foreman of the Bar-20 had seen that precious sheet, but the scene of its finding would never fade from his memory. He stood as if carved from stone, with a look on his face that made the crowd shift uneasily and glance at Trendley.

Frenchy turned to the rustler and regarded him evilly. "You are the hellish brute that wrote that note," pointing to the paper in the hand of his friend. Then, turning again, he spoke: "Buck, read that paper."

The foreman cleared his throat and read distinctly:

"McAllister: Yore wife is to damn good to live. Trendley."

There was a shuffling sound, but Buck and Frenchy, silently backed up by Hopalong and Red, intervened, and the crowd fell back, where it surged in indecision.

"Gentlemen," said Frenchy, "I want you to vote on whether any man here has more right to do with Slippery Trendley as he sees fit than myself. Anyone who thinks so, or that he should be treated like the *others*, step forward. Majority rules."

There was no advance and he spoke again: "Is there anyone here who objects to this man dying?"

Hopalong and Red awkwardly bumped their knuckles against their guns and there was no response.

The prisoner was bound with cowhide to the wall of the cabin and four men sat near and facing him. The noonday meal was eaten in silence, and the punchers rode off to see about rounding up the cattle that grazed over the plain as far as eye could see. Suppertime came and passed, and busy men rode away in all directions. Others came and relieved the guards, and at midnight another squad took up the vigil.

Day broke and the thunder of hoofs as the punchers rounded up the cattle in herds of about five thousand each became very noticeable. One herd swept past toward the south, guarded and guided by fifteen men. Two hours later and another followed, taking a slightly different trail so as to avoid the close-cropped grass left by the first. At irregular intervals during the day other herds swept by, until six had passed and denuded the plain of cattle.

Buck, perspiring and dusty, accompanied by Hopalong and Red, rode up to where the guards smoked and joked. Frenchy came out of the cabin and smiled at his friends. Swinging in his left hand was a newly filled Colt's .45, which was recognized by his friends as the one found in the cabin and it bore a rough "T" gouged in the butt.

Buck looked around and cleared his throat: "We've got th' cows on th' home trail, Frenchy," he suggested.

"Yas?" inquired Frenchy. "Are there many?"

"Six drives of about five thousand to th' drive."

"All th' boys gone?" asked the man with the newly filled Colt's.

"Yas," replied Buck, waving his hand at the guards, ordering them to follow their friends. "It's a good deal for us: we've done right smart this hand. An' it's a good thing we've got so many punchers: thirty thousand's a big contract."

"About five times th' size of th' herd that blamed near made angels out'en me an' yu," responded Frenchy with a smile.

"I hope almighty hard that we don't have no stampedes on this here drive. Thirty thousand locoed cattle would just about wipe up this here territory. If th' last herds go wild they'll pick up th' others, an' then there'll be th' devil to pay."

Frenchy smiled again and shot a glance at where Mr. Trendley was bound to the cabin wall.

Buck looked steadily southward for some time and then flecked a foam-sud from the flank of his horse. "We are goin' south along th' Creek until we gets to Big Spring, where we'll turn right smart to th' west. We won't be able to make more'n twelve miles a day, 'though I'm goin' to drive them hard. How's yore grub?"

"Grub to burn."

"Got yore rope?" asked the foreman of the Bar-20, speaking as if the question had no especial meaning.

Frenchy smiled: "Yes."

Hopalong absentmindedly jabbed his spurs into his mount with the result that when the storm had subsided the spell was broken and he said "So long," and rode south, followed by Buck and Red. As they swept out of sight behind a grove Red turned in his saddle and waved his hat. Buck discussed with assiduity the prospects of a rainfall and was very cheerful about the recovery of the stolen cattle. Red could see a tall, broad-shouldered man standing with his feet spread far apart, swinging a Colt's .45, and Hopalong swore at everything under the sun. Dust arose in streaming clouds far to the south and they spurred forward to overtake the outfits.

Buck Peters, riding over the starlit plain, in his desire to reach the first herd, which slept somewhere to the west of him under the care of Waffles, thought of the events of the past few weeks and gradually became lost in the memories of twenty years before, which crowded up before his mind like the notes of a half-forgotten song. His nature, tempered by two decades of a harsh existence, softened as he lived again the years that had passed and as he thought of the things which had been. He was so completely lost in his reverie that he failed to hear the muffled hoofbeats of a horse that steadily gained upon him, and when Frenchy McAllister placed a friendly hand on his shoulder he started as if from a deep sleep.

The two looked at each other and their hands met. The question which sprang into Buck's eyes found a silent answer in those of his friend. They rode on side by side through the clear night and together drifted back to the days of the Double Y.

After an hour had passed, the foreman of the Bar-20 turned to his companion and then hesitated: "Did, did—was he a cur?"

Frenchy looked off toward the south and, after an interval, replied: "Yas." Then, as an afterthought, he added, "Yu see, he never reckoned it would be that way."

Buck nodded, although he did not fully understand, and the subject was forever closed.

CHAPTER 23

Mr. Cassidy Meets a Woman

The work of separating the cattle into herds of the different brands was a big contract, but with so many men it took but a comparatively short time, and in two weeks all signs of the rustlers had faded. It was then that good news went the rounds and the men looked forward to a week of pleasure, which was all the sharper accentuated by the grim mercilessness of the expedition into the Panhandle. Here was a chance for unlimited hilarity and a whole week in which to give strict attention to celebrating the recent victory.

So one day Mr. Hopalong Cassidy rode rapidly over the plain, thinking about the joys and excitement promised by the carnival to be held at Muddy Wells. With that rivalry so common to Western towns the inhabitants maintained that the carnival was to break all records, this because it was to be held in their town. Perry's Bend and Buckskin had each promoted a similar affair, and if this year's festivities were to be an improvement on those which had gone before, they would most certainly be worth riding miles to see. Perry's Bend had been unfortunate in being the first to hold a carnival, inasmuch as it only set a mark to be improved upon, and Buckskin had taken advantage of this and had added a brass band, and now in turn was to be eclipsed.

The events slated were numerous and varied, the most important being those which dealt directly with the everyday occupations of the inhabitants of that section of the country. Broncho-busting, steer-roping and tying, rifle and revolver shooting, trick riding and fancy roping made up the main features of the programme and were to be set off by horse and foot racing and other county fair necessities. Buckskin's brass band was to be on hand and the climax was to be capped by a scientific exhibition between two real roped-arena stars. Therefore Muddy Wells rubbed its hands and smiled in condescending egotism while the crowded gaming halls and the three-card-monte men on the street corners enriched themselves at the cost of know-it-all visitors.

Hopalong was firmly convinced that his day of hard riding was well worth-while, for the Bar-20 was to be represented in strength. Probably a clearer in-sight into his idea of a carnival can be gained by his definition, grouchily expressed to Red Connors on the day following the last affair: "Raise Hell, go broke, wake up an' begin punching cows all over again." But that was the day after and the day after is always filled with remorse.

Hopalong and Red, having twice in succession won the revolver and rifle competitions, respectively, hoped to make it "three straight." Lanky Smith, the Bar-20 rope expert, had taken first prize in the only contest he had entered. Skinny Thompson had lost and drawn with Lefty Allen, of the O-Bar-O, in the broncho-busting event, but as Skinny had improved greatly in the interval, his friends confidently expected him to "yank first place" for the honor of his ranch. These expectations were backed with all the available Bar-20 money, and, if they were not realized, something in the nature of a calamity would swoop down upon and wrap that ranch in gloom. Since the O-Bar-O was aggressively opti-mistic the betting was at even money, hats and guns, and the losers would begin life anew so far as earthly possessions were concerned. No other competitors were considered in this event, as Skinny and Lefty had so far outclassed all oth-ers that the honor was believed to lie between these two.

Hopalong, blissfully figuring out the chances of the different contestants, galloped around a clump of mesquite only fifteen miles from Muddy Wells and stiffened in his saddle, for twenty rods ahead of him on the trail was a woman. As she heard him approach she turned and waited for him to overtake her, and when she smiled he raised his sombrero and bowed.

"Will you please tell me where I am?" she asked.

"Yu are fifteen miles southeast of Muddy Wells," he replied.

"But which is southeast?"

"Right behind yu," he answered. "Th' town lies right ahead."

"Are you going there?" she asked.

"Yes, ma'am."

"Then you will not care if I ride with you?" she asked. "I am a trifle fright-ened."

"Why, I'd be some pleased if yu do, 'though there ain't nothing out here to be afraid of now."

"I had no intention of getting lost," she assured him, "but I dismounted to pick flowers and cactus leaves and after a while I had no conception of where I was."

"How is it yu are out here?" he asked. "Yu shouldn't get so far from town."

"Why, Papa is an invalid and doesn't like to leave his room, and the town is *so* dull, although the carnival is waking it up somewhat. Having nothing to do I procured a horse and determined to explore the country. Why, this is like Stanley and Livingstone, isn't it? You rescued the explorer!" and she laughed heartily. He wondered who in thunder Stanley and Livingstone were, but said nothing.

"I like the West, it is so big and free," she continued. "But it is very monotonous at times, especially when compared with New York. Papa swears dreadfully at the hotel and declares that the food will drive him insane, but I notice that he eats much more heartily than he did when in the city. And the service!—it is awful. But when one leaves the town behind it is splendid, and I can appreciate it because I had such a hard season in the city last winter—so many balls, parties and theaters that I simply wore myself out."

"I never hankered much for them things," Hopalong replied. "An' I don't like th' towns much, either. Once or twice a year I gets as far as Kansas City, but I soon tires of it an' hits th' back trail. Yu see, I don't like a fence country—I wants lots of room an' air."

She regarded him intently: "I know that you will think me very forward."

He smiled and slowly replied: "I think yu are all O.K."

"There do not appear to be many women in this country," she suggested.

"No, there ain't many," he replied, thinking of the kind to be found in all of the cowtowns. "They don't seem to hanker for this kind of life—they wants parties an' lots of dancin' an' them kind of things. I reckon there ain't a whole lot to tempt 'em to come."

"You evidently regard women as being very frivolous," she replied.

"Well, I'm speakin' from there not being any out here," he responded, "although I don't know much about them, to tell th' truth. Them what are out here can't be counted." Then he flushed and looked away.

She ignored the remark and placed her hand to her hair: "Goodness! My hair must look terrible!"

He turned and looked: "Yore hair is pretty—I allus did like brown hair."

She laughed and put back the straggling locks: "It is terrible! Just look at it! Isn't it awful?"

"Why, no: I reckons not," he replied critically. "It looks sort of free an' easy thataway."

"Well, it's no matter, it cannot be helped," she laughed. "Let's race!" she cried and was off like a shot.

He humored her until he saw that her mount was getting unmanageable, when he quietly overtook her and closed her pony's nostrils with his hand, the operation having a most gratifying effect.

"Joe hadn't oughter let yu had this cayuse," he said.

"Why, how do you know of whom I procured it?" she asked.

"By th' brand: it's a O-Bar-O, canceled, with J. H. over it. He buys all of his cayuses from th' O-Bar-O."

She found out his name, and, after an interval of silence, she turned to him with eyes full of inquiry: "What is that thorny shrub just ahead?" she asked.

"That's mesquite," he replied eagerly.

"Tell me all about it," she commanded.

"Why, there ain't much to tell," he replied, "only it's a valuable tree out here. Th' Apaches use it a whole lot of ways. They get honey from th' blossoms an' glue an' gum, an' they use th' bark for tannin' hide. Th' dried pods an' leaves are used to feed their cattle, an' th' wood makes corrals to keep 'em in. They use th' wood for making other things, too, an' it is of two colors. Th' sap makes a dye what won't wash out, an' th' beans make a bread what won't sour or get hard. Then it makes a barrier that shore is a dandy—coyotes an' men can't get through it, an' it protects a whole lot of birds an' things. Th' snakes hate it like poison, for th' thorns get under their scales an' whoops things up for 'em. It keeps th' sand from shiftin', too. Down South where there is plenty of water, it often grows forty feet high, but up here it squats close to th' ground so it can save th' moisture. In th' night th' temperature sometimes falls thirty degrees, an' that helps it, too."

"How can it live without water?" she asked.

"It gets all th' water it wants," he replied, smiling. "Th' taproots go straight down 'til they find it, sometimes fifty feet. That's why it don't shrivel up in th' sun. Then there are a lot of little roots under it an' they protects th' taproots. Th' shade it gives is th' coolest out here, for th' leaves turn with th' wind an' lets th' breeze through—they're hung on little stems."

"How splendid!" she exclaimed. "Oh! Look there!" she cried, pointing ahead of them. A chaparral cock strutted from its decapitated enemy, a rattlesnake, and disappeared in the chaparral.

Hopalong laughed: "Mr. Scissors-bill Read-runner has great fun with snakes. He runs along th' sand—an' he *can* run, too—an' sees a snake takin' a siesta.

Snip! goes his bill an' th' snake slides over th' Divide. Our fighting friend may stop some coyote's appetite before morning, though, unless he stays where he is."

Just then a gray wolf blundered in sight a few rods ahead of them, and Hopalong fired instantly. His companion shrunk from him and looked at him reproachfully.

"Why did you do that!" she demanded.

"Why, because they costs us big money every year," he replied. "There's a bounty on them because they pull down calves, an' sometimes full-grown cows. I'm shore wonderin' why he got so close—they're usually just out of range, where they stays."

"Promise me that you will shoot no more while I am with you."

"Why, shore: I didn't think yu'd care," he replied. "Yu are like that sky-pilot over to Las Cruces—he preached agin killin' things, which is all right for him, who didn't have no cows."

"Do you go to the missions?" she asked.

He replied that he did, sometimes, but forgot to add that it was usually for the purpose of hilarity, for he regarded sky pilots with humorous toleration.

"Tell me all about yourself—what you do for enjoyment and all about your work," she requested.

He explained in minute detail the art of punching cows, and told her more of the West in half an hour than she could have learned from a year's experience. She showed such keen interest in his words that it was a pleasure to talk to her, and he monopolized the conversation until the town intruded its sprawling collection of unpainted shacks and adobe huts in their field of vision.

CHAPTER 24

The Strategy of Mr. Peters

Hopalong and his companion rode into Muddy Wells at noon, and Red Connors, who leaned with Buck Peters against the side of Tom Lee's saloon, gasped his astonishment. Buck looked twice to be sure, and then muttered incredulously: "What th' hell!" Red repeated the phrase and retreated within the saloon, while Buck stood his ground, having had much experience with women, inasmuch as he had narrowly escaped marrying. He thought that he might as well get all the information possible, and waited for an introduction. It was in vain, however, for the two rode past without noticing him.

Buck watched them turn the corner and then called for Red to come out, but that person, fearing an ordeal, made no reply and the foreman went in after him. The timorous one was corraling bracers at the bar and nearly swallowed down the wrong channel when Buck placed a heavy hand on his broad shoulder.

"G'way!" remarked Red. "I don't want no introduction, none whatever," he asserted. "G'way!" he repeated, backing off suspiciously.

"Better wait 'til yu are asked," suggested Buck. "Better wait 'til yu sees th' rope afore yu duck." Then he laughed: "Yu bashful fellers make me plumb disgusted. Why, I've seen yu face a bunch of guns an' never turn a hair, an' here yore all in because yu fear yu'll have to stand around an' hide yore hands. She won't bite yu. Anyway, from what I saw, Hopalong is due to be her grub—he never saw me at all, th' chump."

"He shore didn't see me, none," replied Red with distinct relief. "Are they gone?"

"Shore," answered Buck. "An' if they wasn't they wouldn't see us, not if we stood in front of them an' yelled. She's a hummer—stands two hands under him an' is a whole lot prettier than that picture Cowan has got over his bar. There's nothing th' matter with his eyesight, but he's plumb locoed, all th' same. He'll go an' get stuck on her an' then she'll hit th' trail for home an' mamma, an' he won't be worth his feed for a year." Then he paused in consternation: "Thunder, Red: he's got to shoot tomorrow!"

"Well, suppose he has?" responded Red. "I don't reckon she'll stampede his gunplay none."

"Yu don't reckon, eh?" queried Buck with much irony. "No, an' that's what's th' matter with yu. Why, do yu expect to see him tomorrow? Yu won't if I knows him an' I reckon I do. Nope, he'll be follerin' her all around."

"He's got sand to burn," remarked Red in awe. "Wonder how he got to know her?"

"Yu can gamble she did th' introducing part—he ain't got th' nerve to do it himself. He saved her life, or she thinks he did, or some romantic nonsense like that. So yu better go around an' get him away, an' keep him away, too."

"Who, *me*?" inquired Red in indignation. "*Me* go around an' tote him off? *I* ain't no wagon: yu go, or send Johnny."

"Johnny would say something real pert an' get knocked into th' middle of next week for it. He won't do, so I reckon yu better go yoreself," responded Buck, smiling broadly and moving off.

"Hey, yu! Wait a minute!" cried Red in consternation. Buck paused and Red groped for an excuse: "Why don't you send Billy?" he blurted in desperation.

The foreman's smile assumed alarming proportions and he slapped his thigh in joy: "Good boy!" he laughed. "Billy's th' man—good Lord, but won't he give Cupid cold feet! Rustle around an' send th' pessimistic soul to me."

Red, grinning and happy, rapidly visited door after door, shouted, "Hey, Billy!" and proceeded to the next one. He was getting pugnacious at his lack of success when he espied Mr. Billy Williams tacking along the accidental street as if he owned it. Mr. Williams was executing fancy steps and was trying to sing many songs at once.

Red stopped and grabbed his bibulous friend as that person veered to starboard: "Yore a peach of a life-preserver, yu are!" he exclaimed.

Billy balanced himself, swayed back and forth and frowned his displeasure at this unwarranted action: "I *ain't* no wife-deserter!" he shouted. "Unrope me an' give me th' trail! No tenderfoot can ride me!" Then he recognized his friend and grinned joyously: "Shore I will, but only one. Jus' one more, jus' one more. Yu see, m' friend, it was all Jimmy's fault. He—"

Red secured a chancery hold and dragged his wailing and remonstrating friend to Buck, who frowned his displeasure.

"This yere," said Red in belligerent disgust, "is th' dod-blasted hero what's a-goin' to save Hopalong from a mournful future. What are we a-goin' to do?"

Buck slipped the Colt's from Billy's holster and yanked the erring one to his feet: "Fill him full of sweet oil, souce him in th' trough, walk him around for awhile an' see what it does," he ordered.

Two hours later Billy walked up to his foreman and weakly asked what was wanted. He looked as though he had just been released from a six-months' stay in a hospital.

"Yu go over to th' hotel an' find Hopalong," said the foreman sternly. "Stay with him all th' time, for there is a plot on foot to wing him on th' sly. If yu ain't mighty spry he'll be dead by night."

Having delivered the above instructions and prevarications, Buck throttled the laugh which threatened to injure him and scowled at Red, who again fled into the saloon for fear of spoiling it all with revealed mirth.

The convalescent stared in open-mouthed astonishment: "What's he doin' in th' hotel, an' who's goin' to plug him?" he asked.

"Yu leave that to me," replied Buck. "All yu has to do is to get on th' job with yore gun," handing the weapons to him, "an' freeze to him like a flea on a cow. Mebby there'll be a woman in th' game, but that ain't none of yore funeral—yu do what I said."

"Damn th' women!" exploded Billy, moving off. When he had entered the hotel Buck went in to Red.

"For God's sake!" moaned that person in senseless reiteration. "Th' Lord help Billy! Holy Mackinaw!" he shouted. "Gimme a drink an' let me tell th' boys."

The members of the outfit were told of the plot and they gave their uproarious sanction, all needing bracers to sustain them.

Billy found the clerk swapping lies with the bartender and, procuring the desired information, climbed the stairs and hunted for room No. 6. Discovering it, he dispensed with formality, pushed open the door and entered.

He found his friend engaged in conversation with a pretty young woman, and on a couch at the far side of the room lay an elderly, white-whiskered gentleman who was reading a magazine. Billy felt like a criminal for a few seconds and then there came to him the thought that his was a mission of great import and he braced himself to face any ordeal. "Anyway," he thought, "th' prettier they are th' more hell they can raise."

"What are *yu* doing here?" cried Hopalong in amazement.

"That's all right," averred the protector, confidentially.

"What's all right?"

"Why, everything," replied Billy, feeling uncomfortable.

The elderly man hastily sat up and dropped his magazine when he saw the armed intruder, his eyes as wide open as his mouth. He felt for his spectacles, but did not need them, for he could see nothing but the Colt's which Billy jabbed at him.

"None of that!" snapped Billy. "'Nds up!" he ordered, and the hands went up so quick that when they stopped the jerk shook the room. Peering over the gentleman's leg, Billy saw the spectacles and backed to the wall as he apologized: "It's shore on me, Stranger—I reckoned yu was contemplatin' some gunplay."

Hopalong, blazing with wrath, arose and shoved Billy toward the hall, when Mr. Johnny Nelson, oozing fight and importance, intruded his person into the zone of action.

"*Lord!*" ejaculated the newcomer, staring at the vision of female loveliness which so suddenly greeted him. "Mamma," he added under his breath. Then he tore off his sombrero: "Come out of this, Billy, yu chump!" he exploded, backing toward the door, being followed by the protector.

Hopalong slammed the door and turned to his hostess, apologizing for the disturbance.

"Who are they?" palpitated Miss Deane.

"What the hell are they doing up here!" blazed her father.

Hopalong disclaimed any knowledge of them and just then Billy opened the door and looked in.

"There he is again!" cried Miss Deane, and her father gasped.

Hopalong ran out into the hall and narrowly missed kicking Billy into Kingdom Come as that person slid down the stairs, surprised and indignant.

Mr. Billy Williams, who sat at the top of the stairs, was feeling hungry and thirsty when he saw his friend, Mr. Pete Wilson, the slow-witted, approaching.

"Hey, Pete," he called, "come up here an' watch this door while I rustles some grub. Keep yore eyes open," he cautioned.

As Pete began to feel restless the door opened and a dignified gentleman with white whiskers came out into the hall and then retreated with great haste and no dignity. Pete got the drop on the door and waited. Hopalong yanked it open and kissed the muzzle of the weapon before he could stop, and Pete grinned.

"Coming to th' fight?" he loudly asked. "It's going to be a hell of a sumptious scrap—just th' kind yu allus like. Come on, th' boys are waitin' for yu."

"Keep quiet!" hissed Hopalong.

"What for?" asked Pete in surprise. "Didn't yu say yu shore wanted to see that scrap?"

"Shut yore face an' get scarce, or yu'll go home in cans!"

As Hopalong seated himself once more Red strolled up to the door and knocked. Hopalong ripped it open and Red, looking as fierce and worried as he could, asked Hopalong if he was all right. Upon being assured by smoking adjectives that he was, the caller looked relieved and turned thoughtfully away.

"Hey, yu! Come here!" called Hopalong.

Red waved his hand and said that he had to meet a man and clattered down the stairs. Hopalong thought that he, also, had to meet a man and, excusing himself, hastened after his friend and overtook him in the street, where he forced a confession. Returning to his hostess he told her of the whole outrage, and she was angry at first, but seeing the humorous side of it, she became convulsed with laughter. Her father re-read his paragraph for the thirteenth time and then, slamming the magazine on the floor, asked how many times he was expected to read ten lines before he knew what was in them, and went down to the bar.

Miss Deane regarded her companion with laughing eyes and then became suddenly sober as he came toward her.

"Go to your foreman and tell him that you will shoot tomorrow, for I will see that you do, and I will bring luck to the Bar-20. Be sure to call for me at one o'clock: I will be ready."

He hesitated, bowed, and slowly departed, making his way to Tom Lee's, where his entrance hushed the hilarity which had reigned. Striding to where Buck stood, he placed his hands on his hips and searched the foreman's eyes.

Buck smiled: "Yu ain't mad, are yu?" he asked.

Hopalong relaxed: "No, but damn near it."

Red and the others grabbed him from the rear, and when he had been "buffaloed" into good humor he threw them from him, laughed and waved his hand toward the bar: "Come up, yu sons-of-guns. Yore a damned nuisance sometimes, but yore a bully gang all th' same."

CHAPTER 25

Mr. Ewalt Draws Cards

Tex Ewalt, cowpuncher, prospector, sometimes a rustler, but always a dude, rode from El Paso in deep disgust at his steady losses at faro and monte. The pecuniary side of these caused him no worry, for he was flush. This pleasing opulence was due to his business ability, for he had recently sold a claim for several thousand dollars. The first operation was simple, being known in Western phraseology as "jumping"; and the second, somewhat more complicated, was known as "salting."

The first of the money spent went for a complete new outfit, and he had parted with just three hundred and seventy dollars to feed his vanity. He desired something contrasty and he procured it. His sombrero, of gray felt a quarter of an inch thick, flaunted a band of black leather, on which was conspicuously displayed a solid silver buckle. His neck was protected by a crimson kerchief of the finest, heaviest silk. His shirt, in pattern the same as those commonly worn in the cow country, was of buckskin, soft as a baby's cheek and impervious to water, and the Angora goatskin chaps, with the long silken hair worn outside, were as white as snow. Around his waist ran loosely a broad, black leather belt supporting a heavy black holster, in which lay its walnut-handled burden, a .44-caliber Remington six-shooter; and fifty center-fire cartridges peeked from their loops, twenty-five on a side. His boots, the soles thin and narrow and the heels high, were black and of the finest leather. Huge spurs, having two-inch rowels, were held in place by buckskin straps, on which, also, were silver buckles. Protecting his hands were heavy buckskin gloves, also waterproof, having wide, black gauntlets.

Each dainty hock of his dainty eight-hundred-pound buckskin pony was black, and a black star graced its forehead. Well groomed, with flowing mane and tail, and with the brand on its flank being almost imperceptible, the animal was far different in appearance from most of the cow-ponies. Vicious and high-spirited, it cavorted just enough to show its lines to the best advantage.

The saddle, a famous Cheyenne and forty pounds in weight, was black, richly embossed, and decorated with bits of beaten silver which flashed back the sunlight. At the pommel hung a thirty-foot coil of braided horsehair rope, and at the rear was a Sharp's .50-caliber, breech-loading rifle, its owner having small use for any other make. The color of the bridle was the same as the saddle and it supported a heavy U bit which was capable of a leverage sufficient to break the animal's jaw.

Tex was proud of his outfit, but his face wore a frown—not there only on account of his losses, but also by reason of his mission, for under all his finery beat a heart as black as any in the cow country. For months he had smothered hot hatred and he was now on his way to ease himself of it.

He and Slim Travennes had once exchanged shots with Hopalong in Santa Fé, and the month which he had spent in bed was not pleasing, and from that encounter had sprung the hatred. That he had been in the wrong made no difference with him. Some months later he had learned of the death of Slim, and it was due to the same man. That Slim had again been in the wrong also made no difference, for he realized the fact and nothing else. Lately he had been told of the death of Slippery Trendley and Deacon Rankin, and he accepted their passing as a personal affront. That they had been caught red-handed in cattle stealing of huge proportions and received only what was customary under the conditions formed no excuse in his mind for their passing. He was now on his way to attend the carnival at Muddy Wells, knowing that his enemy would be sure to be there.

While passing through Las Cruces he met Porous Johnson and Silent Somes, who were thirsty and who proclaimed that fact, whereupon he relieved them of their torment and, looking forward to more treatment of a similar nature, they gladly accompanied him without asking why or where.

As they left the town in their rear Tex turned in his saddle and surveyed them with a cynical smile.

"Have yu heard anything of Trendley?" he asked.

They shook their heads.

"Him an' th' Deacon was killed over in th' Panhandle," he said.

"What!" chorused the pair.

"Jack Dorman, Shorty Danvers, Charley Teale, Stiffhat Bailey, Billy Jackson, Terry Nolan an' Sailor Carson was lynched."

"*What!*" they shouted.

"Fish O'Brien, Pinochle Schmidt, Tom Wilkins, Apache Gordon, Charley of th' Bar Y, Penobscot Hughes an' about twenty others died fightin'."

Porous looked his astonishment: "Cavalry?"

"An' I'm going after th' —— who did it," he continued, ignoring the question. "Are yu with me?—yu used to pal with some of them, didn't yu?"

"We did, an' we're shore with yu!" cried Porous.

"Yore right," endorsed Silent. "But who done it?"

"That gang what's punchin' for th' Bar-20—Hopalong Cassidy is th' one I'm pining for. Yu fellers can take care of Peters an' Connors."

The two stiffened and exchanged glances of uncertainty and apprehension. The outfit of the Bar-20 was too well known to cause exuberant joy to spring from the idea of war with it, and well in the center of all the tales concerning it were the persons Tex had named. To deliberately set forth with the avowed intention of planting these was not at all calculated to induce sweet dreams.

Tex sneered his contempt.

"Yore shore uneasy: yu ain't a-scared, are yu?" he drawled.

Porous relaxed and made a show of subduing his horse: "I reckon I ain't scared plumb to death. Yu can deal me a hand," he asserted.

"I'll draw cards too," hastily announced Silent, buttoning his vest. "Tell us about that jamboree over in th' Panhandle."

Tex repeated the story as he had heard it from a bibulous member of the Barred Horseshoe, and then added a little of torture as a sauce to whet their appetites for revenge.

"How did Trendley cash in?" asked Porous.

"Nobody knows except that bum from th' Tin-Cup. I'll get him later. I'd a got Cassidy up in Santa Fé, too, if it wasn't for th' sun in my eyes. Me an' Slim loosened up on him in th' Plaza, but we couldn't see nothing with him a-standin' against th' sun."

"Where's Slim now?" asked Porous. "I ain't seen him for some time."

"Slim's with Trendley," replied Tex. "Cassidy handed him over to St. Pete at Cactus Springs. Him an' Connors sicked their outfit on him an' his vigilantes, bein' helped some by th' O-Bar-O. They wiped th' town plumb off th' earth, an' now I'm going to do some wipin' of my own account. I'll prune that gang of some of its blossoms afore long. It's cost me seventeen friends so far, an' I'm going to stop th' leak, or make another."

They entered Muddy Wells at sunrise on the day of the carnival and, eating a hearty breakfast, sallied forth to do their share toward making the festivities a success.

The first step considered necessary for the acquirement of ease and polish was begun at the nearest bar, and Tex, being the host, was so liberal that his friends had reached a most auspicious state when they followed him to Tom Lee's.

Tex was too wise to lose his head through drink and had taken only enough to make him careless of consequences. Porous was determined to sing "Annie Laurie," although he hung on the last word of the first line until out of breath and then began anew. Silent, not wishing to be outdone, bawled at the top of his lungs a medley of music-hall words to the air of a hymn.

Tex, walking as awkwardly as any cowpuncher, approached Tom Lee's, his two friends trailing erratically, arm in arm, in his rear. Swinging his arm he struck the door a resounding blow and entered, hand on gun, as it crashed back. Porous and Silent stood in the doorway and quarreled as to what each should drink and, compromising, lurched in and seated themselves on a table and resumed their vocal perpetrations.

Tex swaggered over to the bar and tossed a quarter upon it: "Corn juice," he laconically exclaimed. Tossing off the liquor and glancing at his howling friends, he shrugged his shoulders and strode out by the rear door, slamming it after him. Porous and Silent, recounting friends who had "cashed in" fell to weeping and they were thus occupied when Hopalong and Buck entered, closely followed by the rest of the outfit.

Buck walked to the bar and was followed by Hopalong, who declined his foreman's offer to treat. Tom Lee set a bottle at Buck's elbow and placed his hands against the bar.

"Friend of yourn just hit th' back trail," he remarked to Hopalong. "He was primed some for trouble, too," he added.

"Yaas?" drawled Hopalong with little interest.

The proprietor restacked the few glasses and wiped off the bar.

"Them's his pardners," he said, indicating the pair on the table.

Hopalong turned his head and gravely scrutinized them. Porous was bemoaning the death of Slim Travennes and Hopalong frowned.

"Don't reckon he's no relation of mine," he grunted.

"Well, he ain't yore sister," replied Tom Lee, grinning.

"What's his brand?" asked the puncher.

"I reckon he's a maverick, 'though yu put yore brand on him up to Santa Fé a couple of years back. Since he's throwed back on yore range I reckon he's yourn if yu wants him."

"I reckon Tex is some sore," remarked Hopalong, rolling a cigarette.

"I reckon he is," replied the proprietor, tossing Buck's quarter in the cash box. "But, say, you should oughter see his rig."

"Yaas?"

"He's shore a cowpunch dude—my, but he's some sumptious an' highfalutin'. An' bad? Why, he reckons th' Lord never brewed a more high-toned brand of cussedness than his'n. He shore reckons he's th' baddest man that ever simmered."

"How'd he look as th' leadin' man in a necktie festival?" blazed Johnny from across the room, feeling called upon to help with the conversation.

"He'd be a howlin' success, son," replied Skinny Thompson, "judgin' by his friends what we elevated over in th' Panhandle."

Lanky Smith leaned forward with his elbow on the table, resting his chin in the palm of his hand: "Is Ewalt still a-layin' for yu, Hopalong?" he asked.

Hopalong turned wearily and tossed his half-consumed cigarette into the box of sand which did duty as a cuspidore: "I reckon so; an' he shore can hatch whenever he gets good an' ready, too."

"He's probably a-broodin' over past grievances," offered Johnny, as he suddenly pushed Lanky's elbow from the table, nearly causing a catastrophe.

"Yu'll be broodin' over present grievances if yu don't look out, yu everlastin' nuisance yu," growled Lanky, planting his elbow in its former position with an emphasis which conveyed a warning.

"These bantams ruffle my feathers," remarked Red. "They go around braggin' about th' egg they're goin' to lay an' do enough cacklin' to furnish music for a dozen. Then when th' affair comes off yu'll generally find they's been settin' on a doorknob."

"Did yu ever see a hen leave th' walks of peace an' bugs an' rustle hell-bent across th' trail plumb in front of a cayuse?" asked Buck. "They'll leave off rustlin' grub an' become candidates for th' graveyard just for cussedness. Well, a whole lot of men are th' same way. How many times have I seen them swagger into a gin shop an' try to run things sudden an' hard, an' that with half a dozen better men in th' same room? There's shore a-plenty of trouble a-comin' to every man without rustlin' around for more."

"'Member that time yu an' Frenchy tried to run th' little town of Frozen Nose, up in Montana?" asked Johnny, winking at the rest.

"An' we did run it, for a while," responded Buck. "But that only goes to show that most young men are chumps—we were just about yore age then."

Red laughed at the youngster's discomfiture: "That little squib of yourn shore touched her off—I reckon we irrigates on yu this time, don't we?"

"Th' more th' Kid talks, th' more money he needs," remarked Lanky, placing his glass on the bar. "He had to buy drinks for me an' Skinny twice last night."

"I got two more after yu left," added Skinny. "He shore oughter practice keeping still."

At one o'clock sharp Hopalong walked up to the clerk of the hotel and grinned. The clerk looked up: "Hullo, Cassidy?" he exclaimed, genially. "What was all that fuss about this mornin' when I was away? I haven't seen you for a long time, have I? How are you?"

"That fuss was a fool joke of Buck's, an' I wish they had been throwed out," Hopalong replied. "What I want to know is if Miss Deane is in her room. Yu see, I have a date with her."

The clerk grinned: "So she's roped you, too, has she?"

"What do yu mean?" asked Hopalong in surprise.

"Well, well," laughed the clerk. "You punchers are easy. Any third-rate actress that looks good to eat can rope you fellows, all right. Now look here, Laura, you keep shy of her corral, or you'll be broke so quick you won't believe you ever had a cent: that's straight. This is the third year that she's been here and I know what I'm talking about. How did you come to meet her?"

Hopalong explained the meeting and his friend laughed again: "Why, she knows this country like a book. She can't get lost anywhere around here. But she's damned clever at catching punchers."

"Well, I reckon I'd better take her, go broke or not," replied Hopalong. "Is she in her room?"

"She is, but she is not alone," responded the clerk. "There is a dude puncher up there with her and she left word here that she was indisposed, which means that you are outlawed."

"Who is he?" asked Hopalong, having his suspicions.

"That friend of yours: Ewalt. He sported a wad this morning when she passed him, and she let him make her acquaintance. He's another easy mark. He'll be busted wide open tonight."

"I reckon I'll see Tex," suggested Hopalong, starting for the stairs.

"Come back, you chump!" cried the clerk. "I don't want any shooting here. What do you care about it? Let her have him, for it's an easy way out of it for you. Let him think he's cut you out, for he'll spend all the more freely. Get your crowd and enlighten them—it'll be better than a circus. This may sound like a steer, but it's straight."

Hopalong thought for a minute and then leaned on the cigar case: "I reckon

I'll take about a dozen of yore very best cigars, Charley. Got any real high-toned brands?"

"Cortez panatella—two for a dollar," Charley replied. "But, seein' that it's you, I'll throw off a dollar on a dozen. They're a fool notion of the old man, for we can't sell one in a month."

Hopalong dug up a handful and threw one on the counter, lighting another: "Yu light a Cortez panatella with me," he said, pocketing the remainder. "That's five dollars she didn't get. So long."

He journeyed to Tom Lee's and found his outfit making merry. Passing around his cigars he leaned against the bar and delighted in the first really good smoke he had since he came home from Kansas City.

Johnny Nelson blew a cloud of smoke at the ceiling and paused with a pleased expression on his face: "This is a lalapoloosa of a cigar," he cried. "Where'd yu get it, an' how many's left?"

"I got it from Charley, an' there's more than yu can buy at fifty a shot."

"Well, I'll just take a few for luck," Johnny responded, running out into the street. Returning in five minutes with both hands full of cigars he passed them around and grinned: "They're birds, all right!"

Hopalong smiled, turned to Buck and related his conversation with Charley. "What do yu think of that?" he asked as he finished.

"I think Charley oughter be yore guardian," replied the foreman.

"He was," replied Hopalong.

"If we sees Tex we'll all grin hard," laughed Red, making for the door. "Come on to th' contests—Lanky's gone already."

Muddy Wells streamed to the carnival grounds and relieved itself of its enthusiasm and money at the booths on the way. Cowpunchers, Indians, Mexicans, and the few tourists that were present were delighted with the picturesque scene. The town was full of fakirs and before one of them stood a group of cowpunchers, apparently drinking in the words of a barker.

"Right this way, gents, and see the woman who don't eat. Lived for two years without food, gents. Right this way, gents. Only a quarter of a dollar. Get your tickets, gents, and see—"

Red pushed forward: "What did yu say, Pard?" he asked. "I'm a little off in my near ear. What's that about eatin' a woman for two years?"

"The greatest wonder of the age, gents. The wom—"

"Any discount for th' gang?" asked Buck, gawking.

"Why don't yu quit smokin' an' buy th' lady a meal?" asked Johnny from the center of the group.

"Th' cane yu ring th' cane yu get!" came from the other side of the street and Hopalong purchased rings for the outfit. Twenty-four rings got one cane, and it was divided between them as they wended their way toward the grounds.

"That makes six wheels she didn't get," murmured Hopalong.

As they passed the snake charmer's booth they saw Tex and his companion ahead of them in the crowd, and they grinned broadly. "I like th' front row in th' balcony," remarked Johnny, who had been to Kansas City. "Don't cry in th' second act—it ain't real," laughed Red. "We'll hang John Brown on a sour apple-tree—in th' Panhandle," sang Skinny as they passed them.

Arriving at the grounds they hunted up the registration committee and entered in the contests. As Hopalong signed for the revolver competition he was rudely pushed aside and Tex wrote his name under that of his enemy. Hopalong was about to show quick resentment for the insult, but thought of what Charley had said, and he grinned sympathetically. The seats were filling rapidly, and the outfit went along the ground looking for friends. A bugle sounded and a hush swept over the crowd as the announcement was made for the first event.

"Broncho-busting.—Red Devil, never ridden: Frenchy McAllister, Tin-Cup, Montana; Meteor, killed his man: Skinny Thompson, Bar-20, Texas; Vixen, never ridden: Lefty Allen, O-Bar-O, Texas."

All eyes were focused on the plain where the horse was being led out for the first trial. After the usual preliminaries had been gone through Frenchy walked over to it, vaulted in the saddle and the bandage was torn from the animal's eyes. For ten minutes the onlookers were held spellbound by the fight before them, and then the horse kicked and galloped away and Frenchy was picked up and carried from the field.

"Too bad!" cried Buck, running from the outfit.

"Did yu see it?" asked Johnny excitedly. "Th' cinch busted."

Another horse was led out and Skinny Thompson vaulted to the saddle, and after a fight of half an hour rode the animal from the enclosure to the clamorous shouts of his friends. Lefty Allen also rode his mount from the same gate, but took ten minutes more in which to do it.

The announcer conferred with the timekeepers and then stepped forward: "First, Skinny Thompson, Bar-20, thirty minutes and ten seconds; second, Lefty Allen, O-Bar-O, forty minutes and seven seconds."

Skinny returned to his friends shamefacedly and did not look as if he had just won a championship. They made way for him, and Johnny, who could not restrain his enthusiasm, clapped him on the back and cried: "Yu old son-of-a-gun!"

The announcer again came forward and gave out the competitors for the next contest, steer-roping and tying. Lanky Smith arose and, coiling his rope carefully, disappeared into the crowd. The fun was not so great in this, but when he returned to his outfit with the phenomenal time of six minutes and eight seconds for his string of ten steers, with twenty-two seconds for one of them, they gave him vociferous greeting. Three of his steers had gotten up after he had leaped from his saddle to tie them, but his horse had taken care of that. His nearest rival was one minute over him and Lanky retained the championship.

Red Connors shot with such accuracy in the rifle contest as to run his points twenty per cent higher than Waffles, of the O-Bar-O, and won the new rifle.

The main interest centered in the revolver contest, for it was known that the present champion was to defend his title against an enemy and fears were expressed in the crowd that there would be an "accident." Buck Peters and Red stood just behind the firing line with their hands on hips, and Tex, seeing the precautions, smiled grimly as he advanced to the line.

Six bottles, with their necks an inch above a board, stood twenty paces from him, and he broke them all in as many shots, taking six seconds in which to do it. Hopalong followed him and tied the score. Three tin balls rolling erratically in a blanket supported by two men were sent flying into the air in four shots, Tex taking three seconds. His competitor sent them from the blanket in three shots and in the same time. In slow shooting from sights Tex passed his rival in points and stood to win. There was but one more event to be contested and in it Hopalong found his joy. Shooting from the hip when the draw is timed is not the sport of even good shots, and when Tex made sixty points out of a possible hundred, he felt that he had shot well. When Hopalong went to the line his friends knew that they would now see shooting such as would be almost unbelievable, that the best draw-and-shoot marksman in their State was the man who limped slightly as he advanced and who chewed reflectively on his fifty-cent cigar. He wore two guns and he stepped with confidence before the marshal of the town, who was also judge of the contest.

The tiny spherical bell which lay on the ground was small enough for the use of a rifle and could hardly be seen from the rear seats of the amphitheater. There was a word spoken by the timekeeper, and a gloved hand flashed down and up, and the bell danced and spun and leaped and rolled as shot after shot followed it with a precision and speed which brought the audience to a heavy silence. Taking the gun which Buck tossed to him and throwing it into the empty holster, he awaited the signal, and then smoke poured from his hips and the bell clanged continuously, once while it was in the air. Both guns emptied in the two-hand shooting, he wheeled and jerked loose the guns which the marshal wore, spinning around without a pause, the target hardly ceasing in its ringing. Under his arms he shot, backward and between his legs; leaping from side to side, ducking and dodging, following the bell wherever it went. Reloading his weapons quickly he twirled them on his fingers and enveloped himself in smoke out of which came vivid flashes as the bell gave notice that he shot well. His friends, and there were many in the crowd, torn from their affected nonchalance by shooting the like of which they had not attributed even to him, roared and shouted and danced in a frenzy of delight. Red also threw his guns to Hopalong, who caught them in the air and turning, faced Tex, who stood white of face and completely lost in the forgetfulness of admiration and amazement. The guns spun again on his fingers and a button flew from the buckskin shirt of his enemy; another tore a flower from his breast and another drove it into the ground at his feet as others stirred his hair and cut the buckle off his pretty sombrero. Tex, dazed, but wise enough to stand quiet, felt his belt tear loose and drop to his feet, felt a spur rip from its strap and saw his cigarette leap from his lips. Throwing the guns to Red, Hopalong laughed and abruptly turned and was lost in the crowd.

For several seconds there was silence, but when the dazed minds realized what their eyes had seen, there arose a roar which shook the houses in the town. Roar after roar thundered forth and was sent crashing back again by the distant walls, sweeping down on the discomfited dude and causing him to slink into the crowd to find a place less conspicuous. He was white yet and keen fear gripped his heart as he realized that he had come to the carnival with the expressed purpose of killing his enemy in fair combat. The whole town knew it, for he had taken pains to spread the news. The woman he had been with knew it from words which she had overheard while on her way to the grounds with him. His friends knew it and would laugh him into forgetfulness as the fool who boasted. Now he understood why he had lost so many friends: they had attempted what he had sworn to attempt. Look where he would he could see only a smoke-wrapped demon who moved and shot with a speed incredible. There was reason why Slim had died. There was reason why Porous and Silent had paled when they learned of their mission. He hated his conspicuous clothes and his pretty broncho, and the woman who had gotten him to squander his money, and who was doubtless convulsed with laughter at his expense. He worked himself into a passion which knew no fear and he ran for the streets of the town, there to make good his boast or to die. When he found his enemy he felt himself grasped with a grip of steel and Buck Peters swung him around and grinned maliciously in his face: "Yu plaything!" hoarsely whispered the foreman. "Why don't yu get away while yu can? Why do yu want to throw yoreself against certain death? I don't want my pleasure marred by a murder, an' that is what it will be if yu makes a gunplay at Hopalong. He'll shoot yu as he did yore buttons. Take yore pretty clothes an' yore pretty cayuse an' go where this is not known, an' if ever again yu feels like killing Hopalong, get drunk an' forget it."

Hopalong Cassidy

Affectionately dedicated
to my father

CHAPTER 1

Antonio's Scheme

The raw and mighty West, the greatest stage in all the history of the world for so many deeds of daring which verged on the insane, was seared with grave-lined trails. In many localities the bad-man made history in a terse and business-like way, and also made the first law for the locality—that of the gun.

There were good bad-men and bad bad-men, the killer by necessity and the wanton murderer; and the shifting of these to their proper strata evolved the foundation for the law of to-day. The good bad-man, those in whose souls lived the germs of law and order and justice, gradually became arrayed against the other class, and stood up manfully for their principles, let the odds be what they might; and bitter, indeed, was the struggle, and great the price.

From the gold camps of the Rockies to the shrieking towns of the coast, where wantonness stalked unchecked; from the vast stretches of the cattle ranges to the ever-advancing terminals of the persistent railroads, to the cow towns, boiling and seething in the loosed passions of men who brooked no restraint in their revels, no one section of country ever boasted of such numbers of genuine bad-men of both classes as the great, semi-arid Southwest. Here was one of the worst collections of raw humanity ever broadcast in one locality; it was a word and a shot, a shot and a laugh or a curse.

In this red setting was stuck a town which we will call Eagle, the riffle which caught all the dregs of passing humanity. Unmapped, known only to those who had visited it, reared its flimsy buildings in the face of God and rioted day and night with no thought of reckoning; mad, insane with hellishness unlimited.

Late in the afternoon rode Antonio, "broncho-buster" for the H2, a man of little courage, much avarice, and great capacity for hatred. Crafty, filled with

cunning of the coyote kind, shifty-eyed, gloomy, taciturn, and scowling, he
was well fitted for the part he had elected to play in the range dispute between
his ranch and the Bar-20. He was absolutely without mercy or conscience; indeed, one might aptly say that his conscience, if he had ever known one, had
been pulled out by the roots and its place filled with viciousness. Coldblooded
in his ferocity, easily angered and quick to commit murder if the risk were
small, he embraced within his husk of soul the putrescence of all that was evil.

In Eagle he had friends who were only a shade less evil than himself;
but they had what he lacked and because of it were entitled to a forced respect of small weight—they had courage, that spontaneous, initiative, heed-
less courage which toned the atmosphere of the whole West to a magnificent
crimson. Were it not for the reason that they had drifted to his social level they
would have spurned his acquaintance and shot him for a buzzard; but, while
they secretly held him in great contempt for his cowardice, they admired his
criminal cunning, and profited by it. He was too wise to show himself in the
true light to his foreman and the outfit, knowing full well that death would be
the response, and so lived a lie until he met his friends of the town, when he
threw off his cloak and became himself, and where he plotted against the man
who treated him fairly.

Riding into the town, he stopped before a saloon and slouched in to the
bar, where the proprietor was placing a new stock of liquors on the shelves.

"Where's Benito, an' th' rest?" he asked.

"Back there," replied the other, nodding toward a rear room.

"Who's in there?"

"Benito, Hall, Archer an' Frisco."

"Where's Shaw?"

"Him an' Clausen an' Cavalry went out 'bout ten minutes ago."

"I want to see 'em when they come in," Antonio remarked, headed towards
the door, where he listened, and then went in.

In the small room four men were grouped around a table, drinking and talking, and at his entry they looked up and nodded. He nodded in reply and seated
himself apart from them, where he soon became wrapped in thought.

Benito arose and went to the door. *"Mescal, pronto,"* he said to the man outside.

"Damned *pronto,* too," growled Antonio. "A man would die of alkali in this
place before he's waited on."

The proprietor brought a bottle and filled the glasses, giving Antonio his
drink first, and silently withdrew.

The broncho-buster tossed off the fiery stuff and then turned his shifty eyes on the group. "Where's Shaw?"

"Don't know—back soon," replied Benito.

"Why didn't he wait, when he knowed I was comin' in?"

Hall leaned back from the table and replied, keenly watching the inquisitor, "Because he don't give a damn."

"You—!" Antonio shouted, half rising, but the others interfered and he sank back again, content to let it pass. But not so Hall, whose Colt was half drawn.

"I'll kill you some day," he gritted, but before anything could come of it Shaw and his companions entered the room and the trouble was quelled.

Soon the group was deep in discussion over the merits of a scheme which Antonio unfolded to them, and the more it was weighed the better it appeared. Finally Shaw leaned back and filled his pipe. "You've got th' brains of th' devil,' 'Tony."

"Eet ees not'ing," replied Antonio.

"Oh, drop that lingo an' talk straight—you ain't on th' H2 now," growled Hall.

"Benito, you know this country like a book," Shaw continued. "Where's a good place for us to work from, or ain't there no choice?"

"Thunder Mesa."

"Well, what of it?"

"On the edge of the desert, high, big. The walls are stone, an' so very smooth. Nobody can get up."

"How can we get up then?"

"There's a trail at one end," replied Antonio, crossing his legs and preparing to roll a cigarette. "It's too steep for cayuses, an' too narrow; but we can crawl up. An' once up, all hell can't follow as long as our cartridges hold out."

"Water?" inquired Frisco.

"At th' bottom of th' trail, an' th' spring is on top," Antonio replied. "Not much, but enough."

"Can you work yore end all right?" asked Shaw.

"Yes," laughed the other. "I am 'that fool, Antonio,' on th' ranch. But they're th' fools. We can steal them blind an' if they find it out—well," here he shrugged his shoulders, "th' Bar-20 can take th' blame. I'll fix that, all right. This trouble about th' line is just what I've been waitin' for, an' I'll help it along. If we can get 'em fightin' we'll run off with th' bone *we* want. That'll be easy."

"But can you get 'em fightin'?" asked Cavalry, so called because he had spent several years in that branch of the Government service, and deserted because of the discipline.

Antonio laughed and ordered more *mescal* and for some time took no part in the discussion which went on about him. He was dreaming of success and plenty and a ranch of his own which he would start in Old Mexico, in a place far removed from the border, and where no questions would be asked. He would be a rich man, according to the standards of that locality, and what he said would be law among the peons. He liked to day-dream, for everything came out just as he wished; there was no discordant note. He was so certain of success, so conceited as not to ask himself if any of the Bar-20 or H2 outfits were not his equal or superior in intelligence. It was only a matter of time, he told himself, for he could easily get the two ranches embroiled in a range war, and once embroiled, his plan would succeed and he would be safe.

"What do you want for your share, 'Tony?" suddenly asked Shaw.

"Half."

"What! *Half?*"

"*Si.*"

"You're loco!" cried the other. "Do you reckon we're going to buck up agin th' biggest an' hardest fightin' outfit in this country an' take all sorts of chances for a measly half, to be divided up among seven of us!" He brought his fist down on the table with a resounding thump. "You an' yore game can go to hell first!" he shouted.

"I like a hog, all right," sneered Clausen, angrily.

"I thought it out an' I got to look after th' worst an' most important part of it, an' take three chances to you fellers' one," replied Antonio, frowning. "I said half, an' it goes."

"Run all th' ends, an' keep it all," exclaimed Hall. "An', by God, we've got a hand in it, now. If you try to hog it we'll drop a word where it'll do th' most good, an' don't you forget it, neither."

"Antonio is right," asserted Benito, excitedly. "It's risky for him."

"Keep yore yaller mouth shut," growled Cavalry. "Who gave you any say in this?"

"Half," said Antonio, shrugging his shoulders.

"Look here, you," cried Shaw, who was, in reality, the leader of the crowd, inasmuch as he controlled all the others with the exception of Benito and Antonio, and these at times by the judicious use of flattery. "We'll admit that you've got a right to th' biggest share, but not to no half. You have a chance to get away, because you can watch 'em, but how about us, out there on th' edge of hell? If they come for us we won't know nothing about it till we're surrounded. Now we want to play square with you, and we'll give you twice as much as any one of th' rest of us. That'll make nine shares an' give you two of 'em. What more do you want, when you've got to have us to run th' game at all?"

Antonio laughed ironically. "Yes. I'm where I can watch, an' get killed first. You can hold th' mesa for a month. I ain't as easy as I look. It's my game, not yourn; an' if you don't like what I ask, stay out."

"We will!" cried Hall, arising, followed by the others. His hand rested on the butt of his revolver and trouble seemed imminent. Benito wavered and then slid nearer to Antonio. "You can run yore game all by yore lonesome, as *long* as you *can*!" Hall shouted. "I know a feller what knows Cassidy, an' I'll spoil yore little play right now. You'll look nice at th' end of a rope, won't you? It's this: share like Shaw said or get out of here, and look out for trouble aplenty to-morrow morning. I've put up with yore gall an' swallered yore insultin' actions just as long as I'm going to, and I've got a powerful notion to fix you right here and now!"

"No fightin', you fools!" cried the proprietor, grabbing his Colt and running to the door of the room. "It's up to you fellers to stick together!"

"I'll be damned if I'll stand—" began Frisco.

"They want too much," interrupted Antonio, angrily, keeping close watch over Hall.

"We want a fair share, an' that's all!" retorted Shaw. "Sit down, all of you. We can wrastle this out without no gunplay."

"You-all been yappin' like a set of fools," said the proprietor. "I've heard every word you-all said. If you got a mite of sense you'll be some tender how you shout about it. It's shore risky enough without tellin' everybody this side of sun-up."

"I mean just what I said," asserted Hall. "It's Shaw's offer, or nothin'. We ain't playing fool."

"Here! Here!" cried Shaw, pushing Hall into a seat. "If you two have got anything to settle, wait till some other time."

"That's more like it," growled the proprietor, shuffling back to the bar.

"Good Lord, 'Tony," cried Shaw in a low voice. "That's fair enough; we've got a right to something, ain't we? Don't let a good thing fall through just because you want th' whole earth. Better have a little than none."

"Well, gimme a third, then."

"I'll give you a slug in th' eye, you hog!" promised Hall, starting to rise again, but Shaw held him back. "Sit down, you fool!" he ordered, angrily. Then he turned to Antonio. "Third don't go; take my offer or leave it."

"Gimme a fourth; that's fair enough."

Shaw thought for a moment and then looked up. "Well, that's more like it. What do you say, fellers?"

"No!" cried Hall. "Two-ninths, or nothin'!"

"A fourth is two-eighths, only a little more," Shaw replied.

"Well, all right," muttered Hall, sullenly.

"That's very good," laughed Benito, glad that things were clearing.

The others gave their consent to the division and Shaw smiled. "Well, that's more like it. Now we'll go into this thing an' sift it out. Keep mum about it— there's twenty men in town that would want to join us if they knowed."

"I'm goin' to be boss; what I say goes," spoke up Antonio. "It's my game an' I'm takin' th' most risky end."

"You ain't got sand enough to be boss of anything," sneered Hall. "Yore sand is chalk."

"You'll say too much someday," retorted Antonio, glaring.

"Oh, not to *you*, I reckon," rejoined Hall, easily.

"Shut up, both of you!" snapped Shaw. "You can be boss, 'Tony," he said, winking at Hall. "You've got more brains for a thing like this than any of us. I don't see how you can figger it out like you do."

Antonio laughed but he remembered one thing, and swore to take payment if the plan leaked out; the proprietor had confessed hearing every word, which was not at all to his liking. If Quinn should tell, well, Quinn would die; he would see to that, he and Benito.

CHAPTER 2

Mary Meeker Rides North

Mary Meeker, daughter of the H2 owner and foreman, found pleasure in riding on little tours of investigation. She had given the southern portions her attention first and found, after the newness had worn off, that she did not care for the level, sandy stretches of half-desert land which lay so flat for miles. The prospect was always the same, always uninteresting and wearying and hot. Now she determined upon a step which she had wished to take for a long time, and her father's request that she should not take it grew less and less of a deterrent factor. He had given so much thought and worry to that mysterious valley, that she at last gave rein to her curiosity and made ready to see for herself. It was green and hilly, like the rugged Montana she had quitted to come down to the desert. There were hills of respectable size, for these she saw daily from the ranch house door, and she loved hills; anything would be better than the limitless sand.

She had known little of restraint; her corner of the world had been filled entirely by men and she had absorbed much of their better traits. Self-reliant as a cowgirl should be, expert with either Colt or Winchester, and at home in the saddle, she feared nothing the desert might hold, except thirst. She was not only expert with weapons, but she did not fear to use them against men, as she had proved on one occasion in wild Montana. So she would ride to the hills which called her so insistently and examine the valley.

One bright morning just before the roundup began she went to the corral and looked at her horse, a cross between Kentucky stock and cow-pony and having in a great degree the speed of the first and the hardiness of the last, and sighed to think that she could not ride it for days to come. Teuton was crippled and she must choose some other animal. She had overheard Doc Riley tell Ed Joyce that the piebald in the smaller corral was well broken, and this was the horse she would take. The truth of the matter was that the piebald was crafty and permitted the saddle to be fixed and himself ridden for varying periods of time before showing what he thought of such things. Doc, unprepared for the piebald's sudden change in demeanor, had taken a tumble, which made him anxious to have his wounded conceit soothed by seeing Ed Joyce receive the same treatment.

Mary found no trouble in mounting and riding the animal and she was glad that she had overheard Doc, for now she had two horses which were thoroughly reliable, although, of course, Teuton was the only really good horse on the range. She rode out of the corral and headed for the White Horse Hills, scarcely twelve miles away. What if her father had warned her not to ride near the lawless punchers who rode the northern range? They were only men and she was sure that to a woman they would prove to be gentlemen.

The southern boundary of the Bar-20 ran along the top of the hills and from them east to the river, and it was being patrolled by three Bar-20 punchers, Hopalong, Johnny, and Red, all on the lookout for straying cattle of both ranches. Neither Hopalong nor Red had ever seen Mary Meeker, but Johnny had upon the occasion of his scout over the H2 range, and he had felt eminently qualified to describe her. He had finished his eulogistic monologue by asserting that as soon as his more unfortunate friends saw her they would lose sleep and sigh often, which prophecy was received in various ways and called forth widely differing comment. Red had snorted outright and Pete swore to learn that a woman was on the range; for Pete had been married, and his wife preferred another man. Hopalong, remembering a former experience of his own, smiled in knowing cynicism when told that he again would fall under the feminine spell.

Red was near the river and Johnny half-way to the hills when Hopalong began the ascent of Long Hill, wondering why it was that Meeker had made no attempt to cross the boundary in force and bring on a crisis; and from Meeker his mind turned to the daughter.

"So there's a woman down here now," he muttered, riding down into an arroyo and up the other bank. "This country is gettin' as bad as Kansas, damned if it ain't. First thing we know it'll be nursin' bottles an' school houses, an' hell loose all th' time instead of once in a while."

He heard hoofbeats and glanced up quickly, alert and ready for trouble, for who would be riding where he was but some H2 puncher?

"What th'—!" he exclaimed under his breath, for riding towards him at an angle was Mary Meeker; and Johnny was wrong in his description of her, but, he thought, the Kid had done as well as his limited vocabulary would allow. She *was* pretty, pretty as—she was more than pretty!

She had seen him at the same time and flashed a quick glance which embraced everything; and she was surprised, for he was not only passably good-looking, barring the red hair, but very different from the men her father had told her made up the outfit of the Bar-20. He removed his sombrero instantly and drew up to let her pass, a smile on his face. Yes, he thought, Johnny had wronged her, for no other woman could have such jet-black hair crowning such a face.

"By God!" he whispered, and went no farther, for that was the summing up of his whole opinion of her.

"He *is* a gentleman," she thought triumphantly, for he had proved that she was right in her surmise regarding the men of the northern ranch. She spurred to pass him and then her piebald took part in the proceedings. The prick of the spur awakened in him a sudden desire to assert his rights, and he promptly pitched to make up for his hitherto gentle behavior. So taken up with what the last minute had brought forth she was unprepared for the vicious bucking and when she opened her eyes her head was propped against Hopalong's knee and her face dripping with the contents of his canteen. "Damn yore ugly skin!" he was saying to the piebald, which stood quietly a short distance away, evidently enjoying the result of his activity. "Just you wait! I'll show you what's due to come yore way purty soon!" He turned again to the woman and saw that her eyes were closed as before. "By God, yore—yore beautiful!"

She moved slightly and color came into her cheeks with a sudden rush and he watched her anxiously. Soon she moved again and then, opening her eyes, struggled to gain her feet. He helped her up and held her until she drew away from him.

"What was it?" she asked.

"That ugly cayuse went an' pitched when you wasn't lookin' for it," he told her. "Are you hurt much?"

"No, just dizzy. I don't want to make you trouble," she replied.

"You ain't makin' me any trouble, not a bit," he assured her earnestly. "But I'd like to make some trouble for that ornery cayuse of yourn. Let me tone him down some."

"No; it was my fault. I should'a been lookin—I never rode him before."

"Well, you've got to take my cayuse to get home on," he said. "He's bad, but he's a regular angel when stacked up agin that bronc. I'll ride the festive piebald, an' we can trade when you get home." Under his breath he said: "Oh, just wait till I get on you, pinto! I'll give you what you need, all right!"

"Thank you, but I can ride him now that I know just what he is," she said, her eyes flashing with determination. "I've never let a bronc get th' best of me in th' long run, an' I ain't goin' to begin now. I came up here to look at th' hills an' th' valley, an' I'm not going back home till I've done it."

"That's the way to talk!" he cried in admiration. "I'll get him for you," he finished, swinging into his saddle. He loosened the lariat at the saddle horn while he rode towards the animal, which showed sudden renewed interest in the proceedings, but it tarried too long. Just as it wheeled and leaped forward the rope settled and the next thing it knew was that the sky had somehow slid under its stomach, for it had been thrown over backward and flat on its back. When it had struggled to its feet it found Hopalong astride it, spurring vigorously on the side farthest from Mary, and for five minutes the air was greatly disturbed. At the end of that time he dismounted and led a penitent pony to its mistress, who vaulted lightly into the saddle and waited for her companion to mount. When he had joined her they rode up the hill together side by side.

Johnny wished to smoke and felt for his tobacco pouch, which he found to be empty. He rode on for a short distance, angry with himself for his neglect, and then remembered that Hopalong had a plentiful supply. He could overtake the man on the hill much quicker than he could Red, who had said that he was going to ride south along the river to see if Jumping Bear Creek was dry. If it were, Meeker could be expected to become active in his aggression. Johnny wheeled and cantered back along the boundary trail, alertly watching for trespassing cattle.

It was not long before he came within sight of the thicket which stood a little east of the base of Long Hill, and he nearly fell from the saddle in astonishment, for his friend was on the ground, holding a woman's head on his knee! Johnny didn't care to intrude, and cautiously withdrew to the shelter of the small chaparral, where he waited impatiently. Wishing to stretch his legs, he dismounted and picketed his horse and walked around the thicket until satisfied that he was out of sight of his friend.

Suddenly he fancied that he heard something suspicious and he crept back around the thicket, keeping close to its base. When he turned the corner he saw the head of a man on the other side of the chaparral which lay a little southwest of his position. It was Antonio, and he was intently watching the two on the slope of the hill, and entirely unaware that he was being watched in turn.

Johnny carefully drew his Colt and covered Antonio who he hated instinctively. He had seen the shifty-eyed broncho-buster on more than one occasion and never without struggling with himself to keep from shooting. Now his finger pressed gently against the trigger of the weapon and he wished for a passable excuse to send the other into eternity; but Antonio gave him no cause, only watching eagerly and intently, his face set in such an expression of malignancy as to cause Johnny's finger to tremble.

Johnny arose slightly until he could see Hopalong and his companion and he smothered an exclamation. "Gosh A'mighty!" he whispered, again watching Antonio. "That's Meeker's gal or I'm a liar! Th' son-of-a-gun, keeping quiet about it all this time. An' no wonder Antonio's on th' trail!"

It was not long before Johnny looked again for Hopalong and saw him riding up the hill with his companion. Then he crept forward, watching Antonio closely, his Colt ready for instant use. Antonio slowly drew down until he was lost to sight of the Bar-20 puncher, who ran slightly forward and gained the side of the other thicket, where he again crept forward, and around the chaparral. When he next caught sight of the broncho-buster the latter was walking towards his horse and his back was turned to Johnny.

"Hey, you!" called the Bar-20 puncher, arising and starting after the other.

Antonio wheeled, leaped to one side and half drew his revolver, but he was covered and he let the weapon slide back into the holster.

"What are you doing?"

Antonio's reply was a scowl and his inquisitor continued without waiting for words from the other.

"Never mind that, I saw what you was doing," Johnny said. "An' I shore knew what you wanted to do, because I came near doing it to you. Now it ain't a whole lot healthy for you to go snooping around this line like you was, for I'll plug you on suspicion next time. Get on that cayuse of yourn an' hit th' trail south—go on, make tracks!"

Antonio mounted and slowly wheeled. "You hab drop, now," he said significantly. "Nex' time, *quien sabe?*"

Johnny dropped his Colt into the holster and removed his hand from the butt. "You're a liar!" he shouted, savagely. "I ain't got th' drop. It's an even break, an' what are you going to do about it?"

Antonio shrugged his shoulders and rode on without replying, quite content to let things stand as they were. He had learned something which he might be able to use to advantage later on and he had strained the situation just a little more.

"Huh! Next time!" snorted Johnny in contempt as he turned to go back to his horse. "It'll allus be 'next' time' with him, 'less he gets a good pot shot at me, which he won't. He ain't got sand enough to put up a square fight. Now for Red; he'll shore be riding this way purty soon, an' that'll never do. Hoppy won't want anybody foolin' around th' hills for a while, lucky devil."

More than an hour had passed before he met Red and he forthwith told him that he had caught Antonio scouting on foot along the line.

"I ain't none surprised, Kid," Red replied, frowning. "You've seen how th' H2 cows are being driven north agin us an' that means we'll be tolerable busy purty soon. Th' Jumping Bear is dry as tinder, an' it won't be long before Meeker'll be driving to get in th' valley."

"Well, I'm some glad of that," Johnny replied, frankly. "It's been peaceful too blamed long down here. Come on, we'll ride east an' see if we can find any cows to turn. Hey! Look there!" he cried, spurring forward.

CHAPTER 3

The Roundup

The Texan sky seemed a huge mirror upon which were reflected the white fleecy clouds sailing northward; the warm spring air was full of that magnetism which calls forth from their earthy beds the gramma grass and the flowers; the scant vegetation had taken on new dress and traces of green now showed against the more sombre-colored stems; while in the distance, rippling in glistening patches where, disturbed by the wind, the river sparkled like a tinsel ribbon flung carelessly on the grays and greens of the plain. Birds winged their joyous way and filled the air with song; and far overhead a battalion of tardy geese flew, arrowlike, towards the cool lakes of the north, their faint honking pathetic and continuous. Skulking in the coulees or speeding across the skyline of some distant rise occasionally could be seen a coyote or gray wolf. The cattle, less gregarious than they had been in the colder months, made tentative sorties from the lessening herd, and began to stray off in search of the tender green grass which pushed up recklessly from the closely cropped, withered tufts. Rattlesnakes slid out and uncoiled their sinuous lengths in the warm sunlight, and copperheads raised their burnished armor from their winter retreats. All nature had felt the magic touch of the warm winds, and life in its multitudinous forms was discernible on all sides. The gaunt tragedy of a hard winter for that southern range had added its chilling share to the horrors of the past and now the cattle took heart and lost their weakness in the sunlight, hungry but contented.

The winter had indeed been hard, one to be remembered for years to come, and many cattle had died because of it; many skeletons, stripped clean by coyotes and wolves, dotted the arroyos and coulees. The cold weather had broken suddenly, and several days of rain, followed by sleet, had drenched the cattle thoroughly. Then from out of the north came one of those unusual rages of nature, locally known as a "Norther," freezing pitilessly; and the cattle, weakened by cold and starvation, had dumbly succumbed to this last blow. Their backs were covered with an icy shroud, and the deadly cold gripped their vitals with a power not to be resisted. A glittering sheet formed over the grasses as far as eye could see, and the cattle, unlike the horses, not knowing enough to stamp through it, nosed in vain at the sustenance beneath, until weakness compelled them to lie down in the driving snow, and once down, they never arose. The storm had raged for the greater part of a week, and then suddenly one morning the sun shown down on a velvety plain, blinding in its whiteness; and when spring had sent the snow mantle roaring through the arroyos and water courses in a turmoil of yellow water and driftwood, and when the range riders rode forth to read the losses on the plain, the remaining cattle were staggering weakly in search of food. Skeletons in the coulees told the story of the hopeless fight, how the unfortunate cattle had drifted before the wind to what shelter they could find and how, huddled together for warmth, they had died one by one. The valley along Conroy Creek had provided a rough shelter with its scattered groves and these had stopped the cattle drift, so much dreaded by cowmen.

It had grieved Buck Peters and his men to the heart to see so many cattle swept away in one storm, but they had done all that courage and brains could do to save them. So now, when the plain was green again and the warm air made riding a joy, they were to hold the calf roundup. When Buck left his blanket after the first night spent in the roundup camp and rode off to the horse herd, he smiled from suppressed elation, and was glad that he was alive.

Peaceful as the scene appeared there was trouble brewing, and it was in expectation of this that Buck had begun the roundup earlier than usual. The unreasoning stubbornness of one man, and the cunning machinations of a natural rogue, threatened to bring about, from what should have been only a misunderstanding, as pretty a range war as the Southwest had seen. Those immediately involved were only a few when compared to the number which might eventually be brought into the strife, but if this had been pointed out to Jim Meeker he would have replied that he "didn't give a damn."

Jim Meeker was a Montana man who thought to carry out on the H2 range, of which he was foreman, the same system of things which had served where he had come from. This meant trouble right away, for the Bar-20, already short in range, would not stand idly by and see him encroach upon their land for grass and water, more especially when he broke a solemn compact as to range rights which had been made by the former owners of the H2 with the Bar-20. It meant not only the forcible use of Bar-20 range, but also a great hardship upon the herds for which Buck Peters was responsible.

Meeker's obstinacy was covertly prodded by Antonio for his own personal gains, but this the Bar-20 foreman did not know; if he had known it there might have been much trouble averted.

Buck Peters was probably the only man of all of them who realized just what such a war would mean, to what an extent rustling would flourish while the cowmen fought. His best efforts had been used to avert trouble, so far successfully; but that he would continue to do so was doubtful. He had an outfit which, while meaning to obey him in all things and to turn from any overt act of war, was not of the kind to stand much forcing or personal abuse; their nervous systems were constructed on the hair-trigger plan, and their very loyalty might set the range ablaze with war. However, on this most perfect of mornings Meeker's persistent aggression did not bother him, he was free from worry for the time.

Just north of Big Coulee, in which was a goodly sized water hole, a group of blanket-swathed figures lay about a fire near the chuck wagon, while the sleepy cook prepared breakfast for his own outfit, and for the eight men which the foreman of the C80 and the Double Arrow had insisted upon Buck taking. The sun had not yet risen, but the morning glow showed gray over the plain, and it would not be long before the increasing daylight broke suddenly. The cook fires crackled and blazed steadily, the iron pots hissing under their dancing and noisy lids, while the coffee pots bubbled and sent up an aromatic steam, and the odor of freshly baked biscuits swept forth as the cook uncovered a pan. A pile of tin plates was stacked on the tail-board of the wagon while a large sheet-iron pail contained tin cups. The figures, feet to the fire, looked like huge, grotesque cocoons, for the men had rolled themselves in their blankets, their heads resting on their saddles, and in many cases folded sombreros next to the leather made softer pillows.

Back of the chuck wagon the eastern sky grew rapidly brighter, and suddenly daylight in all its power dissipated the grayish light of the moment before. As the rim of the golden sun arose above the low sand hills to the east the foreman rode into camp. Some distance behind him Harry Jones and two other C80 men drove up the horse herd and enclosed it in a flimsy corral quickly extemporized from lariats; flimsy it was, but it sufficed for cow-ponies that had learned the lesson of the rope.

"All ready, Buck," called Harry before his words were literally true.

With assumed ferocity but real vociferation Buck uttered a shout and watched the effect. The cocoons became animated, stirred and rapidly unrolled, with the exception of one, and the sleepers leaped to their feet and folded the blankets. The exception stirred, subsided, stirred again and then was quiet. Buck and Red stepped forward while the others looked on grinning to see the fun, grasped the free end of the blanket and suddenly straightened up, their hands going high above their heads. Johnny Nelson, squawking, rolled over and over and, with a yell of surprise, sat bolt upright and felt for his gun.

"Huh!" he snorted. "Reckon yo're smart, don't you!"

"Purty near a shore 'nuf pin-wheel, Kid," laughed Red.

"Don't you care, Johnny; you can finish it tonight," consoled Frenchy McAllister, now one of Buck's outfit.

"Breakfast, Kid, breakfast!" sang out Hopalong as he finished drying his face.

The breakfast was speedily out of the way, and pipes were started for a short smoke as the punchers walked over to the horse herd to make their selections. By exercising patience, profanity, and perseverance they roped their horses and began to saddle up. Ed Porter, of the C80, and Skinny Thompson, Bar-20, cast their ropes with a sweeping, preliminary whirl over their heads, but the others used only a quick flit and twist of the wrist. A few mildly exciting struggles for the mastery took place between riders and mounts, for some cow-ponies are not always ready to accept their proper places in the scheme of things.

"Slab-sided jumpin' jack!" yelled Rich Finn, a Double Arrow puncher, as he fought his horse. "Allus raisin' th' devil afore I'm all awake!"

"Lemme hold her head, Rich," jeered Billy Williams.

"Her laigs, Billy, not her head," corrected Lanky Smith, the Bar-20 rope expert, whose own horse had just become sensible.

"Don't hurt him, bronc; we need him," cautioned Red.

"Come on, fellers; gettin' late," called Buck.

Away they went, tearing across the plain, Buck in the lead. After some time had passed the foreman raised his arm and Pete Wilson stopped and filled his pipe anew, the west-end man of the cordon. Again Buck's arm went up and Skinny Thompson dropped out, and so on until the last man had been placed and the line completed. At a signal from Buck the whole line rode forward, gradually converging on a central point and driving the scattered cattle before it.

Hopalong, on the east end of the line, sharing with Billy the posts of honor, was now kept busy dashing here and there, wheeling, stopping, and maneuvering as certain strong-minded cattle, preferring the freedom of the range they had just quitted, tried to break through the cordon. All but branded steers and cows without calves had their labors in vain, although the escape of these often set examples for ambitious cows with calves. Here was where reckless and expert riding saved the day, for the cow-ponies, trained in the art of punching cows, entered into the game with zest and executed quick turns which more than once threatened a catastrophe to themselves and riders. Range cattle can run away from their domesticated kin, covering the ground with an awkward gait that is deceiving; but the ponies can run faster and turn as quickly.

Hopalong, determined to turn back one stubborn mother cow, pushed too hard, and she wheeled to attack him. Again the nimble pony had reasons to move quickly and Hopalong swore as he felt the horns touch his leg.

"On th' prod, hey! Well, stay on it!" he shouted, well knowing that she would. "Pig-headed old fool—*all right*, Johnny; I'm comin'!" and he raced away to turn a handful of cows which were proving too much for his friend. *"Ki-yi-yeow-eow-eow-eow-eow!"* he yelled, imitating the coyote howl.

The cook had moved his wagon as soon as breakfast was over and journeyed southeast with the cavvieyh; and as the cordon neared its objectives the punchers could see his camp about half a mile from the level pasture where the herd would be held for the cutting-out and branding. Cookie regarded himself as the most important unit of the roundup and acted accordingly, and he was not far wrong.

"Hey, Hoppy!" called Johnny through the dust of the herd, "there's Cookie. I was 'most scared he'd get lost."

"Can't you think of anythin' else but grub?" asked Billy Jordan from the rear.

"Can you tell me anything better to think of?"

There were from three to four hundred cattle in the herd when it neared the stopping point, and dust arose in low-hanging clouds above it. Its pattern of differing shades of brown, with yellow and black and white relieving it, constantly shifted like a kaleidoscope as the cattle changed positions; and the rattle of horns on horns and the muffled bellowing could be heard for some distance.

Gradually the cordon surrounded the herd and, when the destination was reached, the punchers rode before the front ranks of cattle and stopped them. There was a sudden tremor, a compactness in the herd, and the cattle in the rear crowded forward against those before; another tremor, and the herd was quiet. Cowpunchers took their places around it, and kept the cattle from breaking out and back to the range, while every second man, told off by the foreman, raced at top speed towards the camp, there to eat a hasty dinner and get a fresh horse from his *remuda*, as his string of from five to seven horses was called. Then he galloped back to the herd and relieved his nearest neighbor. When all had reassembled at the herd the work of cutting-out began.

Lanky Smith, Panhandle Lukins, and two more Bar-20 men rode some distance east of the herd, there to take care of the cow-and-calf cut as it grew by the cutting-out. Hopalong, Red, Johnny, and three others were assigned to the task of getting the mother cows and their calves out of the main herd and into the new one, while the other punchers held the herd and took care of the stray herd when they should be needed. Each of the cutters-out rode after some calf, and the victim, led by its mother, worked its way after her into the very heart of the mass; and in getting the pair out again care must be taken not to unduly excite the other cattle. Wiry, happy, and conceited cow-ponies unerringly and patiently followed mother and calf into the press, nipping the pursued when too slow and gradually forcing them to the outer edge of the herd; and when the mother tried to lead its offspring back into the herd to repeat the performance, she was in almost every case cleverly blocked and driven out on the plain where the other punchers took charge of her and added her to the cow-and-calf cut.

Johnny jammed his sombrero on his head with reckless strength and swore luridly as he wheeled to go back into the herd.

"What's th' matter, Kid?" laughingly asked Skinny as he turned his charges over to another man.

"None of yore damned business!" blazed Johnny. Under his breath he made a resolve. "If I get you two out here again I'll keep you here if I have to shoot you!"

"Are they slippery, Johnny?" jibed Red, whose guess was correct. Johnny refused to heed such asinine remarks and stood on his dignity.

As the cow-and-calf herd grew in size and the main herd dwindled, more punchers were shifted to hold it; and it was not long before the main herd was comprised entirely of cattle without calves, when it was driven off to freedom after being examined for other brands. As soon as the second herd became of any size it was not necessary to drive the cows and the calves to it when they were driven out of the first herd, as they made straight for it. The main herd, driven away, broke up as it would, while the guarded cows stood idly beside their resting offspring awaiting further indignities.

The drive had covered so much ground and taken so much time that approaching darkness warned Buck not to attempt the branding until the morrow, and he divided his force into three shifts. Two of these hastened to the camp, gulped down their supper, and rolling into their blankets, were soon sound asleep. The horse herd was driven off to where the grazing was better, and night soon fell over the plain.

The cook's fires gleamed through the darkness and piles of biscuits were heaped on the tail-board of the wagon, while pots of beef and coffee simmered over the fires, handy for the guards as they rode in during the night to awaken brother punchers, who would take their places while they slept. Soon the cocoons were quiet in the grotesque shadows caused by the fires and a deep silence reigned over the camp. Occasionally some puncher would awaken long enough to look at the sky to see if the weather had changed, and satisfied, return to sleep.

Over the plain sleepy cowboys rode slowly around the herd, glad to be relieved by some other member of the outfit, who always sang as he approached the cattle to reassure them and save a possible stampede. For cattle, if suddenly disturbed at night by anything, even the waving of a slicker in the hands of some careless rider, or a wind-blown paper, will rise in a body—all up at once, frightened and nervous. The sky was clear and the stars bright and when the moon rose it flooded the plain with a silvery light and made fairy patterns in the shadows.

Snatches of song floated down the gentle wind as the riders slowly circled the herd, for the human voice, no matter how discordant, was quieting. A low and plaintive "Don't let this par-ting grieve y-o-u" passed from hearing around the resting cows, soon to be followed by "When-n in thy dream-ing, nights like t-h-e-s-e shall come a-gain—" as another watcher made the circuit. The serene cows, trusting in the prowess and vigilance of these low-voiced centaurs to protect them from danger, dozed and chewed their cuds in peace and quiet, while the natural noises of the night relieved the silence in unobtruding harmony.

Far out on the plain a solitary rider watched the herd from cover and swore because it was guarded so closely. He glanced aloft to see if there was any hope of a storm and finding that there was not, muttered savagely and rode away. It was Antonio, wishing that he could start a stampede and so undo the work of the day and inflict heavy losses on the Bar-20. He did not dare to start a grass fire for at the first flicker of a light he would be charged by one or more of the night riders and if caught, death would be his reward.

While the third shift rode and sang the eastern sky became a dome of light reflected from below and the sunrise, majestic in all its fiery splendor, heralded the birth of another perfect day.

Through the early morning hours the branding continued, and the bleating of cattle told of the hot stamping irons indelibly burning the sign of the Bar-20 on the tender hides of calves. Mother cows fought and plunged and called in reply to the terrified bawling of their offspring, and sympathetically licked the burns when the frightened calves had been allowed to join them. Cowboys were deftly roping calves by their hind legs and dragging them to the fires of the branding men. Two men would hold a calf, one doubling the foreleg back on itself at the knee and the other, planting one booted foot against the calf's under hind leg close to its body, pulled back on the other leg while his companion, who held the foreleg, rested on the animal's head. The third man, drawing the hot iron from the fire, raised and held it suspended for a second over the calf's flank, and then there was an odor and a puff of smoke; and the calf was branded with a mark which neither water nor age would wipe out.

Pete Wilson came riding up dragging a calf at the end of his rope, and turned the captive over to Billy Williams and his two helpers, none of them paying any attention to the cow which followed a short distance behind him. Lanky seized the unfortunate calf and leaned over to secure the belly hold, when someone shouted a warning and he dropped the struggling animal and leaped back and to one side as the mother charged past. Wheeling to return the attack, the cow suddenly flopped over and struck the earth with a thud as Buck's rope went home. He dragged her away and then releasing her, chased her back into the herd.

"*Hi!* Get that little devil!" shouted Billy to Hopalong, pointing to the fleeing calf.

"Why didn't you watch for her," demanded the indignant Lanky of Pete. "Do you think this is a ten-pin alley!"

Hopalong came riding up with the calf, which swiftly became recorded property.

"Bar-20; tally one," sang out the monotonous voice of the tally man. "Why didn't you grab her when she went by, Lanky?" he asked, putting a new point on his pencil.

"Hope th' next one leads yore way!" retorted Lanky, grinning.

"Won't. I ain't abusin' th' kids."

"Bar-20; tally one," droned a voice at the next fire.

All was noise, laughter, dust, and a seeming confusion, but every man knew his work thoroughly and was doing it in a methodical way, and the confusion was confined to the victims and their mothers.

When the herd had been branded and allowed to return to the plain, the outfit moved on into a new territory and the work was repeated until the whole
range, with the exception of the valley, had been covered. When the valley was
worked it required more time in comparison with the amount of ground covered than had been heretofore spent on any part of the range; for the cattle
were far more numerous, and it was no unusual thing to have a herd of great
size before the roundup place had been reached. This heavy increase in the
numbers of the cattle to be herded made a corresponding increase in the time
and labor required for the cutting-out and branding. Five days were required
in working the eastern and central parts of the valley and it took three more
days to clean up around the White Horse Hills, where the ground was rougher
and the riding harder. And at every cutting-out there was a large stray-herd
made up of H2 and Three Triangle cattle. The H2 had been formerly the
Three Triangle. Buck had been earnest in his instructions regarding the strays,
for now was the opportunity to rid his range of Meeker's cattle without especial significance; once over the line it would be a comparatively easy matter to
keep them there.

For taking care of this extra herd and also because Buck courted scrutiny
during the branding, the foreman accepted the services of three H2 men. This
addition to his forces made the work move somewhat more rapidly and when,
at the end of each day's cutting-out, the stray herd was complete, it was driven
south across the boundary line by Meeker's men. When the last stray-herd
started south Buck rode over to the H2 punchers and told them to tell their
foreman to let him know when he could assist in the southern roundup and
thus return the favor.

As the Bar-20 outfit and the C80 and Double Arrow men rode north towards
the ranch house they were met by Lucas, foreman of the C80, who joined them
near Medicine Bend.

"Well, got it all over, hey?" he cried as he rode up.

"Yep; bigger job than I thought, too. It gets bigger every year an' that blizzard
didn't make much difference in th' work, neither," Buck replied. "I'll help you
out when you get ready to drive."

"No you won't; you can help me an' Bartlett more by keeping all yore men
watchin' that line," quickly responded Lucas. "We'll work together, me an'
Bartlett, an' we'll have all th' men we want. You just show that man Meeker that
range grabbin' ain't healthy down here—that's all we want. Did he send you any
help in th' valley?"

"Yes, three men," Buck replied. "But we'll break even on that when he works along the boundary."

"Have any trouble with 'em?"

"Not a bit."

"I sent Wood Wright down to Eagle th' other day, an' he says the town is shore there'll be a big range war," remarked Lucas. "He said there's lots of excitement down there an' they act like they wish th' trouble would hurry up an' happen. We've got to watch that town, all right."

"If there's a war th' rustlers'll flock from all over," interposed Rich Finn.

"Huh!" snorted Hopalong. "They'll flock out again if we get a chance to look for 'em. An' that town'll shore get into trouble if it don't live plumb easy. You know what happened th' last time rustlin' got to be th' style, don't you?"

"Well," replied Lucas, "I've fixed it with Cowan to get news to me an' Bartlett if anything sudden comes up. If you need us just let him know an' we'll be with you in two shakes."

"That's good, but I don't reckon I'll need any help, leastwise not for a long time," Buck responded. "But I tell you what you might do, when you can; make up a vigilance committee from yore outfits an' ride range for rustlers. We can take care of all that comes on us, but we won't have no time to bother about th' rest of th' range. An' if you do that it'll shut 'em out of our north range."

"We'll do it," Lucas promised. "Bartlett is going to watch th' trails north to see if he can catch anybody runnin' cattle to th' railroad construction camps. Every suspicious looking stranger is going to be held up an' asked questions; an' if we find any runnin' irons, you know what that means."

"I reckon we can handle th' situation, all right, no matter how hard it gets," laughed the Bar-20 foreman.

"Well, I'll be leavin' you now," Lucas remarked as they reached the Bar-20 bunk house. "We begin to round up next week, an' there's lots to be done by then. Say, can I use yore chuck wagon? Mine is shore done for."

"Why, of course," replied Buck heartily. "Take it now, if you want, or any time you send for it."

"Much obliged; come on, fellers," Lucas cried to his men. "We're going home."

CHAPTER 4

In West Arroyo

opalong was heading for Lookout Peak, the highest of the White Horse Hills, by way of West Arroyo, which he entered half an hour after he had forded the creek, and was half way to the line when, rounding a sharp turn, he saw Mary Meeker ahead of him. She was off her horse picking flowers when she heard him and she stood erect, smiling.

"Why, I didn't think I'd see you," she said. "I've been picking flowers—see them? Ain't they pretty?" she asked, holding them out for his inspection.

"They shore are," he replied, not looking at the flowers at all, but into her big, brown eyes. "An' they're some lucky, too," he asserted grinning.

She lowered her head, burying her face in the blossoms and then picked a few petals and let them fall one by one from her fingers. "You didn't look at them at all," she chided.

"Oh, yes, I did," he laughed. "But I see flowers all th' time, and not much of you."

"That's nice—they are so pretty. I just love them."

"Yes. I reckon they are," doubtfully.

She looked up at him, her eyes laughing and her white teeth glistening between their red frames. "Why don't you scold me?" she asked.

"Scold you! What for?"

"Why, for being on yore ranch, for being across th' line an' in th' valley."

"Good Lord! Why, there ain't no lines for you! You can go anywhere."

"In th' valley?" she asked, again hiding her face in the flowers.

"Why, of course. What ever made you think you can't?"

"I'm one of th' H2," she responded. "Paw says I run it. But I'm awful glad you won't care."

"Well, as far as riding where you please is concerned, you run this ranch, too."

"There's a pretty flower," she said, looking at the top of the bank. "That purple one; see it?" she asked, pointing.

"Yes. I'll get it for you," he replied, leaping from the saddle and half way up the bank before she knew it. He slid down again and handed the blossom to her. "There."

"Thank you."

"See any more you wants?"

"No; this is enough. Thank you for getting it for me."

"Oh, that was nothing," he laughed, awkwardly. "That was shore easy."

"I'm gong to give it to you for not scolding me about being over th' line," she said, holding it out to him.

"No; not for that," he said slowly. "Can't you think of some other reason?"

"Don't you want it?"

"Want it!" he exclaimed, eagerly. "Shore I want it. But not for what you said."

"Will you wear it because we're friends?"

"Now yo're talking!"

She looked up and laughed, her cheeks dimpling, and then pinned it to his shirt. It was nice to have a flower pinned on one's shirt by a pretty girl.

"There," she laughed, stepping back to look at it.

"You've pinned it up so high I can't see it. Why not put it lower down?"

She changed it while he grinned at how his scheming had born fruit. He was a hog, he knew that, but he did not care.

"Oh, I reckon *I'm* all right!" he exulted. "Shore you don't see no more you want?"

"Yes; an' I must go now," she replied, going towards her horse. "I'll be late with th' dinner if I don't hurry."

"What! Do you cook for that hungry outfit?"

"No, not for them—just for Paw an' me."

"When are you comin' up again for more flowers?"

"I don't know. You see, I'm going to make cookies some day this week, but I don't know just when. Do you like cookies, an' cake?"

"You bet I do! Why?"

"I'll bring some with me th' next time. Paw says they're th' best he ever ate."

"Bet I'll say so, too," he replied, stepping forward to help her into the saddle, but she sprang into it before he reached her side, and he vaulted on his own horse and joined her.

She suddenly turned and looked him straight in the eyes. "Tell me, honest, has yore ranch any right to keep our cows south of that line?"

"Yes, we have. Our boundaries are fixed. We gave th' Three Triangle about eighty square miles of range so our valley would be free from all cows but our own. That's all th' land between th' line an' th' Jumping Bear, an' it was a big price, too. They never drove a cow over on us."

She looked disappointed and toyed with her quirt.

"Why don't you want to let Paw use th' valley?"

"It ain't big enough for our own cows, an' we can't share it. As it is, we'll have to drive ten thousand on leased range next year to give our grass a rest."

"Well—" she stopped and he waited to hear what she would say, and then asked her when she would be up again.

"I don't know! I don't know!" she cried.

"Why, what's the matter?"

"Nothing. I'm foolish—that's all," she replied, smiling, and trying to forget the picture which arose in her mind, a picture of desperate fighting along the line; of her father—and him.

"You scared me then," he said.

"Did I? Why, it wasn't anything."

"Are you shore?"

"Please don't ask me any questions," she requested.

"Will you be up here again soon?"

"If th' baking turns out all right."

"Hang the baking! Come anyway."

"I'll try; but I'm afraid," she faltered.

"Of what?" he demanded, sitting up very straight.

"Why, that I can't," she replied, hurriedly. "You see, it's far coming up here."

"That's easy. I'll meet you west of the hills."

"No, no! I'll come up here."

"Look here," he said, slowly and kindly. "If yo're afraid of bein' seen with me, don't you try it. I want to see you a whole lot, but I don't want you to have no trouble with yore father about it. I can wait till everything is all right if you want me to."

She turned and faced him, her cheeks red. "No, it ain't that, exactly. Don't ask me any more. Don't talk about it. I'll come, all right, just as soon as I can."

They were on the line now and she held out her hand.

"Good-bye."

"Good-bye for now. Try to come up an' see me as soon as you can. If yo're worryin' because Antonio don't like me, stop it. I've been in too many tight places to get piped out where there's elbow room."

"I asked you not to say nothing more about it," she chided. "I'll come when I can. Good-bye."

"Good-bye," he replied, his sombrero under his arm. He watched her until she became lost to sight and then, suspicious, wheeled, and saw Johnny sitting quietly on his horse several hundred yards away. He called his friend to him by one wide sweep of his arm and Johnny spurred forward.

"Follow me, Johnny," he cried, dashing towards the arroyo. "Take th' other side an' look for Antonio. I'll take this side. Edge off; yo're too close. Three hundred yards is about right."

They raced away at top speed, reckless and grim, Johnny not knowing just what it was all about; but the name Antonio needed no sauce to whet his appetite since the day he had caught him watching his friend on the hill, and he scanned the plain eagerly. When they reached the other end of the arroyo Hopalong called to him: "Sweep east an' back to th' line on a circle. If you catch him, shoot off yo're colt an' hold him for *me*. I'm going west."

When they saw each other again it was on the line, and neither had seen any traces of Antonio, to Johnny's vexation and Hopalong's great satisfaction.

"What's up, Hoppy?" shouted Johnny.

"I reckoned that Antonio might a' followed her so he could tell tales to Meeker," Hopalong called.

Johnny swept up recklessly, jauntily, a swagger almost in the very actions of his horse, which seemed to have caught the spirit of its rider.

"Caught you that time," he laughed—and Johnny, when in a teasing mood, could weave into his laughter an affectionate note which found swift pardon for any words he might utter. "You an' her shore make a good—" and then he saw the flower on his friend's shirt and for the moment was rendered speechless by surprise. But in him the faculty of speech was well developed and he recovered quickly. "Sufferin' coyotes! Would you look at that! What's comin' to us down here, anyway? Are you loco? Do you mean to let th' rest of th' outfit see *that*?"

"Calamity is comin' to th' misguided mavericks that get funny about it!" retorted Hopalong. "I wear what I feels like, an' don't you forget it, neither."

"'In thy d-a-r-k eyes splendor, where th' l-o-v-e light longs to dwel-l,'" Johnny hummed, grinning. Then his hand went out. "Good luck, Hoppy! Th' best of luck!" he cried. "She's a dandy, all right, but she ain't too good for you."

"Much obliged," Hopalong replied, shaking hands. "But suppose you tell me what all th' good luck is for. To hear you talk anybody'd think all a feller had to do was to ride with a woman to be married to her."

"Well, then take off that wart of a flower an' come on," Johnny responded.

"What? Not to save yo're spotted soul! An' that ain't no wart of a flower, neither."

Johnny burst out laughing, a laugh from the soul of him, welling up in infectious spontaneity, triumphant and hearty. "Oh, oh! You bit that time! Anybody'd think about right in yo're case, as far as *wantin'* to be married is concerned. Why, yo're hittin' th' lovely trail to matrimony as hard as you can."

In spite of himself Hopalong had to laugh at the jibing of his friend, the Kid. He thumped him heartily across the shoulders to show how he felt about it and Johnny's breath was interfered with at a critical moment.

"Oh, just wait till th' crowd sees that blossom! Just wait," Johnny coughed.

"You keep mum about what you saw, d'y' hear?"

"Shore; but it'll be on my mind all th' time, an' I talk in my sleep when anything's on my mind."

"Then that's why I never heard you talk in yo're sleep."

"Aw, g'wan! But they'll see th' flower, won't they?"

"Shore they will; but as long as they don't know how it got there they can't say much."

"They can't, hey!" Johnny exclaimed. "That's a new one on me. It's usually what they don't know about that they talks of most. What they don't know they can guess in this case, all right. Most of 'em are good on readin' signs, an' that's plain as th' devil."

"But don't you tell 'em!" Hopalong warned.

"No. I won't tell 'em, honest," Johnny replied. He could convey the information in a negative way and he grinned hopefully at the fun there would be.

"I mean it, Kid," Hopalong responded, reading the grin. "I don't care about myself; they can joke all they wants with me. But it ain't nowise right to drag her into it, savvy? She don't want to be talked about like that."

"Yo're right; they won't find out nothin' from me," and Johnny saw his fun slip from him. "I'm goin' east; comin' along?"

"No; th' other way. So long."

"Hey!" cried Johnny anxiously, drawing rein, "Frenchy said Buck was going to put some of us up in Number Five so Frenchy an' his four could ride th' line. Did Buck say anything to you about it?"

Line house Number Five was too far from the zone of excitement, if fighting should break out along the line, to please Johnny.

"He was stringin' you, Kid," Hopalong laughed. "He won't take any of th' old outfit away from here."

"Oh, I knowed that; but I thought I'd ask, that's all," and Johnny cantered away, whistling happily.

Hopalong looked after him and smiled, for Johnny had laughed and fought and teased himself into the heart of every man of the outfit: "He's shore a good Kid; an' how he likes a fight!"

◼▮ ◆ ◆ ◆ ◆ ◆ ▮ ◆ ▮ ◆ ◆ ◆ ◆ ◆ ▮◼

CHAPTER 5

Hopalong Asserts Himself

Paralleling West Arroyo and two miles east of it was another arroyo, through which Hopalong was riding the day following his meeting with Mary. Coming to a place where he could look over the bank he saw a herd of H2 and Three Triangle cows grazing not far away, and Antonio was in charge of them. Hopalong did not know how long they had been in the valley, nor how they had crossed the line, but their presence was enough. It angered him, for here was open and, it appeared, authorized defiance. Not content to let his herds run as they wished, Meeker was actually sending them into the valley under guard, presumably to find out what would be done about it. The H2 foreman would find that out very soon.

Antonio looked around and wheeled sharply to face the danger, his listlessness gone in a flash. He was not there because of any orders from Meeker, but for reasons of his own. So when the Bar-20 puncher raised his arm and swept it towards the line he sat in sullen indifference, alert and crafty.

"You've got gall!" cried Hopalong. "Who told you to herd up here!"

Antonio frowned but did not reply.

"Yo're three miles too far north," continued Hopalong, riding slowly forward until their stirrups almost touched.

Antonio shrugged his shoulders.

"I ain't warbling for my health!" cried Hopalong. "You start them cows south right away."

"I can't."

Hopalong stared. "You can't! Well, I reckon you can, an' will."

"I can't. Boss won't let me."

"Oh, he won't! Well, I feel sorry for yore boss but yo're going to push 'em just th' same."

Antonio again shrugged his shoulders and lifted his hands in a gesture of helplessness.

"How long you been here, an' how'd you get in?"

"'N'our. By de *rio*."

"Oh, yore foreman's goin' to raise hell, ain't he!" Hopalong snorted. "He's going to pasture on us whether we like it or not, is he? He's a land thief, that's what he is!"

"De boss ees all right!" asserted Antonio, heatedly.

"If he is he's lop-sided, but he'll be *left* if he banks on this play going through without a smash-up. You chase them cows home an' keep 'em there. If I find you flittin' around th' ends of th' line or herdin' on this side of it I'll give you something to nurse—an' you'll be lucky if you can nurse it. Come on, get a-going!"

Antonio waved his arm excitedly and was about to expostulate, but Hopalong cut him short by hitting him across the face with his quirt: "Damn you!" he cried, angrily. "Shut yore mouth! Get them cows going! I've a mind to stop you right now. Come on, get a move on!"

Antonio's face grew livid and he tried to back away, swearing. Stung to action by the blow, he jerked at his gun, but found Hopalong's Colt pushing against his neck.

"Drop that gun!" the Bar-20 puncher ordered, his eyes flashing. "Don't you know better'n that? We've put up with yore crowd as long as we're going to, an' th' next thing will be a slaughter if that foreman of yourn don't get some sense, an' get it sudden. Don't talk back! Just start them cows!"

Antonio could do nothing but obey. His triumph at the success of his effort was torn with rabid hatred for the man who had struck him; but he could not fight with the Colt at his neck, and so sullenly obeyed. As they neared the line Hopalong ceased his personal remarks and, smiling grimly, turned to another topic.

"I let you off easy; but no more. Th' next herd we find in our valley will go sudden an' hard. If anybody is guardin' it they'll never know what hit 'em." He paused for a moment and then continued, cold contempt in his voice: "I reckon you had to obey orders, but you won't do it again if you know what's good for you. If yore boss, as you calls him, don't like what I've done, you tell him I said to drive th' next herd hisself. If he ain't man enough to bring 'em in hisself, tell him that Cassidy says to quit orderin' his men to take risks he's a-scared of."

"He ees brafe; he ain't 'fraid," Antonio rejoined. "He weel keel you ef I tell heem what you say."

"Tell him jus' th' same. I'll be riding th' line mostly, an' if he wants to hunt me up an' talk about it he can find me any time."

Antonio shrugged his shoulders and rode south, filled with elation at his success in stirring up hostility between the two ranches, but his heart seethed with murder for the blow. He would carry a message to Meeker that would call for harsh measures, and the war would be on.

As Antonio departed Lanky Smith rode into sight and cantered forward to meet his friend.

"What's up?" he asked.

"I don't know, yet," replied Hopalong. "He could be lying, I don't know what to think," and he related the matter to his companion.

"Lord, but you sent a stiff message to Meeker!" Lanky exclaimed. "You keep yore eyes plumb open from now on. Meeker'll be wild, an' Antonio won't forget that blow."

"Was anybody on th' east end this morning?"

"Shore; me an' Pete," Lanky replied, frowning. "He couldn't get a cow across without us seein' him—he lied."

"Well, it makes no difference how he got across; he was there, an' that's all I care about."

"There's one of his outfit now," Lanky said.

Hopalong looked around and saw an H2 puncher riding slowly past them, about two hundred yards to the south.

"Who is he?" Lanky asked.

"Doc Riley. Meeker got him an' Curley out of a bad scrape up north an' took them both to punch for him. I hear he is some bad with th' Colt. Sort of reckons he's a whole war-party in breech-cloths an' war-paint just 'cause he's got his man."

"He's gettin' close to th' line," Lanky remarked.

"Yes, because we've been turnin' their cows."

"Reckon he won't stop us none to speak of."

Doc had stopped and was watching them and while he looked a cow blundered out of the brush and started to cross the line. Hopalong spurred forward to stop it, followed by Lanky, and Doc rode to intercept them.

"G'wan back, you bone-yard!" Hopalong shouted, firing his Colt in front of the animal, which now turned and ran back.

Doc slid to a stand, his Colt out. "What do you think you're doing with that cow?"

"None of yore business!" Hopalong retorted.

Doc backed away so he could watch Lanky, his hand leaping up, and Hopalong fired. Doc dropped the weapon and grabbed at his right arm, cursing wildly.

Hopalong rode closer. "Next time you gets any curious about what I'm doing, you better write. You're a fine specimen to pull a gun on me, you are!"

"You'll stop turnin' our cows, or you'll get a pass to hell!" retorted Doc. "We won't stand for it no more, an' when th' boys hears about this, you'll have all you can take care of."

"I ain't got nothing to do but ride th' line an' answer questions like I did yourn," Hopalong rejoined. "I will have lots of time to take care of any little trouble that blows up from yore way. But *Meeker's* th' man I want to see. Tell him to take a herd across this line, will you?"

"You'll see him!" snapped Doc, wheeling and riding off.

"Things are movin' so fast you better send for Buck," Lanky suggested. "Hell'll be poppin' down here purty soon."

"I'll tell him what's going on, but there ain't no use of bringing him down here till we has to," Hopalong replied. "We can handle 'em. But I reckon Johnny had better go up an' tell him."

"Johnny ought to be riding this way purty quick; he's coming from th' hills."

"We'll meet him an' get him off."

They met Johnny and when he had learned of his mission he protested against being sent away from the line when things were getting crowded. "I don't want to miss th' fun!" he exclaimed. "Send Red, or Lanky."

"Red's too handy with th' Winchester; we might need him," Hopalong replied, smiling.

"Then you go, Lanky," Johnny suggested. "I'm better'n you with th' Colt."

"You're better'n nothing!' retorted Lanky. "You do what you're told, an' quick. Nothing will happen while you're gone, anyhow."

"Then why don't you want to go?"

"I don't want th' ride," Lanky replied. "It's too fur."

"Huh!" snorted Johnny. "Too bad about you an' th' ride! Poor old man, scared of sixty miles. I'll toss up with you."

"One of you has got to ride to Red an' tell him. He mustn't get caught unexpected," Hopalong remarked.

"What do you call?" asked Johnny, flipping a coin and catching it when it came down.

"All right, that's fair enough. Heads," Lanky replied.

"Whoop! It's tails!" cried Johnny, wheeling. "I'm going for Red," and he was gone before Lanky had time to object.

"Blasted Kid!" Lanky snorted. "How'd I know it was tails?"

"That's yore lookout," laughed Hopalong. "You ought to know him by this time. It's yore own fault."

"I'll tan his hide one of these fine days," Lanky promised. "He's too fresh," and he galloped off to cover the thirty miles between him and the bunk house in the least possible time so as to return as soon as he could.

CHAPTER 6

■ |◆ ◆ ◆ ◆ ◆| ■ |◆◆◆◆◆◆◆◆◆◆◆◆◆◆◆◆◆◆◆◆◆◆◆◆◆| ■ |◆ ◆ ◆ ◆ ◆| ■

Meeker Is Told

When Antonio had covered half of the distance between the line and the H2 bunk house he was hailed from a chaparral and saw Benito ride into view. He told his satellite what had occurred in the valley, gave him a message for Shaw, who was now on the mesa, and cantered on to tell Meeker his version of the morning's happenings.

The H2 foreman was standing by the corral when his broncho-buster rode up, and he stared. "Where'd you get that welt on th' face?" he demanded.

Antonio told him, with many exclamations and angry gestures, that he had ridden through the valley to see if there were any H2 cows grazing on it, that he had found a small herd and was about to return to his own range when he was held up and struck by Hopalong, who accused him of having driven the cattle across the line. When he had denied this he had been called a liar and threatened with death if he was ever again caught on that side of the line.

"By God!" cried the foreman. "That's purty highhanded! I'll give 'em something to beller about when I finds out just what I want to do!"

"He say, 'Tell that boss of yourn to no send you, send heemself nex' time.' He say he weel keel you on sight. I say he can't. He laugh, *so!*" laughing in a bloodcurdling manner. "He say he keel nex' man an' cows that cross line. He ees *uno* devil!"

"He will, hey!" Meeker exclaimed, thoroughly angered. "We'll give him all th' chance he wants when we get things fixed. 'Tony, what did you do about getting those two men you spoke of? You went down to Eagle, didn't you?"

"*Si, si,*" assured Antonio. "They come, *pronto.* They can keel heem. They come to-day; *quien sabe?*"

"I'll do my own killin'—but here comes Doc," Meeker replied. "Looks mad, too. Mebby they was going to kill him an' he objected. Hullo, Doc; what's th' matter?"

"That Cassidy damn near blowed my arm off," Doc replied. "Caught him turnin' back one of our cows an' told him not to. When I backed off so I could keep one eye on his friend he up an' plugs me through my gun arm."

"I see; they owns th' earth!" Meeker roared. "Shootin' up my men 'cause they stick up for me! Come in th' house an' get that arm fixed. We can talk in there," he said, glancing at Antonio. "They cut 'Tony across th' face with a quirt 'cause he was ridin' in their valley!"

"Let's get th' gang together an' wipe 'em off th' earth," Doc suggested, following Meeker towards the house.

Mary looked up when they entered: "What's th' matter, Dad? Why, are you hurt, Doc?"

"Don't ask questions, girl," Meeker ordered. "Get us some hot water an' some clean cloth. Sit down, Doc; we'll fix it in no time."

"We better clean 'em up to-morrow," Doc remarked.

"No; there ain't no use of losin' men fighting if there's any other way. You know there's a good strong line house on th' top of Lookout Peak, don't you?"

"Shore; reg'lar fort. They calls it Number Three."

Mary had returned and was tearing a bandage, listening intently to what was being said.

"What's th' matter with getting in that some day soon an' holdin' it for good?" asked the foreman. "It overlooks a lot of range, an' once we're in it it'll cost 'em a lot of lives to get it back—if they can get it back."

"You're right!" cried Doc, eagerly. "Let me an' Curley get in there to-night an' hold her for you. We can do it."

"You can't do that. Somebody sleeps in it nights. Nope, we've got to work some scheme to get it in th' daylight. They are bound to have it guarded, an' we've got to coax him out somehow. I don't know how, but I will before many hours pass. Hullo, who's this?" he asked, seeing two strangers approach the house.

"The new punchers," grunted Doc.

"Hey, you," cried Meeker through the open door. "You go down to th' corral an' wait for me."

"Sure thing."

"What's th' matter, Dad?" asked Mary. "How did Doc get shot?"

Meeker looked up angrily, but his face softened.

"There's a whole lot th' matter, Mary. That Bar-20 shore is gettin' hot-headed.

Cassidy hit 'Tony across th' face with a quirt an' shot Doc. 'Tony was riding through that valley, an' Doc told Cassidy not to drive back a cow of ourn."

She flushed. "There must 'a been more'n that, Dad. He wouldn't 'a shot for that. I know it."

"You know it!" cried Meeker, astonished. "How do you know it?"

"He ain't that kind. I know he ain't."

"I asked how you knew it!"

She looked down and then faced him. "Because I know him, because he ain't that kind. What did you say to him, Doc?"

Meeker's face was a study and Doc flushed, for she was looking him squarely in the eyes.

"What did you say to him?" she repeated. "Did you make a gun-play?"

"Well, by God!" shouted Meeker, leaping to his feet. "You know him, hey! 'He ain't that kind!' How long have you known him, an' where'd you meet him?"

"This is no time to talk of that," she replied, her spirit aroused. "Ask Doc what he did an' said to get shot. Look at him; he lied when he told you about it."

"I told him to quit driving our cows back," Doc cried. "Of course I had my hand on my gun when I said it. I'd been a fool if I hadn't, wouldn't I?"

"That ain't all," she remarked. "Did you try to use it?"

Meeker was staring first at one and then at the other, not knowing just what to say. Doc looked at him and his mind was made up.

"What'd you do, Doc?" he asked.

"I said: 'What are you doing with that cow?' an' he said it wasn't none of my business. I got mad then an' jerked my gun loose, but he got me first. I wasn't going to shoot. I was only getting ready for him if he tried to."

"How did he know you wasn't going to shoot?" Meeker demanded. "Reckon I can't blame him for that. He must be quick on th' draw."

"Quickest I ever saw. He had his gun out to shoot in front of a cow. At th' time I thought he was going to kill it. That's what made me get in so quick. He slid it back in th' holster an' faced me. I told you what happened then."

"Well, we've got to show them fellers they can't fool with us an' get away with it," Meeker replied. "An' I've got to have th' use of that crick somehow. I'll think of some way to square things."

"Wait, I'll go with you," Doc remarked, following the other towards the door.

"You go in th' bunk house an' wait for me.

"Wonder how much Tony didn't tell," mused the foreman, as he went towards the corral. "But I've got to notice plays like that or they'll think I'm scared of 'em. I'll go up an' have it out, an' when I get ready I'll show them swaggerin' bucks what's what."

When he returned he saw Antonio leaning against his shack, for he was not tolerated by the rest of the outfit and so lived alone. He looked at his foreman and leered knowingly, and then went inside the building, where he laughed silently. "That's a joke, all right! Meeker hiring two of my friends to watch his cows an' do his spying! We'll skin this range before we're through."

Meeker frowned when he caught his broncho-buster's look and he growled: "You never did look good, an' that welt shore makes you look more like th' devil than ever." He glanced at the house and the frown deepened. "So you know Cassidy! That's a *nice* thing to tell me! I'll just go up an' see that coyote, right now," and he went for his horse, muttering and scowling.

Antonio knew of a herd of cows and calves which had not been included in the H2 roundup, and which were fattening on an outlying range. There was also a large herd of Bar-20 cattle growing larger every day on the western range far outside the boundaries. Benito was scouting, Shaw and the others were nearly ready for work on the mesa. Added to this was the constantly growing hostility along the line, and this would blaze before he and Benito had finished their work. Everything considered he was very much pleased and even his personal vengeance was provided for. Doc had more cause for animosity against Hopalong than he had, and if the Bar-20 puncher should be killed some day when Doc rode the northern range, Doc would be blamed for it. But Meeker had not acted as he should have done when two of his men had been hurt on the same day, and that must be remedied. The faster things moved towards fighting the less chance there would be of the plot becoming known.

Antonio was the broncho-buster of the H2 because he was a positive genius at the work, and he was a good, all-around cowman; but he was cruel to a degree with both horses and cattle. Because of his fitness Meeker had overlooked his undesirable qualities, which he had in plenty. He was entirely too fond of liquor and gambling, was uncertain in his hours, and used his time as he saw fit when not engaged in breaking horses. A natural liar, vindictive and with a temper dry as tinder, he was shunned by the other members of the outfit. This filled his heart with hatred for them and for Meeker, who did not interfere. He swore many times that he would square up everything some day, and the day was getting closer.

In appearance he was about medium height, but his sloping shoulders and lax carriage gave his arms the appearance of being abnormally long. His face was sharp and narrow, while his thin, wiry body seemed almost devoid of flesh. Like most cowboys he was a poor walker and his toes turned in. Such was Antonio, who longed to gamble with Fortune in a dangerous game for stakes which to him were large, and who had already suggested to Meeker that the line house on Lookout Peak was the key to the situation. It was the germ, which grew slowly in the foreman's brain and became more feasible and insistent day by day, and it accounted for his fits of abstraction; it would not do to fail if the attempt were made.

CHAPTER 7

Hopalong Meets Meeker

When Meeker was within a mile of the line he met Curley, told him what had occurred and that he was going to find Hopalong. Curley smiled and replied that he had seen that person less than ten minutes ago and that he was riding towards the peak, and alone.

"We'll go after him," Meeker replied. "You come because I want to face him in force so he won't start no gun-play an' make me kill him. That'd set hell to pop."

Hopalong espied Johnny far to the east and he smiled as he remembered the celerity with which that individual had departed after glancing at the coin.

"There ain't no flies on th' Kid, all right," he laughed, riding slowly so Johnny could join him. He saw Curley riding south and looked over the rough plain for other H2 punchers. Some time later as he passed a chaparral he glanced back to see what had become of his friend, but found that he had disappeared. When he wheeled to watch for him he saw Meeker and Curley coming towards him and he shook his holster to be sure his Colt was not jammed in it too tightly.

"Well, here's where th' orchestry tunes up, all right," he muttered grimly. "Licked Antonio, plugged Doc, an' sent word to Meeker to come up if he wasn't scared. He's come, an' now I'll have to lick two more. If they push me I'll shoot to kill!"

The H2 foreman rode ahead of his companion and stopped when fifty yards from the alert line-rider. Pushing his sombrero back on his head, he lost no time in skirmishing. "Did you chase my broncho-buster out of yore valley, cut his face with yore quirt, an' shoot Doc? Did you send word to me that you'd kill me if I showed myself?"

"Was you ever an auctioneer," calmly asked Hopalong, "or a book agent?"

"What's that got to do with it?" Meeker demanded. "You heard what I said."

"I don't know nothing about yore broncho-buster, taking one thing at a time, which is proper."

"What! You didn't drive him out, or cut him?"

"No; why?" asked Hopalong, chuckling.

"He says you did—an' somebody quirted him."

"He's loco—he wasn't in th' valley," Hopalong replied. "Think he could get in that valley? Him, or any other man we didn't want in?"

"You're devilish funny!" retorted Meeker, riding slowly forward, followed by his companion, who began to edge away from his foreman. "Since you are so exact, did you chase him off yore range an' push him over th' line at th' point of yore gun?"

"You've got me. Better not come too close—my cayuse don't like gettin' crowded."

"That's all right," Meeker retorted, not heeding the warning. "Do you mean to tell me you don't know? Yore name's Cassidy, ain't it?" he asked, angrily, his determination to avoid fighting rapidly becoming lost.

"That's my own, shore 'nuf name," Hopalong answered, and then: "Do you mean Antonio, the one I caught stealing our range?"

"Yes!" snapped Meeker, stopping again.

"Why didn't you say so, then, 'stead of calling him yore broncho-buster?" Hopalong demanded. "How do I know who yore broncho-buster is? I don't know what every land pirate does in this country."

"Then you shot Doc—do you know who I mean this time?" sarcastically asked the H2 foreman.

"Oh, shore. He didn't get his gun out quick enough when he went after it, did he? Any more I can tell you before I begins to say things, too?"

Meeker, angered greatly by Hopalong's contemptuous inflection and the reckless assertiveness of his every word and look, began to ride to describe a circle around the Bar-20 puncher, Curley going the other way.

"You said you'd kill me when you saw me, didn't you, you—"

Hopalong was backing away so as to keep both men in front of him, alert, eager, and waiting for the signal to begin his two-handed shooting. "I ain't a whole lot deaf—I can hear you from where you are. You better stop, for I've ridden out of tighter holes than this, an' you'll shore get a pass to hell if you crowd me too much!"

Adown th' road, an' gun in hand,
Comes Whiskey Bill, mad Whiskey Bill—

This fragment of song floated out of a chaparral about twenty yards behind Hopalong, who grinned pleasantly when he heard it. Now he knew where Johnny was, and now he had the whip hand without touching his guns; while the youngster was not in sight he was all the more dangerous, since he presented no target. Johnny knew this and was greatly pleased thereby, and he was more than pleased by the way Hopalong had been talking.

The effect of the singing was instant and marked on Meeker and his companion, for they not only stopped suddenly and swore, but began to back away, glancing around in an endeavor to locate the joker in the deck. This they failed to do because Johnny was far too wise to advertise his exact whereabouts. Meeker looked at Curley and Curley looked at Meeker, both uneasy and angry.

"As I was sayin' before th' concert began," Hopalong remarked, laughing shortly, "it's a pass to hell if you crowd me too much. Now, Meeker, you'll listen to me an' I'll tell you what I didn't have time to say before: I told an Antonio that th' next herd of yourn to cross th' line should be brought in by you, 'less you was scared to run th' risks yore men had to take. He said you'd kill me for that message, an' I told him you knew where you could find me. Now about Doc: When a man pulls a gun on me he wants to be quicker than *he* was or he'll shore get hurt. I could 'a killed him just as easy as to plug his gun arm, an' just as easy as I could 'a plugged both of you if you pulled on me. You came up here looking for my scalp an' if you still wants it I'll go away from th' song bird in the chaparral an' give you th' chance. I'd ruther let things stay as they are, though if you wants, I'll take both you an' Curley, half-mile run together, with Colts."

"No, I didn't come up here after your scalp, but I got mad after I found you. How long is this going to last? I won't stand for it much longer, nohow."

"You'll have to see Buck. I'm obeying orders, which are to hold th' line again you, which I'll do."

"H'm!" replied Meeker, and then: "Do you know my girl?"

Hopalong thought quickly. "Why, I've seen her ridin' around some. But why?"

"She says she knows you," persisted Meeker, frowning.

The frown gave Hopalong his cue, but he hardly knew what to say, not knowing what she had said about it.

"Hey, you!" he suddenly cried to Curley. "Keep yore hand from that gun!"

"I didn't—"

"You're lying! Any more of that an' I'll gimlet you!"

"What in hell are you doing, Curley?" demanded Meeker, the girl question out of his mind instantly. He had been looking closely at Hopalong and didn't know that Curley was innocent of any attempt to use his Colt.

"I tell—"

"Get out of here! I've wasted too much time already. Go home, where that gun won't worry you. You, too, Meeker! Bring an imitation bad-man up here an' sayin' you didn't want my scalp! Flit!"

"I'll go when I'm damn good and ready!" retorted Meeker, angry again. "You're too blasted bossy, you are!" he added, riding towards the man who had shot Doc.

A-looking for some place to land—

floated out of the chaparral and he stiffened in the saddle and stopped.

"Come on, Curley! We can't lick pot-shooters. An' let that gun alone!"

"Damn it! I tell you I wasn't going for my gun!" Curley yelled.

"Get out of here!" blazed Hopalong, riding forward.

They rode away slowly, consulting in low voices. Then the foreman turned and looked back. "You better be careful how you shoot my punchers! They ain't all like Doc."

"Then you're lucky," Hopalong retorted. "You keep yore cows on yore side an' we won't hurt none of yore outfit."

When they had gone Hopalong wheeled to look for Johnny and saw him crawling out of a chaparral, dragging a rifle after him. He capered about, waving the rifle and laughing with joy and Hopalong had to laugh with him. When they were rid of the surplus of the merriment Johnny patted the rifle. "Reckon they was shore up against a marked deck that time! Did you see 'em stiffen when I warbled? Acted like they had roped a puma an' didn't know what to do with it. Gee, it was funny!"

"You're all right, Kid," laughed Hopalong. "It was yore best play—you couldn't 'a done better."

"Shore," replied Johnny. "I had my sights glued to Curley's shirt pocket, an' he'd been plumb disgusted if he'd tried to do what you said he did. I couldn't 'a missed him with a club at that range. I nearly died when you pushed Meeker's girl question up that blind canyon. It was a peach of a throw, all right. Bet he ain't remembered yet that he didn't get no answer to it. We're going to have some blamed fine times down here before everything is settled, ain't we?"

"I reckon so, Kid. I'm going to leave you now an' look around by West Arroyo. You hang around th' line."

"All right—so long."

"Can you catch yore cayuse?"

"Shore I can; he's hobbled," came the reply from behind a spur of the chaparral. *"Stand still, you hen!* All right, Hoppy."

Johnny cantered away and, feeling happy, began singing:

> *Adown th' road, an' gun in hand,*
> *Comes Whiskey Bill, mad Whiskey Bill;*
> *A-looking for some place to land*
> *Comes Whiskey Bill.*
> *An' everybody'd like to be*
> *Ten miles away behind a tree*
> *When on his joyous, achin' spree*
> *Starts Whiskey Bill.*
>
> *Th' times have changed since you made love,*
> *Oh, Whiskey Bill, oh, Whiskey Bill;*
> *Th' happy sun grinned up above*
> *At Whiskey Bill.*
> *An' down th' middle of th' street*
> *Th' sheriff comes on toe-in feet,*
> *A-wishing for one fretful peek*
> *At Whiskey Bill.*
>
> *Th' cows go grazin o'er th' lea—*
> *Pore Whiskey Bill, pore Whiskey Bill,*
> *An' aching thoughts pour in on me*
> *Of Whiskey Bill.*
> *Th' sheriff up an' found his stride,*
> *Bill's soul went shootin' down th' slide—*
> *How are things on th' Great Divide,*
> *Oh, Whiskey Bill?*

CHAPTER 8

On the Edge of the Desert

Thunder Mesa was surrounded by almost impenetrable chaparrals, impenetrable to horse and rider except along certain alleys, but not too dense for a man on foot. These stretched away on all sides as far as the eye could see and made the desolate prospect all the more forbidding. It rose a sheer hundred feet into the air, its sides smooth rock and affording no footing except a narrow, precarious ledge which slanted up the face of the southern end, too broken and narrow to permit of a horse ascending, but passable to a man.

The top of the mesa was about eight acres in extent and was rocky and uneven, cut by several half-filled fissures which did not show on the walls. Uninviting as the top might be considered it had one feature which was uncommon, for the cataclysm of nature which had caused this mass of rock to tower above the plain had given to it a spring which bubbled out of a crack in the rock and into a basin cut by itself; from there it flowed down the wall and into a shallow depression to the rock below, where it made a small water hole before flowing through the chaparrals, where it sank into the sand and became lost half a mile from its source.

At the point where the slanting ledge met the top of the mesa was a hut built of stones and adobe, its rear wall being part of a projecting wall of rock. Narrow, deep loopholes had been made in the other walls and a rough door, massive and tight fitting, closed the small doorway. The roof, laid across cedar poles which ran from wall to wall, was thick and flat and had a generous layer of adobe to repel the rays of the scorching sun. Placed as it was the hut overlooked the trail leading to it from the plain, and should it be defended by determined men, assault by that path would be foolhardy.

On the plain around the mesa extended a belt of sparse grass, some hundreds of feet wide at the narrowest point and nearly a mile at the widest, over which numerous rocks and bowlders and clumps of chaparral lay scattered. On this pasture were about three score cattle, most of them being yearlings, but all bearing the brand HQQ and a diagonal ear cut. These were being watched by a careless cowboy, although it was belittling their scanty intelligence to suppose that they would leave the water and grass, poor as the latter was, to stray off onto the surrounding desert.

At the base of the east wall of the mesa was a rough corral of cedar poles set on end, held together by rawhide strips, which, put on green, tightened with the strength of steel cables when dried by the sun. In its shadow another man watched the cattle while he worked in a desultory way at repairing a saddle. Within the corral a man was bending over a cow while two others held it down. Its feet were tied and it was panting, wild-eyed and frightened. The man above it stepped to a glowing fire a few paces away and took from it a hot iron, with which he carefully traced over the small brand already borne by the animal. With a final flourish he stepped back, regarding the work with approval, and thrust the iron into the sand. Taking a knife from his pocket he trimmed the V notch in its ear to the same slanting cut seen on the cattle outside on the pasture. He tossed the bit of cartilage from him, stepping back and nodding to his companions, who loosened the ropes and leaped back, allowing the animal to escape.

Shaw, who had altered the H2 brand, turned to one of the others and laughed heartily. "Good job, eh Manuel? Th' H2 won't know their cow now!"

Manuel grinned. "*Si, si;* eet ees!" he cried. He was cook for the gang, a bosom friend of Benito and Antonio. In his claw-like fingers he held a husk cigarette, without which he was seldom seen. He spoke very little but watched always, his eyes usually turned eastward. He seemed to be almost as much afraid of the east as Cavalry was of the west, where the desert lay. He ridiculed Cavalry's terror of the desert and explained why the east was to be feared the more, for the eastern danger rode horses and could come to them.

"Hope 'Tony fixes up that line war purty soon, eh, Cavalry?" remarked Shaw, suddenly turning to the third man in the group.

Cavalry was staring moodily towards the desert and did not hear him.

"Cavalry! Get that desert off yore mind! Do you want to go loco? Who's going to take th' next drive an' bring back th' flour, you or Clausen?"

"It's Clausen's turn next."

Manuel slouched away and began to climb the slanting path up the mesa. Shaw watched him reflectively and laughed. "There he goes again. Beats th' devil how scared he is, spending most of his time on th' lookout. Why, he's blamed near as scared of them punchers as you are of that skillet out yonder."

"We ain't got no kick, have we?" retorted Cavalry. "Ain't he looking out for us at th' same time?"

"I don't know about that," Shaw replied, frowning. "I ain't got no love for Manuel. If he saw 'em coming an' could get away he'd sneak off without saying a word. It'd give him a chance to get away while we held 'em."

"We'll see him go, then; there's only one way down."

"Oh, the' devil with him!" Shaw exclaimed. "What do you think of th' chances of startin' that range war?"

"From what Antonio says it looks good."

"Yes. But he'll get caught some day, or night, an' pay for it with his life."

Cavalry shrugged his shoulders. "I reckon so. I'd ruther they'd get him out there than to follow him here. If he goes, I hope it's sudden, so he won't have time to squeal."

"He's a malignant devil, an' he hates that H2 outfit like blazes," replied Shaw. "An' now he's got a pizen grudge agin' th' Bar-20. He might let his hate get th' upper hand an' start in to square things; if he does that he'll over-reach, an' get killed."

"I reckon so; but he's clever as th' devil hisself."

"Well, if he gets too big-headed out here Hall will take care of him, all right," Shaw laughed.

"I don't like them saddled us with," Cavalry remarked. "There's Manuel an' Benito. One of 'em is here all th' time an 'close to you, too, if you remember. Then he's going to put two or three on th' range; why?"

"Suspects we'll steal some of his share, I reckon. An' if he gets in trouble with us they'll be on his side. Oh, he's no fool."

"If he 'tends to business an' forgets his grudges it'll be a good thing for us. That Bar-20 has got an awful number of cows. An' there's th' H2, an' th' other two up north."

"We've tackled th' hardest job first—th' Bar-20," replied Shaw, laughing. "I used to know some fellers what said that outfit couldn't be licked. They died trying to prove themselves liars."

"Wonder how much money 'Tony totes around on him?" asked Cavalry.

"Not much; he's too wise. He's cached it somewhere. Was you reckonin' on takin' it away from him at th' end?"

"No, no. I just wondered what he did with it."

The man at the gate looked up. "Here comes 'Tony."

Shaw and his companion rode forward to meet him.

"What's up?" cried Shaw.

"I have started th' war," Antonio replied, a cruel smile playing over his sharp face. "They'll be fightin' purty soon."

"That's good," responded Shaw. "Tell us about it."

Antonio, with many gestures and much conceit, told of the trick he had played on Hopalong, and he took care to lose no credit in the telling. He passed lightly over the trouble between Doc and the Bar-20 puncher, but intimated that he had caused it. He finished by saying: "You send to th' same place tomorrow an' Benito'll have some cows for you. They'll soon give us our chance, an' it'll be easy then."

"Mebby it will be easy," replied Shaw, "but that rests with you. You've got to play yore cards plumb cautious. You've done fine so far, but if you ain't careful you'll go to hell in a hurry an' take us with you. You can't fool 'em all th' time, someday they'll get suspicious an' swap ideas. An' when they do that it means fight for us."

Antonio smiled and thought how easy it might be, if the outfits grew suspicious and he learned of it in time, to discover tracks and other things and tell Meeker he was sure there was organized rustling and that all tracks pointed to Thunder Mesa. He could ride across the border before any of his partners had time to confess and implicate him. But he assured Shaw that he would be careful, adding: "No, I won't make no mistakes. I hate 'em all too much to grow careless."

"That's just where you'll miss fire," the other rejoined. "You'll pamper your grouch till you forget everything else. You better be satisfied to get square by taking their cows."

"Don't worry about that."

"All right. Here's yore money for th' last herd," he said digging down into his pocket and handing Antonio some gold coins. "You know how to get more?"

Antonio took the money, considered a moment and then pocketed it, laughing. "Good! But I mus' go back now. I won't be out here again very soon; it's too risky. Send me my share by Benito," he called over his shoulder as he started off.

The two rustlers watched him and Cavalry shook his head slowly. "I'm plumb scairt he'll bungle it. If he does we'll get caught like rats in a trap."

"If we're up there we can hold off a thousand," Shaw replied, looking up the wall.

"Here comes Hall," announced the man at the gate.

The newcomer swept up and leaped from his hot and tired horse. "I found them other ranches are keeping their men ridin' over th' range an' along th' trails—I near got caught once," he reported. "We'll have to be careful how we drives to th' construction camps."

"They'll get tired watchin' after a while," replied the leader. " 'Tony was just here."

"I don't care if he's in hell," retorted Hall. "He'll peach on us to save his mangy skin, one of these days."

"We've got to chance it."

"Where's Frisco?"

"Down to Eagle for grub to tide us over for a few days."

"Huh!" exclaimed Hall. "Everything considered we're goin' to fight like th' devil out here someday. Down to Eagle!"

"We can fight!" retorted Shaw. "An' if we has to run for it, there's th' desert."

"I'd ruther die right here fighting than on that desert," remarked Cavalry, shuddering. "When I go I want to go quick, an' not be tortured for 'most a week." He had an insistent and strong horror of that gray void of sand and alkali so near at hand and so far across. He was nervous and superstitious, and it seemed always to be calling him. Many nights he had awakened in a cold sweat because he had dreamed it had him, and often it was all he could do to resist going out to it.

Shaw laughed gratingly. "You don't like it, do you?"

Hall smiled and walked towards the slanting trail.

"Why, it ain't bad," he called over his shoulder.

"It's an earthly hell!" Cavalry exclaimed. He glanced up the mesa wall. "We can hold that till we starve, or run out of cartridges—then what?"

"You're a calamity howler!" snapped Shaw. "That desert has wore a saddle sore on yore nerves somethin' awful. Don't think about it so much! It can't come to you, an' you ain't going to it," he laughed, trying to wipe out the suggestion of fear that had been awakened in him by the thought of the desert as a place of refuge. He had found a wanderer, denuded of clothes, sweating blood and hopelessly mad one day when he and Cavalry had ridden towards the desert; and the sight of the unfortunate's dying agonies had remained with him ever since. "We ain't going to die out here—they won't look for us where they don't think there's any grass or water."

Fragments of Manuel's song floated down to them as they strode towards the trail, and reassured that all would be well, their momentary depression was banished by the courage of their hearts.

The desert lay beyond, quiet; ominous by its very silence and inertia; a ghastly, malevolent aspect in its every hollow; patient, illimitable, scorching; fascinating in its horrible calm, sinister, forbidding, hellish. It had waited through centuries—and was still waiting, like the gigantic web of the Spider of Thirst.

CHAPTER 9

On the Peak

Hopalong Cassidy had the most striking personality of all the men in his outfit; humorous, courageous to the point of foolishness, eager for fight or frolic, nonchalant when one would expect him to be quite otherwise, curious, loyal to a fault, and the best man with a Colt in the Southwest, he was a paradox, and a puzzle even to his most intimate friends. With him life was a humorous recurrence of sensations, a huge pleasant joke instinctively tolerated, but not worth the price cowards pay to keep it. He had come onto the range when a boy and since that time he had laughingly carried his life in his open hand, and although there had been many attempts to snatch it he still carried it there, and just as recklessly.

Quick in decisions and quick to suspect evil designs against him and his ranch, he was different from his foreman, whose temperament was more optimistic. When Buck had made him foreman of the line riders he had no fear that Meeker or his men would take many tricks, for his faith in Hopalong's wits and ability was absolute. He had such faith that he attended to what he had to do about the ranch house and did not appear on the line until he had decided to call on Meeker and put the question before him once and for all. If the H2 foreman did not admit the agreement and promise to abide by it then he would be told to look for trouble.

While Buck rode towards Lookout Peak, Hopalong dismounted at the line house perched on its top and found Red Connors seated on the rough bench by the door. Red, human firebrand both in hair and temper, was Hopalong's loyal chum—in the eyes of the other neither could do wrong. Red was cleaning his rifle, the pride of his heart, a wicked-shooting Winchester which used the Government cartridge containing seventy grains of powder and five hundred grains of lead. With his rifle he was as expert as his friend was with the

Colt, and up to six hundred yards, its limit with accuracy, he could do about what he wished with it.

"Hullo, you," said Red, pleasantly. "You looks peevish."

"An' you look foolish. What you doing?"

"Minding my business."

"Hard work?" sweetly asked Hopalong, carelessly seating himself on the small wooden box which lay close to his friend.

"Hey, you!" cried Red, leaping up and hauling him away. "You bust them sights an' you'll be sorry! Ain't you got no sense?"

"Sights? What are you going to do with 'em?"

"Wear 'em 'round my neck for a charm! What'd you reckon I'd do with 'em!"

"Didn't know. I didn't think you'd put 'em on that thing," Hopalong replied, looking with contempt at his friend's rifle. "Honest, you ain't a-goin' to put 'em on that lead ranch, are you? Yo're like th' Indians—want a lot of shots to waste without re-loadin'."

"I ain't wasting no shots, an' I'm going to put sights on that lead ranch, too. These old ones are too coarse," Red replied, carefully placing the box out of danger. "Now you can sit down."

"Thanks; please can I smoke?"

Red grunted, pushed down the lever of the rifle, and began to re-assemble the parts, his friend watching the operation. When Red tried to slip the barrel into its socket Hopalong laughed and told him to first draw out the magazine, if he wanted to have any success.

The line foreman took a cartridge from the pile on the bench and compared it with one which he took from his belt, a huge, 45-caliber Sharps special, shooting five hundred and fifty grains of lead with one hundred and twenty grains of powder out of a shell over three inches long; a cartridge which shot with terrific force and for a great distance, the weight of the large ball assuring accuracy at long ranges. Besides this four-inch cartridge the Government ammunition appeared dwarfed.

"When are you going to wean yoreself from popping these musket caps, Red?" he asked, tossing the smaller cartridge away and putting his own back in his belt.

"Well, you've got gall!" snorted Red, going out for his cartridge. Returning with it he went back to work on his gun, his friend laughing at his clumsy fingers.

"Yore fingers are all thumbs, an' sore at that."

"Never mind my fingers. Have you seen Johnny around?"

"Yes; he was watching one of them new H2 punchers. He'll go off th' handle one of these days. He reminds me a whole lot of a bull-pup chained with a corral-ful of cats."

Red laughed and nodded. "Where's Lanky?"

"Johnny said he was at Number Four fixin' that saddle again. He ain't done nothin' for th' last month but fix it. Purty soon there won't be none of it left to fix."

"There certainly won't!"

"His saddle an' yore gun make a good pair."

"Let up about the gun. You can't say nothin' more about it without repeatin' yoreself."

"It's a sawed-off carbine. I'd ruther have a Spencer any day."

"You remind me a whole lot of a feller I once knowed," Red retorted.

"That so?" asked Hopalong suspiciously. "Was he so nice?"

"No; he was a fool," Red responded, going into the house.

"Then that's where you got it, for they say it's catching."

Red stuck his head out of the door. "On second thought you remind me of another feller."

"You must'a knowed some good people."

"An' he was a liar."

"Hullo, Hop Wah!" came from the edge of the hilltop and Hopalong wheeled to see Skinny Thompson approaching.

"What you doing?" Skinny asked, using his stock question for beginning a conversation.

"Painting white spots on pink elephants!"

"Where's Red?"

"In th' shack, rubbin' 'em off again."

"Johnny chased that Antonio off'n th' ranch," Skinny offered, grinning.

"Good for him!" cried Hopalong.

"Johnny's all right—here comes Buck," Red said, coming out of the house. "Johnny's with him, too. Hullo, Kid!"

"Hullo, Brick-top!" retorted Johnny, who did not like his nickname. No one treated him as anything but a boy and he resented it at times.

"Did he chase you far?" Hopalong queried.

"I'd like to see anybody chase me!"

Buck smiled. "How are things down here?"

Hopalong related what had occurred and the foreman nodded. "I'm going down to see Meeker—he's th' only man who can tell me what we're to look for. I don't want to keep so many men down here. Frenchy has got all he can handle, an' I want somebody up in Two. So long."

"Let me an' Red go with you, Buck," cried Hopalong.

"Me, too!" exclaimed Johnny, excitedly.

"You stay home, an' don't worry about me," replied the foreman, riding off.

"I don't like to see him go alone," Hopalong muttered. "He may get a raw deal down there. But if he does we'll wipe 'em off'n th' earth."

"Mamma! Look there!" softly cried Johnny, staring towards the other side of the plateau, where Mary Meeker rode past. Red and Skinny were astonished and Johnny and Hopalong pretended to be; but all removed their sombreros while she remained in sight. Johnny was watching Hopalong's face, but when Red glanced around he was staring over the Hill.

"Gosh, ain't she a ripper!" he exclaimed softly.

"She is," admitted Skinny. "She shore is."

Hopalong rubbed his nose reflectively and turned to Red. "Did you ever notice how pretty a freckle is?"

Red stared, and his friend continued: "Take a purty girl an' stick a freckle on her nose an' it sort of takes yore breath."

Red grinned. "I ain't never took a purty girl an' stuck a freckle on her nose, so I can't say."

Hopalong flushed at the laughter and Skinny cried, joyously: "She's got two of us already! Meeker's got us licked if he'll let her show herself once in a while. Oh, these young fellers! Nothing can rope 'em so quick as a female, an' th' purtier she is th' quicker she can do it."

A warning light came into Hopalong's eyes. "Nobody in this outfit'll go back on Buck for all th' purty women in th' world!"

"Good boy!" thought Johnny.

"We've got to watch th' Kid, just th' same," laughed Skinny.

"I'll knock yore head off!" cried Johnny. "You're sore 'cause you know you ain't got no chance with women while me an' Hoppy are around!"

Red looked critically at Hopalong and snickered. "If we've got to look like him to catch th' women, thank God we don't want 'em!"

"Is that so!" retorted Hopalong.

"Say," drawled Skinny. "Wouldn't th' Kid look nice hobbled with matrimony? That is, after he grows up."

"You go to th' devil!"

"Gee, Kid, you look bloodthirsty," laughed Red.

"You go to," Johnny retorted, swinging into the saddle. "I'm going along th' line to see what's loose."

"I'll lick you when I see you again!" shouted Red, grinning.

Johnny turned and twirled his fingers at his red-haired friend. "Yah, you ain't man enough!"

"Johnny's gettin' more hungry for a fight every day," Hopalong remarked. "He's itching for one."

"So was you a few years back, an' you ain't changed none," replied Red. "You used to ride around looking for fights."

"To hear you talk, anybody'd think you was a Angel of Peace," Hopalong retorted.

"One's as bad as th' other, so shut up," Skinny remarked, going into the house for a drink.

CHAPTER 10

Buck Visits Meeker

As Buck rode south he went over the boundary trouble in all its phases, and the more he thought about it the firmer his resolution grew to hold the line at any cost. He had gone to great expense and labor to improve the water supply in the valley and he saw no reason why the H2 could not do the same; and to him an agreement was an agreement, and ran with the land. What Meeker thought about it was not the question—the point at issue was whether or not the H2 could take the line and use the valley, and if they could they were welcome to it.

But while there was any possibility for a peaceable settlement it would be foolish to start fighting, for one range war had spread to alarming proportions and had been costly to life and property. Then there was the certainty that once war had begun, rustling would develop. But, be the consequences what they might, he would fight to the last to hold that which was rightfully his. He was not going to Meeker to beg a compromise, or to beg him to let the valley alone; he was riding to tell the H2 foreman what he could expect if he forced matters.

When he rode past the H2 corrals he was curiously regarded by a group of punchers who lounged near them, and he went straight up to them without heeding their frowns.

"Is Meeker here?"

"No, he ain't here," replied Curley, who was regarded by his companions as being something of a humorist.

"Where is he?"

"Since you asks, I reckon he's in th' bunk house," Curley replied. "Where he ought to be," he added, pointedly, while his companions grinned.

"That's wise," responded Buck. "He ought to stay there more often. I hope his cows will take after him. Much obliged for th' information," he finished, riding on.

"His cows an' his punchers'll do as they wants," asserted Curley, frowning.

"Excuse me. I reckoned *he* was boss around here," Buck apologized, a grim smile playing about his lips. "But you better change that 'will' to 'won't' when you mean th' valley."

"I mean *will*!" Curley retorted, leaping to his feet. "An' what's more, I ain't through with that game laig puncher of yourn, neither."

Buck laughed and rode forward again. "You have my sympathy, then," he called over his shoulder.

Buck stopped before the bunk house and called out, and in response to his hail Jim Meeker came and stood in the door.

The H2 foreman believed he was right, and he was too obstinate to admit that there was any side but his which should be considered. He wanted water and better grass, and both were close at hand. Where he had been raised there had been no boundaries, for it had been free grass and water, and he would not and could not see that it was any different on his new range. He had made no agreement, and if one had been made it did not concern him; it concerned only those who had made it. He did not buy the ranch from the old owners, but from a syndicate, and there had been nothing said about lines or restrictions. When he made any agreements he lived up to them, but he did not propose to observe those made by others.

"How'dy, Meeker," said Buck, nodding.

'How'dy, Peters; come in?"

"I reckon it ain't worth while. I won't stay long," Buck replied. "I came down to tell you that some of yore cows are crossing our line. They're gettin' worse every day."

"That so?" asked Meeker, carelessly.

"Yes."

"Um; well, what's th' reason they shouldn't? An' what is that 'line,' that we shouldn't go over it?"

"Dawson, th' old foreman of th' Three Triangle, told you all about that," Buck replied, his whole mind given to the task of reading what sort of a man he had to deal with. "It's our boundary; an' yourn."

"Yes? But I don't recognize no boundary. What have they got to do with me?"

"It has this much, whether you recognize it or not: It marks th' north limit of yore grazin'. We don't cross it."

"Huh! You don't have to, while you've got that crick."

"We won't have th' crick, nor th' grass, either, if you drive yore cows on us. That valley is our best grazing, an' it ain't in th' agreement that you can eat it all off."

"What agreement?"

"I didn't come down here to tell you what you know," Buck replied, slowly. "I came to tell you to keep yore men an' yore cows on yore own side, that's whatever."

"How do you know my cows are over there?"

"How do I know th' sun is shining?"

"What do you want me to do?" Meeker asked, leaning against the house and grinning.

"Hold yore herds where they belong. Of course some are shore to stray over, but strays don't count—I ain't talkin' about them."

"Well, I've punched a lot of cows in my day," replied Meeker, "an' over a lot of range, but I never seen no boundary lines afore. An' nobody ever told me to keep on one range, if they knowed me. I've run up against a wire fence or two in th' last few years, but they didn't last long when I hit 'em."

"If you want to know what a boundary line looks like I can show you. There's a plain trail along it where my men have rode for years."

"So you say; but I've got to have water."

"You've got it; twenty miles of river. An' if you'll put down a well or two th' Jumping Bear won't go dry.'

"I don't know nothing about wells," Meeker replied. "Natural water's good enough for me without fooling with wet holes in th' ground."

"No; but, by God, yo're willin' enough to use them what *I* put down! Do you think I spent good time an' money just to supply *you* with water? Why don't you get yore own, 'stead of hoggin' mine!"

"There's water enough, an' it ain't yourn, neither."

"It's mine till somebody takes it away from me, an' you can gamble on that."

"Oh, I reckon you'll share it."

"I reckon I won't!" Buck retorted. "Look here; my men have held that range for many years against all kinds of propositions an' we didn't get pushed into th' discard once; an' they'll go right on holding it. Hell has busted loose down here purty often during that time, but we've allus roped an' branded it; an' we hain't forgot how!"

"Well, I don't want no trouble, but I've got to use that water, an' my men are some hard to handle."

"You'll find mine worse to handle before you gets through," Buck rejoined.

"They're restless now, an' once they start, all hell can't stop 'em." Meeker started to reply, but Buck gave him no chance. "Do you know why I haven't driven you back by force? It wasn't because I figgered on what *you'd* do. It was on account of th' rustling that'll blossom on this range just as soon as we get too busy to watch things. That's why, but if yo're willing to take a chance with cow thieves, I am."

"I'm willing. I've got to have water on my northwest corner," Meeker replied. "An' I'm going to have it! If my cows get on yore private reservation, it's up to you to drive 'em off; but I wouldn't be none hasty doing it if I was you. You see, my men are plumb touchy."

"That's final, is it?"

"I ain't never swallered nothing I ever said."

"All right. I can draw on forty men to fill up gaps, an' I'll do it before I let any range jumper cheat me out of what's mine. When you buck that line, come ready for trouble."

"Yore line'll burn you before I'm through," retorted Meeker, angrily.

Meeker laughed, stretched, and slipped his thumbs in the armholes of his vest, watching the Bar-20 foreman ride away. Then he frowned and snapped his fingers angrily. "We'll keep you busy on yore 'line' when I get ready to play th' cards I'm looking for!" he exclaimed. "Th' gall of him! Telling me I can't pasture where I wants! By God, I'll be told I'm using his sunlight an' breathing his air!"

He stepped forward. "Curley! Chick! Dan!"

A moment later the three men stood before him.

"What is it, Jim?" asked Curley.

"You fellers drive north to-morrow. Pick up th' stragglers an' herd 'em close to that infernal line. Don't drive 'em over till I tell you, but don't let none stray south again; savy? If they want to stray north it's none of our business."

"Good!"

"Fine!"

"That's th' way to talk!"

"Don't start nothing, but if trouble comes yore way take care of yoreselves," Meeker remarked. "I'm telling you to herd up on our north range, that's all."

"Shore; we'll do it!" laughed Curley.

"Is that house on th' peak guarded?" Meeker asked.

"Somebody's there most of th' time," replied Dan Morgan.

"Yes; it's their bunk house now," explained Chick.

"All right; don't forget to-morrow."

CHAPTER 11

Three Is a Crowd

When Buck reached the line on his return Hopalong was the first man he met and his orders were to the point: "Hold this line till hell freezes, drive all H2 cows across it, an' don't start a fight; but be shore to finish any that zephyrs up. Keep yore eyes open."

Hopalong grinned and replied that he would hold the line that long and then skate on the ice, that any cow found trying to cross would get indignant, and that he and trouble were old friends. Buck laughed and rode on.

"Red Eagle, old cayuse!" said the line rider, slapping the animal resoundingly. "We're shore ready!" And Red Eagle, to show how ready he was to resent such stinging familiarities, pitched viciously and bit at his rider's leg.

"Hit her up, old devil!" yelled Hopalong, grabbing his sombrero and applying the spurs. Red Eagle settled back to earth and then shot forward at top speed along the line trail, bucking as often as he could.

It was not long before Hopalong saw a small herd of H2 cows on Bar-20 land and he rode off to head them. When he got in front of the herd he wheeled and dashed straight at it, yelling and firing his Colt, the horse squealing and pitching at every jump.

"Ki-yi, yeow-eow-eow-eow!" he yelled, and the herd, terror-stricken, wheeled and dashed towards their ranch. He followed to the line and saw them meet and terrorize another herd, and he gleefully allowed that it would be a "shore 'nuf stampede."

"Look at 'em go, old Skyrocket," he laughed. The horse began to pitch again but he soon convinced it that play time had passed.

"You old, ugly wart of a cayuse!" he cried, fighting it viciously as it reared and plunged a bit. "Don't you know I can lick four like you an' not touch leather! There, that's better. If you bite me again I'll kick yore corrugations in! But we made 'em hit th' high trail, didn't we, old hinge-back?"

He looked up and stiffened, feeling so foolish that he hardly knew enough to tear off his sombrero, for before him, sitting quietly in her saddle and looking clean through him, was Mary Meeker, a contemptuous firmness about her lips.

"Good-afternoon, Miss Meeker," he said, wondering how much she had seen and heard.

"I'll not spoil yore fun," she icily replied, riding away.

He stared after her until she had ridden around a chaparral and out of his sight, and he slammed his sombrero on the ground and swore.

"Damn th' luck!"

Then he spurred to overtake her and when he saw her again she was talking to Antonio, who was all smiles.

Hopalong muttered, savagely, "I'll spill him all over hisself some day, th' squint-eyed mud-image! Th' devil with him, if he don't like my company he can amble."

He swept up to them, his hair stirred by the breeze and his right hand resting on the butt of his Colt. Antonio was talking when he arrived, but he had no regard for him and interrupted without loss of time.

"Miss Meeker," he began, backing his horse so he could watch Antonio. "I shore hope you ain't mad. Are you?"

She looked at him coldly, and her companion muttered something and found Hopalong's eyes looking into his soul.

"Speak up if you've got anything to say, which you ain't," Hopalong commanded and then turned to the woman. "I'm shore sorry you heard me. I didn't think you was anywhere around."

"Which accounts for you terrorizing our cows an' calves," she retorted. "An' for trying to start a stampede."

Antonio stiffened at this, but did nothing because Hopalong was watching him.

"You ought to be ashamed of yoreself!" she cried, her eyes flashing and deep color surging into her cheeks. "You had no right to treat them calves that way, or to start a stampede!"

"I didn't try to start no stampede, honest," he replied, fascinated by the color playing across her face.

"You did!" she insisted, vehemently. "You may think it's funny to scare calves, but it ain't!"

"I was in a hurry," he replied, apologetically. "I shore didn't think nothing about th' calves. They was over on us an' I had to drive 'em back before I went on."

"You have no right to drive 'em back," she retorted. "They have every right to graze where the grass is good an' where they can get water. They can't live without water."

"They shore can't," he replied in swift accord, as if the needs of cattle had never before crossed his mind. "But they can get it at th' river."

"You have no right to drive 'em away from it!"

"I ain't going to argue none with you, Miss," he responded. "My orders are to drive 'em back, which I'll do."

"Do you mean to tell me that you'll keep them from water?" she demanded, her eyes flashing again.

"It ain't my fault that yore men don't hold 'em closer to th' river," he replied. "There's water a-plenty there. Yore father's keeping 'em on a dry range."

"Don't say anything about my father," she angrily retorted. "He knows his business better'n you can tell it to him."

"I'm sorry if I've gone an' said anything to make you mad," he earnestly replied. "I just wanted to show you that I'm only obeying orders. I don't want to argue with you."

"I didn't come here to argue," she quickly retorted. "I don't want you to drive our calves so hard, that's all."

"I'll be plumb tender with 'em," he assured her, grinning. "An' I didn't try to scare that other herd, honest."

"I saw you trying to scare them just before you saw me."

"Oh!" he exclaimed, chuckling as he recalled his fight with Red Eagle. "That was all th' fault of this ornery cayuse. He got th' idea into his fool head that he could throw me, so me an' him had it out right there."

She had been watching his face while he spoke and she remembered that he had fought with his horse, and believed that he was telling the truth. Then suddenly, the humorous side struck her and brought a smile to her face. "I'm sorry I didn't understand," she replied in a low voice.

"Then you ain't mad no more?" he asked eagerly.

"No; not a bit."

"I'm glad of that," he laughed, leaning forward. "You had me plumb scared to death."

"I didn't know I could scare a puncher so easy, 'specially you," she replied, flushing. "But where's yore sombrero?"

"Back where I throwed it," he grinned.

"Where you threw it?"

"Shore. I got sore when you rode away, an' didn't care much what hap-pened," he replied, coolly. Then he transfixed Antonio with his keen eyes. "If yo're so anxious to get that gun out, say so or do it," he said, slowly. "That's th' second time."

Mary watched them breathlessly, but Hopalong didn't intend to have any fighting in her presence.

"You let it alone before I take it away from you," he said. "An' I reckon you better pull out—you ain't needed around here. Go on, flit!"

Antonio glanced at Mary for orders and she nodded her head. "I don't need you; go."

Hopalong watched him depart and turned to his companion. "What's eat-ing him, anyhow?"

"I don't know. I never saw him act that way before."

"H'm. I reckon I know; but he don't want to act that way again," he said, de-cisively.

"All men are funny," she replied. "Th' idea of being scared by me when you ain't afraid of a man like him."

"That's a different kind of a scare, an' I never felt like that before. It made me want to kill somebody. I don't want you to get mad at me. I like you too much. You won't will you?"

She smiled. "No."

"Never? No matter what happens?"

"Do you care?"

"Do I care! You know I do. Look at me, Mary!"

"No; don't come any nearer. I must go—good-bye."

"Don't go; let's ride around for a while."

"But 'Tony may tell Dad; an' if he does Dad'll come up here an' make trouble. No, I must go."

"Tell 'Tony I want to see him," he replied. "If he says anything I'll make him pay for it; an' he won't do it again."

"You mustn't do that! It would make things all th' worse."

"Will you come up again to-morrow?"

She laughed. "That'll be too soon, won't it?"

"Not by a blamed sight."

"Well, I don't know. Good-bye."

"Good-bye," he said, holding out his hand.

She gave him her hand and then tried to push him away. "No, no! No, I say! I won't come any more if you do that!"

Despite her struggles he drew her to him and kissed her again and again.

"I hate you! I hate you!" she cried, her face the color of fire. "What made you do it! You've spoiled everything, an' I'll never see you again! I hate you!" and she wheeled and galloped away.

He spurred in pursuit and when he had overtaken her he grasped her horse by the bridle and stopped her. "Mary! Don't be mad—I love you!"

"Will you let me go?" she demanded, her face crimson.

"Not till you say yo're not mad."

"Please let me go," she replied, looking in his eyes. "I'm not mad at you; but you mustn't do that again. Won't you let me go before some one sees us?"

He released her and she impulsively put her hand on his arm. "Look out—an' watch 'Tony," and she was gone.

"Yo're th' best girl ever rode a cayuse," he muttered, joyously. "'Look out—an' watch 'Tony,'" he cried. "What do I care about him? I can clean out th' whole gang now. Just let 'em start something."

When he neared the place where his sombrero lay he saw Johnny in the act of picking it up, and Johnny might take a notion to make a race out of it before giving it up. "Hey, you!" Hopalong cried, dashing forward, "gimme that cover!"

"Come an' get it; I don't want it," Johnny retorted. "What made you lose it?"

"Fighting."

"Fighting! Fighting who?"

"Just fighting, Kid."

"Ah, come on an' tell me," begged Johnny. Then, like a shot: "Was it Antonio?"

"Nope."

"Who was it?"

"None of yore business," laughed Hopalong, delighted to be able to tease him.

"All right!" Johnny cried. "You wait; th' boys will be glad to learn about you an' her!"

Hopalong's hand shot out and gripped his friend's shoulder. "Don't you say a word about it, do you hear?"

"Shore. I was only fooling," replied Johnny. "Think I tell them kind of things!"

"I was too quick, Kid. I know yo're a thoroughbred. An' now I'll tell you who I was fighting. It was Red Eagle. He got a fit of pitching, an' I had to take it out of him."

"I might 'a knowed it," responded Johnny, eyeing the tracks in the sand. "But I reckoned you might 'a had a run-in with Antonio. I was saving him for myself."

"Why do you hate him so much?"

"Never mind that now. I'll tell you after I get him."

"Have you seen Buck since he came back?"

"No; why?"

Hopalong told him what the foreman had said and his friend grinned. "The good old days are coming back again, Hoppy!" he exulted.

"Shoo, fly! Shoo, fly," laughed Hopalong.

"Where are you going now?" asked Johnny.

"Where I please."

"Shore. I knowed that. That's where you want to go," grinned Johnny. "But where do you want to go?"

"Where I can't go now."

"Ah, shut up! Come on. I'll go with you."

"Well, I'm going east to tell th' fellers what Buck said."

"Go ahead. I'm with you," Johnny said, wheeling.

"I didn't ask you to come.'

"I didn't ask you to go," retorted Johnny. "Here," he said, holding out a cigar and putting another in his mouth. "Have a smoke; they're all right."

"Where the devil did you get 'em?"

"Up in Number Five."

"In Number Five!"

"Shore. Frenchy, th' son-o'-a-gun, had three of 'em hid over th' windy," Johnny explained. "I hooked 'em."

"So I reckoned; did you take 'em all?"

"Was you going up?"

"No; but did you?"

"Well, I looked good, but I didn't see none to leave."

"You wait till he finds it out," Hopalong warned.

"He won't do nothing," assured Johnny, easily. "Anyhow, yo're as guilty as me. He ain't got no right to cache cigars when we can't get to town for any. Besides, he's afraid of me."

"Scared of you! Oh, Lord, that's good!"

"Quit fooling an' get started," Johnny said, kicking his friend's horse.

"You behave, or I'll get that Antonio to lick you good," threatened Hopalong as he quieted Skyrocket.

"Let's get a-going!"

They cantered eastward, driving back Meeker's cows whenever they were found too close to the line or over it, and it was not long before they made out Lanky riding towards them. He had not yet seen them and Johnny eagerly proposed that they prepare an ambush and scare him.

"He don't scare, you fool," replied Hopalong. "A joke is a joke, but there ain't no use getting shot at when you can't shoot back. No use getting killed for a lark."

"He might shoot, mightn't he," Johnny laughed. "I didn't think about that."

Lanky looked around, waved his hand and soon joined them. "I see yo're taking care of th' Kid, Hopalong. Hullo, Kid."

"Go to blazes!" snorted Johnny.

"Has he been a good boy, Hoppy?"

"No more'n usual. He's looking for Antonio."

"*Again?*" asked Lanky, grinning. "Ain't you found him yet?"

"Ah, go on. I'll find him when I want him," Johnny retorted.

When Lanky had heard Buck's orders he frowned.

"We'll hold it all right. Wait for Billy, he'll be along purty soon. I left him chasing some cows."

"Got yore saddle so it'll stay together for more'n ten minutes at a time?" asked Johnny.

"I bought Billy's old one," Lanky replied. "Got anything to say about it?"

Billy Williams, pessimist by nature and choice, rode up and joined them and, laughing and joking, they rode towards the Peak, to see if Buck had any further orders. But they had not gone far before Hopalong stopped and thought. "You go on. I'll stay out here an' watch things."

"I'm with you, Hoppy," Johnny offered. "You fellers go on; me an' Hopalong'll take care of th' line out here."

"All right," replied Lanky. "So long."

A few minutes later Johnny turned in his saddle. "Hey, Billy!" he shouted. "What?"

"Has Lanky paid you for that saddle yet?"

"Shore; why?"

"Oh, nothing. But yo're lucky."

Billy turned and said something to Lanky and they cantered on their way.

"Hey, Hoppy; don't you tell Frenchy about them cigars," Johnny suddenly remarked some time later.

CHAPTER 12

Hobble Burns and Sleepers

The western part of the Bar-20 ranch was poor range and but few cattle were to be found on it until Big Coulee had been reached. This portion of the ranch fed quite a large number of cattle, many of which were outlaws, but because of the heavy work demanded on the more fertile southern and eastern sections it was the custom with Buck to pay little attention to the Big Coulee herds; if a man rode up there once in a while he was satisfied. This time it was Skinny who was to look over the condition of affairs around Number Two, which was not far from Big Coulee.

Detouring here and there he took his own time and followed the general direction of the western line, and about four hours after he had quitted the Peak he passed line house Number Two and shortly afterward stopped on the rim of the coulee, a brush-grown depression of a score of acres in extent, in which was a pond covering half an acre and fed by springs on the bottom, its outlet being a deep gorge cut in the soft stone. Half a mile from the pond the small stream disappeared in the sand and was lost.

He rode through the coulee without seeing a single cow and an exploration lasting over an hour resulted no better. Beyond a bear track or two among the berry bushes he saw no signs of animal life. This did not disturb him because he took it for granted that the herds had wandered back to where the grass was better. Stopping at the line house to eat, he mounted and rode towards the hills to report to Hopalong.

Suddenly it struck him that he had seen no cow tracks in the mud around the water hole and he began to hunt for cattle. Using Pete's glasses constantly to sweep the plain for the missing herds, it was not until he had reached a point half-way to the Peak that his search was rewarded by seeing a calf far to the east of him. Watching it until it stood out boldly to his sight he followed an impulse and rode towards it to examine it at close range.

Upon getting near it he saw that it bore the V notch of the H2 cut in its ear, and that it was not branded. He thought it strange that an H2 "sleeper" should be so far from home, without a mother to lead it astray, and he roped it to look more closely at the notch. His opinion was that it had been done very recently, for the cartilage had not yet dried on the edges. Releasing the animal he mounted and started for the line, muttering to himself.

As he swung into the line trail he saw a lame cow limping around a thicket and he spurred forward, roped and threw it, this time giving no thought to the ears, for its brand was that of the Bar-20. He looked at the hocks and found them swollen and inflamed, and his experience told him that it had been done by hobbles. This, to him, explained why the calf was alone, and it gave him the choice of two explanations for the hobbling and the newly cut ear notch on the calf. Either the H2 was sleepering Bar-20 calves for their irons later on, or rustlers were at work. It seemed incredible that any H2 puncher should come that distance to make a few sleepers—but the herd had not been to the water hole! He was greatly wrought up and it was none the more pleasant to be unable to say where the blame lay. There was only one thing to do and that was to scout around and try to find a clue to the perpetrators—and, perhaps, catch the thieves at work. This proved to be unfruitful until he came to North Hill, where he found a cow dead from gunshot. He put spurs to his horse and rode straight for the Peak, which he reached as night fell and as Hopalong, Red, Pete, and Lanky were eating supper and debating the line conditions.

Skinny joined them and listened to the conversation, wordless, nodding or shaking his head at the points made. When he had finished eating he leaned back against his saddle and fumbled for tobacco and pipe, gazing reflectively into the fire, at which he spat. Hopalong turned in time to see the act and, knowing Skinny's peculiarities, asked abruptly: "What's on yore mind, Skinny?"

"Little piece of hell," was the slow reply, and it gained the attention of the others at once. "I saw a H2 sleeper, up just above th' Bend and half way between it an' th' line."

"That so!" exclaimed Hopalong.

"Long way from home—starting in young to ramble," Red laughed. "Lazy trick, that sleepering."

"This here calf had a brand new V—hadn't healed yet," Skinny remarked, lighting his pipe. "An' it didn't—*puff*—have no—*puff*—mother," he added, significantly.

"Huh, weaned, you chump—but that fresh V is shore funny."

"Go on, Skinny," ordered Hopalong, eagerly.

"I found its mother an hour later—hobble-burned an' limping; an' it wasn't no H2 cow, neither; it was one of ourn."

"Rustling!" cried Hopalong.

"Th' H2 is doing it," contradicted Red, quickly.

"They wouldn't take a chance like that," replied Hopalong.

"There ain't no rule for taking chances," Red rejoined. "Some men'll gamble with hell itself—you, for instance, in gun-play."

"What else?" demanded Hopalong of Skinny.

"That Big Coulee herd ain't up there, an' hain't been near th' water hole for so long th' mud's smooth around the edges of th' pond; kin savvy?"

"It's rustlers, by God!" cried Hopalong, looking triumphantly at Red.

"An' I found a dead cow—shot—on th' upper end of North Hill," Skinny added.

"H2!" Red shouted. "They're doing it!"

"Yes, likely; it was an H2 cow," Skinny placidly explained.

"Why in hell can't you tell things in a herd, 'stead of stringin' 'em out like a stiff reata trailing to soften!" Red cried. "Yo're the damndest talker that ever opened a mouth!"

Skinny took the pipe from his mouth and looked at Red.

"I allus get it all out, don't I? What are you kicking about?"

"Yes, you do; like a five thousand herd filtering through a two-foot gate!"

"Mebby th' herd drifted to th' valley," Pete offered.

"Mebby nothing!" Red retorted. "Why, we can't *drive* 'em down here without 'em acting loco about it."

"Cows are shore fool animals," Pete suggested in defence.

"There's more than cows that are fool animals," Red snapped, while Skinny laughed to see Pete get his share.

Sixteen miles to the southeast of the Peak, Meeker sat on a soap box and listened, with the rest of his outfit, to what Curley was saying—"an' when I got down a good ways south I found two young calves bellering for their maws. They was sleepers; an' an hour later I found them same maws bellering for them calves—they was limping a-plenty an' their hocks looked burned—hobble burns."

Meeker mused for a moment and then arose. "You ride that range regular, an' be cautious. Watch towards Eagle. If you catch any sons-of-skunks gamboling reckless, an' they can't explain why they are flitting over our range, shoot off yore gun accidental—there won't be no inquest."

CHAPTER 13

Hopalong Grows Suspicious

The eastern sky grew brighter and the dim morning light showed a group of men at breakfast on the Peak. They already had been given their orders and as soon as each man finished eating he strode off to where his horse was picketed with the others, mounted, and rode away. Pete had ridden in late the night before and was still sleeping in the house, Hopalong not wishing to awaken him until it was absolutely necessary.

Red Connors, riding back to the house from the horse herd, drew rein for a final word. "I'm going out to watch that unholy drift of Meeker's cows, just this side of th' half-way point. They was purty thick last night when I rode in. I told Johnny to keep on that part of th' line, for I reckon things will get too crowded for one man to handle. Th' two of us can take care of 'em, all right. You knows where you can find us if you need us."

"I don't like that drift, but I'll stay here an' give Pete an hour more sleep," Hopalong replied. "Buck didn't know just when he'd be down again, but I'm looking for him before noon, just th' same."

"Well, me an' Johnny'll stop th' drift. So long," and Red cantered away, whistling softly.

Hopalong kicked out the fire and walked restlessly around the plateau, puzzled by the massing of the H2 cows along the line. The play was obvious enough on its face, for it meant that Meeker, tired of inaction, had decided to force the issue by driving into the valley. But Hopalong, suspicious to a degree, was not satisfied with that solution.

On more than one occasion he had searched past the obvious and found deeper motives, and to this ferment of thought he owed his life many times. He, himself, essentially a schemer and trusting no one but the members of his outfit, accused others of scheming and bent his mind to outwit them. Buck often irritated him greatly, for the foreman, optimistic and believing all men honest until they proved to be otherwise, held that Meeker thought himself to be in the right and so was justified in his attempt to use the valley. Hopalong believed that Meeker was not square, that he knew he had no right to the valley and was trying to steal range; he maintained that the wiser way was to believe all men crooked and put the burden on them of proving otherwise; then he was prepared for anything.

A better cow-man than Buck Peters never lived; he knew the cattle industry thoroughly, was honest, fair, and fearless, maintained an even temper and tried to avoid fighting until the last ditch had been reached. But it was an indisputable fact that Hopalong Cassidy had proved himself to be the best man on the ranch when danger threatened. He grasped situations quickly and clearly and his companions looked to him for suggestions when the sky was clouded by impending conflict. Buck realized that his line-foreman was eminently better qualified to handle the skirmish line than himself, that Hopalong could carry out things which would fall flat if any one else attempted them. Back of Buck's confidence was the pleasing knowledge that no man had ever yet got in the first shot against Hopalong on an "even break," and that when his puncher's gun exploded it was all over; this is why Hopalong could, single-handed, win out in any reasonable situation.

While Hopalong turned the matter over in his mind he thought he saw a figure move among the chaparrals far to the south and he whipped out his glasses, peering long and steadily at the place. Then he put them away and laughed softly. "You can't fool me, by God! I'll let you make yore play—an' if Pete don't kill a few of you I'm a liar. Here are th' shells—pick out th' pea."

Returning to the house he shook Pete. "Hey, get up!"

Pete bounded up, wide awake in an instant. "Yes?"

"Put on yore clothes an' come outside a minute," he ordered, going out.

Pete finished buttoning his vest when he joined his friend, who was pointing south. "Pete, they're playing for this house, an' I can't stay—Red an' Johnny may need me any minute. Down there an H2 rider is watching this house. Meeker is massing his cows along th' line for two reasons; he's trying to draw us away from here so he can get in, an' he's going to push over th' line if he falls down here. You stay in that shack. Don't leave it for a second, understand? Stop anybody that comes up here if you have to kill him. But don't leave this house for nothing, savvy?"

"Go ahead. I savvy."

Hopalong vaulted to his saddle and started away. "I'll get somebody to help you as soon as I can," he called.

"Don't need anybody!" Pete shouted, going inside and barring the door.

Hopalong was elated by the way he had forestalled Meeker, and also because it was Pete who guarded the house. He knew his companions only as a man can know friends with whom he has lived for nearly a score of years. Red was too good a fighter to be cooped up while trouble threatened in the open; Johnny, rash and hot-tempered, could be tempted to leave the house to indulge in personal combat if taunted enough, and he, too, was too good a man in a *mêlée* to remain on the Peak. The man for the house was Pete, for he was accurate enough for that short range, he was unemotional and did not do much thinking for himself when it ran counter to his instructions; he had been told to stay in the house and hold it, and that, Hopalong felt certain, he would do.

"Pete'll hold 'em with one leg in th' air if they happen to be taking a step when he sees 'em," he laughed.

But Pete was to be confronted with a situation so unexpected and of such a nature that for once in his life he was going to forget orders—and small blame to him.

CHAPTER 14

The Compromise

It was night and on the H2 sickly, yellow lights gleamed from the ranch houses. From the bunk house came occasional bursts of song, the swinging choruses thundering out on the night air, deep-toned and strong. In the foreman's quarters the clatter of dishes was soon stilled and shortly afterward the light in the kitchen could be seen no more. A girl stood in the kitchen door for a moment and then, singing, went inside and the door closed. The strumming of a guitar and much laughter came from Antonio's shack, for now he had Juan and Sanchez to help him pass the time.

Meeker emerged from a corral, glanced above him for signs of the morrow's weather, and then stood and gazed at the shack. Turning abruptly on his heel he strode to the bunk house and smiled grimly as the chorus roared out, for he had determined upon measures which might easily change the merriment to mourning before another day passed. He had made up his mind to remain inactive no longer, but to put things to the test—his outfit and himself against the Bar-20.

He entered the building and slamming the door shut behind him, waited until the chorus was finished. When the last note died away he issued his orders for the next day, orders which pleased his men, who had chafed even more than he under the galling inaction, since they did not thoroughly understand the reasons for it.

"I had them cows herded up north for th' last three days so they'd be ready for us when we wanted 'em," he said, and then leaped at the door and jerked it open, peering about outside. Turning, he beckoned Doc Riley to him and the two stepped outside, closing the door behind them. Great noise broke out within the house as his orders were repeated and commented on. Meeker and

Doc moved to the corner of the building and consulted earnestly for several minutes, the foreman gesticulating slowly.

"But Juan said they had a man to guard it," Doc replied.

"Yes; he told me," Meeker responded. "I'm going to fix that before I go to bed—we've got to coax him out on some excuse. Once we get him out of th' house we can cover him, an' th' rest'll be easy. I won't be able to be with you— I'll have to stay outside where I can move around an' look out for th' line trouble, an' where they can see me. But you an' Jack can hold it once you get in. By God, you *must* get in, an' you *must* hold it!"

"We'll do it if it's possible."

"That's th' way to talk. Th' boys seem pleased about it," Meeker laughed, listening to the joy loose in the house.

"Pleased! They're tickled plumb to death. They've got so sore about having to keep their guns quiet that when they cut loose—well, something's due to happen."

"I don't want that if there's any other way," Meeker replied earnestly. "If this thing can be done without wholesale slaughter we've got to do it that way. Remember, Doc, this whole country is backing Peters. He's got thirteen men now, an' he can call on thirty more in two days. Easy is th' way, easy."

"I'll spend th' next hour pounding that into their hot heads," Doc replied. "They're itching for a chance to square up for everything. They're some sore, been so for a couple of days, about that line house being guarded—they get sore plumb easy now, you know."

"Well, good-night, Doc."

"Good-night, Jim."

Meeker went towards his own house and as he neared the kitchen door a deep-throated wolf-hound bayed from the kennels, inciting a clamorous chorus from the others. Meeker shouted and the noise changed to low, deep, rumbling growls which soon became hushed. Chains rattled over wood and the fierce animals returned to their grass beds to snarl at each other. The frightened crickets took up their song again and poured it on the silence of the night.

Meeker opened the door and strode through the kitchen and into the living room, his eyes squinting momentarily because of the light. His daughter was sitting in a rocking chair, sewing industriously, and she looked up, welcoming him. He replied to her and, dexterously tossing his sombrero on a peg in the wall where it caught and hung swinging, walked heavily to the southern window and stood before it, hands clasped behind his back, staring moodily into the star-stabbed darkness. Down the wind came the faint, wailing howl of a wolf, quavering and distant, and the hounds again shattered the peaceful quiet. But he heard neither, so absorbed was he by his thoughts. Mary looked at him for a moment and then took up her work again and resumed sewing, for he had done this before when things had gone wrong, and frequently of late.

He turned suddenly and in response to the movement she looked up, again laying her sewing aside. "What is it?" she asked.

"Trouble, Mary. I want to talk to you."

"I'm always ready to listen, Daddy," she replied. "I wish you wouldn't worry so. That's all you've done since we left Montana."

"I know; but I can't help it," he responded, smiling faintly. "But I don't care much as long as I've got you to talk it over with. Yo're like yore mother that way, Mary; she allus made things easy, somehow. An' she knew more'n most women do about things."

"Yo're my own Daddy," she replied affectionately. "Now tell me all about it."

"Well," he began, sitting on the table, "I'm being cheated out of my rights. I find lines where none exist. I'm hemmed in from water, th' best grazing is held from me, my cows are driven helter-skelter, my pride hurt, an' my men mocked. When I say I must have water I'm told to go to th' river for it, twenty miles from my main range, an' lined with quicksands; an' yet there is water close to me, water enough for double th' number of cows of both ranches! It is good, clean water, unfailing an' over a firm bottom, flowing through thirty miles of th' best grass valley in this whole sun-cursed section. Two hundred miles in any direction won't show another as good. An' yet, I dassn't set my foot in it—I can't drive a cow across that line!"

He paused and then continued: "I'm good an' sick of it all. I ain't going to swaller it no longer, not a day. Peace is all right, but not at th' price I'm paying! I'd ruther die fighting for what's mine than put up with what I have since I came down here."

"What are you going to do?" she asked quietly.

"I'm going to have a force on that line by to-morrow night!" he said, gradually working himself into a temper. "*I'm* going to hold them hills, an' th' springs at th' bottom of 'em. *I'm* going to use that valley an' I'll fight until th' last man goes under!"

"Don't say that, Daddy," she quickly objected. "There ain't no line worth yore life. What good will it do you when yo're dead? You can get along without it if it comes to that. An' what'll happen to me if you get killed?"

"No, girl," he replied. "You've held me back too long. I should 'a struck in th' beginning, before they got so set. It would 'a been easier then. I don't like range wars any more'n anybody, but it's come, an' I've got to hold up my end—an' my head!"

"But th' agreement?" she queried, fearful for his safety. She loved her father with all her heart, for he had been more than a father to her; he had always confided in her and weighed her judgment; they had been companions since her mother died, which was almost beyond her memory; and now he would risk his life in a range war, a vindictive, unmerciful conflict which usually died out when the last opponent died—and perhaps he was in the wrong. She knew the fighting ability of that shaggy, tight-lipped breed of men that mocked Death with derisive, profane words, who jibed whether in *mêlée* or duel with as light hearts as if engaged in nothing more dangerous than dancing. And she had heard, even in Montana, of the fighting qualities of the outfit that rode range for the Bar-20. If they must be fought, then let it be for the right principles and not otherwise. And there was Hopalong!—she knew in her heart that she loved him, and feared it and fought it, but it was true; and he was the active leader of his outfit, the man who was almost the foreman, and who would be in the thickest of the fighting. She didn't purpose to have him killed if he was in the right, or in the wrong, either.

"Agreement!" he cried, hotly. "Agreement! I hear that every time I say anything to that crowd, an' now you give it to me! Agreement be damned! Nason never said nothing about any agreement when he told me he had found a ranch for me. He wouldn't 'a dealt me a hand like that, one that'd give me th' worst of it in a show-down! He found out all about everything before he turned over my check to 'em."

"But they say there is one, an' from th' way they act it looks that way."

"I don't believe anything of th' sort! It's just a trick to hog that grass an' water!"

"Hopalong Cassidy told me there was one—he told me all about it. He was a witness."

"Hopalong hell!" he cried, remembering the day that Doc had been shot, and certain hints which Antonio had let fall.

"Father!" she exclaimed, her eyes flashing.

"Oh, don't mind me," he replied. "I don't know what I'm saying half th' time. I'm all mixed up, now-a-days."

"I believe he was telling the truth—he wouldn't lie to me," she remarked, decisively.

He looked at her sharply. "Well, am I to be tied down by something I don't know about? Am I to swallow everything I hear? *I* don't know about no agreement, except what th' Bar-20 tells me. An' if there was one it was made by th' Three Triangle, wasn't it?—an' not by Nason or me? Am I th' Three Triangle? Am I to walk th' line on something I didn't make? *I* didn't make it!—oh, I'm tired arguing about it."

"Well, even if there wasn't no agreement you can't blame them for trying to keep their land, can you?" she asked, idly fingering her sewing. "The land is theirs, ain't it?"

"Did you ever hear of free grass an' free water?"

"I never heard of nothing else till I came down here," she admitted. "But it may be different here."

"Well, it ain't different!" he retorted. "An' if it is it won't stay so. What goes in Montanny will go down here. Anyhow, I don't want their land—all I want is th' use of it, same as they have. But they're hogs, an' want it all."

"They say it ain't big enough for their herds."

"Thirty-five miles long, and five miles wide, in th' valley alone, an' it ain't big enough! Don't talk to me like that! You know better."

"I'm only trying to show it to you in every light," she responded. "Mebby yo're right, an' mebby you ain't; that's what we've got to find out. I don't want to think of you fightin', 'specially if yo're wrong. Suppose yo're killed—an' you might be. Ain't there some other way to get what you want, if yo're determined to go ahead?"

"Yes, I might be killed, but I won't go alone!" he cried savagely. "Fifty years, man an' boy, I've lived on th' range, taking every kick of fortune, riding hard an' fightin' hard when I had to. I ain't no yearling at any game about cows, girl."

"But can't you think of some other way?" she repeated.

"I've got to get that line house on th' hill," he went on, not heeding her question. "Juan told me three days ago, that they've put a guard in it now—but I'll have it by noon to-morrow, for I've been thinking hard since then. An' once in it, they can't take it from me! With that in my hands I can laugh at 'em, for I can drive my cows over th' line close by it, down th' other side of th' hill, an' into th' valley near th' springs. They'll be under my guns in th' line house, an' let anybody try to drive 'em out again! Two men can hold that house—it was built for defense against Indians. Th' top of th' hill is level as a floor an' only two hundred yards to th' edge. Nobody can cross that space under fire an' live."

"If they can't cross it an' live, how can *you* cross it, when th' house is guarded? An' when th' first shot is fired you'll have th' whole outfit down on you from behind like wild fire. Then what'll you do? You can't fight between two fires."

"By God, yo're right! Yo're th' brains of this ranch," his eyes squinting to hide his elation. He paced back and forth, thinking deeply. Five minutes passed, then ten, and he suddenly turned and faced her, to unfold the plan he had worked out the day before. He had been leading up to it and now he knew how to propose it. "I've got it. I've got it! Not a shot, not a single shot!"

"Tell me," she said smiling.

He slowly unfolded it, telling her of the herds waiting to be driven across the line to draw the Bar-20 men from the Peak, and of the part she was to play. She listened quietly, a troubled frown on her face, and when he had finished and asked her what she thought of it she looked at him earnestly and slowly replied: "Do you think that's fair? Do you want *me* to do that?"

"What's unfair about it? They're yore enemies as much as they are mine, ain't they? Ain't everything fair in love an' war, as th' books say?"

"In war, perhaps; but not in love," she replied in a low voice, thinking of the man who wore her flower.

"Now look here!" he cried, leaning forward. "Don't you go an' get soft on any of that crowd! Do you hear?"

"We won't mix love an' war, Daddy," she said, decisively. "You take care of yore end, that's war; an' let me run my part. I'll do what I want to when it comes to falling in love; an' I'll help you to-morrow. I don't want to do it, but I will; you've got to have th' line house, an' without getting between two fires. I'll do it, Daddy."

"Good girl! Yo're just like yore mother—all grit!" he cried, going towards the door. "An' I reckon I won't have to take no hand in *yore* courting," he said, grabbing his sombrero. "Yo're shore able to run yore own."

"But *promise* me you won't interfere," she said, calmly, hiding her triumph.

"It's a go. I'll keep away from th' sparking game," he promised. "I'm going out to see th' boys for a minute," and the door slammed, inciting the clamor of the kennels again, which he again hushed. "Damn 'em!" he muttered, exultantly. "They tried to hog th' range, an' then they want my girl! But they *won't* hog th' range no more, an' I'll put a stop to th' courting when she plays her cards to-morrow, an' without having any hand in it. Lord, I win every trick!" he laughed.

CHAPTER 15

Antonio Meets Friends

Before daylight the next morning Antonio left the ranch and rode south, bearing slightly to the west, so as not to leave his trail in Curley's path. He was to meet some of Shaw's men who would come for more cattle. When a dozen miles southwest of the ranch house he espied them at work on the edge of an arroyo. They had a fire going and were re-branding a calf. Far out on the plain was a dead cow, the calf's mother, shot because they had become angered by its belligerency when it had gone "on th' prod." They had driven cow and calf hard and when they tried to separate the two the mother had charged viciously, narrowly missing one of them, to die by a shot from the man most concerned. Meanwhile the calf had run back over its trail and they had roped it as it was about to plunge over the bank of the arroyo.

"You fools!" yelled Antonio, galloping towards them. "Don't you know better'n to blot on this range! How many times have I told you that Curley rides south!"

"He never gets this far west—we've watched him," retorted Clausen, angrily.

"Is that any reason why he can't!" demanded Antonio. "How do you know what he'll do?"

"Yes!" rejoined Clausen. "An' I reckon he can find that steep-bank hollow with th' rope gate, can't he? Suppose he finds th' herds you holds in it for us—what then?"

"It's a whole lot farther west than here!" retorted Antonio, hotly. "They never go to Little Muddy, an' if they do, that's a chance we've got to take. But you can wait till you get to th' mesa before you change brands, can't you!"

"Aw, close yore pie-sump!" cried Frisco. "Who th' devil is doing this, anyhow? You make more noise than Cheyenne on th' Fourth of July!"

"What right have you fellers got to take chances an' hobble *me* with trouble?"

"Who's been doing all th' sleepering, hey?" sarcastically demanded Dick Archer. "Let Meeker's gang see the God-forsaken bunch of sleepers running on their range an' you'll be hobbled with trouble, all right."

Through laziness, carelessness, or haste calves might not be branded when found with branded cows. Feeling was strong against the use of the "running iron," a straight iron rod about eighteen inches long which was heated and used as a pencil on the calf's hide, and a man caught with one in his possession could expect to be dealt with harshly; it was a very easy task to light a fire and "run" a brand, and the running iron was easily concealed under the saddle flap. But it was not often that a puncher would carry a stamping iron, for it was cumbersome. With a running iron a brand could be changed, or the wrong mark put on unbranded cattle; but the stamping iron would give only one pattern.

When a puncher came across an unbranded calf with its branded mother, and the number which escaped the roundup was often large, he branded it, if he had an iron; if he did not have the iron he might cut the calf's ear to conform to the notch in its mother's ears. When the calf was again seen it might have attained its full growth. In that case there was no branded mother to show to whom it belonged; but its cut ears would tell.

These unbranded, ear-cut calves were known as "sleepers" and, in localities where cattle stealing was being or had been carried on to any extent, such sleepering was regarded with strong suspicion, and more than one man had paid a dear price for doing the work.

The ear mark of the H2 was a V, while the Bar-20 depended entirely on the brand, and part of its punchers' saddle equipment was a stamping iron.

Cowmen held sleepering in strong disfavor because it was an easy matter for a maverick hunter or a rustler to drive off these sleepers and, after altering the ear cut, to brand them with his own or some strange brand; and it was easy to make sleepers.

In the case of rustling the separation of branded calves and mothers was imperative, for should any one see a cow of one brand with a calf of another, it was very probable that a committee of discretionary powers would look into the matter. Hobbling and laming mothers and then driving away the calves were not the only ways of separating them and of weaning the calves, for a shot was often as good a way as any; but as dead cows, if found, were certain to tell the true story, this was not generally employed.

"Yes," laughed Frisco. "What about th' sleepers?"

They were discreetly silent about the cow they had killed, for they were ashamed of having left such a sign; but they would not stand Antonio's scorn and anger, and that of the other members of the band, and so said nothing about it.

"Where's th' mother of this calf?" demanded Antonio, not heeding the remarks about sleepers.

"Hanged if I know," replied Clausen, easily; "an' hanged if I care—we can leave *one* cow, I reckon."

"Got many for us this time?" asked Archer as they rode west, driving before them the newly branded calf.

"Not many," replied Antonio. "It's risky, with Curley loose. We won't be able to do much till th' fighting starts."

When they reached their destination they came to a deep, steep-walled depression, exit from which was had at only one end where a narrow trail wound up to the plain. Across this trail at its narrowest point was stretched a lariat.

The depression itself was some ten acres in extent and was well covered with grass, while near the southwest corner was a muddy pool providing water for the herd which was now held captive.

Clausen rode down and removed the rope, riding into the basin to hasten the egress of the herd. When the last cow had scrambled out and joined its fellows, Archer and Frisco drove them west, leaving Clausen to say a few final words with Antonio before joining them.

"How's th' range war coming on?"

"Fine!" laughed Antonio. "Meeker's going to attack th' line house on th' Peak, though what good it'll do him is more than I can figure out. I put it in his head because it'll start th' fight. I had to grin when I heard Meeker and Doc planning it last night—they're easy."

"Gee!" laughed Clausen. "It's a stiff play. Who's going to win? Meeker?"

"Meeker's going to get th' licking of his life. I know that Bar-20 gang, every one. I've lived down here for some time, an' I know what they've done. Don't never get in a six-shooter argument with that feller Cassidy; an' if his friend Connors tells you to stop under eight hundred yards, you do it, an' trust to yore tongue, or Colt. He's th' devil hisself with a Winchester."

"Much obliged—but I ain't so bad that way myself. Well, I'm going to ooze west. Got any word for Shaw?"

"I'll sent word by Benito—I'll know more about it tomorrow."

"All right," and Clausen was being jerked over the scenery by his impatient mount.

Antonio wheeled and rode at a gallop, anxious to be found on northern range, and eager to learn the result of his foreman's attack.

"Salem," once a harpooner on a whaling vessel, now cook for the H2, drove home from Eagle in the chuck wagon, which contained food supplies for his ranch. He was in that state hovering between tears and song, which accounted for the winding trail his wagon wheels left, and also for him being late. He had tarried in Eagle longer than he should have, for he was reluctant to quit the society of his several newly made friends, who so pleasantly allowed him to "buy" for them. When he realized how the time had flown and that his outfit would be clamoring for the noonday meal, such clamoring being spicy and personal in its expression, he left the river trail before he should and essayed a shorter way home, chanting a sea song.

A pirate bold, on th' Spanish Main—
Set sail, yo-ho, an' away we go—

"Starboard yore helm, you lubbers!" he shouted when the horses headed towards Mexico. Then he saw a large bulk lying on the sand a short distance ahead and he sat bolt upright.

"There she blows! No, blast me, it's a dead cow!"

He drove closer to it and, stopping the team, staggered over to see what had killed it.

"Damn me, if it ain't shot in th' port eye!" he ejaculated. "If I find the lubber what's sinkin' our cows, I'll send him to Davy Jones' locker!"

He returned to the wagon and steered nor' by nor' east, once more certain of his bearings, for he knew the locality now, and sometime later he saw Curley riding towards him.

"Ahoy!" he yelled. "Ahoy, you wind-jammer!"

"What's eating you? Why are you so late?" demanded Curley, approaching. "You needn't say—I know."

"Foller my wake an' you'll see a dead cow," cried Salem. "Deader'n dead, too! Shot in th' starboard—no, was it starboard? Now, damned if I know—reckon it was in th' port eye, though I didn't see no port light; aye, 'twas in th' port—"

"What in the hell do I care what eye it was!" shouted Curley. "Where is it?"

"Eight knots astern. Shot in th' port eye, an', as I said, deader'n dead. Flew our flag, too."

Curley, believing that the cook had seen what he claimed, wheeled abruptly and galloped away to report it to Meeker.

"Hey! Ain't you going to *see* it?" yelled Salem, and as he received no reply, turned to his team. "Come on, weigh anchor! Think I want to lay out here all night? 'A-sailing out of Salem town—'" he began, and then stopped short and thought. "I *knowed* it!—it *was* th' port eye! Same side th' flag was on!" he exclaimed, triumphantly.

CHAPTER 16

The Feint

On the boundary line alert and eager punchers rode at a canter to and fro, watching the herds to the south of them, and quick to turn back all that strayed across the line. Just east of the middle point of the boundary Red and Johnny met and compared notes, and both reported the same state of affairs, which was that the cattle came constantly nearer.

Johnny removed his field glasses from his eyes.

"There's punchers with that herd, Red. Three of 'em."

"I reckoned so."

"Wonder what they think they're going to do?"

"We'll know purty soon."

"They're coming this way."

"If you had th' brains of a calf you'd know they wouldn't go south."

"Think they're going to rush us?" Johnny asked, eagerly.

"No; course not!" retorted Red. "They're going to make 'em stand on their heads!"

Johnny began to hum—

Joyous Joe got a juniper jag
A-jogging out of Jaytown;
Joyous Joe got a juniper jag—

"We'll show that prickly pear from Montanny some fine points."

"Now, look here, Kid; don't you let 'em get a cow across th' line. Shoot every one, but keep yore eyes on th' gang."

"'Joyous Joe got a juniper jag—' Come on, you fools!"

"Wonder where Hopalong is?" Red asked.

"Up on th' Peak, I reckon. *Hey*, Billy!" he yelled. "Here comes Billy, Red."

"I guessed as much when you yelled; if you don't yell away from my ear next time I'll kick yore pants over yore hat. Damned idiot, you!"

"Hullo, Billy," cried Johnny, ignoring Red's remarks. "Just in time for th' pie. Where's Hopalong?"

"In th' hills."

"You get along an' tell him what's doing out here," ordered Red. "Go lively!"

"Reckon I'd better stay an' give you a hand; you'll need it before long," Billy replied.

"You know what Hopalong said, don't you?" blazed Red. "What do you think me an' th' Kid are made of, anyhow? You go on, an' quick!"

"Send Johnny," Billy suggested, hopefully.

"Why, you coyote!" cried Johnny, excitedly. "Th' idea! You go on!"

"Yo're a pair of hogs," grumbled Billy, riding off. "I'll get square, someday. Hope they lick you!"

"Run along, little boy," jeered Johnny. "Oh, gee! Here they come!" he cried as Billy rode behind the chaparral. "Look at 'em!"

"*Let* 'em come!" cried Billy, returning. "We'll lick 'em!"

"Get out of here!" shouted Red, drawing his Winchester from its sheath. "For God's sake, do what yo're told! Want to let Meeker win out?"

"Nope; so long," and Billy galloped away.

"That ain't a herd!" cried Johnny, elated. "That's only a handful. It's a scrawny looking bunch, men an' all. Come on, you coyotes!" he yelled, waving his rifle.

"You chump; this ain't the real play—it's a blind, a wedge," Red replied. "They're pushing a big one through somewhere else."

"I'm shore glad Billy went, an' not me," Johnny remarked.

"There's Morgan," Red remarked. "I know his riding."

"Bet you won't know it when th' show's over. An' there's Chick, too. He needs a licking. You won't know his riding, neither."

The herd came rapidly forward and the men who were guarding it waved their sombreros and urged it on. Red, knowing that he would be crowded if he waited until the cows were upon him, threw his rifle to his shoulder and began to shoot rapidly, and cow after cow dropped, and the rush was stopped. Before the H2 men could get free from the panic-stricken herd Red and Johnny were within a hundred yards of them and when they looked up it was to see Red covering them, while Johnny, pleased by the reduced range, was dropping more cows.

"Stop!" Red shouted, angrily.

"Huh!" exclaimed Johnny, looking up. "Oh, I thought you was talking to me," he muttered, and then dropped another cow.

"What in hell do you think yo're doing?" yelled Morgan.

"Just practicing," retorted Johnny. He quickly swung his rifle on Chick. "Hands up! No more of that!"

"You've got gall, shooting our cows!" replied Chick.

"Get 'em up, boy!" snapped Johnny, and Chick slowly raised his arms, speaking rapidly.

"What do you take us for!" shouted Ed Joyce, frantic at his helplessness.

"Coyotes," replied Red. "An' since coyotes don't ride, you get off'n them cayuses, *pronto.*"

"Like hell!" retorted Ed.

Johnny's rifle cracked and Ed tumbled off his dead horse, and when he arose the air was blue.

"Nex' gent say 'I,'" called Johnny.

"I'll be damned if I'll stand for that!" yelled Morgan, reaching for his gun. The next thing he knew was that the air was full of comets, and that his horse was dead.

Chick sullenly dismounted and stood watching Red, who was now in vastly better spirits, since the H2 rifles were on the horses and too far away from their owners to be of any use. The range was too great for good revolver shooting even if they could get them into action.

"Watch 'em," said Red, firing. Chick's horse, stung to frenzy by the wound, kicked up its heels and bolted, leaving the three punchers stranded ten miles from home.

"Turn around an' hit th' back trail," ordered Red. "No back talk!"

"I'll bust you wide open, someday, you red-headed wart!" threatened Dan, shaking his fist at the grinning line man. "That's a hell of a thing to do, that is."

"Shut up an' go home. Ain't you got enough?" shouted Red.

"Just wait," yelled Ed Joyce.

"That's two with th' waiting habit," laughed Johnny.

"What do—" began Chick, stepping forward.

"Shut up! Who told you to open yore face!" cried Red, savagely. "Get home! G'wan!"

"Walk, you coyotes, walk!" exulted Johnny.

He and his companions watched the three angry punchers stride off towards the H2 and then Red told Johnny to ride west while he, himself, would go east to help his friends if they should need him. They had just begun to separate when Johnny uttered a shout of joy. Antonio had joined the trio of walkers and they were pulling him from his horse. He waved his arms excitedly, but Chick had him covered. Dan and Ed were already on the animal and they quickly pulled Chick up behind them, narrowly watching Antonio all the while. The horse fought for some time and then started south, the riders shouting while Antonio, still waving his arms, plodded homeward on foot.

Great joy filled Johnny's heart as he gloated over Antonio's predicament. "Hoof it, you snake! Kick up th' dust!"

"They can't get in th' game again for some time, till they get cayuses," remarked Red. "That makes four less to deal with."

"He acts like he had all eternity to get nowhere—look at him! Let's go down an' rope him. He's on th' prod now—we can have a lot of fun."

"If I go down there it'll be to plug him good," Red replied. "You hang around out here for a while. I'm goin' west—Pete's in that house alone—so long, Kid."

Johnny grinned a farewell to Antonio and followed instructions while his friend rode towards the Peak to assist Pete, the lonely, who as it happened, would be very glad to see him.

CHAPTER 17

Pete Is Tricked

Pete Wilson grumbled, for he was tiring of his monotonous vigil, and almost hoped the H2 would take the house because of the excitement incident to its recapture. At first his assignment had pleased, but as hour after hour passed with growing weariness, he chafed more and more and his temper grew constantly shorter.

With the exception of smoking he had exhausted every means of passing the time; he knew to a certainty how many bushes and large stones were on the plateau, the ranges between him and distant objects, and other things, and now he had to fell back on his pipe.

"Wish some son-of-a-thief would zephyr up an' start something," he muttered. "If I stays in this fly-corral much longer I'll go loco. A couple of years back we wouldn't have waited ten minutes in a case like this—we'd 'a chased that crowd off th' range quick. What's getting into us has got me picking out th' festive pea, all right."

He stopped at the east window and scrutinized the line as far as he could see the dim, dusty, winding trail, hoping that some of the outfit would come into sight. Then he slid the Sharps out of the window and held it on an imaginary enemy, whom he pretended was going to try to take the house. While he thought of caustic remarks, with which to greet such a person, he saw the head of a horse push up into view over the edge of the hill.

Sudden hope surged through him and shocked him to action. He cocked the rifle, the metallic clicks sweet to his ears. Then he saw the rider, and it was—Mary Meeker.

Astonishment and quick suspicion filled his mind and he held the weapon ready to use on her escort, should she have one. Her horse reared and plunged and, deciding that she was alone, and ashamed to be covering a woman, he slid the gun back into the room, leaning it against the wall close at his hand, not losing sight of the rider for a moment.

"Now, what th' devil is she doing up here, anyhow?" he puzzled, and then a grin flickered across his face as the possible solution came to him. "Mebby she wants Hopalong," he muttered, and added quickly, "Purty as blazes, too!" And she did make a pretty picture even to his scoffing and woman-hating mind.

She was having trouble with her mount, due to the spurring it was getting on the side farther from the water. It reared and plunged, bucking sideways, up-and-down and fence-cornered, zigzagging over the ground forward and back, and then began to pitch "stiff-legged." Pete's eyes glowed with the appreciation of a master rider and he was filled with admiration, which soon became enthusiastic, over her saddle-ease and cool mastery. She seemed to be a part of the horse.

"She'd 'a been gone long ago if she was fool enough to sit one of them side saddle contraptions," he mused. "A-straddle is th' only—*Good!* All right! Yo're a stayer!" he exclaimed as she stepped from one stirrup and stood up in the other when the animal reared up on its hind legs.

He glanced out of the other windows of the house and fell to watching her again, his face darkening as he saw that she appeared to be tiring, while her mount grew steadily worse. Then she "touched leather," and again and again. Her foot slipped from the stirrup, but found it again, while she frantically clung to the saddle horn.

"Four-legged devil!" Pete exclaimed. "Wish *I* was on you, you ornery dog! Hey! Don't you bite like that! Keep yore teeth away from that leg or I'll blow yore dammed head off!" he cried wrathfully as the animal bit viciously several times at the stirrup leather. "I'll whale th' stuffin' outen you, you wall-eyed claybank! Yo're too bronc for *her* to ride, all right."

Then, during another and more vicious fit of stiff-legged pitching the rider held to the saddle horn with both hands, while her foot, again out of the stirrup, sought for it in vain. She was rapidly losing her grip on the saddle and suddenly she was thrown off, a cry reaching Pete's ears. The victorious animal kicked several times and shook its head vigorously in celebration of its freedom and then buck-jumped across the plateau and out of sight down the hill, Pete strongly tempted to stop its exuberance with a bullet.

Pete glanced at the figure huddled in the dust and then, swearing savagely and fearing the worst, he threw down the bar and jerked open the door and ran as rapidly as his awkward legs would take him to see what he could do for her, his hand still grasping his rifle. As he knelt beside her he remembered that he had been told not to leave the house under any circumstances and he glanced over his shoulder, and just in time to see a chap-covered leg disappear through the doorway. His heart sank as the crash of the bar falling into place told him that he had been unworthy of the trust his best friend had reposed in him. It was plain enough, now, that he had been fooled, to understand it all and to know that as he left the house one or more H2 punchers had sprinted for it from the other side of the plateau.

Red fury filled him in an instant and tearing the revolver from the girl's belt he threw it away and then, grasping her with both hands, he raised her up as though she weighed nothing and threw her over his shoulder, sprinting for the protection of the hillside, which he reached in a few bounds. Throwing her down as he would throw a bag of flour he snarled at her as she arose and brushed her clothes. Years ago in Pete's life a woman had outraged his love and trust and sent him through a very hell of sorrow; and since then he had had no love for the sex—only a bitter, scathing cynicism, which now found its outlet in words. "Yo're a nice one, you are!" he yelled. "You've done yore part! Yo're all alike, every damned one of you—Judas wasn't no man, not by a damned sight! You know a man won't stand by an' see you hurt without trying to help you—an' you play it against him!"

She was about to retort, but smiled instead and went on with her dusting.

"Tickled, hey! Well, you watch an' see what *we* do to coyotes! You'll see what happens to line-thieves down here!"

She looked up quickly and suspected that instead of averting a fight she had precipitated one. Both Hopalong and her father were in as much danger now as if she had taken no part in the trouble.

Pete emptied his revolver into the air as rapidly as he could work the hammer and hurriedly reloaded it, all the time watching his prisoner and the top of the hill. Three quick reports, muffled by distance, replied from Long Hill and he turned to her.

"Now why don't you laugh?" he gritted savagely. He caught sight of her horse grazing calmly further down the hill and his Sharps leaped to his shoulder and crashed. The animal stiffened, erect for a moment, and then sank slowly back on its quivering haunches and dropped.

"*You* won't pitch no more, damn you!" he growled, reloading.

Her eyes snapped with anger and she fought at her holster. "You coward! You coward!" she cried, stamping her foot. "To kill that horse, an' steal my gun—afraid of a woman!" she taunted. "Coward!"

"I'll pull a snake's fangs rather than get bit by one, when I can't shoot 'em!" he retorted, stung by her words. "You'll see how big a coward I am purty soon—an' you'll stay right here an' see it, too!"

"*I* won't run away," she replied, sitting down and tucking her feet under her skirts. "*I'm* not afraid of a coward!"

Another shot rang out just over the top of Stepping Stone Hill and he replied to it. Far to the west a faint report was heard and Pete knew that Skinny was roweling the lathered sides of his straining horse. Yet another sounded flatly from the direction of the dam, the hills multiplying it into a distant fusillade.

"Hear 'em!" he demanded, fierce joy ringing in his voice. "Hear 'em! You've kicked th' dynamite, all right—you'll smell th' smoke of yore little squib clean down to yore ranch house!"

"That's grand—yo're doing it fine," she laughed, strangling the fear which crept slowly through her. "Go on—it's grand!"

"It'll be a whole lot grander when th' boys get here an' find out what's happened," he promised. "There'll be some funerals start out from what's left of yore ranch house purty soon."

"K-i-i-i-e-e-p! Ki-ip ki-ip!" came the hair-raising yell from the top of Stepping Stone Hill, and Pete withheld the rest of his remarks to reply to it in kind. Suddenly Red Connors, his quirt rising and falling, bounded over the top of the hill and shot down the other side at full speed. Close behind him came Billy Williams, who rode as recklessly until his horse stepped into a hole and went down, throwing him forward like a shot out of a catapult. He rolled down the hill some distance before he could check his impetus and then, scrambling to his feet, drew his Colt and put his broken-legged mount out of its misery before hobbling on again.

Red slid to a stand and leaped to the ground, his eyes on the woman, but his first thought was for the house. "What's the matter? Why ain't you in that shack? Didn't Hopalong tell you to hold it?" he demanded. Turning to Mary Meeker he frowned. "What are you doing up here? Don't you know this ain't no place for you today?"

Pete grasped his shoulder and swung him around so sharply that he nearly lost his balance, crying: "Don't talk to her, she's a damned snake!"

Red's hand moved towards his holster and then stopped, for it was a friend who spoke. "What do you mean, damn you? Who's a snake? What's wrong here, anyhow?"

Billy limped up and stood amazed at the strange scene, for besides the presence of the woman, his friends were quarreling and he had never seen that before. Seeing Mary look at him he flushed and sneaked off his sombrero, ashamed because he had forgotten it.

Pete swiftly related all that had occurred, and ended with another curse flung at his prisoner, who looked him over with a keen, critical glance and then smiled contemptuously.

"That's a fine note!" Red cried, his sombrero also coming off. He looked at Mary and saw no fear in her face, no sign of any weakness, but rather a grimness in the firmness of her lips and a battling light in her eyes, which gained her immunity from his tongue, for he admired grit. "Here, you, stop that cussing! You can't cuss no woman while I'm around!" he cried hotly. "Hopalong'll break you wide open if he hears you. Cussing won't do no good; what we want is thinking, an' fighting!" Catching sight of Billy, who looked self-conscious and a little uncomfortable, he cried: "An' what's th' matter with you?"

Billy jerked his thumb over his shoulder in the direction of the dead horse and Red, following the motion, knew. "By th' Lord, you got off easy! Pete, you watch yore prisoner; keep her out of danger, an' there'll be lots of it purty soon. We'll get th' house for you."

"Send up to Cowan's saloon; he had some dynamite, an' if we can get any we can blow them sneaks off th' face of th' earth," Pete exclaimed, his anger and shame urging him against his better nature. "Go ahead. I'll take th' chances using th' stuff—I lost th' house."

The pathetic note of self-condemnation in his last words stopped Red's reprimand and he said, instead: "We'll talk about that later. But don't you lose no sleep—they can't hold it, dynamite or no dynamite. We'll have it before sundown."

Dynamite! Mary caught her breath and sudden fear gripped her heart. Dynamite! And two men were in the house, Doc Riley and Jack Curtis, men who would not be there if she had not made it possible for them—she was responsible.

"Here comes Skinny!" cried Billy, waving his arm.

"An' here's Hopalong!" joyously cried Pete, elated, for he pinned his faith in his line-foreman's ability to get out of any kind of a hole, no matter how deep and wide. "Now things'll happen! We're going to get busy now, all right!"

The two arrived at the same instant and both asked the same question. Then Hopalong saw Mary and he was at her side in a trice.

"Hullo! What are you doing up here?" he cried in astonishment.

"I'm a prisoner—of *that!*" she replied, pointing at Pete.

Hopalong wheeled. "What! What have you been doing to her? Why ain't you in th' house, where you belongs?"

Pete told him, briefly, and he turned to the prisoner, a smile of admiration struggling to get through his frown. She looked at him bravely, for now was the crisis, which she had feared, and welcomed.

"By th' Lord!" he cried, softly. "Yo're a thoroughbred, a fighter from start to finish. But you shouldn't come up here to-day; there's no telling, sometimes, where bullets go after they start." Turning, he said, "Pete, you chump, stay on this side of th' hills an' watch th' house. Billy, lay so you can watch th' door. Red, come with me. An' if anybody gets a shot at them range stealers, shoot to kill. Understand? Shoot to kill—it's time."

"Dynamite?" queried Pete, hopefully. "I'll use it. Cowan—"

Hopalong stared. "Dynamite! Dynamite! We ain't fighting 'em that way, even if they are coyotes. You go an' do what I told you."

"Yes, but—"

"Shut up!" snapped Hopalong. "I know how you feel *now*, but you'll think different to-morrow."

"Let's swap th' girl for th' house," suggested Skinny, grinning. "It's a shore cinch," he added, winking at Billy, who laughed.

Hopalong wheeled to retort, caught Skinny's eye closing, and laughed instead. "I reckon that would work all right, Skinny. It'd be a good joke on 'em to take th' house back with th' same card they got it by. But this ain't no time for joking. Pete, you better stay here an' watch th' window on this side; Billy, take the window on th' south side. Skinny can go around west an' Red'll take th' door. They won't be so joyous after they get what's coming their way. This ain't no picnic; shoot to kill. We've been peaceful too blamed long!"

"That's th' way to talk!" cried Pete. "If we'd acted that way from th' very first day they crossed our line we wouldn't be fighting to capture our own line house! You know how to handle 'em all right!"

"Pete, how much water is in there?" Hopalong asked.

"'Bout a hatful—nobody brought me any this morning, th' lazy cusses."

"All right; they won't hold it for long, then. Take yore places as I said, fellers, an' get busy," he replied, and then turned to Mary. "Where's yore father? Is *he* in that house?"

"I don't know—an' I wouldn't tell if I did!"

"Say, yo're a regular hummer! Th' more you talk th' better I like you," he laughed, admiringly. "You've shore stampeded me worse than ever—I'm so loco I can't wait much longer—when are you going to marry me? Of course you know that you've got to someday."

"Indeed I have *not!*" she retorted, her face crimson. "If you wait for me to marry you you will die of old age! An' I'm shore somebody's listening."

"Then *I'll* marry *you*—of course, that's what I meant."

"Indeed you *won't!*"

"Then th' minister will. After this line fighting is over I won't wait. I'll just rope you an' drive you down to Perry's Bend to th' hobbling man, if you won't go any other way. We'll come back a team. I mean what I say," and she knew that he did, and she was glad at heart that he thought none the less of her for the trick she had played on Pete. He seemed to take everything as a matter of course, and as a matter of course he was going to re-take the house.

"You just *dare* try it! Just *dare!*" she cried, hotly.

"Now you have gone an' done it, for I never take a dare, *never,*" he laughed. "It's us for th' sky pilot, an' then th' same range for life. Yo're shore purty, an' that fighting spunk doubles it. You can begin to practice calling yourself Mrs. Hopalong Cassidy, of th' Bar-20."

Pete fired, swore, and turned his head. "How th' devil can I hit a house with all that fool talk!" and the two, suddenly realizing that Pete had been ordered to remain close by, looked foolish, and both laughed.

"It gets on my nerves," Pete growled, and then: "Here comes Johnny like a greased coyote."

They looked and saw Johnny tearing down Stepping Stone Hill as if he were afraid that the fighting would be over before he could take a hand in it. When he came within hailing distance he stood up in his stirrups, shouting, "What's up?" and then, seeing Pete, understood. Leaping from the saddle he jerked his rifle out of the sheath and ran to him, jeering. "Oh, Pete! Oh you damned fool!"

"Hey, Johnny! How's things east?" Hopalong demanded.

Johnny stopped and hastily recounted how he and Red had driven back the herd, adding: "Her dad is out there now looking at his dead cows—I saw him when I came back from East Arroyo. An' I saw them three punchers ride over that ridge down south; and they shore made good time. Say, how did they get Pete out?" he asked eagerly.

"I'll tell you that later—Pete, you go an' tell Red to come here, an' take his place. We can't swap Mary for th' house, but we can swap her dad! Mary, you better go home—this won't be no place for you in a little while. Where's yore cayuse?" he asked, looking around.

"It's down there—he shot it," she replied, nodding at Pete.

"Shot it? Lord, but he must 'a been mad! Well, you can get square—Pete, where's yore cayuse?"

"How th' devil do *I* know!" Pete blazed, indignantly. "*I* wasn't keeping track of no cayuse after they got th' house!"

"It's down there on th' hill—see it?" volunteered Johnny. "Shall I get it?" he asked, grinning at the disgruntled Pete.

"Yes; an' strip th' fixings off her cayuse while yo're about it—lively."

Johnny vaulted into his saddle and loped down the hill, shortly returning with Mary's saddle and bridle in front of him and Pete's horse at the end of his rope. Hopalong quickly removed Pete's saddle and put the other in its place, Pete eloquent in his silence, and Johnny manifestly pleased by the proceedings.

"Now you can ride," Hopalong smiled, helping her into the saddle. "Pete don't care at all—he ain't saying a word," whereat Pete said a word, several of them in fact, under his breath and vowed that he would kill the men in the house to get square.

"I'll send it back as soon as I can," she promised, and then, when Hopalong leaned closer and whispered something to her, she flushed and spurred the animal, leaving him standing in a cloud of dust, a smile on his face.

Johnny, grinning until his face threatened to be ruptured, wheeled on Pete. "Yo're a lucky fool, even if you did go an' lose th' house for us—wish she'd ride *my* cayuse!"

Pete replied in keeping with his feelings now that there was no woman present, and walked away to change places with Red, who soon came up. Then the three mounted and cantered east to find the H2 foreman, Johnny mauling "Whiskey Bill" in his exuberance. Suddenly he turned in his saddle and slapped his thigh: "I'll bet four cents to a tooth brush that she's telling her dad to get scarce. She heard what you said, Hoppy!"

"Right! Come on!" exclaimed Hopalong, spurring into a gallop, his companions racing behind, spurring and quirting to catch him.

"Say, Red, she's a straight flush," Johnny shouted to his companion. "Can't be beat—if she turns Hoppy down I'm next in th' line-up!"

"You don't want no wife—you wants a nurse!" Red retorted.

CHAPTER 18

The Line House Recaptured

After Chick, Dan Morgan, and Ed Joyce had commandeered Antonio's horse and left him on foot they rode as rapidly as they could to the corrals of their ranch, where they saddled fresh mounts and galloped back to try conclusions with the men who had humbled them. They also wished to find their foreman, who they knew was somewhere along the line. Chick rode to the west, Dan to the east, and Ed Joyce straight ahead; intending to search for Meeker and then ride together again.

Meanwhile Antonio, tired of walking, returned to the line and lay in ambush to waylay the first Bar-20 puncher to ride past him, hoping to get a horse and also leave a dead man for the Bar-20 to find and lay the blame on the H2. He knew that his rustler allies had scouts in the chaparrals and were ready to run off a big herd as soon as conditions were propitious, and he was anxious to give them the word to begin.

It chanced, however, that Ed Joyce was the first man to approach Antonio, and he paid dearly for being a party to taking his horse. The dead man would not inflame the Bar-20, but the H2, and the results would be the same in the end. Mounting Ed's horse Antonio galloped north into the valley through West Arroyo so as to leave tracks in the direction of the Bar-20, intending to describe a semi-circle and return to his ranch by way of the river trail, leaving the horse where the trail crossed the Jumping Bear. By going the remainder of the way on foot he would not be seen on the horse of the murdered puncher, which might naturally enough stray in that direction, and so be free from suspicion.

Lanky Smith, wondering why none of his friends had passed him on the line, followed the trail west to see if things were as they should be. He was almost in sight of a point opposite West Arroyo, his view being obstructed by chaparrals, when he heard a faint shot, and spurred forward, his rifle in the hollow of his arm ready for action. It could mean only one thing—one of his friends was shooting H2 cows, and complications might easily follow. When he had turned out of an arroyo which made part of the line for a short distance he saw a body huddled on the sand several hundred feet ahead of him. At that instant Meeker, with Chick and Dan close at his heels, came into view on the other side, saw the body and, drawing their own conclusions, opened a hot fire on the Bar-20 puncher, riding to encircle him. Surprised for an instant, and then filled with rage because they had killed one of his friends, as he thought, he returned their fire and raced at Chick, who was now some distance from his companions. Dan and Meeker wheeled instantly and rode to the aid of their friend, and Lanky's horse dropped from under him. Luckily for him he felt a warning tremor go through the animal and jerked his feet free from the stirrups as it sank down, quickly crawling behind it for protection.

Immediately thereafter Chick lost his hat, then the use of his right arm, followed by being deprived of the services of a very good cow-pony, for Lanky now had a rest for his rifle and while his markmanship was not equal to that of his friend Red, it was good enough for his present needs. Dan Morgan started to shout to his foreman and then swore luridly instead, for Lanky was pleased to drill him at five hundred yards, the bullet tearing a disconcerting hole in Dan's thigh.

Meeker had been most zealously engaged all this time in making his rifle go off at regular intervals, his bullets kicking up the dust, humming viciously about Lanky's head, and thudding into the carcass of the dead horse. Then Lanky swore and shook the blood from his cheek, telling Meeker what he thought about the matter. Settling down again he determined to husk Meeker's body from its immortal soul, when he found his magazine empty. Reaching to his belt for the wherewithal for the husking he discovered the lamentable fact that he had only three cartridges left for the Winchester, and the Colt was more ornamental than useful at that range. To make matters worse both Chick and Dan were now sitting up wasting cartridges in his direction, while Meeker seemed to have an unending supply. Just then the H2 foreman found his mark again and rendered his enemy's arm useless. At that point the clouds of misfortune parted and Hopalong, Red, and Johnny at his heels, whirled into sight from the west, firing with burning zeal.

Meeker's horse went down, pinning its rider under it; Dan Morgan threw up his arms as he sat in the saddle, for his rifle was shattered; Chick, propping up his good arm first, arose from behind his fleshy breastwork and announced that he could not fight, although he certainly wanted to; but Meeker said nothing.

Riding first to Lanky, his friends joked him into a better humor while they attended to his wounds. Then they divided to extend the wound-dressing courtesy. First they tried to kill a man, then to save him; but, of course, they desired mostly to render him incapable of injuring them and as long as this was accomplished it was not necessary to deprive him of life.

Hopalong, being in command, went over to look at the H2 foreman and found him unconscious. Dragging him from under the body of his horse Hopalong felt along the pinned leg and found it was not broken. Pouring a generous amount of whiskey down the unconscious man's throat he managed to revive him and then immediately disarmed him. Meeker complained of pains in his groin, not by words but by actions. His left leg seemed paralyzed and would not obey him. Hopalong called Red, who took the injured man up in front of him, where Hopalong bound his hands to the pommel of the saddle.

Meeker preserved a stolid silence until Lanky joined them and then his rage poured out in a torrent of abuse and accusations for the killing of Ed Joyce. Lanky retorted by asking who Ed Joyce was, and wanted to know whose body he had found just before Meeker had come onto the scene. When he found that they were the same he explained that he had not seen it before Meeker had, which the H2 foreman would not believe. Red captured Dan Morgan's horse and led it up. After Chick and Dan had been helped to mount the Bar-20 men's horses, placed before the saddles and bound there, all started towards Lookout Peak, Lanky riding Dan's horse.

When they had arrived at their destination Meeker suddenly realized what he was to be used for and stormed impotently against it. He heard the intermittent firing around the plateau and knew that Doc and Jack still held the house, and believed they could continue to hold it, since the thick adobe walls were impenetrable to rifle fire.

"Well, Meeker, it's you for th' house," Hopalong remarked after he had sent Red to stop the fire of the others. "You got off damned lucky to-day; th' next time you raise heck along our line we'll pay yore ranch houses a visit an' give you something to think about. We handled you to-day with six of us up north, an' what th' whole crowd can do you can guess. Now walk up there an' tell them range-jumpers to vamoose th' house!"

"They'll shoot me before they sees who I am," Meeker retorted, sullenly. "If yo're so anxious to get 'em out, do it yoreself—I don't want 'em."

By this time the others were coming up and heard Meeker's words, and

Hopalong, turning to Skinny and Billy, curtly ordered them to mount. "Take this royal fool up to th' bunk house to Buck. Tell Buck what's took place down here, an' also that we're going to shoot hell out of th' fellers in th' house before he sees us. After that those of us who can ride are going down to th' H2 an' clean up that part of th' game, buildings an' all. Go on, lively! Red, Johnny, Pete; cover th' windows an' fill that shack plumb full of lead. It's clouding up now an' when it gets good an' dark we'll bust in th' door an' end it. Skinny, you come back again, quick, with all th' grub an' cartridges you can carry. Meeker started this, but *I'm* going to finish it an' do it right. There won't be no more line fights down here for a long time to come."

"I reckon I'll have to order 'em out," Meeker growled. "What'll you do to 'em if I do?"

"Send 'em home so quick they won't have any time to say 'good-bye,'" Hopalong rejoined. "We've seen too much of you fellers now. An' after I send 'em home you see that they stays away from that line—we'll shoot on sight if they gets within gunshot of it! You've shore had a gall, pushing us, you an' yore hatful of men an' cows! If it wasn't for th' rustling we'd 'a pushed you into th' discard th' day I found yore man herding on us."

Meeker, holding his side because of the pain there from the fall, limped slowly up the hill, waving his sombrero over his head as he advanced.

"What do you want now?—*Meeker!*" cried a voice from the building. "What's wrong?"

"Everything; come on out—we lose," the foreman cried, shame in his voice.

"Don't you tell us that if you wants us to stay here," came the swift reply. "We're game as long as we last, an' we'll last a long time, too."

"I know it, Doc—" his voice broke "—they've killed Ed an' captured Chick, Dan an' me. I'd say fight it out, an' I'd to th' end, only they'll attack th' ranch house if we do. We're licked, *this time!*"

"First sensible words you've said since you've been on this range," growled Lanky. "You was licked before you began, if you only knowed it. An' you'll get licked *every* time, too!"

"Well, we'll come out an' give up if they'll let us all go, including you," called Doc. "I ain't going to get picked off in th' open while I've got this shack to fight in, not by a blamed sight!"

"It's all right, Doc," Meeker replied. "How's Jack?" he asked, anxiously, not having heard Doc's companion speak.

"Wait an' see," was the reply, and the door opened and the two defenders stepped into sight, bandaged with strips torn from their woollen shirts, the remains of which they did not bother to carry away.

"Who played that gun through th' west window?" asked Doc, angrily.

"Me!" cried Skinny, belligerently. "Why?"

"Muzzle th' talk—you can hold yore pow-wow some other time," interposed Hopalong. "You fellers get off this range, an' do it quick. An' stay off, savvy?"

Meeker, his face flushed by rage and hatred for the men who had so humiliated him, climbed up on Dan's horse and Dan was helped up behind. Then Chick was helped to mount in front of his foreman and they rode down the hill, followed by Doc and Jack. The intention was to let Dan ride to the ranch after they had all got off the Bar-20 range, and send up the cook with spare horses. Just then Doc remembered that he and Jack had left their mounts below when they walked up the hill to take the house, and they went after them.

At this instant Curley was seen galloping up and he soon reported what Salem had seen. Meeker flew into a rage at this and swore that he would never give in to either foe. While Curley was learning of the fighting, Doc and his companion returned on foot, reporting that their horses had strayed, whereupon Meeker got off the horse he rode and told Doc and Chick to ride it home, Curley being despatched for mounts, while the others sat down on the ground and waited.

When Curley returned with the horses he was very much excited, crying that during his absence Salem had seen six men run off a herd of several hundred head toward Eagle and had tried to overtake them in the chuck wagon.

"God A'mighty!" cried Meeker, furiously. "Ain't I got enough, *now*! Rustling, an' on a scale like that! Peters was right after all about th' rustling, damn him. A whole herd! Why didn't they take th' rest, an' th' houses, an' th' whole ranch? An' Salem, th' fool, chasing 'em in th' chuck wagon! Wonder they didn't take him, too."

"I reckon he wished he had his harpoon with him," Chick snorted, the ridiculousness of Salem's action bringing a faint grin to his face, angry and wounded as he was. "He's the locoedest thing that wears pants in this section, or any other!"

"It was a shore fizzle all around," Meeker grumbled. "But I ain't through with that line yet—no, by th' Lord, I ain't got started yet! But this rustling has got to be cleaned up first of all—th' line can wait; an' if we don't pay no attention to th' valley for a while they'll think we've given it up an' get off their guard."

"Shore!" cried Dan, whose fury had been aroused almost to madness by the sting of the bitter defeat, and who itched to kill, whether puncher or rustler it little mattered; he only wanted a vent for his rage.

"We'll parade over that south range like buzzards sighting carrion," Meeker continued, leading the way homeward. "I ain't a-going to get robbed all th' time!"

"Wonder if Smith did shoot Ed?" queried Dan, thoughtfully. "There was quite a spell between th' shot I heard an' us seeing him, an' he acted like he had just seen Ed. But it's tough, all right. Ed was a blamed good feller."

"Who did shoot him, then?" snapped Meeker, savagely. "There's no telling what happened out there before we got there. Here, Curley, you ain't full of holes like us—you ride up there and get him while we go home. He's laying near that S arroyo right close to th' line—th' one we scouted through that time."

"Shore, I'll get him," replied Curley, wheeling. "See you later."

CHAPTER 19

Antonio Leaves the H2

On the H2 Jim Meeker rolled and muttered in his sleep, which had been more or less fitful because of his aching groin and strained leg. Gazing confusedly about him he sat bold upright, swearing softly at the pain and then, realizing that he was where he should be, grumbled at the kaleidoscopic dreams that had beset him during his few hours of sleep, and glanced out of the window. Hastily dressing he strode to the kitchen door, calling his daughter as he passed her room, and looked out. The bunk house and the corrals were beginning to loom up in the early light and the noise in the cook shack told him that Salem was preparing breakfast for the men. He did not like the looks of the low, huge, black cloud east of him and as he figured that it would not pass over the ranch houses unless the wind shifted sharply he suddenly stared at a corral and then hastened back to his room for the Colt which lay on the floor beside his bunk. He had seen a man flit past the further corral, speed across the open, and disappear behind the corral nearest to the bunk house. This ordinarily would have provoked no further thought, but his men were crazy-headed enough to do anything, but while rustling flourished, and so audaciously, and while a line war was on, it would stand prompt investigation.

Peering again from the door, Colt in hand, Meeker slipped out silently and ran to the corral wall as rapidly as his injuries would allow. When he reached it he leaned close to it and waited, his gun levelled at the corner not ten feet from him. Half a minute later and without a sound a man suddenly turned it, crouching and alertly watching the bunk house and cook shack at his left, and then stopped with a jerk and reached to his thigh as he became aware that he was being watched at such close range. Straightening up and smothering an exclamation he faced the foreman and laughed, but to Meeker's suspicious ears it sounded very much forced and strained.

"No *sabe* Anton?" asked the prowler, smiling innocently and raising his hand from the gun.

Meeker stood silent and motionless, the Colt as steady as a rock, and a heavy frown covered his face as he searched the evil eyes of his broncho-buster, whose smile remained fixed.

"No *sabe Anton?*" somewhat hastily repeated the other, a faint trace of anxiety in his voice, but the smile did not waver, and his eyes did not shift. He began to realize that it was about time for him to leave the H2, for he knew that few things grow so rapidly as suspicion.

Meeker slowly lowered his weapon and swore; he did not like the prowling any better than he did the smile and the laugh and the treacherous eyes.

"I no savvy why yo're flitting around th' scenery when you should ought to be in bed," he replied, his words ominously low and distant. "I'm curious as to why yo're prowling around so early before breakfast. It ain't a whole lot like you to be out so early before grub time. What dragged you from th' bunk so damned early, anyhow?"

Antonio rolled a cigarette to gain time, being elaborately exacting, and thought quickly for an excuse. Tossing the match in the air and letting the smoke curl slowly from his nostrils he grinned pleasantly. "I no sleep—have bad dreams. I wake up, *uno, dos* times an' teenk someteeng ees wrong. Then I ride to see. Eet ees soon light after that an' I am hungry, so I come back. Eet ees no more, at all."

"Oh, it ain't!" retorted the foreman, still frowning, for he strongly doubted the truth of what he had heard, so strongly that he almost passed the lie. "It's some peculiar how this ranch has been shedding dreams last night, all right. However, since I had some few myself I won't say I had all there was loose. But you listen to me, an' listen good, too. When I want any scouting done before daylight I'll take care of it myself, savvy? An' if yo're any wise you'll cure yoreself of th' habit of being out nights percolating around when you ought to be asleep. You ain't acted none too wide awake lately an' yore string of cayuses has shore been used hard, so I want it stopped, an' stopped *sudden*; hear me? I ain't paying you to work nights an' loaf days an' use up good cayuses riding hell-bent for nothing. You ain't never around no more when I want you, so you get weaned of flitting around in th' night air like a whip-poor-will; you might go an' catch malaria!"

"I no been out bafo'—Juan, he tell you that ees so, *si.*"

"Is that so? I sort of reckon he'd tell me anything you want him to if he thought I'd believe it. Henceforth an' hereafter you mind what *I've* just told *you*. You might run up against some rustler what you don't know very well, an' get shot on suspicion," Meeker hazarded, but he found no change in the other's face, although he had hit Antonio hard, and he limped off to the ranch house to get his breakfast, swearing every time he put his sore leg forward, and at the ranch responsible for his condition.

Antonio leaned against the corral wall and smoked, gazing off into space as the foreman left him, for he had much to think about. He smiled cynically and shrugged his shoulders as he shambled to his shack, making up his mind to leave the H2 and join Shaw on the mesa as soon as he could do so, and the sooner the better. Meeker's remark about meeting strange rustlers, thieves he did not know, was very disquieting, and it was possible that things might happen suddenly to the broncho-buster of the H2. Soon emerging from his hut he walked leisurely to the fartherest corral and returned with his saddle and bridle. After holding a whispered consultation with Juan and Sanchez, who both showed great alarm at what he told them, and who called his attention to the fact that he had lost one of the big brass buttons from the sleeve of his coat, the three walked to the cook shack for their breakfast, where, every morning, they fought with Salem.

"Here comes them Lascars again to fill their holds with grub," the cook growled as he espied them. "If I was th' old man I'd maroon them, or make 'em walk th' plank. Here, *you*! Get away from that bench!" he shouted, running out of the shack. "That's *my* grub! If you ain't good enough to eat longside of th' crew, damned if you can eat with th' cook! Some day I'll slit you open, tail to gills, see if I don't! Here's yore grub—take it out on th' deck an' fight for it," and Salem, mounting guard over the bench, waved a huge butcher knife at them and ordered them off. "Bilgy smelling lubbers! I'll run afoul of 'em some morning an' make shark's food out of th' whole lot!"

Meanwhile Meeker, finding his breakfast not yet ready, went to Antonio's shack and glanced in it. The bunk his broncho-buster used was made up, which struck him as peculiar, since it was well known that Antonio never made up his bunk until after supper. As he turned to leave he espied the saddle and saw that the stirrups were streaked with clay. "Now what was he doing over at th' river last night?" he soliloquized. Shrugging his shoulders he wheeled and went to the bunk house, where he stumbled over a box, whacking his shins soundly. His heartfelt and extemporaneous remarks regarding stiff legs and malicious boxes awakened Curley, who sat up and vigorously rubbed his eyes with his rough knuckles. Grunts and profanity came from the other bunks, Dan swearing with exceptional loquacity and fervor at his wounded thigh.

"Somebody'll shore have to lift me out like a baby," he grumbled. "I'll get square for this, all right!"

"Aw, what you cussing about?" demanded Chick, whose arm throbbed with renewed energy when he sat up. "How'd you like to have an arm like mine so you can't use it for grub, hey?"

"You an' yore arm can—"

"What's matter, Jim?" interrupted Curley, dropping his feet to the floor and groping for his trousers. "You got my pants?" he asked Dan, whereupon Dan told him many things, ending with: "In th' name of heaven what do I want with pants on this leg! I can't get my own on, let alone yourn. Mebby Chick has put 'em on his scratched wing!" he added, with great sarcasm, whereupon Curley found them under his bunk and muttered a profane request to be told why they had crawled so far back.

"Yo're a hard luck bunch if yo're as sore as me," growled Meeker, kicking the offending box out of doors. "I cuss every time I hobble."

"Oh, I ain't sore, not a bit—I'm feeling fine," exulted Curley, putting one foot into a twisted trouser leg while he hopped recklessly about to keep his balance, Dan watching him enviously. He grabbed Chick's shoulder to steady himself and then arose from the floor to find Chick calling him every name in the language and offering to whip him with one hand if he grabbed the wounded arm again.

"Aw, what's th' matter with you!" he demanded, getting the foot through without further trouble. "I didn't stop to think, you chump!"

"Why didn't you?" snapped Chick, aggressively.

"Curley, yo're a plain, damned nuisance—get outside where you'll have plenty of room to get that other leg in," remarked Dan.

"Not satisfied with keeping us all awake by his cussed snoring an' talking, he goes an' hops right on my bad arm!" Chick remarked. "He snores something awful, Jim; like a wagon rumbling over a wooden bridge; an' he whistles every lap."

"You keep away from me, you cow!" warned Doc, weighing a Colt in his hand by the muzzle. "I'll shore bend this right around yore face if you don't!"

"Aw, go to th' devil! Yo're a bunch of sore-heads, just a bunch of—" Curley snapped, his words becoming inaudible as he went out to the wash bench, where Meeker followed him, glad to get away from the grunting, swearing crowd inside.

"Curley," the foreman began, leaning against the house to ease his thigh and groin, "Antonio is either going *loco*, or he is up to some devilment, an' I a whole lot favors th' devilment. I thought of telling him to clean out, get off th' range an' stay off, but I reckon I'll let him hang around a while longer to see just what his game is. Of course if he is crooked, it's rustling. I'd like an awful lot to ketch him rustling; it'd wipe out a lot of guessing, an' him at th' same time."

"All three of 'em crooked," Curley replied, refilling the basin. "Every blasted one, an' he's worse than th' others—he's a coyote!"

"Yes, I reckon you ain't far from right," replied Meeker. "Well, anyway, I put in a bad night an' rolled out earlier'n usual. I looked out an' saw somebody sneaking around th' corral, an', gettin' my gun, I went after him hot foot. It was Antonio, an' when I asks for whys an' wherefores, he gives me a fool yarn about having a dream. He woke up an' was plumb scared to death somebody was running off with th' ranch, an', being so all-fired worried about th' safety of th' ranch he's too lazy to work for, he just couldn't sleep, but had to get up an' *saddle his cayuse* an' *ride* around th' corrals to see if it was here. Now, what do you think of that?"

"Huh!" snorted Curley. "He don't care a continental cuss about this ranch or anybody on it, an' never did."

"Which same I endorses; it shore was a sudden change," Meeker replied, glancing at his shack. "I looked in his hut an' saw his bunk hadn't been used since night afore last, so he must 'a had his dreams then. There was yaller clay on his stirrups—he must 'a been scared somebody was going to run off with th' river, too. Now he shore was rampaging all over creation last night—he didn't have no dreams nor no sleep in that bunk last night, nohow. Now, th' question is, where was he, an' what th' devil was he doing? I'd give twenty-five dollars if I knowed for shore."

"That's easy!" snorted Curley, trying to get water out of his ear. "Where'd I 'a been last night if I wasn't broke? Why, down in Eagle having a good time— there's lots of good times in that town if you've got th' price of more than a look-in. Or, mebby, he was off seeing his girl. That's a good way to pass th' evening, too." Then, seeing the frown on Meeker's face he swiftly contradicted himself, realizing that it was no time for jesting. "Why, it looks to me like he might be a little interested in some of th' promiscuous cattle lifting that's going on 'round here. I'll pump him easy so he won't know what I'm driving at."

"Yes, you might do that if yo're shore you won't scare him away, but I want you to pass th' horse corral, anyhow, an' see what horse he rode. See how hard he pushed it riding around th' corrals, an' if there's any yellow clay on its legs. Don't let him see you doing it or he'll get gun-shy an' jump th' country. I'm going up to breakfast—Mary's calling me."

Curley looked up. "Shore I'll do it. It's raining some on th' hills, all right. Look yonder!"

"Yes. I saw it this morning early. It passed to th' northeast of us. I'll be back soon," and the foreman limped away. "Hey, Curley," he called over his shoulder for Antonio's benefit, "take a look at them sore yearlings in th' corral," referring to several calves they had quarantined.

"All right, Jim. They was some better last night. I don't think it's anything that's catching."

"O-o-h!" yawned Jack in the doorway. "Seems like I just turned in—gosh, but I'm sleepy."

"Nothing like cold water for that feeling," laughed Curley. "We stayed up too late last night talking it over. Hullo, Chick; still going to lick me one-handed?"

"You get away from that water, so I can wash one-handed," replied Chick. "But you shouldn't ought to 'a done that. No, Jack—go ahead; but I'm next. Hey, Dan!" he cried, laughing, "shall I bring some water in to you?"

"I won't stay here an' listen to such language as Dan's ripping off," Curley grinned, starting away. "I'm going up to look at them sick yearlings in Number Two corral."

True to his word Curley looked the animals over thoroughly and then dodged into the horse corral, where he quickly examined the horses as he passed them, alert for trouble, for a man on foot takes chances when he goes among cow-ponies in a corral. Not one of the animals forming Antonio's *remuda* appeared to have been ridden and it was not until he espied Pete, Doc's favorite horse, that he found any signs. Pete's hair was roughened and still wet from perspiration, there was a streak of yellow clay along its belly on one side but none on its hoofs, and dried lather still clung to its jaws. Pete made no effort to get away, for he was one of the best trained and most intelligent animals on the ranch, a veteran of many roundups and drives, and he knew from experience that he would not be called on to do double duty; he had done his trick while the others rested.

"An' you know I ain't a-going to ride you, hey?" Curley muttered. "You've had yore turn, an' you know you won't be called on to-day, you wise old devil.

Pete, some people say cayuses ain't got no sense, that they can't reason—they never knowed you, did they? Well, boy, you'll have yore turn grazing with th' rest purty soon."

He returned to the bunk house and spent a few minutes inside and then sauntered easily towards the ranch house, where the foreman met him.

"So there wasn't no clay on his hoofs, hey?" Meeker exclaimed. "Some on his belly, an' none on his hoofs. Hum! I reckon Pete was left by hisself while Antonio wrastled with th' mud. Must 'a thought he was prospecting. Well, he's a liar, an' a sneak; watch him close, an' tell th' rest to do th' same. Mebby we'll get th' chance soon of stretching his neck some bright morning. I'll be down purty soon to tell you fellers where to ride."

Curley returned to the wash bench and cleansed his hands, and because the cold water felt so good, he dipped his face into it again, blowing like a porpoise. As he squilgeed his face to lessen the duty of the overworked towel, he heard a step and looked up quickly. Antonio was leaning against the house and scowling at him, for he had looked through a crack in the corral wall and had seen Pete being examined.

"Eet ees *bueno* thees mornin'," Antonio offered.

"What's good?" Curley retorted, staring because of Antonio's unusual loquacity.

"*Madre de Dios*, de weatha."

"Oh, salubrious," replied Curley, evading a hole in the towel. "Plumb sumptuous an' highfalutin', so to speak. You had a nice night in Eagle, all right. Who-all was down there?"

"Antone not en Eagle—he no leev de rancho," Antonio replied. He hesitated as if to continue and Curley noticed it.

"What's on yore mind, 'Tony? What's eating you? *Pronto*, I'm hungry."

Antonio hesitated again. "What you do een de corral thees mornin'?"

"Oh, I was looking at them yearlings—they were purty bad, but they're gettin' along all right. What do you think about 'em?"

"No; een de *beeg* corral."

"Oh, you do!" snapped Curley. "Well, I remembered you was riding around this morning before sunup so I reckoned I'd look in an' see if you rid my cayuse, which you didn't, an' which is good for you. I ain't a whole lot intending to go moping about on no tired-out bronc, an' don't you forget it, neither. An' seeing as how it ain't none of your damned business what I do or where I go, that's about all for you."

"You no spik true—*Pah*! eet ees a lie!" cried Antonio excitedly, advancing a step, and running into the wash water and a fist, both of which met him in the face. Curley, reaching for his holster and finding that he had forgotten to buckle it on, snatched the Remington from Antonio's sheath while the fallen man was half dazed. Pointing it at his stomach, he ordered him up and then told him things.

"I reckon you got off easy—th' next time you calls me a liar shoot first, or there'll be one less, shifty-eyed coyote to ride range nights."

Antonio, drenched and seething with fury, his discolored face working with passion and his small, cruel eyes snapping, sprang to the wall and glared at the man who had knocked him down. But for the gun in Curley's hand there would have been the flash of a knife, but the Remington was master of the situation. Knife throwing is a useful art at times, but it has its limitations. Cursing, he backed away and slunk into his shack as Doc Riley stuck his head out of the bunk house doorway, hoping to be entertained.

"Worth while hanging 'round, Curley? Any chance of seeing a scrap?" Doc asked, eyeing the gun in his friend's hand.

"You could 'a seen th' beginning of a scrap a couple of minutes earlier," Curley replied. "I didn't give him a chance to throw. Why, he was out all night on Pete, yore cayuse—rode him hard, too. He said—"

"My Pete! Out all night on Pete!" yelled Doc, taking a quick step towards Antonio's hut, the door of which slammed shut, whereupon Doc shouted out his opinions of Antonio. "Is that right?" he asked, turning to Curley. "Was he out on Pete?"

"He shore was—used him up, too."

"I'll break every bone in his yaller carcass!" Doc shouted, shaking his fist at the hut. "Every time I see him I want to get my gun going, an' it's getting worse all th' time. I'll fill him full of lead pills surer than anything one of these days."

"If you don't I will," replied Curley. "I just don't know why I didn't then because—"

"Four bells—grub pile!" rang out the stentorian voice of Salem, who could shout louder than any man on the ranch, and the conversation came to an abrupt end, to be renewed at the table.

When Antonio heard the cook's shout he opened the door a trifle and then, seeing that the coast was clear, picked up the bundle which contained his belongings, shouldered his saddle, slipped his rifle under his arm, and ran to the corral. Juan and Sanchez had been there before him and he found that they not only had taken four of the best horses, but that they had also picketed two good ones for him, and had driven off the remainder to graze, which would delay pursuit should it be instituted. Saddling the better of the two, he left the other and cantered northwest until hidden from the sight of any one at the ranch, and then galloped for safety.

Meeker, returning to the bunk house, found his men in far better humor than they were in when he left them, although the death and burial of Ed Joyce and the other misfortunes of the day before had quieted them a little. As he entered the room he heard Salem in the cook shack, droning a mournful dirge-like air as he slammed things about.

"Hey, cook!" shouted the foreman, standing in the door of the gallery. "Cook!"

"Aye, aye, sir!"

"You are shore you didn't recognize none of them thieves that ran off our herd yesterday?"

"Nary a one, sir. They was running with all sails set two points off my port bow, which left me astern of 'em. I was in that water-logged, four-wheeled hunk of a chuck wagon an' I couldn't overhaul 'em, sir, 'though I gave chase. I tried a shot with th' chaser, but I was rolling so hard I couldn't hull 'em. But I'll try again when I'm sober, sir."

"All right, Salem," laughed Meeker. "Curley, you take yore regular range. Doc, suppose you take th' west, next to Curley? Chick an' Dan will have to stay here till they get well enough to ride, an' I'll need somebody on th' ranch after yesterday, anyhow. Jack, how do you feel? Good! Ride between here an' Eagle. I'm going to go down to that town an' see what I can find out."

"But I can ride, Jim," offered Chick, eagerly. "This arm won't bother me much. Let me stick close to Doc, or one of th' boys. Maybe they might need me, Jim."

"You stay right here, like I said. We'll have to wait till we're all right before we can get down to work in earnest. An' every one of you look out for trouble—shoot first an' talk after." He turned again to the gallery. "Salem, kill a cow an' sun cure th' meat; we might want it in a hurry sometime soon. That'll be one cow they don't get, anyway."

"Who's going to ride north, Jim?" asked Doc.

"Nobody; th' Bar-20 has been so damned anxious to turn our cows an' do our herding for us, an' run th' earth, we'll just let 'em for a while. Not much danger of any rustlers buzzing reckless around *that* neighborhood; they'll earn all they steal if they get away with it."

I saw her face grow cold in death,
I saw her—

came Salem's voice in a new wail. Meeker grabbed a quirt and, leaping to the gallery, threw it. The song stopped short and other words, less tuneful, finished the cook's efforts.

"You never mind what you saw!" shouted the foreman. "If you can't sing anything but graveyard howls, you shut up yore singer!"

CHAPTER 20

What the Dam Told

About the time Meeker caught Antonio prowling around the corral, Hopalong stepped out of the line house on the Peak and saw the approaching storm, which gladdened him, notwithstanding the fact that he and Red would ride through it to the bunk house. The range was fast drying up, the grass was burning under the fierce heat of the sun, and the reservoir, evaporating as rapidly as it was supplied, sent but little water down the creek through the valley. This storm, if it broke over the valley, promised to be almost a flood, and would not only replenish the water supply, but would fortify the range for quite a while against the merciless sun.

After he had sent Meeker and his men on their homeward journey he ordered all but Red to report to Buck at the bunk house, believing that the line fighting was at an end for a while, at least. But to circumvent any contingency to the contrary, he and Red remained to guard the house and discuss the situation. The rest of the line riders were glad to get away for a day, as there was washing and mending to be done, clothes to be changed, and their supply of cartridges and tobacco to be replenished.

After throwing his saddle on his horse he went back to the house to get his "slicker," a yellow water-proof coat, and saw Red gathering up their few belongings.

"Going to rain like th' devil, Red," he said. "We'll get soaked before we reach th' dam, but it'll give th' grass a chance, all right. It's due us, an' we're going to get it."

Red glanced out of the window and saw the onrushing, low black mass of clouds. "I reckon yes. Going to be some fireworks, too."

Hopalong, slipping into the hideous slicker, followed Red outside and watched him saddle up. "It'll seem good to be in th' house again with all th' boys, an' eat cook's grub once more. I reckon Frenchy an' some of his squad will drift in—Johnny said he was going to ride out that way on his way back an' tell 'em all th' news."

"Yes. Mind yore business, Ginger!" Red added as his horse turned its head and nipped at his arm, half in earnest and half in playful expostulation. Ginger could not accustom himself to the broad, hind cinch which gripped his soft stomach, and he was wont to object to it in his own way. "Yes, it's going to be a shore enough cloud-burst!" Red exclaimed, glancing apprehensively at the storm. "Mebby we better take th' hill trail—we won't have no cinch fording at th' Bend if *that* lets loose before we get there. We should 'a gone home with th' crowd last night, 'stead of staying up here. I knowed they wouldn't try it again—it's all yore fault."

"Oh, yo're a regular old woman!" retorted Hopalong. "A wetting will do us good—an' as for th' ford, I feel like having a swim."

The close, humid air stirred and moaned, and fitful gusts bent the sparse grass and rustled across the plateau, picking up dust and sending it eddying along the ground. A sudden current of air whined around the corners of the line house, slamming the door violently and awakening the embers of the fire into a mass of glowing coals, which crackled and gave off flying sparks. Several larger embers burst into flame and tumbled end over end across the ground, and Hopalong, running them down, stamped them out, returning and kicking dust over the fire, actuated by the plainsman's instinct. Red watched him and grinned.

"Of course that cloud-burst won't put the fire out," he remarked, sarcastically, although he would have done the same thing if his friend had not.

"Never go away an' leave a fire lit," Hopalong replied, sententiously, closing the banging door and fastening it shut. A streak of lightning quivered between earth and clouds and the thunder rolled in many reverberations along the cliffs of the valley's edge, to die out on the flat void to the west. Down the wind came the haunting wail of a coyote, sounding so close at hand that Red instinctively reached for his rifle and looked around.

"Take *mine!*" jeered Hopalong, mounting, having in mind the greater range of his weapon. "You'll shore need it if you want to get that feller. Gee, but it's dark!"

It was dark and the air was so charged with electricity that blue points of flame quivered on the ears of their horses.

"We're going to get hell!" shouted Red above the roar of the storm. "Every time I spits I make a streak in th' air—an' ain't it hot!"

One minute it was dark; another, the lightning showed things in a ghastly light, crackling and booming like a huge fireworks exhibition. The two men could feel the hearts of their horses pounding against their sides, and the animals, nervous as cats, kept their ears moving back and forth, the blue sparks ghostly in the darkness.

"Come on, get out of this," shouted Hopalong. "Damn, there goes my hat!" and he shot after it.

For reply Red spurred forward and they rode down the steep hill at a canter, which soon changed to a gallop, then to a dead run. Suddenly there came a roar that shook them and the storm broke in earnest, the rain pouring down in slanting sheets, drenching them to the skin in a minute, for their slickers were no protection against that deluge. Hopalong stripped his off, to see it torn from his grasp and disappear in the darkness like a frightened thing.

"Go, then!" he snapped. "I was roasting in you, anyhow! I won't have no clothes left by th' time I hits th' Bend—which is all th' better for swimming."

Red slackened pace, rode at his friend's side, their stirrups almost touching, for it was safer to canter than to gallop when they could not see ahead of them. The darkness gradually lessened and when they got close to the dam they could see as well as they could on any dull day, except for a distance—the sheets of water forbade that.

"What's that?" Hopalong suddenly demanded, drawing rein and listening. A dull roar came from the dam and he instinctively felt that something was radically wrong.

"Water, of course," Red replied, impatiently. "This is a *storm*," he explained.

Hopalong rode out along the dam, followed by Red, peering ahead. Suddenly he stopped and swore.

"She's *busted*! Look there!"

A turbulent flood poured through a cut ten feet wide and roared down the other side of the embankment, roiled and yellow.

"Good God! She's a goner shore!" cried Red excitedly.

"It shore is—*No*, Red! It's over th' stone work—see where that ripple runs? We can save it if we hustle," Hopalong replied, wheeling. "Come on! Dead cows'll choke it—get a move on!"

When Buck had decided to build the dam he had sent for an engineer to come out and look the valley over and to lay out the lines to be followed. The west end, which would be built against the bluff, would be strong; but Buck was advised to build a core of rubble masonry for a hundred feet east of the centre, where the embankment must run almost straight to avoid a quicksand bottom. This had been done at a great increase over the original estimate of the cost of the dam, but now it more than paid for itself, for Antonio had dug his trench over the rubble core—had he gone down a foot deeper he would have struck it and discovered his mistake.

Hopalong and Red raced along the dam and separated when they struck the plain, soon returning with a cow apiece dragging from their lariats, which they released and pushed into the torrent. Their bodies floated with the stream and both men feared their efforts were in vain. Then Hopalong uttered a shout of joy, for the carcasses, stranding against the top of the masonry core, stopped, the water surging over them. Racing away again they dragged up more cows until the bodies choked the gap, when they brought up armfuls of brush and threw them before the bodies. Then Red espied a shovel, swore furiously at what it told him, and fell to throwing dirt into the breach before the brush. He had to take it from different places so as not to weaken the damn, and an hour elapsed before they stopped work and regarded the results of their efforts with satisfaction.

"Well, she's there yet, and she'll stay, all right. Good thing we didn't take th' hill trail," Hopalong remarked.

"Somebody cut it, all right," Red avowed, looking at the shovel in his hands. "*H2*! Hoppy, see here! This is *their* work!"

"Shore enough H2 on th' handle, but Meeker an' his crowd never did that," Hopalong replied. "I ain't got no love for any of 'em, but they're too square for this sort of a thing. Besides, they want to use this water too much to cheat themselves out of every chance to get it."

"You may be right—but it's damned funny that we find their shovel on th' job," Red rejoined, scowling at the brand burned into the wooden handle.

"What's that yo're treading on?" Hopalong asked, pointing to a bright object on the ground.

Red stooped and then shouted, holding up the object so his friend could see it. "It's a brass button as big as a half-dollar—bet it belonged to th' snake that used this shovel!"

"Yo're safe. I won't bet you—an' Antonio was th' only one I've seen wearing buttons like that in these parts," Hopalong replied. "I'm going to kill him on sight!" and he meant what he said.

"Same here, th' ornery coyote!" Red gritted.

"Antonio had me guessing, but I'm beginning to see a great big light," Hopalong remarked, taking the button and looking it over. "Yep, it's hissn, all right."

"Well, we've filled her," Red remarked after a final inspection.

"She'll hold until to-morrow, anyhow, or till we can bring th' chuck wagon full of tools an' rocks down here," Hopalong replied. "We'll make her solid for keeps. You better take th' evidence with you, Red, an' let Buck look 'em over. It's a good thing Buck spent that extra money putting in that stone core! Besides losing th' reservoir we'd have had plenty of dead cows by this time if it wasn't for that."

"An' that Antonio went an' picked out the weakest spot in th' whole thing, or th' spot what would be th' weakest if that wall wasn't there," Red remarked. "He ain't no fool, but a stacked deck can beat a good head time after time."

When they reached the ford they found a driftwood-dotted flood roaring around the bend, three times as wide as it was ordinarily, for the hills made a watershed that gave quick results in such a rain.

"Now Red Eagle, old cayuse, here's where you swim," Hopalong laughed, riding up stream so he would not be carried past the bottom of the hill trail on the farther side. Plunging in the two horses swam gallantly across, landing within a few feet of the point aimed at, and scrambled up the slippery path, down which poured a stream of water.

When they reached the half-way point between the ford and the ranch houses the storm slackened, evolving into an ordinary rain, which Hopalong remarked would last all day. Red nodded and then pointed to a miserable, rain-soaked calf, which moved away at their approach.

"Do you see that!" he exclaimed. "Our brand, an' Meeker's ear notch!"

"That explains th' shovel being left on th' dam," quickly replied Hopalong. "It would be plumb crazy for th' H2 to make a combination like that ear notch an' our brand, an' you can gamble they don't know nothing bout it. Th' gent that left Meeker's shovel *for us to find* did that, too. You know if any of th' H2 cut th' dam they wouldn't forget to take th' shovel with 'em, Red. It's Antonio, that's who it is. He's trying to make a bigger fight along th' line an' stir things up generally so he can rustle promiscuous. Well, we'll give all our time to th' rustling end from now on, if I have got any voice in th' matter. An' I hope to th' Lord I can get within gun range of that coyote. Why, by th' A'mighty, I'll go down an' plug him on his own ground just as soon as I can get away, which will be to-morrow! That's just what I'll do! I'll stop his plays or know th' reason why."

"An' I'm with you—you'll take a big chance going down there alone," Red replied. "*After* Meeker hears what we've got to say he'll be blamed glad we came."

An hour later they stopped at the ranch house, a squat, square building, flat of roof, its adobe walls three feet thick and impenetrable to heat. Stripping saddles and bridles from their streaming mounts, they drove the animals into a large corral and ran to the bunk house, where laughter greeted their appearance.

"Swimming?" queried Johnny, putting aside his harmonica.

"Hey, you! Get out of here an' lean up against th' corral till you shed some of that water!" yelled Lanky, the wounded, watching the streams from their clothes run over the floor. "We'll be afloat in a minute if you don't get out—we ain't no fishes."

"You shut up," retorted Red. "We'll put you out there to catch what water we missed if you gets funny," he threatened, stripping as rapidly as he could. He hung the saturated garments on pegs in the gallery wall and had Pete rub him down briskly, while Billy did the same for his soaked companion.

Around them were their best friends, all laughing and contented, chaffing and exchanging personal banter with each other, engaged in various occupations, from sewing buttons on shirts to playing cards and mending riding gear. Snatches of songs burst forth at odd intervals, while laughter was continually heard. This was the atmosphere they loved, this repaid them for their hard work, this and the unswerving loyalty, the true, deep affection, and good-natured banter that pricked but left no sting. Here was one of the lures of the range, the perfect fellowship that long acquaintance and the sharing of hard work and ubiquitous danger breeds among the members of a good, square outfit. Not one of them ever counted personal safety before duty to his ranch and his companions, taking his hard life laughingly and without complaint, generous to a fault, truthful and loyal and considerate. There was manhood for you, there was contempt for restricting conventions, for danger; there was a unity of thought and purpose that set the rough-spoken, ready-fighting men of the saddle and rope in a niche by themselves, a niche where fair play, unselfishness, and a rough but sterling honor abides always. Their occupation gave more than it exacted and they loved it and the open, windswept range where they were the dominating living forces.

Buck came in with Frenchy McAllister and Pie Willis and grinned at his crowd of happy "boys," who gave warm welcome. The foreman was not their "boss," their taskmaster, but he was their best friend, and he shared with them the dangers and joys which were their lot, sympathetic in his rough way, kind and trusting.

Hopalong struggling to get his head through a dry shirt, succeeded, and swiftly related to his foreman the occurrences of the morning, pointing to the shovel and button as the total exhibit of his proofs against Antonio. The laughter died out, the banter was hushed, and the atmosphere became that of tense hostility and anger. When he had ceased speaking angry exclamations and threats filled the room, coming from men who always "made good." When Red had told of the H2-Bar-20 calf, an air of finality, of conviction, settled on them; and it behooved Antonio to hunt a new range, for his death would be sudden and merciless if he met any of the Bar-20 outfit, no matter when or where. They never forgot.

After a brief argument they came to the decision that he was connected with the rustling going on around them, and this clenched his fate. Several, from the evidence and from things which they had observed and now understood, were of the opinion that he was the ringleader of the cattle thieves.

"Boys," Buck remarked, "we won't bother about th' line very much for a while. It's been a peaceable sort of a fracas, anyhow, an' I don't expect much further trouble. If H2 cows straggle across an' yo're right handy to 'em an' ain't got nothing pressing to do, drive 'em back; but don't look for 'em particularly. There won't be no more drives against us for a long time. We've got to hunt rustlers from now on, an' hunt hard, or they'll get too numerous to handle very easy. Let th' cows take care of themselves along th' river, Frenchy, an' put your men up near Big Coulee, staying nights in Number Two. Pete an' Billy will go with you. That'll protect th' west, an' there won't be no rustling going on from the river, nohow. Don't waste no time herding—put it all in hunting. Hopalong, you, Johnny, Red, an' Skinny take th' hills country an' make yore headquarters in Number Three an' Four. Lanky will stay up here until he can handle hisself good again. I'll ride promiscuous, but if any of you learn anything you want me to know, leave it with Lanky or th' cook if you can't find me. Just as soon as we have anything to go on, we'll start on th' war path hot foot an' clean things up right an' proper."

"What'll we do if we catches anybody rustling?" asked Johnny, assuming an air of ignorance and curiosity, and ducking quickly as Red swung at him.

"Give 'em ten dollars reward an' let 'em go," Buck grinned.

"Give me ten if I brings Antonio to you?"

"I'll fine you twenty if you waste that much time over him," Buck replied.

"Whoop!" Johnny exulted. "Th' good old times are coming back again! Remember Bye-an'-Bye an' Cactus Springs, Buckskin an' Slippery Trendley? Remember th' good old scraps? Now we'll have something else to do besides chasing cows an' wiping th' rust off our guns!"

Lanky, who took keen delight in teasing the youngster, frowned severely.

"Yo're just a fool kid, just a happy idiot!" he snorted, and Johnny looked at him, surprised but grinning. "Yes, you are! I never seen such a bloody-minded animal in all my born days as you! After all th' fighting you've gone an' got mixed up in, you still yap for more! You makes me plumb disgusted, you do!"

"He *is* awful gory," remarked Hopalong soberly. "Just a animated massacre in pants."

"Regular Comanche," amended Red, frowning. "What do you think about him, Frenchy?"

"I'd ruther not say it," Frenchy replied. "You ask Pie—he ain't scared of nothing, massacre *or* Comanche."

Johnny looked around the room and blurted out, "You all think th' same as me, every one of you, even if you are a lot of pussy-cats, an' you know it, too!"

"Crazy as a locoed cow!" Red whispered across the room to Buck, who nodded sorrowfully and went into the cook shack.

"You wait till I sees Antonio an' you'll find out how crazy I am!" promised Johnny.

"I shore hopes he spanks you an' sends you home a-bawling," Lanky snorted. "You needs a good licking, you young cub!"

"Yah, yah!" jibed Johnny. "Needing an' getting are two different tunes, grand-pop!"

"You wasn't down here, was you, Frenchy, when Johnny managed to rope a sleepy gray wolf that was two years old, an' tried to make a pet out of him?" asked Hopalong, grinning at his recollection of the affair.

"No!" exclaimed Frenchy in surprise. "Did he do it?"

"Oh, yes, he did it; with a gun, after th' pet had torn his pants off an' chewed him up real well. He's looking for another, because he says that was too mean a beast to have any luck with."

Buck stepped into the room again. "Who wants to go with me to th' dam in th' wagon?" he asked. "I want to look at that cut an' fix it for keeps if it needs fixing. All right! All right! Anybody'd think I asked you to go to a dance," he laughed. "Pete, you an' Billy an' Pie will be enough."

"Can't we ride alongside?" asked Pie. "Do we have to sit in that thing?"

"You can walk, if you want to. I don't care how you go," Buck replied, stepping into the rain with the three men close behind him. Soon the rattling of the wagon was heard growing fainter on the plain.

The banter and the laughter ran on all the rest of the morning. After dinner Hopalong built a fire in the huge stove and put a ladleful of lead on the coals, while Frenchy and Skinny re-sized and re-capped shells from the boxes on the wall. Hopalong watched the fire and smoked the bullet moulds, while Lanky managed to measure powder and fill the shells after Frenchy and Skinny had finished with them. Hopalong filled the moulds rapidly while Johnny took out the bullets and cooled them by dropping them into cold rain water, being cautioned by Hopalong not to splash any water into the row of moulds. As soon as he found them cool enough, Johnny wiped them dry and passed them on to Red, who crimped them into the charged shells. Soon the piles of cartridges grew to a goodly size, and when the last one had been finished the crowd fell to playing cards until supper was ready. Hopalong, who had kept on running bullets, sorted them, and then dropped them into the boxes made for each size. Finally he stopped and went to the door to look for signs of the morrow's weather.

"Clearing up in th' west an' south—here comes Buck an' th' others," he called over his shoulder. "How was it, Buck?" he shouted, and out of the gathering dusk came the happy reply: "Bully!"

CHAPTER 21

Hopalong Rides South

The morning broke clear and showed a clean, freshened plain to the men who rode to the line house on the Peak, there to take up their quarters and from there to ride as scouts. Hopalong sent Red to ride along the line for the purpose of seeing how things were in that vicinity and, leaving the others to go where they wished, struck south down the side of the hill, intending to hunt Antonio on his own ground. Tied to his saddle was the shovel and in his pocket he carried the brass button, his evidence for Meeker. As he rode at an easy lope he kept a constant lookout for signs of rustling. Suddenly he leaned forward and tightened his knee grip, the horse responding by breaking into a gallop, while its rider took up his lariat, shaking it into a long loop, his twisting right wrist imparting enough motion to it to keep it clear of the vegetation and rocks.

A distant cow wheeled sharply and watched him for a moment and then, snorting, its head down and its tail up, galloped away at a speed not to be found among domesticated cattle. It was bent upon only one thing—to escape that dreaded, whirling loop of rawhide, so pliant and yet so strong. Hopalong, not as expert as Lanky, who carried a rope nearly sixty feet long and who could place it where he wished, used one longer than the more common lariats.

The cow did its best, but the pony steadily gained, nimbly executing quick turns and jumping gullies, up one side of a hill and down the other, threading its way with precision through the chaparrals and deftly avoiding the holes in its path. Closer and closer together came the pursued and pursuers, and then the long rope shot out and sailed through the air, straight for the animal's hind legs. As it settled, a quick upward jerk of the arm did the rest and there was a snubbing of rope around the saddle horn, a sudden stopping and dropping back on haunches on the part of the pony, and the cow went down heavily.

The rider did not wait for the horse to get set, but left the saddle as soon as the rope had been securely snubbed, and ran to the side of his victim.

The cow was absolutely helpless, for the rope was taut, the intelligent pony leaning back and being too well trained to allow the least amount of slack to bow the rawhide closer to the earth. Therefore Hopalong gave no thought to his horse, for while cinches, pommel, and rope held, the small, wiry, wild-eyed bundle of galvanic cussedness would hold the cow despite all its efforts to get up.

"Never saw *that* brand before, an' I've rid all over this country for a good many years, too," he soliloquized. "There sure ain't no HQQ herd down this way, nor no place close enough for a stray. Somebody is shore starting a herd on his own hook; from th' cows on this range, too.

"By th' great horned spoon! I can see Bar-20 in them marks!" he cried, bending closer. "All he had to do was to make a H out of th' Bar, close up th' 2, an' put a tail on th' O! Hum—whoop! There is H2 in it, too! Close th' 2 an' add a Q, an' there you are! I don't mind a hog once in a while, but working both ranches to a common mark is shore too much for me. Stealing from both ranches an' markin' 'em all HQQ!"

He moved up to look at the ears and swore when he saw them. "Damn it! That's all I want to know! Mebby a sheriff wouldn't get busy on th' evidence, but I ain't no sheriff—I'm just a plain cow-punch with good common sense. Meeker's cut is a V in one ear—here I finds a slant like Skinny saw, an' in both ears. If that don't cut under Meeker's notch I'm a liar! All framed up to make a new herd out of our cows. Just let me catch some coyote with a running iron under his saddle flap an' see what happens!"

He quickly slacked the rope and slipped off the noose, running as fast as he could go to his pony, for some cows get "on the prod" very easily, and few cows are afraid of a man on foot; and when a long-horned Texas cow has "its dander up," it is not safe for an unmounted man to take a chance with its horns, unless he is willing to shoot it down. This Hopalong would not do, for he did not want to let the rustlers know that the new brand had been discovered. Vaulting into his saddle he eluded the charge of the indignant cow and loped south, coiling up his rope as he went.

Half an hour after leaving the HQQ cow he saw a horseman ahead of him, threading his way through a chaparral. As Hopalong overtook him the other emerged and stopped, uncertain whether to reach for his gun or not. It was Juan, who had not gone to Mesa overnight, scouting to learn if any new developments had taken place along the boundary. Juan looked at the shovel and then at the puncher, his face expressionless.

Hopalong glanced at the other's cuff, found it was all right, and then forced himself to smile. "Looking for rustlers?" he bantered.

"*Si.*"

"What! There ain't no rustlers loose on this range, is there?" asked Hopalong, surprised.

"*Quien sabe?*"

"Oh, them sleepers were made by yore own, lazy outfit, an' you might as well own up to it," Hopalong grinned, deprecatingly. "You can fool Meeker, all right, he's easy; but you can't throw dust in my eyes like that. On th' level, now, ain't I right? Didn't you fellers make them sleepers?"

Juan shrugged his shoulders. "*Quien sabe?*"

"That '*Quien sabe*' is th' handiest an' most used pair of words in yore cussed language," replied Hopalong grinning. "Ask one of you fellers something you don't want to tell an' its '*Quien sabe?*' ain't it?"

"*Si,*" laughed Juan.

"I thought so," Hopalong retorted. "You can't tell me that any gang that would cut a dam like they did ourn wouldn't sleeper, an' don't you forget it, neither!"

Juan's face cleared for a moment as he gloated over how Antonio's scheme had worked out, and he laughed. "No can fool you, hey?" Then he pressed his knee tighter against his saddle skirt and a worried look came into his eyes.

Hopalong took no apparent notice of the action, but he saw it, and it sent one word burning through his brain. They were riding at a walk now and Hopalong, not knowing that Juan had left the H2, suggested that they ride to the ranch together. He was watching Juan closely, for it would not be unusual for a man in his position to try to get out of it by shooting. Juan refused to ride south and Hopalong, who was determined to stay with his companion until he found out what he wanted to know, proposed a race to a barranca that cut into the plain several hundred yards ahead. He would let Juan beat him, and all the way, so he could watch the saddle flap, and if this failed he would waste no more time in strategy, but would find out about it quickly. Juan also declined to race, and very hurriedly, for the less his saddle was jolted the better it would be for him. He knew Hopalong's reputation as a revolver fighter and would take no chances.

"That ain't a bad cayuse you got there. I was wondering it it could beat mine, what's purty good itself. Is it very bronc?" he asked, kicking the animal in the ribs, whereupon it reared and pranced. Juan's left hand went to the assistance of his knee, his right grasped the cantle of his saddle, where it was nearer the butt of his Colt, and a look of fear came into his eyes.

Hopalong watched his chance and as the restive animal swung towards him he spurred it viciously, at the same time crying: "Take yore hand from off that flap, you damned cowlifter!"

The command was unnecessary, for a thin, straight rod of iron slipped down and stuck in the sand, having worked loose from its lashings. Juan had put off until to-morrow to heat it and bend a loop in one end for more secure fastening.

At the instant it fell Juan leaned back and dropped over on the far side of his horse, his right leg coming up level with his enemy, and reached for his gun, intending to shoot through the end of the holster and save time. But he went farther than he had intended, not stopping until he struck the earth, his bullet missing Hopalong by only a few inches.

The Bar-20 puncher slipped his Colt back into the sheath and, leaning down, deftly picked up the iron and fastened it to his saddle. Roping Juan's horse he continued on his way to the H2, leaving Juan where he had fallen.

When he arrived at the ranch he turned the horse into the corral and started to ride to the bunk house; but Salem, enjoying a respite from cooking and washing dishes, saw him and started for him on an awkward run, crying: "Where'd you git that hoss? Where'd you clear from, an' who are you?"

"Th' cayuse belongs to Meeker—Juan was riding it. Is anybody around?"

"I'm around, ain't I, you fog-eyed lubber! Where's th' Lascar? Who are you?"

"Well, Duke, I'm from th' Bar-20, an' my name is Hop—"

"Weigh anchor an' 'bout ship! You can't make this port, you wind-jamming pirate!"

"I want to see yore foreman. This is his shovel, an' I—"

"Then where'd you get it, hey? How'd you get his—"

"Hang it!" interrupted Hopalong, losing his patience. "I tell you I want to see Meeker! I want to see him about some—"

"An' where's th' man that rid that hoss?" demanded the cook, belligerently.

"You won't see that thief no more. That's one of th' things I want to—"

"Hooray!" cried Salem. "Was he drowned, or shanghaied?"

"Was he what? What are you talking about, anyhow? Where did you ever learn how to talk Chinese?"

"What! Chinese! You whale-bellied, barnacle-brained bilge pirate, I've got a good notion—"

"Say, is there anybody around here that ain't loco? Are they all as crazy as you?" Hopalong asked.

Salem grabbed up one of the bars of the corral gate and, roaring strange oaths, ran at the stranger, but Hopalong spurred his horse and kept clear of the pole while Salem grew short winded and more profane. Then the puncher thought of Mary and cantered towards the ranch house intending to ask her where he could find her father, thus combining business with pleasure. Salem shook the pole at him and then espied the saddled horse in the corral. He disliked horses as much as they disliked him, so much, in fact, that he said the only reason he did not get out of the country and go back to the sea was because he had to ride a horse to do it. But any way was acceptable under the present exigencies, so he clambered into the saddle after more or less effort and found it not quite roomy enough for one of his growing corpulency. Shouting "Let fall!" he cantered after the invader of his ranch, waving the pole valiantly. He did not see that the ears of his mount were flattened or that its eyes were growing murderous in their expression, and he did not know that the lower end of the pole was pounding lustily against the horse's legs every time he waved the weapon. All he thought about was getting his pleasant duty over with as soon as possible, and he gripped the pole more firmly.

Hopalong looked around curiously to see what the cook was doing to make all that noise, and when he saw he held his sides. "Well, if th' locoed son-of-a-gun ain't after me! Lord! Hey, stranger," he shouted, "if you want him to run fast, take hold of his tail an' pull it three times!"

He was not averse to having a little fun at the tenderfoot's expense and he deferred his visit to the house to circle around the angry cook and shout advice. Instead of laying the reins against his mount's neck to turn it, Salem jerked on them, which the indignant animal instantly resented. It had felt all along that it was being made a fool of and imposed upon, but now it would have a sweet revenge. Leaping forward suddenly it stopped stiff-legged and arched its back several times with all the force it was capable of; but it could have stopped immediately after the first pitch, for Salem, still holding to the pole, executed a more or less graceful parabola and landed in a sitting posture amid much dust.

"*Whoof!* What'd we strike?" he demanded dazedly. Then, catching sight of the cause of his flight, which was at that moment cropping an overlooked tuft of grass as if it were accustomed to upsetting pole-waving cooks, Salem scrambled to his feet and ran at it, getting in one good whack before the indignant and groping pony could move.

"There, blast you!" he yelled. "I'll show you what you get for a trick like that!" Turning, and seeing Hopalong laughing until the tears ran down his face, he roared, "What are you laughing at, damn you?"

A rope sailed out and tightened around Salem's feet and he once more sat down, unable to arise this time, because of Hopalong's horse, which backed slowly, step by step, dragging the captive, who was now absolutely helpless.

"Now I want to talk to you for a few minutes, an' I'm going to," Hopalong remarked. "Will you listen quietly or will you risk losing th' seat of yore pants? You've *got* to listen, anyhow."

"Wha—what—go ahead, only stop th' headway of yore craft! Lay to! I'm on th' rocks!"

Laughing, Hopalong rode closer to him. "Where's Antonio?"

"In hell, I hope, leastwise that's where he ought to be."

"Well, I just sent his friend Juan there—had to; he toted a running iron an'—"

"Did you? Did you?" cried Salem in accents of joy. "Why didn't you say so before! Come in an' splice th' main brace, shipmate! Juan is in Davy Jones' locker, is he? Hey, wait till I get these lashings cast off—yo're a good hand after all. Come in an' have some grog—best stuff this side of Kentucky, where it was made."

"I ain't got time," replied Hopalong, smiling. "Where's that Antonio?"

"Going to send *him* down too? Damn my tops'ls, wish I knowed! He deserted, took shore leave, an' ain't reported since. Yo're clipper-rigged, a regular AB, you are! Spin us th' yarn, matey."

Hopalong told him about the dam and the shooting of Juan and gave him the shovel and button for Meeker, Salem's mouth wide open at the recital. When he had finished the cook grabbed his stirrup and urged him towards the grog, but Hopalong laughingly declined and, looking towards the ranch house, saw Jim Meeker riding like mad in their direction.

"What do you want?" blazed the foreman, drawing rein, his face dark with anger.

"I want to plug Antonio, an' his friend Sanchez," Hopalong replied calmly. "I just caught Juan with a running iron under his saddle flap an' I drilled him for good. Here's th' iron."

"Good for you!" cried Meeker, taking the rod. "They've jumped, all of 'em.

I'm looking for 'em myself, an' we're all looking for coyotes toting these irons. I'm glad you got one of 'em!"

"Antonio scuttled their dike—here's th' shovel he did it with," interrupted Salem eagerly. "An' here's th' button off Antonio's jacket. He left it by th' shovel. My mate, here, is cruising to fall in with 'em, an' when he does there'll be—"

"Why, that's *my* shovel!" cried Meeker. "An' that's his button, all right."

Hopalong told him all about the attempt to cut the dam and when he had ceased Meeker swore angrily. "Antonio and his men are on th' rustle, for shore! They're trying to keep th' fighting going on along th' line so we'll be too busy to bother 'em in their stealing. I've been losing cows right an' left—why, they run off a herd of beef right here by th' houses. Salem saw 'em. They killed cows down south an' covered my range with sleepers an' lame mothers. How did you come to guess he had an iron?"

Hopalong told of the HQQ cow he had found and, dismounting, traced the brand in the sand, Meeker bending over eagerly.

"You see this Bar-20?" he asked, pointing it out, and his interested companion interrupted him with a curse.

"Yes, I do; an' do *you* see this H2?" he demanded. "They've merged our brands into one—stealing from both of us!"

"Yes. I figgered that out when I saw th' mark; that's one of th' things I came down to tell you about," Hopalong replied, mounting again. "An' Red an' me found a Bar-20 calf with a V ear notch, too. That proves what th' dam was cut for, don't it?"

"Why didn't I drop that coyote when I caught him skulking th' other morning!" growled Meeker, regretfully. "He had just come back from yore dam then—had yaller mud on his cayuse an' his stirrups. Out all night on a played-out bronc, an' me too thick to guess he was up to some devilment an' shoot him for it! Oh, hell! I thought purty hard of you, Cassidy, but I reckon we all make mistakes. Any man what would stop to think out th' real play when he found that shovel is square."

"Oh, that's all right. I allus did hate Antonio, an' mebby that was why I suspected him, that an' th' button."

Meeker turned to the cook. "Where's Chick an' Dan?" he asked, impatiently. "I ain't seen 'em around."

"Why, Chick rid off down south an' Dan cleared about an hour ago."

"What! With that leg of hissen!"

"Aye, aye, sir; he couldn't leave it behind, you know, sir."

"All right, Cassidy; much obliged. I'll put a stop to th' rustling on *my* range, or know th' reason why. Damn th' day I ever left Montanny!" Meeker swore, riding towards the ranch house.

"Say, I hope you find them Lascars," remarked Salem. "Yo're th' boy that'll give 'em what they needs. Wish you had caught 'em all four instead of only one."

Hopalong smiled. "Then they might 'a got me instead."

"No, no, siree!" exclaimed the cook. "You can lick 'em all, an' I'll gamble on it, too! But you better come in an' have a swig o' grog before you weighs anchor, matey. As I was saying, it's th' best grog west of Kentucky. Come on in!"

CHAPTER 22

Lucas Visits the Peak

When Hopalong returned to the line house on the Peak he saw Johnny and Skinny talking with Lucas, the C80 foreman, and he hailed them.

"Hello, Lucas!" he cried. "What are you doing down here?"

"Glad to see you, Hopalong," Lucas replied, shaking hands. "Came down to see Buck, but Lanky, up in th' bunk house, said he was off somewhere scouting. From what Lanky said I reckon you fellers had a little joke down here last week."

"Yes," responded Hopalong, dismounting. "It was a sort of a joke, except that somebody killed one of Meeker's men. I'll be blamed if I know who done it. Lanky says he didn't an' he don't have to deny a thing like that neither. Looks to me like he caught some brand-blotter dead to rights, like I did a little while ago, an' like he got th' worst of th' argument."

"What's that about catching somebody dead to rights?" eagerly asked Johnny.

"Who was it?" asked Skinny.

"Juan. He toted a running iron an' I caught him just after I looked over a cow with a new brand—"

"Did you get him good?" quickly asked Johnny. "Did he put up a fight?"

"Yes; an' what was th' brand?" Skinny interposed.

"Here, here!" laughed Hopalong. "I reckon I'll save time if I tell you th' whole story," and he gave a short account of his ride, interrupted often by the inquisitive and insistent Johnny.

"An' who is Salem?" Johnny asked.

"Meeker's cook."

"What did Meeker say about it when you told him?"

"Gimme a chance to talk an' I'll tell you!" and Johnny remained silent for a moment. Finally the story was told and Johnny, asked one more question, grinning broadly: "An' what did Mary say?"

"You say Meeker lost a whole herd?" asked Lucas. "Let me tell you there's more people mixed up in this rustling than we think. But I'll tell you one thing; that herd didn't go north, unless they drove ten miles east or west of our range."

"Well, I reckon it's under one man, all right," Hopalong replied. "If it was a lot of separate fellers running it by themselves there'd 'a been a lot of blunders an' some few of 'em would 'a been shot before Juan went. It's a gang, all right. But why th' devil did they turn loose that H2 rebranded cow, that HQQ that I found? They might 'a knowed it would cause some hot thinking when it was found. That cow is just about going to lick 'em."

"Stray," sententiously remarked Skinny.

"Shore, that's what it was," Lucas endorsed.

"An' do you know what that means?" asked Hopalong, looking from face to face. "It means that they can't be holding their heads very far away. It's three to one that I'm right."

"Mebby they're down in Eagle," suggested Johnny hopefully, for Eagle would be a good, exciting proposition in a fight.

"No, it ain't there," Hopalong replied. "There's too many people down there. They would all know about it an' want a share in th' profits; but it ain't a whole lot foolish to say that Eagle men are in it."

"Look here!" cried Skinny. "Mebby that HQQ is their road brand—that cow might 'a strayed from their drive. They've got to have some brand on cows they sell, an' they can't have ours on an' get back alive."

"You are right, but not necessarily so about th' road brand," Hopalong rejoined. "But that don't tell us where they are, does it?"

"We've got to hunt HQQ cows on th' drive," Johnny interposed as Skinny was about to speak. "I'll go down to Eagle an' see if I can't get on to a drive. Then I'll trail th' gang all th' way an' back to where they hangs out. That'll tell us where to go, all right."

"You keep out of Eagle—you'd be shot before you reached Quinn's saloon," Hopalong said. "No; it ain't Eagle, not at all. See here, Lucas; have you watched them construction camps along that railroad? There ain't a better market nowhere than them layouts; they don't ask no questions if th' beef is cheap."

"Yes, I've watched th' trails leading to 'em."

"Why, they wouldn't cross yore range!" Hopalong cried. "They'd drive around you an' hit th' camp from above; they ain't fools. Hey! I've got it! They can't go around th' Double Arrow unless they are willing to cross th' Staked Plain, an' you can bet they ain't. That leaves th' west, an' there's a desert out there they wouldn't want to tackle. They drive between th' desert an yore range."

"If they drive to th' camps, yo're right without a doubt," Skinny remarked. "But mebby they are driving south—mebby they're starting a ranch along th' Grande, or across it."

"Well, we'll take th' camps first," Hopalong replied. "Lucas, can you spare a man to look them camps over? Somebody that can live in 'em a month, if he has to?"

"Shore. Wood Wright is just th' man."

"No, he ain't th' man," contradicted Hopalong quickly. "Anybody that wears chaps, or walks like he does would arouse suspicion in no time, an' get piped out in one night. This man had got to have business up there, like looking for a job. Say! Can you get along without yore cook for a while? If you can't we will!"

"You bet yore life I can!" exulted Lucas. "That's good. He can get a job right where th' meat is used, an' where th' hides will be kicking around. He goes tomorrow!"

"That's th' way; th' sooner th' better," Hopalong responded. "But we won't wait for him. We'll scout around lively down here an' if we don't find anything he may. But for th' Lord's sake, don't let him ride a cayuse into that camp that has brands of this section. Cowan will be glad to lend you his cayuse; he got it up north too far to make them suspicious."

"Yes; I reckon that'll be about the thing."

"Here comes Red," Johnny remarked. "Hey, Red, Hoppy got Juan this morning. Caught him toting a straight iron!"

"Johnny, you get away lively an' tell Frenchy to scout west," Hopalong ordered. "You can stay up in Number Two with them to-night, but come down here again in th' morning. Red, to-morrow at daylight we go west an' comb that country.

"That's th' way," remarked Lucas, mounting. "Get right at it. Have you got any word for Buck? I'll go past th' house an' leave it if you have."

"Yes; tell him what we've talked over. An' you might send yore outfit further west, too," Hopalong responded. "I'll bet a month's pay we end this cow-lifting before two weeks roll by.

"Oh, yes; I near forgot it—Bartlett thinks we-all ought to get together after th' rustling is stopped an' shoot that town of Eagle plumb off th' earth," Lucas said. "It's only a hell hole, anyhow, an' it won't do no harm to wipe it out." He looked around the group. "What do you fellers think about it?" he asked.

"Well, we might, then; we've got too many irons in th' fire now, though," Hopalong replied. "Hey, Johnny! Get a-going! We'll talk about Eagle later."

"I'm forgetting lots of things," laughed Lucas. "We had a little fight up our way th' other day. Caught a feller skinning one of Bartlett's cows, what had strayed over on us. Got him dead to rights, too. He put up a fight while he lasted. Said his name was Hawkins."

"Hawkins!" exclaimed Hopalong. "I've heard that name somewhere."

"Why, that's th' name on th' notice of reward posted in Cowan's," Red supplied. "He's wanted for desertion from th' army, an' for other things. They want him bad up at Roswell, an' they'll pay for him, dead or alive."

"Well, they won't get him; he ain't keeping good enough," Lucas replied. "An' we don't want that kind of money. So long," and he was off.

"So you got Juan," Red remarked. "You ought to have took him alive—we could get it all out of him an' find out where his friends are hanging out."

"He went after his gun, an' he had an iron," Hopalong replied. "I didn't know he had left Meeker, an' I didn't stop to think. He was a brand-blotter."

"What's Meeker going to do about th' line?" Red asked.

"Nothing for a while; he's too worried an' busy looking after his sleepers. He ain't so bad, after all."

"Say," remarked Skinny, thoughtfully. "Mebby that gang is over east, like Trendley was. There's lots of water thereabouts, an' good grass, too, in th' Panhandle. Look how close it is to Fort Worth an' th' railroad."

"Too many people over there," Hopalong replied. "An' *they* know all about th' time we killed Trendley an' wiped out his gang. They won't go where they are shore we'll look."

"If I can get sight of one of them I'll find out where they are," Red growled. "I'll put green rawhide around his face if I have to, an' when he savvys what th' sun is going to do to that hide an' him, he'll talk, all right, an' be glad of th' chance."

"To hear you, anybody would think you'd do a thing like that," Hopalong laughed. "I reckon he'd drop at eight hundred, clean an' at th' first shot. But, say, green rawhide wouldn't do a thing to a man's face, would it! When it shrunk he'd know it, all right."

"Crush it to a pulp," Skinny remarked. "But who is going to cook th' supper? I'm starved."

·   ·   ·

Hopalong awakened suddenly and listened and found Red also awake. Hoofbeats were coming towards the house and Hopalong peered out into the darkness to see who it was, his Colt ready.

"Who's that?" he challenged, sharply, the clicks of his gun ringing clear in the night air.

"Why, me," replied a well-known voice. "Who'd you think it was?"

"Why didn't you stay up in Number Two, like I told you? What's wrong?"

"Nothing," Johnny replied, stripping off his saddle and bridle.

"An' you came all th' way down here in th' dark, just to wake us up?" Hopalong asked, incredulously. "Twenty miles just for that!"

"No. I ain't got here yet—I'm only half way," Johnny retorted. "Can't you see I'm here? An' I didn't care about you waking up. I wanted to get here, an' here I am."

"In the name of heaven, are you drunk, or crazy?" asked Red. "Of all th' damn fools I ever—"

"Oh, shut up, all of you!" growled Skinny, turning over in his bunk. "Lot of locoed cusses that don't know enough to keep still! Let th' Kid alone, why don't you!" he muttered and was sound asleep again.

"No, I ain't drunk or crazy! Think I was going to stay up there when you two fellers are going off scouting to-morrow? Not by a jugful! I ain't letting nothing get past me, all right?" Johnny rejoined.

"Well, you ain't a-going, anyhow," muttered Hopalong, crawling into his bunk again. "You've got to stay with Skinny—" he did not speak very loud, because he knew it would cause an argument, and he wished to sleep instead of talk.

"What'd you say?" demanded Johnny.

"For God's sake!" marvelled Red. "Can't nobody go an' scratch 'emselves unless th' Kid is on th' ground? Come in here an' get to sleep."

Adown th' road, his gun in hand,
Comes Whiskey Bill, mad Whiskey—

Johnny hummed. "Hey! What you doing?" he yelled, leaping back.

"You heave any more guns on my face an' you'll find out!" roared Skinny, sitting up and throwing Johnny's Colt and belt to the floor. "Fool infant!"

"Tumble in an' shut up!" cried Red. "We want some sleep."

"Yo're a lot of tumble-bugs!" retorted Johnny, indignantly. "How did I know

Skinny had his face where I threw my gun! He's so cussed thin I can't hardly see him in daylight, th' chalk mark! Why didn't he say so? Think I can see in th' dark?"

"I don't talk in my sleep!" retorted Skinny, "or go flea-hopping around in th' dark like a—"

"*Shut up!*" shouted Hopalong, and silence at last ensued.

CHAPTER 23

Hopalong and Red Go Scouting

As Hopalong and Red rode down the slope of the Peak the rays of the sun flashed over the hills, giving promise of a very hot day. They were prepared to stay several days, if need be, on the semi-arid plain to the west of them, for it would be combed thoroughly before they returned. On they loped, looking keenly over the plain and occasionally using their field glasses to more closely scrutinize distant objects, searching the barrancas and coulees and threading through mesquite and cactus growths. Hopalong momentarily expected to find signs of what they were looking for, while Red, according to his habit, was consistently contradictory in his words and disproportionately pessimistic.

Moving forward at a swinging lope they began to circle to the west and as they advanced Hopalong became eager and hopeful, while his companion grumbled more and more. In his heart he believed as Hopalong did, but there had to be something to talk about to pass the time more pleasantly; so when they met in some barranca to ride together for a short distance they exchanged pleasantries.

"Yore showing even more than yore usual amount of pigheaded ignorance today," Hopalong grumbled. "Yore blasted, ingrowing disposition has been shedding cussedness at every step. I'll own up to being some curious as to when it's going to peter out."

"As if that's any of yore business," retorted Red. "But I'll just tell you, since you asks; it's going to stop when I get good an' ready, savvy?"

"Yo're awful cheerful at times," sarcastically snorted his companion.

Red's eyes had been roving over the plain and now he raised his glasses and looked steadily ahead.

"What's that out there? Dead cow?" he asked, calmly.

Hopalong put his glasses on it instantly, "Cow?" he asked, witheringly. "No; it's an over-grown lizard! Come on," he cried, spurring forward, Red close behind him.

Riding around it they saw that it bore the brand of the H2, and Hopalong, dismounting, glanced it over quickly and swore.

"Shot in th' head—what did I tell you!"

"You didn't have to get off yore cayuse to see that," retorted Red. "But get on again, an' come along. There's more out here. I'll take th' south end of this—don't get out of hearing."

"Wait! Wonder why they shot it, instead of driving it off after they got it this far?" Hopalong mused.

"Got on th' prod, I reckon, leaving its calf an' being run so hard. I've seen many a one I'd like to have shot. Looks to me like they hang out around that water hole—they drove it that way."

"You can bet yore head they didn't drive it straight to their hangout—they ain't doing nothing like that," Hopalong replied. "They struck south after they thought they had throwed off any pursuit. They drove it almost north, so far; savvy?"

"Well, they've got to have water if they're holding cows out on this stove," Red rejoined. "An' I just told you where th' water is."

"G'wan! Ten cows would drain that hole in two days!" Hopalong responded. "They've also got to have grass, though mebby you never knew that. An' what about that herd Meeker lost? They wouldn't circle so far to a one-by-nothing water hole like that one is."

"Well, then, where'll they find grass an' water out here?" demanded Red, impatiently. "Th' desert's west, though mebby you never knew that!"

"Red, we've been a pair of fools!" Hopalong cried, slapping his thigh by way of emphasis. "Here we are skating around up here when Thunder Mesa lays south, with plenty of water an' a fair pasture on all sides of it! That's where we'll go."

"Hoppy, once in a great while you do show some intelligence, but we better go up to that water hole first," Red replied. "We can swing south then. We're so close to it now that there ain't nothing to be gained by not taking a look at it. Mebby we'll find a trail, or something."

"Right you are; come on. There ain't no use of us riding separate no more."

Half an hour later Hopalong pointed to one side, to a few half-burned greasewood and mesquite sticks which radiated like the spokes of a wheel.

"Yes, I saw 'em," Red remarked. "They couldn't wait till they got home before they changed th' brand, blamed fools."

"Yes, an' that explains th' HQQ cow I discovered," Hopalong quickly replied. "They got too blamed hasty to blot it an' it got away from 'em."

"Well, it shore beats th' devil how Meeker had to go an' stir up this nest of rattlers," Red grumbled, angrily.

"If these fellers hang out at Thunder Mesa an' drive to th' railroad camps we ought to strike their trail purty close to th' water hole," Hopalong remarked. "It's right in their path."

Red nodded his head. "Yes, we ought to."

An hour later they rode around a chaparral and came within sight of the water hole, which lay a few hundred yards away. As they did so a man rode up out of the depression and started north, unconscious of his danger.

The two men spurred to overtake him, both drawing their rifles and getting ready for action. He turned in his saddle, saw them, and heading westward, quirted and spurred his horse into a dead run, both of his pursuers shouting for him to stop as they followed at top speed. He glanced around again and, seeing that they were slowly but surely gaining, whipped up his rifle and fired at them several times, both replying. He kept bearing more and more to the west and Red rode away at an angle to intercept him. Ten minutes later the fleeing man turned and rode north again, but Red had gained fifty yards over Hopalong and suddenly stopping his horse to permit better shooting, he took quick aim and fired. The pursued man found that his horse was useful only as a breastwork as Red's report died away, and hastily picked himself up and crawled behind it.

"Look out, Red!" warned Hopalong as he flung himself off his horse and led it down into a deep coulee for protection. "That's Dick Archer, an' he can shoot like th' very devil!"

Red, already in a gully, laughed. "An' so can I."

"Hey, I'm going around on th' other side—look out for him," Hopalong called, starting away. "We can't waste no more time up here than we has to."

"All right; go ahead," Red replied, pushing his sombrero over the edge of the gully where the rustler could see it; and he laughed softly when he saw the new hole in it. "He shore can shoot, all right," he muttered. Working down the gully until he came to a clump of greasewood he crawled up the bank and looked out at the man behind the dead horse, who was intently watching the place where he had seen Red's sombrero. "I knowed Eagle was holding cards in this game," Red remarked, smiling grimly. "Wonder how many are in it, anyhow?"

Hearing the crack of a gun he squinted along the sights of his Winchester and waited patiently for a chance to shoot. Then he heard another shot and saw the rustler raise himself to change his position, and Red fired. "I knowed, too, that Hoppy would drive him into range for me, even if he didn't hit him. Wonder what Mr. Dick Archer thinks about *my* shooting about now? Ah!" he cried as the smoke from his second shot drifted away. "Got you again!" he grunted. Then he dropped below the edge of the gully and grinned as he listened to the bullets whining overhead, for the rustler, wounded twice inside of a minute by one man, was greatly incensed thereby and petulantly bombarded the greasewood clump. He knew that he was done for, but that was no reason why he shouldn't do as much damage as he could while he was able.

"Bet he's mad," grinned Red. "An' there goes that Sharps—I could tell Hoppy's gun in a fusillade."

Crawling back up the gully to his first position Red peered out between some gramma grass tufts and again slid his rifle to his shoulder, laughing softly at the regular reports of the Sharps.

A puff of smoke enveloped his head and drifted behind him as he worked the lever of his rifle and, arising, he walked out towards the prostrate man and waved for his friend to join him. As he drew near the rustler struggled up on one elbow, and Red, running forward with his gun raised half-way to his shoulder, cried: "Don't make no gun-play, or I'll blow you apart! Where's th' rest of yore gang?"

"Go to hell!" coughed the other, trying to get his Colt out, for his rifle was empty. He stiffened and fell flat.

Ten minutes later Hopalong and Red were riding southwest along a plain and well beaten trail, both silent and thoughtful. And at the end of an hour they saw the ragged top of Thunder Mesa towering against the horizon. They went forward cautiously now and took advantage of the unevenness of the plain, riding through barrancas and keeping close to chaparrals.

"Well, Red, I reckon we better stop," Hopalong remarked at last, his glasses glued to his eyes. "No use letting them see us."

"Is that smoke up there?" asked Red.

"Yes; an' there's somebody moving around near th' edge."

"I see him now."

"I reckon we know all that's necessary," Hopalong remarked. "That trail is enough, anyhow. Now we've got to get back to th' ranch without letting them fellers see us."

"We can lead th' cayuses till we can get in that barranca back there," Red replied. "We won't stick up so prominent if we do that. After we make it we'll find it easy to keep from being seen if we've any caution."

Hopalong threw himself out of the saddle. "Dismount!" he cried. "That feller up there is coming towards this end. He's their lookout, I bet."

They remained hidden and quiet for an hour while the lookout gazed around the plain, both impatient and angry at the time he gave to his examination. When he turned and disappeared they waited for a few minutes to see if he was coming back, and satisfied that the way was clear, led their horses to the barranca and rode through it until far enough away to be safe from observation.

Darkness caught them before they had covered half of the distance between the mesa and the ranch, and there being no moon to light the way, they picketed their mounts, had supper, and rolling up in their blankets, spent the night on the open plain.

CHAPTER 24

Red's Discomfiture

On their return they separated and Red, coming to an arroyo, rode along its edge for a mile and then turned north. Ten minutes after he had changed his course he espied an indistinct black speck moving among a clump of cottonwoods over half a mile ahead of him, and as he swung his glasses on it a cloud of smoke spurted out. His horse reared, plunged, and then sank to earth where it kicked spasmodically and lay quiet. As the horse died Red, who had dismounted at the first tremor, threw himself down behind it and shoved his rifle across the body, swearing at the range, for at that distance his Winchester was useless. A small handful of sand flew into the air close beside him with a vicious spat, and the bullet hummed away into the brush as a small pebble struck him sharply on the cheek. A few seconds later he heard the faint, flat report.

"It's a clean thousand, an' more," he growled. "Wish I had Hopalong's gun. I'd make that feller jump!"

He looked around to see how close he was to cover and when he glanced again at the cottonwoods they seemed to be free of an enemy. Then a shot came from a point to the north of the trees and thudded into the carcass of the horse. Red suddenly gave way to his accumulated anger which now seethed at a white heat and, scrambling to his feet, ran to the brush behind him. When he gained it he plunged forward to top speed, leaping from cover to cover as he zig-zagged towards the man who had killed Ginger, and who had tried his best to kill him.

He ran on and on, his rifle balanced in his right hand and ready for instant use, his breath coming sharply now. Red was in no way at home out of the saddle. His high-heeled, tight-fitting boots cramped his toes and the sand made running doubly hard. He was not far from the cottonwoods; they lay before him and to his right.

Turning quickly he went north, so as to go around the plot of ground on which he hoped to find his accurate, long-range assailant, and as he came to a break in the hitherto close-growing brush he stopped short and dropped to one knee behind a hillock of sand, the rifle going to his shoulder as part of the movement.

Several hundred yards east of him he saw two men, who were hastily mounting, and running from them was a frightened calf. One of the pair waved an arm towards the place where Ginger lay and as he did so a puff of smoke lazily arose from behind the hillock of sand to the west and he jumped up in his saddle, his left arm falling to his side. Another puff of smoke arose and his companion fought his wounded and frightened horse, and then suddenly grasped his side and groaned. The puffs were rising rapidly behind the hillock and bullets sang sharply about them; the horse of the first man hit leaped forward with a bullet-stung rump. Spurring madly the two rustlers dashed into the brush, lying close along the necks of their mounts, and soon were lost to the sight of the angry marksman.

Red leaped up, mechanically re-filling the magazine of his rifle, and watched them out of sight, helpless either to stop or pursue them. He shook his rifle, almost blind with rage, crying: "I hope you get to Thunder Mesa before we do, an' stay there; or run into Frenchy an' his men on yore way back! If I could get to Number Two ahead of you you'd never cross that boundary."

As he returned to his horse his rage cooled and left him, a quiet, deep animosity taking its place, and he even smiled with savage elation when he thought how he had shot at eight hundred yards—they had not escaped entirely free from punishment and his accuracy had impressed them so much that they had not lingered to have it out with him, even as they were two to one, mounted, and armed with long-range rifles. And he could well allow them to escape, for he would find them again at the mesa, if they managed to cross the line unseen by his friends, and he could pay the debt there.

He swore when he came to the body of his horse and anger again took possession of him. Ginger had been the peer of any animal on the range and, contrary to custom, he had felt no little affection for it. At cutting out it had been unequalled and made the work a pleasure to its rider; at stopping when the rope went home and turning short when on the dead run it had not been excelled by any horse on the ranch. He had taught it several tricks, such as coming to him in response to a whistle, lying down quickly at a slap on the shoulder, and bucking with whole-hearted zeal and viciousness when mounted by a stranger. Now he slapped the carcass and removed the saddle and bridle which had so often displeased it.

"Ginger, old boy," he said, slinging the forty-pound saddle to his shoulder and turning to begin his long tramp toward the dam, "I shore hate to hoof it, but I'd do it with a lot better temper if I knowed you was munching grass with th' rest of the cavvieyh. You've been a good old friend, an' I hates to leave you; but if I get any kind of a chance at th' thief that plugged you I'll square up for you good an' plenty."

To the most zealous for exercise, carrying a forty-pound double-cinch saddle for over five miles across a hot, sandy plain and under a blazing, scorching sun, with the cinches all the time working loose and falling to drag behind and catch in the vegetation, was no pleasant task; and add to that a bridle, full magazine rifle, field glasses, canteen, and a three-pound Colt revolver swinging from a belt heavily weighted with cartridges, and it becomes decidedly irksome, to say the least. Red's temper can be excused when it is remembered that for years his walking had been restricted to getting to his horse, that his footwear was unsuited for walking, that he had been shot at and had lost his best horse. Each mile added greatly to his weariness and temper and by the time he caught sight of Hopalong, who rode recklessly over the range blazing at a panic-stricken coyote, he was near the point of spontaneous combustion.

He heaved the saddle from him, kicked savagely at it as it dropped, for which he was instantly sorry, and straightened his back slowly for fear that any sudden exertion would break it. His rifle exploded, twice, thrice; and Hopalong sat bolt upright and turned, his rifle going instinctively to his shoulder before he saw his friend's waving sombrero.

The coyote-chaser slid the smoking Sharps into its sheath and galloped to meet his friend who, filling the air with sulphurous remarks, now seated himself on the roundly cursed saddle.

Hopalong swept up and stopped, grinning expectantly and, to Red, exasperatingly. "Where's yore cayuse?" he asked. "Why are you toting yore possessions on th' hoof? Are you emigrating?"

Red's reply was a look wonderfully expressive of all the evils in human nature; it was fairly crowded with murder and torture, and Hopalong held his head on one side while he weighed it.

"Phew!" he exclaimed in wondering awe. "Yo're shore mad! You'd freeze old Geronimo's blood if he saw that look!"

"An' I'll freeze yourn; I'll let it soak into th' sand if you don't change yore front!" blazed Red.

"What's the matter? Where's Ginger?"

A rapid-fire string of expletives replied and then Hopalong began to hear sensible words, which more and more interspersed the profanity, and it was not long before he learned of Red's ride along the arroyo's rim.

"When I turned north," Red continued, wrathfully, "I saw something in them dozen cottonwoods around that come-an'-go spring; an' then what do you think happened?" he cried. Not waiting for any reply he continued hastily: "Why, some murdering squaw's dog went an' squibbed at me at long range! With me on my own ranch, too! An' he killed Ginger first shot. He missed me three straight an' *I* couldn't do nothing at a thousand an' over with this gun."

"Th' damn pirate!" exclaimed Hopalong, hotly.

"I was a whole lot mad by that time, so I jumped back into th' brush an' ran for th' grove, hoping to get square when I got in range. After I'd run about a thousand miles I came to th' edge of th' clearing west of th' trees an' damned if I didn't see two fellers climbing on their cayuses, an' some hasty, too. Reckon they didn't know how many friends I might have behind me. Well, I was some shaky from running like I did, an' they was a good eight hundred away, but I let drive just th' same an' got one in th' arm, th' other somewhere else, an' hit both of their cayuses. I wish I'd 'a filled 'em so full of holes they couldn't hang together, th' thieves!"

"I'd shore like to go after them, Red," Hopalong remarked. "We could ride west an' get 'em when they pass that water hole if you had a cayuse."

"Oh, we'll get 'em, all right—at th' mesa," Red rejoined. "I'm so tired I wouldn't go now if I could. Walking all th' way down here with that saddle! You get off that cayuse an' let me ride him," he suggested, mopping his face with his sleeve.

"What! Me? *Me* get off an' walk! I reckon not!" replied Hopalong, and then his face softened. "You pore, unfortunate cowpunch," he said, sympathetically. "You toss up yore belongings an' climb up here behind me. I'll take you to th' dam, where Johnny has picketed his cayuse. Th' Kid's going in for a swim; said he didn't know how soon he'd get a chance to take a bath. We can rustle his cayuse for a joke—come on."

"Oh, wait a minute, can't you?" Red replied, wearily. "I can't lift my legs high enough to get up there—they're like lead. That trail was hell strung out."

"You should 'a cached yore saddle an' everything but th' gun an' come down light," Hopalong remarked. "Or you could 'a gone to th' line an' waited for somebody to come along. Why didn't you do that?"

"I ain't leaving that saddle nowhere," Red responded. "Besides I was too blamed mad to stop an' think."

"Well, don't wait very long—Johnny may skin out if you do," Hopalong replied, and then, suddenly: "Just where was it you shot at them snakes?"

Red told him and Hopalong wheeled as if to ride after them.

"Here, you!" cried Red, the horseless. "Where th' devil are you going so sudden?"

"Up to get them cow-lifters that you couldn't, of course," his companion replied. "I'm shore going to show you how easy it is when you know how."

"Like hell you are!" Red cried, springing up, his lariat in his hand. "Yo're going to stay right here with me, that's what yo're going to do! I've got something for you to do, you compact bundle of gall! You try to get away without me and I'll make you look like an interrupted spasm, you wart-head!"

"Do you want 'em to get plumb away?" cried the man in the saddle, concealing his mirth.

"I want you to stick right here an' tote me to a cayuse!" Red retorted, swinging the rope. "*I'm* going to be around when anybody goes after them Siwashes, an' don't you forget it. There ain't no hurry—we'll get 'em quick enough when we starts west. An' if you try any get-away play an' leave me out here on my two feet with all these contraptions, I'll pick you off'n that pie-bald like hell greased with calamity!"

Hopalong laughed heartily. "Why, I was only a-fooling, Red. Do you reckon I'd go away an' leave you standing out here like a busted-down pack mule?"

"I hoped you was only fooling, but I wasn't taking no chances with a cuss like you," Red replied, grinning. "Not with this load of woe, you bet."

"Say, it's too bad you didn't have my gun up there," Hopalong said, regretfully. "You could 'a got 'em both then, an' had two cayuses to ride home on."

"Well, *I* could 'a got 'em with it," Red replied, grinning, his good nature returning under the chaffing. "But you can't hit th' mesa with it over six hundred. They'd 'a got away from you without getting hit."

Hopalong laughed derisively and then sobered. "Yo're right, Red, yo're right. Now you get right up here behind me an' I'll take you to th' dam where th' Kid is. Pore feller," he sighed. "Well, I ain't a-wondering after all you've been through. It was enough to make a *strong*-minded man loco." He smiled reassuringly. "Now climb right up behind me, Reddie. Gimme yore little saddle an' yore no-account gun—Ouch!"

"I'll give you th' butt of it again if you don't act like you've made th' best of them gravy brains!" Red snorted. "Here, you lop-eared cow-wrastler—catch this!" throwing the saddle so sudden and hard that Hopalong almost lost his balance from the impact. "Now you gimme a little room in front of th' tail—I ain't no blasted fly."

Hopalong gave his friend a hand and Red landed across the horse's back, to the instant and strong dislike of that animal, which showed its displeasure by bucking mildly.

"Glory be!" cried Hopalong, laughing. "Riding double on a bucking hinge ain't no play, is it? Suppose he felt like pitching real strong—where would you be with that tail holt?"

"You bump my nose again with th' back of yore head an' you'll see how much play it is!" Red retorted. "Come on—pull out. We ain't glued fast. Th' world moves, all right, but if yo're counting on it sliding under you till th' dam comes around yo're way off; it ain't moving that way. Hey! Stop that spurring!"

"I'll hook 'em in you again if you don't shut up!" Hopalong promised, jabbing them into the horse, which gave one farewell kick, to Red's disgust, and cantered south with ears flattened.

"Whoop! I'm riding again!" Red exulted.

"I'm glad it wasn't Red Eagle they went an' killed," Hopalong remarked.

"Red Eagle!" snorted Red, indignantly. "What good is this cayuse, anyhow? Ginger was worth three like this."

"Well, if you don't like this cayuse you can get off an' hoof it, you know," Hopalong retorted. "But I'll tell you what you know a'ready; there ain't no cayuse in this part of th' country that can lose him in long-distance running. He ain't no fancy parlor animal like Ginger was; he don't know how to smoke a cig or wash dishes, or do any of th' fool things yore cayuse did, but he's right on th' job when it comes to going hard an' long. An' it's them two things that tell how much a cayuse is worth, down here in this country. If I could 'a jumped on him up there when they made their get-away from you, me an' th' Sharps would 'a fixed 'em. They wouldn't be laughing now at how easy you was."

"They ain't laughing, not a bit of it—an' they won't even be able to swear after I get out to th' mesa," Red asserted. "Have you seen Buck, or anybody 'cept th' Kid?"

"Yes. I told Buck an' Frenchy about it, an' Skinny, too," Hopalong replied. "Buck an' Frenchy went north along th' west line to get th' boys from Number Two. Buck says we'll go after 'em just as soon as we can get ready, which most of us are now. Pore Lanky; he's got to stay home an' pet his wounds—Buck said he couldn't go."

"Did Buck say who was going an' who was going to stay home?"

"Yes; you, Johnny, Billy, Pete, Skinny, Frenchy, me, Buck, an' Pie Willis are going—th' rest will have to watch th' ranch. That makes nine of us. Wonder how many are up at the mesa?"

"There'll be plenty, don't you worry," Red replied. "When we go after anybody we generally has to mix up with a whole company. I wouldn't be a whole lot surprised if they give us an awful fight before they peter out. They'll be up in th' air a hundred feet. We'll have plenty to do, all right."

"Well, two won't be there, anyhow—Archer an' Juan. I bet we'll find most of th' people of Eagle up there waiting for us."

"Lord, I hope they are!" cried Red. "Then we can clean up everything at once, town an' all."

"There's th' Kid—see th' splash?" Hopalong laughed. "He shore is stuck on swimming. He don't care if there's cottonmouths in there with him. One of them snakes will get him some day, an' if one does, then we'll plant him, quick."

"Oh, I dunno. I ain't seen none at th' dam," Red replied. "They don't like th' sand there as much as they do th' mud up at th' other end, an' along th' sides. Gee! There's his cayuse!"

Johnny dove out of sight, turned over and came up again, happy as a lark, and saw his friends riding towards him, and he trod water and grinned. "Hullo, fellers. Coming in?—it's fine! Hey, Red. We're all going out to Thunder Mesa as soon as we can! But what are you riding double for? Where's yore cayuse?" Something in Red's expression made him suspicious of his friends' intentions and, fearing that he might have to do some walking, he made a few quick strokes and climbed out, dressing as rapidly as his wet skin would permit.

Red briefly related his experience and Johnny swore as he struggled through his shirt. "What are you going to do?" he asked, poking his head out into sight.

"I'm going to ride yore cayuse to th' line house—you ain't as tired as me," replied Red.

"Not while I'm alive, you ain't!" cried Johnny, running to his horse. Then he grinned and went back to his clothes. "You take him an' rope th' cayuse I saw down in that barranca—there's two of 'em there, both belonging to Meeker. But you be shore to come back!"

"Shore, Kid," Red replied, vaulting into the saddle and riding away.

Johnny fastened his belt around him and looked up. "Say, Hoppy," he laughed, "Buck said Cowan sent my new gun down to th' bunk house yesterday. He's going to bring it with him when he comes down to-morrow. But I only got fifty cartridges for it—will you lend me some of yourn if I run short?"

"Where did Cowan get it?"

"Why, don't you remember he said he'd get me one like yourn th' next time he went north? He got back yesterday—bought it off some feller up on th' XS. Cost me twenty-five dollars without th' cartridges. But I've got fifty empties I can load when I get time, so I'll be all right later on. Will you lend me some?"

"Fifty is enough, you chump," laughed Hopalong. "You won't get that many good chances out there."

"I know; but I want to practice a little. It'll shoot flatter than my Winchester," Johnny grinned, hardly able to keep from riding to the bunk house to get his new gun.

Red rode up leading a horse. "That's a good rope, Kid, 'though th' hondo is purty heavy," he said, saddling the captured animal. "Is Buck going to bring down any food an' cartridges when he comes?" he asked.

"Yes; three cayuses will pack 'em. We can send back for more if we stay out there long enough to need more. Buck says that freak spring up on top flows about half a mile through th' chaparral before it peters out. What do you know about it, Red?" Hopalong asked.

"Seems to me that he's right. I think it flows through a twisting arroyo. But there'll be water enough for us, all right."

"I got a .45–120 Sharps just like Hopalong's, Red," Johnny grinned. "He said he'd lend me fifty cartridges for it, didn't you, Hoppy?"

"Well, I'll be blamed!" exclaimed Hopalong. "First thing I knowed about it, if I did. I tell you you won't need 'em.

"Where'd you get it?" asked Red.

"Cowan got it. I told you all about it three weeks ago."

"Well, you better give it back an' use yore Winchester," replied Red. "It ain't no good, an' you'll shoot some of us with it, too. What do you want with a gun that'll shoot eighteen hundred? You can't hit anything now above three hundred."

"Yo're another—I can, an' you know it, too. Three hundred!" he snorted. "Huh! Here comes Skinny!"

Skinny rode up and joined them, all going to the Peak. Finally he turned and winked at Johnny.

"Hey, Kid. Hopalong ought to go right down to th' H2 while he's got time. He hadn't ought to go off fighting without saying good-bye to his girl, had he?"

"She'd keep him home—wouldn't let him take no chances of getting shot," Red asserted. "Anyhow, if he went down there he'd forget to come back."

"Ow-wow!" cried Johnny. "You hit him! You hit him! Look at his face!"

"He shore can't do no courting while he's away," Skinny remarked. "He wouldn't let Red go with him when he went to give Meeker th' shovel, an' I didn't know why till just now."

"You go to blazes, all of you!" exclaimed Hopalong, red and uncomfortable. "I ain't doing no courting, you chump! An' Red knows why I went down there alone.

"Yes; you gave me a fool reason, an' went alone," Red retorted. "An' if that ain't courting, for th' Lords sake what is it? Or is she doing all of it, you being bashful?"

"Yes, Hoppy; tell us what it is," asked Skinny.

"Oh, don't mind them, Hoppy; they're jealous," Johnny interposed. Don't you make no excuses, not one. Admit that yo're courting an' tell 'em that yo're going to keep right on a-doing it an' get all th' honey you can."

Red and Skinny grinned and Hopalong, swearing at Johnny, made a quick grab for him, but missed, for Johnny knew the strength of that grip. "I ain't courting! I'm only trying to—trying to be—sociable; that's all!"

"Sociable!" yelled Red. "Oh, Lord!"

"It must be nice to be sociable," replied Johnny. "Since you ain't courting, an' are only trying to be sociable, then you won't care if we go down an' try it!"

"You bet; an' I'm going down, too," asserted Red, who was very much afraid of women, and who wouldn't have called on Mary Meeker for a hundred dollars.

Hopalong knew his friend's weakness and he quickly replied: "Red, I dare you to do that. I dare you to go down there an' talk to her for five minutes. When I say talk, I don't mean stammer. I dare you!"

"Do you dare *me*?" asked Johnny, quickly, glancing at the sun to see how much time he had.

"Oh, I ain't got time," replied Red, grinning.

"You ain't got th' nerve, you mean," jeered Skinny.

"I dare you, Red," Hopalong repeated, grimly.

"I asked you if you dared *me*?" hastily repeated Johnny.

"*You*! Not on yore life, Kid. But you stay away from there!" Hopalong warned.

"Gee—wish you'd lend me them cartridges," sighed Johnny. "Mebbe Meeker has got some he ain't so stingy with," he added, thoughtfully.

"I'll lend you th' cartridges, Kid," Hopalong offered. "But you stay away from th' H2. D'y hear?"

CHAPTER 25

Antonio's Revenge

While Red had been trudging southward under his saddle and other possessions a scene was being enacted on a remote part of the H2 range which showed how completely a cowboy leased his very life to the man who paid him his monthly wage, one which serves to illustrate in a way how a ranchman was almost a feudal lord. There are songs of men who gave up their lives to save their fellows, one life for many, and they are well sung; but what of him who risks his life to save one small, insignificantly small portion of his employer's possessions, risks it without hesitation or fear, as a part of his daily work? What of the man who, not content with taking his share of danger in blizzard, fire, and stampede, on drive, roundup, and range-riding, leaps fearlessly at the risk of his life to save a paltry head or two of cattle to his ranch's tally sheet? Such men were the rule, and such a one was Curley, who, with all his faults, was a man as a man should be.

Following out his orders he rode his part of the range with alertness, and decided to explore the more remote southwestern angle of the ranch. Doc had left him an hour before to search the range nearer Eagle and would not be back again until time to return to the ranch house for the night. This was against Meeker's order, for they had been told to keep together for their own protection, but they had agreed that there was little risk and that it would be better to separate and cover more ground.

The day was bright and, with the exception of the heat, all he could desire. His spirits bubbled over in snatches of song, but all the time moving in the general direction of the little-ridden territory. On all sides stretched the same monotonous view, sage brush, mesquite, cactus, scattered tufts of grass, and the brown plain, endless, flat, wearying.

The surroundings did not depress him, but only gradually slowed the exultant surge of his blood and, as he hummed at random, an old favorite came to him out of the past, and he sung it joyously:

My taste is that of an aristocrat,
    My purse that of a pauper:
I scorn the gold her parents hold—
    But shore I love their daughter.
Hey de diddle de, hey de dee,
    But shore I love their daughter.

When silvery nights my courting light
    An' souls of flowers wander,
Then who's to blame if I loved th' game
    An' did not pause to ponder?
Hey de diddle de, hey de dee,
    An' did not pause to ponder.

Her eyes are blue, an' oh, so true—
    Th' words were said ere thought, Lad.
Her father swore we'd meet no more—
    But I am not distraught, Lad.
Hey de diddle de, hey de de—
    But I am not distraught, Lad.

He ceased abruptly, rigidly erect, staring straight ahead as the significance of the well trodden trail impressed itself on his mind. He was close to the edge of a steep-walled basin; and leading to it was a narrow, steep gully, down which the beaten trail went. Riding closer he saw that two poles were set close to the wall of the gully, and from one of them dangled a short, frayed hempen rope. There was a water hole in the basin, surrounded by a muddy flat, and everywhere were the tracks of cattle.

As he hesitated to decide whether or not it would be worth while to ride through the depression he chanced to look south, and the question decided itself. Spurring savagely, he leaned forward in the saddle, the wind playing a stern song in his ears, a call to battle for his ranch, his pride, and his hatred for foul work. He felt the peculiar, compelling delight, the surging, irresistible intoxication of his kind for fighting, the ecstasy of the blood lust, handed down from his Saxon forefathers.

A mile ahead of him was a small herd of cattle, being driven west by two men. Did he stop to return to the ranch for assistance? Did he count the odds? Not he, for he saw the perpetrators of the insults he and his companions had chafed under—the way was clear, the quarry plain, and he asked naught else.

They saw him coming—one of them raised a pair of glasses to his eyes and looked closely at him and from him all around the plain. All the time they were driving the cattle harder, shouting and whipping about them with their rawhide quirts; and constantly nearer came the cowboy, now standing up in his stirrups and lashing his straining mount without mercy. Soon he thought he recognized one of the herders, and he flung the name on the whistling wind in one contemptuous shout: "*Antonio!* Damn his soul!" and fell to beating the horse all the harder.

It was Antonio, and a puff of smoke arose from the Mexican's shoulder, and streaked behind, soon followed by another. Curley knew the rifle, a .40–90 Sharps, and did not waste a shot, for he must be on equal terms before he could hope to cope with it. Another puff, then another and another, but still he was not hit. Now he drew his own rifle from his holster and hazarded a shot, but to no avail. Then the second herder, who had not as yet fired, snatching the rifle from Antonio's hands and, checking his horse, leaped off and rested the weapon across the saddle. Taking deliberate aim, he fired, and Curley pitched out of the saddle as his horse stumbled and fell. The rider scrambled to his feet, dazed and hurt, and ran to his horse, but one look told the story and he ended the animal's misery with a shot from his Colt.

The herder and the cattle were rapidly growing smaller in the distance but the Mexican rode slowly around the man on foot, following the circumference of a large circle and shooting with calm deliberation. The bullets hummed and whined viciously past the H2 puncher, kicking up the dust in little spurts, and cold ferocity filled his heart as he realized the rustler's purpose. He raised his own rifle and fired—and leaded the barrel. When he had fallen the barrel had become choked with sand and dust and he was at the mercy of his gloating enemy, who would now wipe out the insult put upon him at the bunk house. Slowly Antonio rode and carefully he fired and then, seeing that there was something wrong with Curley's rifle, which the puncher threw aside, he drew closer, determined to shoot him to pieces.

Curley was stung with rage now. He knew that it was only a question of waiting until the right bullet came, and scorning to hug the sand for the man he held in such contempt, and vaguely realizing that such an act would not change the result, he put all his faith in a dash. He ran swiftly towards his astonished enemy, who expected him to seek what cover the dead horse would give him, Colt in hand, cursing at every jump and hoping to be spared long enough to get within range with his six-shooter, if only for one shot. Antonio did not like this close work and cantered away, glancing back from time to time. When Curley finally was forced to stop because of exhaustion the rider also stopped and slipped off his horse to have a rest for the rifle. Curley emptied the Colt in a futile, enraged effort to make a lucky hit while his enemy had now aimed from across the saddle. Hastily reloading the Colt as he ran, the puncher dashed forward again, zig-zagging to avoid being hit. There was a puff of gray smoke, but Curley did not hear the report. He threw one arm half up as if to ward off the shot and pitched forward, face down in the dust, free from all pain and strife.

Antonio fired again and then cautiously drew nearer to his victim, the rifle at the ready. Turning shortly he made a quick grab at his horse, fearing that it might leave him on foot to be caught by some wandering H2 puncher. Springing into the saddle he rode forward warily to get a closer look at the man he had murdered, proud of his work, but fearful that Curley was playing dead.

When assured that he had nothing to fear from the prostrate form, he rode close. "Knock me down, will you!" he gritted, urging the horse to trample on the body, which the animal refused to do. "Come out looking for us, did you? Well, you found us, all right, but a hell of a lot of good it did you. You ain't saying a word, are you, you carrion? You ain't got no smart come-back now, an' you ain't throwing no wash water on me, are you?"

He started and looked around nervously, fearful that he might be caught and left lying on the sand as he had left Curley. One or two of the H2 outfit carried single-shot rifles which shot as far if not farther than his own, and the owners of them knew how to shoot. Wheeling abruptly he galloped after the herd, looking back constantly and thinking only of putting as great a distance as possible between himself and the scene of the killing.

A lizard crawled out of a hillock and stared steadily at the quiet figure and then, making a tentative sortie, disappeared under the sand; but the man who had sung so buoyantly did not mind it, he lay wrapped in the Sleep Eternal. He had died as he had lived, fearlessly and without a whimper.

Late in the afternoon Doc Riley, sweeping on a circling course, rode through chaparrals, alert even after his fruitless search, looking around on all sides, and wondered if Curley and he would meet before they reached the ranch proper. Suddenly something caught his eye and he stood up in the stirrups to see it better, a ready curse leaping from his lips. He could not make out who it was, but he had fears and he spurred forward as hard as he could go. Then he saw the horse and knew.

Riding close to the figure so as to be absolutely sure, he knew beyond a hope of mistake and looked around the plain, his expression malevolent and murderous.

"Curley! Curley!" he cried, leaping off his horse and placing a heavy, kindly hand on the broad, sloping shoulder of the man who had been his best friend for years. "So they got you, lad! They got you! In God's name, why did I leave you?" he cried in bitter self-condemnation. "It's my fault, it's my fault, lad!" He straightened up suddenly and glared around through tear-dimmed eyes. "*But by th' living God I'll pay them for this*, I'll pay them for this! Damn their murdering souls!"

He caught sight of an empty cartridge shell and snatched it up eagerly. "Forty–ninety, by God! That's Antonio's! Curley, my lad, I'll get him for you— an' when I *do*! I'll send his soul to th' blackest pit in hell, an' send it *slow*!"

He noticed and followed the tracks in the sand, reading them easily. He found the Winchester and quickly learned its story, which told him the whole thing. Returning to the body of his friend he sat by it quietly, looking down at it for several minutes, his sombrero in his hand.

"Well, wishing won't do no good," he muttered, dismounting. "I'll take you home, lad, an' see you put down too deep for coyotes to bother you. An' I'll square yore scores or join you trying."

He lifted the body across the withers of his horse and picked up the Colt. Mounting, he rode at a walk toward the bunk house, afire with rage and sorrow.

For the third time Meeker strode to the door of the bunk house and looked out into the darkness, uneasy and anxious. Chick sauntered over to him and leaned against the frame of the door. "They'll show up purty soon, Jim," he remarked.

"Yes. I reckon so—Salem!" the foreman called. "Put their grub where it'll keep warm."

"Aye, aye, sir. I was just thinking I ought to. They're late, ain't they, sir?" he asked. "An' it's dark, too," he added, gratis.

"Why, is it, Salem?" queried Dan, winking at Jack Curtis, but Salem disappeared into the gallery.

"Listen!—I hear 'em!" exclaimed Chick.

"You hear one of 'em," corrected Meeker, turning to the table to finish drinking his coffee. "Hey, Salem! Never mind warming that grub—rustle it in here. One of 'em's here, an' he'll be starved, too."

Suddenly Chick started back with an exclamation as Doc Riley loomed up in the light of the door, carrying a body over his shoulder. Stepping into the room while his friends leaped to their feet in amazement and incredulity, he lowered his burden to a bench and faced them, bloody and furious.

"What's th' matter?" exclaimed Meeker, the first to find his voice, leaping forward and dropping the cup to the floor. "Who did that?"

Doc placed his sombrero over the upturned face and ripped out a savage reply. "Antonio! Yore broncho-buster! Th' snake that's raising all th' devil on this range! Here—see for yoreself!" tossing the cartridge shell to his foreman, who caught it clumsily, looked at it, and then handed it to Dan. Exclamations and short, fierce questions burst from the others, who crowded up to see the shell.

"Tell me about it, Doc," requested Meeker, pacing from wall to wall.

"He was shot down like a dog!" Doc cried, his rage sweeping over him anew in all its savagery. "I saw th' whole thing in th' sand, plain as day. Antonio got his cayuse first an' then rode rings around him, keeping out of range of Curley's Colt, for Curley had leaded his rifle. It was Colt against Sharps at five hundred, that was what it was! He didn't have a show, not a measly show for his life! Shot down like a *dog*!"

"Where'd it happen?" asked Chick, breathlessly, while the low-voiced threats and imprecations swelled to an angry, humming chorus.

"Away down in th' southwest corner," replied Doc, and he continued almost inaudibly, speaking to himself and forgetful of the others. "Me an' him went to school together an' I used to lick every kid that bullied him till he got big enough to do it hisself. We run away together an' shared th' same hard luck. We went through that Sioux campaign together, side by side, an' to think that after he pulled out of *that* alive he had to be murdered by a yaller coward. If he'd been killed in fair fight it would be all right; but by that coyote—it don't seem possible, not noway. I licked th' feller that hurt him on his first day at school—I'm going to kill th' last!"

"Meeker," he said, coming to himself and facing the angry foreman, "I'm quitting to-night. I won't punch no more till I get that murderer. I take up that trail at daylight an' push it to a finish. It's got to be him or me, now."

"You don't have to quit to do that, an' you *know* it! I don't care if yore gone for six months—yore pay goes on just th' same. He went down fighting for me, an' I'll be everlastingly condemned if I don't have a hand in squaring up for it. Yo're going on special duty for th' H2, Doc, an' yore orders are to get Antonio. Why, by th' Lord, I'll take up th' trail with you, Doc, an' with th' rest of th' boys behind me. This ranch can go galley-west an' crooked till we get that snake. Dan an' Salem stays with my girl an' to watch th' ranch—th' rest of us are with you—we're as anxious as you to push him Yonder, Doc."

"If I can get him alive, get my two hands on his skinny neck," Doc muttered, his fingers twitching. "I'll kill him slow, so he'll feel it longer, so he'll be shore to know why he's going. I want to *feel* his murdering soul dribble hell-wards, an' let him come back a couple of times so I can laugh in his yaller face when he begs! I want to get him—*so!*" and Chick shuddered as the knotted, steel-like fingers opened and shut, for Doc was half devil now. While Chick stared, the transformed man walked over to the bench and picked up the body in his brawny arms and strode into the blackness—Curley was going to lie in the open, with the stars and the sky and the sighing wind.

"God!" breathed Chick, looking around, "I never saw a man like *that* before!"

"I hope he gets what he wants!" exclaimed Dan, fiercely.

"You fellers get yore traps ready for a chase," Meeker ordered as he strode to the door of the gallery. "Fifty rounds for six-shooters an' fifty for rifle, an' plenty of grub. It's a whole lot likely that killer's headed for his gang, an' we've got to be ready to handle everything that comes up. Hey, Salem!" he shouted.

"Aye, aye, sir!" replied Salem, who had just come in from one of the corrals and knew nothing of what had occurred.

"Did you cure that beef I told you to?" demanded the foreman.

"Yes, sir; but it ain't had time to cure—th' weather's not been right. How-somever, I smoked some. That'll be ship-shape."

"Well, have it on our cayuses at daylight. Did you cut this beef in strips, or in twenty-pound chunks, like you did th' last?"

"Strips, *little* strips—I ain't trying to sun-cure no more big hunks, not me, sir."

Meeker turned and went towards the outer door.

"Don't waste no time, boys," he said. "Get all th' sleep you can to-night—you'll need it if I reckon right. Goodnight," and he stepped out into the dark-ness. "Damn them dogs!" he muttered, disappearing in the direction of the kennels, from which came quavering, long-drawn howls.

CHAPTER 26

Frisco Visits Eagle

Eagle did not thoroughly awaken until the sun began to set, for it was not until dark that its inhabitants, largely transient, cared to venture forth. Then it was that the town seethed, boldly, openly, restrained by nothing save the might of the individual.

Prosperity had blessed the town, for there had been an abrupt and pleasing change in local conditions since the disagreement between the two ranches north of the town had assumed warlike aspect. Men who heretofore had no standing with the proprietors of the town's places of amusement and who had seldom been able to pay for as much liquor as they were capable of drinking, now swaggered importantly where they pleased, and found welcome where formerly it had been denied them; for their hands were thrust deep into pockets from which came the cheerful and open-sesame clinking of gold. Even Big Sandy, who had earned his food by sweeping out the saloons and doing odd jobs about them, and was popularly believed to be too lazy to earn a better living by real work, now drank his fill and failed to recognize a broom when he saw it. While the inhabitants could not "get in" on the big plums which they were certain were being shaken down on the range, they could and did take care of the windfalls, and thrived well. They would stay in town until their money was gone and then disappear for a week, and return to spend recklessly. It is not out of place to state, in passing, that numerous small herds bearing strange brands frequently passed around the town at a speed greater than that common to drives, and left clouds of dust on the southeastern horizon.

The town debated the probable whereabouts of ten men who had suddenly disappeared in a body, along with Antonio of the H2. It was obvious what they were doing and the conjectures were limited as to their whereabouts and success. For a while after they had left one or two had ridden in occasionally to buy flour and other necessities, and at that time they had caused no particular thought. But now even these visits had ceased. It was common belief that Quinn knew all about them, but Quinn for good reasons was not urged to talk about the matter. Big Sandy acted as though he knew, which increased his importance for a time, and discredited him thereafter.

While the citizens had been able to rustle as they pleased they had given but little thought to the ten men, being too busy to trail. But now that the H2 punchers rode range with rifles across their arms rustling had become very risky and had fallen off. Then it was that the idlers renewed their conjectures about Shaw and his men and thrashed that matter over and over again. The majority being, as we have said, transients, knew nothing about Thunder Mesa, and those who did know of it were silent, for Shaw and some of his companions knew only one way to close a man's mouth, and were very capable.

So it happened that about noon of the day Curley lost his life six men met in the shadow cast by the front of the "Rawhide" a hundred yards from Quinn's, and exercised squatter sovereignty on the bench just outside the door, while inside the saloon Big Sandy and Nevada played cards close to the bar and talked in low tones. When they were aware of the presence of those on the bench they played silently and listened. The six men outside made up one of the groups of the town's society, having ridden in together and stuck together ever since they had arrived, which was wise.

Big Sandy and Nevada made a team more feared than any other combination. The former, while fair with weapons, was endowed with prodigious strength; by some it was hailed as being greater than that of Pete Wilson, the squat giant of the Bar-20, whose strength was proverbial, as it had good right to be. Nevada was the opposite type, short, wiry, and soft-spoken, but the quickest man in the draw and of uncertain temper.

Chet Bates, on the bench, replied to a companion and gave vent to his soft, Southern laugh. "Yuh still wondering 'bout thet man Shaw, an' th' othas?"

"Nothing else to do, is there?" retorted Dal Gilbert. "We can't run no more cattle, can we?"

"I reckon we can't."

"They're running a big game an' I want to get in it," remarked John Elder. "Frisco was allus friendly. We've got to go trailing for 'em."

"Yes; an' get shot," interposed George Lewis. "They're ten to our six. An' that ain't all of our troubles, neither. We'll find ourselves in a big fight some day, an' right here. Them ranches will wake up, patch up their troubles, an' come down here. You remember what Quinn said about th' time Peters led a lot of mad punchers agin Trendley an' his crowd, don't you? In a day he can raise men enough to wipe this town off th' map."

"Yuh forget, suh, that they are fighting foh principles, an' men who fight foh principles don't call truces," said Chet Bates.

"You've said that till it's old," laughed Sam Austin.

"*I* say we've got to keep our eyes open," warned Lewis.

"Th' devil with that!" broke in Con Irwin. "What *I* want to know is how we're going to get some of th' easy money Shaw's getting."

"We'll have to wait for one of his men to come to town an' trail him back," replied Gilbert.

"What do you say that we try to run one more good herd an' then scout for them, or their trails?" asked Irwin.

"Heah comes somebody," remarked Chet, listening.

The sound of galloping grew rapidly louder and soon they saw Frisco turn into the street and ride towards them. As they saw him a quiet voice was heard behind them and looking up, they saw Nevada smiling at them. "Get him drunk an' keep him away from Quinn's," he counselled.

They exchanged looks and then Elder stepped out into the street and held up his hand. "Hullo, Frisco!" he cried.

"Where yuh been keeping yuhself foh so long?" asked Chet, affably. "Holed up som'ers?"

"Hullo, fellers," grinned Frisco, drawing rein.

"Everybody have a drink on me," laughed Chet. "Ah'm pow'ful thirsty."

Frisco was escorted inside to the bar, where Chet did the honors, and where such a spirit of hospitality and joviality surrounded him that he forgot how many drinks he had taken. He dug up a handful of gold and silver and spread it out on the bar and waved at the bartender. "Bes' you got—ver' bes'," he grinned. "Me an' my fren's want th' ver' bes'; don't we, fellers? I got money—helluva lot of money—an' thersh more where it came from, ain't that so, boys?"

When the noise had subsided he turned around and levelled an unsteady finger at the bartender. "I never go—back onsh fren', never. An' we're all frensh—ain't we, fellers? Tha's right. I got s'more frensh—good fellesh, an' lots of money cached in sand."

"Ah'll bet yuh have!" cried Chet.

"You allus could find pay-dirt," marvelled Nevada, glancing warningly around him. "Yo're a fine prospector, all right."

Frisco stared for a moment and then laughed loudly and leaned against the bar for support. "Proshpector! Proshpector! W'y, we earned tha's money—run a helluva lot of risks. Mebbe tha's Bar-20 outfit'll jump us an' make us fight 'em. No; they can't jump us—they can't get up at us!"

"On a mesa, shore!" whispered Elder to Lewis.

"Wha's you shay?"

"Said they couldn't lick you."

"Who couldn't—lick us?"

"Th' Bar-20," explained Elder.

Frisco rubbed his head and drew himself up, suspicion percolating through his muddled brain. "Never shaid nozzing 'bout no Bar-Twensh!" he asserted, angrily. "Nozzing 'tall. I'm going out of here—don't like you! Gotta get some flour an' ozzer stuff. Never shaid nozzing 'bout—" he muttered, staggering out.

Nevada turned to Elder. "You go with him an' quiet his suspicions. Keep him away from Quinn, for that coyote'll hold him till he gets sober if you don't. This is the chance we've been wanting. Don't try to pump him—his trail will be all we need."

"Wonder what mesa they're on?" asked Lewis.

"Don't know, an' don't care," Nevada replied. "We'll find out quick enough. There's eight of us an' we can put up a stiff argument if they won't take us in. You know they ain't going to welcome us, don't you?"

"Hey, go out th' back way," growled Big Sandy interposing his huge hulk between Bates and the door. "An' don't let Frisco see you near a cayuse, neither," he added.

Nevada walked quickly over to his friend and said a few hurried words in a low voice and Big Sandy nodded. "Shore, Nevada; he might try that, but I'll watch him. If he tries to speak I'll let you know hasty. We're in this to stay," and he followed the others to the door.

Nevada turned and faced the bartender. "Mike, you keep quiet about what you saw an' heard to-day; understand? If you don't, me an' you won't fit in this town at th' same time."

Mike grinned. "I forgot how to talk after one exciting day up in Cheyenne, an' I ain't been drunk since, neither."

"Yo're a wise man," replied the other, stepping out by the back door and hastening up the street where he could keep watch over Quinn's saloon. It was an hour before he caught sight of Frisco, and he was riding west, singing at the top of his lungs. Then Quinn slipped into his corral and threw a saddle on a horse.

"Drop it!" said a quiet voice behind him and he turned to see Nevada watching him.

"What do you mean?" demanded Quinn, ominously.

"Let loose of that cayuse an' go back inside," was the reply.

"You get th' hell out of here an mind yore own—" Quinn leaped aside and jerked at his Colt; but was too late, and he fell, badly wounded. Nevada sprang forward and disarmed him and then, mounting, galloped off to join his friends.

CHAPTER 27

Shaw Has Visitors

When Frisco reached the edge of the clearing around the mesa he saw Antonio and Shaw toiling cautiously up the steep, precarious trail leading to the top, and he hailed vociferously. Both looked around, Antonio scowling and his companion swearing at their friend's condition. Frisco's pack horse, which he had sense enough to bring back, was loaded down with bags and packages which had been put on recklessly, inasmuch as a slab of bacon hung from the animal's neck and swayed to and fro with each step; and the animal he rode had a bartender's apron hanging down before its shoulders.

"Had a rip-snorting time—rip-snorting time," he announced pleasantly, in a roar. "Salubrious—rip-snorting—helluva time!"

"Nobody'd guess it!" retorted Shaw. "Look at them bundles! An' him an expert pack-horse man, too. An' that cayuse with a shirt! For anybody that can throw as neat a diamond hitch as him, that pack horse is a howling disgrace!"

"Hang th' pack horse!" growled Antonio. "I bet th' whole town knows our business now! He ought to be shot. Where you going?"

"Down to help him up," Shaw replied. "He'll bust his fool neck if he wrestles with that trail alone. You go on up an' send a couple of th' boys down to bring up th' grub," he ordered, starting down the path.

"Let him bust his fool neck!" replied Antonio. "He should 'a done that before he left."

"What's th' ruction?" asked Clausen, looking down over the edge.

"Oh, Frisco's come back howling drunk. Go down an' help him tote th' grub up. Shaw said for somebody else to help you."

"Hey, Cavalry," cried Clausen. "Come on an' gimme a hand," and the two disappeared down the trail.

The leader returned, heralded by singing and swearing, and pushed Frisco over the mesa top to sprawl full-length on the ground. Shaw looked down at him with an expression of anger and anxiety and then turned abruptly on his heel as a quavering snore floated up from the other.

"Here, Manuel!" he called, sharply. "Take my glasses an' go out to yore lookout rock. Look towards Eagle an' call me if you see anybody."

Manuel moved away as Cavalry and Clausen, loaded down, appeared over the edge of the mesa wall and dropped their loads at Shaw's feet.

"What did you tell him to get?" asked Clausen, marvelling.

"What do you think I told him to get?" snapped Shaw.

"I don't know, seeing what he brought back," was the reply.

Shaw examined the pile. "God's name, what's all this stuff?" he roared. "Bacon! An' all th' meat we want is down below. Canned milk! Two bottles XXX Cough Syrup, four bottles of whiskey, bottle vaniller extract, plug tobacco, an' three harmonicas! Is *that* flour!" he yelled, glaring at a small bag. "Twenty pounds! Five pounds of salt!"

"I reckon he bought all th' cartridges in town," Cavalry announced, staggering into sight with a box on his shoulder. "Lord, but it's heavy!"

"Twenty pounds of flour to last nine men a month!" Shaw shouted, kicking at the bag. "An' look at this coffee—two pounds! I'll teach him a lesson when he gets sober."

"Well, he made up th' weight in th' cartridges," Cavalry grinned. He grasped Shaw's arm. "What's got into Manuel?"

The leader looked and sprinted to the lookout rock, where Manuel was gesticulating, and took the glasses. Half a minute later he returned them and rejoined his companions near the pile of supplies.

"What is it?" asked Cavalry.

"Some of our Eagle friends. Mebby they want cards in this game, but we'll waste little time with 'em. Post th' fellers along th' edge, Clausen, an' you watch th' trail up. Keep 'em covered while I talks with 'em. Don't be slow to burn powder if they gets to pushing things."

"They trailed Frisco," growled Cavalry.

"Shore; oh, he was a great success!" snapped Shaw, going to the edge of the mesa to await the eight newcomers, his men finding convenient places along the top of the wall, their rifles ready for action.

They did not have long to wait for soon Nevada and Chet Bates rode into the clearing and made for the trail.

"That's far enough, Nevada!" shouted Shaw, holding up his hand.

"Why, hullo, Shaw!" cried the man below. "Yo're up a good tree, all right," he laughed.

"Yes."

"Can we ride up, or do we have to take shank's mare?"

"Neither."

"Well, we want some water after that ride," replied Nevada.

"Plenty of it below. Nobody asked you to take that ride. What do you want, anyhow?"

"Why, when Frisco said you was out here we thought we'd drop in on you an' pay you a little visit."

"You have paid us a little visit. Call again next summer."

"Running many cows?" asked Nevada.

"Nope; educating coyotes. Didn't see none, did you?"

Nevada exchanged a few words with his companion and then looked up again. "I reckon you need us, Shaw. Eight more men means twice as many cows; an' we can all fight a little if th' ranches get busy out here."

"We're crowded now. Better water up an' hit th' back trail. It's hard riding in th' dark."

"We didn't come out here for a drink," replied Nevada. "We came out to help you rustle, which same we'll do. I tell you that you need us, man!"

"When I need you I'll send for you. *Adios.*"

"You ain't going to let us come up?"

"Not a little bit. Pull yore stakes an' hit th' back trail. *Adios!*"

"Well, we'll hang around to-night an' talk it over again to-morrow. Mebby you'll change yore mind. So long," and the two wheeled and disappeared into the chaparrals, Nevada chuckling. "I didn't spring that little joker, Chet, because it's a good card to play last. When we tell him that we won't let nobody come down off'n th' mesa it'll be after we can't do nothing else. No use making him mad."

Up on the mesa Shaw wheeled, scowling. "I knowed that fool would fire off something big! Why can't he get drunk out here, where it's all right?"

"That Nevada is a shore bad proposition," Clausen remarked.

"So'm I!" snapped Shaw. "He can't come up, an' pursooant to that idee I reckon you an' Hall better arrange to watch th' trail to-night."

He walked away and paced slowly along the edge of the wall, studying every yard of it. He had done this thing before and had decided that no man set a saddle who could scale the sheer hundred feet of rock which dropped so straight below him. But somehow he felt oppressed, and the sinking sun threw into bold relief the furrows of his weather-beaten, leathery face and showed the trouble marks which sat above his eyes. At one part of the wall he stopped and peered over, marshalling imaginative forces in attack after attack against it. But at the end he smiled and moved on—that was the weakest point in his defense, but he would consider himself fortunate if he should find no weaker defense in future conflicts. As he returned to the hut he glanced at the lookout rock and saw Manuel in his characteristic pose, unmoving, silent, watchful.

"I'm getting as bad as Cavalry and his desert," he grumbled. "Still, they can't lick us while we stay up here."

CHAPTER 28

Nevada Joins Shaw

Late in the forenoon of the day after Nevada had argued with Shaw, Manuel shifted his position on the lookout rock and turned to face the hut. "Señor! Señor Shaw! He ees here."

Shaw strode to the edge of the mesa and looked down, seeing Nevada sitting quietly on a horse and looking up at him. Manuel, his duty performed, turned and looked eastward, shrinking back as Shaw stepped close to him. Lying prone along the edge half a dozen men idly fingered rifles as they covered the man below, Antonio's face in particular showing intense aversion to any more recruits.

"Morning, Shaw," shouted Nevada. "Going to let us come up?"

The leader was about to reply when he felt a tug at his ankle and saw Manuel's lips moving. "What is it"

"Look, Señor, look!" whispered the frightened Mexican, pointing eastward. "Eet ees de Bar-20! They be here *poco tiempo!*"

"Shut up!" retorted Shaw in a whisper, glancing east, and what he saw changed his reply to the man below. "Well, Nevada, we are purty crowded up here as it is, but I'll ask th' boys about it. They ain't quite decided. Be back in a minute," and he stepped back out of sight of those below and waved his companions to him. Briefly stating the facts he asked that Nevada and his force be allowed up to help repulse the Bar-20, and the men who only a short time before had sworn that they would take in no partners nodded assent and talked over the new conditions while their leader again went to the edge.

"We can get along without you fellers," he called down, "but we don't reckon you'll cut any hole in our profits as long as you do yore share of work. If yo're willin' to share an' share alike, in work, grub, profits, an' fighting, why

I reckon you can come up. But I'm leader here an' what I says goes: are you agreeable?"

"That's fair," Nevada replied. "Th' harder you work th' bigger th' pay—come on, boys," he cried, turning and waving his arm. "We're in!"

While the newcomers put their horses in the corral and toiled carefully up the steep trail Manuel stared steadily into the east and again saw the force that had filled him with fear. Hall, who was now watching with him, abruptly arose and returned to the hut, reporting: "Seven men out there—it's th' Bar-20, all right, I reckon;" and almost immediately afterward Manuel found a moving speck far to the east which Shaw's powerful glasses soon showed to be three pack horses driven by two men.

Nevada looked curiously about him as he gained his goal and then sought a place in the hut for his bunk. This, however, was full, and he cast around outside to find the best place for his blankets. Finding it, he stepped to the spring and had just quenched his thirst when he saw Shaw standing on a ledge of rock above him, looking down. "What is it, Shaw?" he asked.

"Well, you fellers shore enough raised hell, now didn't you!" demanded the leader, a rising anger in his voice. "Yo're a fine collection of fools, you are—"

"What do—"

"—Leading that Bar-20 gang out here by th' nice, plain trail you left," Shaw continued, sarcastically, not heeding the other's explosive interjection. "That's a nice thing to saddle us with! Damn it, don't you know you've queered th' game for good?"

"Yo're drunk!" retorted Nevada, heatedly. "We came up from th' south! How th' devil could that crowd hit *our* trail?"

"They must 'a hit southwest on a circle," lied Shaw. "Manuel just now saw 'em pass a clearing an' heading this way—nine of 'em!"

"Th' devil!" exclaimed Nevada. "How many are up here now?" he asked quickly.

"Sixteen."

"All right! Let 'em come!" cried the other. "Sixteen to nine—it's easy!" he laughed. "Look here; we can clean up them fellers an' then raid their ranch, for there's only four left at home. We can run off a whopping big herd, sell 'em, an' divvy even. Then we separates, savvy? Why, it couldn't be better!"

Shaw showed his astonishment and his companion continued. "Th' H2 is shy men, an' th' C80 and th' Double Arrow is too far away to bother us. As soon as we lick this aggregation of trouble hunters, what's left will ride hell-bent for that valley. Then th' biggest herd ever rustled in these parts, a trip to a new range, an' plenty of money to spend there."

"That sounds good—but this pleasing cleaning-up is due to be full of knots," Shaw rejoined. "Them nine men come from th' craggiest outfit of high-toned gun-artists in these parts, an' you can bet that they are th' pick of th' crowd! Cassidy, Connors, Peters—an' they've got forty friends purty nigh as bad, an' eager to join in. I ain't no ways a quitter, but this looks to me like Custer's last stand, us being th' Custers."

"Ah, yo're loco!" retorted Nevada. "Look here! Send a dozen picked men down quick an' let 'em lose 'emselves in th' chaparral, far back. When th' terrible man-killers of th' great Bar-20 get plugging this way, our trouble-gang slips up from behind an' it's all over! Go on, before it's too late! Or one of us will ride like th' devil to Eagle for help—but it's got to be quick! You say I got you in this, which I know well I didn't, but now I'll get you out an' put you in th' way of a bar-rel of money."

The crack of a rifle sounded from the plain and the next instant Clausen dashed up, crying, "Manuel tried to cut an' run, but somebody down below dropped him off'n th' trail. They're all around us!"

"Good for th' somebody!" cried Shaw. "I'll kill th' next man that tries to leave us—that goes, so pass it along." Then he turned to Nevada, a sneer on his face. "That means anybody riding for help, too!" and he backed away.

Hall turned the corner, looking Nevada squarely in the eyes. "Say, Shaw, wonder what's got into Archer? He's been gone a long time for that trip."

"Reckon he's got tired an' quit," replied Shaw.

"You know he ain't that kind!" Hall cried, angrily.

"All right, all right. If he comes back an' finds out what's up he'll probably hustle to Eagle for some of th' boys," Shaw responded. Neither would ever see Dick Archer again—his bones were whitening near a small water hole miles to the north, as Hopalong and Red could testify.

"As long as one of us is outside we've got a chance," Nevada remarked. "How're we fixed for grub, Hall?"

"Got enough jerked beef to last us a month," and Hall departed.

A shot hummed over Nevada's head and, ducking quickly, he followed Hall. Close behind him went Shaw, muttering. "Well, it had to come sometime—an' we're better fixed than I ever reckoned we'd be. Now we'll see who gets wiped out!"

CHAPTER 29

Surrounded

Above, a pale, hot sky with only a wisp of cloud; below, a semi-arid "pasture," scant in grass, seamed by tortuous gullies and studded with small, compact thickets and bulky boulders. A wall of chaparral, appearing solid when viewed from a distance, fenced the pasture, and rising boldly from the southwest end of the clearing a towering mass of rock flung its rugged ramparts skyward. Nature had been in a sullen mood when this scene had been perpetrated and there was no need of men trying to heighten the gloomy aspect by killing each other. Yet they were trying and had been for a week, and they could have found no surroundings more in keeping with their occupation.

Minute clouds of smoke spurted from the top of the wall and from the many points of vantage on the pasture to hang wavering for an instant before lazily dissipating in the hot, close air. In such a sombre setting men had elected to joke and curse and kill, perhaps to die; men hot with passion and blood-lust plied rifles with deliberate intent to kill. On one side there was fierce, deep joy, an exultation in forcing the issue, much as if they had tugged vainly at a leash and suddenly found themselves free. They had been baited, tricked, robbed, and fired upon and now, their tormentors penned before them, there would be no cessation in their efforts to wipe out the indignities under which they had chafed for so long a time.

On the other side, high up on a natural fortress which was considered impregnable, lay those who had brought this angry pack about them. There was no joy there, no glad eagerness to force the battle, no jokes nor laughter, but only a grim desperation, a tenacious holding to that which the others would try to take. On one side aggression; on the other, defense. Fighters all, they now were inspired by the merciless end always in their minds; they were trapped like rats and would fight while mind could lay a plan or move a muscle. Of the type which had out-roughed, out-fought for so long even the sturdy, rough men who had laid the foundation for an inland empire amid dangers superlative, they knew nothing of yielding; and to yield was to die. It was survivor against survivor in an even game.

"Ah, God!" moaned a man on the mesa's lofty rim, staggering back aimlessly before he fell, never to rise again. His companions regarded him curiously, stolidly, without sympathy, as is often the case where death is constantly expected. Dal Gilbert turned back to his rifle and the problems before him. "So you've gone, too. An' I reckon we'll follow"—such was Chet Bates' obituary.

In a thicket two hundred yards south of the mesa Red Connors worked the lever of his rifle, a frown on his face. "I got him, all right. Do you know who he is?"

"No; but I've seen him in Eagle," replied Hopalong, lowering the glasses. "What's worrying me is water—my throat's drying awful."

"You shouldn't 'a forgot it," chided Red. "Now we've got to go without it all day."

Hopalong ducked and swore as he felt of his bleeding face. "Purty close, that!"

"Mind what yo're doing!" replied Red. "Get off my hand."

"This scrap is shore slow," Hopalong growled. "Here we've been doing this for a whole week, all of us shot up, an' only got two of them fellers."

"Well, yo're right; but there ain't a man up there that ain't got a few bullet holes in him," Red replied. "But it is slow, that's shore."

"I've got to get a drink, an' that's all about it," Hopalong asserted. "I can crawl in that gully most of th' way, an' then trust a side-hopping dash. Anyhow, I'm tired of this place. Johnny's got th' place for me."

"You better stay here till it's dark, you fool."

"Aw, stay nothing—so long," and Hopalong, rifle in hand, crawled towards the gully. Red watched the mesa intently, hoping to be able to stop some of the firing his rash friend was sure to call forth.

Twenty minutes passed and then two puffs of smoke sailed against the sky, Red replying. Then half a dozen puffs burst into sight. A faint shout came to Red's ears and he smiled, for his friend was safe.

As Hopalong gained the chaparral he felt himself heartily kicked and, wheeling pugnaciously, looked into Buck Peters' scowling face. "Yo're a healthy fool!" growled the foreman. "Ain't you got no sense at all? Hereafter you flit over that pasture after dark, d'y hear!"

"He's th' biggest fool I ever saw, an' th' coolest," said a voice in the chaparral at the left.

"Why, hullo, Meeker," Hopalong laughed, turning from Buck. "How do you like our little party now?"

"I'm getting tired of it, an' it's some costly for me," grumbled the H2 foreman. "Bet them skunks in Eagle have cleaned out every head I owned." Then he added as an afterthought: "But I don't care a whole lot if I can see this gang wiped out—*Antonio* is th' coyote *I'm* itching to stop."

"He'll be stopped," replied Hopalong. "Hey, Buck, Red's shore thirsty."

"He can stay thirsty, then. An' don't you try to take no water to him. You stay off that pasture during daylight."

"But it was all my fault—" Hopalong began, and then he was off like a shot across the open, leaping gullies and dodging around bowlders.

"Here you!" roared Buck, and started to stare, Meeker at his side. A man was staggering in circles near a thicket which lay a hundred yards from them. He dropped and began to crawl aimlessly about, a good target for the eager rifles on the mesa. Bullets whined and shrilled and kicked up the dust on the plain, but still the rushing Bar-20 puncher was unhit. From the mesa came the faint cracking of rifle fire and clouds of smoke hovered over the cover sheltering Red Connors. Here and there over the pasture and along the chaparral's rim rifles cracked in hot endeavor to drive the rustlers from their positions long enough to save the reckless puncher. Buck and Meeker both were firing now, rapidly but carefully, muttering words of hope and anxiety as they worked the levers of their spurting guns. Then they saw Hopalong gain the prostrate man's side, drag him back to cover, and wave his arm. The fire from the mesa was growing weaker and as it stopped Hopalong, with the wounded man on his back, ran to the shelter of a gully and called for water.

"He's th' best man in this whole country!" cried Meeker, grabbing up a canteen and starting to go through the chaparral to give them water. "To do that for one of *my* men!"

"I've knowed that for nigh onto fifteen years," replied Buck.

Near the Eagle trail Billy Williams and Doc Riley lay side by side, friendly now.

"I tell you we've been shooting high," Doc grumbled. "It's no cinch picking range against that skyline."

"Hey! Look at Hopalong!" cried Billy, excited. "Blamed idiot—why, he's going out to that feller. Lord. Get busy!"

"That's Curtis out there!" ejaculated Doc, angrily. "They've got him, damn 'em!"

"My gun's jammed!" cursed Billy, in his excitement and anger standing up to tear at the cartridge. "I allus go an'—" he pitched sideways to the sand, where he lay quiet.

Doc dropped his rifle and leaped to drag his companion back to the shelter of the cover. As he did so his left arm was hit, but he accomplished his purpose and as he reached for his canteen the Bar-20 pessimist saved him the trouble by opening his eyes and staring around. "Oh, my head! It's shore burning up, Doc!" he groaned. "What th' devil happened that time, anyhow?"

"Here; swaller this," Doc replied, handing him the canteen.

"Who got me?" asked Billy, laying the vessel aside.

"How do I know? Whoever he was he creased you nice. His friends got me in th' arm, too. You can help me fix it soon."

"Shore I will! We can lick them thieves, Doc," Billy expounded without much interest. "Yessir," he added.

"You make me tired," Doc retorted. "You talking about being careful when you stand up in plain sight of them fellers like you just did."

"Yes, I know. I was mad, an' sort of forgot about 'em being able to shoot me—but what happened out there, anyhow?"

Doc craned his neck. "There's Cassidy now, in that gully—Meeker's just joined him. Good men, both of 'em."

"You bet," replied Billy, satisfied. "Yessir, we can lick 'em—we've got to."

On the west side of the mesa, and out of sight of the rustlers, Pie Willis lay face down in the sand, quiet. Near him lay Frenchy McAllister, firing at intervals, aflame with anger and a desire to kill. Opposite him on the mesa, a scant three hundred yards away, two rustlers gloated and fired, eager to kill the other puncher, who shot so well.

"That other feller knows his business, Elder," remarked Nevada as a slug ricochetted past his head. "Wonder who he is."

"Wonder *where* he is," growled Elder, firing at a new place.

"He's been shifting a lot. Anyhow, we got one. There's so much smoke down there I can't seem to place him. Mebby—" he fell back, limp, his rifle clattering down a hundred feet of rock.

Nevada looked at him closely and now drew back to a more secure position. "We're even, stranger, but we ain't quits, by a good deal!" He swore. *Zing-ing-ing!* "Oh, you know I moved, do you!" he gritted. "Well, how's *that!*" *Spat!* a new, bright leaden splotch showed on the rock above his head and hot lead stung his neck and face as the bullets spattered. "I'll get you yet, you coyote!" he muttered, changing his position again. "Ah, *hell!*" he sobbed and dropped his rifle to grasp his right elbow, shattered by a Winchester .45. Pain shot through every fibre of his body and weakened him so he could not crawl for shelter or assistance. He swayed, lost his balance and swayed further, and as his side showed beyond the edge of his rocky rampart he quivered and sank back, helpless, pain-racked, and bleeding to death from two desperate wounds.

"We was—tricked—up here!" he moaned. "That must—be Red—Connors out there. Ah!" *Spat! Chug! Spat!* But Nevada did not hear them now.

Down in the chaparral, Frenchy, getting no response to his shots, picked up his glasses and examined the mesa. A moment later he put them back in the case, picked up his rifle and crawled towards his companion.

"Pie!" he called, touching the body. "Pie, old feller! I got 'em both for you, Pie—got 'em—" Screened by the surrounding chaparral he stood up and shook a clenched fist at the sombre, smoke-wreathed pile of rock and shouted: "An' they won't be all! Do you hear, you thieves? *They won't be all!*"

Lying in a crack on the apex of a pinnacle of rock a hundred yards northwest of the mesa Johnny Nelson cursed the sun and squirmed around on the hot stone, vainly trying to find a spot comparatively cool, while two panic-stricken lizards huddled miserably as far back in the crack as they could force themselves. Long bright splotches marked the stone all around the youthful puncher and shrill whinings came to him out of the air, to hurtle away in the distance ten times as loud and high-pitched. For an hour he had not dared to raise his head to aim, and his sombrero, which he had used as a dummy, was shot full of holes. Johnny, at first elated because of his aerial position, now cursed it fervently and was filled with disgust. When he had begun firing at sunrise he had only one man to face. But the news went around among the rustlers that a fool had volunteered to be a target and now three good shots vied with each other to get the work over with quickly, and return to their former positions.

"I reckon I can squirm over th' edge an' drop down that split," Johnny soliloquized, eying a ragged, sharp edge in the rock close at hand. "Don't know where it goes to, or how far down, but it's cool, that's shore."

He wriggled over to it, flattened as much as possible, and looked over the edge, seeing a four-inch ledge ten feet below him. From the ledge it was ten feet more to the bottom, but the ledge was what interested him.

"Shore I can—just land on that shelf, hug th' wall an' they can't touch me," he grinned, slipping over and hanging for an instant until he stopped swinging.

The rock bulged out between him and the ledge, but he did not give that any thought. Letting go he dropped down the face of the rock, shot out along the bulge and over his cherished ledge, and landed with a grunt on a mass of sand and debris twenty feet below. As he pitched forward to his hands he heard the metallic warning of a rattlesnake and all his fears of being shot were knocked out of his head by the sound. When he landed from his jump he was on the wrong side of the crevice and among hot lead. Ducking and dodging he worked back to the right side and then blew off the offending rattler's head with his Colt. Other rattlers now became prominent and Johnny, realizing that he was an unwelcome guest in a rattlesnake den, made good use of his eyes and Colt as he edged towards the mouth of the crevice. Behind him were rattlers; before him, rustlers who could and would shoot. To say that he was disgusted is to put it mildly.

"Cussed joint!" he grunted. "This is a measly place for me. If I stay I get bit to death; if I leave I get shot. Wonder if I can get to that ledge—ugh!" he cried as the tip of a rattler's tail hung down from it for an instant. "Come on! Bring 'em all out! Trot cut th' tarantulas, copper heads, an' Gilas! Th' more th' merrier! Blasted snake hangout!"

He glanced about him rapidly, apprehensively, and shivered. "No more of this for Little Johnny! I'll chance th' sharp-shooters," he yelled, and dashed out and around the pile so quickly as to be unhit. But he was not hit for another reason, also. Skinny Thompson and Pete Wilson, having grown restless, were encircling the mesa by keeping inside the chaparral and came opposite the pinnacle about the time Johnny discovered his reptilian neighbors. Hearing the noise they both stopped and threw their rifles to their shoulders. Here was a fine opportunity to lessen the numbers of the enemy, for the rustlers, careless for the moment, were peering over their breastwork to see what all the noise was about, not dreaming that two pairs of eyes three hundred yards away were calculating the range. Two puffs of smoke burst from the chaparral and the rustlers ducked out of sight, one of them hard hit. At that moment Johnny made his dash and caused smiles to flit across the faces of his friends.

"We might 'a knowed it was him!" laughed Skinny. "Nobody else would be loco enough to pick out that thing."

"Yes; but now what's he doing?" asked Pete, seeing Johnny poking around among the rocks, Colt in hand.

"Hunting rustlers, I reckon," Skinny replied. "Thinks they are tunnelling an' coming up under him. I suppose. Hey! Johnny!"

Johnny turned, peering at the chaparral.

"What are you doing?" yelled Skinny.

"Hunting snakes."

Skinny laughed and turned to watch the mesa, from which lead was coming.

"Can you cover me if I make a break?" shouted Johnny, hopefully.

"No; stay where you are!" shouted Pete, and then ducked.

"Stop yelling and move about some or you'll get us both hit," ordered Skinny. "Them fellers can *shoot!*"

"Come on; let's go ahead. Johnny can stay out there till dark an' hunt snakes," Pete was getting sarcastic. "Wonder if he reckons we came here to get shot at just to hunt snakes!"

"No; we'll help him in," Skinny replied. "You'll find th' rattlers made it too hot for him up there. Start shooting."

Johnny, hearing the rapid firing of his friends, ran backwards, keeping the pinnacle between him and his enemies as long as he could. Then, once out of its shelter, he leaped erratically over the plain and gained a clump of chaparral. He now had only about a hundred yards to go, and Johnny could sprint when need was. He sprinted. Joining his friends the three disappeared in the chaparral and two disgusted rustlers helped a badly wounded companion to the rough hospital in the hut at the top of the mesa trail.

Johnny and his friends had not gone far before Johnny, eager to find a rustler to shoot at, left them to go to the edge of the chaparral and while he was away his friends stumbled on the body of Pie Willis. Johnny, moving cautiously along the edge of the chaparral, soon met Buck and Hopalong, who were examining every square foot of the mesa wall for a way up.

"Hullo, Johnny!" cried Hopalong. "What you doing here? Thought you were plumb stuck on that freak rock up north."

"I was—an' *stuck*, for shore," grinned Johnny. "That rock is a nest of snakes, besides being a fine place to get plugged by them fellers. An' hot!"

"How'd you get away?"

"Pete an' Skinny drove 'em back an' I made my getaway. They're in th' chaparral somewhere close," Johnny replied. "But why are you telescoping at th' joker? Think you see money out there?"

"Looking for a place to climb it," Hopalong responded. "We're disgusted with this long-range squibbing. You didn't see no breaks in th' wall up where you was, did you?"

"Lemme see," and Johnny cogitated for a moment. Then his face cleared. "Shore I did; there's lots of cracks in it, running up an' down, an' a couple of ledges. I ain't so shore about th' ledges, though—you see I was too busy to look for ledges during th' first part of th' seance, and I dassn't look during th' last of it. There was three of 'em a-popping at me!"

"Hey, Johnny!" came a hail; "Johnny!"

"That's Pete an' Skinny—Hullo!" Johnny shouted.

"Come here—Pie Willis is done for!"

"What?"

"Pie—Willis—is—done—for!"

The three turned and hastened towards the voice, shouting questions. They found Skinny and Pete standing over the body and sombreros came off as the foreman knelt to examine it. Pie had been greatly liked by the members of the outfit he had lately joined, having been known to them for years.

"Clean temple shot," Buck remarked, covering the face and arising. "There's some fine shots up on that rock. Well, here's another reason why we've got to get up there an' wipe 'em out quick. Pie was square as a die and a good puncher—I wouldn't have asked for a better pardner. You fellers take him to camp—we're going to find a way to square things if there is one. No, Pete, you an' Johnny carry him in—Skinny is going with us."

Buck, Hopalong, and Skinny returned to the edge of the pasture and the foreman again swept the wall through his glasses. "Hey! What's that? A body?"

Hopalong looked. "Yes, two of 'em! I reckon Pie died game, all right."

"Well, come on—we've got to move along," and Buck led the way north, Skinny bringing up the rear. Next to Lanky Smith, at present nursing wounds at the ranch, Skinny was the best man with a rope in the Bar-20 outfit and the lariat he used so deftly was one hundred and fifty feet in length, much longer than any used by those around the mesa. Buck had asked him to go with them because he wished to have his opinion as to the possibility of getting a rope up the mesa wall.

When they came opposite the rock which had sheltered Johnny they sortied to see if that part of the mesa was guarded, but there was no sign of life upon it. Then, separating, they dashed to the midway cover, the thicket, which they reached without incident. From there they continued to the pinnacle and now could see every rock and seam of the wall with their naked eyes. But they used the glasses and after a few minutes' examination of the ledges Hopalong turned to his companions. "Just as Johnny said. Skinny, do you reckon if you was under them tonight that you could get yore rope fast to th' bottom one?"

"Shore; that's easy. But it won't be no cinch roping th' other," Skinny replied. "She sticks out over th' first by two feet. It'll be hard to jerk a rope from that narrow foothold."

"Somebody can hang onto you so you can lean out," Buck replied. "Pete can hold you easy."

"But what'll he hold on to?"

Hopalong pointed. "See that spur up there, close to th' first ledge? He can hitch a rope around that an' hang on th' rope. I tell you it's *got* to be done. We can't lose no more men in this everlasting pot-shooting game. We've got to get close an' clean up!"

"Well, I ain't saying nothing different, am I?" snapped Skinny. "I'm saying it'll be hard, an' it will. Now suppose one of them fellers goes on sentry duty along this end; what then?"

"We'll solve that when we come to it," Hopalong replied. "I reckon if Red lays on this rock in th' moonlight that he can drop any sentry that stands up against th' sky at a hundred yards. We're got to try it, anyhow."

"*Down!*" whispered Buck, warningly. "Don't let 'em know we're here. Drop that gun, Hoppy!"

They dropped down behind the loose boulders while the rustler passed along the edge, his face turned towards the pinnacle. Then, deciding that Johnny had not returned, he swept the chaparral with a pair of glasses. Satisfied at length that all was well he turned and disappeared over a rocky ledge ten feet from the edge of the wall.

"I could 'a dropped him easy," grumbled Hopalong, regretfully, and Skinny backed him up.

"Shore you could; but I don't want them to think we are looking at this end," Buck replied. "We'll have th' boys raise th' devil down south till dark an' keep that gang away from this end."

"I reckon they read yore mind—hear th' shooting?" Skinny queried.

"That must be Red out there—I can see half of him from here," Hopalong remarked, lowering his glasses. "Look at th' smoke he's making! Wonder what's up? Hear th' others, too!"

"Come on—we'll get out of this," Buck responded. "We'll go to camp an' plan for to-night, an' talk it over with th' rest. I want to hear what Meeker's going to do about it an' how we can place his men."

"By thunder! If we *can* get up there, half a dozen of us with Colts, an' sneak up on 'em, we'll have this fight tied up in a bag so quick they won't know what's up," Skinny remarked. "You can bet yore life that if there's any way to get a rope up that wall I'll do it!"

CHAPTER 30

Up the Wall

Pipes were glowing in the shadows away from the fire, where men lay in various attitudes of ease. A few were examining wounds while others cleaned rifles and saw that their revolvers were in good condition. Around the fire but well back from it four men sat cross-legged, two others stretched out on their elbows and stomachs near them.

"You say everything is all right on th' ranch?" asked Buck of a man who, covered with alkali, had just come from the Bar-20. "No trouble, hey?"

"Nope; no trouble at all," replied Cross, tossing his sombrero aside. "Lucas an' Bartlett each sent us four men to help out when they learned you had come out here. We shipped four of 'em right on to th' H2, which is too short-handed to do any damage to rustlers."

"Much obliged for that," spoke up Meeker, relief in his voice. "I'm blamed glad to hear things are quiet back home—but I don't know how long they'll stay that way with Eagle so close."

"Well, Eagle ain't a whole lot anxious to dip in no more," laughed Cross, looking at the H2 foreman. "Leastawise, that's what Lucas said. He sent a delegation down there which made a good impression. There was ten men in it an' they let it be known that if they came back again there would be ten more with 'em. In that case Eagle wouldn't be no more than a charred memory. Since Quinn died, being shot hard by Nevada, who I reckons is out here, th' town ain't got nobody to tell it how to do things right, which is shore pleasant."

"You bring blamed good news—I'm glad Lucas went down there," Buck replied. "I can't tell of good news about us out here, yet. We've had a hard time for a week. They got Pie to-day, an' most of us are shot up plentiful. Yo're just in time for th' festival, Cross—we're going to try to rush 'em to-night an' get it over. We reckon Skinny an' Pete can get us a way up that wall before dawn."

"Me for th' rush," laughed Cross. "I'm fresh as a daisy, which most of you fellers ain't. How many of 'em have you got so far? Are there many still up there?"

"We've got four of 'em that I knows of, an' how many of 'em died from their wounds I can't say," replied Hopalong. "But a whole lot of 'em have been plugged, an' plugged hard."

"But how many are up there still able to fight?"

"I should say about nine," Hopalong remarked, thoughtfully.

"Ten," corrected Red. "I've been watching th' positions an' I know."

"About nine or ten—they shift so nobody can really tell," Buck replied. "I reckon we've seen 'em all in Eagle, too."

"Frenchy got Nevada an' another to-day, on th' west side," Johnny interposed.

"I'm glad Nevada is gone—he's a terror in a mixup," Cross rejoined. "Best two-handed gun man in Eagle, he was."

"Huh!" snorted Johnny. "Stack him up against Hoppy an' see how long he'd last!"

"I said in Eagle!" retorted Cross.

Buck suddenly stood up and stretched. "You fellers all turn in now an' snatch some sleep. I'm going out to see how things are with Billy. I'll call you in time. Doc, you an' Curtis are too shot up to do any climbing—you turn in too. When I come back I'll wake you an' send you out to help Billy watch th' trail. Where's Red?"

"Over here—what do you want?" came from the shadows.

"Nothing, only get to sleep. I reckoned you might be off somewheres scouting. Skinny, where's yore rope? Got that manilla one? Good! Put three more hemp lariats out here where I can find 'em when I come back. Now don't none of you waste no time; turn in right now!" He started to walk away and then hesitated, turning around. "Doc, you an' Curtis better come with me now so you won't lose no time hunting Billy in th' dark when yore eyes are sleepy—it's hard enough to find him now in th' dark, when I'm wide awake. You can get yore sleep out there—he'll wake you when yo're needed."

The two punchers arose and joined him, Doc with his left arm bandaged and his companion with three bandages on him. When they joined Buck Doc protested. "Let me go with you an' th' rest of th' boys, Peters, when you go up that wall. I came out here to get th' man that murdered Curley, an' I hate to miss him now. If I can't climb th' boys will be glad to pull me up, an' it won't take no time to speak of. My gun arm is sound as a dollar—*I* want that murderer!"

Buck glanced at Meeker, who refused to give any sign of his thoughts on the matter. "Well, all right, Doc. But if we should have to fight as soon as we get up an' don't have no time to pull you after us, you'll miss everything. But you can do what you want."

"I'll just gamble on that. I ain't hurt much, an' if I can't climb I'll manage to get in th' scrap someway, even if I has to hunt up Billy," replied Doc, contentedly, returning to the fire.

Buck and his companion moved away into the darkness while those around the fire lay down to get a few hours' rest, which they needed badly. George Cross, who was not sleepy, remained awake in a shadow and kept guard, although none was needed.

Buck and Curtis found Billy by whistling and the wounded H2 puncher found a place to lie down and was soon asleep, while the foreman and his friend sat up, watching the faint glow on the mesa, the camp-fire of the besieged. Once they heard the clatter of a rifle from the head of the trail and later they saw a dim figure pass quickly across the lighted space. They were content to watch on such a night, for the air had cooled rapidly after the sun went down and the sky was one twinkling mass of stars.

Twice during the wait Buck disappeared into the black chaparral close at hand and struck a match under his coat to see the time, and on the last occasion he returned to Billy, remarking: "Got half an hour yet before I leave you. Are you sleepy?"

"No, not very; my head hurts too much to sleep," Billy replied, re-crossing his legs and settling himself in a more comfortable position. "When you leave I'll get up on my hoofs so I won't feel like dosing off. I won't wake Curtis unless I have to—he's about played out."

"You wake him when you think I've been gone half an hour," Buck ordered. "It'll take him some time to get his eyes open—we mustn't let any get away. They've got friends in Eagle, you know."

"Wish I could smoke," Billy remarked, wistfully.

"Why, you can," replied Buck, quickly. "Go back there in th' chaparral an' get away with a pipeful. I'll watch things till you come back an' if I need you quick I can call. You've got near half an hour—make th' best of it."

"Here's th' gun—much obliged, Buck," and Billy disappeared, leaving the foreman to plan and watch. Buck glanced at the sleeping man occasionally when he heard him toss or mutter and wished he could let him sleep on undisturbed.

Suddenly a flash lighted up the top of the trail for an instant and the sharp report of a rifle rang out loudly on the still, night air. Buck, grabbing the Winchester, sprang to his feet as an excited chorus came from the rustlers' stronghold. Then he heard laughter and a few curses and quiet again ensued.

"What was that, Buck?" came a low, anxious hail from behind.

The foreman laughed softly and said: "Nothing, Billy, except that th' guard up there reckoned he saw something to shoot at. It's funny how staring at th' dark will get a feller seeing things that ain't. Why, had yore smoke so soon?" he asked in surprise as Billy sat down beside him.

"Shore," replied Billy. "Two of 'em. I reckon yore time is about up. Gimme th' gun now."

"Well, good luck, Billy. Better move up closer to th' trail if you can find any cover. You don't want to miss none. So long," and Billy was alone with his sleeping companion.

When the foreman returned to the camp he was challenged, and stopped, surprised. "It's Peters," he called.

"Oh, all right. Time to go yet?" asked Cross, emerging from the darkness.

"Purty near; but I thought I told you to go to sleep?"

"I know, but I ain't sleepy, not a bit. So I reckoned I'd keep watch over th' rest of th' gang."

"Well, since yo're wide awake, you help me knot these ropes an' let th' others have a few minutes more," Buck responded, picking up Skinny's fifty-foot lariat and placing it to one side. He picked up the three shorter ropes and threw one to his companion. "Put a knot every foot an' a half—make 'em tight an' big."

In a few minutes the work was finished and Buck awakened the sleeping men, who groped their way to the little stream close by and washed the sleep out of their tired eyes, grabbing a bit of food on their return to the fire.

"Now, fellers," said the foreman, "leave yore rifles here—it's Colts this trip, except in Red's case. Got plenty of cartridges? Everybody had a drink an' some grub? All right; single file after me an' don't make no noise."

When the moon came up an hour later Red Connors, lying full length on the apex of the pinnacle which Johnny had tried and found wanting, watched an indistinct blur of men in the shadow of the mesa wall. He saw one of them step out into the moonlight, lean back and then straighten up suddenly, his arm going above his head. The silence was so intense that Red could faintly hear the falling rope as it struck the ground. Another cast, and yet another, both unsuccessful, and then the fourth, which held. The puncher stepped back into the shadow again and another figure appeared, to go jerking himself up the face of the wall. While he watched the scaling operations Red was not missing anything on top of the mesa, where the moon bathed everything in a silvery light.

Then he saw another figure follow the first and kick energetically as it clambered over onto the ledge. Soon a rope fell to the plain and the last man up, who was Skinny, leaned far out and cast at the second ledge, Pete holding him. After some time he was successful and again he and his companion went up the wall. Pete climbed rapidly, his heavy body but small weight for the huge, muscular arms which rose and fell so rapidly. On the second ledge the same casting was gone through with, but it was not until the eighth attempt that the rope stayed up. Then Red, rising on his elbows, put his head closer to the stock of his rifle and peered into the shadows back of the lighted space on the rocky pile. He saw Pete pull his companion back to safety and then, leaping forward, grasp the rope and climb to the top. Already one of the others was part way up the second rope while another was squirming over the lower ledge, and below him a third kicked and hauled, half way up the first lariat.

"String of monkeys," chuckled Red. "But they can't none of 'em touch Pete in that sort of a game. Wonder what Pete's doing?" he queried as he saw the man on the top of the mesa bend, fumble around for a moment, and then toss his arm out over the edge. "Oh, it's a knotted rope—he's throwing it down for th' others. Well, Pete, old feller, you was th' first man to get—*Lord!*"

He saw Pete wheel, leap forward into a shadow, and then a heaving, twisting, bending bulk emerged into the moonlight. It swayed back and forth, separated into two figures and then became one again.

"They're fighting, rough an' tumble!" Red exclaimed. "Lord have mercy on th' man who's closing with that Pete of ourn!"

He could hear the scuffling and he knew that the others had heard it, too, for Skinny was desperately anxious to wriggle over the edge, while down the line of ropes the others acted like men crazed. Still the pair on the mesa top swayed back and forth, this way and that, bending, twisting, and Red imagined he could hear their labored breathing. Then Skinny managed to pull himself to the top of the wall and sprang forward, to sink down from a kick in the stomach.

"God A'mighty!" cried Red excitedly. "Who is it that can give Pete a fight like that? Well, I'm glad he's so busy he can't use his gun!"

Skinny was crawling around on his hands and knees as Buck's head arose over the edge. The foreman, well along in years, and heavy, was too tired to draw himself over the rim without a moment's rest. He had no fear for Pete, but he was worried lest some rustler might sound an alarm. Skinny now sat up and felt for his Colt, but the foreman's voice stopped him. "No shooting, yet! Want to tell 'em what's up! You let them fellers alone for a minute, an' give me a hand here."

Pete, his steel-like fingers darting in for hold after hold, managed to jerk his opponent's gun from its sheath and throw it aside, where Skinny quickly picked it up. He was astonished by the skill and strength of his adversary, who blocked every move, every attempt to get a dangerous hold. Pete, for a man reputed as being slow, which he was in some things, was darting his arms in and out with remarkable quickness, but without avail. Then, realizing that his cleaner living was standing him in good stead, and hearing the labored breathing of the rustler, he leaped in and clinched. By this time Hopalong and three more of the attacking force had gained the mesa top and were sent forward by the foreman, who was now intent upon the struggle at hand.

"It's Big Sandy!" Hopalong whispered to Skinny, pausing to watch for a moment before he disappeared into the shadows.

He was right, and Big Sandy, breathless and tired, was fighting a splendid fight for his life against a younger, fresher, and stronger man. The rustler tried several times for a throat hold but in vain, and in a fury of rage threw his weight against his opponent to bear him to the ground, incautiously bringing his feet close together as he felt the other yield. In that instant Pete dropped to a crouch, his vice-like hands tightened about Big Sandy's ankles, and with a sudden, great surge of his powerful back and shoulders he straightened up and Sandy plunged forward to a crashing fall on the very edge of the mesa, scrambled to his feet, staggered, lost his balance, and fell backwards a hundred feet to the rocks below.

The victor would have followed him but for Buck, who grasped him in time. Pete, steady on his feet again, threw Buck from him by one sweep of his arms and wheeled to renew the fight, surprise flashing across his face at not seeing his opponent.

"He's down below, Pete," Buck cried as Johnny, white-faced, crawled over the edge.

"What was that?" exclaimed the Kid. "Who fell?"

"Big Sandy," replied the foreman. "He—" the report of a shot cut him short. "Come on!" he called. "They're at it!" and he dashed away, closely followed by Johnny and Pete as Jim Meeker came into view. The H2 foreman slid over the mesa rim, leaped to his feet and sprinted forward, Colt in hand, to be quickly lost in the shadows, and after him came Red Connors, the last.

Down below Doc, hearing a thud not far from him, hurried around a spur of rock in the wall, sick at heart when he saw the body. Bending over quickly he recognized the mass as once having been Big Sandy, and he forthwith returned to the rope to be pulled up. When he at last realized that his friends had forgotten him there was loud, lurid cursing and he stamped around like a wild man, waving a Colt in his right hand. Finally he dropped heavily on a rock, too enraged to think, and called the attacking force, collectively and individually, every name that sprang to his lips. As he grew calmer he arose from the rock, intending to join Billy and Curtis at the other end of the pasture, and as he took a step in that direction he heard a sharp click and a pebble bounced past him. He stepped backwards quickly and looked up, seeing a figure sliding rapidly down the highest rope. He was immediately filled with satisfaction and easily forgave his companions for the anxiety they had caused him, and as he was about to call out he heard something spoken in Spanish. Slipping quickly and noiselessly into the deeper shadow at the base of the wall he flattened himself behind the spur of rock close to the rope, where he waited tensely, a grim smile transforming his face. He knew that voice.

CHAPTER 31

Fortune Snickers at Doc

Antonio was restless and could not sleep. He turned from side to side on the ground near the fire before the hut and was one of the first to run to the top of the trail when the guard there discharged his rifle at nothing. Returning to his blanket he tried to compose himself to rest, but was unsuccessful. Finally, he arose, picked up his rifle, and slouched off into the shadows to wander about from point to point.

Cavalry, coming in from his post to get a drink, caught sight of Antonio before he was swallowed up by the darkness and, suspicious as ever of Antonio, forgot the drink and followed.

After wandering about all unconscious of espionage Antonio finally drifted to the western edge and seated himself comfortably against a boulder, Cavalry not fifty feet away in a shadow. Time passed slowly and as Antonio was about to return to the fire he chanced to glance across the mesa along a moon-lighted path and stiffened at what he saw. A figure ran across the lighted space, silently, cautiously, Colt in hand, and then another, then two together, and he knew that the enemy had found a way up the wall and were hurrying forward to fight at close quarters, to effect a surprise on the unsuspecting men about the fire and in the hut. There remained, perhaps, time enough for him to escape and he arose and ran north, crouching as he zigzagged from cover to cover, cautious and alert.

Cavalry, because of his position, had not seen the flitting punchers and, his suspicions now fully aroused, he slipped after Antonio to find out just what he was going to do. When the firing burst out behind him he paused and stood up, amazed. As he struggled to understand what it meant he saw three men run past a boulder at his left and then he knew, and still hesitated. He was not a man who thought quickly and his first natural impulse, due to his army training, was to join his friends, but gradually the true situation came to him. How many men there were in the attacking force he did not know, but he had seen three after the fighting had begun; and it was evident that the cowmen would not rush into the lion's jaws unless they were strong enough to batter down all resistance. Four of his friends were dead, another had evidently deserted, and the remainder were all more or less severely wounded—there could be no hope of driving the ranchmen back, and small chance of him being able to work through their line to join his friends. There remained only one thing to be done, to save himself while he might.

As he moved forward slowly and cautiously to find a way down the wall he remembered Antonio's peculiar actions and wondered if he had a hand in helping the cowmen up.

Meanwhile Antonio, reaching the edge of the open space where Pete and Big Sandy had fought, saw Red Connors appear over the rim and dash away to join in the fighting. Waiting long enough to assure himself that there were none following Red he ran to the edge and knelt by the rope. Leaving his rifle behind and seeing that the flap of his holster was fastened securely, he lowered himself over, sliding rapidly down to the first ledge. Here he spent a minute, a minute that seemed an eternity, hunting for the second rope in the shadows, found it and went on.

Sliding and bumping down the rough wall he at last reached the plain and, with a sigh of relief, turned to run. At that instant a figure leaped upon him from behind and a hand gripped his throat and jerked him over backwards. Antonio instinctively reached for his Colt with one hand while he tore at the gripping fingers with the other, but he found himself pinned down between two rocks in such a manner that his whole weight and that of his enemy was on the holster and made his effort useless. Then, terrified and choking for breath, he dug wildly at the vise-like fingers which not for a moment relaxed, but in vain, for he was growing weaker with each passing second.

Doc leaned forward, peering into the face before him, his fingers gripping with all their power, gripping with a force which made the muscles of the brawny forearm stand out like cords, his face malevolent and his heart full of savage joy. Here was the end of his hunt, here was the man who had murdered Curley in cold blood, cowardly, deliberately. The face, already dark, was turning black and the eyes were growing wide open and bulging out. He felt the surge of Antonio's pulse, steadily growing weaker. But he said no word as he watched and gloated, he was too intent to speak, too centered upon the man under him, too busy keeping his fingers tight-gripped. He would make good his threat, he would keep his word and kill the murderer of his best friend with his naked hands, as he had sworn.

Up above the two Cavalry, working along the edge, had come across Antonio's rifle and then as he glanced about, saw the rope. Here was where the cowmen had come up and here was where he could go down. From the way the shooting continued he knew that the fight was desperate and he believed himself to be cut off from his friends. He hated to desert in the face of the enemy, to leave his companions of a dangerous business to fight for their lives without him, but there was only one thing to do since he could not help them—he must save himself.

Dropping his rifle beside the other he lowered himself over the edge and slid rapidly down. When halfway down the last rope his burning hands slipped and he fell head over heels, and landed on Doc, knocking him over and partially stunning him. Cavalry's only idea now was to get from the men who, as he thought, were guarding the rope and, hastily picking himself up, he dashed towards the chaparral to the west as fast as he could run, every moment expecting to feel the hot sting of a bullet. At last, when the chaparral closed about him he plunged through it recklessly and ran until sheer exhaustion made him drop insensible to the sand. He had run far, much farther than he could have gone were it not for the stimulus of the fear which gripped him; and had he noticed where he was going he would have known that he was running up a slope, a slope which eventually reached a level higher than the top of the mesa. And when he dropped if he had been capable of observation he would have found himself in a chaparral which arose above his head, and seen the narrow lane through it which led to a great expanse of sand, tawney and blotched with ash-colored alkali, an expanse which stretched away to the desolate horizon.

Shortly after Cavalry's descent Antonio stirred, opened his eyes, stared vaguely about him and, feeling his bruised and aching throat, staggered to his feet and stumbled to the east, hardly conscious of what he was doing. As he proceeded his breath came easier and he began to remember having seen Doc lying quiet against a rock. He hesitated a moment as he wondered if Doc was dead and if so, who had killed him. Then he swore because he had not given him a shot to make sure that he would not rejoin his friends. Hesitating a moment he suddenly decided that he would be better off if he put a good distance between himself and the mesa, and ran on again, eager to gain the shelter of the chaparral.

When Doc opened his eyes and groped around he slowly remembered what had occurred and his first conscious act was to look to see if his expected victim were dead or alive. It did not take him long to realize that he was alone and his hand leaped for his Colt as he peered around. Limping out on the plain he caught sight of Antonio running, rapidly growing indistinct, and hazarded two shots after him. Antonio leaped into a new speed as though struck with a whip and cursed himself for not having killed the H2 puncher when he had the chance. A moment more and he was lost in the thickets. Doc tried to follow, but his leg, hurt by Cavalry's meteoric descent, was not equal to any great demand for speed and so, turning, he made his way towards the camp to get a horse and return to take up Antonio's trail.

He lost an hour in this, a feverishly impatient hour, punctuated with curses as he limped along and with an unsparing quirt once he was astride. What devilish Humpty Dumpty had cheated him this time? "All the king's horses and all the king's men couldn't put Humpty Dumpty together again." He laughed grimly and swore again as the cranky beast beneath him shied a pain into his sore leg. "Go on, you!" he yelled, as he swept up to where the ropes still dangled against the wall. The world was not big enough to hide the murderer of Curley, to save him from his just deserts. The two trails lay plain before him in the brilliant moonlight and his pony sprang forward toward the spot where Antonio had disappeared in the chaparral.

CHAPTER 32

Nature Takes a Hand

When Hopalong caught up with his four companions he was astonished by the conditions on the mesa. Instead of a boulder-strewn, rocky plain as he had believed it to be he found himself on a table-land cut and barred by fissures which ran in all directions. At one time these had been open almost to the level of the surrounding pasture but the winds had swept sand and debris into the gashes until now none were much more than ten feet deep. Narrow alleyways which led in every direction, twisting and turning, now blocked and now open for many feet in depth, their walls sand-beaten to a smoothness baffling the grip of one who would scale them, were not the same in a fight as a comparatively flat plain broken only by miscellaneous bowlders and hummocks. There could be no concerted dash for the reason that one group of the attacking force might be delayed until after another had begun to fight. And it was possible, even probable, that the turns in the alleyways might be guarded; and once separated in the heat of battle it would be easy enough to shoot each other. Instead of a dashing fight soon to be over, it looked as though it would be a deadly game of hide and seek to wear out the players and which might last for an indefinite length of time. It was disconcerting to find that what had been regarded as the hardest part of the whole affair, the gaining of the mesa top, was the easiest.

"Here, fellows!" Hopalong growled. "We'll stick together till we get right close, an' then if we have time an' these infernal gorges don't stop us, we may be able to spread out. We've got to move easy, too. If we go galloping reckless we'll run into some guard an' there won't be no surprise party on Thunder Mesa. We can count on having light, though not as much as we might have, for th' moon won't go back on us till th' sun fades it."

"It's light enough," growled Skinny. "Come on—we've got to go ahead an' every minute counts. *I* don't think we'd lose so much time roping them knobs an' getting up."

They moved forward cautiously in single file, alert and straining eyes and ears, and had covered half of the distance when a shot was heard ahead and they listened, expecting an uproar. Waiting a minute and hearing nothing further, they moved on again, angry and disgruntled. Then another shot rang out and they heard Billy and Curtis reply.

"Shooting before daylight, before they get their morning's grub," grumbled George Cross.

"Yes; sort of eye-opener, I reckon," softly laughed Chick Travers, who was nervous and impatient. "Get a move on an' let's start something," he added.

As they separated to take advantage of a spoke-like radiation of several intersecting fissures another shot rang out ahead and there was an angry *spat!* close to Hopalong's head. Another shot and then a rattling volley sent the punchers hunting cover on the run, but they were moving forward all the time. It was a case of getting close or be killed at a range too great for Colts, and their rifles were in the camp. Had the light been better the invaders might have paid dearly right there for the attack.

Confusion was rife among the defenders and the noise of the shouts and firing made one jumble of sound. Bullets whistled along the fissures in the dim light and hummed and whizzed as they ricochetted from wall to wall. As yet the attacking force had made no reply, being too busily occupied in getting close to lose time in wasting lead at that range, and being only five against an unknown number protected by a stone hut and who knew every boulder, crevice, and other points of vantage.

Hopalong slid over a bowlder which choked his particular and personal fissure and saw Jim Meeker sliding down the wall in front of it. And as Meeker picked himself up Skinny Thompson slid down the other wall.

"Well, I'm hanged!" grunted Hopalong in astonishment.

"Same here," retorted Skinny. "What you doing 'way over here?"

"Thought you was going to lead th' other end of th' line!" rejoined Hopalong.

"This is it—yo're off yore range."

"Well, I reckon not!" Hopalong responded, indignantly.

"An' say, Meeker, how'd you get over here so quick?" Skinny asked, turning to the other. "You was down below when I saw you last."

"*Me?* Why, I just follered my nose, that's all," Meeker replied, surprised.

"You've got a blamed crooked nose, then," Skinny snorted, and turned to

Hopalong. "Why don't you untangle yoreself an' go where you belong, you carrot-headed blunderer!"

"Hang it! I tell you—" Hopalong began, and then ducked quickly. "Lord, but somebody's got us mapped out good!"

"Well, some of our fellers have started up—hear 'em over there?" exclaimed Skinny as firing broke out on the east. "Them's Colts, all right. Mebby it's plumb lucky for us it *ain't* so blamed light, after all; we'll have time to pick our places before they can see us real good."

"Pick our places!" snorted Hopalong. "Get tangled up, you mean!" he added.

"Hullo! What you doing, fellers?" asked a pained and surprised voice above them. "Why ain't you in it?"

"For th' love of heaven—it's Frenchy!" cried Hopalong. "Skinny, I reckon them Colts you heard belonged to th' rustlers. *We're* all here but a couple."

"Didn't I leave you over east five minutes ago, Frenchy?" demanded Skinny, his mouth almost refusing to shut.

"Shore. I'm east—what's eating at you?" asked Frenchy.

"Come on—get out of this!" ordered Hopalong, scrambling ahead. "You foller me an' you'll be all right."

"We'll be back to th' ropes if we foller you," growled Skinny. "Of all th' lo-coed layouts I ever run up against this here mesa top takes th' prize," he finished in disgust.

Bullets whined and droned above them and frequently hummed down the fissure to search them out, the high, falsetto whine changing quickly to an angry *spang*! as they struck the wall a slanting blow. They seemed to spring away again with renewed strength as they sang the loud, whirring hum of the ricochette, not the almost musical, sad note of the uninterrupted bullet, but venomous, assertive, insistent. The shots could be distinguished now, for on one side were the sharp cracks of rifles; on the other a different note, the roar of Colts.

"This ain't no fit society for six-shooters," Meeker remarked in a low voice as they slid over a ridge, and dropped ten feet before they knew it.

"For th' Lord's sake!" ejaculated Hopalong as he arose to his feet. "Step over a rock an' you need wings! Foller a nice trail an you can't get out of th' cussed thing! Go west an' you land east, say 'solong' to a friend an' you meet him a minute later!"

"We ought to have rifles in this game," Meeker remarked, rubbing his knee-cap ruefully.

"Yes; an' ladders, ropes, an' balloons," snorted Skinny.

"Send somebody back for th' guns," suggested Frenchy.

"Who?" demanded Hopalong. "Will *you* go?"

"Me? Why, I don't want no rifle."

"Huh! Neither do I," remarked Skinny. "Here, Frenchy, give me a boost up this wall—take my hand."

"Well, don't wiggle so, you!"

"That's right! Walk backwards. I ain't no folding stepladder! How do you think I'm going to grab that edge if you takes me ten feet away from it?"

Spang! Spang! Zing-ing-ing!

"Here, you! Lemme down! Want me to get plugged!" yelled Skinny, executing ungraceful and rapid contortions. "Lower me, you fool!"

"Let go that ridge, then!" retorted Frenchy.

During the comedy Hopalong had been crawling up a rough part of the wall and he fired before he lost his balance. As he landed on Meeker a yell rang out and the sound of a rifle clattering on rock came to them. "I got him, Skinny—go ahead now," he grunted, picking himself up.

It was not long until they were out of the fissure and crawling down a boulder-strewn slope. As they came to the bottom they saw a rustler trying to drag himself to cover and Meeker fired instantly, stopping the other short.

"Why, I thought *I* stopped him!" exclaimed Hopalong.

"Reckon you won't rustle no more cows, you thief," growled Meeker, rising to his knees.

Hopalong pulled him down again as a bullet whizzed through the space just occupied by his head. "Don't you get so curious," he warned. "Come on— I see Red. He's got his rifle, lucky cuss."

"Good for him! Wish I had mine," replied Meeker, grinning at Red, who wriggled an elbow as a salutation. In his position Red could hardly be expected to do much more, since two men were waiting for a shot at him.

"Well, you can get that gun down there an' have a rifle," Hopalong suggested, pointing to the Winchester lying close to its former owner. "You can do it, all right."

"Good idea—shoot 'em with their own lead," and the H2 foreman departed on his hands and knees for the weapon.

"I hit one—he's trying to put his shoulder together," hollered Red, grinning. "What makes you so late—I was th' last one up, an' I've been here a couple of hours."

"You're a sinful liar!" retorted Hopalong. "We stopped to pick blackberries back at that farm house," he finished with withering sarcasm.

"You fellers had time to get married an' raise a family," Red replied. He ducked and looked around. "Ah, you coyote—hit him, but not very hard, I reckon."

It was daylight when Pete, on the other end of the line, turned and scourged Johnny. "Ain't you got no sense in yore fool head? How can I see to shoot when you kick around like that an' fill my eyes with dirt! Come down from up there or I'll lick you!"

"Ah, shut up!" retorted Johnny with a curse. "You'd kick around if somebody nicked *yore* ear!"

"Well, it serves you right for being so unholy curious!" Pete replied. "You come down before he nicks yore eye!"

"Not before I get square—*Wow!*" and Johnny came down rapidly.

"Where'd he get you that time?"

"None of yore business!" growled Johnny.

"I told you to come—"

"Shut up!" roared Johnny, glaring at him. "Wish I had that new Sharps of mine!"

"Go an' get it, Kid. Yo're nimble," Pete responded. "An' bring up some of th' others, too, while yo're about it."

"But how long will this fight last, do you reckon?" the other asked, with an air of weighing something.

"All day with rifles—a week without 'em."

"Shore yo're right?"

"Yes; go ahead. There'll be some of th' scrap left for you when you get back."

"All right—but don't you get that feller. I want him for what he did to me," and Johnny hastened away. He returned in fifteen minutes with two rifles and gave one of them to his companion.

"They're .45–70's—an' full, too," he remarked. "But I ain't got no more cartridges for 'em."

"How'd you get 'em so quick?"

"Found 'em by th' rope where we came up—didn't have to stop; just picked 'em up an' came right back," Johnny laughed. "But I wonder how they got there?"

"Bet four dollars an' a tooth-pick they means that two thieves got away down them ropes. Where's Doc?"

"Don't know—but I don't think anybody pulled him up here."

"Then he might 'a stopped them two what owned th' rifles—he would be mad enough to stay there a month if Red forgot him."

"Yes; waiting to lick Red when he came down," and Johnny crawled up again to his former position. "Now, you cow-stealing coyote, watch out!" As he settled down he caught sight of his foreman. "Hullo, Buck! What yo doing?"

"Stringing beads for my night shirt," retorted Buck. "You get down from up there, you fool!"

"Can't. I got to pay for—" He ducked, and then fired twice. "Just missed th' other ear, Pete. But I made him jump a foot—plugged him where he sits down. He was moving away."

"Yes; an' you took two shots to do it, when cartridges are so scarce," Pete grumbled.

At first several of the rustlers had defended the hut but the concentrated fire of the attacking force had poured through its north window from so many angles that evacuation became necessary. This was accomplished through the south window, which opened behind the natural breastwork, and at a great cost, for Con Irwin and Sam Austin were killed in the move.

The high, steep ridge which formed the rear wall of the hut and overlooked the roof of the building ran at right angles to the low breastwork and extended from the north end of the hut to the edge of the mesa, a distance of perhaps fifty feet. On the side farthest from the breastwork it sloped to the stream made by the spring and its surface was covered with bowlders. The rustlers, if they attempted to scale its steep face, would be picked off at short range, but they realized that once the enemy gained its top their position would be untenable except around the turn in the breastwork at the other side of the mesa. In order to keep the punchers from gaining this position they covered the wide cut which separated the ridge from the enemy's line and so long as they could command this they were safe.

After wandering from point to point Hopalong finally came to the edge of the cut and found Red Connors ensconced in a narrow, shallow depression on a comparatively high hummock. While they talked his eyes rested on the ridge across the cut and took in the possibilities that holding it would give.

"Say, Red, if we could get up on that hill behind th' shack we'd have this fight over in no time—see how it overlooks everything?"

"Yes," slowly replied Red. "But we can't cross this barranca—they sweep it from end to end. I tried to get over there, an' I know."

"But we can try again," Hopalong replied. "You cover me."

"Now don't be a fool, Hoppy!" his friend retorted. "We can't afford to lose you for no gang of rustlers. It's shore death to try it."

"Well, you can bet I ain't going to be fool enough to run twenty yards in th' open," Hopalong replied, starting away. "But I'm going to look for a way across, just th' same. Keep me covered."

"All right, I'll do my best—but don't you try no dash!"

But the rustlers had not given up the idea of holding the ridge themselves, and there was another and just as important reason why they must have it; their only water was in the hut and the spring. To enter the building was certain death, but if they could command the ridge it would be possible to get water, for the spring and rivulet lay on the other side at its base. Hall, well knowing the folly of trying to scale the steep bank under fire, set about finding another way to gain the coveted position. He found a narrow ledge on the face of the mesa wall, at no place more than eight inches wide, and he believed that it led to the rear of the ridge. Finding that the wall above the narrow foothold was rough and offered precarious finger holds, he began to edge along it, a hundred feet above the plain. When he had almost reached the end of his trying labors he was discovered by Billy and Curtis, who lay four hundred yards away in the chaparral, and at once became the target for their rifles. Were it not for the fact that they could not shoot at their best because of their wounds Hall would never have finished his attempt, and as it was the bullets flattened against the wall so close to him that on two occasions he was struck by spattering lead and flecks of stone. Then he moved around the turn and was free from that danger, but found that he must get fifty yards north before he could gain the plateau again. To make matters worse the ledge he was on began to grow narrower and at one place disappeared altogether. When he got to the gap he had to cling to the rough wall and move forward inch by inch, twice narrowly missing a drop to the plain below. But he managed to get across it and strike the ledge again and in a few minutes more he stepped into a crevice and sat down to rest before he pushed on. When he looked around he found that the crevice led northeast and did not run to the ridge, and he swore as he realized that he must go through the enemy's line to gain the position. He would not risk going back the way he had come, for he was pretty well tired out. He thought of trying to get to the other end of the mesa so as to escape by the way the attacking force had come up, but immediately put it out of his mind as being too contemptible for further consideration. He arose and moved forward, seeking a way up the wall of the crevice—and turning a corner, bumped into Jim Meeker.

There was no time for weapons and they clinched. Meeker scorned to call for help and Hall dared make no unnecessary noise while in the enemy's line and so they fought silently. Both tried to draw their Colts, Meeker to use his either as a gun or a club, Hall as a club only, and neither succeeded. Both were getting tired when Hall slipped and fell, the H2 foreman on top of him. At that instant Buck Peters peered down at them from the edge of the fissure and then dropped lightly. He struck Hall over the head with the butt of his Colt and stepped back, grinning.

"There'll be a lot more of these duets if this fight drags out very long," Buck said. "This layout is shore loco with all its hidden trails. Have you got a rope, Jim? We'll tie this gent so he won't hurt hisself if you can find one."

"No. Much obliged, Peters," Meeker replied. "Why, yes I have, too. Here, use this," and he quickly untied his neck-kerchief and gave it to his friend. Buck took the one from around Hall's neck and the two foremen gave a deft and practical exhibition of how to tie a man so he cannot get loose. Meeker took the Winchester from Hall's back, the Colt and the cartridge belt, and gave them to Buck, laughing.

"Seventy-three model; .44 caliber," he explained. "You'll find it better than th' six-shooter, an' you'll have plenty of cartridges for it, too."

"But don't you want it?" asked Buck, hesitating.

"Nope. I left one around th' corner here. I can get along with it till I get my own from th' camp."

"All right, Jim. I'll be glad to keep this—it'll come in handy."

"Tough luck, finding them fellers in such a strong layout," Meeker growled, glancing around at the prisoner. "Ah, got yore eyes open, hey?" he ejaculated as Hall glared at him. "How many of you fellers are up here, anyhow?"

"Five thousand!" snapped Hall. "It took two of you to get me!" he blazed. "Got my guns, too, ain't you? Hope they bust an' blow yore cussed heads off!"

"Thanks, stranger, thanks," Buck replied, turning to leave. "But Meeker had you licked good—I only hurried it to save time. Coming, Jim?"

"Shore. But do you think this thief can get loose?"

Buck paused, searching his pockets, and smiled as he brought to light a small, tight roll of rawhide thongs. "Here, this'll keep him down," and when they had finished their prisoner could move neither hands nor feet. They looked at him critically and then went away towards the firing, the rustler cursing them heartily.

"What's the matter, Meeker?" asked Buck suddenly, noticing a drawn look on his companion's face.

"Oh, I can't help worrying about my girl. She ain't scared of nothing an' she likes to ride. She's too pretty to go breezing over a range that's covered with rustling skunks. I told her to stay in th' house, but—"

"Well, why in thunder don't you go back where you can take care of her?" Buck demanded, sharply. "She's worth more than all th' cows an' rustlers on earth. You ain't needed bad out here, for we can clean this up, all right. You know as long as there are fellers like us to handle a thing like this no man with a girl depending on him has really got any right to take chances. I never thought of it before, or I'd 'a told you so. You cut loose for home to-day, an' leave us to finish this."

"Well, I'll see how things go to-morrow, then. I can pull out th' next morning if everything is all right out here." He hesitated a moment, looking Buck steadily in the eyes, a peculiar expression on his face. "Peters, yo're a good man, one of th' best I ever met, an' you've got a good outfit. I don't reckon we'll have no more trouble about that line of yourn, not nohow. When we settle down to peace an' punching again I'm going to let you show me how to put down some wells at th' southern base of yore hills, like you said one day. If I can get water, a half as much as you got in th' Jumping Bear, I'll be fixed all right. But I want to ask you a fair question, man to man. I ain't no real fool an' I've seen more than I'm sup-posed to, but I want to be shore about this, dead shore. What kind of a man is Hopalong Cassidy when it comes to women?"

Buck looked at him frankly. "If I had a daughter I wouldn't want a better man for her."

CHAPTER 33

Doc Trails

oc had not gone far into the chaparral before he realized that his work was going to be hard. The trail was much fainter than it would have been if the man he followed were mounted; the moonlight failed to penetrate the chaparral except in irregular patches which made the surrounding shadows all the deeper by contrast; what little he saw of the trail led through places far too small and turning too sharply to permit being followed by a man on horseback, and lastly, he expected every minute to be fired upon, and at close range. He paused and thought a while—Antonio would head for Eagle, that being the only place where he could get assistance, and there he would find friends. Doc picked his way out of the labyrinth of tortuous alleys and finally came to a comparatively wide lane leading southeast. He rode at a canter now and planned how he would strike the fugitive's trail further down, and after he had ridden a few miles he was struck by a thought that stopped him at once.

"Hang it all, he might 'a headed for them construction camps or for one of th' north ranches, to steal a cayuse," he muttered. "Th' only safe thing for me to do is to jump his trail an' stop guessing, an' even then mebby he'll get me before I get him. That's a clean gamble, an' so here goes," wheeling and retracing his course. When he again found the trail at the place he had quit in, he dismounted and crawled along on his hands and knees in order to follow the footprints among the shadows. Then some animal bounded up in front of him and leaped away, and as he turned to look after it he caught sight of his horse standing on its hind legs, and the next instant it was crashing through the chaparral. Drawing his Colt and cursing he ran back in time to see the horse gain an alleyway and gallop off. Angered thoroughly he sent a shot after it and then followed it, finally capturing it in a blind alley. Roundly cursing the frightened beast he led it back to where he had left the trail and, keeping one hand on the reins, continued to follow the foot-prints. Day broke when he had reached the edge of the chaparral and he mounted with a sigh of relief and rode forward along the now plainly marked trail.

As he cantered along he kept his eyes searching every possible cover ahead of and on both sides of him, watching the trail as far ahead as he could see it, for Antonio might have doubled back to get a pursuer as he rode past. After an hour of this caution he slapped his thigh and grinned at his foolishness.

"Now ain't I a cussed fool!" he exclaimed. "A regular, old-woman of a cow-puncher! He won't do no doubling back or ambushing. He'll shore reckon on being trailed by a bunch an' not by a locoed, prize-winning idiot. Why, he's making th' best time he can, an' that's aplenty, too. Besides he ain't got no rifle. Lift yore feet, you four-legged sage hen," he cried, spurring his horse into a lope. He mechanically felt at the long rifle holster at the saddle flap and then looked at it quickly. "An' no rifle for *me*, neither! Oh, well, that's all right, too. I don't need any better gun than he's got, th' coyote. Canteen full of water an' saddle flaps stuffed with grub. Why, old cayuse, if you can do without drinking till we get back to th' mesa we'll be plumb happy. Wonder when you was watered last?"

The trail had been swinging to the north more and more and when Doc noted this fact he grinned again.

"Nice fool I'd 'a been hunting for these tracks down towards Eagle, wouldn't I? But I wonder where he reckons he's going, anyhow?"

Sometime later he had his answers for he found himself riding towards a water hole and then he knew the reason for the trail swinging north. He let his mare drink its fill and while he waited he noticed a torn sombrero, then a spur, and further away the skeleton of a horse. Looking further he saw the skeleton of a man, all that the coyotes had left of the body of Dick Archer, the man killed by Red on the day when he and Hopalong had discovered that Thunder Mesa was inhabited. He pushed around the water hole and then caught sight of something in the sand. Edging his mount over to it he leaned down from the saddle and picked up a Colt's revolver, fully leaded and as good as the day Archer died. That air contained no moisture. As he slipped it in a saddle bag he spurred forward at top speed, for on the other side of a hummock he saw the head and then the full figure of a man plodding away from him, and it was Antonio.

The fugitive, hearing hoof-beats, looked back and then dropped to one knee, his rifle going to his shoulder with the movement.

"Where in the hell did *he* get a rifle?" ejaculated Doc, forcing his horse to buck-jump and pitch so as to be an erratic target. "He didn't have none when *I* grabbed him! Th' devil! That cussed skeleton back there gave *me* a six-shooter, an' *him* a rifle!"

There was a dull smothered report and he saw Antonio drop the gun and rock back and forth, apparently in agony, and he rode forward at top speed. Jerking his horse to its haunches he leaped off it just as Antonio wiped the blood from his eyes and jerked loose his Remington six-shooter. But his first shot missed and before he could fire again Doc grappled with him.

This time it was nearly an even break and Doc found that the slim figure of his enemy was made up of muscles of steel, that the lazy rider of the H2 ranch was, when necessary, quick as a cat and filled with the courage of desperation. It required all of Doc's attention and skill to keep himself from being shot by the other's gun and when he finally managed to wrest the weapon loose he was forced to drop it quickly and grab the same hand, which by some miracle of speed and dexterity now held a knife, a weapon far more deadly in hand-to-hand fighting. Once when believing himself to be gone the buckle of his belt stayed the slashing thrust and he again fought until the knife was above his head. Then, suddenly, two fingers flashed at his eyes and missed by so close a margin that Doc's eyebrows were torn open and his eyes blinded with blood. Instinct stronger than the effect of the disconcerting blindness made him hold his grip on the knife hand, else he would have been missing when his foreman looked for him at the mesa. He dug the fingers of his left hand, that had gripped around the waist, into his enemy's side and squeezed the writhing man tighter to him, wiping the blood from his eyes on the shirt of the other. As he did so he felt Antonio's teeth sink into his shoulder and a sudden great burst of rage swept over him and turned a man already desperate into a berserker, a mad man.

The grip tightened and then the brawny, bandaged left arm quickly slipped up and around Antonio's neck, pressing against the back of it with all the power of the swelling, knotted muscles. A smothered cry sobbed into his chest and he bent the knife hand back until the muscles were handicapped by their unnatural position and then, suddenly releasing both neck and hand, leaped back a step and the next instant his heavy boot thudded into the other's stomach and he watched the gasping, ghastly-faced rustler sink down in a nerveless heap, fighting desperately for the breath that almost refused to return.

Doc wiped his eyes free of blood and hastily bound his neck-kerchief around the bleeding eyebrows. As he knotted the bandage he stepped forward and picked up both the revolver and knife and threw them far from him. Glancing at the rifle he saw that it had burst and knew that the greased, dirty barrel had been choked with sand. He remembered how Curley's rifle had been leaded by the same cause and fierce joy surged through him at this act of retributive justice. He waited patiently, sneering and taunting him until the desperate man had gained his feet.

Doc stepped back a pace, tossing the burst rifle from him, and grinned malignantly. "Take yore own time. Get all yore wind an' strength. *I* ain't no murderer— I don't ride circles around a man an' potshoot him. I'm going to kill you fair, with my hands, like I said. Th' stronger you are th' better I'll feel when I leave you. An' if you should leave me out here on th' sand, all right—but it's got to be fair."

When fully recovered Antonio began the struggle by leaping forward, thinking his enemy unprepared. Doc faced him like a flash and bent low, barely escaping the other's kick. They clinched and swayed to and fro, panting, straining, every ounce of strength called into play. Then Doc got the throat hold again and took a shower of blows unflinchingly. His eyebrows, bleeding again, blinded him, but he could feel if he could not see. Slowly the resistance weakened and finally Doc wrestled Antonio to his knees, bending, and slowly tightening his grip; and the man who had murdered Curley went through all he had felt at the base of the mesa wall, at last paying with his life for his career of murder, theft, fear, and hypocrisy.

Doc arose and went to his horse. Leading the animal back to the scene of the struggle he stood a while, quietly watching for any sign of life, although he knew there would be none.

"Well, bronc, Curley's squared," he muttered, swinging into the saddle and turning the animal's head. "Come on, get out of this!" he exclaimed, quirting hard. As he passed the water hole he bowed to the broken skeleton. "Much obliged, stranger, whoever you was. Yore last play was a good one."

◆◆◆◆◆◆ ◆◆◆◆◆◆◆◆◆◆◆◆◆◆◆◆◆◆◆◆◆◆◆◆◆◆◆◆ ◆◆◆◆◆◆

CHAPTER 34

Discoveries

When the two foremen entered the firing line again they saw Red Connors and they cautiously went towards him. As they came within twenty feet of him Buck chanced to glance across the cut and what he saw brought a sudden smile to his face.

"Meeker, Red has got that spring under his gun!" he exclaimed in a low voice. "They can't get within ten feet of it or within ten feet of th' water at any point along its course. This is too good to bungle—wait for me," and he ran out of sight around a bend in the crevice, Meeker staring across at the spring, his eyes following the rivulet until it flowed into the deep, narrow cut it had worn in the side of the mesa.

Red looked around. "Why, hullo, Meeker! Where's Buck? Thought I heard him a minute ago. If you have any water to spare I can use some of it. Some thief drilled my canteen when I went fooling along this barranca, an' I ain't got a drop left."

Meeker began to move closer to him, Red warning him to be careful, and adding, "Three of them fellers ain't doing nothing but watch this cut. Scared we'll get across it an' flank 'em, I reckon."

"Do you know that yo're covering their water supply?" Meeker asked, handing his canteen to his thirsty companion. "They can't get to it as long as you stay here. That's why they're after you so hard."

Red wiped his lips on his sleeve and sighed contentedly. "It's blamed hot, but it's wet. But is that right? Am I keeping 'em thirsty? Where's th' water?"

"Shore you are! It's right over there—see that little ditch?" Meeker replied, pointing.

Bing! Spat!

The H2 foreman dropped his arm and grinned. "They're watching us purty close, ain't they? Didn't miss me far, at that," showing his companion a torn sleeve and a lead splotch on the rock behind him.

"Not a whole lot. Two of them fellers can shoot like blazes. Yo're plumb lucky," Red responded. "If you'd showed more'n your sleeve that time they'd 'a hit you." He looked across the cut and puckered his brow. "Well, if that's where their water is they don't get none. Mebby we can force 'em out if we watches that spring right smart."

"Here comes Buck now, with Skinny."

"It's too good a card to lose, Skinny," the Bar-20 foreman was saying as he approached. "You settle some place near there where you can pot anybody that tries for a drink. Mebby this little trick wins th' game for us—*quien sabe?* Hullo, Red; where's yore side pardner?"

"Oh, he went prospecting along this barranca to see if he could get across," Red replied. "He wants to get up on top of that ridge behind th' shack. Says if he can do it th' fight won't last long. See how it overlooks their layout?"

Buck looked and his eyes glistened. "An' he's right, too, like he is generally. That's th' key, an' it lies between them an' th' spring. Beats all how quick that feller can size up a hand. If he could play poker as well as he can fight he could quit working for a living."

"Yes; yo're shore right," Red replied.

Several shots rang out from the breastwork and the bullets hummed past them down the cut. A burst of derisive laughter replied fifty yards to their right and a taunt followed it. More shots were fired and answered by another laugh and taunt, inducing profanity from the marksman, and then Hopalong called to Red. "Six out of seven went plumb through my sombrero, Red, when I poked it out to find out if they was looking. They was. Purty good for 'em, eh?"

"Too blamed good to suit me—lucky yore head wasn't in it," Red replied.

Hopalong, singing in stentorian voice an original version of "Mary and Her Little Lamb" in which it seemed he aspired to be the lamb, finally came into view with a perforated sombrero in his hand, which he eyed ruefully. "A good roof gone up, but I didn't reckon everybody was looking my way," he grumbled. "Somebody shore has got to pay for that lid, too," then he glanced up, saw Meeker, and looked foolish. "Howd'y, Meeker; what's new, Buck?"

"Hey, Hoppy! Did you know I was covering their drinking water?" asked Red, triumphantly.

"I knowed you was covering some of it, but you needn't take on no airs about it, for you didn't know it," Hopalong retorted. "What *I* want to know is why you wasn't covering *me*, like you said you would! It's all yore fault that my Stetson's bust wide open, an' that being so, we'll just swap, right now, too!" suiting the action to the words.

"Hey! Gimme that war-bonnet, you bunch of gall!" yelled Red kicking at his tormentor and missing. "Gimme that, d'y hear!"

"Give you a punch in th' eye, you sheep!" retorted Hopalong, backing away. "Think you can get away with a play like that after saying you was going to cover me? *I* ain't no papoose, you animated carrot!"

"Gimme that Stetson!" Red commanded, starting to risc. There was a sharp hum and he dropped back again, blood flowing from his cheek, that being the extent of his person he had so inadvertently exposed. "There, blank you! See what you made me do! Going to drop that hat?"

"Why don't you give 'em a good shot at you? That ain't no way to treat 'em— but honest, Red, you shouldn't get so excited over a little thing like that," Hopalong replied. "Now, I'll leave it to Meeker, here—hadn't I ought to take his roof?"

Meeker laughed. "Th' Court reserves its decision, but possession is nine points in law."

"Huh! Possession is everything. Since I can keep it, why, then, according to th' Court, th' hat belongs to me. Hear that, Red?"

"Yes, I hear it! An' if I wasn't so cussed busy I'd show you how long you'd keep it," Red rejoined. "I'll bet you a hat you don't keep it a day after we get this off'n our hands. Bow-legged cuss, you!"

"Done—then I'll have two hats; one for work an' one to wear when I'm visiting." Hopalong laughed. "But you've got th' best of th' swap, anyhow. That new lid of yourn, holes an' all, is worth twice as much as this wool thing I'm getting for it. My old one is a *hat*!"

Red refused to lower his dignity by replying and soon fired. "Huh! Reckon that feller won't shoot no more with his right hand."

"Say, I near forgot to tell you Meeker captured one of them fellers out back; got him tied up now," Buck remarked, relating the incident, Meeker interrupting to give the Bar-20 foreman all the credit.

"Good!" exclaimed Red. "It's a rope necktie for him. An' one less to shoot at me."

"An' *you* here, Buck!" cried Hopalong in surprise. "Come on, lead th' way! How do you know he was th' only one to get behind us! Good Lord!"

"Gosh, yo're right!" Buck exclaimed, running off. "Come on, Jim. We're a pair of fools, after all!"

At the other end of the line Chick Travers and George Cross did as well as they could with their Colts, but found their efforts unavailing. Their positions were marked by the rustlers and they had several narrow escapes, both being wounded, Cross twice. Ten yards west of them Frenchy McAllister was crawling forward a foot at a time from cover to cover and so far he had not been hit. His position also had been marked and he was now trying to find a new one unobserved, where he could have a chance to shoot once without instantly being fired upon. Pete and Johnny had separated, the latter having given up his attempt to make the rustler pay for his wounded ear. He had emptied the magazine of the rifle he had found and now only used his Colt. As he worked along the firing line he saw Frenchy ten yards in front of him, covered nicely by a steep rise in the ground.

"How are you doing out there, Frenchy?" he asked in a low voice.

"Not very good; wish I had my rifle," came the soft-spoken reply.

"I had one that I found, but I used up all th' cartridges there was in th' magazine."

"What kind an' caliber?"

"Forty-five–seventy Winchester. I found it by th' ropes. Pete says he reckoned some rustler must have left it behind an' got away down th'—"

"Get it for me, Kid, will you?" interrupted Frenchy, eagerly. "I plumb forgot to leave my belt of rifle cartridges back in th' camp. Got it on now, an' it's chock full, too. Hurry up, an' I'll work back to you for it."

"What luck! In a second," Johnny exulted, disappearing. Returning with the rifle he handed it to his friend and gazed longingly at the beltful of rifle cartridges. "Say, Frenchy," he began. "You know we'll all have our rifles tonight, an' you've got more cartridges for that than you can use before then. It won't be more than three hours before we send for ours. Suppose you gimme some of them for Pete—he's got th' mate to that gun, an' can't use it no more because it's empty."

"Shore, Kid," and Frenchy slipped a handful of cartridges out of his belt and gave them to Johnny. "With my compliments to Pete. What was that you was saying about rustlers an' th' ropes?"

Johnny told of Pete's deductions regarding the finding of the rifles and Frenchy agreed with them, and also that Doc had taken care of the owners of the weapons when they had reached the plain.

"Well, I'm going further away from them thieves now that I've got something to shoot with," Frenchy asserted. "They won't be looking for any of us a hundred yards or more farther back. Mebbe I can catch some of 'em un-awares."

"I'll chase off an' give Pete these pills," Johnny replied. "He'll be tickled plumb to death. He was cussing bad when I left him."

George Cross, crawling along a steep, smooth rock barely under the shelter of a bowlder, endeavored to grasp the top, but under-reached and slipped, rolling down to the bottom and in plain sight of the rustlers. As his companion, Chick Travers, tried to help him two shots rang out and Cross, sitting up with his hands to his head, toppled back to arise no more. Chick leaped up and fired twice at one of the marksmen, and missed. His actions had been so sudden and unexpected that he escaped the return shot which passed over him by a foot as he dropped back to cover. Somehow the whole line seemed to feel that there had been a death among them, as evidenced by the burst of firing along it. And the whole line felt another thing; that the cartridges of the rustlers were getting low, for they seemed to be saving their shots. But it was Hopalong who found the cause of the diminishing fire. After hunting fruitlessly with the two foremen and finding that Hall was the only man to get back of the firing line he left his two companions in order to learn the condition of his friends. As he made his way along the line he chanced to look towards the hut and saw four rifles on the floor of it, and back of them, piled against the wall, was the rustlers' main supply of ammunition. Calling out, he was answered by Pete, who soon joined him.

"Pete, you lucky devil, turn that rifle through th' door of th' shack an' keep it on them cartridges," he ordered. "They ain't been shooting as fast as they was at first, an' there's th' reason for it. Oh, just wait till daylight to-morrow! They won't last long after that!"

"They won't get them cartridges, anyhow," Pete replied with conviction.

"Hey, fellers," cried a voice, and they looked around to see Chick Travers coming towards them. "Yore man Cross has passed. He rolled off his ledge an' couldn't stop. They got him when he hit th' bottom of it."

"Damn 'em!" growled Hopalong. "We'll square our accounts to-morrow morning. Pete, you watch them cartridges."

"Shore—" *Bang!* "Did you see that?" Pete asked, frantically pumping the lever of his rifle.

"Yes!" cried Chick. "Some feller tried to get in that south window! Bet he won't try again after that hint. Hear him cuss? There—Red must 'a fired then, too!"

"Good boy, Pete!—keep 'em out. We'll have somebody in there after dark,"

Hopalong responded. "They've got th' best covers now, but we'll turn th' table on 'em when th' sun comes up to-morrow."

"Here comes Buck an' Meeker," remarked Chick. "Them two are getting a whole lot chummy lately, all right. They're allus together."

"That's good, too. They're both of 'em all right," Hopalong replied, running to meet them. Chick saw the three engage in a consultation and look towards the hut and the ridge behind it, Buck and Meeker nodding slowly at what Hopalong was saying. Then they moved off towards the west where they could examine the building at closer range.

CHAPTER 35

Johnny Takes the Hut

As the day waned the dropping shots became less and less frequent and the increasing darkness began to work its magic. The unsightly plain with its crevices and boulders and scrawny vegetation would soon be changed into one smooth blot, to be lighted with the lurid flashes of rifles as Red and Pete fired at irregular intervals through the south windows of the hut to keep back any rustler who tried to get the ammunition within its walls. Two were trying and had approached the window just as a bullet hummed through it. They stopped and looked at each other and moved forward again. Then a bullet from Pete's rifle, entering through the open door, hummed out the window and struck against the rocky ridge.

"Say! Them coyotes can see us through that windy," remarked Clausen. 'Th' sky at our backs is too light yet."

"They can't see us standing here," objected Shaw.

"Then what are they shooting at?"

"Cuss me if I know. Looks like they was using th' winder for a target. Reckon we better wait till it gets darker."

"If we wait till it's dark we can sneak in through th' door," suggested Clausen. "If we go in crawling we ain't likely to stop no shot high enough to go through that windy."

"You can if you wants, but I ain't taking no chances like that, none whatever."

Another shot whined through the window and stopped with an angry spat against the ridge. Shaw scratched his head reflectively. "It shore beats me why they keeps that up. There ain't no sense to it," he declared in aggrieved tones. "They don't know nothing about them cartridges in there."

"That's it!" exclaimed Clausen, excitedly. "I bet a stack of blues they do know. An' they're covering somebody going in to steal 'em. Oh, hell!" and he slammed his hat to the ground in bitter anger. "An' us a-standing here like a couple of mired cows! I'm going to risk it."

"Wait," advised Shaw. "Let's try a hat an' see if they plug it."

"Wait be damned! My feet are growing roots right now. I'm going in," and Clausen broke away from his friend and ran towards the hut, a crouching run, comical to look at but effective because it kept his head below the level of the window; without pausing in his stride his body lengthened into a supple curve as he plunged head foremost through the window, landing on the cabin floor with hands and feet bunched under him, his passing seen only as a fleeting puzzling shadow, by the watchful eyes outside.

Across the cut Johnny was giving Red instructions and turned to leave. "Th' cut is full of shadows an' th' moon ain't up yet. Now, remember, one more shot through that window—I'm going to foller it right in. Get word to Pete as soon as you can, though I won't pass th' door. He's only got three cartridges left an' he'll be getting some anxious about now. So long."

"So long, an' good luck, Kid," Red replied.

Johnny wriggled across the cut on his stomach, picking out the shadows and gaining the shelter of the opposite bank, stood up, and ran to the hut. Red fired and then Johnny cautiously climbed through the window and dropped to the floor.

He had anticipated Clausen by the fraction of a second. As his feet touched the floor the noise of Clausen's arrival saluted him and the startled Johnny jerked his gun loose and sent a shot in the other's direction, leaping aside on the instant. The flash of the discharge was gone too quickly for him to distinguish anything and the scrambling sound that followed mystified him further. That there had been no return shot did not cause him to dance with joy, far otherwise; it made him drop silently to his stomach and hunt the darkest part of the hut, the west wall. He lay still for a minute, eyes and ears strained for a sound to tell him where to shoot. Then Red called to him and wanted an answer, whereupon Johnny thought of things he ached to call Red. Then he heard a low voice outside the south window, and it called: "Clausen, Clausen—what happened? Why don't you answer?"

"Oh, so my guest is Clausen, hey?" Johnny thought. "Wonder if Clausen can see in th' dark?' Nother damned fool wanting an answer! I'll bet Clausen is hugging th' dark spots, too. Wonder if I scared him as much as he scared me?"

The suspense was becoming too much of a strain and, poking his Colt out in front of him, he began to move forward, his eyes staring ahead of him at the place where Clausen ought to be.

Inch by inch he advanced, holding his breath as well as he could, every moment expecting to have Clausen salute him in the face with a hot .45. Johnny was scared, and well scared, but it only proves courage to go on when scared stiff, and Johnny went on and along the wall he thought Clausen was using for a highway.

"Wonder how it feels to have yore brains blowed out," he shivered. "For God's sake, Clausen, make a noise—sneeze, cough, choke, yell, anything!" he prayed, but Clausen remained ominously silent. Johnny pushed his Colt out farther and poked it all around. Touching the wall it made a slight scraping sound and Johnny's blood froze. Still no move from Clausen, and his fright went down a notch—Clausen was evidently even more scared than he was. That was consoling. Perhaps he was so scared that he couldn't pull a trigger, which would be more consoling.

"Johnny! Johnny! Answer, can't you!" came Red's stentorian voice, causing Johnny to jump a few inches off the floor.

"Clausen! Clausen!" came another voice.

"For God sake, answer, Clausen! Tell 'em yo're here!" prayed Johnny. "Yo're damned unpolite, anyhow."

By this time he was opposite the door and he wondered if Pete had been told not to bombard it. He stopped and looked, and stared. What was that thing on the floor? Or was it anything at all? He blinked and moved closer. It looked like a head, but Johnny was taking no chances. He stared steadily into the blackest part of the hut for a moment and then looked again at the object. He could see it a little plainer now, for it was not quite as dark outside as it was in the building; but he was not sure about it.

"Can't fool me, you coyote," he thought. "Yo're hugging this wall as tight as a tick on a cow, a blamed sight tighter than I am, an' in about a minute I'm going to shoot along it about four inches from th' floor. I'd just as soon get shot as be scared to death, anyhow. Mebby we've passed each other! An' Holy Medicine! Mebby there's two of 'em!"

He regarded the object again. "That shore looks like a head, all right." He felt a pebble under his hand and drawing back a little he covered the questionable object and then tossed the pebble at it. "Huh, if it's a head, why in thunder didn't it move?"

There were footsteps outside the south window and he listened, the Colt ready to stop any one rash enough to look in, Clausen or no Clausen.

"Where's Clausen, Shaw?" said a voice, and the reply was so low Johnny could not make it out.

"Yes; that's just what I want to know," and Johnny stared in frowning intentness at the supposed head. He moved closer to the object and by dint of staring thought he saw the head and shoulders of a man face down in a black, shallow pool. Then his hand became wet and he jerked it back and wiped it on his sleeve; he could hardly believe his senses. As he grasped the significance of his discovery he grinned sheepishly and moved back to the north wall, where no rustler's bullet could find him. "Lord! An' I got him th' first crack! Got him shooting by ear!"

"Johnny! Johnny!" came Red's roar, anxious and querulous.

Johnny wheeled and shook his Colt out of the window, for the moment forgetting the peril of losing sight of the opening in the other wall. "I'll Johnny *you*, you blankety-blank fool!" he shouted. Then he heard a curse at the south window and turned quickly, his Colt covering the opening. "An' I'll Johnny you too, you cow-stealing coyotes! Stick yore thieving heads in that windy an' holler for yore Clausen! *I* can show you where he is, an' send you after him if you'll just take a look! Want them cartridges, hey? Well, come an' get 'em!"

A bullet, fired at an angle through the window, was the reply and several hummed through the open door and glanced off the steep sides of the ridge. Waiting until they stopped coming he dropped and wriggled forward along the west wall, feeling in front of him until he touched a box. Grasping it he dragged the important cartridges to him and then backed to the north window with them.

He fell to stuffing his pockets with the captured ammunition and then stopped short and grinned happily. "Might as well *hold* this shack an' wait for somebody to look in that windy. They can't get me."

He dropped the box and walked to the heavy plank door, slamming it shut. He heard the thud of bullets in it as he propped it, and laughed. "Can't shoot through them planks, they're double thick." He smelled his sticky fingers. "An' they're full of resin, besides."

He stopped suddenly and frowned as a fear entered his mind; and then smiled, reassured. "Nope; no rustling snake can climb up that ridge—not with Red an' Pete watching it."

CHAPTER 36

The Last Night

Fifty yards behind the firing line of the besiegers a small fire burned brightly in a steep-walled basin, casting grotesque shadows on the rock walls as men passed and re-passed. Overhead a silvery moon looked down at the cheerful blaze and from the cracks and crevices of the plain came the tuneful chorus of Nature's tiny musicians, sounding startlingly out of place where men were killing and dying. A little aside from the others three men in consultation reached a mutual understanding and turned to face their waiting friends just as Pete Wilson ran into the lighted circle.

"Hey, Johnny is in th' hut with th' cartridges," he exclaimed, telling the story in a few words.

"Good for th' Kid!"

"It's easy now, thanks to him."

"Why didn't he tell us he was going to try that?" demanded Buck. "Taking a chance like that on his own hook!"

"Scared you wouldn't let him," Pete laughed. "Red an' me backed him up with our rifles th' best we could. He had a fight in there, too, judging from th' shot. He had me an' Red worried, thinking he might 'a been hit, but he was cussing Red when I left."

"Well, that helps us a lot," Buck replied. "Now I want three of you to go to camp an' bring back grub, rifles, an' cartridges. Pete, Skinny, Chick—yo're th' ones. Leave yore canteens here an' hustle! Hopalong, you an' Meeker go off somewhere an' get some sleep. I'll call you before it gets light. Frenchy, me an' you will take all th' canteens at hand an' fill 'em while we've got time. They won't be able to see us now. We'll pass Red an' get his, too. Come on."

When they returned they dropped the dripping vessels and began cleaning their Colts. That done they filled their pipes and sat cross-legged, staring into the fire. A snatch of Johnny's exultant song floated to them and Buck smiled, laying his pipe aside and rising. "Well, Frenchy, things'll happen in chunks when th' sun comes up. Something like old times, eh? There ain't no Deacon Rankin or Slippery Trendley here—" He stopped, having mentioned a name he had promised himself never to say in Frenchy's presence, and then continued in a subdued voice, bitterly scourging himself for his blunder. "They're stronger than I thought, an' they've shot us up purty well, killed Willis an' Cross, an' made fools of us for weeks on th' range; but this is th' end of it all. *We* deal to-morrow, an' we cut th' cards to-night."

Frenchy was strangely silent, staring fixedly at the fire. Buck glanced at him in strong sympathy, for he knew what his slip of the tongue had awakened in his friend's heart. Frenchy had adored his young wife and since the day he had found her murdered in his cabin on the Double Y he had been another man. When the moment of his vengeance had come, when he had her murderer in his power and saw his friends ride away to leave him alone with Trendley that day over in the Panhandle, to exact what payment he wished, then he had become his old self for a while, but it was not long before he again sank into his habitual carelessness, waiting patiently for death to remove his burden and make him free. His vengeance did not bring him back his wife.

Buck shook his head slowly and affectionately placed a heavy hand on his friend's shoulder. "Frenchy, won't you ever forget it? It hurts me to see you this way so much. It's over twenty years now an' day after day I've grieved to see you so unhappy. You paid him for it in yore own way. Can't you forget it now?"

"Yes; I killed him, an' slow. He never thought a man could make th' payment so hard, not even his black heart could realize it till he felt it," Frenchy replied, slowly and calmly. "He took th' heart out of me; he killed my wife and made my life a living hell. All I had worth living for went that day, an' if I could kill him over again every day for a year it wouldn't square th' score. I reckon I ain't built like other men. You never heard me whimper. I kept my poison to myself an' tried to do the best that was in me. An' you ain't never heard me say what I'm going to tell you now. I never believed in hunches, but something tells me that I'll leave all this behind me before another day passes. I felt it somehow when we left th' ranch an' it's been growing stronger every hour since. If I do pass out to-morrow, I want you to be glad of it, same as I would be if I could know. I'm going back to th' line now an' watch them fellers. So long."

The two men, bosom friends for thirty years, looked in each other's eyes as they grasped hands, and it was Buck's eyes that grew moist and dropped first. "So long, Frenchy—an' good luck, as you see it."

The foreman watched his friend until lost in the darkness and he thought he heard him singing, but of this he was not sure. He turned and stared at the fire for a minute, silent, immovable, and then breathed heavily.

"I never saw anybody carry a grief so long, never. I reckon it sort of turned his brain, coming so sudden an' in such a damnable way. I know it made me see red for a week. If I had only stayed there that day! When he got Trendley in th' Panhandle I hoped he would change, an' he did for a while, but that was all. He lived for that alone, an' since then I reckon he's felt he hadn't nothing to do with his life. He has been mixed up in a bunch of gun-arguments since then; but he didn't have no luck. Well, Frenchy, I hate to lose a friend like you, but here's better luck to-morrow, luck as you see it, friend!"

He kicked the fire together and was about to add fuel when he heard two quick shots and raised his head to listen. Then a ringing whoop came from the front and he recognized Johnny's voice. He heard Red call out and Johnny reply and he smiled grimly as he went towards the sounds. "Reckon somebody tried to get in that shack, like a fool. He must 'a been disgusted. How that Kid shore does love to fight!"

Joyous Joe got a juniper jag,
A jogging out of Jaytown,

came down the wind.

"Did you get him, Kid?" cried Buck from the firing line.

"Nope; got his hat, though—but I shore got Clausen an' all of their cartridges!"

"Can you keep them shells alone?"

"*Can I? Wow,* ask th' other fellers! An' I'm eating jerked beef—sorry I can't give you some."

"Shut up about eating, you pig!" blazed Red, who was hungry.

"You'll eat hot lead to-morrow, all of you!" jeered a rustler's voice.

Red fired at the sound. "Take yourn now!" he shouted.

"You can't hit a cow!" came the taunt, while other strange voices joined in.

Buck found Red and ordered him to camp to get some sleep before Pete and the others returned, feeling that he and Frenchy were enough to watch. Red demurred sleepily and finally compromised by lying down at Buck's side, where

he would be handy in case of trouble. Buck waited patiently, too heavily laden
with responsibility to feel the need of rest, and when he judged that three hours
had passed began to worry about the men he had sent to camp. Drawing back
into a crevice he struck a match and looked at him.

"Twelve o'clock!" he muttered. "I'll wake Red an' see how Frenchy is getting on. Time them fellers were back too."

Frenchy changed his position uneasily and peered at the distant breastwork, hearing the low murmur of voices behind it. All night he had heard their
curses, but a new note made him sit up and watch more closely. The moon
was coming up now and he could see better. Suddenly he caught the soft flash
of a silver sombrero buckle and fired instantly. Curses and a few shots replied
and a new, querulous voice was added to the murmur, a voice expressing pain.

"I reckon you got him," remarked a quiet voice at his side as Buck lay down
beside him. The foreman had lost some time in wandering along the whole
line of defense and was later than he had expected.

"Yes; I reckon so," Frenchy replied without interest, and they lapsed into silence, the eloquent silence of men who understand each other. They heard a
shot from below and knew that Billy or Curtis was about and smiled grimly at
the rising murmur it caused among the rustlers. Buck glanced at the sky and
frowned. "There can't be more'n five or six left by now, an' if it wasn't for th'
moon I'd get th' boys together an' rush that bunch." He was silent for a moment and then added, half to himself, "but it won't be long now, an' we can
wait."

Distant voices heralded the return of Pete and his companions and the
foreman arose. "Frenchy, I'm going to place th' boys an' start things right away.
We've been quiet too long."

"Might as well," Frenchy replied, "I'm getting sleepy—straining my eyes
too much, I reckon, trying to see a little better than I can."

"Here's th' stuff, Buck," Skinny remarked as the foreman entered the circle
of light. "Two day's fighting rations, fifty rounds for th' rifles an' fifty for th'
Colts. Chick is coming back there with th' rifles."

"Good. Had yore grub yet?" Buck asked. "All right—didn't reckon you'd
wait for it. What kept you so long? You've been gone over three hours."

"We was talking to Bill an' Curtis," Skinny remarked. "They're anxious to
have it over. They've been spelling each other an' getting some sleep. We saw
Doc's saddle piled on top of th' grub when we got to camp. It wasn't there when
we all left th' other night. Billy says Doc came running past last night, saddled
up an' rode off. He got back this afternoon wearing a bandage around his head.

He didn't say where he had been, but now he is at th' bottom of th' trail waiting for a shot, so Billy says. Pete reckons he went after somebody that got down last night, one of them fellers that left their rifles up here by th' ropes."

"Mebby yo're right," replied Buck, hurriedly. "Get ready to fight. I ain't going to wait for daylight when this moonlight will answer. Pete, Skinny, Chick—you get settled out on th' east end, where me an' Frenchy will join you. We'll have this game over before long."

He strode away and returned with Hopalong and Meeker, who hastily ate and drank and, filling their belts with cartridges and taking their own rifles from the pile Chick had brought, departed toward the cut with orders for Red to come in.

Pete and his companions moved away as Frenchy, shortly followed by Red, came in and reported.

"Eat an' drink, lively. Red, you get back to yore place an' take care of th' cut," Buck ordered. "Frenchy, you come out east with th' rest. There's cartridges for you both an' there's yore own rifle, Frenchy."

"Glad yo're going to start things," chewed Red through a mouthful of food. "It's about time we show them fellers we can live up to our reputation. Any of 'em coming my way won't go far."

Frenchy filled his pipe and lighted it from a stick he took out of the fire and as it began to draw well he stepped quickly forward and held out his hand. "Good luck, Red. They can't fight long."

"Same to you, Frenchy. You look plumb wide awake, like Buck—how'd you do it?"

Frenchy laughed and strode after his foreman, Red watching him. "He's acting funny—reckon it's th' sleep he's missed. Well, here goes," and he, too, went off to the firing line.

> —An' aching thoughts pour in on me,
>   Of Whiskey Bill,

came Johnny's song from the hut—and the fight began again.

CHAPTER 37

Their Last Fight

A figure suddenly appeared on the top of the flanking ridge, outlined against the sky, and flashes of flame spurted from its hands, while kneeling beside it was another, rapidly working a rifle, the roar of the guns deafening because of the silence which preceded it. Shouts, curses, and a few random, futile shots replied from the breastworks, its defenders, panic-stricken by the surprise and the deadly accuracy of the two marksmen, scurrying around the bend in their fortifications, so busy in seeking shelter that they failed to make their shots tell. Two men, riddled by bullets, lay where they had fallen and the remaining three, each of them wounded more than once, crouched under cover and turned their weapons against the new factors; but these had already slid down the face of the ridge and were crawling along the breastwork, alert and cautious.

In front of the rustlers heavy firing burst out along the cowmen's line and Red Connors, from his old position above the cut, swung part way around and turned his rifle against the remnant of the defenders at another angle, and fired at every mark, whether it was hand, foot, or head; while Johnny, tumbling out of the south window of the hut, followed in the wake of Hopalong and Meeker. The east end of the line was wrapped in smoke, where Buck and his companions labored zealously.

Along the narrow trail up the mesa's face a man toiled heavily and it was not long before Doc Riley opened fire from the rear. The three rustlers, besieged from all sides, found their positions to be most desperate and knew then that only a few minutes intervened between them and eternity. They had three choices—to surrender, to die fighting, or to leap from the mesa to instant death below.

Shaw, to his credit, chose the second and like a cornered wolf goaded to despair leaped up and forward to take a gambler's chance of gaining the hut. Before him were Hopalong, Meeker, Johnny, and Doc. Doc was hastily reloading his Colt, Johnny was temporarily out of sight as he crawled around a boulder, and Hopalong was greatly worried by ricochettes and wild shots from the rifles of his friends which threatened to end his career. Meeker alone was watching at that moment but his attention was held by the rustler near the edge of the mesa who was trying to shrink himself to fit the small rock in front of him and to use his gun at the same time.

Shaw sprang from his cover and straight at the H2 foreman, his foot slipping slightly as he fired. The bullet grazed Meeker's waist, but the second, fired as the rustler was recovering his balance, bored through Meeker's shoulder. The H2 foreman, bending forward for a shot at the man behind the small rock, was caught unawares and his balance, already strained, was destroyed by the shock of the second bullet, and he flopped down to all fours. Shaw sprang over him just as Hopalong and Johnny caught sight of him and he swung his revolver on Hopalong at the moment when the latter's bullet crashed through his brain.

Buck Peters, trying for a better position, slipped on the rock which had been the cause of the death of George Cross and before he could gain his feet a figure leaped down in front of him and raised a Colt in his defense, but spun half way around and fell, shot through the head. A cry of rage went up at this and a rush was made against the breast works from front and side. Frenchy McAllister's forebodings had come true.

Sanchez, finding his revolver empty and no time to reload, held up his hands. Frisco, blinded by blood, wounded in half a dozen places, desperate, snarling, and still unbeaten, wheeled viciously, but before he could pull his trigger, Hopalong grasped him and hurled him down, Johnny going with them. Doc, a second too late, waved his sombrero. "Come on, it's all over!"

In another second the rushing punchers from the front slid and rolled and plunged over the breastwork and eyed the results of their fire.

Meeker staggered around the corner and leaned against Buck for support. "My God! This is awful! I didn't think we were doing so much damage."

"I did!" retorted Buck. "I know what happens when my outfit burns powder. Where's Red?" he asked anxiously.

"Here I am," replied a voice behind him.

"All right; take that feller to the hut," the foreman ordered. "Johnny, you an Pete take the other," pointing to Frisco. "He's th' one that killed Frenchy. Hopalong, take Red, an' bring in that feller me an' Meeker tied up in that crevice, if he ain't got away."

CHAPTER 38

■ ❖ ❖ ❖ ❖ ❖ ■ ❖ ■ ❖ ❖ ❖ ❖ ❖ ■

A Disagreeable Task

Two men, Hall and Frisco, sat with their backs against the wall of the hut, weaponless, wounded, nervous, one sullen and enraged, the other growling querulously to himself about his numerous wounds. The third prisoner, was pacing to and fro with restless strides, vicious and defiant, his burning eyes quick, searching, calculating. It seemed as though he was filled with a tremendous amount of energy which would not let him remain quiet. When his companions spoke to him he flashed them a quick glance but did not answer; thinking, scheming, plotting, he missed not the slightest movement of those about him. Wounded as he was he did not appear to know it, so intent was he upon his thoughts.

Hall, saved from the dangers of the last night's fight, loosed his cumulative rage frequently in caustic and profane verbal abuse of his captors, his defeat, his companions, and the guard. Frisco, courageous as any under fire, was dejected because of the wait; merely a difference of temperament.

The guard, seated carelessly on a nearby rock, kept watch over the three and cogitated upon the whole affair, his Colt swinging from a hand between his knees. Twenty paces to his right was a stack of rifles and Sanchez, lengthening his panther stride with barely perceptible effort, drew nearer to them on each northward lap. He typified the class of men who never give up hope, and as he gained each yard he glanced furtively at the guard and then estimated the number of leaps necessary to reach the coveted rifles. His rippling muscles were bunching up for the desperate attempt when the guard interfered, the sharp clicks of his Colt bringing the Mexican to an abrupt stop. Sanchez shrugged his shoulders and wheeling, resumed his restless walk, being careful to keep it within safe limits.

Hall, lighting his pipe, blew a cloud of smoke into the air and looked at the guard, who was still cogitating.

"How did you fools finally figger we was out here?"

Hopalong looked up and smiled. "Oh, we just figgered you fools would be here, and would stay up here. Yore friend Antonio worked too hard."

Hall carefully packed his pipe and puffed quietly. "I knowed he'd bungle it."

"What happened to Cavalry an' Antonio?" asked Hall. "Did you get 'em when you came up?"

"They got down th' way we came up—Doc trailed Antonio an' got him at that water hole up north," Hopalong replied. "Don't know nothing about th' other feller. Reckon he got away, but one don't make much difference, anyhow. He'll never come back to this country."

"Say, how much longer will it take yore friends to do th' buryin' act?" asked Frisco irritably. "I'm plumb tired of waiting—these wounds hurt like blazes, too."

"Reckon they're coming now," was the reply. "I hear—yes, here they are."

"I owe you ten dollars, Hall," Frisco remarked, trivial thing now entering his mind. "Reckon you won't get it, neither."

"Oh, pay me in hell!" Hall snapped.

"Yes," Buck was saying, "He knowed he was going an' he went like th' man he was—saving a friend. 'Tain't th' first time Frenchy McAllister's saved my life, neither."

Frisco glanced around and his face flashed with a look of recognition, but he held his tongue; not so with Curtis, who stared at him in surprise and stepped forward.

"Good God! It's Davis! What ever got you into this?"

"Easy money an' a gun fight," Davis, alias Frisco, replied.

"Tough luck, tough luck," Curtis muttered slowly.

"Damn tough, if you asks me," Frisco growled.

"What happened to th' others?" Curtis asked, referring to three men with whom he and Frisco had punched and prospected several years before.

"Little Dan went out in that same gun fight, Joe Baird was got by th' posse next day, an' George Wild an' I got into th' mountains an' was separated. I got free after a sixty-mile chase, but I don't know how George made out. We had stuck up a gold caravan an' killed two men what was with it. They was th' only fellers to pull their guns against us."

"Well, I'm damned!" ejaculated Curtis. "An' so that crowd went bad!"

"Say, for th' Lord's sake, get things moving," cried Hall, angrily. "If we've got to die make it quick. Wish I'd a' gone with Shaw 'stead of waiting for my own funeral."

Buck surveyed them. "Got anything to say?"

"Not me—I've had mine," replied Frisco, toying with a bandage. Then he started to say something but changed his mind. "Oh, well what's th' use! Go ahead."

"Don't drag it out," growled Hall. "Say, you got *my* rope there?" he demanded suddenly, eyeing the coils slung over Skinny's shoulder. "No, you ain't, I want my own, savvy?"

"Oh, we ain't got time to hunt for no ropes," rejoined Skinny. "One's as good as another, ain't it."

"Yes, I reckon so—hustle it through," Hall replied, sullenly.

"Go ahead, you fellers," ordered Hopalong as some of his friends went first down the trail after the two sent to the camp for the horses. "Come, on, Sanchez! Fall in there!"

When the procession reached the bottom of the trail Buck halted it to wait for the horses and his prisoners took one more look around.

"Say, Peters, where's th' cayuses we had in that corral?" asked Hall, surprised.

"Oh, we got them out th' first night—we wasn't taking no chances," replied the foreman. "They're somewhere near th' camp now."

As the horse herd was driven up Sanchez made his last play. All were intent upon tightening cinches, the more intent because of the impending and disagreeable task, when he slipped like a shadow through the group and throwing himself across a pinto, headed in a circular track for the not too distant chaparral.

"*Take* him, Red!" shouted Buck, who was the first to recover.

Red's rifle leaped to his shoulder and steadied; in three more jumps the speedy pinto would have shielded Sanchez, clinging like a burr to the further side; but the rifle spoke once and he dropped and lay quiet on the sand.

Hopalong rode out to him and glancing at the still form, wheeled and returned. "Got him clean, Red."

A group of horsemen rode eastward towards the chaparral and as it was about to enclose them one of the riders bringing up the rear turned in his saddle and looked back at two dangling forms outlined against the darker background of the frowning mesa, two where he had expected to see three.

"Well, th' rustling is over," he remarked.

CHAPTER 39

Thirst

The stars grow dim and a streak of color paints the eastern sky, sweeping through the upper reaches of the darkness and tingeing the earth's curtain until the dim gray light outlines spectral yuccas and twisted, grotesque cacti leaning in the hushed air like drunken sentries of some monstrous army. The dark carpet which stretched away on all sides begins to show its characteristics and soon develops into greasewood brush. As if curtains were drawn aside objects which a moment before were lost to sight in the darkness emerge out of the light like ghosts, bulky, indistinct, grotesque, and array themselves to complete the scene.

The silence seems to deepen and become strained, as if in fear of what is to come; the dark ground is now gray and tawny in places and the vegetation is plain to the eye. Then out of the east comes a flash and a red, coppery sun flares above the horizon, molten, quivering, blinding; the cool of the night swiftly departs and a caldron-like heat bursts upon the plain. The silence seems almost to shrink and become portentous with evil, the air is hushed, the plants stand without the movement of a leaf, and nowhere is seen any living creature. The whole is unreal, a panorama, with vegetation of wax and a painted, faded blue sky, the only movement being the shortening shadows and the rising sun.

Across the sand is an erratic trail of shoe prints, coming from the east. For a dozen yards it runs evenly and straight, then a few close prints straggle to and fro, zigzagging for a distance, finally going on straight again. But the erratic prints grow more frequent and become more pronounced as they go on, circling and weaving, crossing, recrossing and doubling back as their maker staggered hopelessly on his way, urged only by the instinct of thirst, to find water, if it were only a mouthful. The trail is here blurred, for he fell, and the prints of his hands and knees and shoe-tips tell how he went on for some distance. He gained his feet here and threw away his Colt, and later his holster and belt.

The sun is overhead now and the sand shimmers, the heated air quivering and glistening, and the desolate void takes on an air of mystery and fear, and death. No living thing moves across the heat-cursed sand, but here is a tangled mass of sand and clay and greasewood twigs, in the heart of which mice sleep and wait for night, and over there is a hillock sheltering lizards. Stay! Under that greasewood bush a foolish gray wolf is waiting for night—but he has little to fear, for he can cover forty miles between dark and dawn, and his instinct is infallible; no wandering trail will mark his passing, but one as straight as the flight of a bullet. The shadows shrink close to the stems of the plants and the thin air dances with heat.

Behind that clump of greasewood, back beyond those crippled cacti, a man staggers on and on. His hair is matted, his fingers bleeding from digging frantically in the sand for water; his lips, cracked and bleeding and swollen, hide the shrivelled, stiff tongue which clicks against his teeth at every painful step. His eyelids are stiff and the staring, unblinking eyes are set and swollen. He clutches at his throat time and time again—a drowning sensation is there. Ha! He drops to his knees and digs frantically again, for the sand is moist! A few days ago a water hole lay there. He throws off his shirt and finally staggers on again.

His tongue begins to swell and forces itself beyond the swollen, festering lips; the eyelids split and the protruding eyeballs weep tears of blood. His skin cracks and curls up, the clefts going constantly deeper into the flesh, and the exuding blood quickly dries and leaves a tough coating over the wounds. Wherever the exudation touches it stings and burns, and the cracks and clefts, irritated more and more each minute, deepen and widen and lengthen, smarting and nerve-racking with their pain.

There! A grove of beautiful green trees is before him, and in it a fountain splashes with musical babbling. He yells and dances and then, casting aside the rest of his clothes, staggers towards it. Water, water, at last! Water and shade! It grows indistinct, wavers—and is gone! But it must be there. It was there only a moment ago—and on and on he runs, hands tearing at his choking, drowning throat. Here is water—close at hand—a purling, cold brook, whispering and tinkling over its rocky bed—he jumps into it—it moved! It's over there, ten paces to his right. On and on he staggers, the stream just ahead. He falls more frequently and wavers now. Oh, for just a canteen of water, just a swallow, just a drop! The gold of the world would not buy it from him—just a drop of water!

He is dying from within, from the inside out. The liquids of his body exude through the clefts and evaporate. His brain burns and bands of white-hot steel crush his throbbing head and his burning lungs. No amount of water will save him now—only death, merciful death can end his sufferings.

Water at last! Real water, a pool of stagnant liquid lies at the bottom of a slight depression, the dregs of a larger pool concentrated by evaporation. Around it are the prints of many kinds of feet. It is water, water!—he plunges forward into it and lies motionless, half submerged. A grayback lizard darts out of the grease-wood near at hand, blinks rapidly and darts back again, glad to escape the intolerable heat.

Cavalry had escaped.

CHAPTER 40

Changes

With the passing of the weeks the two ranches had settled down to routine duty. On the H2 conditions were changed greatly for the better and Meeker gloated over his gushing wells and the dam which gave him a reservoir on his north range, the early completion of which he owed largely to the experience and willing assistance of Buck and the Bar-20 outfit.

It was getting along towards fall when a letter came to the Bar-20 addressed to John McAllister. Buck looked at it long and curiously. "Wonder who's writing to Frenchy?" he mused. "Well, I've got to find out," and he opened the envelope and looked at the signature; it made him stare still more and he read the letter carefully. George McAllister, through the aid of the courts, had gained possession of the old Double Y in the name of its owners and was going to put an outfit on the ground to evict and hold off those who had jumped it. He knew nothing about ranching and wanted Frenchy McAllister, who owned half of it, to take charge of it and to give him the address of Buck Peters the other half-owner. He advised that Peters' share be bought because the range was near a railroad and was growing more valuable every day.

Buck's decision was taken instantly. Much as he disliked to leave the old outfit here was the chance he had been waiting for without knowing it. He would never have set foot on the Double Y during Frenchy's lifetime because of loyalty to his old friend. Had he at any time desired possession of the property he and his friends could have taken it and left court actions to the other side. But Frenchy was gone, and he still owned half of a valuable piece of property and one that he could make pay well. He was getting on in years and it would be pleasant to have his cherished dream come true, to be the over-lord and half-owner of a good cattle ranch and to know that when he became too old to work with any degree of pleasure he need not worry about his remaining years. If he left the Bar-20 one of his friends would take his place and he was sure it would be Hopalong. The advancement in pay and authority would please the man whom he had looked upon as his son. And perhaps it would bring to Hopalong that which now kept his eyes turned towards the H2. Yes, it was time to go to his own and let another man come into *his* own; to move along and give a younger man a chance.

He replied to George McAllister at length, covering everything, and took the letter to the bunk house to have it mailed.

"Billy," he said, "here's a letter to go to Cowan's first thing to-morrow. Don't forget."

Buck started the fall work early and pushed it harder than usual for he wished to have everything done before the new foreman took charge. The beef roundup and drives were over with quickly, considering the time and labor involved, and when the chill blasts of early winter swept across the range and whined around the ranch buildings Buck smiled with the satisfaction which comes with work well done. George McAllister, failing to buy Buck's interest, now implored him to go to the Double Y at once and take charge, which he had promised to do in time to become familiar with conditions on the winterbound northern range before the new herds were driven to it.

As yet he had told his men nothing of his plans for fear they would persuade him to stay where he was, but he could tell Meeker, and one crisp morning he called at the H2 and led its foreman aside. When he had finished Meeker grasped his hand, told him how sorry he was to lose so good a friend and neighbor, and how glad he was at the friend's good fortune.

"I hope Cassidy *is* th' man to take yore place, Peters," he remarked, thoughtfully. "He's a good man, th' best in th'country, strong, square, and nervy. I've had my eyes on him for some time an' I'll back him to bust anything he throws his rope on. He can handle that ranch easy an' well."

"Yo're right," replied Buck, slowly. "He ain't never failed to make good yet. Whoever th' boys pick out to be foreman will be foreman, for th' owners have left that question with me. But Meeker, it's like pulling teeth for me to go up to Montana without him. I can't take him 'less I take 'em all, an' I've got reasons why I can't do that. An' I ain't quite shore he'd go with me now—yore ranch holds something that ties him tight to this range. He'll be lonely up in our ranch house, an' it's plenty big enough for two," he finished, smiling interrogatively at his companion.

"Well, I reckon it'll not be lonely if he wants to change it," laughed Meeker. "Leastawise, them's th' symptoms plentiful enough down here. I was dead set agin it at first, but now I don't want nothing else but to see my girl fixed for life. An' when I pass out, all I have is hers."

CHAPTER 41

Hopalong's Reward

Seven men loitered about the line house on Lookout Peak, wondering why they, the old outfit, had been told to await their foreman there. Why were the others, all good fellows, excluded? What could it mean? Foreboding grew upon them as they talked the matter over and when Buck approached they waited eagerly for him to speak.

He dismounted and looked at them with pride and affection and a trace of sorrow showed in his voice and face when he began to talk.

"Boys," he said, slowly, "We've got things ready for snow when it comes. Th' cattle are strong an' fat, there's plenty of grass curing on th' range, an' th' biggest drive ever sent north from this ranch has been taken care of. There's seven of you here, two on th' north range, an' four more good men coming next week; an' thirteen men can handle this ranch with some time to spare.

"I've been with you for a long time now. Some of you I've had for over twelve years, an' no man ever had a better outfit. You've never turned back on any game, an' you've never had no trouble among yoreselves. You've seen me sending an' getting letters purty regular for some time, an' you've been surprised at how I've pushed you to get ready for winter. I'm going to tell you all about it now, an' when I've finished I want you to vote on something," and they listened in dumb surprise and sorrow while he told them of his decision. When he had finished they crowded about him and begged him to stay with them, telling him they would not allow him to leave. But if he must go, then they, too, must go and help him whip a wild and lawless range into submission. He would need them badly in Montana, and nowhere could he get men who would work and fight so hard and cheerfully for him as his old outfit. They would not let him talk and he could not if they would, for there was something in his throat which choked and pained him. Johnny Nelson and

Hopalong were tugging at his shoulders and the others stormed and pleaded and swore, tears in the eyes of all. He wavered and would have thrown away all his resolutions, when he thought of Hopalong and the girl. Pushing them back he told them he could not stay and begged them, as they loved him to consider his future. They looked at one another strangely and then realized how selfish they were, and said so profanely.

"*Now* yo're my old outfit," he cried, striking while the iron was hot. "I've told you why I must go, an' why I can't take *all* of you with me, an' why I won't take a few an' leave th' rest. Don't think I don't want you! Why, with you at my back I'd buck that range into shape in no time, an' chase th' festive gunfighters off th' earth. Mebby some day you can come up to me, but not now. Now I want th' new foreman of th' Bar-20 to be one of th' men who worked so hard an' loyally an' long for me an' th' ranch. I want one of you to take my place. Th' owners have left th' choice to me, an' say th' man I appoint will be their choice; an' I ain't a-going to do it—I can't do it. One last favor, boys; go in that house an' pick yore foreman. Go now, an' I'll wait for you here."

"We'll do it right here—Red Connors!" cried Hopalong.

"Hopalong!" yelled Red and Johnny in the same voice, and only a breath ahead of the others. "Hopalong! Hopalong!" was the cry, his own voice lost, buried, swept under. He tried to argue, but he could make no headway, for his exploits were shouted to convince him. As fast as he tried to speak someone remembered something else he had done—they ranged over a period of ten years and from Mexico to Cheyenne; from Dodge City and Leavenworth to the Rockies.

Buck laughed and clapped his hands on Hopalong's shoulders. "I appoint you foreman, an' you can't get out of it, nohow! Lemme shake hands with th' new foreman of th' Bar-20—I'm one of th' boys now, an' glad to get rid of th' responsibility for a while. Good luck, son!"

"No you ain't going to get rid of 'em," laughed Hopalong, but serious withal. "Yo're th' foreman of this ranch till you leave us—ain't he, boys?" he appealed.

Buck put his hands to his ears and yelled for less noise. "All right, I'll play at breaking you in—'though th' Lord knows I can't show you nothing you don't know now. My first order under these conditions is that you ride south, Hopalong, an' tell th' news to Meeker, an' to his girl. An' tell 'em separate, too. An' don't forget I want to see you hobbled before I leave next month—tell her to make it soon!"

Hopalong reddened and grinned under the rapid-fire advice and chaffing of his friends and tried to retort.

Johnny sprang forward. "Come on, fellers! Put him on his cayuse an' start him south! We've got to have *some* hand in his courting, anyhow!"

"Right!"

"Good idea!"

"Look out! *Grab* him, Red!"

"Up with him!"

"We ought to escort him on his first love trail," yelled Skinny above the uproar. "Come on! *Saddles*, boys!"

"Like hell!" cried Hopalong, spurring forward his nettlesome mount. "You've got to grow wings to catch me an' Red Eagle! *Go, bronc!*" and he shot forward, cheers and good wishes thundering after him.

Buck moved about restlessly in his sleep and then awakened suddenly and lay quiet as a hand touched his shoulder. "What is it? Who are you?" he demanded, ominously.

"I reckoned you'd like to know that yo're going to be best man in two weeks, Buck," said a happy voice. "She said a month, but I told her you was going away before then, an' you *might*, you know. I shore feel joyous!"

The huge hand of the elder man closed over his in a grip which made him wince. "Good boy, an' good luck, Hoppy! It was due you. Good luck, an' happiness, son!"